Tales of the
Dissolutionverse

Tales of the Dissolutionverse

TEN STORIES OF MUSIC AND MAGIC

William C. Tracy

Space Wizard Science Fantasy
Raleigh, NC
www.spacewizardsciencefantasy.com

Cover art by Luisa Preissler
Art and illustrations by Micah Epstein, Justin Donaldson, and Luisa Preissler
Map by Damijan
Editing by Heather Tracy
Book Layout © 2015 BookDesignTemplates.com

Author's website: www. spacewizardsciencefantasy.com

CONTENTS

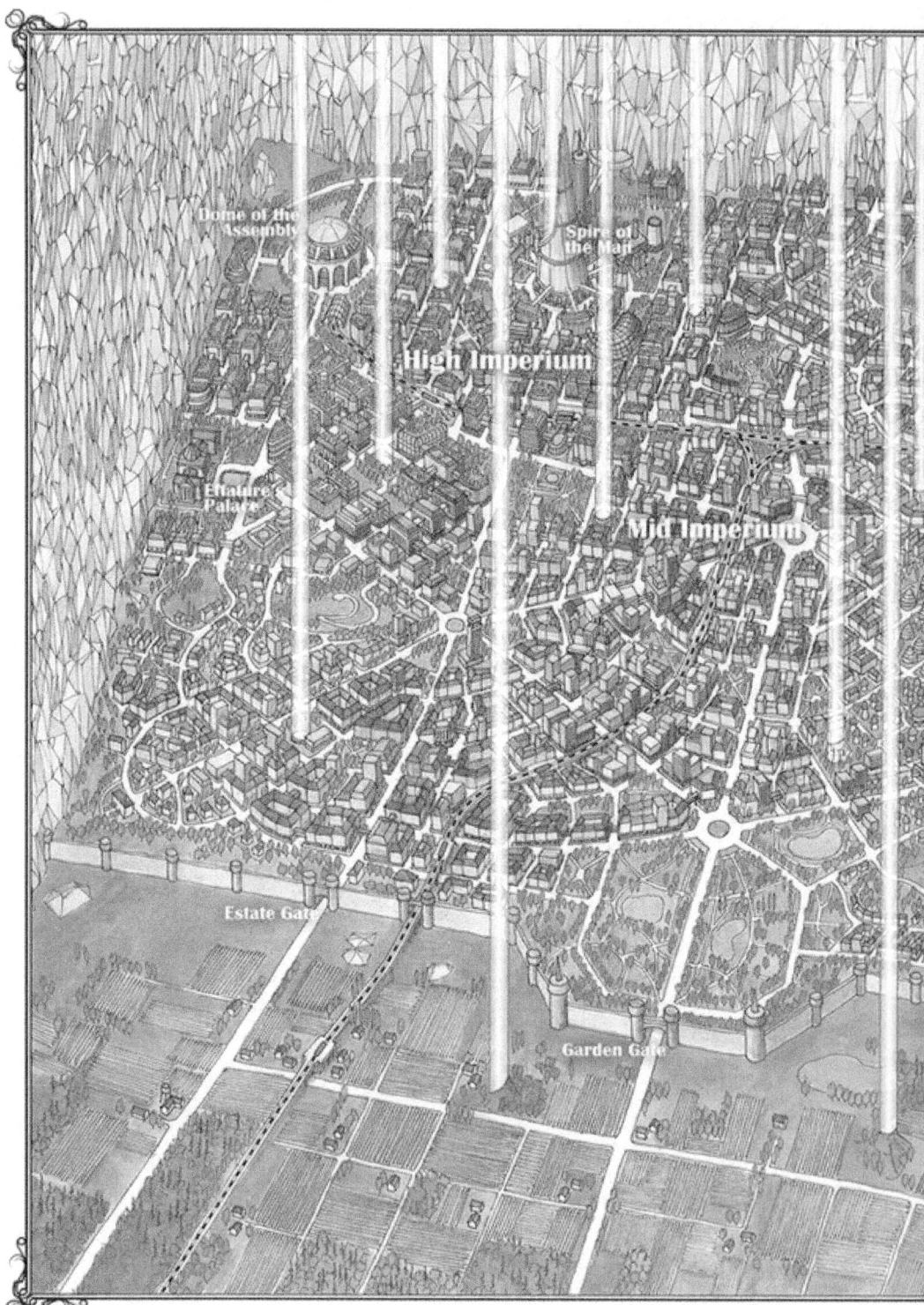

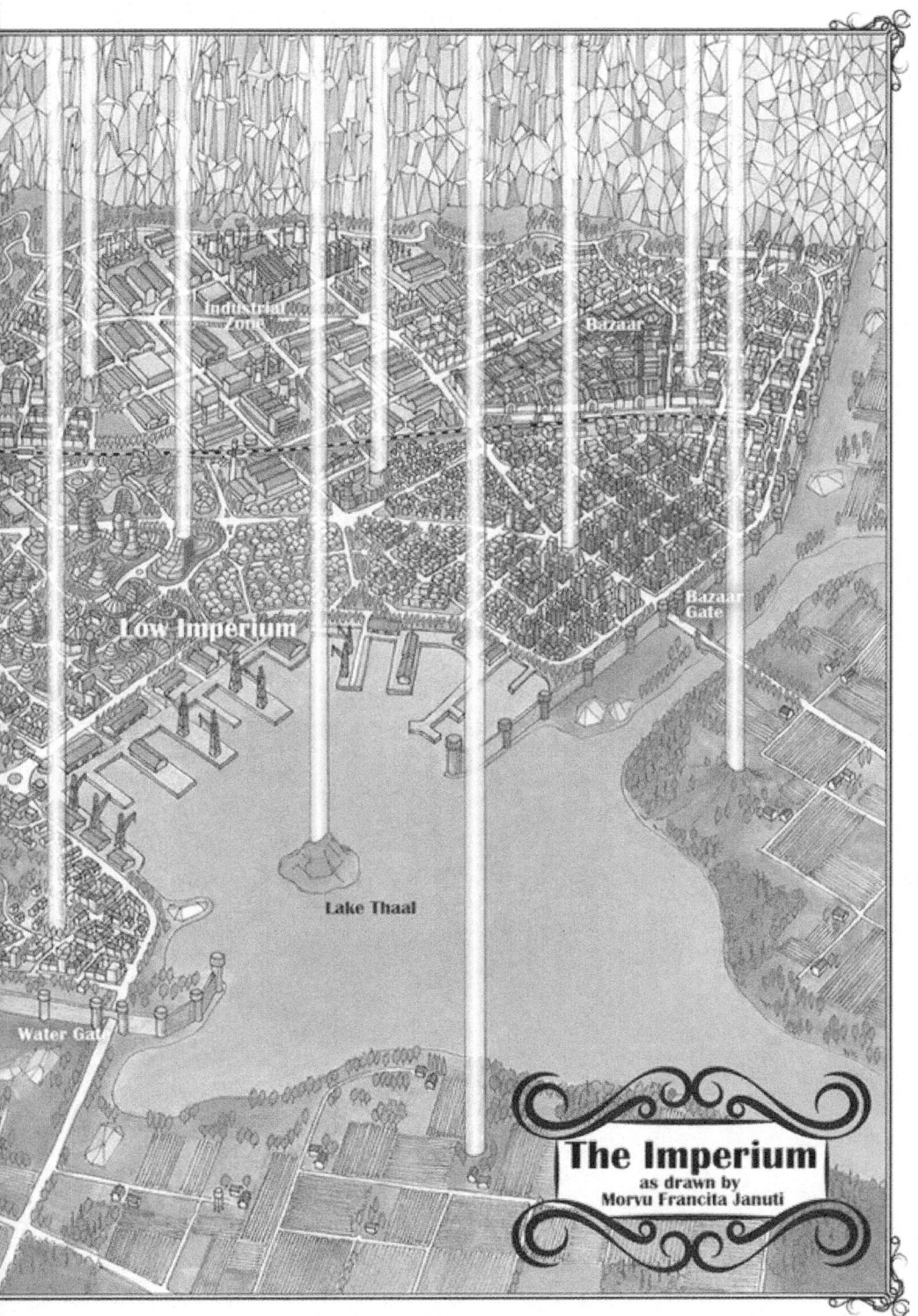

Industrial Zone

Bazaar

Low Imperium

Bazaar Gate

Lake Thaal

Water Gate

The Imperium
as drawn by
Morvu Francita Januti

The Five Hive Plateau
964 A.A.W.

Origon Cyrysi pushed open the door to the Council's chambers, ignoring the bleats of the Methiemum guards. Weren't they supposed to prevent anyone unauthorized getting in? But then, that was the whole problem, wasn't it? The Council of the Maji wasn't helping the Assembly of Species like it used to. They told new maji like him to mind their business and stay in the Nether rather than seeing the profundity of the homeworlds.

He shook off the guard's hand catching at the sleeve of his robe, though the hand fell away as the guards hastily returned to their posts. They saw what he did.

Origon's steps slowed as the six councilors of the maji—one for each house—stared up at him. They had been in the middle of arguing about something, gathered around the table from which they presided over the rest of the maji. Trills and glissandos in the House of Power reflected the vestiges of the argument before the Symphony escaped his perception. He grasped after the fading notes, but if he was truthful—and he always was—those gazes unnerved him. His fingers crumpled the newsprint he held in his left hand. It was the latest example of the Council refusing to send maji where they were needed. There had been three natural disasters in the last two cycles where the Council did nothing to help. They cited the force of maji was spread too thin already.

"Majus Cyrysi, why are you to be breaking into our meeting, unannounced, in a dirty robe? Again." Mareveluchi Karendi looked down her hooked nose at him, her crest spreading in an intimidating display. The leader of the Council, and the head of his primary house—the House of Communication—was a Kirian like him, and seemed always to think he was lacking. He still hadn't figured out why. He only wanted the Council to afford him a little recognition.

"Speaker Karendi, I was reading the latest report from one of the local newspapers of the continuing conflict on the Pixie homeworld." He brandished the print, sparing a glance for the sleeve of his robe as he did. A stain from his breakfast of meal grubs in broth ran between lines of crimson and purple. The stain was nearly hidden against the background. Speaker Karendi must have the eyes of an eagle. Or, she was looking for some deficiency, more likely. Origon's own crest drooped under her stare.

"And what of this story, pup?" asked the head of the House of Strength. Jasrimopobt Huar, Grower was a large Festuour woman, her fur decked with silver rings worked into braids, and an enormous pink hat perched on her head. Her bright blue eyes glared at him from underneath. She was usually even tempered. He must have caught them at something important then. The only way through was forward. Origon pushed his crest back up, propping up his confidence. If the Council accepted his case, it would be something to share with the other maji.

"Well, why is the Council not sending a representative to end the fight?" He waved the newsprint for emphasis, and several sets of eyes followed the movement. "Another hive outpost was burned yesterday, and two hundred Pixies killed. The Pixie speakers are livid. They—"

"The Council, we do attend the Assembly meetings," Councilor Zsaana, head of the House of Healing, said. He was bolt upright in his chair as if to show off every spec of his diminutive height. The cowl that hid his face shifted as he spoke. "Yes, certain Pixie representatives, they have asked for aid. But the Council has determined this, it is a local matter for the Pixies—not big enough for the maji to step in."

"What could the maji be doing that an army could not, hmm?" Speaker Karendi added. "Maji are not trained for war. Maji are trained to spread knowledge, to teach, and to be providing relief from natural disasters."

"But this—" he started.

"Is *not* a natural disaster, Majus Cyrysi," Councilor Huar said, sitting back with one hand on her hat to keep it from flapping off her head like a deranged bird. "This is pure social conflict between two different philosophical factions. The maji cannot get involved. It would show favor to one species over another. Everyone would want us to win their wars for them."

Origon's hands flexed, crumping the newsprint further. When the Luthenia Dam on Etan burst not six months ago, which *had* been a natural disaster, the Council sent no maji. Twenty-eight Etanela perished. If *he* had been there...well, he wasn't certain what he would have done, but he would have at least tried.

He stared down at the carving on the front of the huge table—a relief of all the species of the Great Assembly, working in harmony to raise a tower. The species who joined later surrounded the six original species who formed the Assembly. Kirians were one of the first, along with

Methiemum and Festuour. The Pixies, however, were on the outskirts of the carving. The only species farther away from the central work was a figure of a Lobhl. That strange species only joined the Assembly twelve cycles past.

"It is not escaping my attention that there has never been a Pixie on the Council of the Maji," Origon said. "Would such a councilor be having a differing opinion?" It was a common stereotype to think Pixies were little smarter than animals. Their buzzing wings and high energy did not help that perception. But it was the warrior caste of the Pixies—the ones who were now killing their kind on Mother Hive—who were the most vicious of their species. Many Pixies were hardworking, quick-thinking, sparks of energy. He had spoken to dozens, some of whom rightly belonged in the research labs connected to the House of Power. But he found them when he walked at the docks of the Imperium. It was the only place many Pixies could get work.

"We ain't sending anyone, so stop asking," Councilor Huar grumped.

"The people in the Nether are to be prejudiced against Pixies," Origon pleaded. He really had to control his crest. "They are not all like the ruffians who have been vandalizing the shops in Mid Imperium. Those are the warrior-minded variety. There are at least—" He stopped and checked the news article again. "Fifteen known aspirations of Pixie. It is how they are to be organizing their society. But the warriors have been culling the other classes somehow on the Five Hive Plateau. That is why the Council should be sending—"

"Enough, Majus Cyrysi," Councilor Zsaana said, his voice rising. The councilors for the Houses of Grace and Potential on his right and left—both Methiemum—rolled their eyes in unison. Origon felt his crest bristle. This was not some joke.

"Even two or three maji would be making a diff—"

"You are excused, *Majus* Cyrysi," Speaker Karendi broke in. Her crest was dangerously low, her eyes narrowed. The other five councilors stared him down, flanking her. Their abandoned papers nearly covered the top of the table.

"Well. I would not be wishing to take any more of your *precious* time," he shot back. "Speaker, Councilors." Origon gave a mocking bow, twirled, and stomped out of the chamber.

* * *

Origon stumped down the steps of the Spire of the Maji, where the Council chambers were. It was a colossal building, even taller than the House of Communication, built around one of the sparkling, semi-transparent columns that held up the crystal expanse of the Nether.

Once outside, Origon took in a deep breath of the clear air of the Nether. He opened himself up to the music underlying the universe as he crossed the grounds from the Spire of the Maji to the House of Communication. It was almost midday, and the titanic walls encasing two sides of the Nether's capital city of the Imperium were at their maximum brightness. They reflected off the other houses of the maji—six in total—that circled the Spire. Strength, Communication, Power, Grace, Healing, and Potential. The maji lived like royalty because they protected and helped the ten species of the Assembly. They were supposed to, anyway. Yet pleas from the maji to their councilors as often as not went unheard. Origon spared a glance down at the arm of his robe. So what if it was dirty? It was typical for the councilors to focus on the wrong problem when the more urgent one was staring them in the face. They wouldn't be able to solve the Assembly's problem if their ancestors led them by the nose.

Origon stopped in the middle of the sculpted grounds between the Spire and the House of Communication. He'd recently found an apartment on the second floor, after moving out of his old mentor's rooms, but now he looked upward, along the many floors of the tower. It was the tallest of the houses, reflecting the Symphony of Communication's connection to matters of the air. Someday, when he had a little more authority, he'd get a more auspicious room. He belonged to two Houses, not just one like most maji. He could have lived in the House of Power if he really wanted to, but it was his second house, after all. He spared a glance for the low, sturdy structure of the House of Power. It was next door to the House of Communication.

His choice was not just because the new maji in the House of Power thought his grasp of the connections of power were "basic" and "worse than an apprentice's." He'd like to see those maji try to separate two of the fractal Symphonies that made up the universe. They only had to deal with one. He should start a club or something to help support the few other maji who could hear two aspects of the Grand Symphony. There weren't many, but he felt there should be more attention paid to them. There were so many possibilities, when hearing more of the Grand Symphony.

Origon's crest flexed in remembered embarrassment, and he tried unsuccessfully to rein it in. The other species did not have such an expressive means of communication as the crests which graced Kirian heads. However, that also meant it was easier for them to hide their feelings. Origon pushed back several out-of-place feathers.

Now his eyes swept across the carefully-tended grounds around the Spire, with peaceful streams, thought-provoking sculptures, and surprise turns in the rolling walkways leading to scenic views. How unlike the war-torn homeworld of the Pixies.

Well, was he a majus, or wasn't he? Origon turned away from the House of Communication.

* * *

He stalked up to the majus attendant at the portal ground. The Spire had its own portal ground, another privilege given to the maji. The attendant was a wari Lobath, the third gender of that species, though he wasn't familiar with hir personally. Zie was an older majus.

"I want to go here." He pointed at the drawing in the newsprint, of a high plateau between giant mounds of dirt, reaching as high as the Spire of the Maji, from what he could tell.

The majus on duty peered at the picture, though hir eyes did not narrow. Lobath's silvery eyes always looked surprised to him.

To be a portal ground attendant required an extensive knowledge of locations on the ten homeworlds—to provide travel to wherever the customer required. Someday, Origon hoped to amass that sort of knowledge. Of course, as a majus, he could travel for free by portal to wherever he wished. Non-maji had to pay a fee, to cover the majus' time in operating the ground. Maji were expected to fill in that role, once they had enough knowledge of places to go. One could only make a portal to a place one previously visited, or a place to which another majus communicated the coordinates.

"That's the Five Hive Plateau," the majus said. Hir head-tentacles were wound tight around the top of hir head. "There's a war going on amongst the Pixies. I wouldn't want to be caught in the middle."

"That is why you are not to be going," Origon told hir. "None of the other maji seem to care either, so I am going to help."

The Lobath shrugged. "It's your head. If the Council gave you permission to go there, who am I to argue?"

Origon desperately forced his crest down so he wouldn't look like a juvenile, caught outside the hatchery after curfew. "I was just to be coming from the Council chamber," he said evasively.

The Lobath shrugged again—impressive for one with practically no neck—and turned around, an oblong of black forming behind hir, ringed in blue and amber. Origon could just hear notes at the edge of his perception. The majus was of the House of Grace, an aspect of the Grand Symphony he couldn't hear, but portals were common to all maji—somehow—and there was a little overlap when a majus of another house opened one.

Origon stepped through the oval of blackness and immediately felt the feathers on his head separate in the dryness and heat. It was a good thing he had decided not to grow a moustache. It would have been severely itchy in this weather. The portal closed behind him with a little *pop* and he looked around the desolate, reddish plane of Mother Hive. There was no majus attendant on this side.

He could see the hives in the distance—towering things, unlike the picture in the newsprint. That had shown mounds of dirt, like an animal could have piled up. The reality was much different. Even from this distance, he could see exquisite carvings on the outside of the hives. They were a history, he thought, a progression of figures and places parading around the circumference, with some aspects coated in paint or precious metals. The carvings made way for the multitude of entrances around the hive and as Origon took a few steps closer, peering, he could make out dozens, no, *hundreds* of figures swarming around the outside of the hive. A growing roar made him pause.

He turned to find another hive to his left, and behind him...

Was an army of Pixies, coming his way.

There was no time to react. Origon yelped and crouched down as a swarm of buzzing wings and shoving arms engulfed him. He dodged to one side as a sword as big as the Pixie wielding it sliced through the space where his crest had been a moment before.

Fortunately, the combatants were too focused on battling each other to pay him much attention. He was treated mostly as an obstacle, though he had to shake off a Pixie who landed on his back and tried to use him as a shield. There were no colors surrounding people or objects that would signal maji were involved. These must all be common soldiers, but their weapons were still sharp. A pair of the bluish, buzzing creatures, half his height, flew over his head. Their shortswords flashed faster than he could follow, pinging off each other like a pair of giant, enraged hornets.

What could he do? Eventually, he'd get skewered and then how would he help these people in their battle?

He fell into the Symphony of Communication, which was a riot of sound, with chords playing over each other and cadenzas doing as much battle musically as the bodies around him. Fighting was a means of communication, and so was the air around them. Origon frantically took notes from the core of his being—generated by everything he experienced—and stuffed them between separations in the measures. A shield of air puffed into existence around him, and the sounds of the battle died away to a muted rumble. The yellow of the House of Communication, visible only to maji, swirled along the outside of the shield.

Origon slumped, brushing dust off his robe, though more landed even as he did. The wings of the Pixies generated strangely tall twists of air, but at least they were outside his bubble. He watched the ballet of death around him, in a circle of empty space.

Except now he labored for every breath. Origon's feathers felt like they might burst into flame. Sweat soaked him. Why was it so hot?

A spear thrust through the side of the shield and Origon jigged away, narrowly avoiding another hole in his robe, and in his side. This shield of air was not nearly as effective as his mentor implied.

Ah. Origon's crest rose in triumph. It was the pressure! Simple thermodynamics. Another thing he hadn't been told when shown the trick with the shield of air.

Well, he could hear more than just the Symphony of Communication, couldn't he? Origon took more of his notes, this time listening to the

Symphony of Power. It was concerned with the connections between things, and one of those things was how heat moved around.

He waded through measures detailing the shifting flows of the battle. One side was definitely winning, though he didn't know who or what they represented.

Origon found the legato phrases, slow and stagnant, defining the inside of the sphere, and changed the tempo of several measures, pushing the heat away from him and into the wall of air until it was even cooler inside than it was on the plateau. Quite by coincidence, it further opened the spaces in the music of the air, and Origon stuffed more notes into the Symphony of Communication. His shield now had another aura of orange, for the House of Power, to match the yellow. It indicated where his circle of protection ended.

This time, when a spear stabbed at the shield, it skidded off the hardened air, dragging the Pixie wielding it off balance. Her compound eyes flashed in anger.

Success! The shield wouldn't last forever—Origon heard degradation of the notes when the spear impacted—but he could take a moment to figure out what was going on without his robe gaining more holes than greens attacked by grubs.

Origon tugged his sleeves down so his wrists were properly covered and spun in a circle, observing the fight.

Now he had a moment to watch, he noted the phenotypical differences of the two parties fighting. One faction was brighter blue, and the chitinous places covering their skin had natural sharpened points. The other, smaller, faction was smoother-looking, and he thought their compound eyes might be larger. The spikier ones also had better armor— harnesses around their chests and shoulders with purple metallic plates. The others had nothing so organized, and many lacked armor at all, relying on their naturally hard skin.

The better clad ones were winning, and Origon would make a wager they were the warrior caste who'd been causing so much trouble. But that meant the fight was spreading dangerously fast through the plateau. If only the Council had listened to him.

He called out to the nearest non-warrior, hoping she could understand the common tongue. He wasn't in the Nether anymore, with its inherent translation between species.

"Which is to be the correct way to your hive?"

The Pixie started, turning multifaceted eyes toward him. Evidently she understood. "Why here, majus? We applied for help. None came. Now you plop down in the middle of a battle we lose?"

"I am to be here now," Origon answered. He tried to keep his crest level as a warrior banged on the top of his shield with a hefty warhammer. He could hear the blows banging notes out of existence, crumpling them from eighth to sixteenth to thirty-second notes. "Simply tell me what to do and I will be helping." If the warriors didn't kill him first, that was.

The Pixie sneered at him and buzzed away, running face-first into a knot of warriors. Origon winced as blades came at her from three sides, then dug into the Symphony of Communication. It was farther away, but he could still hear the melody of the air, tumbling around them in a violent caprice. He redirected a few phrases with his notes and wind caught the flats of blades, moving them enough to narrowly miss her. The Pixie countered and thrust back, hitting one warrior in her armored breastplate, but the Pixie's strike slid off.

Origon could see the blades coming in again, and again he tried to change the Symphony, but it resisted his efforts. What he attempted was too similar to what he had done before. The Symphony was getting muddy with his alterations. Origon watched in horror as the Pixie he addressed was cut down in seconds.

He could do little from where he was. He was no warrior, though he could handle himself in a fight. Still, he alone would not make a difference in this battle. If the Council sent more maji, however...

The warhammer was still knocking notes from their places in his shield and Origon turned a glare upward, his crest expanding. He delved back into the Symphony of Power. This music was fresher than the music of Communication. A few more of his notes to increase the tempo of the warhammer's melody and it heated until it glowed. The Pixie warrior swore and dropped her weapon. Origon reversed the change he'd made to the Symphony, taking his notes back into his core. He breathed easier, feeling less spent. He'd need to make sure he didn't overreach. That had always been a failing of his in university. Change too many things at once, use too many notes, and what was left?

No, this fight didn't need him. It was already lost. The warriors were chasing down the remnants of the smaller army. He looked toward his original objective—the hive with the elaborate carvings around its circumference. He was nearly sure it was the one to host a scientific-minded faction of the five hives. As he recalled, the warriors had taken over several others already. If the Pixie's history was accurate, they developed this part of their homeworld twenty-five hundred cycles past, long before they were part of the Assembly, when one hive mother birthed an unheard-of five hive daughters at once. The plateau where they settled became a hub for commerce with the other species of the Assembly, until this war started. If he stopped it, commerce from Mother Hive would flow again. The Council would have to acknowledge what he'd done.

The hive mother was the key. From what he knew, she was the way to influence the hive. He definitely couldn't reach the warrior mother, but he might reach the mother for the losing side.

Origon listened to the music defining his shield. The Pixies couldn't harm him right now, but if he left the shield's protection, he wouldn't last long. The only answer was to take it with him. As another spear pinged off the shield, he composed a wandering refrain from his notes and attached it beneath the score of the shield. Then he began walking. To his relief, the shield traveled with him, though the effort of putting one boot in front of the other was exhausting. How many of his notes were in his constructs? The Symphony did not like to be changed twice in the same manner, and the farther a majus moved a change in the music from its starting point, the harder it was to hold.

Fortunately the pull from the ground was far less here than in the Nether. It was the reason one rarely saw Pixies flying in the Imperium. Here, however, he bounced along, though each jump tugged at the muscles in his legs. He was breathing far faster than he should be. He'd have to take back the notes of his change soon, and that would leave him defenseless.

He was nearing the edge of the battle. Forty more paces. Thirty. Twenty-five. He huffed like an asthmatic Festuour. The Symphony's resistance to his shield was growing.

Origon looked around. There were still twenty or more warrior Pixies close enough to catch him. They were busy chasing the last of their opponents, but once they did that, he knew they would be after him. He heaved his feet forward in another half-hop. Fifteen paces farther. Ten.

The shield of heated air compressed in on him, and it grew hotter again in his little bubble. Eight more paces.

By all the ancestors, enough!

He dropped the shield, taking his notes back with a rush of energy, and sprang forward. There were warriors nearby but his jump caught them off guard. He got three more jumps in before they gave chase.

Origon picked up his robe and ran across the dusty plateau toward the ornamented hive.

* * *

"Who comes here?" called a sentry at the hive entrance.

"Origon...Cyrysi..." Origon gasped, holding a stitch in his side. "Majus of the...Houses of Communication and Power...I come to aid you in your war."

The Pixie considered him a moment with her large, dark compound eyes, then the pack of warriors closing swiftly behind him. Origon knew his crest was spread in all directions, and tried not to clench his hands. They might be chasing him, but this was their eventual destination. He and this sentry had a common cause.

"You may pass."

Origon jumped through the entrance to the hive as a horde of guards rushed to meet the warriors who had chased him. Origon collapsed against the inside wall of the hive. This was not how he thought helping the Pixies would go. Thoughts of being welcomed with a stately ceremony flew from his mind.

Thump. The sound was right next to his ear, on the other side of the hive wall.

He bolted upright, then glanced out the entrance to see the group that had been chasing him engaged with the less-equipped guards from the hive. They weren't the ones making the noise.

A shaft of stone thrust through the wall next to his left ear, and Origon screeched, his crest as wild as if one of his ancestors had appeared in front of him.

"What are these walls to be made of?" he said, hopping several steps farther into the hive. Behind him, the stone battering ram jerked and disappeared through the hole it made. He didn't want to know what it had done to the relief sculptures on the outside.

He fled inward, to repeated thumpings on the walls of the hive. The force he encountered on the plateau must have made their way here after him.

The inside of the hive was dry and roomy, cooler than outside, though Origon still felt his feathers separate from the lack of humidity. The halls were tight for him, and his crest brushed the ceiling, but that was understandable. After all, the standard Pixie only came up to his waist. Passages branched off to his left and right, but he headed inward and down. From what little he knew of Pixie habitation, the hive mothers were usually at the bottom, and she was the person with whom he needed to speak. Why were they not mobilizing defenses faster?

Then he saw the inhabitants, and his steps slowed. He passed through an open area, and the Pixies there were dressed in simple coverings—tunics that left their wings free, and belts or harnesses to hold tools and personal items. Many more had leggings crafted from some flat fiber, like overlapping leaves stitched together. They looked comfortable. These people were not ready for war, and might not even have the capability to fight competently. His thoughts went to the Pixie he'd talked to, cut down with almost no effort from the warrior faction.

Another *boom* sounded through the hive, and rock and dirt rained down from the ceiling. Pixies yelled and scrambled for the relative safety of the smaller passages—save for one. Around her, an aura of blue and orange bloomed, and she moved around falling rocks, the orange glow leaving her outstretched hands and gluing sections of the ceiling together. Her extended arms showed that one of her wings was a prosthetic, connected to her body by a set of harnesses wrapping around her torso. Origon could hear the changes in the Symphony of Power—they shared that house. Her notes were bolstering the connections amid the particles making up walls and ceiling of the hive. It was as if she was awaking connections the rocks remembered, telling them where they should stay.

Origon stepped toward the majus—and a majus of two houses at that! He clumsily followed her example in the Symphony, but the music would resist him if he tried to make the same change. Instead, he devoted notes to energizing the connections in the ceiling. Increasing the friction between the separate rocks might be enough to fuse them back into a solid surface.

The Pixie spared him one glance as they worked. The ceiling of this room was a lost cause for permanent inhabitation, but they could make certain all the civilians escaped to safer parts of the hive. He watched the other Pixies flit from the room.

When the ceiling was stabilized, Origon lowered his arms, pulling the sleeves of his now dusty robe down to cover his arms. He'd raised them to the ceiling at some point, though the location of his hands did not actually affect how he changed the Symphony.

"Good work," the Pixie majus said. "But you come here why? What does Kirian have to do with hive of engineering-minded Pixies?"

"To help," Origon said. He tried to catch his breath. Most of those changes had been permanent, not reversible. He wouldn't be getting those notes back unless he wanted the ceiling to fall in on him. "The Council is refusing to send anyone to be helping stop this genocide."

The Pixie grunted and tilted her head as if to observe a curious specimen of grub, her fingers twitching. Her wings were a blur on her back—the prosthetic seemed just as functional as the flesh and blood one—and she shifted around him in the air, almost too fast for him to follow. Finally, she said, "You have two houses."

That was not what Origon expected, but he remembered using the Symphony of Communication somewhere in there to keep a chunk of rock from falling on his head. This Pixie did not miss much. From the gnarled edges of the chitinous plates on her head and shoulders, she was older than him, and considering the short lives of the species, that meant she was likely a senior member of the hive.

He stumbled to the left as something larger shook the hive. Had that been an explosion? He glanced at their recent work, but the ceiling held.

"Come. Need to find Mother," The Pixie said, and buzzed to one of the many entrances to the open area. "Two maji may be enough to change tide of what will happen. One will not."

Origon was caught flat-footed, but leaned forward and half-ran, half-jumped to catch up. At last, someone who moved as fast as the situation warranted!

He caught up with her a few paces down the corridor, and noticed the carvings along the tops of the walls. They were heading in the right direction—which would have taken him too long to figure out, alone.

"Kratithakanipoulitekaveya," the Pixie said, and Origon tried to catch the intricacies of the Pixie name. Judging by the number of syllables, this one was highly esteemed in her hive.

She spun in the air, flying backwards as she observed him. "Common name is Kratitha. You are Origon Cyrysi, yes?"

For the second time, Origon was caught off guard. She'd heard of him?

"I—yes, that is to be accurate," he said. "I am afraid I am not to be familiar with you."

Kratitha waved a small hand as if to dismiss the comment. "No matter. Good to work with another two-house majus again. Probably shouldn't have come. This is internal matter to Pixies, but since you came—"

"I want to help," Origon broke in. "The Council will not be treating this matter with the attention it deserves. Let me know what I can be doing to help." He let his crest curl up to show his determination. At least speaking with another majus, there were no barriers in communication.

Kratitha turned, picking one corridor out of a three-way split. Origon had to admit, he would have been completely lost. They'd passed countless doorways, though glimpses of Pixies hurrying this way or that were getting less frequent the farther in and down they went.

"Must secure Mother and one other. Many engineers will be turned today, but as long as Mother is safe, still have chance at our way of life."

"I must be admitting, I am not fully versed on Pixie social customs," Origon admitted.

"Yet still barged in thinking could be a hero, hm?" Kratitha said. Her voice didn't have the sting of accusation, just stating fact.

"Er, yes," Origon said. Fortunately Kratitha's back was still toward him so she couldn't see his crest droop in embarrassment.

"This way." The Pixie took another side passage, which looped into a sloped circular tunnel, spiraling sharply down. She explained as Origon hurried along behind her, "Pixies are still hive-minded beings, yes?"

Origon nodded, though she wasn't looking. Kratitha seemed to take his silence for agreement and continued. "We wage war less by death and more by...ah...." She paused and swung around in the air to watch him, her compound eyes glittering in the little lights placed in recesses in the rock ceiling. "More by mind control, if you accept flawed comparison."

"You are having a collective of like-minded individuals," Origon said, and Kratitha cocked a tiny finger at him.

"Yes. When warriors take over, as have in other hives on the plateau, many engineering-minded members here will ally. Sort of peer pressure."

"But the hive mother?" Origon prompted.

"Stronger-willed. Different genotype from children," Kratitha offered. She landed, then walked through a small opening in the tunnel. Origon had to bend almost double to fit through.

"And you are her child?" he asked. He would have to talk with other maji in the House of Communication when he returned to the Nether. There were several who would be fascinated with Pixie sociology.

"All here are," Kratitha answered. "Though will join warrior mother, when there are more of that influence than of this hive mother."

"So we must be taking the hive mother from this place to somewhere safe?" Origon asked.

Kratitha flew to a doorway trimmed in carvings, coated with what looked like gold and copper, in the glow from bioluminescent lights recessed into the ceiling. She turned, half-barring the doorway, then seemed to force herself to relax.

"Must rescue two members of hive to propagate." she said. Her fingers fidgeted and she shifted from foot to foot.

"There is to be something you are not telling me," Origon said. He had always wondered how an all-female species reproduced, though some of the others of the ten species had even stranger ways of reproduction— not something easy and normal, like the way Kirians laid eggs.

"There is," Kratitha agreed. "Shown to very few not of Pixies species— few *of* our species, in fact." She moved through the doorway, then beckoned Origon closer. "These are his quarters."

Origon cocked his head at the pronoun use, his crest rising in anticipation. He stepped forward into the room.

Inside was a brightly lit mess. There were piles of papers as tall as him, a highly detailed miniature of the hive—including its many layers below ground—a pile of scrolls, and a collection of various drinking vases stacked haphazardly on a table. There were also surgical implements in a glass-fronted cabinet.

The occupant of the room was—not quite a Pixie, or at least not one Origon was familiar with. Where most Pixies had interlocking sections of carapace on their skin, this individual was completely smooth-skinned, and where Pixie coloring was in the light blue and green range, this person was beet red and lacked Pixie wings. He was hunched over an unrolled scroll, scribbling a line of characters.

"Up, Lauka," Kratitha called, slapping her wings together to get the individual's attention. "Mother needs you. Whole hive needs you."

Lauka ducked his head farther into the scroll, as if by not looking at them, they couldn't see him.

"Warriors coming," Kratitha said. "Dangerous time. We must all move to save Mother."

Lauka continued to write as Kratitha spoke, not even glancing up. Origon's crest flattened and curved outward. There was something else different about this Pixie. Not only that he was a male.

"Must finish calculation. Then save Mother," Lauka mumbled.

Kratitha took a step into the chamber, but Lauka scooted backwards, curling around the scroll, still writing. Kratitha huffed, her wings buzzing in annoyance though she stood on the floor.

"Males cannot be indoctrinated to another Mother," she explained to Origon. "Unfortunately, also means he's useless to warriors. With lack of connection to larger consciousness, means males are harder to deal with. Mystery to all but hive mothers. Often killed when hives taken over."

Origon was watching Lauka while Kratitha spoke. He was writing furiously, but now he began to beat one hand rhythmically against the wall. Nothing about the gesture showed on his face.

"Have to finish last calculation. Not right yet. Can't leave." He continued to pound his fist into the wall, even as the other hand wrote.

"If I may help?" Origon asked. Kratitha waved a hand for him to continue, as Lauka made no indication he'd heard.

There was a growing spot of brownish blood on the wall where the Pixie beat his fist into it. There was no emotion shown, but that did not mean there was a *lack* of emotion. The Pixie was likely distressed by them asking him to leave before he finished his work. Origon dug into the Symphony of Communication, rearranging notes to remove the rests, and make the air thicker. Lauka's hand still thudded against the wall and he would still receive the satisfaction of the pressure against his hand, but it was harder for him to get up speed. He could still express his concern, but without so much damage.

Origon moved quietly into the room, ducking so he was closer in height to the male Pixie. Lauka was even shorter than the female Pixies, and with the lack of solid chitinous plates, Origon guessed he would be more vulnerable to the warriors.

When they were little more than hatchlings, Origon's younger brother Delphorus had a friend similar in some respects to Lauka, though Kirians differed in presentation.

"Can hear sounds from above," Kratitha said. "Must leave quickly."

Origon raised a hand to hush her, though she was a senior majus. Kratitha was trying reason, but Lauka had his own priorities. Delphorus learned to work with his friend. It was part of the motivation for Origon's brother to enter the police academy on Kiria, though their grandmother nearly disowned him in response. Origon only talked her down by virtue of being trained as an apprentice majus, though even that did not carry the weight he thought it should have with a lauded public speaker like his grandmother. Spiteful old turtle.

"Are you to be familiar with the trader's tongue?" Origon asked the Pixie, keeping his voice level and calm.

Lauka's hand paused for a moment. He nodded, still writing.

"Lauka speaks at least one tongue from every homeworld," Kratitha put in. So Origon might have even been able to speak his native Kirian dialect. He stayed with the more common trader's tongue.

Origon bent down near Lauka, trying to see the scroll crumpled in his hands, though he wouldn't understand the Pixie script. "Can you be completing this while we walk?"

Lauka made one more mark. "Efficiency schedule. Not perfect yet. Will come after perfect." Origon frowned, his crest flaring out. There wasn't time for that.

"Males very good at scheduling and regulation tasks," Kratitha offered. "Important to take burden off Mother. Act as secretaries and planners for hive."

"Perhaps if you can be explaining the listed schedule modifications to me we can work on a solution?" Origon said. In the back of his mind, he was counting down the seconds until the warriors would find the most protected part of the hive. "The warriors are close."

Lauka finally looked up, pointing his multifaceted eyes over Origon's shoulder. "Might help. Can explain. Want to know?"

"Very much," Origon said. It was an effort to keep his voice level. A Kirian might pick up on increased agitation, though with Kratitha flitting around as she was, perhaps Pixies were not as sensitive.

"What is the problem with the schedule?" As he spoke, Origon listened to the changes he'd made in the Symphony of Communication, taking notes back and rearranging them to move the blanket of air around Lauka. It would provide the feeling of pressure the Pixie seemed to want. Origon added several more notes to the wafting rhythms of the Symphony of Power, similar to what he discovered in the first attack. He changed the pressure of the air by redirecting the heat, making it thicken into a close blanket. It now covered Lauka's lower body, gently pressing in. Origon could see Lauka relax as he did so. Behind him, Kratitha had her head cocked, likely listening to the changes he'd made in the House of Power—that aspect of the Grand Symphony they shared.

"Have not tried that," she said. "Some others can work with males. Never had time around studies to learn."

"Yes. Finish on the way," Lauka said, and as he didn't have wings, he pushed to his feet. Origon shuffled a few of the notes so the blanket of air would follow him. He didn't know how long he would need to hold the change to the Symphony, but he was already feeling fatigued. It would only get worse as they traveled from the origin of the change.

"Must take all my papers and equipment," Lauka said, shuffling around the room, gathering scrolls until his arms were overloaded and he tottered on his short legs. "Might have needed equations."

"Don't need all these, surely," Kratitha said. She was buzzing and flitting from spot to spot. "Only most important ones."

Lauka paused, and shook his head, as if trying to clear a thought from it. Origon wondered how often females interacted with male Pixies. Kratitha seemed unprepared at best. The females must truly have little to do with the male of the hive.

"Are you having a sack to carry your papers in? Maybe then we can be transporting them all with us." Origon carefully kept his crest neutral, and turned to give Kratitha a knowing look. He'd want to take all his equations with him, too.

It took far too long, but Origon finally got Lauka out of the chamber, with a satchel on his back, filled with scrolls, blueprints, equipment, and papers. He still held his scroll, and Origon listened with one ear to the explanations of statistical deviations in the modal averages of Pixie work times. Occasionally, he offered a suggestion, and Lauka scribbled it down.

Kratitha zipped out of the male's room, leading the way to the hive mother's chamber. There were distant thumps as they walked, and Origon heard the resonances in both the Symphonies of Communication and Power. All of them twitched at the noises, and he stumbled on the flat surface of the tunnel, far more tired than he should be. He needed to take his notes back, but he also knew how much the comfort of a blanket of warm air could help Lauka. Still, if Origon waited too long, the notes would be lost forever. He hoped he could tell when that was. Rarely in his training in the Nether had he been required to make so many complicated changes so close together. But this was what he had wanted! Although he was tired, this was far more exciting than struggling under what the Council said he could and could not do. *This* was being a majus.

Kratitha led them ever deeper, and Lauka followed without looking up except to ask a question here and there of Origon. Lauka was close to saving three seconds on each Pixie's routine, and Origon would have stopped to delve into the equations deeper himself, if the noises had not been getting closer. Instead, he bled off the notes he'd used to make the blanket of air. His strength grew as he did, and Lauka didn't seem to notice.

"Many pathways down to Mother," Kratitha said as they walked. These corridors were cooler than the hot dry air outside, as they were deep within the base of the Five Hive Plateau. The thumps echoing down from above were less common this deep in the corridors, but they still caused the three of them to hunch in at each sound.

There were no other Pixies in these passages, whether because they were all higher in the hive, fighting the warriors, or down near the mother, Origon didn't know. In any case, they weren't here.

The distance from Lauka's chamber to the hive mother's was not great, and Origon tried to picture the little wingless Pixie scurrying along these passageways to report a discrepancy in this month's work schedule to the mother.

The booming and thumping grew louder again as the corridors of the hive grew increasingly extravagant. Origon drew one thumbnail along a plate of what he thought was pure gold, bolted to the wall.

Kratitha put out a hand and the three of them slowed. "Hush. Close now. Possible that warriors found quicker way down, while we were diverted."

"Will the mother fight?" Origon asked. He tried to imagine a single Pixie holding her own. Certainly there would be guards with her.

But Kratitha shook her head. "Mother is concerned only with governing and creating new Pixies. No time for combat, and...would not be easy anyway. Mother is constantly gestating new grubs. Fortunate she is between litters, but means she is gravid."

Origon could see a doorway a few paces down the hallway, outlined in precious metals and stones. He could only spare a moment to appreciate it as Kratitha pulled him toward and then through. He saw with whom they shared the room.

Close to the door were a pile of engineer-type Pixies, their wings broken. They lay still in death, and puddles of brown blood pooled under them.

"Would have resisted switching allegiance," Kratitha explained. "Too close to Mother." Lauka hunched along behind them, a low groan coming from him at the carnage.

This chamber, in contrast to Lauka's room, was gigantic—easily the biggest in the hive. It was big enough to warrant pillars to keep the ceiling from collapsing.

They crept forward, listening to sounds of metal on metal.

Then a group of Pixies burst from the columns to the left. Origon saw the same differences from the battle above ground. The engineer Pixies were badly outnumbered, outclassed, and outarmed. Before Origon could do anything more than listen to the Symphony, the warrior Pixies cut down the last few guards. He and Kratitha might still have an element of surprise if—

The warriors turned to them, and Lauka shrieked in surprise.

"Hide!" Origon told him. The male Pixie wouldn't be able to stand up to those weapons. Origon wasn't sure he could, either.

Lauka bolted for the cover of the nearest columns as the warriors closed in. They were heavily armored with segmented leather and metal scales over top of their chitin. As they approached, Origon looked at

Kratitha. Her large multifaceted eyes showed little emotion in the way a Kirian's would, but Origon knew she was ready for this fight. Her hands spread, as if feeling the air.

They changed the Symphony at the same time. Origon could hear Kratitha modifying the Symphony of Power, but what she was doing was deeper in the music than he was used to adjusting, the notes passing by too fast. She charged at the soldiers, the blue of the House of Grace around her feet, hands, and wings, and the orange of the House of Power around her body. She was tweaking connections of some sort between the warriors, and they fell out of formation as she barreled through them, slashing out with one hand to knock a cutlass from one warrior's grip.

But she hadn't attracted the attention of all the attackers, and a group turned toward him. Origon raised his hands, though he had never been formally trained in any of the martial arts some beings favored, like the *Fading Hands* or *Dancing Step* schools. Instead he groped through the music of Communication.

These Pixies were organized, and embellished musical phrases showed the coordination in their small hand and wing signals to each other.

Origon backed up, staying a constant distance from the warriors and gauging the notes available to him. He had an idea. It was something he'd first thought of in his university physics class. Most of the species in the Assembly—except maybe the Benish, as their flesh was of a different makeup than the other species—were vulnerable to rapid changes in air pressure. Especially these Pixies, who depended on the air for movement and respiration.

Origon found the melody of the air around the nearest warrior, a turbulent measure, and stripped the notes from it, moving them to a register three octaves higher by dint of a few well-placed notes from his core. It was a rapid change—almost too quick for him to handle, but his notes snapped into place.

There was an instant where the Symphony rang almost painfully inside Origon's head.

By the ancestors, what have I done?

The warrior exploded in a burst of freezing blue flesh, and Origon fell back.

The two nearest to her remains wobbled in the air, as brown blood leaked from their ear-holes and eyes. Both fell to the floor with a crash and didn't move.

Origon sucked in a deep breath. The cold that chilled him had little to do with the sudden change in the air. He tried and failed to push his crest down, then reached up with a shaking hand and flicked a freezing chunk of...something...from his cheek.

I will not be throwing up.

He hadn't meant to make such a large difference in pressure. He hadn't meant to kill them, just to disorient and maybe knock them out.

If you had not been killing them, they would have killed you.

He knew what went wrong. He only had to lessen the difference in the notes' frequency, and there would not be so much pressure difference, especially *inside* a person. If he ever tried that again, he'd be prepared. He wouldn't kill anyone else.

Origon contemplated fainting for a moment, then straightened. Kratitha and Lauka were still in danger. He should have thought of the possibility of death before coming here, but that feather was already plucked. His crest fanned out wildly as his breathing sped up.

He held his breath, then blew it out, turning away from the remains on the floor. This scene would haunt his dreams, but he couldn't dwell on it now. He'd suffer through those nightmares later.

Origon watched Kratitha, who was halfway down the immense hall, a trail of bodies behind her. She was certainly no stranger to death. He had to move. Origon lifted one boot and half walked, half leaped forward in the homeworld's weak pull. It got easier the farther he got from the death.

The Mother's throne was a hulk at the other end of a long hall. As he watched, Kratitha spun in the air, wings buzzing, as a pike thrust through the space where she'd been. She landed in an aura of blue, caught the weapon, and spun it toward a second attacker. The pike glowed an orange visible only to a majus, and Kratitha jammed it through the smallest crack in the warrior's scale armor. It opened the way as it went in, plunging through her body and exiting out the other side. Origon swallowed at her violence.

Kratitha dropped the handle of the pike as she spun back to the first attacker, jamming one hand tensed like a knife through one of the warrior's compound eyes. The warrior shrieked and fell back.

Origon glanced around. Out of the original nine warriors, none were left near him. He had beaten—killed—three, and Kratitha took another five in the same time period.

Which meant there was one more. Kratitha jerked and sped forward. He followed. She must have reached the same conclusion.

As they got closer, Origon realized what he thought was the mother's throne was the hive mother herself, sitting on an ornamented stool. She was nearly as large as Origon—twice as big as the Pixies he was familiar with. Behind her she had another appendage, like a stubby tail, but it throbbed under the blade of a sharp-looking cutlass, held by the last warrior, standing behind the mother on her throne. From the extra tassels and silver highlights on her armor, she must be the leader of this invasion. The mother had not called out, as the warrior also had a short knife pressed under her chin.

"Drop weapons. Will render her sterile," the warrior leader threatened, tightening her grip on the hilts of both blades. That explained what the appendage was. Origon wondered why the threat was to her egg-producing section, and not about the knife under her throat, but Kratitha dropped the dagger she'd picked up. This fierce majus was capitulating so easily?

"Can grow it back," Kratitha whispered to him, perhaps seeing his confusion. "But new Pixies she makes will be based on attitude at time of growth. Will no longer be the hive of engineers."

Well that would never work. Origon pushed away thoughts of the bodies lying in the hall on the way here. He had to do something.

He addressed the warrior in the trader's tongue. "Will the official censure of the Council of the Maji not be dissuading you from taking over this hive? Both of us are maji." He gestured between himself and Kratitha. She spared him a look, but he had not said he represented the Council. Let the warrior draw her own conclusions.

The warrior rubbed her wings together, making a disparaging sound. "Have no time for Council. They do not play in Pixie politics. Have our own maji, anyway. Warrior's hive is strong."

"Mother, are you unharmed?" Kratitha asked. She glared at the warrior. "Let her speak. Won't sing while you threaten gestation section."

The warrior hesitated only a moment before nodding and removing the knife from the mother's throat. "No singing, or I cut this off." The cutlass waved toward the appendage behind the mother.

"Daughter," the hive mother said in a deep, resonant voice, and Kratitha snapped to attention. "Can rebuild, in another place. Give sister's daughter what she wants."

"But new sisters will not be engineers, Mother," Kratitha said. "Will be civil war until one side wins."

"Yet we will live," the mother said. Her voice was low and soothing. Origon felt it in his toes, and listened to the Symphony of Communication. There was a turbulent cadenza buried deep within. Was this the control the hive mother had over Pixies in her vicinity? What did they mean about singing?

Even the warrior paid attention when the mother spoke. Yes, Kratitha spoke of the members of this hive "converting" to the viewpoint of whichever mother controlled them. It must be how so many hives fell under the warrior's influence. Origon would have to study this later, preferably with a majus of the House of Healing. Origon stilled one shaking hand on his leg. The analysis helped him forget the sight of the Pixie exploding into bits of flesh.

Don't think about it.

He watched the warrior leader sway just slightly. How long could she keep her loyalty in this inner sanctum of the engineer's hive?

"Make choices quickly," the warrior said, and lifted her blade for the strike that would sever the gestation section of the mother. Aha. Not long, it seemed. Everyone here but him knew exactly how long it took to convert an enemy soldier. It was like when another species tried to compete in a Kirian philosophical debate. They did not understand the unspoken rules.

"Will not let you take yet another hive," Kratitha said, "No matter what Mother tells you." The aura of the House of Grace surrounded her, though the other two wouldn't be able to see it. She must have a plan. Origon could give her time with a distraction.

"Why is the warrior hive to be attacking the others anyway?" he asked.

"Is their drive," the mother said. "Seek to protect, as we strive to build and understand. But has grown and warped over the centuries. Used to be a good thing. But protection has grown into conquering." The mother's voice was soothing. Origon could see the warrior struggling not to fall under its sway. "Warriors first clashed with religious-minded hive. Won, but the feedback and conflict between two mothers mutated. After, warriors expanded too far, too fast. Now they come for us. Think with technology the Assembly of Species offers, no need for engineering Pixies any longer."

The glow around Kratitha centered on her prosthetic wing, and straps slackened. The House of Grace was best at making things more efficient and making objects operate easier. But in this case, he had no idea why she would be loosening her wing.

"Make choices now," the warrior called, and waited only a split-second before raising her cutlass. "Too long!"

As the blade swung down, time slowed for Origon. Several things happened at once.

Kratitha spun, throwing the loose wing with the momentum of her body. Origon just barely got to the correct measure in the Symphony of Communication in time. He plucked one more of the notes from his core to make a breeze. The wing was designed to fly, and it took little effort to control the surface as a projectile.

The wing struck the warrior, knocking her backward, the cutlass shimmering in the lights of the hall as it rose into the air. It reached the top of its arc, hung, and plunged down toward the hive mother's gestation section. Origon's eyes widened, his crest spiking in fear. He imagined a sword piercing the belly of a Kirian woman, gravid with an egg.

But none of them were paying attention to Lauka. The male Pixie sprang with a scream from cover behind a thick, carved bench, his satchel clasped in both hands above his head. There was equipment inside, not just papers, for it contacted the falling cutlass solidly, diverting the weapon with a meaty *thunk* into the warrior's belly. She twitched, and dropped, wriggling around the metal pinning her to the floor.

Lauka stumbled toward the corpse as if he would fall on it, his bag raised again, but the Mother turned with more speed than Origon would have thought possible, and brought her clawed foot down on the warrior's head with a *crunch*. Her leg blocked the male Pixie from coming any closer.

"Come to me," she said, and Lauka looked from the corpse to the hive mother, then sprang into her arms, the top of his head pressed firmly against hers. They stayed that way for a long moment, until Kratitha moved to retrieve her wing, and Origon discovered he could breathe once again.

"Not safe yet," she said. Origon helped her tie the wing back on, tracing the harnesses which coiled around her body. This close, he could see the veins of blue, green, white, and brown in the prosthetic. There were at least four houses of the maji included in this architecture. It was a fantastically complicated System—a collection of changes to the Symphony held in place by the House of Potential. "More warriors coming," Kratitha said, shooing his hands from their investigation of the contraption. "This was surprise strike, meant to decimate Mother, but larger army will arrive and convert."

"We will go. The back passage." The Mother rose to her feet and Origon, for once in his life, found he had to look *up* to make eye contact with a standing Pixie. His crest flared in nervousness.

She put Lauka down, and the male Pixie patted her hand affectionately, gathering the satchel onto his shoulder again. "Must retune efficiency calculations," he said. "Intrusion of warriors will interfere with response times."

"I fear you may have to redo all your calculations," Origon told him. "I cannot be certain how long until you will be able to return here."

Lauka frowned, for once looking into Origon's face. "Then calculations will take quite a while."

The mother did not fly, though her wings buzzed. There were not much larger than a normal-sized Pixie's. Maybe they helped her keep her feet, even in the lesser pull from this homeworld. There was little question why hive mothers never visited the Nether. She would collapse under her own weight.

Kratitha, her wing now reattached, flew in front of the mother and spun in the air. "Maji first. Will be more warriors at the back passage, surely." She looked over the Mother's shoulder to Origon. "You will help, yes?"

She was relying on him. Finally, recognition. Once Origon returned with the grateful hive mother's thanks, the Council would have to listen to his pleas for them to be more involved with the ten species. His crest rose, and he stumped around the hive mother and Lauka. "I will help. It was to be my intention from the beginning to stop this senseless war as much as I was able."

"Good," Kratitha answered. "Keep alert."

They left the back of the mother's chamber and up a sloping tunnel just big enough for Origon and the mother to pass through. It was steep, aiming directly for the surface. At first, there were intersecting corridors, then only dirt and stone, with little ornamentation to tell this connected to the hive mother's chamber.

"Made for quick passage," Kratitha said as they half-crawled up the passage. The mother was making good time, though her gravid appendage throbbed in time with her labored breathing. Origon hoped he wouldn't be required to carry the giant Pixie. It wouldn't be...dignified.

Fortunately, they rose quickly, with neither incident from outside forces nor from the mother and Lauka. The male Pixie seemed contented to walk by the hive mother, occasionally touching her hand or shoulder as if to confirm she was still there. At least he had resigned himself to completing his calculations later.

"Not hurt?" he asked at one point, and the mother responded with a negative. "Have surgical tools with me, in case."

Origon's hopes rose as they did. Perhaps they would escape without incident. Now that would be a story to tell the other maji back at the Spire.

Above them, a square of orange light grew, and the tunnel grew warmer. Origon could practically feel the sun beating down on his crest. Dry and scratchy feathers would be worth seeing the hive mother off to safety. He was visualizing how Kratitha might sponsor some of his ideas to the Council. Surely the elder majus had more clout in the House of Power than he did...

They emerged from the tunnel to find a thousand waiting warriors.

Origon froze, his crest spiking. His dreams of showing the Council what he had done evaporated as quickly as the moisture in his feathers. He looked to Kratitha, whose hands were clenched in front of her. She looked as if she might dive directly into the army, but not even the House of Grace could save her from that.

Origon felt himself pushed to the side as the mother strode out from their protection. Lauka was riding on her shoulders, yelling at the warriors. He brandished a short dagger he'd gotten somewhere.

Kratitha was the first to move, but Origon found his feet and surged after her, letting the notes of the Symphony of Communication flow through his mind. There was so much going on. Should he try the pressure trick from the mother's chamber? He knew how to adjust it so it wasn't fatal—he'd never make *that* mistake again.

Origon began the change, then stopped, shaking his head. There were too many soldiers, and the Symphony wouldn't let him repeat the pressure difference too close in time or space. He'd have to find another offensive use of the Symphony. Maji were not taught those.

Then a low soothing cadenza flowed up from the bottom of the Symphony. It wasn't his doing. Was there a majus among the warriors?

He realized what it was. The hive mother was *singing*.

It was a powerful song, though in a range Origon could not physically hear. He tracked its effect in the Symphony as the nearest warriors fell from the air, crashing to their knees, their weapons clattering around them. They were genuflecting. No wonder the warrior kept her from singing in the mother's chamber.

But the song did not penetrate the entire army, and the warriors farther away drew bows, and cocked spears to throw.

"Defend me!" The mother sang, and the words were low enough for Origon to comprehend. Seven warriors sprang into the air, one catching two arrows with her body, only to fall back dead to the ground.

Origon took the opportunity to close the distance, Kratitha buzzing right beside him.

"You take left!" she shouted, and Origon gave a sharp nod, veering to one side of the mother, who was already moving.

The mother cleaved a path through kneeling warriors, some of whom popped back up to defend her. Others stayed on the ground, and still others shook their heads and took up their weapons again when the mother passed.

Origon conducted the Symphonies of Communication and Power with the notes from his core. He could hear Kratitha in the music with him, wrapping connections between warriors in perpetual loops of notes. When they shot projectiles, or slashed at the mother's new honor guard, half the attacks went wide. The rest felled their former sisters.

The air around Origon was wild with his attempts to divert the showers of arrows flying toward them. He felt his chest tighten with the effort of tracking two Symphonies, keeping up with the mother, and not getting stabbed by overzealous Pixies.

He glanced toward the edge of the army. They were making good time, but the mother's stride lessened with each step. What else could he do? The Symphony was resisting his changes. He could only think of so many ways to divert the air. There were only so many combinations of notes.

He twisted at a yell from Lauka. He was bent over the mother's shoulders, and she was holding her middle. The shaft of a spear was sticking from her. The male Pixie reached down, but his arms were too short to touch the spear from his perch. Faster than thought, Kratitha was in front of her, catching her. The mother's song stopped, and the warriors in her impromptu honor guard were slowing, some already shaking their heads.

"The shield!" Origon crowed. He knew there was something he had done, but his travels through the hive had driven it completely out of his head.

He reached deep into the rhythms of the Symphony of Communication to find the melody of a patch of air he hadn't yet touched. The Symphony of Power was easier, as he'd used it less during their fight to give Kratitha free reign.

Origon pressed the heat away from them and into the growing bubble of air as he poured notes into the music. A spear and then a patter of arrows clattered off the hardened air.

"Get her moving!" he yelled, and pushed the mother—carefully—from behind. The shield was just big enough to encapsulate all of them, and it scooted Pixies out of the way as it moved with him.

Lauka hopped down from the mother and pulled at her hand. She was bent forward, limping, but Kratitha held her upright.

Once they shoved past the edge of the army, the going was easier, though Origon felt as if he had lumps of lead attached to his boots. The warrior Pixies largely didn't follow, though a few buzzed around the shield at all times. He risked a look back and saw the ones nearest the hive rising in the air to stab at something beneath. He hoped the engineer-minded Pixies were putting up enough of a fight to let their mother get away.

The next stretch of time was the longest in Origon's life. The effort to keep the shield of air up while they moved was extraordinary. Partway through he felt Kratitha layering her notes on his, bolstering the effect of his change. Even with her help, there would be a point where he could no longer hold the change.

It was another eternity before Kratitha held up a hand. "Enough."

There were only two warriors still buzzing nearby, and Origon kept an eye on them as he gratefully dropped the shield of air and heat. Notes rushed back to him, and he regained a little of his strength, but that was like comparing walking the length of the Nether to doing it twice. Either one was enough to drain you.

Kratitha levered the mother to the ground, then buzzed like a shot toward the warriors. They backed away, turned, and ran. Kratitha came back to them.

"Must attend to her," Kratitha told him. "She is...everything."

Origon bent to the mother's wound. If only he had someone from the House of Healing with him.

Lauka crawled forward, taking a complicated looking device out of his satchel. Origon had last seen it in the glass-fronted case in his room. Lauka raised it to one compound eye and leaned into the shaft piercing the mother's belly.

"Hands here," he said, then when no one moved, he waved an arm toward Kratitha. "Hands here." He pointed to a spot just beside the shaft.

"Can heal her, Lauka?" Kratitha asked as she pressed small hands to the mother's belly.

"Possible," Lauka said, then fell silent. His whole attention was focused on the mother's injury. Origon stood up, watching for more warriors. From the discussion about his efficiency calculation, Origon knew the male Pixie would not rush into something unless he knew he could finish it. They had only to wait until Lauka saved the hive mother. Then Origon could return to the Nether, confident he'd helped.

* * *

"The mother was to be saved, though Kratitha and Lauka were not telling me where they would take her," Origon said. "They advised me to return before they left our improvised campsite that night." His hands were clasped behind his back to hide their nervous twitching. He hoped his crest wasn't lifting again. His gaze flitted down to the carved image on the front of the table. He wondered if the species of the Assembly ever actually worked together as in the depiction. Probably not, as the new figure representing a Lobhl balanced the void where a figure on the other side had been removed by chisel. People regarded the Aridori as little more than terror stories these days.

"I see," said Speaker Karendi, peering down at him from behind the large table in the Spire of the Maji. Her crest was flared out in displeasure.

"We have complaints coming in from the hive mother of the Five Hive Plateau," Councilor Huar grumbled. "Seems they don't much like maji interferin' in their business. As we told you." She pulled her floppy hat tighter on her head

"The warrior hive mother is not to be fully recognized yet by the other hive mounds." Origon raised a finger. "With the engineering hive mother to be safe, there is precedent to—"

Speaker Karendi banged a fist on the top of the table, making the jug of ice water rattle.

"There is *no* precedent for a majus to interfere in a homeworld's internal politics!"

"The maji cannot always stand apart," Origon shot back. "Majus Kratitha—"

"Majus Kratitha, she already has certain...issues in her past record," Councilor Zsaana interrupted, and two of the other six councilors nodded along with him. "She, we do not believe is a good influence, especially for one of your...attitude."

There went any hope of Kratitha sponsoring him in the House of Power.

"Then my good work in this case is to be erased?" Origon asked. "The Council will simply ignore that a Pixie hive mother would have been murdered if I was not to be *interfering*?"

"The Council *cannot* recognize such a flagrant abuse of power," Speaker Karendi said. "Fortunate the Pixie government is not to be bringing a formal complaint before the Assembly. Yet."

Origon leaned onto the front of the table, his hands gripping the top. His curved nails bit into the wood. "So I may be clear: the Council says it does not recognize an act of altruism save if there is political gain from it? Is that the official stance of the maji now?"

"If it serves the greater peace of the Assembly? Yes." Speaker Karendi's crest rose with her voice.

"You are despicable," Origon spat, and as his fingers clenched, he felt a part of the carving crumble under his thumb.

Fitting that the construction is as shoddy as the Council's makeup.

"Be clear, majus," the Speaker said. Her tone was warning, but Origon was past caring. That he had made her crest rise was proof of how much he'd twisted her feathers. "If the Pixie government *does* bring grievances against the maji for this...disaster...you will be addressing them on your own. Without the Council's backing."

Origon only shook his head. He wasn't afraid of the Council or the Pixie government. From what he'd seen, both had too much to fix internally to bother going after one majus.

"For you, there will be a permanent note going in the Council records of your actions," Councilor Zsaana added. "You, you are young. The Council, we hope you will grow out of this...phase."

A phase. Origon pushed away from the table with a bark of a laugh. That's what they thought this was. He'd show them how much of a *phase* wanting to help the homeworlds was.

"Then if we have nothing more to discuss, I will take my leave," he said, letting his crest fluff out in disdain.

"Off with you, pup," Councilor Huar said, and waved a hand at him. "Don't come back here without a good reason."

Origon turned and left silently, his hands clenched into knots. Now he knew the true heart of the Council. But they were old, and he was still young. He had many cycles ahead of him as a majus, and plenty of time to find other maji who shared his views. Other councilors would rise in time. He'd be there to make sure they served the Great Assembly of Species, and not just themselves.

* * *

Back in his apartment, Origon placed the detailed model of the hive on his shelf. It was a gift from Lauka, when the mother came through her field surgery successfully. Why Lauka lugged it from his room, Origon didn't know, but the little Pixie's hands trembled when he'd given it away. Pixies didn't cry—not with those compound eyes—but if they did, he was sure Lauka would have been.

Kratitha promised to see the hive mother to a new place, where she could begin anew. It had been a surprise to see the extra section the mother carried dispense a mass of squirming grubs into the dusty plateau. The stress of the surgery was too much to keep the gravid sack and to keep breathing.

They held a burial for Kratitha's unborn sisters, but Lauka promised the mother would be well after that. The hive mother added her own thanks, her voice weak, but resonant in the Symphony.

Origon hoped a new generation of engineer Pixies could challenge the warriors of the Five Hive Plateau, but it would be many cycles coming. Considering Pixies' life spans, it might even be the mother's successor who came back into the political scene. It wasn't Origon's fight. However, showing the maji the true stripe of the Council's feathers *was*.

Origon had too many eyes on him now to keep track of the Pixies, but he wouldn't have traded this adventure for anything. He knew what maji should do, even if many others didn't. He'd just have to search out the others like him—the ones willing to go out into the ten homeworlds rather than sitting like turtles in their shells here in the Nether.

Tuning the Symphony

984 A.A.W.

PART ONE

Majus

Maji have a long tradition of training suitable apprentices and, after many years of dedication, testing them in pairs to determine the better candidate. There is no rule saying one who can change the Grand Symphony must belong to the maji, but where else would they go? The maji control passage between the ten homeworlds, regulate disputes, and give aid during natural disasters. It is an honor to belong to their order.

—From "The Houses of the Maji," by Ribothari Tan, Knower, later of the Council of the Maji

Rilan Ayama stood at the great crystal wall. It stretched both left and right, taking up the entire fourth side of the testing room, like a tremendous shop window. She was in the largest single chamber in the Spire of the Maji, occupying nearly the entire twenty-first floor, but the room on the other side of the wall was even larger.

Hesitantly, she placed one hand against the cool surface. On the other side, the six councilmembers stood, waiting on the wood floor constructed inside the hollow crystal column adjacent to the Spire. They were the highest ranking maji among the ten species. And they would all be testing her today. Her and Vethis. Only one would come out a full majus after today. The other would wait until the next quarter, though with another apprentice as a challenger. Rilan had heard of poorly testing apprentices waiting for three or four cycles while others were raised in favor of them.

She looked down at the crumpled piece of paper in her other hand. The note had been terse, unsigned, but she knew it was from Origon. How could the man write such a cryptic note, when he talked so much?

Just received news of family matter. May be late. Come see me after. Important decision to discuss.

As if she was raised to majus already, when she still had to test.

She was alone in the testing room, for now. Vethis was late as usual. The audience would file in later, including her and Vethis' mentors. It was a tradition. In a society of ten alien species, coexisting in the

Nether—the common place to which all ten homeworlds connected—traditions were important.

Rilan had read the note over and over since a panting apprentice delivered it to her while she climbed to the testing floor, but hadn't been able to untangle any new information. She shook her head and stuffed the paper back into the pouch at her belt. Origon had promised to watch her test. She hoped he wouldn't be too late. Her insides were twisted in nervous knots quite enough. Vethis was lazy and narcissistic, but he had areas where he outshone her, if she was being honest.

Zsaana, the old councilmember for the House of Healing, her house, beckoned with a gloved claw. It was a perfunctory gesture for her to enter the immense crystal column standing adjacent to the Spire of the Maji, like a tree supporting a slumped bear. Many rooms of the Spire opened to the column. But the column vanished out of sight in the distance above. The Spire was merely forty-two stories tall.

Rilan took a deep breath and pushed her hand gently against the crystal surface, dark flesh against unbreakable material, willing it to give way. She had only passed twice before into one of the columns, big around as buildings, that supported the expanse of the Nether. It was a thing only maji could do, ensuring they were the only ones present inside the column at an apprentice's testing. She listened for the Grand Symphony of the universe, or that portion she could hear. It came after the briefest moment, a single high vibrato string that split into an entire orchestra, and then an orchestra of orchestras. Most of the notes rushed past far faster than she could comprehend. It was the music that underlay the universe. Change one chord, one note of the Symphony, and the universe changed with it.

She let the sound fill her, listening to individual notes and phrases in the melody of the House of Healing. She heard music defining her breath and movement, her skin, and her thoughts. Her senses extended to everything biological within range, from the shifting rhythms and accelerandos of the Councilors, to the brisk notes describing insects living in the wood and stone walls of the Spire. She heard her own song—that composition which both defined her existence and let her change the Grand Symphony of the universe—blend with the column as her hand sank into the crystal surface. Harder than diamond, yet yielding to her, she heard snatches of music making up the essence of the Nether itself.

It was, in some part, also a biological entity. No one knew where it came from, or even where it was located, in relation to the ten homeworlds, but it was where the early maji met others of their kind and began relations between the different alien races. Now it was the heart of the Great Assembly of Species.

She pushed into the outer wall of the column, its material parting before her. Colors sprang into existence, running along invisible paths. Emerald green for the House of Strength. Diamond yellow for the House of Communication. Blazing orange for the House of Power. Cool blue for the House of Grace. Pure white for the House of Healing—her house. And finally Rusty brown for the House of Potential. The column wall was several strides thick and she passed through as if walking through thick syrup.

As Rilan emerged into the open interior column, she sucked in air, though she hadn't felt the need within the wall. A smell of old wood and stale air tickled her nose as she stepped onto the floor built inside the column. It was high above the ground, but there were other floors in the column, above and below, each with its own specific purpose, connecting to a floor in the Spire of the Maji. The bottom of the floor above her was several stories overhead.

The councilmembers were arrayed in a line twenty strides away, and she crossed the distance to them, wiping sweaty palms against her dark leather pants. It was a pair her father made for her by hand. Her dark hair fanned out down her back and she swept a hand along it, trying to coax it to lie in a single bunch. She really should have tied it, but hated the feeling of it all bound up.

Speaker Karendi, head of the House of Communication and de-facto voice for the Council, stepped forward. The Kirian's garish robe flowed across bare knees, her crest of feathery hair flaring to show her welcome.

"I am believing there should be two apprentices testing this day, not just...ah."

Rilan looked over her shoulder to see Fernand Vethis pushing through the wall of the column, looking for a moment like a man suspended in ice. Once through, he tugged at his sleeves, straightening the blue-black crushed velvet coat. He was dressed as if he had just come from a party in High Imperium, with striped pants, white cuffs and cravat. It was a wholly unpractical thing to wear to a test designed to mentally and physically wear out the participant. But fitting, for him.

Vethis grinned as if he had already been chosen to become a majus today. They had been rivals since the first time they met as apprentices. Vethis was from a wealthy family, she from a poor one. He believed the maji were better than everyone. She just wanted to serve the Great Assembly. He was a social-climbing, toadying, power monger. The only reason he hadn't tested before now was he was unforgivably lazy, and preferred to cheat off his peers. He was everything that could be wrong with a majus.

Rilan showed her teeth in what could be construed as a smile by someone who didn't know her. As Vethis came abreast of them, smoothing back his long and oily black hair, Speaker Karendi continued.

"Only one of you will be leaving this chamber as a majus. Apprentice Ayama, Apprentice Vethis, it has been a pleasure for us to be devising these challenges specifically for each of you. Remember, there is always a way to pass each test, even though you are to be pitted against councilmembers." The Kirian's speech was less convoluted than most of her species, trained by cycles of acting as the Council's Speaker to the Great Assembly of Species.

"If you both will be stepping this way, Councilor Huar will be testing Apprentice Ayama first, against the House of Strength. On the other side of the column, Councilor Feldo will be testing Apprentice Vethis, against the House of Potential. The rest of us shall be observing, from a safe distance, of course." Speaker Karendi flashed her pointed teeth, her feathery hair rippling in what the Nether interpreted as anticipation. The Nether's translation of social gestures and language fostered cooperation and understanding, for the most part, keeping all ten species in relative peace.

Rilan drew in a shaky breath. The councilors made the tests unique to each aspiring apprentice, so she and Vethis would not have the same challenges. She didn't want hers to be easy, of course, but she also wanted to pass and become a full majus. Vethis gave her a self-satisfied smirk.

"May the best man win," he told her. Rilan stared back. She hated his clipped, affected accent.

"Or woman." Maybe she wouldn't mind if her tests were easier than his. She turned away. Better to concentrate on her own evaluation. Put the irritating man out of her mind.

Rilan found the head of the House of Strength and bowed. Councilor Huar bowed back slightly, then smiled, teeth open and tongue out. The massive Festuour was dressed in only a bandolier of pockets across her furry green-brown chest, a pair of glasses perched on her long snout in front of bright blue eyes, and a massive floppy pink hat sitting astride her ears.

"Come on girl. We have a match. I wanted to get yours in special, before I retire."

Huar led Rilan to a large table with two chairs, set near the far wall of the hollow column. Across its diameter, larger than most buildings, Rilan saw the other councilors watching, each at their own post. Vethis was chatting comfortably at Councilor Feldo, who seemed to be frowning back. Behind them, she could see foggy glimpses of the Imperium city, capital of the Nether, outside the translucent walls opposite the Spire of the Maji. She chewed her lower lip, heart hammering against her ribs.

"Now, I suppose we should do this formal-like." The Festuour settled her girth in the chair on the far side of the table, behind a collection of tiny pots and vines. "Sit, sit. Don't stand there gawking."

Rilan sat on a wooden chair opposite the councilor, somewhat heavily. She wrinkled her nose at the smell of dirt and decay. On her side of the table was a collection of vermin, tiny furry or scaled jaws gaping in death, collected from alleys of Imperium city. There were ten of them, each fitted with a small humming talisman.

The councilor touched a button on the side of the board and the little vermin started to twitch, crawling spastically forward. Rilan started at the sudden animation. "I, Councilor Jasrimopobt Huar, Grower, head of the House of Strength, challenge you to overcome my test and show yourself worthy of the House of Healing. Break my defenses."

Councilor Huar gestured three-fingered hands, her ears cocking forward, sliding across her pink hat's brim. An emerald green aura enveloped her as she changed notes in that part of the Grand Symphony she could hear. Rilan knew the House of Strength dealt with physical strength, of course, but also constitution, growth, and sustenance. It also dealt with living beings, overlapping somewhat with musical phrases from Rilan's house.

The plants in front of the councilor perked up as she adjusted the Symphony. A vine stretched forward and snapped at a crawling lizard that spasmed in range, throwing it back to Rilan's side of the table. She narrowed her eyes at the board, nervousness fleeing.

As vines reached forward, grabbed a furry scrounger, and tore it in half, Rilan opened herself to the Symphony. Fractal orchestras tumbled through her mind and she waded through the musical phrases. Some were too fast for her to understand before the tune played out. Her skill lay more in the mental side than the physical. She was training to become a psychologist, not a medical doctor, as Vethis was.

There was a complex musical phrase controlling the dead things. Since she could hear it, it must be of the House of Healing. Rilan guessed it had been stored by a majus of the House of Potential in the talismans attached to the creatures' backs. Otherwise, the music would have faded away by now.

A large flower scooped down, holding another lizard hostage. Down two creatures. Rilan found the melody defining musculature and bone density, taking a moment to understand the tempo and rhythm. Without doing so, a majus might fail to effect a change correctly. She inserted notes taken from her own song into the Symphony, increasing the tempo, making notes forte that were previously piano, increasing their intensity. The white glow of the House of Healing encircled her fingers as the creatures crawled faster, dodging the snapping vines. Rilan spared a glance to see Councilor Huar's large tongue caught between her fleshy lips. The plants sped up in response.

Rilan would not be able to make the same change twice in the same way, but neither could the councilor. The universe resisted changes to the Symphony, and if a majus tried to repeat the same change either before enough time had passed or while too close to the original change, it would fail.

Instead, she flexed her fingers like she was grabbing something, and caught the music defining the creatures' skin, using her song to change it. The white aura around her fingers was joined by her secondary color, only just starting to appear. The colors, indicative of the house, were only visible to a majus. Flecks of dull olive green sparkled in the white aura.

The lizard-like creatures shuddered, scales growing and toughening to protect against vines and sticky flowers. Huar's green of the House of Strength began to show her own secondary color, the hue of peach flesh, as she put forth more effort. Each majus had a secondary color, and as the majus grew in experience, the unique color grew bolder, like a magical personality.

The vines thickened in response. Rilan grew sharper teeth on her rodents. The flowers reactions became more efficient.

Another lizard was plucked away and thrown off the table.

Evolve, defend, repeat.

Rilan adjusted the vermin's response to her commands, but they were thrown back again.

Her mentor told her never to go against the House of Strength head-on, and now she believed him. She couldn't win that way. But she threw six of her seven remaining creatures into a desperate rush, straight toward the plants.

Huar watched them so intently Rilan saw her miss the seventh creature, a little furry thing, scamper under the side of the table. She worked furiously to change the melody, rearranging internal organs, making room for chemicals to mix in ratios a body should never have.

As the vines and flowers pushed her vermin back, the little furry saboteur crawled over the far side of the table, behind Huar's line of plants. Its body shifted, muscles squirming under flesh. It stopped behind the center of the councilor's defense, and with a tiny squeak, exploded.

Rilan's other creatures rushed through the hole of burnt plant fiber.

Councilor Huar sat back with a puff of air. Rilan reversed the changes she had made to the Symphony, feeling her song flow back to her, and the rest of the vermin began drifting aimlessly, back to their original condition. Each person had their own song, and each song only had so many notes. Maji were careful to make changes that could be reversed. If a majus instead made permanent changes to the music, notes of their song would be lost until they slowly grew back, based on individual experiences. Until then, the majus would be less able to effect complex changes, their song no longer whole.

"Mighty fine," the councilor said. She swept her massive hat off and dabbed at the fur underneath, patting it back into place. "That's me beaten, fair. Go on now, see what the speaker has in store for you."

Rilan stood up shakily and nodded to the councilor. She glanced past to see the light outside the column was darker than before. Vethis was already with the head of their house, Councilor Zsaana. The two were bent over a table, and though she could see flashes of white light, they were too far away for her to hear the changes in the Symphony. What mattered was that he was ahead of her. Did that mean he had done better?

She walked toward Speaker Karendi where she stood at a podium, slowing her steps to sneak a look into the Spire of the Maji. The room on the other side of the column wall was starting to fill up with maji and other apprentices. She didn't see Origon, and made an effort to relax her shoulders.

Come on, Origon, you've been waiting for this test as much as I have. His tardiness was not helping her stress level.

The head of the Council coughed to get her attention, and Rilan looked away from the crystal wall. "I am to be the Speaker Mareveluchi Karendi, head of the House of Communication. I am challenging you to defeat my test and show yourself as being worthy of the House of Healing. Overcome my speech." She stepped behind the podium, looming over Rilan. It hid her bright robe, pink and brown with yellow accents. The Kirians, of which the speaker and Origon were both members, were known for their garish dress.

Rilan felt a knot of worry forming in her stomach. Kirians were also famous for their public speaking and discourses on philosophy.

"Why are you here?"

"Um." Rilan adjusted to the new test as she looked into the speaker's gray eyes and pointy smile. "To become a majus."

"Why?"

Rilan swallowed. Her throat was constricted. A subtle yellow light, flecked with dark brown specks, surrounded the speaker. Yellow for the House of Communication, brown for the majus' personal color. "I want to use my ability to help...people." She had to swallow in between words. How was this a test of her house? "I'm going to become a psychologist."

Was it a mental challenge of some sort? That was her strength, and Speaker Karendi knew it.

"Do you think the House of Healing is needing one of your abilities? Why are you unique? Would not Apprentice Vethis be a better choice?"

Rilan fought to push words out. It was getting hotter and the air felt like molasses. "I'm the...best in my class...I can change the Symphony...in ways they can only imagine..." She sagged. It was a strain merely to speak. She could barely draw breath and her vision was fogging. The speaker was doing something to the Symphony of the air, the medium of communication, changing its density or—

"Are you so arrogant to think you are being better than maji who have studied longer than you have been alive?"

The words had a force behind them, driving into her brain. What was she worth, really? Speaker Karendi was affecting her, persuading her. A two pronged attack. She struggled to hear the Symphony.

"Why are you able to hear the music when there are so many who cannot do this?"

She *could* hear the Symphony. She had since she was a child. Focus.

"I can...hear the Symphony...because I am unique...I—" Her words choked off and Rilan diverted effort into listening. There it was, very faint, the cloud of impulses that was Speaker Karendi. Chords flashed by, almost too quick to hear.

"If you are being so unique, give me the correct answer to this question. You are Speaker for the Council. Your species has gone to war against the Lobath, but you know they are in the wrong. How do you advise the Great Assembly?"

Rilan shook her head. She thought furiously over the answer while she put the notes of her song into in a Symphony the speaker couldn't hear.

"I must stay neutral in my answer, not favoring either side."

Pheromones were the answer, subtly influencing. She could do pheromones.

"You did not answer the question. Give me a definite solution."

The speaker pounded her with unsolvable dilemmas, unfair rulings, and tempting but unethical situations. Rilan devoted as much of her mental attention as she dared to the questions, answering as best as she could, gasping through the alternating thin and thick atmosphere. With the other part of her attention, she changed notes. Attraction. Distrust. Fight. Flight. Fear. Confusion. The notes were familiar to her. She had worked with many other apprentices, practicing her skill at mental healing.

"A Sathssn has been caught killing another of her species..." Speaker Karendi shook her head. "...But there is evidence that points to..." She raised a liverspotted hand to her head, smoothing back the crest of feathery hair that popped up in sudden apprehension. Rilan took a quick step forward, closing the distance between them. She touched the speaker, and a new Symphony exploded in her head, the kind that was only available in very close quarters. Rilan changed the speaker's mind.

Karendi's stern demeanor fell away at once and the pressure against Rilan's vocal chords ceased.

"I find I am unable to be competitive against you." She smiled pointily. Rilan had momentarily blocked her sense of ambition, simply a matter of changing notes defining the way the brain's receptors fired. "Well done." The smile faltered. "I am assuming this will dissipate soon?"

"In a few moments, Speaker," Rilan said. She began disassembling the changes she had made, regaining the phrases of her song. That little bit that was not reversible would replenish with a good night's sleep.

"Then you will be testing against the House of Power. I believe I will be checking with Councilor Zsaana just in case, to make sure there are no lasting effects."

Rilan bowed and moved on, walking around the perimeter of the column. Two down, four to go. She wondered if that was the way she had been supposed to complete the test. It had taken less time than the first. Vethis was just finishing his test with Zsaana. Had he done better than her? *Was* there a right way?

She looked to the other side of the column again. Had their whole class of apprentices showed? Certainly Vethis' gambling and drinking buddies were there. Were any there for her, or had they all come to cheer Vethis on? She had fewer friends than he, and fewer her own age. One in particular was still missing. Where was Origon?

Her next challenge was from the head of the House of Power, a corpulent Lobath who had occupied the post since before she was born. Though he was near sixty cycles old, he was still the craftiest on the

Council. It was appropriate, as the House of Power dealt with connections, relations, power structure, as well as heat and fire.

This time, she was to beat the house head at Hidden Chaturan, something specifically suited to the House of Power. One who could see the relations between things had a much easier time of determining where the pieces were hidden under the board.

Rilan struggled against the crafty Councilor while the light outside the column slowly died. Where was Vethis? Was he doing better than she? A quick glance around told her the oily man was finishing up with the councilor for the House of Grace. She was lagging behind. And on top of that, Origon was still not here.

The councilor moved another piece off Rilan's edge of the board. "That is not your test, apprentice, this is. Stop looking away."

Rilan pulled her gaze away from the wall, and back to the board. Of course the councilor would see that connection as well—her nervousness about Vethis and Origon. She tried to hold the whole board in her mind, but it was impossible, with the confounded rotating hatches hiding pieces.

Finally, she beat the Councilor, barely, and only by using the Symphony of Healing to follow the Lobath's movement impulses. He sat back with a groan, wiping a bead of sweat from between the base of his head-tentacles. "A rousing game, apprentice. If you are up for another game of Hidden Chaturan in the future, look me up. Now, off to the House of Grace."

Rilan stood, stretching, and took a few steps to wake up her legs. She had no idea how long she had been sitting at the little table, and turned to find Vethis in front of her. They were both standing near the center of the column.

"Finally done, Ayama? Took you long enough." Vethis adjusted his crushed velvet coat, though it looked in better order than her shirt, wrinkled from sitting at the table for so long. "I don't see that ratty old professor you hang around—the one no one likes?" Vethis made a show of looking around in surprise. "In fact, did anyone come here to see you besides your own mentor?"

Rilan resisted the urge to hit him. The best way to deal with Vethis was to ignore him. Anything else would only rile up the fop.

"At least I didn't have to pay my friends to attend." *So much for staying silent.*

"Aaahaha." Vethis gave his fake laugh to go with his affected accent. It was the way the richer echelons of High Imperium spoke. "Well, as they say, at least I can *afford* to have friends." He gave her a condescending smile. "Tests going well for you? Fortunately I got the harder part done first. Just need to coast through the rest. Watch out for Councilor Zsaana—I think the old snake has it in for those of his own House. He did some things with the House of Healing I'd never seen before."

Rilan thought of the way she passed the speaker's test, and how she barely scraped by against the House of Power. Surely Vethis wouldn't do better than her, but then the tests were different for each apprentice.

"I'll do just fine," she told him. "After all, I studied for this."

"Yes, top marks in the class and all that. Of course, sleeping with your philosophy professor probably helped."

"I didn't—" Rilan clenched her fists. Vethis would take anything she said about Origon the wrong way. "At least my father didn't buy my grades for me."

"No, I don't believe he's ever seen that much money in his life." Vethis waved his hand as if to shoo her along, the lace at his wrist fluttering limply. "Can't stay to talk, I'm due to be raised a majus, after all." He headed to the table where the head of the House of Power still sat.

"You can't bribe the councilors," Rilan called after him. She *hoped* he couldn't bribe the councilors. She sighed.

Rilan glanced across the translucent column and saw the crowd in the connecting room in the Spire of the Maji. As she moved to the next station, the figures on the other side became clearer. Her eyes flicked over Farha Meyta, her mentor, and she frowned. Where was Origon? He should have been front and center at her test. He had been talking about her transition to full majus since her graduation from university. Surely news of his family could wait a little longer.

She pursed her lips and gathered her hair back with both hands. She was distracted, and in addition, Vethis had made her doubt herself. She knew it objectively, but that didn't actually help the queasy feeling in her stomach. Her psychology training wasn't helping her now.

She had to put all this out of her mind, or it would hinder her test. Either Origon would show or he wouldn't. And if he didn't, she prayed Vish would give him strength to heal quickly from what she would do to him.

The Etanela who was head of the House of Grace was immensely tall, even for one of her species. Rilan felt her back straighten as she strained for an extra finger's-breadth of height. The councilor bowed down to speak to Rilan, the bluish cast of her skin transitioning to the pale blue-blond mane of hair all around her head and long neck.

"Are you ready, apprentice?" she asked. Rilan nodded. They were at a roped obstacle course, dotted with little paper flags. The Etanela crouched down and smoothed her mane of hair, affixing it with a short length of string behind her neck. Her fingers tied a complex knot in the string with ease, fingers glowing slightly with the blue of her house.

Showoff.

Rilan crouched next to her, wondering what the signal would be to start. Would there be a—

A horn blared and the councilor was off, long legs taking steps five times hers. Rilan puffed after her. *Did Vethis have to do this? He couldn't have been so put together if he'd just run a race.*

This was a test of the physical, how the efficiency of the House of Grace could compare against the body-changing aspects of the House of Healing. Just like the other tests, she would not win if she stayed on the defensive. Rilan reached mentally while she ran, trying to hear the chords defining the councilor's legs. They jangled and went in and out of hearing. She grabbed at the notes as she could, trying to slow the Etanela down. Physical changes from a distance with the House of Healing were not her specialty. She was better at the mental aspect. At least training with her father prepared her for the exertion. Breathe in through the nose, controlled pulse out through the mouth. Repeat.

The obstacle course was not easy, and she barely stayed abreast of the councilor, even with the changes she effected. The councilor flowed through the obstacles, meanwhile, she bumbled through, moments behind, looking like a horse swimming next to a dolphin.

When the end of the course came up, she tried to tally things in her head. Had she hit five flags or six? She was nearly certain the councilor had touched nine, all with her help. Otherwise the tall woman wouldn't have touched one.

Speaker Karendi was waiting at the exit to the race. Rilan bent forward, resting hands on knees to get her wind back. She took in long sweet breaths, then undid the changes she still held, regaining her song. The Etanela wasn't even breathing hard. Her long arms were clasped behind her back. Who knew the councilor had such a competitive streak, especially for one of her placid race? At least it had kept Rilan from thinking about who was—and was not—watching. She looked over to the table at the House of Power. Vethis was still bent over the board with the Lobath Councilor. Maybe she didn't do too badly.

"You were having a lag of six seconds, apprentice," Speaker Karendi said, "However, the Head of the House of *Grace,*" she gave a sardonic pointy smile, "touched four more flags. I will be calling this test a tie. Your next challenger is Councilor Zsaana."

Rilan bowed to the two councilors, still panting a little, and straightened. Three wins and one tie, out of six houses. How had Vethis done? The final decision could go against her, even with all wins. A tie wasn't good. The next house was hers, but Vethis' warning flashed through her head. She had hoped for an easy win from the House of Healing.

She glanced to her growing audience. Still no Origon. This was more than just lateness, but she couldn't afford to think about him. After the test. Then she would find out what was going on. She tried to concentrate, but her stomach felt like it was twisting into knots.

Councilor Zsaana was standing in the middle of a circle painted on the floor, ten paces across. His face, as always, was hidden under his deep black cowl. Personally, she found his cat eyes and scaly skin unnerving, though the last time she had seen him without a hood was cycles ago. The shorter councilor stood with a hunch from age, gloved hands clasped behind his back, not a bit of skin showing. The only bright color on him was the small patch on the breast of his cloak, marked with the white of the House of Healing and the turquoise of his personal color.

As she stepped in the circle, his gravelly voice issued from the depths of his cowl: "I, Councilor Zsaana, head of the House of Healing, challenge you to overcome me. In this test, show yourself worthy of my house. Move me out of the ring."

He stepped back, front heel lifting, toe of his boot just touching. One gloved hand came forward, raised, palm up in front of his chest. The other now pointed down, warding off a blow. Rilan recognized the stance from the art called *Dancing Step* and automatically moved into the form of *Fading Hands*, the art she studied, her hands ready to catch or twist.

After the race? Really? Breathe in through the nose, out through the mouth. Conserve energy. Don't think about Origon. The familiar fighting form comforted and relaxed her. Maybe this wouldn't be so hard after all.

She moved forward in a straight line, but the councilor shifted off at an angle. This would not be a normal sparring match, not between two members of her house.

White and turquoise surrounded the councilor, but Rilan could hear the changes in the Symphony this time. Did those notes describe balance? Yes, and leg strength, she decided. The councilor was quick, shifting through measure after measure of the melody describing his body faster than she could even process the notes. He had cycles of experience over her. The speaker said the tests were made to be passed, but this was pure experience and skill. Rilan pushed the worry away— pushed all her worries away.

The councilor sprang, quicker than thought. One hand locked against hers, forcing it out while the other popped against her chest. She exhaled as she was pushed back, stopping just at the edge of the circle.

Rilan shook her head, adjusting her stance and then the Symphony, tightening musical phrases to freshen muscles tired from the race. It was a permanent use of notes from her song, and she would only be able to do it once, but it would give her more endurance for this fight. Losing that bit of her song was worth it. She stalked forward and the councilor moved back, keeping the distance between them the same. Rilan leapt.

Bone crunched against bone, hardened like steel.

The two circled, reassessing strengths and weaknesses.

The councilor's arm lengthened, muscles stretching past their normal limits to land a strike.

The straight lines of *Fading Hands* intersected the circular arc of *Dancing Step*.

Rilan caught a boot before it contacted her sternum, but only by increasing her reaction time.

Her hand moved a punch aside, twisting it so the councilor went backwards. But he snapped straight up, black cloak flapping, driving a punch that just brushed her nose as she pulled away from it.

Rilan staggered back, nose stinging and eyes watering. She sniffed back blood, then countered. Councilor Zsaana sidestepped it easily.

She was on the defensive again. This was her house, but she had to be better than its leader, who had forty cycles more experience. She scowled and ducked a backfist.

This wasn't a physical challenge. It was a mental one.

She studied the melody defining her opponent's mental state. This was her specialty, and she could understand more of the music from a distance than most. Add to that the closeness and understanding of sparring with someone, and she had a clear picture of what the councilor was thinking. They circled, trading blows that tested the other's defense.

He was calm, collected, and completely in charge of his situation. There was no place for her to start making changes without him noticing instantly. He'd either counter it or shrug it off.

She adjusted melodies in her body, the white and olive glow around her brightening. Councilor Zsaana's attacks increased, seeking every hole in her defense as he saw her rewriting the Symphony. She had to hope he was not as familiar with mental changes as physical ones.

Rilan's perceptions began to slow as she inserted the adjusted music made of her own song back into the Symphony. Zsaana's movement sped up to her eyes. She felt a rib creak as his gloved hand struck, palm forward. She was pushed back, but managed to recover, her thoughts fuzzy. Zsaana was moving like a projection at double speed and she backed up farther, desperately warding off strikes.

A booted toe touched a pressure point in her leg and she wavered to that side with a grunt. He circled and the next punch came at an oblique angle, just grazing his glove's leather against her chin. One of her teeth bit into her cheek.

She saw him gather for the last strike—the one that would push her backward out of the circle. Her mind was foggy now, and slow, like cold honey. There was something she had to remember, more important than anything else. It was a simple sequence of notes.

Oh yes.

She reversed what she had done, gaining the phrases of her song back.

As the councilor sprang forward, her mind cleared, her reactions increased, and she saw the opening she would not have before.

Councilor Zsaana struck, but Rilan spun to the side much faster than she had moved before, taking a stance from *Dancing Step*. She caught a flash of surprise in the cat's eyes deep under his hood as Zsaana flew past her, landing with the toe of one boot outside the circle.

Rilan turned to him and bowed. Councilor Zsaana gave a respectful tilt of his cowled head in return.

"Your technique, it has improved, but do not depend on such deception to save your life. It is risky. You are ready for your last test, apprentice."

Rilan walked to the only section of the testing area she hadn't yet visited, near where the Spire of the Maji met the wall of the column. Back across its width, Vethis was face to face with Speaker Karendi. She held on to the hope that he couldn't find a way to cheat his way through this test.

Outside, it was nearly full dark in the city. In the Spire of the Maji, she saw the crowd of onlookers craning to see her actions. Her eyes roamed the various maji and apprentices in vain.

Where is he?

She directed a raised eyebrow to Farha Meyta, but her mentor only shook his balding head. He didn't know either.

Rilan faced the last councilor.

The head of the House of Potential stared back impassively from under bushy black eyebrows, and Rilan finally looked away from the intense gaze. She had to stop thinking about Origon.

"This is the last one, apprentice," he cautioned, his voice resonant. "Keep your wits about you. You will need them."

Rilan glanced down at the worktable between them, holding a contraption made of interwoven gears, levers, and springs. Many separate pieces were clasped together, some with vials of fluids held between metal pistons.

"I, Councilor Mandamon Feldo, head of the House of Potential, challenge you to overcome my puzzle and show yourself worthy of the House of Healing. Disarm my bomb."

Her head jerked back up. Though he was the only councilor of her species, he was harder to read than some of the aliens.

"Time is wasting, apprentice."

Rilan focused on the contraption—the bomb—and swallowed. There were no biological pieces. There was nothing for her to affect with the Symphony. The parts were obviously artifacts made with the House of Potential, many with faint brown auras, storing energy and action in different combinations. They might also store effects from other houses. Each artifact could do something as sinister as suck the air from her lungs, or merely slip from her grasp. There was one way to tell, though she had rarely used that facet of the House of Healing.

Rilan dove into the Symphony, tracing the architecture of the convoluted thing with a finger, listening for the traces every person left in their wake. Far down in the melody there was a crumbling cadenza, the music deteriorated with age. But there was still evidence of fingers and breath touching it in the past, marking its construction. As she was only listening, and not changing, she would be able to do this multiple times. But the moment she used her song to change notes, the universe would close down on that potential for variation.

Rilan closed her eyes, listening to the story the notes told. There was a switch, carefully placed with bare fingers when arming the mechanism, just...there.

She pushed a point on a cubical piece, identical to every other part, and the pistons hissed, releasing the cube's grasp. She risked a glance up, to see Councilor Feldo's eyes trained on her, no expression on his face. His arms were crossed in front of his dark brown suitcoat.

"Do you imagine he'll arrive before you finish your test?"

Rilan frowned. "I have no idea." That wasn't fair. She bent back to her task, trying to focus on the notes. Her mind wandered to all the reasons Origon could be late. Of all the people not to be at her test. He was scattered when he chose to be, but whatever he was to her now; professor, friend...something more...she deserved more respect than this.

Origon, I'm going to kill you when this is over.

She became aware of the councilor's finger, tapping against his other arm, and shook her head, pushing the arrogant man from her mind.

The next part to the puzzle was more complex, having changed hands several times. Finally, she traced down the answer and pressed the correct combination of buttons on its side.

"I imagine even apprentice Vethis could finish this faster." Rilan tried to ignore the councilor's voice.

The next piece was shaped like a clenched hand, fingers closed into the palm. Bare skin had never touched it, and she darted an irritated look at the councilor. He stared back.

She dug even farther into the Symphony. This far down, chords and musical phrases sped by, faster than she could follow. Pieces were incomplete, like listening to one instrument playing something meant for a full orchestra.

She kept on, thoughts of Origon sliding into her concentration, disrupting her test.

So he isn't here. Why should that matter? Maybe he was only interested in a good student. Maybe I read his attentions wrong.

"Focus, apprentice. This is why inter-species relationships are frowned upon. Too much miscommunication."

What did the councilor know about it? Maybe he thought she should be with Vethis instead, just because he was near her own age and her same species? Rilan scowled up at him. Was that worry on his face? She snapped back to her task. Which piece was next?

There were several left, but this puzzle had many dead ends. She chose a clasp holding a box in its middle. It was the most likely to be her objective.

Something held the clasp closed, some infused air pressure captured by a member of the House of Communication. She looked into the Symphony to determine its source, peering past crumbling chords.

Origon had created it.

Her mind whirled, trying to understand. He had even contributed to her test. Why was he not here to see her succeed? Why wasn't—

Something inside the box began smoking.

Councilor Feldo reached out quickly, his hand ringed with the rust-brown color of the House of Potential. As he made contact with the box, the smoke died away, its energy transferred before it could explode.

The councilor flicked the air with a hand and a miniature firework shone sun-bright for a moment as the air heated incandescent, then faded.

"And that would be time, apprentice."

Rilan hung her head.

A few minutes later, she stood in the middle of the circular floor. To her right, lights were shining in the vast city outside the crystal column, especially in the High Imperium, where money and fashion were prevalent. The sons and daughters of senators, speakers, and other diplomats would be playing at cards, drinking wine, and dancing at balls. Vethis was beside her, seeming at ease, his velvet suit as unwrinkled as if he had just put it on.

To her left Farha Meyta still watched her eagerly from the Spire of the Maji, though some of the other spectators were playing card games or talking amongst themselves. Probably Vethis' friends who had grown bored of the tests. All six members of the Council of the Maji spoke amongst themselves in a little circle not far away, but no sound came to them.

"Concerned, Ayama?" Vethis asked. Only one of them would leave this column a full majus. The other would have to wait until the next rising apprentice from the House of Healing was ready.

"Of course not," she answered, though she felt as if she might be sick. Honestly, she was a good student. She shouldn't be worried. The tests were made to be passed. Otherwise she would have no chance to win against the senior maji who had become the heads of their respective houses. Yet she had tied one—barely—and lost another. She had no idea how well Vethis did. He could have been a good student if he applied himself instead of lazing about with his rich friends. It was one of the things about him that annoyed her most.

She looked up as rustling came to her. The councilors filed in a semicircle around her and Vethis, a vast difference in shapes and sizes, from the diminutive Councilor Zsaana to the towering Etanela councilor.

Speaker Karendi stepped forward just a little, used to being the voice of the Council. Her crest of feathery hair bristled, and the Nether translated it to an impression of someone settling a jacket. "We have been discussing your tests, apprentices. Your skills are not being in question. Both of you are having enough talent in the House of Healing to work with any of the other houses in our service of the Great Assembly."

Speaker Karendi looked at Vethis first. "Your natural skill in healing is impressive to several of the councilmembers." Vethis stood straighter at that, smiling.

The speaker turned to Rilan. "And with your talent for hearing and changing the Grand Symphony, you could rise far one day—maybe even to the heights of the Council."

Rilan felt a thrill rise through her. They thought she was that good? Then why were there frowns on some councilors' faces? She waited for the 'but.'

"But," Speaker Karendi continued, "the maji are servants of the ten species. We are creating the portals that connect the ten homeworlds with the Nether and with each other. Without us, there could be no Great Assembly of Species."

Her crest of feathery hair waved as if in a breeze. "Neither of you are yet willing to serve, to ignore distractions that take you away from your work. Apprentice Ayama, you go your own way, around the rules that hold our society together. You must be finding out what it means to be helping its inhabitants, instead. Apprentice Vethis, you are, bluntly, arrogant. You must learn to listen to those who know more than you. You would do well to study with Apprentice Ayama, and vice versa. Each of you could teach the other something. Now, I will be giving over to my fellow councilors."

Rilan frowned at Vethis, and saw the same expression mirrored on his face. *That's never going to happen.* She looked back to the house heads.

Councilor Huar gave a big pink smile, tongue lolling in a Festuour smile. "You passed in my eyes, dear," she said to Rilan. "I'll be up for a rematch anytime." She turned to Vethis, not smiling so broadly. "You passed as well, though next time I wager you'll remember not to challenge the House of Strength head on." Rilan wondered what his test had been. It sounded like the Festuour favored her over Vethis.

Speaker Karendi's crest made a single flat line down the middle of her head. Decisive. "Apprentice Ayama, while your technique may be suspect—I am not enjoying being mentally adjusted—I must pass you on merit alone." She crossed bare liverspotted arms. "Apprentice Vethis, I am afraid you did not measure up to what I expected."

A straight win for her. Rilan felt a little bit of tension leave.

The councilor for the House of Power rubbed at his rubbery mouth with long fingers, watching Rilan. The tips of his three head-tentacles twitched around his shoulders. "Try not to keep the company of *that man* so much. Nothing good will come of such an inter-species dalliance."

Rilan felt her eyebrows climb. How widely known was their relationship? This was the Nether, not a backwards homeworld. Still, she caught a nod of agreement from some of the other councilors out of the corner of her eye. The Lobath councilor looked to his left and the next councilor. It seemed that was all he had to say. What did that mean? Did she pass or did Vethis? She caught her rival frowning as well.

The head of the House of Grace paused for a moment, looking upward from her great height. "A pass for both. There are not many who can rival me at the obstacle course. I am frankly surprised either of you came as close as you did."

Yep. Still an ass. And still no help to decide who would become majus. The twisting feeling in Rilan's stomach returned.

Councilor Zsaana folded gloved hands together, the opening of his hood pointing to Rilan. "Today, I am afraid I cannot pass you." She gaped, and some of the other councilors even looked surprised. "Your technique, it is good, but ineffective. In real combat, with intent to injure, your technique would be impractical and you would be quickly defeated. My vote, it is going to Apprentice Vethis." And after Vethis' report to her, she was sure she had that one locked down. What test had the councilor set for Vethis?

Councilor Feldo glared at her under his bushy eyebrows. His eyes flicked to Zsaana and back to her. "My vote was to fail you and pass Vethis. Before I do that, one question. Apprentice, why did you fail to defuse my bomb?"

Rilan opened her mouth, hesitated. Her first inclination was to say she should have used some better method, but she knew that was untrue. She could tell the way she answered this question would be important, maybe to her future as a majus.

"The truth, apprentice," Feldo warned.

Rilan forced the answer out, but kept her eyes on the floor. "My attachments...no...my *attachment* got the better of me."

"And this is how it will always be." Rilan looked up to Feldo in surprise, and saw Speaker Karendi frown. "Keep that in mind. A pass for Apprentice Ayama."

Rilan blinked.

Speaker Karendi looked her councilors over. "If I am understanding your votes correctly, both Apprentices have passed four of their tests and failed two. In everything, the Council must be unanimous. Which apprentice shall we pass? Please be giving your vote to one or the other."

In turn, each of the councilors gave their answer.

"The House of Strength passes Apprentice Ayama."

"The House of Communication is also passing Apprentice Ayama."

"The House of Power passes Apprentice Vethis."

The tall Etanela councilor hesitated, hands smoothing back her mane of hair. She had been one to pass both of them. Then, "The House of Grace passes Apprentice Vethis."

"The House of Healing passes Apprentice Vethis," Councilor Zsaana growled beneath his dark cowl.

"And the House of Potential passes Apprentice Ayama." Councilor Feldo crossed his arms. "I believe we are tied again, Councilors. Is someone willing to change their vote?"

Several hundred ages of the universe went by, and no one spoke. Rilan's stomach felt like lead, and she pressed her hands to her leather pants to keep them from shaking. She saw Vethis smoothing his coat again and again, though it was as straight as it was going to be.

Gradually, Rilan got the impression of eyes staring at her from under Councilor Zsaana's hood. "My vote, I will be willing to change. Pass for Apprentice Ayama."

Rilan sagged. She heard Vethis stamp a foot, and for once, couldn't blame him. He must be surprisingly competent when testing for them to be tied. He had never been a good student at university.

"Welcome, Majus Rilan Ayama, to the House of Healing," Speaker Karendi intoned. "Henceforth you will be granted all privileges of majus status, including rooms, stipend, and a seat in the Great Assembly. You will also be required to fulfill all duties, including operating portals to the various homeworlds in equal portion to other maji." The speaker let a smile show her pointy teeth. "Congratulations." She turned to Vethis. "Do not let this be disheartening you, apprentice. With such a close test, I am sure you will be making majus next time."

The others followed suit, congratulating her in their various manners, and offering condolences to Vethis. One by one they passed through the wall of the column back into the Spire of the Maji proper, to the applause and commiseration of the waiting crowd.

After that, it was all smiles, and handshakes, and back pats for Rilan. She spoke to all those who had watched from outside the column. Even some of Vethis' friends came over to congratulate her, seeming sincere.

Rilan returned every smile she got, even going so far as to shake hands with Vethis, though he did try to squeeze her knuckles off. Afterward he went to talk with his mentor, a small majus of the House of Healing who earned his living as a medical doctor.

Her own mentor, Farha Meyta, gave her a gift of a small white bell, imbued with a permanent investment of his own song and the Symphony of Healing, held to the bell by the craft of the House of Potential. He said it would ward off disease.

"It has been a pleasure, dear," he said.

"But now please get out of your apartment?"

Farha laughed good naturedly at her joke. "I'll admit, I am ready to be on my own again."

"Maybe you'll finally find a wife," she ribbed.

"Or another insufferable apprentice. I used to have hair before I took you on, you know." They clasped hands again. "Good luck, Rilan—Majus Ayama," he said. "I'm sure we will be seeing each other across the Great Assembly."

Rilan took her leave of her mentor—former mentor, and slowly started pressing toward the exit. She took one last look back at Vethis, who was now talking animatedly with a large Festuour she didn't recognize. He would become a majus eventually, and maybe this would inspire the lazy man to pay attention to his work, but she doubted it.

She headed for stairs down and out of the Spire of the Maji. Despite her forced calm, she was about to jump out of her own head. By Shiv's ponderous earlobes, where *was* that man?

PART TWO

Origon

Inter-species relationships have been contentious since the species initially met in the Nether. From the first time an adventurous Methiemum flirted with an Etanela or a Festuour, these relationships have occurred. The xenophobic of the ten species deride such activities, though the majority are neutral. Few encourage such romantic ties even in the Nether, though it has more active long-lasting inter-species relationships than all ten homeworlds combined. On the worlds, a more conservative philosophy is the norm.

—Excerpt from "A Dissertation on the Ten Species, Book I: Overview"

Rilan trudged up the spiral steps in the House of Communication, grumbling. Because of their connection with the air, some egotistical idiot many cycles in the past decided the physical House would be second in height to only the Spire itself. The House of Strength had it right, with half their headquarters at ground level, spread out in a vast circle. Even the House of Healing was only a few stories tall, connecting their members to the Imperium's medical research center.

But no, this had to be the tallest house and the arrogant ass that lived on the top floor was the one she was going to see. The climb only stoked her anger.

She paused for breath, leaning back on the carved balustrade dividing the top floor from a plunge to the ground floor far below. A hallway stretched out in front of her, wood and stone panels lit by lamps containing ever-glowing fires courtesy of the House of Power. The window at the end of the hall gave little light this late at night.

Rilan trudged down the hall, still muttering under her breath. If she wasn't so concerned over her former philosophy professor's absence at her testing, she might have just stewed at home.

She patted her pouch, with the note still in it. *No, I would have come anyway. At least be truthful to myself.*

Rilan knocked on Origon's door. Why he insisted on this particular apartment was beyond her. It was a waste of time just to run up and down the flights. She waited.

"Come on, Origon," she said to the door. There was a small card affixed in the middle with the majus' name, but aside from that, no decoration. "You have a lot of explaining to do, and I know you're at home." She was leaning into another knock when the door opened like a cork from a bottle.

Rilan nearly fell, but turned it into a stumble, right into his skinny arms. Origon looked terrible. His crest was drooping, feathery hair languid. There were circles under his large dark eyes, and his liverspotted Kirian skin looked more pale and wrinkled than usual. Even his feathery moustaches drooped, beneath the edge of his chin. The bright orange fabric of his robe only made him look worse.

Rilan resisted showing sympathy. "Why weren't you there? What was that note about?" She could see him pull himself together, pasting a false smile above the wisps of his feathery beard.

"I was knowing you would pass, wasn't I? No need to be there just to be distracting you." Origon paused. "You did pass, yes?"

"I very nearly didn't, thanks to you." She pushed at his chest and he stepped back, closing the door behind her with one foot. "You would have had to call Vethis majus, otherwise. Maybe I should take the councilors' advice and keep away from you." She saw the flash of irritation that crossed his face before he hid it. The Council and he were never on the best terms.

"Your father wasn't there either." He retreated as she stalked forward.

"My father is an indigent craftsman in the middle of the poorest city on Methiem. He flatly refused to 'embarrass' me by coming to the 'rich' Imperium, despite the fact I had special permission to create a portal directly to his house instead of using the portal ground. He's stubborn as a stone and I promised I would visit him as soon as I got my first vacation. What's your excuse?"

He was stalling. There was something else.

"I—" There was only a half second of pause before he answered, but she knew him well enough to catch it. "It is not really to be important..."

"Not buying it." Rilan kept moving forward, pushing Origon backward with the tip of one finger. He stumbled over a low yellow ottoman.

"The councilors were not wanting me there anyway—"

"I'll believe that, except maybe for Councilor Feldo." Thoughts of the artifact Origon contributed to flashed through her mind. "But when has the Council's displeasure *ever* kept you from doing exactly what you wanted?"

Origon's back hit the wall of his apartment and he sagged against it, face crumpling. Rilan's anger disappeared in a flash. Was that a tear?

"My brother...he is...I was just receiving the news before your test. I could not..."

She had never seen Origon so defenseless. She took the last step toward him and enfolded his larger frame. He buried his head in her shoulder.

Well, this wasn't how she expected to celebrate her graduation from apprentice to majus. She gently stroked the tiny gray feathers that made up the Kirian's hair. She loved the way pink and blue tufts fluttered in and out of sight as his crest responded to her touch. But his face was still buried against her best shirt.

"Want to tell me about it?" she ventured. She was, after all, the one training to be a psychologist. Although she didn't think her first real case would be comforting a man more than twenty cycles her senior, both her professor and her close friend.

Origon straightened, running a long finger along his cheek. She was always surprised he didn't poke himself in the eye with his claw-like fingernails. "I am sorry to be missing your testing, Rilan," he said, more contrite than she had ever heard. "Sit. I have something to ask."

She took a seat on the yellow couch, matching the ottoman he had tripped over. Origon sat beside her, straightening his garish robe's sleeves and length to cover ankles and wrists. It was a cultural thing for the Kirians, for the males to hide their legs and arms. She still didn't understand why, as the females showed so much skin. Origon had told her it wasn't anything religious. Just one of those customs that didn't translate well between species.

Origon picked up a little statue from a side table; a token from one of his many travels among the ten homeworlds. He idly fondled it, running fingers along the length. It was some animal she didn't recognize. His whole apartment was filled with knick-knacks, and as little time as he spent here, they were always covered with a layer of dust.

He didn't look at her as he spoke. "I will be having to leave tomorrow morning. It is another reason I could not be attending your testing." He waved a hand to where a small bag was half-full of clothes in a corner. "I must be discovering what happened."

"What did happen?" Rilan asked. She folded her hands in her lap. At least that explained the note. "What about your brother?"

Origon's face went through permutations of sadness, then straightened, becoming almost haughty. His hair slicked back to a neutral position. That was the man she knew.

"He is dead."

Origon didn't talk about his family much. Rilan knew he had the one brother, though both his parents had gone back to the Great Wheel of life and death before she met him.

"Oh. I'm so sorry," she said. She could only think how inconvenient a time it was for this to happen. She buried the thought.

It's a normal reaction to a message of grief. Stop focusing on yourself and help him.

"Will you be going back home to Kiria to handle his affairs?"

Origon, still fiddling with the carving, looked up at that. "No, I am going to Festuour."

"Festuour?" She had never been to the furry aliens' home world, though of all the homeworlds, it was the friendliest with her own. "What's there?"

"His body, so I am told."

Now she was confused. "He is not a majus, is he?"

"No. I am the only one of all my relations having that ability. And doubly fortunate in being able to hear the Symphony of two houses."

Rilan waved the fact away. Origon never grew tired of mentioning that he was a member of both the Houses of Communication *and* Power. "What business did he have on Festuour?"

"That I do not know." Origon's crest spiked and separated, the Nether translating it as confusion. "The communication was sent to me through a portal from a little city on Festuour being called Martflen."

"Never heard of it." But that wasn't very odd. She had only ever been on Methiem—her homeworld—and in the Nether, as it was the hub of communications between the homeworlds, and the headquarters of the maji.

"Nor I." That was stranger. Origon knew just about every nook and cranny of all ten homeworlds. His face showed pain for an instant, and Rilan knew his brother's death was eating at him far more than he would show. The emotions she saw when she arrived were likely the most she would get. It wasn't good for him to suppress that emotion, but he would never even admit he was doing it.

"Are you knowing what my brother did?" Rilan shook her head. "He was a lawman on Kiria—and very good at it. The last communication I was getting from him mentioned a far reaching case he had started, but gave no information except that someone had been killed."

"And Festuour?"

Origon shook his head, feathery hair flattening in negation. "That is something I will be discovering."

Rilan sighed. She had hoped they could spend more time together. "I'll let you get back to packing," she said, rising, then paused, searching his face. "When will I see you again?"

Origon's crest suddenly fluttered in agitation, and he put the little carving down, but continued to move his fingers restlessly. "That is to be the other part I wanted to talk with you about."

Rilan stood this time, turned to face him as he sat on the couch. "What is that?"

"Come with me tomorrow."

"To Festuour?"

"Yes." Origon leaned forward, pleading, his words coming out in a rush. "And after I am finishing this ancestor's cursed business with my brother, stay with me. Travel with me. We will be seeing all the homeworlds and their cultures, disagreements, religions, and secrets. Share it with me." He looked away. "I had meant to ask before, and then at your test, but then..." he trailed off.

"But—Origon." Rilan was speechless for a moment. "What about everything here?" Her hands took in not just the apartment, but the Nether itself. "I am only a majus as of today. I have to..."

"Have to what? Be finding a profession to please the people of the Great Assembly? Scraping your nose on the ground before the Council? Solving petty problems?"

The speaker's words about skirting the rules came back to her. "The Council is there for a reason," she answered, her voice hotter than she meant. "It directs the maji how to best help all of us."

Origon made a rude noise. "They are being a bunch of blowhards. What better time to see the universe? Come with me."

"This isn't an idle jaunt. Your own brother was killed!" Rilan stepped forward and poked him in the chest again. The man was still in denial.

"Well, yes." She caught another flash of sadness, but Origon was fast hiding it, becoming his usual blustery self. She knew if he didn't let it out now, it would come out later.

"Let us adventure through the jungles of Festuour. Even if I am not discovering what happened, it will be a time of solitude, and reflection."

"Solitude? With me in tow?"

"Reflection, then."

"You're impossible." But now the thought nagged at her. What would she do here? Wait until Vethis tested up to antagonize her? Find some psychologist to work with, using the House of Healing to diagnose petty issues in ten different species? Deal with stares from those who knew about her and Origon? She hadn't thought news of their relationship had spread that far. Vethis knew, of course, because all through university he made it his business to know anything that might be damaging to her image. Maybe he had spread it around in hopes of sabotaging her test.

And if she hung around the Nether, when would she get to see the homeworlds like she wanted?

"You are wanting to. I can tell."

"I...do." The words felt almost dragged from her, yet she found they were true. "But I have responsibilities here. And your brother..."

"I will be welcoming the help, and your responsibilities can wait for a time, can they not?"

"Well...yes."

"Do this for me. Come with me this one time. I will show you all I have lectured about in your classes, all I have told you of when we met alone. See if this is what you are wanting to do with your life." He paused, watching his hands for a moment before looking up at her. "With our lives." Once again, he looked vulnerable. "You will be...helping me past this period. And if you find it is not to your tastes, then come back here and find another path."

Rilan searched Origon's face, but she could feel the certainty bubbling up within her. Maybe she *could* help distract him, at least for the moment. Slowly, she leaned forward, lips close to his, and turned her head so she didn't bump his long nose.

They kissed, and Rilan pushed him back into the horrible yellow couch.

* * *

Some time later, Origon set the ottoman back aright, while Rilan picked up several of his little knick-knacks that had been knocked off.

"I am assuming that was a 'yes?'" Origon didn't take his eyes from a small rip in the hem of the ottoman.

"I only need to get a few things from my apartment—or Majus Meyta's apartment, rather." She adjusted a painting of a distinguished Kirian hanging above an ornamental side table. "What time is it, anyway?"

Origon squinted through to his kitchen, which had a small outside window—a testament to his ability to complain until he got what he wanted. He ran long fingers down his drooping moustaches. "It is looking to be around second lightening."

Rilan groaned. "I need some sleep, especially if we'll be up at fifth or sixth lightening."

Origon raised a feathery eyebrow, like an angular caterpillar over his eye. "There is my bedroom. You do not want to be disturbing your mentor at this hour."

"I suppose not." And it wasn't like the bed was any different than the... She looked at the couch. And the floor. And ottoman. Then her glance caught a picture of Origon and another Kirian—she assumed his brother—on the mantle, and she cringed.

"Really, are you sure? I shouldn't have... I didn't mean to take advantage of you right after..." She trailed off.

Origon actually laughed. It was a welcome sound. "I will be letting you know the first time you are taking advantage of *me*." His face grew serious. "Please. Come be with me for a little while longer. I will be welcoming the company. It is...helping while I cannot do anything else."

She followed Origon to his bedroom.

* * *

Rilan stretched, and looked out the window beside the bed. She swished her legs under the covers. Had she known he had silk sheets, she would have tried this earlier. Origon was up already, puttering in his washroom. He did seem to be better for having her sleep—and they did actually sleep this time—next to him. She listened to sounds of running water and questioned whether there was anything else that would have helped Origon deal with his grief in a better way. He was a complex man. Finally, she gave up the thought. Time would tell.

Without us, there could be no Great Assembly of Species, Speaker Karendi had said. Was she doing the right thing, going with him? What would her mentor say when she packed a few changes of clothes and left the apartment empty until she and Origon returned? When would that be? Days? Weeks? Yes, she deserved a vacation after studying for so long. She had finished both her testing and her graduation from university less than a ten-day apart. Not many did that. Yes, she could afford time off before transitioning to the life of a majus, and an apprentice psychologist. She already had recommendations to several places that might accept her. Would the lost time hurt her? Probably not. But on the other hand, was she just doing this to skirt the rules, like the speaker had said?

"Are you ready?" Origon poked his head out of the washroom.

"Just a moment," she answered, rolling out of his bed and pushing her rambling thoughts to the back of her mind.

They went out for breakfast. She strolled next to Origon, matching his long strides with quicker steps. It was a clear day in the Nether, bright and warm, with the light cascading down on them from the great walls. She looked across their length to where they met above the palace and Great Assembly, like some giant had shoved two slabs of translucent marble together. The walls, the same crystal substance as the columns, disappeared overhead, out of the range of her vision. Just as someday she would visit all ten homeworlds, someday she would travel to the top of the Nether. There were stories of course, but no one had ever brought back proof of what was up there, higher even than the birds and beasts flew. She had to make time to do those things. Otherwise she would be pinned to one place for the rest of her life.

"You are sure about this?" Origon brought her focus down to the ground. The area around the Spire of the Maji and between the houses of the maji encircling it was the largest continuous green plot in the Imperium. It was decorated with trees and bushes and tended by an army of groundskeepers. Specially trained birds and beasts prowled its circumference, never leaving the influence of the maji. It was far different from the warren of buildings that made up the rest of the Imperium.

"I'm surer by the minute," she answered. She pushed down a twinge of panic. It was just the feeling of worms in her belly because she was doing something new.

And totally insane.

"Is your brother in Martflen?" She redirected her thoughts.

"His body is, though I am not knowing how he was caught in such a place, especially to inconvenience me with having to travel there and finish his business." She snuck a glance at his face, but his expression—and crest—was carefully controlled. She wouldn't see another display like last night.

They walked in silence the rest of the way to the restaurant, a little corner establishment tucked between two busy thoroughfares and across from the campus of the medical research center. On the way, Rilan was almost positive she saw Vethis walking next to the hairy mass of a Festuour, possibly the same one as from last night. She shook her head. The oily man wasn't worth the effort. She needed to get him out of her head. Just wait and see if he passed his second testing.

The owner of the restaurant, a Lobath, lived above it and beneath a higher roadway serviced by the Imperium tram line.

"Come in, come in," Methle a'Tru, the owner, enthused at them when they opened the door. "Finally a majus, then? Will I expect more or less business from you in the future?" He kept up his steady flow of one-sided conversation, large silvery eyes staring unblinkingly as his head-tentacles twitched with delight. Methle had served generations of apprentices and maji.

Rilan and Origon got their usual—her, a fruit yogurt and spiced flatbread, and he a bowl of wiggling worms, with a tall container of hot tea. They discussed the logistics of getting to Festuour later that morning. Rilan watched the older man, his pointed features relaxed as he ate. Was this really the beginning of something lasting, or just a young woman's crush? She feared she was over-analyzing, but he was the one pushing for her to come. He wouldn't do that if he thought she was a mere fling, would he?

His brother's death certainly weighed on him. She wanted to help him—draw the pain from him, but she knew it would take time. Though she had known him for several cycles, much of Origon's past was still a mystery to her. Maybe she would learn more on this trip. She hoped so.

Afterwards, they stood outside the restaurant. "I'll meet you at the portal ground," she told him.

"I can easily be coming with you," he said. "I can help you carry your bags."

"I'll be traveling light," Rilan told him. Since when did Origon offer to carry someone else's things? "You just wait at the portal ground."

"You are sure? It is no problem."

"Quite." She searched his face, but could find no hint of amusement. His crest was calm, at ease.

As if telling her mentor—former mentor—that she was off on a wild adventure with one of the Council's least favorite maji wasn't bad enough. She shuddered to think about Origon being there.

"I am thinking Farha Meyta will not be minding much if I just—"

"Go." Rilan pointed away. Now she saw the crease next to his eyes. The Shiv-cursed man was laughing at her! He brushed his moustaches down, obviously hiding a smile.

She waited while he sauntered off, whistling through his pointy teeth, before she went in the other direction, toward the House of Healing. At least he felt better enough this morning to joke. She didn't think his humor would continue when they got to Martflen.

Majus Meyta was not at home—praises to all the gods—and she hurriedly packed what she needed. That only meant she looked more like she was running away when the door opened. Rilan's eyes darted around, but she knew there was no other exit. He must have been out at breakfast too.

"Have you found an apartment already?" her former mentor asked, removing his bowler hat and setting it on the stand next to the door. His tufts of white hair stood out like errant vegetation.

"Not...exactly."

Farha Meyta only raised his eyebrows, his face bland—an expression she knew from long experience meant, 'Yes? Tell me more.'

"I'm taking a quick vacation before starting my career as a majus."

"I see. With Origon Cyrysi, I suppose?"

Her mouth worked, but no sound came out.

"The Council will not be happy with this." His tone said he wasn't pleased either.

"It's only a few days. The Council doesn't need to know. I'll be back and starting my promising career before they figure anything out." She was babbling, but Majus Meyta had a certain way of looking at people.

"Hm." His mouth tightened, just a little.

Rilan took that as a form of acceptance and scurried past him to the door.

"Majus Ayama." The new title brought her up short. She looked back over a shoulder.

"I assume he wouldn't be satisfied with just visiting your home city or some other part of Methiem. Where are you going, if I may ask?"

She paused, but she owed him that much. "Festuour."

"Wear the bell I gave you. No knowing what diseases you could pick up on the first trip to another homeworld. I won't be there to heal you like when you decided to tangle with that nest of ratwolves in Low Imperium. And healing yourself is not your best skill, as we both know."

"Yes sir."

"On your way then." Rilan fled. Old obediences died hard.

* * *

The Spire of the Maji was the center of their presence in the Nether, surrounded by all six houses, and it had its own private portal ground, used almost exclusively by the maji. The ground was enclosed by an oasis of hedges and trees, obstructing the view of the rest of the city. When maji traveled there, it was like they were stepping out into a well-manicured estate, not a city crawling with millions.

This portal ground, just as with every other one on every homeworld, was tended by a majus, one of the less glorious jobs of the maji. Just as any majus, no matter which house, could create a portal, so everyone took their turn to tend them.

Origon was waiting. This early in the day there were few travelers, and a Benish majus she didn't recognize was tending the ground. The massive creature's skin had the hue of polished oak, and they stood three times as wide as she, though only slightly taller.

"There is no portal ground near Martflen," Origon told her. "The nearest is to be a week's journey away. I was given the information for the town's location, so I will be providing it to the majus. Do you have all you need?"

"I'm ready," Rilan said. She took the little white bell out of a pocket in her leather vest. Did it need to be touching her skin to work? Majus Meyta hadn't told her.

Origon went to the Benish, who watched him with pupil-less yellow eyes from a craggy face. Rilan followed.

"We are going to a location on Festuour," he told the Benish. "I will be communicating the exact coordinates, by your leave."

The Benish nodded their head with a creak. "This one will accept the information."

Origon raised a hand, the yellow of the House of Communication visible in rings around it. His house was the best at transferring the half scientific, half intuitive coordinates to make a portal reaching across the universe. One could only make a portal to where one had been, unless the location was transferred in this manner. So information about the maji's network of portals spread through their ranks.

Origon's hand touched the Benish's head, and the color moved from his hand to the other's craggy skin as he adjusted the Symphony of Communication. Rilan could not hear the change, of course, any more than she could hear the Symphony of any other house. The Benish's eyes dimmed at the wash of new information.

"This one has the location," they confirmed, and turned to the center of the ground. Thick arms with skin like old bark lifted and before them, a hole, pitch black, appeared in the air. As all maji shared the ability to make portals, Rilan caught hints of the melody of this place merging with another one: humid and dappled with light.

The hole, ringed in the blue of the House of Grace and a drab rust color, grew until it would accept Origon's height. Rilan pushed away the twinge of panic that always rose when she approached one of the pitch black holes between locations. She had to trust the majus who made the portal.

"Let us be going." Origon stepped into the blackness of the portal without even blinking.

Rilan gave the Benish a little wave, sighed, and entered after him.

PART THREE

Festuour

Festuour is almost an anomaly among the ten homeworlds with its dense air and crushing weight. Where one would feel light and graceful on Etan, that same person would drag their feet on the Festuour homeworld. Perhaps this is why it is inhabited by such fearsome predators. In contrast, the folk of this homeworld tend to be lighthearted, inquisitive, and jovial.

—Excerpt from "A Dissertation on the Ten Species, Book IV: Festuour"

Rilan's foot hit the dirt with more force than she expected. She turned, clumsy, just in time to see the portal close behind them. The blue and rust rings around it compressed, squeezing it into a droplet, and then to nothing at all. Behind where it vanished, trees filled the sky.

Rilan adjusted her shirt, dark green under her leather vest. Both hung heavily on her. She was lighter in the Nether than on her home world of Methiem. But this was like walking with a heavy bag slung around her waist. The heat didn't help. It was almost as oppressive as her extra weight. It hung over her.

There was no breeze to lessen the heat, but there were trees everywhere—massive things, twice as wide as she was tall. Rather than the teaks, beeches, and banyans of her home, these had no leaves, but something like cilia in place of bark. Their branches divided like fingers, pointing nearly vertical. Small furry things nested in the branches, and glided from tree to tree.

"The town is to be this way."

As she turned, her loose black hair whipped her in the face. It was like little steel wires on this world.

"Phaw." She spit it out and went to draw it behind her back, but realized she still had something in her hand. The little bell. She looked back to Origon. He was pointing to a road cleared between the trees.

"Is it far?"

"A walk of a few minutes. I was placing the portal far enough from the town to be out of danger of passersby." There was a reason there were designated portal grounds.

"Then I'm putting my hair up in a braid while we walk. It feels like I have a bunch of wet socks tied to my head."

"My robes are being as much a bother." Today Origon wore orange and purple checks, with silver filigree and a green belt. A long collar stuck out behind his neck, but even it was drooping. It was very nearly coordinated colors, for a Kirian.

"You could always roll up your sleeves," Rilan suggested while they walked, "Show off a little arm." Origon scowled at her, making the ends of his moustaches twitch.

"There is no need to be indecent." But he swept a fold in the excess fabric of his robe and tucked it into his belt.

Soon they passed a massive wooden and metal construct ringed around a tree. The cilia-bark was stripped in thin spirals, leaving a fair bit still attached to the tree. Sheets of bark lay between massive swaths of oilcloth. Rilan spotted another scaffold, and another. Every alternate tree had something around it, though none seemed damaged or dying.

Festuour swarmed over the platforms, at least five to a tree. Most of the stocky furred creatures had iron-rimmed goggles and large wooden hats like circular shields. Besides that, they wore nothing but bandoliers filled with tools. They slotted curved spades in between the tree and its bark, and pulled off sloughs of material.

Rilan and Origon passed hundreds of trees being harvested before the dirt road dumped them into a bare expanse in the forest, holding a sizeable town. Rilan, her new braid in one hand, tied the little white bell to the tip with a bit of string she had in one pocket. It was almost impossible for a majus to see the glow of the House of Healing around it, it was so slight. She let it fall, like a pendulum down her back.

"Do you even know who we're meeting here?" she asked. Origon looked to her, his crest ruffling. The Nether didn't put the translation in her head on the homeworlds, of course, but she could tell curiosity in a Kirian.

"I am not certain. I am assuming a local law officer, if there is even one here." He looked around, arrogant as usual, no sign of his recent grief.

It was a funny thing, but maji, as if they carried a bit of the Nether around with them, had no trouble communicating with each other on the homeworlds, and she would be able to hear and translate the local language. Communicating *to* the non-maji inhabitants, on the other hand, was another matter. She ran through phrases in her head, hoping the Festuour in this little backwater town spoke the Trader's Tongue.

As they passed through, Rilan saw the town was laid out in a spiral, stores and warehouses on the outer arms nearest the trees they harvested, and residences in the middle. Anyone—or anything—coming out of the forest surrounding them would have to go through low, curved, wooden buildings containing tools easily adaptable to weaponry.

They saw no species but Festuour as they walked through the town, and the usually jolly creatures stared back suspiciously. Their brown and green fur looked bedraggled and matted in the humid heat. A mother in a frilly lace hat pulled her cub close to her as they passed, watching them through narrowed blue eyes behind spectacles. A male in a high top hat and monocle peered down his snout at them.

"Cheery lot," Rilan murmured. "This is a wonderful reception for my first visit to another homeworld."

"I do not believe Festuour prefer this environment. They must live here for the textiles they make from the trees." Origon motioned to a factory as they walked by, stacks of the raw cilia-bark on one side, and folded sheets of sheer fabric on the other. They had passed several others like it.

The local law house was mid-way through the town, dividing the residences from the factories and stores. A large Festuour was standing outside, his protruding belly circumnavigated by a bandolier of pockets with paper, writing utensils, a short sword, and even a small projectile weapon—one of the newer ideas to come from Methiem. Rilan usually admired her homeworld's inventions, but not in this case. The slugs they shot moved so fast even a majus didn't have time to react. Maji were the servants and protectors of the Great Assembly. They should be harder to hurt than a non-majus.

"You all are here for the feather-head, I expect?" the Festuour drawled. He was wearing a large hat, the sides curled up and a metal emblem on the front. He was the local equivalent of the sheriff, Rilan guessed. The bit of the Nether left in her mind made his words clear, even if his body language was strange.

His blue eyes took in Origon. "No offense, meant, naturally."

Rilan watched her friend, noting the tightening of his mouth, the way his crest bunched and curled. Kirians in general were a stoic lot—but Origon was affected, not just by the epithet, but by the reminder of his brother's death, she guessed. She put a hand on his sleeved arm, but he didn't look at her.

"I am Origon Cyrysi," he said, and there was a yellow aura around him, more concentrated about his throat. He must have been putting his song into the Symphony of this place to make his words easier to understand. She would be able to comprehend him either way, so it was hard to tell if he was speaking in the Trader's Tongue.

The Festuour's bright eyes widened. He was one of the few of his species who didn't wear some form of spectacles. "And I'm Hantamoptigor Wint, Guarder. Then y'all're related, I reckon. About the only thing I've found out about this fellow is his name, and that has a 'Cyrysi' in it too."

Origon nodded, and Rilan heard his sharp teeth grind together beneath his moustache. The aura was still around him. "He is to be my brother. Delphorus Cyrysi."

"Yep. That's the name he gave us, when he was still alive. Best you folks come in. We've got him laid out." The sheriff turned his bulk through an arched doorway, waving a three-fingered paw lazily over his shoulder.

Rilan tried to catch Origon's arm as they went inside, to say something—anything—to show she would support him, but he brushed past her, his crest twitching.

The inside of the law house was sparse, but clean. Wint took them through several rooms with various desks, piles of paper, wooden cabinets, and Festuour clerks scribbling notes. In the back of the building was a closed and locked door. Wint produced a ring of circular keys from a pouch on his bandolier and unlocked it.

"In here. We keep a special room for any dead in our town. Got to keep 'em chill, on account of the heat here. Turns 'em to slush otherways."

The room was freezing. Rilan's eyes automatically went to several devices fastened to the ceiling, walls, and floor. They were small bundles of wire, with an aura of blue, orange, and brown around them. The Houses of Grace, to control the humidity, Power, to control the heat, and Potential, to fashion the artifact. Physically the wires glowed a soft yellow-red, melting the ice that gathered around them. They were hot, busy removing the heat and humidity from the air.

Delphorus Cyrysi was laid out on a wooden table in the middle of the room, and Origon was already at his side. The body was still dressed in a dull brown robe—the least colorful she had seen on a Kirian. It was filled with pockets, inside and out, and a line of Kirian hieroglyphics was stitched on the right breast, probably giving his name. Rilan stuck her hands in her pockets to warm them.

She could see similarities in the face—the long nose, and triangular feathered eyebrows—though Delphorus hadn't worn a moustache. His face was relaxed in death, but Origon's was fixed. He gently ran his liverspotted hands down his brother's robe, as if looking for something.

"His work as an officer was meaning much to him. Female Kirians were never holding much interest for him. We were alike in some ways." He gave her a shaky smile, filled with sharp teeth. It didn't reach his eyes.

"Y'all lookin' for this?" Wint held up a leather-bound book. "He requested some help on a case of his, even though I told him this was a smidge out of his jurisdiction. He wouldn't listen and went off into the jungle." The sheriff shook his head, blue eyes fixed on Origon. "One of the harvesters found him a couple days later, sprawled out. He was dead, but still fresh. No animals got to him. That's when we sent off a message to his kin. Guess it found you."

Origon took the book, slowly opening it.

"Can I?" Rilan gestured toward the body. Investigating it—him—felt wrong, but it was the only way she could think to help. At least she might be able to determine what happened. Origon waved a hand at her to proceed and she went to the table.

She closed her eyes and delved into the Symphony. Near the top were the reactions in her body, and those in Origon's and the Festuour's.

She mentally pushed those aside and listened deeper. Everything organic in the room had some signature, but now that Delphorus was dead it was harder to find his song instead of that of the wooden table he lay on. Every living—and once living—thing had one. Maji were just able to tap into theirs.

There.

Signs of decay permeated already, even in the chilly room. Parts of the song that once defined him were missing, or breaking down, with notes and phrases dissonant. But that wasn't what killed him. She was looking for something specific, violent. An animal attack, or a natural occurrence. It should show up in the Symphony, but there was nothing.

"I can't find how he was killed," she said.

"What's she sayin'?" The Festuour cocked an ear at her. She had forgotten to speak in the Trader's Tongue. It was so natural in the Nether simply to speak in her native language. She tried again.

"I..not am...finding death cause..." She spoke in broken phrases.

"I don't think he died of a cold, girlie, if that's what you're trying to say." Wint squinted at her.

Rilan tried not to get frustrated. "I said he has no having any wounds."

Wint just looked confused. "No what now? Why would he do that?"

"Wounds!"

"He was insulted?"

She growled in annoyance. "Origon?"

But Origon was staring at his brother's body. She touched his shoulder and he jumped.

"She means my brother was not killed in a manner that is obvious."

"Well why didn't she say so?" Wint scratched at his snout. "I could have told you that. Don't know what he died from, and we'd rather not have a big incident in our little town. We're quiet here. Don't like folks from the big city coming down, messing things up. Figured we could handle it quiet-like." He gestured to Delphorus' notebook. "Don't have a translator 'round here for Kirian languages, neither."

Origon looked down at the notebook, still open in his hand. It was filled with the same style hieroglyphics as were stitched into Delphorus' robe. If they were still in the Nether, Rilan would have been able to read them with the aid of its translation. Her friend didn't look like he was taking in any of the words.

"What does it say?" she prompted.

Origon started again. "It is to be his journal log," he said. The yellow aura still hung at his throat. He was not taking his brother's death well. She thought it was just his normal aloofness, back at his apartment in the Nether, but now she could tell he was shaken. If his concentration slipped enough, his change to the Symphony might reverse, and then he wouldn't be able to reproduce it until either some time had passed, or they moved a distance through the town. It would take even longer to find what they needed from Wint. She needed to get him away from here.

"Maybe there's something later in the book," Rilan suggested gently. "Perhaps near the end." Origon was holding it open at the front, where presumably it held some sort of identification of his brother.

He grunted, crest flat and unmoving, and flipped through the log. Several minutes passed, and Rilan tried not to fidget. Her teeth were starting to chatter with the cold. She didn't look at the sheriff, though she knew the Festuour was watching them. It was best for Origon to come to terms with this on his own, but they needed some information on what happened.

"He was investigating," Origon said finally. His face showed a little more animation as he read. "There were to be several homicides in his jurisdiction on Bhuontifontona—the capitol of our home province." He turned a page. "All victims were displaying the same identifying marks—strange circular wounds in their heads and necks." He looked through a few more pages. "He was suspecting a Festuour, for some reason. It does not say why. He traced the suspect's movements to near this town, bought passage through the nearest portal ground, and traveled here, one ten-day ago."

"That tells me what I needed, folks," Wint said, unheeding of Origon's state. "There was a madman brought down in a big city up north, just after he got here." He waved a paw at the table, "That must've been who he was looking for, but he went the wrong direction in his investigation and ran himself afoul of something local that didn't agree with him. We have a mighty dangerous world for those unfamiliar."

But that didn't make sense. Only an idiot would go to a little manufacturing village when their target was in a larger metropolis. Origon's relatives might be arrogant, but she doubted they were stupid. Had Delphorus found some other clue?

She was about to argue with Wint, who obviously wanted them out of his quiet town with the least fuss, and didn't particularly care about Kirians, when Origon turned back to his brother on the table, gently arranging his robe. He was in no state to reach logical conclusions.

"So will ya'll be takin' the body back with you?" Wint asked.

"Give us one moment," Rilan said, slowly enunciating her words so Wint could understand her poor speech. He nodded.

"Origon, tell him you need to make an offering to your ancestors over your brother's body," she said, in her native tongue.

"But I do not practice..." he cut off at her glare, blinked, and repeated her words to the sheriff. At least he was together enough to take her hint.

The Festuour exhaled a cloud of mist. "Don't take long now. It's cold in here." He shut the door behind him.

"What were you—" Origon looked more clearheaded.

"There's something wrong here. I couldn't find how your brother was...what happened to him." She went back to the table. "The portal ground is up there, so why would he come down here if the one he was after was in the city up north? He must have had some other objective."

Origon cocked his head to the side. "You are correct. See if you are being able to find anything else," he gestured to his brother's body.

She leaned close to Delphorus, searching deep into the Symphony. It resisted, as she had done the same thing just recently. But she hadn't actually used her song to make a change, so it was possible to perform the same action. There was no sign of trauma in the body's past, and she searched deeper, to where the Symphony divided into smaller and smaller parts, like repeating solos that made up the body. Something was off at this level. Parts of the music seemed to be missing, as if Delphorus' life had been leeched away. The music felt wrong, as if it had been...

"Origon," she said. He looked at her, catching her mood. "Can the House of Power tell you how his life energy was connected to his body? I think something stole it."

He moved slowly, looking thoughtful, paused, then, reached out with long fingers to hover over his brother's chest. His face was set in a frown. An orange aura appeared, moving down from his fingertips to the body's chest. Origon was using his secondary house. Those maji's specialty was to hear how the Symphony connected one thing to another.

The orange glow spread to Delphorus' body, as Origon closed his eyes, tilting his head as if listening intently. Finally, he opened them again.

"There are to be changes, very deep in the Symphony. The way my...the way this body was connected together has been changed at a basic level."

"That's what I suspected. I think your brother was killed by a majus." Rilan held his eyes for a long moment. "We need to find who did this."

Origon nodded in agreement. "For more than one reason." His face was dark.

Rilan almost expected the cold surface of the door to resist her as she pushed, but it opened easily, and they exited into the hot and humid interior of the law office.

The big Festuour was holding a sheaf of paper over his belly, a length of charcoal gripped in his paw. "We can pack that body up for y'all, if you like. Just give us an address. I'm assuming y'all came from the Nether, seein' as you're maji. We can request a special portal for it."

"Thank you," Rilan told him slowly, since Origon was silent. "But we will come tomorrow. Tonight, we must find lodgings."

Wint's long snout lowered and his charcoal drooped in disappointment. "Ah—of course. The Harvester's Stump can offer accommodation. Tomorrow, then? We're a quiet town, best to button this all up before it causes more hubbub around here."

Maybe the sheriff's idea of a "hubbub" was different than hers. Rilan thought for a moment, but her language skills weren't up to the task. She whispered to Origon, who translated, the glow still hanging around his neck.

"Are there any local maji in Martflen?"

Wint looked confused for a moment. "Just you two. The nearest is up north, and she only makes an appearance here once in a bear's age." He frowned. "Haven't seen her for about three cycles now, in fact."

"And in which direction was my brother's body found?"

Wint frowned, but pointed across the town with his charcoal. "East of town, right where the forest starts. Why do you ask?"

Rilan waved the question away, smiled at him tightly, and dragged Origon with her out of the law office. She hoped she hadn't given the sheriff any offense while she was here. She couldn't remember nuances of Festuour body language. How did people live outside the Nether? No wonder one didn't see alien species on other homeworlds often.

Once in the street, they turned in the direction the sheriff pointed.

"We can be purchasing a room at the local common house later." Origon said. "I want to see the place where it happened."

"Yes. Something's off here." She walked along beside him, shorter legs taking more steps to keep up with his stride.

"Are you thinking Wint is keeping something back?"

"No," she answered slowly. "I think he really is just trying to protect his little town from scandal. I don't think he knows about this other majus."

Origon looked back to the law office, stopping in the middle of the street.

"There's nothing you can do for your brother now," Rilan insisted. "But you can honor him by finding out why he's on that table." She had to keep him moving or he would stop like he did in the morgue.

"They'll thank us after we bring back the majus responsible for this. Come on. You love wandering out in the wild. It will help you feel better." She caught one of his hands, his long curved nails sliding along her skin; hard, and with an edge. She pulled, and finally he came with her. They headed through the town.

They stopped in a general store on the way out, at her insistence. Origon would have been happy to go off into the forest with nothing at all, but she wanted supplies. The Festuour had always been allies to her species, and over the cycles, there had been cross-pollination of foods and other cultural likes. That meant she could find dried jerky to eat. She also bought several canteens of fresh water, rope, and a pack to carry them in. She even found a folding tent, but Origon stopped her from buying that for some reason. She was surprised how little it cost. This town must have been poorer than she thought. She used only a few small clear chips of the Nether's currency, and still got several sticks of local currency back in change.

Soon after leaving the store, they faced a wall of the cilia-bark trees. The town was not that large. "You will be more tired for carrying that pack," Origon told her. His voice was the one he adopted lecturing to freshmen, and Rilan rolled her eyes. She had it strapped to her back, her leather vest providing some padding between the rough fabric of the pack and her linen shirt. The yellow glow had faded from his throat sometime in the past few minutes as he reversed the change he made to his speech and reabsorbed the notes of his song. They shouldn't need translation in the woods.

"I'll be fine. You just worry about helping me track where Delphorus went." She knelt down at the treeline, hands just above the ground. Chords and whole musical phrases of the Symphony flew past her, containing the many biological changes in the forest. There were numerous creatures hidden around them. However, there had not been harvesters at these trees recently, so any sentient disturbance would stand out. People made their own very definite impact on the music of the universe. She used her song to make a minor chord major and the differences popped to the forefront. There was something to their left, and she went that direction, Origon following.

They went a few hundred paces. "Here. There's a footprint." It was partially buried in the dusty shavings the trees dropped from the end of their cilia—probably some form of waste product. She reclaimed her notes and the obvious signs faded from her perception. No matter, they had the trail now. "What can you find?"

Origon bent down next to her, the orange glow of the House of Power already forming about his arms as he laid his hand in the footprint. It had been made by the large three-toed foot of a Festuour, facing toward town. The aura transferred to the footprint, tracing the outline, uncovering how this one piece was connected to its surroundings. Two orange lines spread from the print, one back to the town, the other into the woods, outlining another footprint nearby.

"This way." Origon stood, still concentrating on the ground. Rilan followed, watching her friend for any sign of distress. Yes, tracking work would be good for him. It would keep him busy.

They followed the footprints backwards, until they reached a larger disturbance, not far into the treeline. The ground was trampled, and several of the trees had patches of bark scraped off.

"This is to be the place." Origon rolled his shoulders, and the orange glow disappeared again, reabsorbed.

"Can you figure out what happened, or is that too similar for another change to the Symphony?" Rilan asked, referring to tracking the footprints.

Origon drew up, lifting his long nose, ends of his moustaches twitching. "Of course I can be figuring out what happened. I was tracking through the wilds of the homeworlds—"

"While I was still a child. You don't need to remind me how much older you are." It was somewhat of a sore point to her, but Origon didn't seem to notice. He blinked at her blankly.

"Never mind. Go on." Rilan waved a hand at their surroundings. She was trying too hard to keep him busy, to not think about his brother, and it was showing. Origon mumbled something, his crest rippling. He went to a nearby tree, listening, then made a tying motion with his hands. As he left one tree to go to another, strands of yellow light fluttered as if a breeze were blowing them, but it was not the same slight breeze that blew through the trees today. The etheric light fluttered to a different wind. He went from tree to tree, and the light trailed after him as if he were making a giant spider web of ribbons. Soon all the nearby surfaces were covered, strands of light all shifting and pointing in the same otherworldly breeze.

Origon stepped back, cocking his head, as if observing the streamers of light. "It is not to be complete. Can you tell exactly where my...the body was found?"

Rilan watched what he was doing. She knew he was very good with the House of Communication, which the yellow ribbons indicated. He was harnessing wind currents of some sort, she thought, but didn't know for what purpose. Still, she nodded and knelt, hands out again. The Symphony resisted. She couldn't make the same change she had to discover the footprint. It was a novice mistake. She should have held on to the change instead of letting it go the first chance she got. She shook her head, frustrated with herself.

After a moment, she listened to her own Symphony, using a few notes of her song to increase her sense of smell. The faded scents of the Festuour harvesters appeared as large hazy masses in the air. The body was easy to find as well, especially since it didn't move on its own.

Origon's brother. Not just a body. But she pushed the thought away. Find the answers first.

"It was right here." She outlined where Delphorus had fallen, one arm outstretched. She sniffed. "There were four Festuour as well." She waved her hands to indicate where they would have gathered around Delphorus.

Origon nodded, laying a hand in the center of each of the masses, then wordlessly touching the center of where his brother's body lay with one finger.

The ribbons of light around them flapped crazily in a nonexistent wind, then died, then flapped again, and the streamers lengthened and joined together. Rilan stepped back, trying to see what Origon had done.

The streamers of light outlined a scene frozen in time, a body made of yellow light laying on the ground and four larger shapes around it, identifiable as the outlines of Festuour. They were frozen in the act of gesturing to each other and to Delphorus. No lines passed through the phantom bodies. Origon had mapped the air itself in that moment in time.

"That's incredible," Rilan breathed. "How did you learn..." But Origon walked past her, to another shape, vaguer than the others, captured as it hid behind a tree, observing. It was on all fours.

Rilan raised her head and sniffed. "Someone, or something, was here with them."

"The majus?" Origon cocked his head, watching the fuzzy shape.

"I...don't know. The smell is heavy, almost like an animal. It came from deeper in the forest, in this direction." Rilan pointed, and Origon raised a hand and twisted. The yellow streamers moved along their paths, creating a funnel aimed farther into the woods.

They moved in that direction, Origon controlling his captured breeze. While walking, Rilan sank farther into the detritus of the trees than expected, and she slowed her pace. No sense tripping over a root and breaking her leg on this heavy world. The woods were strange. Unlike the forests of her home where many types of trees grew together, this forest was all cilia-bark trees, branches like reaching fingers. Rilan wondered if it was planted or if the trees pushed out any other organism. Light got to the ground, but aside from a few scrubby bushes here and there, nothing grew underneath. The floor of the forest was deep with the shaving-like waste of the trees.

There was animal life hiding nearby, despite the lack of leaves or ground cover. She caught glances of the same gliding creatures they saw on the way in, and once in a while saw a tuft of fur or tail of ground creatures the size of the forest cats they had back near her home city. These seemed skittish and were camouflaged, and Rilan guessed they were prey creatures, not predators, even though they were rather large.

Every so often, Origon paused for a few minutes while touching a tree, mapping another point in the complex web of air movement he was building. Sometimes she saw the shapes of animals outlined in the false breeze. Once or twice she saw a man-sized shape. Was he going farther back in time, mapping the air around where his brother had walked?

Rilan kept the change to her sense of smell, though she felt it wearing on her. Holding a change contrary to the Grand Symphony of the universe took effort. Many other new maji would be struggling more than she did. Take that oaf Vethis, for example. Well, he wouldn't even be out here in the first place.

Origon was sweating, and she watched a bead of water roll into his feathery moustache. It wasn't just the humidity. If it was hard for her, it was amazing he could hold such a complex change over this length of time. She rarely had a chance to observe how talented he was, especially with the House of Communication, and it gave her new appreciation for the tests the house heads set for her. Of course she had been meant to pass them. Otherwise she would have had no chance.

"How long can you hold on to the air map?" she asked. They were already some distance away from the source of the change and traveling farther by the moment.

"Long enough." The terseness of his speech spoke volumes. She let the matter drop as a scent caught at her.

"What's that?" It was sharp, and pungent. Similar to the smell at the site of the disturbance, but from a different individual. She couldn't place it. It wasn't the musty scent of the ground creatures.

"There are predators on Festuour," Origon said, watching her sniff the air. "On this homeworld, the dominant species is having a massive build, thick fur to repel fangs and claws, and a mouth full of sharp teeth. Imagine what their wild fauna is like."

Rilan was leading, and forced her Kirian friend to stop as she slowed. "You decided to mention this only after we entered the deep dark forest without telling anyone where we were going?"

Origon shrugged. "It was to be your idea."

Rilan growled. "You are—" *Arrogant. Stuck up. A thrill seeker.* "—going to take the first watch when we camp for the night."

It was getting dark, and her change to the Symphony was progressively harder to maintain. The longer she used her new sense of smell, the more likely she wouldn't be able to reverse the change, and thus lose those notes from her song forever as the change became permanent. There was a good reason she didn't have the sense of smell of a dog. It would mess up her other senses, eventually.

She knew Origon was suffering, though he would never admit it.

"Let's find somewhere to stop."

They walked until they found a space between the ever-present cilia-barked trees large enough to camp for the night. Origon touched one last trunk, watched how the line of yellow streamers blew, and nodded to himself. The yellow light vanished from around them and he stood straighter, as if putting down a rucksack full of bricks.

Rilan reversed her own change and felt the notes of her song come back to her. It was never completely perfect—one always lost one or two in the transition—but it was much less than if she had made the change permanent. She'd feel better tomorrow.

She took in a long breath of the warm, humid air, and began making a little bed among the roots of one of the trees, grumbling about Origon keeping her from getting a tent. It wouldn't have cost much more.

"What are you to be doing?" She turned to find his head cocked to one side.

"I'm trying to make a place to sleep, since someone insisted we didn't need tents." She stood, and put her hands on her hips.

"That is to be solved easily." Origon even gave her a little smile as he came over. He set his stance, feet planted firmly, and raised both hands. Yellow and orange auras, mixing together like pools of paint, extended from his outstretched hands. She could tell he was listening intently. He shook his hands and the aura flexed out like a sheet. It fell slowly, draping over an area big enough for two people to sleep comfortably together. As if there was a tent pole, the center hung in the air, the sides of the sheet of aura draping to the ground, the back of it resting against the tree she had chosen.

Rilan raised her eyebrows. She didn't know he could do that. Being born with access to more than one house invited combinations she had never really considered.

"What is it?" she asked.

"It is the mixture of air and heat, compressed to be forming a tactile surface." He brought a fist down on the surface, invisible to non-maji except for a faint glimmer in the air. Something resisted him.

"And you can hold that all night?" And after mapping miles of air currents, too.

"It is staying in one place. I will be nearby. It is no matter."

Rilan ducked under the sheet of compressed air. Origon had left an entrance, clearly visible to a majus by a break in the yellow and orange aura. She lay back on the ground, her pack making a suitable pillow against the tree base. Shavings drifted down from the tree above her, and gently landed on the invisible surface above. There would be a thin layer by the morning, she expected. At least they wouldn't be on her.

Origon took first watch, sitting outside the impromptu tent. Rilan watched the unfamiliar stars, trying to find similarities. Festuour was the closest homeworld to her own, but she could find none of the constellations she knew.

She was almost asleep when Origon began to speak.

"I was always closest to Delphorus, out of all of my family members." Rilan propped herself up on elbows, leaning forward to hear better. He didn't look at her, but she saw the outline of his head turn in the darkness. He knew she was listening.

"Neither of us got along with the rest. Our grandmother was being an eminent stateswoman in her youth, and expected her descendants to be following in her trail. My father, her son, was deeply religious, and was trained in the priesthood, leading the family in their regard of our ancestors. He was using his talent for speech, but not in the manner my grandmother preferred. She never had any regard for our mother. When I was found to be able to hear the Grand Symphony, I was sent to the Nether, of course, for training. I could only be accessing the House of Communication then. My second house, that of Power, came later. I think my grandmother expected me to be serving on the Council in a few cycles. She was disappointed.

"Delphorus was younger than me. He showed no inclination for the maji or for public speech, which as you know is highly prized on Kiria." He waved a shadowy hand, as if the point was self-evident. Rilan crept closer to the entrance of the tent, pulling herself into a ball.

"The position of lawman, especially one devoted to ferreting out wrongdoers, is viewed as a necessary evil in my province, but is never a prestigious job anywhere on Kiria. When my brother chose such a base job, my grandmother was near to be disowning him. She died a few cycles after he started his profession." Origon's voice dipped alarmingly at the last sentence, and Rilan resisted the urge to hug the man. She wanted to hear more.

"He confessed to me later he felt he failed our family, though I never did." Origon left unsaid whether he considered himself a success. Rilan had an idea, considering his standing with the Council.

"We kept in contact, sending messages to each other about our work. I was visiting him when I had the chance, as he never had much money. My father joined the ancestors a few cycles after our grandmother and our mother was long departed. It was a sign of their feelings for us that the family house and all the accumulated wealth was left to the descendants of a cousin of our grandmother—a noted public speaker, I might be adding."

"That's awful," Rilan said. The shadow of Origon's head nodded. She saw his crest rise.

"It is to be somewhat traditional on Kiria, in our province."

Rilan moved out of the tent, snuggling up next to him, now that he seemed to be done with his story. One of the moons of Festuour was up, and she thought she could see tears on Origon's cheeks, reflecting its faint light.

"We had not spoken for several months before...before I got the communication."

Rilan touched his cheek, wiping a tear away. "I'm sorry," she said. She was an only child. "I can't imagine what it would be like to lose—"

Something cracked, above them and to the right.

"What was that?" Rilan searched the branches above them. She started to push up, but a shape dropped with a thud in front of Origon. The same sharp scent hit her, strong now, like metal and rotting meat.

"Back!" He pushed her and she fell against the sheet of air making their tent. It flexed slightly at her weight, and she slipped underneath it. Origon scooted in after her.

"Ancestor of a turtle!" he cursed. "I cannot be creating another shield over the entrance." His body was blocking a clear view of whatever was out there. In the dark, it was only a massive shape under the starlight. It stood over them, now they were inside the tent.

She saw the yellow of the House of Communication blossom in his hands, and a blast of air blew the scent of the thing out of the tent. There was a deep snort and the shadow shook its head, which seemed half as big as the tent. Something smashed against the sheet of air, pressing Origon back into her. He grunted and the colors intensified. He was putting more of his song into holding the change. She caught a glimpse of a massive razor-sharp claw bearing down on them. It ran over the top of the tent of air, the surface bowing alarmingly.

"That didn't do anything," she said. "How do we get rid of it?" She jumped as the creature grunted at them, loud and deep.

"I am open to any suggestions, provided they are quick." Origon scooted back farther as something swiped across the opening with a hiss of air.

"I can't see it clearly," Rilan said. "I don't know what its biology is, and I don't know how to affect it." The Symphony seemed remote and hard to hear. She had never been in a situation like this before. Even her testing had been a controlled environment. The beast swiped again and its sharp smell flowed back. It couldn't seem to figure out why something resisted it.

"I'm going to adjust my eyes," Rilan told Origon. It was the only thing she could think of. He only grunted, not turning. He was pressed into her, her back to the tree, her pack under her. The orange and yellow outline of the sheet of air was moving. He was trying to adjust it between them and the thing.

Rilan listened for the Symphony, but it was spotty and far away. She closed her eyes and focused on her own body, one of the easiest actions for her house.

Come on. Focus. She couldn't fail them now. She had tested under pressure a hundred times. Another deep grunt made her pop an eye open before closing it again.

She listened for the melody of her visual system. This was familiar. The tune floated by, faster than usual, in time with her heartbeat. Change the tempo slightly, use her song to adjust the cadence and brighten her night vision.

"I can see it now. Move out of the way." She peered past Origon, trying to get a good look at their attacker.

The second one landed on top of them.

Rilan looked up and screamed. Above her, two sets of serrated jaws sawed at the air inches above her face. She felt the sheet of air push her to the ground. Triangular teeth vied with three large tusks jutting at angles from a face that seemed half mouth. The shaggy body was larger than the now flat tent.

She flinched back into the ground, but its full weight was on them. She could barely see Origon, on his stomach beside her, not moving. The sheet of air above her pressed in, pushing both of them down into the ground. Jaws snapped so close above her she couldn't focus on them.

On the positive side, the other one couldn't get at them, now the opening was squashed flat.

Her arms were pinned, and Origon's face was being crushed into the debris of the forest floor. He wasn't moving, but he was breathing. Unconscious. His tent would only last a few minutes without him holding it in place. When it dissolved, there would be no barrier between her and the teeth above her.

This was not the time to crack under pressure.

Rilan closed her eyes again, and tried to ignore the wet sounds and grunts from above her. *Assess the situation. Make a decision. Follow through.* Words her mentor had taught her long ago snapped into her head.

She delved into the Symphony. There was no problem finding it this time. Pure adrenaline brought the music to her, beating in time with her fear. She blocked out the Symphonies of her body and Origon's, focusing on the two creatures. If she could only touch them, it would be easy. She could affect their bodies or minds, make them docile. But if she could touch them, they could touch her.

She concentrated on the pheromones traveling back and forth, along with grunts and snarls. They were a mated hunting pair, she realized.

She adjusted notes, hoping the sheet of air was porous enough to pass scents through. Copied pheromones might confuse them.

A few moments later, the snarling stopped and she cracked open an eye. The jaws were still, and the massive head was tilted, watching her. An eye the size of her fist took her in. Shaggy black hair surrounded it.

The pressure on her increased and another head joined the first, watching. She felt a root digging into her leg. Origon was pressed almost completely into the shavings.

There was no snarling now, but twice the weight—not the solution she wanted. The tent dissipated much of the creature's weight, or they would both be crushed to death. Still, the air was getting thick and her head felt fuzzy. She wouldn't get another chance. The next change had to be right.

She took back the notes of her song and searched the Symphony again for anything that would draw the beasts away. Free from the confusing pheromones, a paw the size of her chest bounced off the blanket of air, just above her. Rilan exhaled sharply as something gave with a muted crack. Probably a rib. Pain flooded through her.

Concentrate! She would not cry out.

She poured through the melodies. What were the strongest urges? Food and sex, and she was food. Sex, then. She grabbed at notes as they flew by, and missed more than she caught.

Change!

The Symphony resisted, but these pheromones were different from the last change. Finally, she captured enough of the notes to create a phrase of the music, and used her song to push it into place, melding it with the beast's natural instincts.

One of the creatures snorted in response, a massive blast of air. The other one cuffed it on its head and Rilan grunted when the pressure on her increased.

She realized she could feel fur tickling her wrist. The pressure was increasing because the blanket of air was dissolving. Her vision contracted to a tunnel.

Come on, take the bait.

The first beast sniffed in her direction, smelling alluring pheromones.

The second one swatted the first in the head again. It responded with a growl that shook her eardrums, but its head turned back to her.

A foot pressed her pelvis into the ground cover and her muscles protested. The blanket was going faster.

Another cuff, and this time the beast responded to its mate, stepping away to growl. The other growled back, and suddenly the weight was off her.

The ground shook as the two beasts cantered off into the woods, one chasing the other like cats the size of wagons. A nearby tree creaked as the first caught a low branch with wicked curved claws and pulled itself up. The second followed.

Rilan let out a breath, looked around with her augmented eyes, then turned to Origon. He wasn't breathing. She snaked an arm beneath him, pulled him around, and cried out as her rib protested.

Definitely broken.

She tried again, slower this time, and got him turned over, brushed shavings off his face and out of his moustaches. She knew basic medicine, but it wasn't her thing. Her forte was mental, not physical. Some of those in the House of Healing could repair flesh itself, though it was strangely not that common.

She pressed an ear to his chest. The heartbeat was strong, and fast. Kirians' hearts beat harder than her own species. So why wasn't he breathing?

She dived into the Symphony again, counting tempos to find the music of Origon's breath. A foreign melody clashed with the one that kept him alive.

An obstruction.

"Shiv's eyes," she swore, and hooked a finger past the Kirian's sharp teeth. She found the collection of tree shavings that was blocking his throat and pried them out. With a snort, Origon gasped in a breath.

Rilan inhaled, clutched a hand to her chest, and exhaled slowly, around her broken rib. *Only a majus would listen to the Symphony before checking to see if someone was choking.*

"What...is happening?" Origon's voice was weak and hoarse. Rilan took in their trampled supplies and the trees around them. The last yellow and orange of the tent faded as Origon reabsorbed its notes.

"Nothing I couldn't handle. I'll take the next watch." Origon snorted something, but was soon asleep, curled up in the tree roots.

Rilan watched the sky the rest of the night, thinking of what he told her about his brother. The forest sounds had returned to normal, but just in case, she copied the scent of the tree she rested against, replacing her own and Origon's so they didn't attract any more attention. And she kept the change to her eyes until just before the sun rose.

Origon was limping when they started out the next day, though he insisted he was fine. The extra weight on this world would not help his injury, or hers. They would be slower to heal. There was not much to do for her rib except to lace her leather vest as tight as she could. It still burned with every step, making it harder to breathe.

"My canteen is empty," he said, shaking his leather pouch.

"And mine spilled last night," Rilan answered. She closed her eyes and felt the Symphony of the forest spill past her, like a warm summer wind. The trees soaked up water stored beneath the ground, but they were better fed in one direction.

"This way. I think there's a stream nearby. We can both get more water."

"Were you hearing...ah...anything else?" Origon didn't look at her.

"There are no more of those creatures close." She answered his unasked question. "This ecosystem wouldn't be able to support many more of them anyway." She glanced to the trees where she could see bits of fur slide out of sight. The prey animals on the ground were well hidden.

The morning was still warm, and humid. Condensation beaded on the bark of the trees. The land rose gently as they made their way to the stream, and Origon was silent.

"I'm sorry," she finally said, trying to ignore the pain in her chest. Origon looked up.

"For what?"

She gestured at his leg. "I'm not very good with healing. It's like the notes just slide away when I try to do it. I can understand the music of a mental state, or a set of pheromones, or even change the way a body works, but to actually grow new cells?" She shook her head.

Origon shrugged. "Some are to be better at certain things. It is natural."

"It's about the only thing Vethis is good at," Rilan continued, hardly hearing her friend's response. "He always held that over me."

"Your testing rival? I am seeming to remember the two of you arguing through one of my classes."

Rilan snorted. "Rivals. He's the lazy son of rich parents. He had everything I didn't growing up. He barely got through University, and most of that was from cheating off his friends. Yet he tested with me. It's so rare to have the ability to change the Symphony, and it's wasted on him."

"But he can heal," Origon offered. "We are always needing good physicians." Rilan rolled her eyes.

"Yes, he's decent at it. He would be better if he practiced it rather than mooching off his parents."

"Surely he is to be proficient at some things."

Rilan waved the comment off. "Maybe, if he applied himself to them." She thought about their test, how he passed just as many challenges as she did. "If he had been my brother growing up, I would have forced him to work for..." she broke off as she realized what she had said.

"I didn't think." She felt her cheeks redden. "Here I am, complaining about that waste of space, when we should be concentrating on where Delphorus went."

The stream came into view in front of them.

"Yes, well, he could not have traveled much farther on his own." Origon finally said.

"Whatever he found must have been a few days walk or less," Rilan agreed. She pressed a hand to the side of her chest. The hike this morning had taken more out of her than she liked. "He was close to death when he fell near the edge of the forest. He wouldn't have traveled far like that." She glanced to Origon. "Sorry."

He nodded, bent, and filled his canteen. Rilan did likewise.

"Give yours to me," he said. When she did, he took the caps off and held both, an orange aura springing up around his hands and the containers. Steam rose for a moment from the open caps, then disappeared. When he gave her back her canteen, the water was just as cool as the flowing stream.

"There were small creatures in the water that would be causing sickness," he said. "Now there are not."

Rilan took her canteen back. She would have known that, if she thought about it. But Origon had much more experience traveling through the wilderness. If she had somehow changed the creatures so they were not toxic, it would have taken a permanent investment from her, and she would have lost those notes of her song. It would have taken a few days to build them back up. But Origon merely applied heat, then took the heat back—a reversible change. The houses of the maji had many ways to accomplish the same goals, but some were better than others.

She took a sip of water, grunting, as raising her arm pulled on her rib. Clean and clear. "Can you tell which way your brother came from?"

"Last night, the air remembered him passing this direction," he said, gesturing with a long finger past the stream. "But I cannot be forming another map to trace him from here. The connections are too sporadic."

"Then we continue in that direction until we find another clue." Rilan pulled a strip of jerky out of her bag and began to chew it, moistening the meat with water from her canteen. If there were any berries or nuts in the woods she would have eaten those instead, after using the House of Healing to make sure they weren't toxic. But it didn't seem to be the season for fruit, if the scrubby bushes even fruited here. She wasn't sure what season it was locally, though the air was hot.

Origon limped along behind her, occasionally reaching out with one finger, smoking in the humid morning air and ringed with an orange aura.

"What are you doing?"

"Breakfast." As he answered, Origon reached out and Rilan saw a large beetle fall out of the air—faster than she expected—crisping from the heat coming off the Kirian's finger. He caught it with his other hand and popped it in his mouth.

Rilan shook her head, then stopped when it hurt too much. "One of these days, you're going to catch a disease from eating foreign bugs."

Origon only smiled, chewing. "The heat is sterilizing the insects, just as it did the water." He caught another delicate flying thing with the finger and it fell from the air, smoking. "Even if they are to be overcooked."

Rilan opened her mouth to argue, but an odd shape on the ground ahead caught her eye. "What's that?"

She moved to the shape, holding her chest, then called Origon over.

"It's the ones from last night," she said. In front of them were two large carcasses, insects already buzzing around. The sharp metallic smell was strong, but mixed with others now; blood, and effluent, and death.

"Are you sure?" Origon toasted one of the flies that got too close to him.

"Positive. I copied their pheromones. I can tell these are the same. Besides, these are apex predators. There wouldn't be others so close."

"It is like they were tearing each other to pieces." Origon gingerly poked at a strip of flesh hanging from the nearest beast. In the daylight, they looked like a cross between the jaguars that frequented the jungles near Rilan's home city of Dalhni and some sort of hulking, hairy bear. They had long hooked claws to allow them to catch branches of the bare trees around them. She didn't look closely at the mouth. She had seen quite enough of that the night before.

"Which pheromones were you using?" Origon asked the question casually, but she caught him glancing at her.

It looked like the beasts had died from the deep clawed wounds. There was a trail of guts from one of the beasts. "Unless they like to kill each other while mating, I don't think I caused this."

"Then why are they dead?"

Rilan looked closer. There were more wounds on the creature's backs, but these were half-closed, and scabbed over. "Something isn't right. Look here." She pointed to a long slash of purple down one of the beasts' backs. She listened for the Symphony.

The music was slowing, becoming lethargic. They hadn't been dead long, but there was another melody underneath, something running counter to the creature's natural tendencies.

"Someone changed them," she said. "And not very well."

"The majus?" Origon's crest rose with interest.

"It must be, but not a very good one."

"It is to be one of the House of Healing, then."

"Ye-es," Rilan hedged. "There was a component of my house involved, but there was something else, too. I can't hear what it is."

"So our majus might be a member of two houses, as I am."

"Isn't that rare?" Rilan looked at Origon. "An order of magnitude higher than those born able to hear one Symphony? You're the only one I know of."

Origon shrugged. She knew he was trying to look humble. He wasn't succeeding. "You know others. We are tending not to advertise our other abilities, rare though we are."

"Still, they aren't common," Rilan said. "Why would a majus be in the middle of nowhere modifying wild animals?" She gestured at the nearest corpse. "Why don't you give a listen. Maybe you can hear other changes."

He looked surprised by her request, only for a moment. "That is to be...a good idea."

"I do have them sometimes."

He bent over the beasts, head cocked, crest fluttering. "I cannot hear any changes to the Symphony."

"Then the other ability was the House of Strength, Grace, or Potential," Rilan concluded.

"Most likely Potential, to be able to store changes to the Symphony," Origon said.

"So what did this have to do with your brother?"

The Kirian's face fell, crest drooping. "I do not know." His large eyes met hers. "But I will be finding out."

A shiver ran down her back at his expression.

"Are there enough clues here to determine where they came from before they attacked us?" Rilan could potentially trace their biological footprint, but she wanted to give Origon something to focus on with the House of Power.

"I will try." As he moved again to the bodies, a deep grunt rang through the forest. Rilan jerked her head and bit back a curse at the pain. She felt her braid hit her shoulder, the little bell at the end chiming.

"Origon."

"I am seeing it." Origon rose, very slowly, his robe clinging around his legs. Another beast stood not twenty paces away, a deep rumbling coming from it. It was either purring or growling, and Rilan didn't want to find out which.

It roared, and its two tiers of serrated teeth shone between its tusks.

"No more apex predators?" Origon asked.

"So maybe we were near the edge of their territory," Rilan snapped, looking for anything to use against the thing. Aside from dead branches, there was nothing. She scooped one up, holding it in both hands. It wouldn't do much, but might give her enough time to make contact with it without losing an arm. Or her face.

It charged.

Origon's skinny arms rotated forward like he was trying to flourish a handkerchief toward the creature.

"Exhale!" he shouted, and Rilan felt the air pressure drop around her, like a storm was approaching. She blew out the air in her lungs. Her rib screamed at her.

There was a deep *thump* and her ears popped. The beast skidded to a stop, shaking its great head as if confused. She saw a trickle of bright purple blood flow from one large ear, and then from the gash of a nose above its teeth. It gave an almost pitiful moan and flopped to its side.

"Is it dead?" Rilan edged closer to the mound of fur. There was something very wrong here.

"I am sincerely hoping so. I cannot be generating so big a change in air pressure for a long time, or unless we are far away from here."

"There can't be that many predators nearby, not this large. And I doubt we're on their regular diet, since we're not even from this homeworld." She stepped closer still. She didn't see any movement.

"You are right." She looked back. Origon was listening to something again. "There is to be some connection here, in tune with the structure of the ecosystem. I can almost tell—"

He was interrupted by another grunt, followed by a snarl.

Four more beasts moved out from behind trees, one far bigger than the others, with fur black as pitch. The others were in shades of gray and brown. With a *whump* of displaced shavings, a fifth dropped from the trees behind her and Origon. They were surrounded, the corpse of the beast Origon had killed blocking their only exit.

"Are you sure you can't make the pressure change again?" Rilan hoped her voice didn't shake. The Symphony came to her, and she followed the unspoken pheromone exchange between the beasts:

Food.

Hungry.

Prey.

Origon cried out, and all the creatures turned toward him. Heedless, he limped in a run toward the one he had felled. Rilan rotated in a circle, falling into the steps of *Fading Hands*, though it would do little good against this crowd. She wouldn't even be able to use her hands effectively with her broken rib. She began to pick apart the notes of the pheromones, hoping to create something to buy them more time.

"I have it!" Origon cried, holding up something that had been strapped to the creature's back. The rest watched him, heads tilting, their motion stopped for the moment by confusion or interest.

Then their heads snapped back to her, almost in unison. She felt their stares boring into her.

"They are all connected!" Origon called, and twisted the thing in his hands, arms held above his head like a madman. Rilan could only spare a small section of her attention to what he was doing.

There was a snap like wood splitting and the pheromones in the air suddenly changed. The beasts looked at each other, grunting and calling. Then one turned and stalked away.

Another caught a tree and pulled itself into the branches. Two more traded cuffs, knocking each other's heads with their wicked claws, then scampered away, catching branches at a distance.

The last, the great black-furred one, circled her. She could hear it snorting and sniffing. The three tusks pointed toward her, away, toward her again...and then it turned with a *whuff* of air, kicking shavings back toward her as if she wasn't worth the effort.

It wandered off.

Rilan let out a breath she didn't know she had been holding, her arms slowly drooping from her guard position. Her legs were nearly locked into a stance of *Fading Hands*. It would have done no good with her muscles so tight. Her ribs complained at the movement, as her adrenaline rush faded.

"This is the key!" Origon called, gesturing with something. Rilan stalked toward him, fists clenched.

"What was that? Are you insane? We could have been killed and you just run off like you're chasing butterflies!"

Origon fell back, his crest flattening at her admonishment. He held the pieces of something out in both hands as if it explained his actions.

"What. What is it?" Rilan gestured impatiently for him to hand over the objects. He did, with a look of trepidation.

It once was a medallion made of wood, with lines carved into it in a now unreadable pattern. Origon had shattered it into five uneven pieces, each of which held the fading orange and brown auras of two of the houses.

"You heard the change from the House of Power." It wasn't a question.

Origon nodded. "That was the connection I was hearing. It became louder as more of the creatures came closer. They are solitary, but their hierarchy was adjusted with my house so they were becoming a pack, tracking intruders. I am believing each of them has one of these."

"Why did breaking one medallion destroy the pack bond?" Rilan wasn't questioning their good fortune, but it did seem odd.

"The web of Power between them was very fine," Origon answered. He brushed his moustaches down, smoothing them. "Each one was to be connected to each other. The medallions might have been created together, though I cannot tell. The creation was using the House of Potential. Breaking one must have tangled enough strings of the web to be bringing the entire construct down. To rewrite a Symphony of such complexity and size would use many notes of one's song. There are many parts I cannot hear, or I would be knowing more."

Rilan lifted one of the pieces. She could barely make out discordant notes, fading rapidly. "My house was used in the medallion too. It adjusted their behavior so they could live together for long periods of time. I must have disrupted that when I increased the mated pair's sex drive."

Origon nodded. "It is quite ingenious. Despite the change in the House of Healing being sloppy, the overall change was to be well crafted."

Rilan frowned as she tucked the broken pieces of what had been an artifact into her vest pocket. Something still didn't add up. "Three houses, and used in a harmony and precision that rivals some of the Council's workings. Are there two maji?"

Now Origon frowned. "You are correct. Even if one majus was of two houses, that person would have had help to craft this."

"You've never heard of someone belonging to three houses, have you?" Rilan asked. It was a silly question. Everyone knew the answer.

But Origon took it seriously, pacing through shavings on the forest floor. "There are schools of thought among the houses—especially with those who are members of more than one—postulating why there are to be maji who can hear two Symphonies. There has never been any recorded case where a majus has heard more than two. The prevailing thought is to be that the strain on the mind is too great. Those who would hear more than two aspects of the Grand Symphony die before they are born."

Visions of secret societies and meetings in the dark flitted through Rilan's imagination. She was only beginning her path to become a majus, and there were still many secrets to unlock in the houses. She looked at her friend, her lover, her old teacher in a new light. How long had he been steeped in that even more rarified atmosphere?

"Can you determine who has touched it?" he asked, breaking through her reverie. His face was questioning; no hint of any secrets.

"Touched...what?" Rilan shook her head, carefully, to keep her rib from taking offense at the action. "Oh, the artifact." She drew one of the larger pieces out of her pocket, hearing the topmost layer of the Symphony even as she did. She banished the thought of secret societies to the back of her mind, assigning a mnemonic to it so she wouldn't forget.

The overwhelming sense of the broken medallion was of the beast to which it had been attached. Muscles bunching and loosening, prey caught, and several wild sprints through the branches.

It had only been attached for two days, and she could still feel the residue of the one who had created it.

The *one*.

She frowned. "This has only been touched by one majus."

Origon's crest fluttered in alarm and he stopped pacing. "Are you sure?"

"I think...yes, though there is interference behind it. But only one majus put notes of their song into this medallion—permanently." Doing so would make the change to the Symphony last much longer, but would weaken the majus for days afterward.

"Are we to be speaking of a majus with access to more than two Symphonies?"

"I'll only believe it if I see it," Rilan answered.

"How are we to be finding them?" Origon looked around as if one might just pop out of the scenery.

Rilan thought for a moment. There was plenty of data here, between the remains of the beast, the medallion, and the change in the group structure of the beasts. But they would need to work together.

"I think we can take a page from our mystery majus' book," she said. "Can you find the connections between the group of beasts that ambushed us? I can add a biological tracker with my house."

Origon thumbed his wispy moustache for a moment, then listened to something hidden from her. "I am having a better idea." He gestured to the air with one hand, as if pulling ropes, and lines of yellow formed, twisting paths following where the beasts had been. Rilan watched him work. He was doing something with the House of Communication, tracking the air currents and communication between the animals. It took time to identify the correct chords of the Symphony. If they were too fast or too strong, it would be harder to change, more prone to failure. But Origon was quick, and decisive. His other hand came forward and orange light flashed between the yellow ropes, lightning strikes of the interchanges of power and hierarchy between the group. He began to walk forward, favoring his good leg, not even looking to see if Rilan was behind him.

"Or you could do it yourself," Rilan mumbled. "So the maji of the Great Assembly work for the good of all..."

She followed Origon, one hand on her aching rib.

PART FOUR

Hidden Chords

Upon answering the Lobath's summons, I found his mate near death in childbirth with severe complications. After a lengthy procedure, I saved the female Lobath's life. The child, however was stillborn and disfigured in strange ways, as if its body skipped some stages of growth and accelerated others. Medically, I cannot say what happened. One of my colleagues in the House of Healing believes the infant was actively changing three of the six Symphonies. This is, of course, impossible. Nevertheless, the House of Healing followed the woman's progress for several cycles until she birthed two completely healthy, and otherwise unremarkable, children.

—Fragment of a medical diagnosis found in the archives of the House of Healing, 506 AAW

The land rose steadily until they found the entrance to the cave. It was set amidst a cluster of giant cilia-bark trees, and if Origon's ropes of yellow and orange hadn't pointed directly to the entrance, Rilan would have missed it.

The entrance was low, but soon opened up into a larger cavern, tall enough even for Origon to stand straight. Rilan was thankful for that, as bending didn't help her rib any. The walls were natural, a crack in the crust of the earth. Small animals had made their mark here and there. She wondered if the sabretooth beasts used this cave too.

"Look." She pointed toward a covered lantern hanging from a hook in the wall. An orange aura surrounded it, but it gave physical light as well— a soft yellow glow. Rilan knew it would give that light for many cycles, notes from the House of Power stored by one of the House of Potential. They were common in the Nether. Not so much in the wilds of Festuour.

"This is to be the correct location." Origon made a dismissive motion. The yellow and orange ropes around them vanished as he sucked in a long breath, his music returning to him, the changes to the Symphony reversed. He limped forward, and Rilan followed him with a grunt. Either standing or walking was fine, but her rib didn't like changing between the two.

They followed the chain of lights, set in crevices in the walls. The rough floor descended steadily down, while the roof soared far overhead. In places where the walls would be too narrow to pass through, there were marks of tools, expanding the passage.

"There are to be many lights," Origon remarked. At first Rilan wondered what he meant, but then she saw. The majus lights were set at regular intervals, no more than a few paces apart. Each had their faint aura of orange, with hints of brown to show the work of one of the House of Potential, though the aura gave no real light. They lit the passage very well. Too well. There was more than enough to keep good footing along the passage.

"Why would a majus expend so much of their song on a permanent investment?" Rilan asked. Origon nodded in agreement.

"It is as if this majus does not understand the costs of making permanent changes to the Symphony." Before long, the majus would become weak, unable to craft the larger changes more complicated works required.

They followed the passage until the first pipes began to appear.

"What are those?" Rilan whispered as she pointed to a brace holding two long cylinders, one of a thin beaten metal, and the other of what looked to be stiff oiled fabric. Their voices dropped in volume the farther they went.

"Vents?" Origon offered. "Maybe there is to be no good source of air deep in the cavern."

"Hmm." Rilan watched another pipe emerge from above and join the other two as they walked. "Or maybe there is something below generating fumes that need ventilation." She sniffed, but the air was still fresh, if a little musty.

"Perhaps we should be moving more quietly," Origon suggested. The cave was alive with little noises; drips, creaks, and rustlings. It covered the sounds of a person moving slowly and carefully. Still, best to be safe.

"I don't think I'm the problem." She glanced down at Origon's thick boots, just peeping from underneath the edge of his now filthy robe hem. He was clumping along louder than usual, with his limp, but he made an effort to reduce his noise. She tried to silence the sound of her labored breathing.

The cavern passage split several times, but always the lights went one direction, and they followed. More pipes joined the three, until there was a bundle on each side, above their heads. There was more metal now, though a few pipes were still made of oiled fabric. Rilan could see valves, gears, and pressure catches in the light from the lamps. Origon was paying careful attention to them, and she wondered if he was listening to the Symphony of Power. What would it tell him about the forces directed along the pipes?

Before long, another sound began to intrude on the other ambient noises. It was continuous, a hissing tick every few seconds like a large clock run by steam. Rilan traded glances with Origon. There was a brighter glow ahead, where the passage took a turn to the left.

"Someone has been here a long time," Origon whispered.

Rilan positioned herself just before the turn in the corridor, gesturing Origon beside her. The rough wall poked her back. She could see marks around the bright entrance, as if someone made an effort to make the opening regular.

She held up three fingers, then two, then—

Origon silently turned into the room ahead of her. Rilan rolled her eyes and followed him, her cracked rib complaining at resuming movement.

The room was illuminated by many majus lights, and Rilan shielded her eyes until they adjusted. The run of pipes in the corridor had nothing on this room. Bunches of them reduced to smaller, thicker tubes, feeding into cabinets filled with whirring gears, pistons, and bellows. Dials and readouts fluctuated above them. Machinery lined the walls of the cavern, twenty or thirty paces across. Some of the equipment was mechanical, while other tables held chemical reagents. A large cabinet near the far wall was the source of the hiss-tick they heard in the hallway. Puffs of steam left it with every beat, and dials spun in the body of the thing. In the middle of the room was a table, obscured by the furry figure bent over it. It was a Festuour.

Origon was in the middle of the doorway, Rilan positioned behind him. They hadn't been seen, and she was just about to pull Origon back when the figure turned.

"Oh! You're early." The Festuour—Rilan was pretty sure it was female, and somehow familiar, at that—was draped in an apron filled with pockets holding calipers, pencils, rulers, and scientific looking devices for which she had no name. The Festuour glanced at a dial on the wall through three pairs of spectacles set at various distances down her snout. "I was sure as punch you would get here twenty minutes later. No matter." She drew one of the devices from her apron—a tube with a piston on one end and a dial on the other. She waved it in Rilan's direction and it made a whistling noise, creating a strange harmonic with the Symphony. Rilan shook her head. "House of Healing. Fine." The Festuour waved her device at Origon and Rilan saw his crest flare. He swayed back in surprise. "And House of Power. Have one of those already." She lifted the middle pair of spectacles and peered through the other two, then turned the dial on the side of the device. "And the House of Communication! That's much better."

Rilan tensed.

"I don't have many visitors out here, as you must imagine," the Festuour told them. Her voice was high, her fur brown and green in patches. She was not old, from what Rilan could tell. Was this their fearsome adversary?

"And so many these last few days!" the Festuour continued. "Well, you must admit, that's surprising as can be. Still, I try to be a hospitable host."

Rilan looked at Origon again. More visitors.

"Someone else has been here? Another Kirian?" she asked. The Festuour blinked at her, seeming not to hear.

"You must excuse my manners. Let me introduce myself. I am Aptibontigon Ket, Maker. Fernand Vethis has told me much about you."

"Wait. *Vethis?*" Rilan wondered if she heard wrong, then realized why the Festuour looked familiar. It was the one she had seen him with after their test.

Ket moved her mass to one side. "Yes. Didn't he tell you he was coming? Let me guess. Wanted to keep all the fun for himself." The Festuour was certainly a majus. They had no trouble communicating, and Rilan was making no effort to translate her words.

There was a body on the table Ket had been leaning over. Rilan saw enough of the dark hair and a hint of his face to recognize her classmate. What had he gotten into now, and how? Was he even still alive?

"What about my brother?" Origon's hands were at his side, clenched. His crest rose like a fan. He spoke before she could ask more about her rival classmate, motionless on the table.

Ket blinked again. "I'm afraid I don't know anything about him. You must explain. What house does he belong to?"

"He is not a majus."

Ket pulled her middle set of spectacles off again. Glancing down at the strange instrument she still held, she fiddled with it, then pointed it at Origon. "Curious. You are older than he, I gather." She seemed unconcerned they had found her.

"I..." Origon stopped short, his hands loosening. "I am. How are you knowing that?" Rilan took advantage of their conversation to sidle slightly to one side. Maybe she could get close enough to see what Ket had done to Vethis. If he was here now, he must have left around the same time they did. She *had* seen them again the morning they left. Ket could have brought him directly here, of course, but why? What did he have to do with this?

"You belong to two houses," Ket said, as if it were self-explanatory. Then she made an annoyed click of her tongue. "I forget others haven't studied the theory of the Grand Symphony as much as I have. I studied acoustics when I was young, you know. Still do."

Rilan concentrated on getting out of the Festuour's field of view, using slow footwork from *Fading Hands*, though the creature was as good as ignoring her. Maybe it would have been better to go on the offensive immediately and incapacitate the majus, but something in her protested against such violence when their opponent was so calm. And, her rib hurt too much.

"I have studied several maji belonging to two houses. In all cases, their birth was followed soon after by a younger brother or sister, devoid of any talent with the Symphony." Ket spoke earnestly to Origon, as if delivering a thesis to the Council.

"This is not to be unusual," Origon countered. "Many maji have siblings. The ability is rare enough that it often does not show in families." Rilan would have laughed if she wasn't so tense. Just like a Kirian to start debating a point when faced with a potentially lethal adversary in a hidden underground lab.

"Yes, but in these cases, the sibling was usually sickly, did not make much of themselves, and often perished young."

Rilan could see Origon's face tighten. She was almost around the room now, and had a better view of the table. It was definitely Vethis, and he was merely unconscious, not dead. He had some sort of fabric mask over his mouth, and a tube was inserted beneath the skin of his left wrist. That triggered another memory. Something about circular marks.

"It is my theory," Ket continued, "That the elder sibling sometimes takes the potential that would be passed on to the second child. The older one robs the younger one, if you will, of its future as a majus." Her voice was easy and calm, as if speaking over a casual lunch.

When Origon started forward, Rilan took the chance to move closer to the table, tracing the tube under Vethis' wrist. "I did not rob my brother! I was caring for him, his whole life." His voice rose, his hands trembling as they reached forward. "I was going to visit him again soon, before I was getting the message—"

"Yes, and you see what happened to him," Ket interrupted. "Maybe if he had access to that second house you wield, he would have lived. Maybe he could have fended off the thrycovolars that followed him. They don't usually hunt people, whatever species."

"You—!" Origon's normally pale skin was growing more flushed by the moment. Rilan glanced between them. The Festuour knew about Delphorus. She had killed him, or let him be killed.

But Delphorus hadn't had any marks on him. She remembered the strips of flesh ripped off the beasts—the thrycovolars. They wouldn't have been able to recognize Origon's brother if the creatures had killed him. She watched Ket through narrowed eyes. What was the Festuour doing?

Origon had both hands up, a yellow and orange glow mixing around them. He was going to do something, and though the heads of the houses forbade maji to fight each other, Rilan wasn't sure she wanted to stop him. She traced where the other end of Vethis' tube vanished into a machine and guessed at the most likely off switch, stabbing down at a carved rocker. The Festuour was ignoring her, for whatever reason, focusing only on Origon. She could use that time to her advantage.

"It is truly a shame about your brother," Ket remarked, hurrying to the hissing machine on the other side of the room. She switched topics. "You must tell me how the mixture of the Houses of Communication and Power changes the way the Symphony is heard." She twisted dials and flipped knobs, glancing back at Origon every few moments.

Rilan's machine sighed, and some life went out of it. She went back to Vethis, sparing a glance at Origon, who was having some difficulty, the aura around him pulsing and fading. The change he was preparing must be particularly complex.

"I'll need that information after all," Ket said, "when I get used to the new house."

Connections bloomed in Rilan's mind. Ket *wanted* Origon to attack her. She reached a hand out, wincing at the ache. "Ori—"

Something beeped near Vethis and Ket spun. "Oh, you mustn't do that." She gestured, and a brown aura flashed across the room. The House of Potential. The machine behind Rilan started back up. Rilan watched with wide eyes. To rewrite the Symphony of a complex machine was a difficult thing, nearly as hard as rewriting the Symphony of a living thing. And the Festuour had done it at a distance without hesitation. Rilan would have needed several moments to catch the measure and tone of a person's music. Ket was fast, and powerful.

Then she saw Origon, slowly sinking to the floor. She was too late. The orange haze was still around him, but the yellow one was gone, or very faint. Across the room, another yellow aura hovered near the hiss-tick machine by Ket. She had transferred it somehow; stolen the change he made to the Symphony. Origon would lose those notes of his song. No wonder he had buckled.

Rilan pressed the rocker switch again. Anything Ket didn't want her to do was a good thing. When the beep sounded once more, the rogue majus was buried in the dials and didn't seem to hear it. Rilan patted at Vethis' cheek, while keeping an eye on Origon. The Kirian was pale and gasping, but still conscious.

"Wake up!" she hissed. Any ally would be an asset, even an arrogant fop like Vethis. He murmured something and his eyelids fluttered. Origon was on his knees, and Ket was still at the controls, doing something. Rilan made eye contact with her friend and made a motion toward him. He shook his head, very slightly, and gestured her back to the table. He wanted her to wake Vethis up too.

Gently, Rilan pulled the tube back out of Vethis' wrist. It wasn't in deep, but the diameter narrowed to a point. It was probably injecting some concoction straight into his veins. She only just had it out, blotting the small wound, when Ket turned back, taking in the whole situation with one look.

She tsked. "Really now, that's rude of you. Do you know how long it took me to prep him? I only perfected the technique a ten-day ago, and I haven't had the chance to complete the transfer." The Festuour pushed out with both hands and something glowed between them, both giving off real orange light and ringed with the orange of the House of Power.

Her second house. She had already demonstrated the House of Potential. Rilan had no idea what the majus was capable of. She began to time the beat of her own song, getting ready.

As Ket pushed outward, the ring of orange expanded forward, leaving her fingers and moving toward Rilan. She guessed the majus was manipulating heat and changed notes to toughen her skin. Her eyes flicked to Vethis. She didn't have time to change his melody too.

Origon, from his knees, curved his fingers through an arc in the air, then slumped again. The wave of orange bowed away from her, toward the high ceiling of the cavern.

Rilan felt an intense drying heat frizzle her hair and shivered involuntarily. Her change would not have stopped that. She quickly reversed what she had done, regaining that part of her song. She would need it.

Ket snapped her long jaws together—a sign of irritation in Festuour—and began some other change in the Symphony of Power. Too late she realized what Rilan saw. Origon hadn't just deflected the wave of heat, he had taken the change from her—a permanent investment on his part. Her friend had a hand on the floor, holding himself up. Oddly, Ket didn't seem to notice. Rilan winced at his loss, even as the orange wave curved back down.

Ket followed Rilan's involuntary glance upward and the haze around her graduated from orange to a brilliant white in a split second. Rilan heard chords change, almost quicker than she could register. Origon's eyes widened. The wave of heat washed over Ket and her fur crinkled, but there was no other effect. The brilliant white faded.

The Festuour had switched Symphonies, mid-tune. To her *third* house.

"I have few notes of that kind of song left to waste," Ket said. "Either of you two can provide me with more." She gestured beside Rilan. Vethis had his eyes open, and was pulling the mask from his face.

"She has a machine that steals a majus' song," Vethis said, his voice hoarse, his clipped, affected accent barely showing through. "She stole those notes from me. And she stole something from that other Kirian."

"Is that even possible?" Rilan asked.

Vethis glared up at her. "I thought you were supposed to be the smart one." His accent was already clearer.

"Of course it is," Ket put in. "I had experimented on Kiria with the energy transfer before I was...interrupted." She looked annoyed.

Origon regained his feet, shaking his head as if clearing it. He growled something, and his crest looked like he had been struck by lightning. Rilan helped Vethis sit up, gathering her song and planning how best to disable Ket. She only needed a moment to—

"You must excuse me. I'm afraid I won't be a very good host to three maji." Ket walked, fast, to the only other blank section of wall. There was a medallion hanging on it, like the ones they had seen on the creatures outside. They must have been artifacts of the House of Potential— storing larger systems of changes to the Symphony.

"My brother!" Origon rushed forward at the same time as Rilan. The room wasn't big, but Ket moved faster. A bright aura erupted from her, brown and orange and white all together. The yellow aura around the hiss-tick machine flew to her and joined the mix. The medallion flashed in response, glowing incandescent. Just as Rilan got to the Festuour, gritting her teeth against the pain in her chest, the wall in front of her dissolved into nothingness and Ket scooted through.

Rilan skidded to a stop as the wall re-solidified in front of her nose. She fell against the hard surface as Origon bumped into her from behind. She made a pained sound, one hand going to her ribs.

"What was that?" he said over her shoulder. He reached out a long finger and scraped down the wall. It was hard as stone. There was no way they could burrow through in time.

Rilan could only shake her head. "I have no idea. Solidified air and fire, made organic? Pure kinetic energy converted to solid matter? With four houses mixed together, the possibilities are endless. Ket must have heard almost the entire Grand Symphony underlying the universe, all at once. It's enough to make anyone mad." Ket was definitely not operating on the same tune as the rest of them.

She turned around as Origon backed away. Vethis was shakily getting to his feet, one hand already preening his hair. "We can't relax," she said. "No telling when she'll come back. We must keep watch." Rilan frowned, looking around the cavern, trying to think of a way to get to the majus.

"I think she was using up most of the notes she stole from me. Luckily, she was not taking all of them. She could be limited to only three houses now." As he spoke, Origon stepped toward the medallion, eyeing it while one hand stroked his moustaches meditatively.

"Or two," Vethis added. "She might not have much left from the House of Healing after what she put into those horrible beasts." His affected accent was back full force—something popular with the other aristocratic prats where he hailed from, some city far to the north of Rilan's birth town.

Rilan crossed to the apprentice. He shouldn't even be out of the Nether before he tested. She wondered when she had started taking for granted that she was a majus. "Speaking of which, what, by Shiv's labyrinthine guts, are *you* doing here?"

Vethis flinched back, raising a velvet sleeve. He was still dressed in the clothes from their test, black-blue velvet coat, striped pants, and white cuffs. A deep blue collar—his secondary color—set off his dark hair.

"I might ask you the same," he returned, peering down his thin nose at her. "Shouldn't you be doing some great deed with the rest of the maji, now you're one of them? Too good for the rest of us—the second best— eh?"

"Answer the question, *apprentice*," Origon said from behind her. "How were you getting here ahead of us? What were you seeing of my brother? Are you knowing where Ket went?"

"I can't tell you much." Vethis sniffed. "The other Kirian was already dead when I got here. That wretched pretend majus drained the life right out of him. It was a terrible experiment on her part. She said something about paying him back for interrupting her." He closed his mouth, eyeing them. When Origon's crest flared and he limped forward, Vethis backed up and began speaking again.

"As to how I got here, the despicable creature invited me. First she wanted information. She picked the right person to come to, of course." Rilan rolled her eyes and motioned for him to continue. "The strange thing was, she wanted information on *him*." Vethis pointed at Origon. "Of course, now I know she wanted him because of his brother. At the time, I thought she had some other purpose, so I was very willing to share what I knew of *you two*." He grinned at her and she wondered how much of the Nether was talking about her and Origon. Then Vethis frowned. "But she wasn't interested in what I had to offer. She started on about a new source of power for all maji, so I went with her. I had no clue the source would be *me*." Origon turned away from Vethis, his wrinkled face twisting in a grimace.

Of course her classmate jumped at that chance. Any whisper of power or influence and he was on it like a Kirian on a grub. He must have been an easy target for the rogue majus, especially after failing his test. Another thought struck her. Ket had been *at* their test. If Rilan had been the one to fail, would Ket have come after her instead? Of course she wouldn't have taken the bait. That feeling of dread when she thought she might fail rose up within her. She hoped she wouldn't have taken it.

Origon grunted behind her and Rilan turned to him too quickly. The heaviness of this world made her rib feel like it was cracking all over again whenever she moved.

"I cannot hear a large enough part of the melody." He was fiddling with the medallion now, yellow and orange sparking between his fingers. "The music is to be too fast for me to catch, and there is too much of at least one other house in it." He shifted, and almost fell as his leg gave out under him.

"Oh for the sake of all that's holy," Vethis said. "Are you still that terrible with healing, Rilan? It's in the *name* of our house, you know."

Rilan glared at him, even as he reached for her. If he touched anything but her ribs, he was drawing back a nub.

But Vethis' fingers were strangely gentle, white and the dark blue of his personal color extending from his hands to the outline of her ribcage. Rilan couldn't quite make out what he did. The melody for encouraging pure healing was almost impossible for her to change, like trying to whistle a base drumbeat. Each majus had areas where they were more skilled.

"There. That should feel better." Vethis watched her until she gave a grudging nod, rotating an arm. It did feel better, but he wasn't getting out of this that easy. He gave her a knowing half-smile and went to Origon, who received Vethis' attentions with a grunt of thanks, still investigating the medallion.

"Don't thank me," Vethis responded, straightening his hair again. "Healing you two means I have a better chance of getting out alive. That crazy bear is tough."

"And she may be coming back at any point," Origon put in. "Do you know where she went? Why was she needing my stolen notes to create the door it if it was there previously?"

Vethis shook his head. "I didn't even know it *was* there. I've been on that table most of the last two days." He pointed with a limp finger toward the table in the middle of the room. "I suspect you're not going to let me make a portal back to the Nether and be done with this mess." Rilan glared at him. Origon's crest had gone all spiky again. "Didn't think so."

"We cannot be letting this criminal loose again," Origon said. "She has already killed several times."

"What is she doing in there?" Rilan smacked the wall with one palm where the doorway had been. It was hard, unyielding. Origon began to investigate each machine in turn.

Vethis watched them both, arms crossed. "Is she even in there any longer? She could have made a portal to anywhere by now. As *we* should."

Rilan ignored him, grasping her braid and pulling it around front. She tapped the bell into her palm with a tiny jingle. *Think.*

"Should we be destroying her equipment?" Origon asked from halfway across the room.

"We don't even know what it does," Rilan told him, watching his progress over one shoulder. "It could all be to vent chemicals to the outside, for what we know."

Vethis pointed at the hiss-tick machine. "That one steals the song from a majus. Or were you not paying attention again? I wonder how you even passed your test."

Origon shrugged and went for the machine, but Rilan waved him away. "And what happens if we beat it to pieces? Have you ever heard of any machine like that? It could suck the rest of our songs away if it malfunctions. We should be figuring out how to get to Ket."

"But what if the design is getting out?" Origon asked. "Imagine if more people could be arbitrarily stealing one's house and song."

Rilan almost missed the gleam in Vethis' eye. She stared him down, daring him to move toward the machine. "Maybe it is better to destroy it." She started to turn away from where Ket had disappeared.

At that moment the wall in front of her dissolved.

Ket snarled, flinging something glowing white, orange and brown at her. It was another medallion. It stuck to her chest, and a searing pain coursed through her. She stumbled back, gasping, hearing Origon yell something. All her senses were going black.

Then there was an intense white light. As Rilan fell back into the table, she saw her hand glowing. Was she changing the Symphony without knowing it? What was happening?

Origon was beside her as her eyes cleared and she saw the little bell in her hand, now devoid of any aura.

It will ward off disease. Thank you, Majus Meyta. Whatever the majus had thrown at her had some element of the House of Healing holding it together, and not a pleasant one.

For once, Ket looked surprised. "You should be dead," she complained, as she closed the distance between them.

"You're not actually very good, are you?" Rilan said, backpedaling. "Fast, yes, and you have lots of power. I would too if I stole it from others." She got back to her feet, Origon beside her. "Are you even a majus? I've never heard of you." Out of the corner of her eye she saw Vethis bolt for the secret room, getting away from the fight. *Coward.*

Ket looked uncertain for only a moment, then her long face twisted up. "I'll be the most powerful majus ever," she said. She started some change, orange and yellow flaring around her arms, but Origon stepped in front of Rilan, hands moving. The air rippled as a curve of compressed air came into being, like the tent when they camped.

Ket's changes beat against the shield, making it wobble. "You must be pleased. Your kind is so smug, controlling the Assembly and all the species. Just because someone is a majus, they're automatically at the top of their field." She flung a hand out, orange and brown ringing it, and it passed completely through Origon's shield. Rilan gasped, something burning in her chest, but only for a moment. Origon had both hands out, his head cocked like he was trying to get a note just right. His crest came to a point in concentration, then relaxed. The heat left her.

"The maji are to be providing for all species," he said. "If some are renowned for their jobs as well, it is because they worked hard to get there." He was brewing another change as he spoke, yellow and orange roiling around his hands. Yet he still kept the shield in place. It would take more concentration, but if he let it fall, he would not be able to make another one for a while. Rilan fell into her own Symphony, listening to all the music of life in the room. Ket's music was off, tempo jerking and stopping. Accessing that many houses was not good for her body. Rilan tried to find a way to incapacitate her.

"*I* worked hard," the Festuour said. "*I* should have been at the top of my field. Why should only maji study the Grand Symphony? It's a beautiful thing. Did you know there are ways to hear the notes mechanically? It's only science. But you maji don't quantify it—you don't study it. You *worship* it."

A glow surrounded Ket suddenly, appearing all at once. It was a large change to the Symphony, and made quickly. Rilan finally understood. Everything Ket did was a permanent change to the Symphony. She wasn't trying to regain any notes, so of course her changes were more powerful—she didn't have to be careful to make reversible changes, the way other maji did. And why not? Everything she was using was stolen. If she ran out, she could just steal more.

All this passed through Rilan's mind in a fraction of a second, while she watched Origon's hands rise slowly, starting to glow. He was making a change in both the House of Communication and Power, maybe another change to the air, maybe something else to defend against what was coming. Rilan began her own change, using her song to heighten her reactions. If she could get around Origon's shield in time to touch the Festuour, she could start destroying muscle and tissue. It wasn't pleasant, but it was quick. Entropy always was.

Though her senses processed faster, the Symphony was unchanged. It still played at its own pace, and she struggled to gather together all the phrases she would change to affect her opponent. She watched Ket's aura, orange and brown, spear toward her and too late to stop it, felt her contact with the Symphony falter. Her opponent was using the Houses of Power and Potential in combination to sap Rilan's connection with the Symphony. This must be what Origon felt before.

Indeed, his yellow and orange construction was flickering too. Rilan saw bits of her own white and olive floating away from her, crossing the room to that terrible hiss-tick machine. She poured more concentration into her change but the notes slipped away, like the music was in another room, and then in another building. Her enhanced senses were slipping away too, the change stolen from her. The very notes making her song were leaving.

Rilan's knees buckled, and she saw Origon slump.

Then there was a hollow sound, like a melon being slapped, and Ket's blue eyes rolled back in their sockets. The suction stopped and Rilan stood, weakly.

Ket fell back to reveal Vethis, a hollow metal pipe dangling from his hands. He dropped it with a clang.

"Never liked the idea of fighting with the Symphony," he said, brushing his hands off with distaste. "It feels so crass."

PART FIVE

Re-Tuning

4th of the Protector's Month, 979 AAW
Waveform function experiments performing well. I have determined there is a certain progression of chords in the Grand Symphony which may characterize one house of the maji from another.

32nd of the Protector's Month, 979 AAW
The House of Strength seems to exhibit the lowest notes of the Grand Symphony, often dipping below the lower threshold of my instruments. Made note to create a second set of connections in the resonancy chamber.

16th of the Watcher's Month, 979 AAW
The House of Healing is a very delicate Symphony compared to those of the other houses. Might be able to use harmonics to create a set of defining patterns. Similar to House of Potential in some aspects?

—From the journal of Aptibontigon Ket, Maker.

"The room back there is absolutely filled with equipment," Vethis said. "I ducked in to see what I could find. There are a fair number of those blasted medallions, for one thing. And journals of notes, and lots of spare parts. I'm certain it takes an effort to keep these things running." Vethis gestured vaguely to the humming machinery.

Rilan stood erect, then pressed her hands against her legs to stop them shaking. She felt weak, drained.

"Thank you." It was one of the hardest things she had ever said. Vethis gave a tiny bow, smirking.

Origon had his hands on his knees, his purple and orange checked robe bunching around his skinny legs. "What shall we be doing with her?"

"We'll take her back to the Council, of course," Rilan said.

Vethis looked between both of them, one hand on his chin. "There are...other... things we can do, you know. No one need ever hear of this."

Rilan shook her head. "Absolutely not." She would have to be a whole lot weaker before she let Vethis get away with something like that.

Once she got her breath back, she leaned over the fallen Festuour, listening to the Symphony of Healing play out. She touched Ket's brow with one finger, sparking white and olive as she picked the right notes and changed them so the false majus would sleep. She didn't have to do much with the head injury. There was blood in her fur where Vethis hit her, still flowing. Rilan could tell from the Symphony it wouldn't kill her, but Ket would be out for a while.

She stood back up, wincing as pain spiked through her own head. "Let's see this room." She gestured Vethis forward, who led with a frown. She knew what he wanted, and he wasn't getting it if she got her way. Origon followed behind them.

The journals were the largest part of Ket's collection. They dated back nearly fifteen cycles. They spent some time looking through them, during which she and Origon both kept an eye on Vethis.

"Look here." Rilan waved a sheet. They had been reading for several minutes. "She was working with a majus from the House of Potential." She read the journal entry again. "One I don't recognize. Sounds like he had a heart attack and...the equipment somehow transferred his ability to her. She doesn't even know how it happened. I was right. She wasn't a majus, to begin with. Can that even happen?"

"I have never heard of it," Origon answered. "If it is possible, it would be shaking the maji to the very core. Our entire institution is depending on the scarcity of maji. Imagine if everyone could be changing the Symphony." Rilan saw Vethis give a dramatic shiver.

"What would that many changes to the Symphony do?"

"Most likely unravel the universe," Vethis said. He hefted a sheaf of notes. "But I believe the ability can only be stolen, or given away. She believed there was a natural constant to the maximum number of maji, a universal constant, if you will."

"She was beginning as merely an acoustic scientist," Origon added, reading his own pages. "She was to be working on a way to channel the Grand Symphony." He gestured to another page. "This is to be from three cycles ago. Are you remembering the majus north of Martflen that the sheriff mentioned?" Rilan nodded, recalling the Festuour's words, a chill running through her. He hadn't seen her for three cycles.

"That was to be her second victim," Origon said. "A majus of the House of Power. It was at the same time she made this lab." His face tightened, his crest hanging limply. "And then she began testing the apparatus on Kirians. Probably to keep the focus away from this location. Delphorus found out about her and began investigating. I believe he was merely in the wrong place at the wrong time, doing his duty. I am wondering if she even received any benefit from draining his energy away." He paused, as if unwilling to say his next words. "Maybe I was doing that long ago."

"You can't believe that," Rilan told him. "You can hear two of the six Symphonies that make up the universe. You didn't steal them. *She* did."

Origon nodded, but she could tell his heart wasn't in it. This would take a long time to heal, but it would, with her help.

Vethis didn't seem interested in the journals any longer, putting down his papers to poke through the spare parts. Pouting, more likely. He would have been the next victim. Ket must have only drained enough of his song to create the system making the beasts into her guard dogs. Why had she waited so long in between the majus north of Martflen and Vethis? Training her new powers, maybe, and building her equipment. It might explain why those changes were so well put together while the one from the House of Healing was so sloppy.

"How did she handle so many houses at once?" Rilan asked, both to change the subject, and out of curiosity. She hadn't found anything to explain that yet.

To her surprise, Vethis answered. "It's something that horrible machine does," he said, fingering a steam valve. "She created it. It lets the recipient keep from losing his or her mind, as well as stealing notes from maji. Otherwise she would have been dead by now." He looked up suddenly. "She, ah, mentioned something about it while I was lying on that table."

They finished looking through the notes, and took them back to the main room. They would take them to the Council along with Ket. This was too important to leave to any one majus.

Origon dusted his hands. "Are we ready to be going? I will open a portal from here and you can be taking the rogue majus through."

Of course he would give her the dirty work. "Come over here and help me," she called to Vethis. She wasn't picking up Ket all on her own. Festuour weren't light.

"One moment." Vethis' voice was airy, distracted. "Just one more thing."

Rilan heard the faint click at the same time as Origon. Both of them spun to the other side of the room, where Vethis was quietly adjusting dials on the hiss-tick machine.

"No!" Rilan reached out a hand, but it was too late. Something was already rising from Ket—a blob of orange and brown. She ran to the Festuour, but before she could gain the full score of the other's music, Ket had breathed her last.

"She deserved that," Vethis spat. "No one steals from me." He spun back to the machine, pulling levers and pushing buttons. "Now let's see how far behind I am, with three houses at my disposal. Give me only a few moments. I'll even be fair. You can try it after I do." How had he learned to use the machine? She knew the man wasn't stupid, just lazy. He must have observed Ket or seen instructions when he was in the secret room alone.

"Vethis, stop this!" Rilan shouted.

"No chance." He darted a look back at them, then toward the machine. "You can't stop me. I know this location. If you drag me away now, I'll merely come back later, when you aren't looking. You cannot have eyes on me all the time. This will take but a moment. Think of the benefits when we know how this works."

Surely he didn't think they would let him get away with this? Rilan looked to Origon, to Vethis, and back. She had to do something, quickly.

Origon locked eyes with her, pointed to her, to Vethis, and then tapped his temple. Rilan looked aghast at him. Was he saying what she thought? It was an intrusion of the worst kind.

Origon raised his bushy eyebrows and pointed to the man's back.

Rilan took a deep breath, stepping quietly across the floor, using training her father taught her in her youth to step silently. Vethis hadn't looked a second time, absorbed in the details of the hiss-tick machine, hands moving quickly over the controls. She heard the Symphony of his body come into clarity as she got closer, then the more subtle Symphony of his mind. She would need to touch him for this to work, but she gathered the pieces of the Symphony in her mind beforehand, noting where she would use her song to make adjustments to chemicals in his brain.

She hesitated only for a moment, standing behind him. He was still adjusting dials, directing the machine to give him the stolen abilities. Hers were not the heroic actions the Council championed, but she was still serving the people of the Great Assembly. She couldn't imagine a Nether with Vethis in control of three houses, any more than Ket, or anyone else, for that matter.

He must have finally heard or felt something, but he turned too late. Rilan put her open palm on his glossy black hair.

She changed his mind.

It was a complex adjustment, burning away memories of the last few days. Much of it she had to do quickly as she encountered the deeper levels of the Symphony defining his mind, catching notes and musical phrases as they flew past. Many sections went almost too fast, but she kept on, her lips pressing together. He fought back, weakly, but he was surprised and she had the full measure of his Symphony. She merely brushed his efforts away. This was her discipline. She was a psychologist. And she was a majus of the House of Healing.

She was supposed to help people with mental issues, not take advantage of them. It was so easy to slide into rationalizing that this was necessary. This would be the first and last time she did such a thing.

Rilan found his hatred of her along the way, burning as brightly as hers of him. She peeked at the chords, surprised to recognize jealousy and shame among them, even more than the hatred. She could just...

No. She resisted the urge to remove it, and gave that tiny win to her conscience. She understood a little better now why he antagonized her. But why was he jealous? If he just applied himself, he could be every bit as effective as she was in the House of Healing.

From now on, every time he looked at her, every time he spoke, she would remember she had the opportunity to change that view of her, and hadn't. She would be the better person.

When she was done, Vethis sank down into a sleep similar to the one Ket had been in. Before he killed her. She wanted him to answer to the Council for his actions, but that was impossible now. He would recall nothing of the past three days. That was more important even than bringing this to the Council.

Rilan found her hands shaking, and not with fatigue. She looked to Origon and something in her face must have told him what she was thinking.

"This was to be the right thing to do," he said. "And this is what being a majus truly is. Are you understanding, now, why I spend so much time on the homeworlds and away from the Nether?"

Rilan thought she did, just a bit. Things happened out here. Things with no right or wrong answer. The Council, for all its power, could not control everything. It was up to the individual majus to do that. But too many maji stayed in the Nether, preferring to turn a blind eye. His words sank in, and her next question became clear.

"With Ket dead, there's no proof here any longer." After the results of Vethis' betrayal, they must get rid of this threat forever. "Should we really give the research to the Council?"

Origon gave her a lopsided half-smile, several pointy teeth showing on one side. "What do you think they will be doing with the knowledge?"

Rilan thought for several moments on that, listening to the hiss-tick that filled the silent room. She eyed Vethis, curled up on the floor.

"Even if they kept it secret, sooner or later someone would come along with more ambition than sense."

"Someone like him?" Origon nodded at the slumbering Vethis.

Rilan grimaced at the thought of Vethis ever being on the Council. That would be the day.

"So what do we do with it?" She looked around the cavern.

"We destroy it," Origon answered, as if that had been his plan all along.

It took time, but they disconnected all the machinery from the pipes and from the steam generators. Rilan bent the ends of the pipes so they wouldn't connect to the machines again easily. Origon was the one to destroy the research. She thought he might make some grand change to the House of Power to cause them to combust, but instead he produced a set of matches from somewhere in his robe.

"Sometimes easier is to be better." He set the pile of notes alight.

Rilan watched the journals burn. "Someday I'll be on the Council. I'll make it so these things don't happen anymore."

Origon only smiled at her. "But first, I am hoping you'll travel with me. This has been...exciting."

Rilan thought over the last several days and shook her head. "Exciting" wouldn't have been her first choice of words.

"We should hide the cave entrance, too," she said.

* * *

Councilor Feldo was manning the portal ground at the Spire of the Maji when they came back to the Nether. Rilan knew even the councilors were not exempt from this duty, but she had never actually *seen* one at the post.

"Celebrating your success?" the councilor asked, arching an eyebrow at the limp form of Vethis slung between them. They had left Ket's body in the cave with her equipment, under a pile of rubble. Origon had been adept at exploiting hidden faults in the cave system with the House of Power. It was unlikely anyone would find it now. "I am surprised Apprentice Vethis accompanied you."

"Merely a short trip to be exploring the possibilities inherent in becoming a majus," Origon said.

"You did suggest we should work together," Rilan added, smiling innocently.

Councilor Feldo only grunted at them, his bushy black beard pointing accusingly until they left the portal ground.

They dropped Vethis off in his room. He would wake up thinking he had celebrated far too heavily the night before with his rich cronies. Rilan knew it wasn't an uncommon thing for him, and his friends likely wouldn't be able to remember either. Another few days lost to intoxicants.

They collapsed at Origon's apartment. They both needed to use his bath.

"I'll need to find another place to live, now that I'm a majus," Rilan told him.

"You were never giving me an answer, before," he said.

"Will I travel with you?"

Origon nodded.

Rilan found she didn't have to think as hard about that as she expected. "Will there be more like this?"

"Much more," he said, his crest fluttering in excitement.

"Then maybe next time we can find a proper inn or hostel to stay in while we travel," Rilan told him.

Origon gave her a full pointy smile—the one that disconcerted most of her species, but not her. "With a comfy bed."

Rilan smiled back. "I'll bring my things up tonight, then." She started to get up from one of his overstuffed chairs.

"I will be needing to contact Wint, to send my brother's body back," Origon said, getting up as well. "He is likely wondering where we went and hoping we also are not going to turn up dead in the forest."

"They do like to avoid hubbub," Rilan added, and was rewarded with a sad smile from Origon.

He went to the mantle, pulling one piece of paper from his pocket, and picking up a portrait. It was the same one she had seen before, of him and his brother, both looking much younger.

"What is that?" Rilan asked.

Origon looked guilty only for a moment. "A memento. I was going to be saving it to remind me of this."

Rilan crossed to him quickly and snatched the paper from him. Her eyes widened as she realized what it was.

"What are you doing?" she cried. The paper was one of Ket's journal entries, describing how the abilities of the majus of the House of Potential transferred to her. "If this became public, someone could replicate Ket's work. I didn't attack a colleague and erase his memory just for you to mess it up!"

Origon's jaw worked, but he said nothing. Gently, he put the picture back on the mantle. His hand went to his moustaches, running down their length. Slowly, Rilan looked around his apartment, filled with knick-knacks and trinkets from all over the ten homeworlds. What else was hidden here?

She thrust the paper back at him. "Burn it," she said. "Burn it, or you can have adventures by yourself."

Origon took the paper back, sighed, and nodded at her. "I like to keep...items to remind me of my travels. But you are to be correct. I am not thinking straight, still." He glanced to the picture, then back to her.

"This is to be why I need you with me. I have been too long by myself, traveling among the homeworlds." He concentrated on the paper between his fingertips. An orange aura swept up it, followed by flame. The paper crumpled, but Origon watched her.

Rilan understood. The fire was not a reversible change. Origon would lose notes of his song by making it, but he wanted her to know he was serious.

"You will come with me now?" he asked.

"Yes," she answered.

"Then there is to be one more thing. You must call me 'Ori' from now on," he told her.

Well, it's shorter, Rilan thought. *It will be easier to get his attention, the next time we're fighting for our lives.*

"It was something only Delphorus called me," he continued. "I was never to be fond of it, but now I am thinking I will be wanting to hear the term again, to remind me of him. I am also thinking you would be the only one I could bear to call me that." He was looking down, at the paper crumbling to ash, but she could hear his voice shake.

Rilan couldn't speak for a moment, fighting around the lump in her throat. She wasn't an emotional woman.

"I would be honored, Ori," she said.

Thorns and Fur

989 A.A.W.

Cooperation Island, the great Festuour Ocean

I stared down at the crumpled and bloody Festuour lying prone in the vine-ridden ditch in front of me. She saw me at the same time and, hands shaking, took aim at my head with a set of large handcannons. I gritted my teeth. Another hostile patient. I raised my hands, hoped the white medic's circle on my headwrap was straight, and picked my way between trees and down the hill to patch up one of my enemies.

This stupid spat between the Methiemum and Festuour was over stupid reasons and I was stupid for being here. Again. I'd avoided two Festuour patrols today dodging through the flora, only to come across this solitary female. She must have been separated from her squad. The sooner my fellow Methiemum recognized grabbing land on a previously undiscovered island in the Festuour Ocean was ridiculous, the better. An inter-species crew had discovered Cooperation Island, but when its potential was revealed, both halves laid claim even though it was obviously Festuour territory. If only things had gone differently. But two cycles later and here I was, a biologist doing double duty as a field medic, inching toward an injured, enraged, young, and...very pretty...soldier in a ditch. It was fortunate we were alone out here in the forest, for now. No telling when her squad would find her.

"You're as likely to shoot your own fingers off with those handcannons as hit me," I said as I clambered down the side of the ditch, hoping she would lower them. Climbing down the slope hid how much my knees were shaking. I didn't *think* she would fire if she hadn't already.

"And I also might take out both of us," the Festuour answered. Her big furry paws were drenched with mud and blood, and she had a gash down one leg. A nasty-looking thorn as long as my arm protruded from her other thigh, and she trembled all over. I hoped her fingers were steadier, or this was going to be a very quick examination.

She looked like she'd been in a fight, but it might not have been one of the Methiemum soldiers. The plants here were almost as vicious as the Festuour, but that was why the survey group originally came to this island several cycles back. The flora was ridiculously efficacious for medical products, and my fellow researchers were discovering more species by the day. Both sides were in a rush to gather as much as they could and take the medical benefits for themselves. Otherwise scientists like me wouldn't have been in a war zone. Of course, there wouldn't have been a reason to call in the armies at all if certain mistakes hadn't been made. I pushed the thought away.

"You need help, and I'm willing to give it," I said, holding my hands out and attempting not to wince at the weapons following my movements. "Just relax and I'll take that—"

"Watch out!" The Festuour dropped her handcannons to shield her muzzle as my foot connected with a plum-sized growth on the ground.

Then my vision went white as I was thrown forward and a spear of pain ripped up my back.

I blinked and darkness replaced the white. Fuzzy, *soft*, darkness—as if I had fallen between two of the firm but malleable fruiting bodies I'd tripped over. I reached to get them away from my face without activating them, and realized what they really were...

"Oh! I'm sorry!" I pushed myself up from where I was wedged face-first into the prone Festuour's generous cleavage, trying not to touch her wounds. Trying not to touch *anything*. If I could have levitated up, I would have, but I *had* to touch her to clamber off her. My face burned.

As a rule, Festuour wore little, and this one was no exception. My hands brushed down incredibly soft fur. It wasn't easy to see what was underneath, but it was certainly easy to *feel*.

Oddly, my embarrassing actions seemed to relax my patient. Her mouth opened in a Festuour laugh, tongue lolling out one side.

"Don't hurt that bad." Her shaking gave away the truth. "Guess your side ain't any more aware of the dangers here than we are. Will save me the trouble of killing you. Those little puffballs make a big boom. Got some sort of trunk under the ground that shoots out spines long enough to pierce straight through a body." She nudged me back to a kneeling position and I winced at a sudden shock of pain up my back. "Did one get you? Look around."

I did so, hissing. It felt like someone had stripped a patch of skin off my back from my shoulders to my waist. My eyes widened at the nest of arm-length thorns sticking into the dirt on both sides of me. They hadn't been there before. The puffball must have shot them out when my foot hit it. How were we both not pincushions? Then I remembered the uncomfortable leather armor Faloua insisted I wear when I left camp. I twisted one arm, but couldn't reach the rear of my leather armor.

Something restricted my movement, and I paused, muscles tensing at air against flesh stripped of skin.

It didn't feel like the spines had torn through my muscle, but my armor was shot, hanging around my arms and keeping me from bringing them all the way together. And it *stung*.

I looked down to see another spine stuck through the side of my boot. The fibrous plant matter pressed against my shin. I swallowed, pulled the spine out, tensing my jaw at the fire along my back, and threw the thing away.

The Festuour interrupted my inspection, holding out an open, furry three-fingered paw to me. I stared at it. That paw had been pointing a gun at me moments before.

"That puffball coulda killed both of us. Heard at least four of the things rip through your vest. Lucky you were wearing it, and acting as my shield." She looked down her chest and her long tongue lolled again. "Shrimasharimsa Bhon, Guarder. Might as well introduce ourselves before I shoot you." Hesitantly, I took her paw. It dwarfed my own, and I had large hands for a woman.

"Kamuli Balion," I answered. "Biologist for the Methiemum, though I'm also working in the field hospital."

Still kneeling, I tried to keep my eyes from her chest, instead watching her handcannons, dropped near enough to reach. Bhon scraped one up, not pointing it directly at me, but at the ready. I swallowed, scenarios running through my head of how to get away. Except no. She was injured and I had a duty to heal—and to continue apologizing for how I landed.

Festuour and Methiemum—the trader species—had known each other a long time. As long as the furry Festuour had pockets to hold their tools, they were happy. And hats. Never seen a species that liked hats so much. This close, I could see the muscles in her arms, under the fur.

"Well, even if you are going to shoot me, let me patch you up first. I just need to..." I struggled to reach the medical bag strapped to my belt. My leather armor was blocking me. It was bent in a way it shouldn't be from the spines hitting it. I had no chance if Bhon decided to attack, even with the thorn through her leg and her paws shaking in pain. She was shorter than me, but nearly twice as thick, and armed. I only had my medical and sample bags.

Bhon strained to see over my shoulder. "That thorn ripped you up worse than a tree shark after a leafnipper. Makes that leather look like paper. Takes the fun out of the chase, don't it?" She reached out. "So let me help. Then we'll be more of an even match and we can get to the important killing part."

"I must apologize again for where my hands—"

She removed my armor and had my shirt unbuttoned and half off before I could finish my apology. Festuour had little regard for clothing. I made a hasty grab for my shirt as Bhon whipped it up over my shoulders, but missed. I barely kept from crossing my arms over my chest.

"Uh. We should not both be naked in a pit of spines in the undiscovered wilds of this blighted island." I made another grab for my shirt, catching it from her paws this time and settling it around my shoulders. I grimaced at the touch of cloth against the shredded skin of my back, but I didn't like showing off my chest even to those I knew very well, being a bit handicapped in that area, and I certainly couldn't compare to...

I forced my eyes back to her face. This close, her fur hid little and...I would not stare. "I'm with the Methiemum scientific party classifying the new plants. We've found another deadly one and I want to take a sample back to the camp to see if it has any other benefits aside from skewering people."

"Not with the Thrandishar army then," said Bhon. "Explains why you were willing to help me. Afraid I'll still have to kill you, though. Orders. But you can heal me up first."

Bhon was a strange mix of pleasant affability and murderous indifference. Would her squad be coming back for her? Soldiers on both sides killed opposing scientists just to keep them from recording a new discovery.

"Generous of you." I rotated my arms, testing mobility for a quick exit while I kept an eye on the bear-like soldier so close I could touch her snout. I'd say she reminded me of my childhood teddy bear, but mine didn't have sharp teeth and two handcannons ready to put holes in me.

I could feel hot blood dripping down my back, but her wounds came first. I drew my field knife, watching her eyes shine with the challenge. I didn't think it was a real contest, but it might keep her wary. She twitched her handcannons up, but I pointed the knife's tip downward. "Let's look at that thigh, shall we? I think you have it worse than I do."

Bhon bared her canines. I gently probed the wound in her thigh with my knife, one of her handcannons now pointed at my head. The spiraling thorn was deep enough I guessed it was scraping her femur, and the tip was almost all the way through the leg.

"It will do too much damage if I pull it out. I'll have to push it through. This will hurt," I told her as I gripped the shaft. Bhon nodded and clenched her paws so tightly the fur stood out straight. "Maybe point that blunderbuss away from my head while I get this out...just in case?"

Bhon thought about it for a moment, then shook her head.

I thought about leaving her there, but decided that was a good way to get shot in the back. This way there might be a chance to talk afterward. I closed my eyes just for a moment, hoping she had a high pain threshold, then twisted and pushed.

"Son of a mangy treesloth!" Bhon growled as the spine exited the other side of her leg. The paw holding the gun shook dangerously, but it didn't go off. I already had my other palm over the entry wound, keeping pressure on it.

"Do you have anything to tie this with?" I asked. Of course she was wearing nothing but a bandolier and a belt. They were both too bulky to work well.

"I've got to concentrate on not pulling this trigger, as much as I want to. Won't do to bleed out once I shoot you. What about that fancy rag you're wearing instead?" Bhon asked.

I eyed the shaking gun nervously, but nodded. "Put your other thumb there. I think one gun pointed at me is quite enough."

She did as I asked, clenching her teeth and flaring her wide nostrils as she bore down on the wound. While she wasn't concentrating quite so much on me, I used my knife to cut a strip from the bottom of my shirt. After an estimating glance, I cut a second strip. Bhon's thigh was as big around as I was, as Festuour were thicker than Methiemum.

Her eyes roamed down to my revealed stomach.

"Shame we're enemies. I like a woman with a bit of hair on her chest." Bhon smiled, but I frowned. I hadn't had time to shave what with being in this wilderness. I tried ineffectually to pull the remains of my shirt down to cover my stomach, but to little effect. Naturally my shirt was the white of the medical team, standing out against my much darker skin.

Bhon's smile fell. "Sorry. Did I say something wrong? I didn't mean to give offense. Killing isn't personal. Offense is."

I almost laughed. "How many Methiemum women have you met who you didn't kill?"

Bhon looked confused. "A few, why?"

"How many do you think have this much body hair? Most Methiemum are not as furry as Festuour."

Bhon's smile returned. "So you're telling me you're as unique as you are pretty."

I was glad my blush didn't show, though my cheeks felt hot. "Well, I'm certainly not the norm for a Methiemum woman, but I'm not unique."

Now Bhon looked curious, but I didn't elaborate. I finished the bandage, cinching the knot tight around her fuzzy thigh, trying not to tangle my fingers in her velvety fur.

"It's really a shame I'll have to shoot you. The rest of my squad will come looking eventually. I'm scouting ahead, but they're expecting me back soon. It would be awkward if you were here and alive," Bhon said, wrinkling her snout as she tried bending her leg. Her ears drew back in pain. She still held the handcannon trained on me.

"Well, what if I'm not here? I could simply return to my camp," I stepped back as Bhon struggled to her feet and gingerly put pressure on the leg, nodding as it held her weight. She'd have to hobble, but if her squad wasn't far, she could manage. Another reason for me to leave.

"And what about this?" Bhon gestured to the makeshift bandage. "How do I explain it?"

"You cut it from the uniform of the last Methiemum you killed," I supplied. "A big strapping soldier who stabbed you with his spear in the leg before you shot him."

Bhon snorted a laugh. "Certainly a better story than shooting an unarmed medic." Finally, the handcannon drooped.

"Then I can go?"

"I reckon so, but you know if I see you again, I'll have to shoot you on sight." Bhon sounded almost regretful. "So go on, turn around and get out of here quick, before I change my mind." Bhon made a twirling motion with her free paw. Obediently, I turned.

"Oowweee!" Bhon said.

I tensed, expecting a gunshot, but there was only the raw throbbing in my back. I looked over one shoulder. "What? Am I still bleeding?"

"Naw, you got a nasty scrape up your spine, but I was taking in that fine view below."

I ducked my head. Festuour culture didn't ascribe as much sensitivity to body parts, and I didn't mind being flirted with, but she *had* wanted to murder me moments ago.

"Well, get on with it and walk away before I change my mind," Bhon said.

Right. I held my head high and climbed out of the ditch. I would not look back. I wouldn't.

I lasted almost until the safety of the taller trees, then snuck a glance over my shoulder. Bhon was staring, eyes roaming, her handcannon cocked over one shoulder and a smug smile on her face. Her other paw was on her generous hip.

She gave me a tilt of her head before I looked forward and ran. Hopefully I'd avoid any other Festuour patrols before I got back to my camp.

* * *

The next day I found myself wondering whether Bhon had found the rest of her squad, and whether they had believed her tale. I was listening to the colonel of our little army drone on about why we were here and what we were supposed to do.

"I will have no fraternizing with the enemy here," Colonel Rhati grumbled. "Many Methiemum say they are friends with these bears, but don't let that fool you. They are ferocious fighters, and if they do not get their way, they will tear us apart. We must defend the new technologies and innovations this island promises. We will grasp its potential for ourselves before they do!"

No word about this island being on the Festuour homeworld, in the middle of their ocean, or how if we had only worked with them, we both would be reaping the benefits already, rather than delaying the plants' medical aid to both species. I wondered whether Bhon's leg was any better, and my mind drifted to the feel of her thigh muscles under my hand.

"Another few ten-days of successful engagements, and we will have the upper hand! Even you scientists—" he directed a sneer at those few of us behind the soldiers, "—if you see one of these bears on the island, during your studies, show them no mercy! We are going to be here for the long haul, and we are going to win."

The soldiers cheered, though I heard botanists and mycologists grumbling. It was telling that there were more grunts on the island than scientists, who had little interest in fighting. They just wanted to get their samples.

I fell in beside Faloua, the head doctor and an old friend, as we all trudged back to our tents.

"Another rousing speech, yes?" Faloua said, and I rolled my eyes as I adjusted my headscarf. She had never lost her outland accent. Mine was much softer, from my time at a university on the northern continent.

"It's a wonder we haven't lost yet," I answered.

"Well, come with me, and we will change the dressing on that wound on your back. Looks like you were attacked by a cheese grater. Maybe this time you will tell me how you got it."

"I did tell you," I said. "Tripping over one of those damnable plants."

Faloua shook her finger at me. She was an old, squat woman, her wrap the same green as the forest. Though her short curly hair was white, it would have been a mistake to dismiss her capability. She'd taught me many of my best medical techniques, as well as how to blaze a path through the jungle.

"I can tell by the look on your face that you are not telling me everything."

I stole a glance around. None of the other scientists were nearby, and more importantly, none of the soldiers. I had to tell *someone* or my mind would go in circles thinking about Bhon's arms, her chest, her easy laugh. The way she held a handcannon.

"Let's get in the tent," I said. "Fewer ears around." I pushed the oiled canvas aside and stalked into Faloua's medical tent.

"Come on, come on, spill the goods," Faloua said as she turned me around and pulled up my shirt to prod the bandage running along my spine. I hunched forward, making sure my chest, and lack of any appreciable breasts, was still covered. The motion pulled on the scab forming on my back. I trusted Faloua, who was the only one I would allow to do medical examinations on me. Not because anyone here cared, but because I was still working on how I wanted to look as a woman. It wasn't a question many male-assigned Methiemum had to reflect on.

"Hmmm, no infection, sides are good." She slowly peeled the bandage away.

"It's only, I happened to run into someone while I was out collecting specimens," I began.

"Finally! I have been telling you to meet more people." Faloua laughed at her own joke as she ran a finger down the slice on my back. "I assume you were victorious, since you are here. Now, tell me who, and what happened for them give you this scrape. Angry scientist, or an enemy soldier? Those Festuour scientists can be competitive."

I paused, figuring out how to word my answer. "I think she's a soldier," I said.

"Got into a fight then? Barely escaped with a wound?" Faloua asked while preparing a new bandage.

I hesitated only for a second before saying, "In a sense."

I felt her tense behind me. She pressed the bandage onto my wound, and ran her fingers down the sides to seal it to my skin. It would last for another day. She turned me back around, her old eyes bright in her wrinkled face.

"No more hiding. I want the whole story this time, or next time I change that bandage I am putting itchgrass in it."

I held up my hands. Faloua knew my history—one of the only ones who did. She would understand my churning thoughts and why the potential of cooperation between our species was a spot of hope.

"All right, I'll tell all. I was looking for another specimen of that sap-producing fern we found last ten-day. I used all of it in the first round of testing, but I think it has potential for altering brain chemicals. If we find some more this ten-day, we might secure a patent before the Festuour have anything."

Faloua rolled her hands for me to get on with it.

"I found an injured Festuour with a corkscrew rasp stuck through her leg, bigger than any I've seen before. It's from another new and deadly plant." I paused as Faloua raised a hand to her mouth in thought.

"No, no, go on," she said. Then she squinted at me. "It was a similar thorn that made that wound on your back, was it not?"

I nodded. "Several, actually. As I came close to her to help tend her wound, I tripped over a puffball mushroom about the size of my hand." I held my fist up for an example. "I need to give you a description to make sure no one else runs into them. They must have a defensive body below ground containing a store of thorns, which spring out on impact."

"But that is not the important part," Faloua said, not so patiently.

"Yes, well, after I tripped, I sort of ended up in her...cleavage. And found out my rear was cute enough that she didn't shoot me."

Faloua hooted with laughter. "And the rest is history, as they say."

"I hope her squad found her. I can't stop thinking about her."

"Huh. I think you should find her again," Faloua said, a twinkle in her eye, as if Methiemum and Festuour together was something commonplace. Maybe it was in the Nether, where all the species lived in harmony, but not on the home worlds. Our struggle here had deepened that divide.

"But we're fighting them, which is never what I wanted!" I said. "She nearly killed me! Finding her again might not be a problem in another cycle, but under Colonel Rhati, that's a recipe for disaster."

Faloua shook her head. "While this mess might *technically* be your fault, the conflict will not be over while the militaries are here. The more we fight, the more Methiemum and Festuour will see each other with animosity. I have old friends among our opposites in the Festuour scientists. We must work to change our perceptions." She paused, looking me over. "And you could do with being less of a grump, you know."

"I am not a grump!"

Faloua waved her hands at me. "Take a chance. Perhaps she will not kill you because of your backside, and you will both skip and hold hands and all the fighting will stop. Methiemum and Festuour living in happiness, like when we were still scouting this island. Or maybe she *will* shoot you and I'll be done with an irritating colleague."

I scowled at her. "I'm not going to look for an enemy combatant who wanted me *dead*. I'm going to stick to my samples. The faster we catalog the plants, the faster we get out of the fight and leave the soldiers to kill each other. We're on the edge of several medical breakthroughs!"

"Do what you wish," Faloua shrugged. She waited until I was exiting the tent before adding, "But try no to get too distracted by that 'ample cleavage.'"

I sighed and kept walking.

* * *

Four days later, I was near the center of the island on a solo expedition, where even the original scientific team had not penetrated. It wasn't generally a good idea to explore solo, but I had more knowledge of the terrain than many here, and I regarded my little expeditions as a method of atonement.

Over the last day, I'd run from a vine that crawled faster than I could walk, had my ankles bitten by tangled underbrush with grasping spiny teeth, and barely escaped falling into a huge funnel plant growing beneath a fragile mesh of leaf-covered vines. The bottom of the funnel was filled with stinking acid. I sharpened my machete daily.

I'd also spotted several suspicious shadows moving parallel to me. I was pretty sure I'd avoided the Festuour patrols, seeing as I hadn't been attacked, and there weren't supposed to be any large creatures on this island, but then, this was Festuour. I stayed alert.

On the plus side, I'd also seen specimens of my target, a fern with a smaller, parasitic plant attached to the underside of the leaves. The ones that grew where the two factions had explored were small and underdeveloped, but toward the interior, the ferns were more than twice my height, and the parasite grew into a fleshy bromeliad with stalks as long as my arm.

The canteens clanking around my waist each held a fern frond in water, both boasting a bromeliad. Contact with their sap caused the skin to tingle and go numb, and breathing in the fumes made my head swim. I suspected I could distil them into an anesthetic, but I needed a larger sample.

"Aha!" I looked up into a massive fern blocking out the neighboring plants. Bromeliads dripped from its fronds, making the plant look like a weeping willow from back on Methiem. I placed my canteens carefully against a bush, making sure the water didn't spill, as the caps were off to make holders for my samples. I hefted my machete and looked for an appropriate frond to cut off from the towering fern.

"Watch out!" A rough voice called from behind me, and I was bowled over in a rush of fur and two scents: one like spices kept in a cupboard, and the other like meat set out in the sun too long. The world toppled and rolled, and I reached for anything to stop it from spinning.

Behind me, two assailants blurred into a mass of green and yellow and brown. I felt the *crack* ring through my head as my skull intersected a tree and blinked, trying to bring the world back into focus. I reached up to straighten my head wrap.

The two fighting were of equal size, but I gradually realized one was a Festuour, and one was not. The fight was quick, but brutal. Fur literally flew, and I heard a rip of skin and bone followed by a shrill screech. The not-Festuour dropped to the ground and I saw it was like a rat, but as large as a Methiemum, with teeth longer than my hand. One of its six legs dangled uselessly as it galloped off.

I turned from the sight to find Bhon staring at me, a deadly-looking knife drawn.

"How did you get here?" I asked, scooting my aching back against the tree. It was not, perhaps, the best question, considering she had promised to kill me the next time we met, but it was all I could think of. She was a vision, standing triumphantly after her victory. The weaponry pointed at me had to be part of my attraction to her. No Methiemum could manage quite that cock of a hip while holding a knife as long as my forearm.

Bhon looked a little embarrassed. "I may have been tracking you. A little. I caught your scent earlier," she confessed. And I thought I'd avoided the patrols with my superior knowledge of the geography.

The knife wobbled and I realized it was covered in rodent blood. "But only for the glory of killing you personally! Our army is camped not far away, and we lost several soldiers to those things. I wasn't going to let them get to you first." She straightened. "That's my job."

"Well...thank you, I think," I said. I dusted myself off and took a quick inventory of my limbs to make sure I wasn't missing any. Yet. My head swam from the impact. "I wasn't aware there were large animals on this island."

Bhon shook her head. "We didn't know either, until two days ago."

We stood awkwardly for a few moments.

"Where's your squad?"

Bhon tilted her head to one side. "I sent them off in the other direction when I smelled you. Got them chasing after the nest of those things." She took a step forward, raising the knife, and I tensed. "That means I get to finish what I promised and—"

The ground opened under Bhon's feet and she plunged from my view.

"Bhon!" I called, rushing to the hole. It was oddly square, as if there had been a tile there, but this was the center of a newly discovered island. There weren't any square edges here. I peered down into the dark hole, feeling stupid at coming to the aid, once again, of one who had promised to kill me. She had *started* to attack before she fell.

"Are you dead?"

"Not yet," came the reply.

"Then stay that way," I called down. "I'll get a torch."

I lit one of the branches I'd brought—treated with pitch—with a pocket flint, and thrust the burning torch down into the darkness, squinting against the oily smoke. Why was I not running away? Why was I once again helping this lethal Festuour? Vish take this attraction and scientific curiosity, *and* fuzzy bear people.

There was what looked oddly like a room down there, and Bhon was sitting in the middle, her legs splayed out. Now I had a moment to take stock, I saw the tatters of my shirt on her thigh. Had she not changed the bandage? It had been days since I last saw her. A memento to remember me by, or just a convenient place for an item with my scent?

"I'm going to find a way down," I said, and started to pull away from the hole. This was stupid. I should be running. I should fill in the hole with Bhon in it.

"Wait!" Bhon called, and I stopped. I assumed she would say something about how I should leave her to die because she'd just try to kill me again. "Can you throw the torch down? It's dark..."

My tension melted. The big scary soldier was afraid of the dark. Wasn't that charming? I kept my mouth shut and held the torch out, then dropped it.

I scrubbed vines and dirt away from the sides of the opening, then noticed the rotten edges of a timber trailing away into the dark, supporting whatever I was standing on. I backed up, even as I heard the crack beneath my feet. Too late to run.

I only had time to call, "Watch your head!" before a section of ground gave way and I rolled forward and down.

I heard Bhon cough in the explosion of dirt and plant matter accompanying my landing. The torch had gone out, but with the new ramp I'd created, enough light filtered through the canopy to illuminate us. I could see large shapes, but everything else was dim.

Bhon held out the stump of the torch. "Try again?" she asked, and there was a worried edge to her voice.

There was also a distinct lack of trying to kill me. I needed to get Bhon alone in the dark more often. Once the torch flared to life again I tucked my flint away.

"Well, you certainly found a new way down," Bhon commented. She had come through near the center of this room, and my weight must have triggered the rest of the collapse. We had a way back up, but it wouldn't be easy, picking through the rotten beams to reach the surface. Certainly not a clear path to run from my new closest enemy.

"Should we explore? If you promise you won't stick that in me?" I nodded at the knife Bhon still held. She'd managed to keep hold of it through the fall.

"I'll give you a pass for now, seeing as you came to help me again," Bhon allowed, her chin high. Her eyes drifted down. "Go ahead."

"Oh no, I don't want you behind me, for multiple reasons," I said. I couldn't tell if her eyes were undressing me or determining the best way to butcher me.

"Just remember who has the knife," Bhon said, taking the lead, and Shiv strike me down if she didn't twitch her hips as she walked—no, sauntered—around the little room. Teddy bears with sashaying hips.

"This has to be constructed," I said, taking the torch from her and holding it close to a wall. It was packed dirt, possibly a natural burrow.

Could those giant rats have made it? But I had seen a beam holding the ceiling up. Why had no one on the original survey team found this?

"It can't be. This island is uninhabited," Bhon said.

"I agree. The survey team mapped the island extensively and saw no signs of inhabitants. It's the whole reason the Methiemum expedition head decided to make his claim. *The* claim. Vish take me." I closed my mouth before I said anything else.

"And why we're in this fight," Bhon said, turning back to me. "Which reminds me, I should take advantage of these closed-in walls. One less Methiemum scientist to steal our resources." But she didn't make a move.

"It wasn't my choice to start this war," I said. Not entirely true, but the full story would really make Bhon tear me to pieces. "I'd rather work with the Festuour so everyone has access to the advances this island will provide." I deliberately turned from her to investigate the new ramp leading to ground level. The whole room was five or six paces to a side—not tiny, but it also didn't seem like a burrow.

I squatted down, brushing aside dirt and vines on the collapsed ceiling until my hand found a hard surface. I turned to Bhon, only to find her snout close to mine, bright blue eyes staring into mine. I jerked, but she wasn't plunging the knife into my breast. She was just...close. Her presence was almost overpowering, and I swallowed, my mouth suddenly dry.

"I, uh, there's something under here," I said. "Help me get it clear."

Bhon's lips twisted up in a smile and she reached out a furry paw to help, her digits brushing mine. Together we cleared the plants that had clogged this patch of ground. I bit my lip as we touched, trying not to notice her strong fingers, each bigger than two of mine. Trying not to imagine them elsewhere on my body.

I shook my head. That was crazy. She already said she was going to kill me, multiple times. Even tried to do so. Yet the way she acted...Was she lying or did Festuour mating rituals have commonalties with homicide?

"Is that a...slate tile?" Bhon asked, seemingly oblivious to my confused thoughts.

"I think so," I said. The square we had uncovered was large enough for a Festuour to pass through, gray and mottled in the torchlight. "This can't be natural."

"No way," Bhon agreed.

"Which means someone lived here, or at least built this."

"And it's old," Bhon added. "Must have been here way before the survey team arrived."

I poked at the slate, then rose to my feet and passed the torch in an arc to better see the rest of the room. My jaw was tense, waiting for Bhon to take any opportunity to lunge at me. "This room's construction is solid. It could be anywhere from fifty to three hundred cycles old."

"However old it is, it means neither side has a claim to the island," Bhon said. "Someone else already claimed it."

"Maybe they're dead?" I watched Bhon's knife.

"We don't know that," she insisted. "They might have a friend group they've told about this place. They might still live here somewhere! What if there are more buildings? We need to explore."

I wrinkled my nose. She was right. Whether the builders were alive or dead, the fighting had to stop. I let a sliver of hope drive through me. Could I actually correct my mistakes? Perhaps Bhon and I didn't need to be on opposite sides. This was a perfect way get Colonel Rhati and his soldiers out of our hair so we could get to the real reason we were here— bettering the life of the ten species.

"You're right. Let's take a look around, if you can keep from gutting me for that long." I held both hands up, palms out.

Bhon's tongue lolled in a laugh. "Enough adventure for me in exploring. We're in an enclosed space. I can always take care of you later."

"I see." We surveyed the cellar, if that's what this room was. We found nothing more than a few broken barrels. It was too hard to see under the collapsed ceiling, so we scrambled up the slope.

Halfway up, my foot went through another tile, and I would have fallen if Bhon didn't clasp her paws around my waist quicker than I thought possible. A shiver passed through me at her touch, the strength in her arms. The flat of the knife, still in her paw, was a cold presence, leaking through the fabric of my shirt. Bhon could have snapped my spine, but she only pulled me back up. We scrambled the rest of the way to the surface. I definitely had a thing for danger.

"Thank you," I panted, looking down at the collapsed cellar.

"Won't do to have you fall and break your neck—that's my job." I sat on the rim of the ramp and Bhon sat down next to me, a furry menace, her toes kicking over the edge of the opening. "You saved me, so now I saved you."

"Does that make us even?" I said.

Bhon rolled her eyes. "You Methiemum and your crazy trading brains. You think everything is a bargain. If we save each other, it means we might want to stay around each other to see if the other needs saving again." She reached out to place a paw on my thigh, resting it lightly, as if in ownership. My muscles contracted, despite me attempting to relax. Her bright blue eyes stared directly into mine, and I swallowed. "That doesn't mean I won't kill you if it serves the purpose of my people."

"I understand," I said, and her paw rested a little heavier. It was odd, but I think she meant everything she said. The Festuour didn't have families, as such. They put little stock into who caused another Festuour to be born, instead relying on close-knit groups of friends. And just like friends, sometimes those relationships fell apart.

Frequently, offspring did come from friend groups, but once old enough, the children were free to choose any group to live with. Any member could invite another to join, but there was a big difference between being a friend with a Festuour and being part of a Festuour's friend group.

"You seem to know a lot about the original expedition," Bhon said suddenly, and I tensed again. "You know any of the original members? Mayhaps we can talk to them to find out if anyone else discovered this building."

I pushed to my feet, letting Bhon's paw slide off, and stared around the clearing dominated by the huge fern. "Several scientists on both sides were on the original survey team," I said. Now I knew what I was looking for, I could pick out bits of rotting timber and surfaces too flat to be natural. "They didn't know about this place."

"Look there," Bhon said, pointing out my fern. "I've never seen one of those get that big. You think it was grown here intentionally?"

My eyes widened. I hadn't even considered that. I led her to it, not even concerned I had my back to her. I was too excited to care. We passed the canteens I'd set down on the way to the giant plant, and once there, I began pulling vines away from the bottom.

"It was," I confirmed, pointing out the remains of a planter box, which the fern had nearly destroyed. "Whoever was here must have been farming it for medicinal purposes. I must add it to my collection."

"Good find? Not bad for a lowpaw in the army, then," Bhon said, paws on hips, knife a malevolent gleam in the sunlight filtering through the trees.

"Not bad at all," I said, as I rooted around the area. I cast a glance up toward her. She was positioned to block my easy escape. Purposeful, or accidental? Either way, I had to investigate this farm. There were the remains of an irrigation system here, and more beds, and more plants, smaller than the fern. Several were ones I'd taken samples of, but there were some I hadn't encountered or thought to investigate.

"This site could shortcut our scientific research on this island by ten-days, or even months." I crawled along the ground, paying little attention to the dirt and old boards snagging my pants. "There are more plants over there, growing in straight rows."

Bhon turned in a circle, but ended up facing me before I could think of escaping. "Or I could lead the Festuour scientists here. Give my people the advantage they deserve. Now I know what to look for, I can see others, all around us."

I shook my head. "There's more than enough for all, and if the attributes of these plants have already been discovered and perhaps even documented, there's absolutely no reason for us to be fighting over them." I got to my feet, stepping closer to her. "We must return to our respective camps and tell them to stop fighting. We can share what we found."

"The soldiers ain't gonna believe me, whatever I tell them," Bhon said. "I'm just a squad second."

"Then help me gather some samples," I suggested. "We'll take them to our respective scientists. Both sides will have plenty to occupy them."

Bhon twisted the knife in the air as she considered. "I guess it won't hurt to help, but don't get too far away. I'm good with my paws and I've got good aim."

I pointed out where she could take samples, then took out my machete, under her watchful gaze, and turned to the fern. Parts of it looked like animals had chewed on it. I supposed they used the medicinal properties too.

"Do these plants make you...feel funny?" Bhon said after a few minutes.

"Oh!" I said, turning to her. "The sap has a relaxing effect." I looked down at where she was cutting a bromeliad from the fern, liquid dripping on her paws. I'd been careful to drop the stalks in my canteen without touching the cut end.

"Gooey," Bhon giggled, and the knife dropped from her fingers.

I froze, torn between going to her and laughing. My deadly, and now high teddy bear.

I placed my cutting in a canteen and went to her, taking a rag from my pocket. "We've got to get this off you. I don't know what the sap will do, undistilled." I wiped at her paws while Bhon watched me, her tongue hanging out one side of her mouth in a Festuour grin.

"Nosso bad," she slurred. "Tingly."

"It's already taking effect, and quickly, too. I've never seen anything work this fast," I said, rubbing furiously. The sap was stuck in her fur.

"Couldn't decide whether to kill you or kiss you," Bhon said, and smeared a dripping paw on my cheek. "Glad I hadn't decided yet."

The tingling started on my cheek, like someone brushing me with a feather. I twitched, but finished getting a patch of sap from between her digits, then took the time to absently swipe at the goo on my face. I blinked, my head feeling fuzzy. What had I been doing?

Oh yes. I went back to rubbing Bhon's paws. Except wasn't I holding something before? My hands buzzed, but not in a bad way. Tickly. Pleasant. I pulled on Bhon's large fingers, grasping each one with my hand and caressing them. She rumbled deep in her throat and stepped into me, her bandolier pressing into my chest. I needed to escape, didn't I? I had to run away because she was trying to...kill me? Kiss me? Steal my ferns?

"What are we...?"

"Maybe 'kiss' is better'n 'kill' after all," Bhon mumbled. She was so close.

"But we're...affected? Influenced?" All I knew was I wanted to nestle into her fur. So I did.

"Mmmm. 'Saright. 'Sa good kinda sap," Bhon said. She brought her hands up, bringing mine with them, and brushed them across my chest, stopping at my hardening nipples. My mind shouted at me to collapse in and protect myself, but I found I couldn't care about whether or not my chest looked "right." Maybe...that was for the best?

I let go, leaning down, my mouth searching for hers. Bhon was wider than me, but shorter. Her muzzle was long, and her teeth sharp, but she tasted like cinnamon. After we broke apart, I said, "Bet it can make all kinds of places tingly." The sap couldn't be that bad. There was some small part of my mind taking notes on the effect. Another small part screamed that this was a bad idea, but the larger part overrode it.

"Like here?" Bhon reached down. I gasped and all other thoughts disappeared. Her mouth opened in a pleased smile. "You *are* different than other Methiemum women. Haven't played around with one of *these* before."

The same warning against others touching me like that slid through my mind, but it was as if it was underneath a block of thick ice, for once muffled. Bhon didn't care what parts I had or whether I was like other Methiemum women. I *was* a woman, and that's what mattered. My shoulders relaxed and I let my hands run down her body, feeling the powerful muscle under her fur, groaning as every place she touched erupted into a warm glow.

She was still stroking and playing and I reached between her legs. I wasn't completely sure how Festuour genitals worked, but I was fairly certain *where* they were.

She grabbed my hand. Hard.

"Oh, Kamuli," Bhon groaned, and the pressure on my hand increased. *"Do not stop!"*

* * *

The sun was just rising when I blinked my eyes open. Had I been asleep?

I was tangled together with Bhon. What had happened? Had we fought? I had hazy memories of our hands on each other. Maybe I'd tried to wrestle her knife away and hit my head?

As I rose to my feet, I realized her bandolier was missing and so were my clothes. I felt strangely refreshed, as if I'd had a long night's sleep, and spotted our belongings piled together in a heap.

Bhon groaned and sat up, then watched me gather my clothes.

"Well that's a pleasant view. Don't you folks usually wear fabric draped around you?"

"We must have passed out because of the sap. I need to get back to my camp and report the structures here." I jerked my pants on as quickly as possible. I felt like something else might have happened, but I only remembered bits and pieces of the night before.

"Now, I never said you could go," Bhon complained, rolling to her feet and plucking her bandolier, knife, and handcannons off the ground. She draped the leather belt diagonally across her shoulder. "Funny though. Can't quite remember what happened last night. Guess I didn't shoot you after all. I wonder why—"

Bhon froze, one paw on a handcannon, which wasn't yet primed. Her eyes stared over my shoulder.

"What?" I asked.

"Don't make any sudden movements. One of those critters that tried to eat you yesterday is sneaking up on us like a branchslider after a nest of chicklings."

Carefully, she pressed a set of buttons on the side of one handcannon, raising it just a hair. I could hear snuffling as a presence approached, ready any moment for the sting of teeth.

Then Bhon paused, her face showing confusion. I turned, slowly and smoothly, to see one of the giant rodents approaching the last canteen left on the ground. It pulled the bromeliad out with its mouth, tipping the container over. I opened a hand, low, to keep Bhon from moving. Last night, I remembered seeing teeth marks on the plants, though not much after that.

The rodent sniffed at the end of the bromeliad, dripping sap, then rubbed its muzzle in it and scooted forward, driving the cutting under its body. It rolled gleefully on the squashed plant.

Bhon tensed as it sprang to its feet, but it only ran around in a circle, then flopped on the cutting again, rolling onto its back, its toes kneading the air.

"Looks like it enjoys the stuff," I said.

"Then I guess I don't need to shoot it," Bhon said. She holstered her handcannon, but tilted her head, blue eyes searching nothing.

"I can get more cuttings," I said.

Bhon shook her head. "That's not it. Do you...remember much from last night?"

"Not much." I watched the giant rodent, then my eyes widened as I saw the kneading paws, the quivering tail, and the rodent's obvious other signs of arousal. My head spun to where the pile of clothes had been, but I ended up staring Bhon in the face.

"Did we...?" Bhon asked, one paw half coming up toward me.

"We couldn't have," I answered. "We're enemies. You're trying to kill me. Maybe."

"I guess not too hard." Bhon shrugged. "But if we did, I can't go back. There's a strict no-fraternizing rule."

"Don't tell them," I said. "We don't even remember what we did."

Bhon grabbed my shoulders and leaned into me. I tensed, unable to avoid her lunge as she inhaled near me, then breathed out a huge gust of Festuour-flavored air. She let me go and bent one arm, sniffing her fur, then bent lower, as if searching for something in her fur.

"Oh, they'll know," Bhon said as she straightened, her eyes wide. "You're all over me. We, ah, I think we..."

"No," I said.

Bhon nodded. "A *lot*. I can't go back to my camp like this. The scent won't fade for days, even with bathing in a stream."

I tried to remember the last night. Bits were coming back, when I...I stared at Bhon's chest. And she...I smoothed my pants. Oh, and then I...My eyes moved downward on Bhon. Fur covered her belly and thighs. I remembered its touch on my skin.

From Bhon's expression, she was going through a similar experience. The rat wriggled in the sap, oblivious.

"Well, if you can't go to your camp, you'll come with me," I said. Colonel Rhati had pushed his troops the last ten-day, claiming he was close to overcoming the Festuour. I was afraid he might be right. With proof of a prior claim on this island, I could end this fight. I could redeem myself, at least in my own eyes.

"Won't they kill me just like my side would kill you?" Bhon asked. Her bright blue eyes caught mine. "Will we get another chance like last night?"

"I think we might, but perhaps without mind-altering substances. Make it a true choice for both of us," I said. Now I was the one in control, with the leverage. I had hedged around the truth for over two cycles. It was time to let the truth come out. "I won't let them hurt you. I can convince the colonel of the army, once he knows who I am. The scientists will follow my lead, if I say so. I'd...like you by my side, Bhon."

She picked up one of my sample canisters, hooking it on her bandolier. Then her eyes narrowed. "You really have that much influence? You said you knew ones who were here on the survey team. How...Kamuli! Were you on the original survey team that came here?"

I should have been ready, but lightning still pulsed through me at telling the truth. "I wasn't on the original team...I led it."

Her eyes were deep with hurt. "Then you let the Methiemum make their claim. Or did you try to claim this island yourself?" Bhon stepped back, away from me. "Two members of my friend group died here." Her lip twisted up to reveal sharp teeth, her ears laid back. "Is Kamuli Balion even your real name, or are you hiding? We know the names of all of the surveyors. Why isn't yours among them?"

I reached a hand out to her, but she took another step back. "Bhon, that was two cycles ago. The name I used, the way I presented myself—it wasn't me, not the real me." I hesitated, but she was watching me, waiting for the rest. "I made changes to my life. Good changes, to my body and my name. But this island *was* a mistake.

"I was angry with the Festuour team. They were dragging their feet, reluctant to verify our results. I thought *they* were trying to steal the research. I threatened and blustered, and I assumed the Festuour scientists would back down. I know your people a lot better now than I did then."

Bhon crossed her arms, waiting.

"My embarrassment about who I was—*what* I was—led me to do stupid things. I put in the request for exclusivity for the discoveries we'd made. I thought it would force us all to talk about it, but I didn't understand how much our militaries *wanted* this fight. By the time the armies arrived, I had no control over the situation."

"So you hid. You hid your name, your body, and your motives."

"No!" I shook my head. "Well, yes. But not how you're thinking. I was afraid of my transition, but *this* is the real me—Kamuli Balion."

Bhon still frowned, but didn't pull farther away. "Why didn't you tell me?"

"I...I meant to, when we first met, when you tried to take my shirt off—" I stopped as Bhon swiped a paw through the air.

"Not that you're trans. I don't care about that. It doesn't matter what set of bits you got. I mean, not as if we're the same species in the first case. We've gotta be inventive if you want to smash 'em together. I think we did a pretty good job, from what I remember."

I blinked at the statement, though I agreed with her.

But Bhon was still talking. "No—why didn't you tell me you *led* the original survey team? You lied to me, and friends don't lie to each other, no matter how hard the truth. It's how a friend group survives."

That...was not the complaint I was expecting. *There's a big difference between being a friend with a Festuour and being part of a Festuour's friend group.*

What was she saying?

Bhon unconsciously re-centered her bandolier. "Maybe you could have prevented this whole thing, maybe it would have happened anyway. But you can't change any of that now." She took a step toward me, her eyes intense. "Are you willing to stop this fight now, with me?"

I straightened. "Every moment I've been on this island, I've been atoning for my mistake. First by finding more plants than the team knew what to do with, so they would have to work with the Festuour, but with this claim, I can—*we* can—finally make a difference, even if everyone ends up knowing my story. We can end this fight."

I scanned the abandoned farm, or research station, or whatever it was. It could have been a hundred cycles old, the original inhabitants dead from old age, or disease, or eaten by giant rats. It didn't matter whether their discoveries were lost, or never even finished. It only mattered that someone else had been here first.

I reached for Bhon's paw, and she gave it. I lifted it with both of mine, raising it to my mouth to kiss her fingertips.

"Let's go sort this out, together."

We left the giant rodent to its fern.

* * *

"She's with me!"

I help up both hands to ward off the soldiers guarding the entrance to the Methiemum camp. I tried to stay in front of Bhon as much as possible, but she was a lot wider than I was. "She's come here to negotiate for a cessation of hostilities."

One soldier—likely a sergeant—stepped forward, looking unimpressed. I wasn't familiar with her, as I knew more scientists than soldiers, but she looked like she had been around a battlefield more than once. A nasty-looking scar crossed from the remains of one ear down to her neck.

"She's just a grunt. She doesn't have authority to negotiate. I'm reporting this." The sergeant gestured to her companion, who went running. I gritted my teeth, but at least Bhon hadn't drawn her handcannons. Yet.

"She was with me when we discovered information that changes this whole fight. That's why she has authority to negotiate. We—both of us— chose to come to the Methiemum camp first. Our side will have the advantage, but you have to let me pass to see Colonel Rhati. Now."

I could feel Bhon pressing close behind me. I didn't dare turn to see her expression, but I hoped she wasn't snarling.

The woman at the gate pursed her lips, making the scar on her neck pucker. I needed her to bend only a little, and let us through. Once in the camp, I'd have enough clout to see the Colonel. Faloua would help. She was one of the only ones who knew my whole story.

The sergeant slowly inclined her head. "Just to the Colonel. And I'm coming with you to keep the gunbear under guard. I'll need all of her weapons." Now when I looked back, Bhon *was* snarling. I shot her a glare, but it did nothing, and I tried not to sigh as Bhon's growl became audible.

"They'll have to shoot me before they shoot you, Bhon," I said. "And they won't do anything to your weapons."

"Do you promise on the life of your oldest friend?" Bhon asked, and I only belatedly realized the depth of what she was asking. I hesitated, thinking back to a boy I had known when I was young, running around the tiny town where I grew up. I still traded letters with him and his family.

"I do. They will not interfere with you or your weapons, or they will answer to me." I gave the woman a stern look, and she nodded back. She at least understood honor between opponents. "I'm leaving my canteens here too." I set down the samples I'd taken, leaving only a small sample case attached to my belt, containing some of the sap squeezed from a stalk. I'd need it to prove its medical use to the colonel.

Bhon's handcannons were only the start. By the time the scarred sergeant finished emptying her bandolier, belt, and patting her down, there was an impressive pile of knives, garrotes, vials, blades, ammunition, and other deadly knick-knacks on top of her two handcannons. The sergeant placed them in a crate near the entrance to the camp, and locked it, showing us the key she put in a pouch on her belt.

"No one can touch them but me," she said.

I made for the medical tent, but she was having none of it. "This way," she said firmly, as the subordinate she had sent running arrived with four more in tow. At a hand gesture, they fell into step behind us, heading straight for Colonel Rhati's pavilion.

I took in quick breaths through my nose, pushing the air out through pursed lips. I wasn't nervous. I could handle him, even if I'd never dared a direct confrontation. Colonel Rhati was just the jumped-up son of some general back in Thrandishar. He'd probably never seen fighting. He'd likely had his command bought for him.

"You sure you can convince the leader of these stone faces?" Bhon whispered in my ear.

"They have to listen to reason," I answered. "Once we tell them what we found, we'll have leverage to make them call this off." I clenched a hand, not sure if I was trying to convince myself or Bhon. I didn't think it was working either way. I'd avoided the colonel in the past because I was hiding from my mistake. And because he was a blustering bigot. But maybe if I had confronted him, I would have reckoned with my guilt sooner. Or if I'd retained control of the original survey team instead of sneaking away to lick my wounds, I might have more influence with Colonel Rhati. Too late for that now.

We stopped outside his pavilion, a huge tent made, ironically, of imported Festuour cloth. Nothing else would have resisted the elements like this material did.

"Wait here," the sergeant with the scar said, and stepped through the flap. I could hear indistinct voices, and looked back to Bhon. Surely with those ears, she could hear more? But she only shrugged.

"He'll see you now," the sergeant said, re-emerging. "But he has limited time for an enemy combatant. Be quick. We'll be close by, so don't try anything." This last was directed at Bhon, who bared her teeth.

I stomped past the roadblock of a woman and into the pavilion, finding the colonel seated behind a desk of dark brown Methiemum heartwood. Vast sheets of blank paper covered the plans he'd obviously been working on, and he glared at Bhon, his elegantly-styled moustache bristling at the interruption.

"What is the meaning of this?" Colonel Rhati asked, before I could speak. "You want us to give in, now we're winning this engagement? We've almost got these filthy bears pushed off this island. What could possibly make us withdraw?"

I felt Bhon tense—I had tensed, for that matter, at his insult—and I reached back, finding her paw, squeezing her fingers.

"There is ample evidence this entire endeavor is illegal from the start, and I should know." I jabbed my forefinger into my breastbone.

The Colonel broke in before I could say more. "I'm well aware of who you used to be. You gave up any entitlement to making decisions for the Methiemum here when you gave up your role."

I shouldn't be surprised he knew. "No matter what I did, there's a prior claim on this island, and that invalidates any agreement made. Both sides must draw back until we can determine who has the true rights to this land. There doesn't need to be any more fighting."

"A prior claim? Absurd. No one else knows about this island— otherwise those weeds you're studying would be in use already."

"Want me to hit him?" Bhon whispered, and I squeezed her paw to quiet her. It would be therapeutic, but not helpful.

"Those 'weeds' are the whole reason we're here, and you know it," I told him. "You just want your military to have a reason to fight. Well, we found a settlement, where the inhabitants studied the same plants we are. They probably used the same properties."

"Fine then." Colonel Rhati sat forward, fingers lightly touching, like a predator about to strike. "Produce this alleged settlement's builders and we'll get this sorted out."

"We, ah, don't have 'em," Bhon said quietly.

"Then how do you intend to prove this prior claim?"

"That's what I'm trying to tell you," I said. I took another step forward, putting myself in the center of the Colonel's space. "*You* need to organize a ceasefire so the *scientists* can discover who built the settlement. *Then* we can find out who has the rights."

Colonel Rhati only stared at me. I didn't like the set of his eyes. "You don't even know if the original claimants are alive, do you? And no one else knows of this place, except you, the bear, and me, yes?"

"That...is correct." Bhon nudged my back with a finger. She didn't like it any better than I did.

"I have a better idea," the Colonel said, with a smile like a knife. "I'll send the troops through this farm. Destroy the evidence." He spread his hands. "No evidence, no problem."

"That's a terrible solution!" I yelled. Bhon's paws held me back and I realized my fingers were in claws, reaching for the vile man's face. But the colonel sat straight, a smug expression creasing his face. "You'd throw away cycles of research, just to win a stupid fight with our closest allies?"

"The bears have diluted our trading rights for cycles, cozying up to the Methiemum so they can share in our profits. Cut them back out, and we rise to being the most powerful of the ten species. As such, I'm afraid you, and your prisoner of war, are liabilities to our plans, and my orders." The colonel looked over my head and made a quick gesture. Hands landed on my shoulders and I tried to shrug them off, but they held fast.

"You will both be imprisoned, and the bear will be executed tomorrow morning to show our superiority before the army. You may be as well, depending on your conduct. Take them away."

"If I had my handcannons—" Bhon started.

"But you don't." The sergeant cut her off. "They're back at the gate, and it's a good thing I took them."

"The bears' cannons are fine work," the colonel said. "You may keep them or distribute them to a subordinate, as you see fit."

"Thank you sir," the scarred sergeant said over Bhon's growls. So much for honor. I tightened my grip on my new friend, though the soldiers were doing most of the work. If she attacked the colonel, they'd kill her without hesitation. I had to make them think she was cowed.

"Let them go," I hissed to her, but Bhon's face swung to me, teeth bared, and I flinched back at the sight, though I didn't look away. "I'll get them back to you. I promise. Just go with them now, and I'll get us out."

Bhon's lips dropped back down over her teeth. "I trust you," she said. She held my eyes, pleading for my promise to be true. I stared back, until the soldiers jerked us around and marched us out of the tent.

* * *

"Let me talk to Faloua first," I told the sergeant. "She deserves to know this research exists. Maybe she can save some before you destroy it all. It can only be an advantage for us. Please let me talk to her. You can lock me up after."

The scarred woman steadfastly ignored me, and her soldiers continued to drag us to the tiny cells where they kept the few prisoners they didn't kill. The three metal cages in the center of the camp were currently empty. They hadn't been when I left.

"Save your breath," Bhon said, and I looked curiously at her. She wasn't the type to give up. When I met her eyes, she stared back, flicked her eyes to the medical tents, then back to me. "If they're going to kill us tomorrow, it doesn't matter what we do."

What was she...?

"So do it!" Bhon cried as she threw her substantial weight to one side. Festuour had more bulk than Methiemum on average, and the three soldiers holding her were no match for the power of Bhon's thighs. She pulled them away from our little procession, and one of the two soldiers holding me leapt to help them.

I spun on the remaining soldier, twisting him around and throwing him to the ground. I had my share of martial training, and had more muscle than people suspected.

I ran to the medical tents. I wouldn't waste Bhon's gift of time.

They were a short sprint away, separated slightly from the main section of scientist's tents. Close enough I could get there quickly with my small head start, far enough to have a moment to warn Faloua. When I reached her tent, I glanced back to see if the soldier was following. He was just rising from the scrubby ground, as the other soldiers threw Bhon into an empty cage. It was too small for her to sit, and too short for her to stand upright. The door clanged shut behind her.

"Go!" she shouted, and I ducked inside the tent, yanking the door ties in a quick knot. It wouldn't keep others out for long, but would buy me a few seconds. I whirled to Faloua, who was tending a nasty cut on a soldier's arm. Her mouth was open and thread dangled from where she had been stitching the wound. I ignored her patient.

"Faloua, listen carefully. West of where we were studying the batch of sapfern plants, check for an abandoned research building. Someone's been here before. Colonel Rhati's going to raze it when he sends soldiers through."

Faloua opened her mouth, but I gave a minute shake of my head. "They've already locked *Bhon* up, and will execute her tomorrow, and possibly me as well." She'd get the implication from the Festuour name.

There was a rustling at the tent before a machete sliced through the ties and half the door, followed by the soldier I'd thrown to the ground.

I gave no resistance as he grabbed my arms. I'd said what I needed to. Faloua would draw the right conclusions from the existence of an abandoned facility on a supposedly deserted island, but my real message was in the last thing I'd said. Faloua was my only hope for freedom, and keeping Bhon from death. My own neck I was less worried about. For all of the colonel's threats, I was still a Methiemum, and killing someone on our own side had consequences. Maybe Faloua could convince the other scientists, or get word to Methiem.

"You be careful with her!" Faloua yelled at the soldier dragging me backward. "You have more of a handful than you know. It will cost you your career to do this, I promise." The soldier hesitated for one step, then continued to tow me to the cages.

When we returned to the middle of the camp, Bhon was alone, her broad shoulders stretching from one side of the cage to the other, her back bent. The soldier directed me to the one next to her, and opened the door. I knew enough not to argue. I'd done the best I could with the time I had.

I had to bend even lower, and my headscarf pressed against the top of the bars. Bhon looked compressed in her cell, barely able to move.

"You got a message out?" she asked. I nodded.

"Right now we must wait." I held a hand out through the bars, and the end of her digits touched mine. We were at least close enough to touch, though I could hardly even squeeze her furry paw.

"You could have run," Bhon said. "In fact, you could have turned me in when you saw how the colonel acted. You could have let them raze that place we found. You didn't have to be stuck here."

I shrugged. "But that's not what a friend group does." I found her eyes with mine. She was staring back, and as I watched, her face relaxed.

The words poured out of me. "I've only known you for a few days, but I can't stop thinking about you. Your touch sparks lighting through me. You're fierce, a protector, and I want to know you better."

Bhon reached out her other paw and I took it with my fingertips. We were separated by cold iron, but still connected. "I had orders to kill any Methiemum I saw. I should have shot you rather than let you get close the first time, but I just couldn't," Bhon said. "I've wanted to kiss you instead, since you first fell into my arms—literally."

There were soldiers around us, but we didn't care. We talked for hours—while the sun set—about our families and friends, our backgrounds, and how we got to this situation. This time, we weren't under the influence of psychotropic sap, and were separated from any real physical action. It was just me and Bhon, talking. I felt I had known her for cycles. It felt perfect.

Festuour's moons were rising when one of the guards perked up.

"What was that?"

"Dunno," the other said. "But it's almost shift change and I'm bored of listening to these two spill their guts to each other. Those cages are locked tight and our replacements will be here in a few minutes. Let's check it out."

The other guard nodded and followed him away from the cages as a shadow slipped through the camp. I recognized the fringe of white hair reflecting moonlight.

"A majus is scheduled to check in on the camp tonight," Faloua whispered to me when she got to my cage. "She is delivering medical equipment from Thrandishar, and chemicals for breaking down compounds. I will try to direct her here. When she sees the abuses the colonel has directed against the Festuour, I'm certain she will demand you are set free."

"You got a bit of metal or anything?" Bhon asked. "I'm a fair paw with locks."

Faloua hesitated, scanning the area. I saw lights coming near. Likely the replacement guard. Faloua straightened. "You know what? Vish take it all. Here."

She took a small pack from her pocket, glanced around again, and tossed it underhand toward Bhon, who caught it and made it disappear in her fur.

"I will send the majus as soon as I can," Faloua promised. I gave her a grateful nod, and she slunk off.

Bhon investigated the pouch, pulling out what looked like tweezers and small metal probes. Perfect for arranging slides and small samples without contamination. Perfect for lock picking as well, if one knew how to use them.

I winced at each tiny clink as Bhon fiddled with the metal implements. The angle was wrong for her to get her paws around to the lock, since it was on the outside of the cage. I tried to give her whispered directions, but she finally huffed out a breath and withdrew the implements as the replacement soldiers took their stations.

"No use. I can't see enough of what I'm doing, and your lock is too far away to reach." She tucked the pieces back in their pouch and secreted it somewhere around her person. "We're gonna have to see what this majus can do, though I don't know why one so high and mighty as all that would rescue us."

I'd seen a few maji before—they were a rare sight, lauded wherever they went, treated like celebrities. Without them, we'd have no portals to link trade between the homeworlds. I didn't know why one would bother with us either.

We stood there for what felt like hours, but probably wasn't. Bhon and I exchanged a few more words, but we'd said most of what we had to say. I hoped Bhon would attempt the lock picks again, but every time she moved, the guards shifted and looked around. I racked my mind for something—*anything*—I could do, but came up empty.

Then, there was a commotion off in the dark.

"The majus?" I wondered. Bhon shook her head. She couldn't see either.

The noise resolved into Colonel Rhati himself, leading the scarred sergeant and several other subordinates. They marched straight to Bhon's cage.

"You're letting us go?" I asked. Maybe the majus had spoken to him.

"Hardly," the colonel snorted. "Moving up the timetables. We're pushing through your accidental discovery and into the Festuour camp tonight instead of tomorrow. Now's a perfect time to tie up loose ends. We'll let *you* out tomorrow, after we settle things."

My plans crashed down around me as I saw Bhon's face go slack, her eyes finding mine.

"What happened to tomorrow morning?" I said.

"And give her a chance to ponder a way to escape?" the Colonel asked. "We've had enough attempts in the past."

They unlocked the cage and pulled Bhon out, then turned to the center of the camp.

"No!" I shouted. "Take me instead. She's done nothing. I got her into this."

"Then you should have thought of that before. Though few remember who you are, I can't execute you right out, but there will be a trial very soon. Any career you hoped to have with the scientists will be long gone." He looked between Bhon and me. "No, I won't have you working with the enemy."

They left me alone. I could just see them, at the edge of the pit where they'd shot other prisoners. A few soldiers came out of their tents to watch the show. The colonel would stall the actual execution for a few minutes to let a crowd gather. What could I do in that time? I'd come up with nothing in the hours I'd been stuck in this cage.

"Come back!" I shouted. An ocean of rage rose up in me and I shook the bars. Could I turn the cage over? Roll it toward the stage? There had to be a way to get closer.

Cold seeped into my hands, and I pulled them back from the bars with a gasp. This was a tropical island, yet frost crept up the iron. The majus? I huddled as far into the center as I could, which wasn't much.

The iron lock groaned. I shook the door and something cracked within the mechanism. I shook it harder. The lock popped off and I stumbled out, searching for the cause of my escape.

I scanned the shadows as I stepped free, but saw nothing in the deepening gloom. The two guards were slumped on the ground, and I heard one snore.

A voice came from the trees, not far away. "Find your friend quickly. The maji cannot directly involve themselves in this campaign without hard evidence. It was approved in the Assembly, but has strong opposition, and I do not appreciate what is happening here."

I couldn't see the speaker, or tell what species they were, though the voice sounded Methiemum. I didn't have time to question their sudden appearance. I ran through the darkness to where the soldiers had Bhon tied up.

I stopped just short of the circle of torchlight, thinking of any advantages I had. No weapons, and there were too many soldiers to overpower. Bhon still had Faloua's tools, little good they could do now.

My hands stopped as they found one small vial, still attached to my belt. The soldiers likely thought it was water—harmless. I shook it, thinking of the giant rodent rolling in the sap. Thinking of Bhon and me.

Maybe I did have a weapon.

I opened the vial, and waved it under my nose. No appreciable smell, but a wave of lassitude radiated through me. I jerked the vial away. I'd have to be careful not to get any on my hands.

I scanned around for anything I could use, then sighed, and tore a patch from the bottom of my shirt. I'd be out of clothes soon at this rate. I doused the center of the strip with some sap, careful not to let it touch my skin, then snuck up behind a soldier emerging from his tent. I had spent a fair amount of time in the jungle, and could move quietly when I needed to.

I slapped the cloth around the soldier's face, hoping he wouldn't cry out. He spun toward me. Even as he did, the scowl I could barely see faded to a slack grin.

"Oh hey there," he said. "I didn't see you. Did something hit me?"

"No, nothing," I said. Was this actually working? "What is going on over there?"

"Oh, they're about to shoot one of the bears. Not really nice, if you ask me." His amiable grin faded.

I had tested the sap's strength. This was just another scientific study. One that would get me killed if I didn't proceed cautiously. "Can you take me over to see it?"

"Oh yeah sure," the soldier said. He reached for my hand, but I used it to point.

"This way?"

"That's right, just gotta follow me."

We did not go far before seeing another soldier coming from her tent. I tried to keep my face in the shadows. Not many had witnessed Bhon and my capture, but it was better to be cautious. "Going to the execution?" the new soldier asked.

"Yeah, showin' this scientist the way to watch the fun." My convert frowned. "Though not really fun if you ask me. It's unfair—"

"Yes, I'm with the scientists, and I'm testing a new serum I think can make soldiers more effective," I interrupted. "It's a great time to test it, while everyone's watching the execution. We were saying it smells like fruit. Take a sniff and see if you agree." I proffered the piece of cloth.

The second soldier took the cloth and put it to her nose. "No, not like fruit at all..." she trailed off. "You know, I haven't had fruit in a few days. They have good stuff in the Festuour tropics. I should—"

"Let's go this way first," I said, directing the soldiers, who were now arguing about which Festuour fruit tasted best. How many more times could I get away with this?

Five, it turned out, intercepting soldiers coming from their tents like rabbits emerging from their burrows in the spring. The last took the dregs of sap in my canteen.

My small group of soldiers, now flirting with each other while arguing the best way to make a chilled fruit drink in this weather, made an impressive force backing me up. I wasn't convinced they'd be effective fighting, or even if they would fight *for* me, but it would give Colonel Rhati and the others pause.

"Stop!" I called when I got close. Bhon's paws and feet were tied, and she stood at the lip of a pit with the scarred sergeant watching over her.

The sergeant's squad of four was nearby, though the soldiers watching were a little ways off. It was five against seven, though my little drugged squad perhaps wouldn't count for too much.

The colonel swung toward me at my shout. "How did you get out...? No matter. It seems we have other insubordinates in this camp." He gestured to the sergeant, who hulked toward me, her large shoulders blocking light from the surrounding torches. Her squad followed her.

"Form up!" she shouted. "Separate the traitor from the soldiers."

"Get 'em guys!" I yelled. There was general confusion behind me, and then three of the seven stumbled forward. They seemed to have forgotten they were armed, and spread their arms wide to catch the scarred soldier. Better reaction than I anticipated, really. I added a mental note to the little experiment I was running.

The scarred sergeant looked confused, then fell into a fighting stance herself. "Take them down, but try not to kill. We will interrogate these traitors later!" Her squad positioned themselves around her.

"Why don't you help them?" I suggested to the other four behind me, gesturing to Bhon. "You can ask them what they think about the morals of shooting a Festuour with no trial."

The first soldier I had drugged, who was the most philosophical, staggered forward, yelling, "Hey, can soldiers can stand in for unbiased judges when we are inherently biased ourselves? I mean, think about it!"

With everyone near me engaged, and the soldiers farther away confused for a few seconds, I skirted around the group toward Bhon.

"Get these ropes off me, and I'll take them all on," she growled. I cast around for anything sharp.

"No more of this, Kamuli," came a harsh voice behind me, and I spun to face Colonel Rhati. "You're interfering with a military venture."

"One which *I* started as a cooperative research mission," I countered.

"Beside the point. I was brought in to protect Methiemum interests, and that is what I'm doing." The colonel pointed at Bhon. "If I have to kill every Festuour on this island, I will."

"This is in the interest of all ten homeworlds, you arrogant prig," I said, and punched him in the face.

I shook my hand out as the colonel slumped to the ground. I must have hit harder than I thought, because he was out cold. As I suspected, a bureaucrat with no training, stuck here to get him out of the way.

I snuck a glance around. The soldiers were in an argument, though one was trying to give the sergeant a hug—or something more. We had a few more seconds of confusion before any newcomers separated them.

"I hope Colonel Rhati keeps his knife sharp," I said, disarming him and slicing through Bhon's bonds. He did.

I barely got the knife out of the way before warm fur surrounded me, paws crushing me in—yes—a giant bear hug.

"Thanks, love," Bhon said, and kissed me.

I came up for air a few moments later, gasped, and looked around again.

"Why don't we take this reunion away from the soldiers?" I asked.

"Out of the camp?" Bhon suggested.

"Good idea," I said. Whatever happened, we needed to find somewhere safe from Colonel Rhati. "The majus is here," I said as we ran. "She said she needs hard evidence to stop this war, and I know where to get it. Would your people help us?"

Bhon shook her head. "They're madder than pollen sippers with their stingers on fire. Too many friends have been lost, and they're not likely to forgive."

"Then I hope the majus can convince our sides to make peace," I said, as we hurried through the gloom. We neared the cluster of scientific tents and I slowed. Maybe Faloua would know how to find her.

"Faloua, are you here—" I froze as I saw what her tent contained. She wasn't alone.

"Ah, you got your friend free. Excellent," said the tall and striking woman next to Faloua, as she rearranged her wrap to cover her legs again. A blue gloss so bright it almost glowed decorated her fingernails. "I couldn't be seen to take sides yet, but I knew you would come through, with a little help."

I stared back. I *thought* the soldiers had helped me too easily. Had the majus influenced them somehow, along with the sap?

"I confess I took a few minutes to...enjoy the scenery while you escaped," the majus continued. I stole a glance at Faloua, who was busily buttoning up her shirt. It was hard to tell, as she had her face turned away, but I suspected she was blushing furiously.

"You must be the majus," Bhon said over my stammering.

"I am that." The majus took Bhon's paw, bowing over it and planting a kiss on her hairy knuckle. "Dihari Silcasta, at your command. And you must be Shrimasharimsa Bhon, Guarder. Faloua told me much about you two in the last few minutes. Between other...vocalizations. She and I are old friends." She spared a glance for me. I couldn't take my eyes off the way her nail polish flashed. No one on this island wore nail polish.

"Only the best Galaxy Gloss, dear," Dihari said. "Blue Snowball. You should try it. Goes with your complexion."

"Ah. Any way you or your majus compatriots can stop this fighting?" Bhon asked.

Dihari pursed her lips. "I can if you get me concrete proof. The Thrandishar government asked me not to interfere, despite my repeated protests of this fiasco. But Faloua warned me when I arrived that proof might actually be a possibility."

"That's where we're going now!" I said. I'd finally found my voice. This majus had legs that went on for *days*.

Bhon nudged me. "Feeling left out."

I dragged my gaze away from Dihari's legs and back to Bhon. "Just distracted, love," I said. I squeezed her ample triceps.

"I can smooth our way a bit if you can give directions," Dihari said.

"I'm coming too," Faloua said. "I packed while you were gabbing."

We slipped out of the camp with no one seeing us. It was something Dihari did, and our way back through the dense jungle was surprisingly free from complications. The whole time, Dihari was in front, waving her fingers as if about to break into a dance step. I swear she did a little two-step a couple times around particularly dense clumps of vines, but once I got to them I saw there was an easy way through—it just hadn't been visible from where I was standing. But even with our time advantage, the forest wouldn't slow down the soldiers fully outfitted with trailblazing gear.

As we broke into the clearing dominated by the huge fern and its bromeliads, we split paths, each to the place we'd assigned ourselves on the way. I gathered more of the bromeliad sap while Bhon searched the perimeter for ways to defend the area. Faloua went to the other plants in the old garden boxes, determining their uses. Dihari did...something. I presume she was doing majus-stuff, as it looked like she was conducting an invisible orchestra.

"Is this enough proof for you to interfere?" I asked, after we showed the majus the abandoned buildings.

"Plenty, dear," Dihari answered, beaming in my direction. "We just need to keep it intact."

Soldiers crashed through the underbrush an hour later.

"Stay together," Bhon called. She'd taken command of the military side of our little encounter.

"Go get them, my little friends," Dihari gestured to our new allies, and the row of giant rodents, the largest the size of a Methiemum, surged forward, to surprised cries from the soldiers.

Since we learned the sap was like catnip to the rodents, we'd forged a sort of bond. They greatly appreciated my collecting it for them, and the majus 'encouraged' our cooperation. Now the beasts were helping us rather than trying to bite our faces off.

"Our turn," I told Bhon, and we waded into the disillusioned soldiers. Bhon was a tempest of fur and fists, dropping soldiers on all sides. I'd convinced her to leave her handcannons—which she had swiped on the way out of the camp—with the rest of our supplies. This was to be a non-lethal confrontation, if at all possible. Dihari even insisted the rats would be careful.

Faloua had found a crop of cultivated plants which we'd already categorized as an anesthetic, and she squirted what she'd prepared into the soldier's faces. A few seconds after dosing, the victim would stagger and fall, paralyzed for the next few hours. If she'd gotten the dosage right.

I used my trusty sap, which was both a drug for the rodents and an aphrodisiac for Methiemum. Through Dihari's efforts, waving her arms behind us, we sidestepped what would have been lethal thrusts of the soldier's swords and axes. Their shots similarly went wild, bullets careening off into the forest.

We'd made some real progress, a score of soldiers paralyzed or knocked out, and I'd convinced four more to fight with us.

"Enough!" called a voice. I recognized Colonel Rhati by his unique bellow. He stepped out of the jungle on our flank, surrounded by a squad of eight soldiers with loaded blunderbusses covering Dihari. She frowned and raised her hands, stopping whatever majus activity she'd been doing, and the rats scampered back into the jungle.

"I could take 'em," Bhon grumbled, but she backed down too. Faloua had already retreated near the majus.

"You are not supposed to affect our activities here, majus," Colonel Rhati accused. "Last I checked, we had approval from the Thrandishar government." He gestured to the soldiers surrounding him. "Prepare to raze this farm—"

"Hold!" came a rough voice from behind us. We spun to see close to twenty Festuour step from the trees, melting to visibility. Their fur was daubed with streaks of jungle green and black, augmenting their natural green-brown fur coloring.

I shot a look at Bhon, who shook her head and shrugged.

"Klot, fancy meeting you here," Colonel Rhati said. "Saves the time for us to march all the way to your camp to finish you off."

"Partifalgunari Klot, Leader," Bhon supplied in an undertone. "She heads the Festuour expeditionary force on this island." She wasn't the Festuour scientist I'd worked with, so there must have been a similar military takeover on their side.

"If we remove you from command, your soldiers will be directionless," Klot returned. Several of her soldiers stepped farther into the clearing.

"Even if you kill me, you'll still lose," the colonel spat. "Why not surrender?"

"Try us, Methiemum!" Klot growled.

"I might just—"

"Stop this childishness!" A ring of ice spread across the clearing, reaching both Klot's feet and Rhati's boots. They both stepped back and I turned to see Dihari, her arms held wide, water dripping from her fingertips. She gave me a tiny wink.

"I am calling a halt to these hostilities. I have seen plenty of evidence of prior inhabitation of this island." She turned, her outstretched arms taking in the clearing, the plants, and the remains of the underground room.

"By what authorization?" Colonel Rhati asked.

"Aye, who put you in charge?" Leader Klot said. She traded a look with Rhati, scowling.

"By authorization of the Council of the Maji," Dihari answered. "A majus brought you to this island, and supplies your troops. Another does the same for the Festuour side. Unless you want to build a boat and paddle back to the mainland, you will cease your fighting. And since none of you know *anything* about shipbuilding, I suspect you will starve to death." She glared at the colonel. "You *may* take that all the way to the Council, if you can get ahold of them without a majus to take you there."

Colonel Rhati and Leader Klot both puffed up, more arguments ready.

I took Bhon's paw. "I'm guessing there's going to be a lot of arguing, negotiations, and grumbling, but I think the majus has this one. She doesn't need us, anyway."

Bhon nodded.

"Which means you won't be ordered to kill me any longer," I suggested.

"That is true." Bhon looked contemplative and her eyes flicked down to the vial of sap I'd collected.

I smiled. I'd been thinking the same thing. "Want to sneak away?"

"Definitely."

While the two leaders spoke over each other and their soldiers struck intimidating poses, Bhon and I found another path through the jungle. It was surprisingly easy to make our way, and I looked back once to see Dihari watching the two of us, hand in hand with Faloua.

We found a bower of leaves I was certain didn't have any effect on Methiemum or Festuour physiology, and Bhon pushed me down.

"Now, I think it's time for another in-depth conversation about how you're a very unique Methiemum woman," Bhon said, her furry chest a handsbreadth from my face. She ran a paw down my chest and over my belly. "I've had a lot of friends, but none like you in my friend group. And since we *are* in the same friend group now, I think we need to do some serious exploration to find *all* the little differences."

"And maybe some big ones?" My nipples were brushing the fabric of my shirt. Her friend group. I still didn't quite believe it. I didn't know the signs of arousal on Festuour that well, but Bhon's heavy panting was probably one of them.

"Don't really care," Bhon said, before she leaned in for a long kiss. Her big paws ran down my chest, across my groin, and down my legs. I gasped as her tongue found mine.

My hands gripped clumps of her fur, but I forced myself to stop for a moment, reaching into my pocket. "How about a little extra assistance?" I offered the vial of sap.

"Yeah, we should find out what all this stuff does," Bhon said, as I uncorked the vial and dipped a finger in.

"After this is all over," I began, and stroked a sap-laden finger across one of her sensitive areas. Bhon shuddered. "How about we stick around each other for a while? With your mercenary skills and my science, we could even keep ourselves comfortable."

"As long as this is one of the perks," Bhon breathed, and I kept up my stroking.

I stopped just a moment, long enough to search those big blue eyes. I was part of Bhon's friend group. And she was more than a friend to me. The majus would track down the island's original discoverer, and for the first time in over two cycles, I could put this accursed island out of my thoughts. I'd never dreamed it was possible, but now I couldn't dream of anything but the two of us.

"Your homeworld or mine?" I asked.

"Wherever you are," Bhon whispered, before she resumed kissing me.

Last Delivery

999 A.A.W.

Plots and Deals

In recent years, some merchants have cried foul against the maji raising prices on portal creation. While the portals are the only way to link our homeworlds together, they are also a drain on the already overworked houses of the maji. But I feel passing this cost on may have a worse result. By driving away the traveling merchants who connect our different cultures, I believe we may generate much more contention and even war among the ten species that make up our coalition of worlds.

—From a travelogue of Morvu Francita Januti, Etanela explorer and big game hunter

From the safety of my metal transport, I eyed the natives around the market's foreign district. The group of Sureriaj was bigger than it had been five minutes ago, and some of them were holding signs. Others were holding sticks.

"We need to go," I told Amra.

She handed local coinage in change over the table to the gangly Sureri buying spices. "Why? Go where?"

In answer, I pointed one finger to my left, aimed at the growing mob of aliens through the windshield of the transport we used to carry and sell goods. Our market table was set up in the pilot section of the transport, looking out through the open side hatch.

"I don't think they're here to buy our marshfern seed, Prot," Amra said. She moved a protective hand over the colorful piles displayed for maximum scent and visual effect. Past the table and through the hatch, I could see other marketgoers perking up at the disruption.

"Maybe they want the *Ibora labat*," I suggested. "It was the best deal on the Lobath homeworld at the time."

"The dried crushed redcap has been selling better," Amra said, but she was already standing, dusting off her yellow wrap.

I let our joke pull the edges of my mouth up, trying not to let her know how concerned I was. I had seen things like this before, and they could get ugly, fast. "Get this packed up. I'm going to get the others moving."

My accountant, and the love of my life, pulled her wrap close to shift her chair out of the way, face tightening. She scraped spare change into a pouch, then reached for the cover to the spice boxes, economical of motion.

I slipped around the edge of the table and down to the ground, calling for my bodyguards and mechanic. "Kamuli! Bhon! Saart! Time to get moving." I waited for a response, shivering in the chilled air. In addition to the growing throng in the market, other Sureriaj wandered through their cold and faded port town like hairy long-legged gargoyles. So many of them in one place had me on edge, though it *was* their homeworld. I could vaguely hear the crowd abusing a Kirian merchant farther down the line of stalls. Her feathery crest was flattened in fear.

No one answered. I pulled myself up into the engine section of the low domed transport, waving away the stink of burning coal. "Saart—what are you doing? We've got a group of Sureriaj ready to—"

"Where's the fire?" rumbled a deep voice. A hairy shape loomed in the corridor. Mogflaratan Saart, Maker, held a massive wrench in one three-fingered paw, pushing up his glasses with the other. There were grease stains in his graying fur and on the belts of pouches across his belly. Working on one of the turrets again. His pet project.

"The fire might be us, in a few more minutes." I told the Festuour. "There's a mob of locals out there who don't look like they want to do business."

Saart wrinkled his long snout, blue eyes peering at me. "I thought the Naiyul port was neutral territory for the families? Won't the constabulary thugs take care of it?"

"I don't want to chance it." I ducked my head back out the door. The mob was chanting something now, with feeling. "Get this thing moving instead of arguing." Saart hrumphed at me, but turned awkwardly in the narrow corridor, grumbling back to the engine.

"Who's arguing?" came another voice. The other Festuour member of my team rounded a nearby building, her mate in tow. "And why aren't I part of it?"

"You and Kamuli get the chocks out from the wheels," I told her. "And keep your handcannons ready." I pointed at the crowd of Sureriaj again. One sign was close enough for me to make out a word in their spidery script: 'go.' I didn't need to be able to read the rest of it.

Bhon grinned up at me with pointy teeth, excited at any prospect of violence. "You got it, boss. We saw them a few minutes ago. We were coming to tell you all, but maybe we can pick off a few on the way out." She sprinted toward the third and fourth sections of the transport—the living and cargo sections—on stumpy furry feet. Kamuli was right behind her, brilliant white teeth and headwrap flashing against her dark skin.

I clambered back to the pilot section, all four sections of the transport rumbling as the engine clanked to life. Amra had the spices back in their boxes, and was clutching the money purse and her ledger where she kept all our expenses. No time to pack this inventory with the rest in the cargo section.

"Everyone ready?" I called into the speaking tubes placed around the pilot's chair. Amra closed the side hatch with a clang, the table and chairs thrust hurriedly out of the way. She climbed into the co-pilot's chair.

"Engine's running," came Saart's voice, tinny, from the speaker.

"Bhon and I are set," Kamuli said from the living quarters.

"Ready," said Amra, jotting down numbers in her ledger, no doubt calculating our losses from closing up early today. She curled a strand of dark hair behind one ear. We had been here less than a week, but I already knew we needed to get off Sureri and to a homeworld less detrimental to our health.

I pushed on one of many levers before me, and the transport crept forward. It was slow to start, but once it got moving, it was hard to stop. The mob blocked the exit to the market road, and there was no way I could turn the transport around without taking half of the sun-bleached buildings with us. More merchant stalls blocked the other end of the road, and my transport didn't do reverse well. I'd rather run into the wall of inhospitable Sureriaj than my fellow merchants, who were packing in a hurry at the rising discontent.

Amra tensed as I made my decision and accelerated. "We'll have to go through them. Hang on!" I yelled into the speakers, and pushed the lever farther. The transport sped up. Several of the mob were pointing now, and I could just make out a couple words of their language filtering through the metal sides of the transport, mostly things like "thief" and "go."

I gritted my teeth and kept moving forward, faster than a walk, not quite fast enough that the group couldn't get out of my way. I didn't want to hurt anyone, especially merchants. Even the liberal families would be quick to revoke our merchant license if that happened. But if an offworlder got injured on Sureriaj? Well, that was their fault.

The transport pressed into the mob now, and several of them banged on the sides. I tried to ignore the metallic pounding.

Then something hit the windshield with a thump. Amra cried out and ducked, and I jerked in my chair. A leafy vegetable of some sort rolled away.

"Boss," came Bhon's voice through the speaker. "These gargoyles are gettin' fresh with the sides of the transport. Want me to pick a few off?"

"No!" I shouted, and ducked again as another rotten vegetable squished into the glass. Amra shook her fist at the offending alien.

"What did we do to you?" she shouted. Then to me, "Why are they all so pale?"

I looked through bat-like faces as I drove. "I think they're all from one of the northern families. Roftun, or perhaps the Baldek family." Both were conservative and isolationist, even for Sureriaj.

"Shove them away if they get too close," I shouted into the speaker, a death grip on the motive lever. I heard the clang of a hatch opening. "No killing!" I hoped Kamuli would rein her fiery mate in, though the large woman held her own share of knives along with her medical pouch. She was as skilled in taking people apart as putting them back together.

The mob crowded close, pushing back as much as the transport pushed them. I heard the engine whine as the mass of people slowed the wheels. I moved the motive lever farther up, giving it more juice.

There was a shout and a clang from outside, and Amra jumped as a curse shot through the speaker system.

"Was that Kamuli?" she asked, and I grunted agreement. The composed woman spoke little and swore almost never.

"Everything alright back there?" I called. I tried to ignore the hostile faces pressed against the windshield.

"Kamuli got hit with a rock!" Bhon growled. "I'm gonna kill those..."

"No!" Amra and I shouted in unison.

"Kamuli?" I asked. If the big woman was down, her mate would go ballistic.

"I am well," Kamuli said through the speaker, though she sounded shaken. "Only bruised."

"We've got to clear a path," Amra said, getting up from her chair. "They're going to stop the transport before we get through, and Bhon won't last that long without shooting one of them." Her dark eyes cast around for objects in the pilot's section. There weren't many. I tried to concentrate on not crushing any angry Sureriaj.

"Aha!" I heard Amra shift something behind the merchandise table.

"What—" I looked around in time to see a spice tray pass by at head height. Fine particles of the orange spice floated through a beam of bright sunlight. My mouth screwed up and I directed a fantastic sneeze into my shoulder.

"This should work fine," Amra said. She jerked the hatch open and flung the stuff out into the crowd.

The reaction was immediate. Sureriaj grabbed at their eyes and mouths, and the pressure on the transport lessened. I pushed the motive lever forward, blinking through tear-filled eyes.

The heavy steel transport was originally made for much bloodier pursuits, and drove through the sneezing and crying Sureriaj with ease. When the last of the four linked sections—our space for cargo—was clear of the mob, I put the transport to full speed, its small wheels churning, leaving the crowd far behind.

"Anyone following?" I asked Amra a few moments later.

She got up again, balancing against the rough roads, and opened the side hatch to peer out. "There's a couple running after us, but they're slowing down. The rest are going after that group of Methiemum who were selling two kiosks down."

I let out a long breath, blinking the last of the spice away. She would have chosen the *Ibora labat*. That stuff was potent. "I don't envy them." I slowed enough to make a wide turn and Amra clung to her seat to keep from falling. Once down a few more side streets, I stopped the transport completely.

"Everyone up front," I called.

We clumped together outside the pilot section. The four parts of the transport were linked together with large coupling rods and pins, but that meant the only way to travel between them was by going outside. Perhaps a flaw of the original designers.

"What the hell was all that about?" said Bhon. Younger than Saart, our other resident Festuour, Bhon was short, covered in light green-yellow hair, and had a snout full of teeth and bright blue eyes. She was also deadly with a handcannon or a crossbow—both hung from the bandoliers crossing her chest—which lent a lot of weight to her words. Or at least a lot of violence. I was glad none of the mob of Sureri had gotten the wrong end of one of her guns, or I would be dealing with a lot more than a shaken crew. Right now, she was dabbing tenderly at a shallow cut on her mate's forehead.

"It was one of the conservative families—Roftun or Baldeks," I said, "though I have no idea why. The Naiyuls are going to be livid they interfered in their trading port affairs."

Sureri was run by the major families of the Sureriaj, each as large as one of the ruling nations on Methiem. The Sureriaj took families seriously. With two males and one female to conceive a child, and with a slow rate of reproduction, the family was the most important social unit to a Sureri. Neither rewards, nor work, nor money, nor love would make a Sureri abandon or betray their family. For the most part.

That was where the disgraced family came in—the Naiyul. It consisted of those Sureriaj from all families, large and small, who had been disowned for crimes and indiscretions. They made a small family all of their own, and ran the one trading port—Naiyul Montufal Desretre—where aliens were tolerated, barely, and bargained with.

"The city is dangerous enough already," Kamuli said. She brushed Bhon away, though with an appreciative smile for her mate. Unmodified by the speaking tube, Kamuli's voice was rich, with thoroughly pronounced vowels. "Should not the gangs in charge be ready to protect their sections of the port?"

There was a thin line the criminal clans toed, as none of the Sureriaj liked outsiders, but it was also the one place on their planet where goods could arrive from offworld. So merchants, if not welcomed, were at least not attacked and robbed on sight. Until today.

"They'll be ready next time," Bhon said, cracking her knuckles. "And there's gonna be turf wars in the next few days over this." Her grin was malicious, and her mate slapped the Festuour's shoulder with the back of her hand.

"Behave."

"Our sales will be terrible until this dies down," Amra said. She looked down at her ledger like a favorite pet. "We might as well throw the rest of the spices in the gutter, except we haven't made enough to buy passage off this world yet." Her skin and dark brown hair had respectively tanned and bleached in the brutal sun that favored the Sureriaj homeworld. The trading town was dry and dusty, and one would think the blazing rays would at least take the time to heat the ground on the way to burning our skin. No such luck. It froze during the night and was merely cold during the day. I was told it was the height of summer.

Saart had been watching the whole exchange, arms crossed, a wrench grasped in one paw. "At least if we dump them, my food won't taste like greenwort mushrooms anymore." He looked between us, then down at Amra's ledger. "If I have to make another flapjack reeking of a squidhead's foot, I may stop cooking altogether. But if we can't sell them, won't that eat into our money like a rat in a seedbag? How much do we have left?"

"I, too, would be interested in seeing return for our hard work with the Lobath," Kamuli spoke up, adjusting her headscarf away from her wound.

"Yeah, we were on Loba for four months to gather this stuff! The transport still stinks of those squiddies." Bhon looked affronted, though that was similar to her usual expression.

I looked between the two. Kamuli Balion and Shrimasharimsa Bhon, Guarder. They couldn't have been happy on Sureri, where they had to hide their attachment from the xenophobic locals, but they were right that we needed to sell our cargo to leave.

"I know." I spread my hands out, palms up. "These are the best tasting spices we've found in years."

"It didn't help the mushroom farmers of Sa'Lob had very little appreciation of our finer trinkets." Amra put in. "We barely made enough to schedule a portal here."

"To this washed-out excuse for a town," Saart said.

"What can I say? Sureriaj love Lobath spices." I shrugged. Still, I had hoped to make a quick sale and be off to a friendlier homeworld before now.

"The market will be a ghost town for weeks," Kamuli added helpfully.

I ran a hand down my face, and answered Saart's original question. "Like Amra says, we won't have enough for a portal without selling the rest of this." I waved a hand at the cargo section, farther down the road. After several unprofitable ventures, we were living from trade to trade. We hadn't been back to Methiem, where Amra and I hailed from, in almost a full cycle. "Bloody maji, hiking up fees on their portals."

"You can't blame them for everything. Let's pack up for today and find a safe spot to park the transport overnight," Amra suggested.

I nodded. "I'll see if I can run down any good deals tomorrow morning."

"And we'll sell these spices like they're grown from the Nether crystal itself," Bhon said.

* * *

The next morning, back at the market, I sat with Amra, leafing through my notes on merchant contracts. Some dated back all the way to when Saart and I started the business together, many cycles ago. We could have been mercenaries, except the strange fellow we bought the transport from insisted any ordnance was gone, any stored energy dissipated. Saart's pet turrets might have been useful yesterday. I wondered how much mercenaries made.

There had to be someone else on Sureri who wanted to take a transport full of spices.

Wearing a rich wrap the color of the crushed redcap, Amra presided over the trays of fragrant powders displayed like so much colored sand, but we had made only one sale so far.

I flung the sheets down. "There's nothing here. All the smart merchants *know* to avoid Sureri. If I had listened to you the last time we made a big sale, we could be sitting in a little shop on Methiem right now, waiting for the customers to come to us."

"You didn't know the frost radish market was going to tank so soon. Besides, you like traveling in this old thing." She patted a metallic wall companionably.

"But you don't."

"I love you, and that's enough. I just—" She cut off and I sighed.

"I won't subject a child to this life. There's time for that when we're settled."

"You're always set on children. What about time for an actual marriage, and a shop, and the money to keep it running? Kamuli and Bhon make a life together, even traveling with us." She was warming up to the old argument.

I did want children, even if Amra wasn't sure. And while I loved my transport, I didn't want to raise a family in it. "We'll get off this world," I said, "and the next time we hit a good deal, we can sell the transport and open a shop on Methiem rather than sitting in a cold and dusty market stall on another homeworld." I gestured to the deserted market, our only prospective customers a trio of Sureriaj beggars huddled in thin blankets. The two males had lost their mate somehow, but they sheltered a thin child beside them, trying to keep her warm.

Besides our stall, there was one run by two balding Etanela, both half again my height, and one with a lone Kirian woman, crest ruffled and wrinkled arms and legs bare even in the cold. Was she the same one the mob yelled at the day before? She must be even more desperate than us.

"And how long until that deal comes along, Prot?" Amra asked, pulling my attention back. "We've been together six cycles."

I searched for an answer, but was fortunately distracted by a Sureri in a top hat walking purposefully our way, tailored leather coat and tails swishing around wool breeches. He didn't even spare a glance for the other merchants. Bhon materialized from somewhere, hand on one of her holsters, and I caught a glimpse of Kamuli's tall frame through the windscreen, taking in the newcomer's clothes.

"I am thinking yer and yer crew are ready to depart our fine world soonish?" he said in a passable version of the Trader's Tongue. Like all Sureriaj, his legs were longer than mine, his torso shorter, though he was of a height with me. Despite a smaller chest, his arms dangled longer than my own.

"After what happened yesterday? You bet we are." Amra scowled at the well-dressed Sureri and I laid a hand on her leg beneath the table. My accountant was an excellent records keeper, and kept our enterprise afloat, but she had no sense for a good deal.

But he only bobbed his hairy bat-like head in her direction. His hat cast a shadow in the morning sun, enough to obscure his eyes. "Yer mate, I assume? I wish yer family great bounty. Eyah, yesterday's events were...unfortunate-like. Some of our people are a little excitable with aliens forcin' their way into our world, sellin' foreign wares we donna need." His accent became thicker, and his lip curled up for a moment. Then he smiled, and Amra sat back at the sight. Sureriaj were not pretty to begin with.

"Are you looking for spices?" I asked, directing his attention to our table. And off Amra.

The Sureri opened a hand, palm out. "Nay, but I do have an opportunity for yer."

My eyes rose back to him. "I'm listening."

"If yer will come with me a shortish way, and speak with me grand-dame, I think we can benefit each other greatly."

My eyebrows shot up, despite myself. A grand-dame? It was rare to see Suereri women, given they were outnumbered by the males two to one, though they ran most of the businesses behind closed doors.

"I'll be happy to accompany you," I said. I very carefully didn't leap over the table before he changed his mind. "Let me get one of my guards and we'll be—"

"Just yer self, I am afraid," the gentleman Sureri said, with another of his frightening grins.

I paused, taking into account Bhon, Kamuli, and Amra. Saart was tinkering somewhere. Amra was staring at the alien in disbelief, and I could tell she was about to protest.

"That will be...acceptable," I said quickly, and held Amra's eyes with mine until she closed her mouth, frowning. "My crew will continue to sell our wares here." I crooked a finger for Kamuli to come sit with Amra. The tall woman was the second best negotiator, next to myself.

"Be careful. I don't like this man," Amra whispered. She got up as I did, making for the pouch holding small change. "But I can at least make myself useful and give those beggars some money. Their child looks half frozen."

* * *

The Sureri gentleman led me out of the foreign market and around the first corner. They must have rented out one of the unused buildings.

Though the outside was gray like the rest of the town, once through the front door, the décor changed dramatically. There were fine carpets and tapestries from Festuour, sculptures and paintings from Kiria and Etan, and an immense chandelier, which unless I missed my guess, was studded with precious gems mined on Loba.

Lighted by the fixture was an ancient female Sureri, with several males and a few females surrounding her—certainly all children, nieces, and nephews. She was clothed in a voluminous orange silk dress, overflowing the padded chair she sat in. Her thin white hair had been teased and piled into an enormous pouf larger than her head, hung with feathers and a silky net. Unfortunately, her attire did nothing to reduce the ghastliness of her face. The female Sureriaj were just as ugly as the males.

"Sit down, Prot," the grand-dame said. She had done her homework. She pointed with a gloved hand to a small chair on her right and I obediently sat, followed by the gentleman Sureri. This was no small scion sub-family, but surely very close to the main family line—whichever family that was.

"I have heard yer crew is one of the best around to carry cargo in a quick-like fashion." Her accent was light.

"It is that, ma'am," I replied. I tried to judge their lineage from the selection of aliens in the room. They all had similar features, delicate, with pale hair, though I couldn't tell how much was cosmetics and how much was natural. Sureriaj were funny about giving out their names, especially to offworlders, and it was considered rude to ask. They of course knew their own families by sight.

"That is good. Eyah, we know yer must be wantin' to leave our fair homeworld. We have an urgent delivery for Methiem. Would yer be willing to take it?"

I tried to make my expression accommodating, but firm. "If the price is right."

The grand-dame named a sum.

"Ahh...that would...do nicely," I said, trying to keep my jaw from the floor. I wasn't going to get another chance like this, not in twenty cycles of trading. "May I ask what the cargo is, and where it will be received?"

"Nothing illegal, or harmful, if that is what yer imaginin'. Have yer not heard of the epidemic o' the Shudders invading yer own homeworld?" the grand-dame asked. I shook my head. "Eyah, the Methiemum government pays us well for medicine for those sufferin'. It is quite desperately needed. Within the next twenty hours." She made a small gesture and the gentleman stepped forward, giving me a paper with a set of directions.

"This is the location of our warehouse here, as well as the one yer will take the medicine to on Methiem, near Kashidur City." The gentleman handed me a contract, which I scanned. Standard boilerplate, the party of the first part and so on. I read it to the end. The Frente family. I tried to remember my history lessons. They were a fairly liberal family, if I remembered correctly, which may have been why they were helping us escape the recent protests. They couldn't have been happy with the interference in offworld trading.

Someone produced a quill and ink from somewhere, but I hesitated. "I hate to be a bother," I started, but the grand-dame smiled slightly, motioning for me to continue. "I still have a transport full of spices to sell, and I will need something up front to pay for an expedited portal to Methiem."

"Eyah, we happen to have a family feast day comin' up soon. The spices will be perfect like," the grand-dame said. "Yer may sell them at the following location." She nodded to the gentleman, who took my set of directions back and scribbled words barely legible at the bottom. "As to yer fee, yer may negotiate with me relatives at the warehouse. I'm sure they will accommodate yer." The grand-dame folded gloved hands and sat back lightly. It was obvious my chance for questions was at an end.

I looked down. If I didn't sign this contract now, another group would get it within the hour, and this was a sure way to get off this planet. Normally the entire crew made the decision on what to trade. Normally

Amra was with me, writing in her ledger and figuring out the plusses and minuses. But this was a good deal—a great bargain, really. One of a kind.

I signed the paper.

* * *

Amra's eyes narrowed, one hand tightening on her ledger. "I'm sure you didn't seal the contract without the approval of the rest of the crew, did you?" The other three crewmembers stood in a circle around us.

"There was no time," I told her, trying to keep my voice level. "By the time I got your nod it would have been gone. And we've got to pick up the new cargo and take it to Methiem in a standard Sureri day."

"Impossible. Scheduling the portal off-world will take longer than that. The one contract can't pay for everything." Amra raised an eyebrow at me.

I showed her the contract, and both eyes went wide. Bhon craned her neck to see.

I could see Amra calculating. "With the profit from this, we could start saving enough to look at places near Kashidur City—"

"Later," I said, though she was probably right. "For now we need to get moving."

"And what about all these spices?" Saart asked. He pushed his glasses farther up his snout. The older Festuour hated wasting anything that might be used in food or repairs. Privately, I agreed with him, but the Sureriaj were not known for their patience, especially with aliens.

"We'll have to sell them at-cost, most likely."

There was a collective groan. Kamuli showed her teeth in something that definitely wasn't a smile.

"I already have a buyer. We'll just have to—" I swallowed, "—let Kamuli sell these off while I negotiate at the pickup site." I didn't look at Amra. If I had let my love run our little shop-on-wheels, we wouldn't have sold enough to get off Methiem in the first place, let alone travel through the ten homeworlds. She would have ended up giving half our profits to needy families. I wasn't uncharitable, but I wanted to support myself before I supported others.

"Can we all agree to follow through with this? We have to move fast, and don't have time for bickering."

Now I did watch Amra. Her eyes were down, focused on her ledger. Reluctantly, she nodded. I looked at the others. Saart had folded his furry arms, tapping his wrench on his shoulder. He shrugged. Bhon rolled her blue eyes, bouncing one of her handcannons off the other paw. She didn't care where we went, as long as she got to shoot something every once in a while. Kamuli looked dubious, but then turned to regard the marketplace. I saw her glance to the merchants not of this homeworld. She wasn't even able to walk hand in hand with her mate. Conservatives like the Sureriaj still frowned on cross-species attachments. She looked back at me, her eyes hard.

I stood, and picked up my stool. "It's settled." As if I hadn't already signed a contract in front of several well-dressed, possibly royal, Sureriaj. "Let's get this place packed up. We have to be at the warehouse as soon as possible."

Packing consisted of breaking down the table, stowing the chairs, and repacking the spices. Saart began stoking the coal furnace that powered the transport, and Kamuli and Bhon shuttered the windows and removed the wheel chocks.

We would have to split the transport for this endeavor, with Kamuli and Bhon driving the living section, which had its own small turbine, towing the cargo section. Saart, Amra, and I would travel in the pilot and engine sections, negotiate the contract, then wait for the empty cargo section at the warehouse.

I passed Amra in the hallway, doing the little dance we all adopted to move around each other in the long, narrow transport sections. She still looked pained, and I knew what she wanted. She was a fabulous accountant, but a lousy negotiator. On the other hand, I had a good sense of market values, but when they were written down, they always got the best of me. That was why we made a good team.

"I could try..." she began as we moved around each other, my hands on her hips, hers on my arms. Her red wrap swirled around my feet.

"No." I wasn't going to be swayed again.

"Come on," she wheedled, "you never let me sell anything off the transport. I can bring in revenue on the spices, no matter how small."

"That's because you don't turn a profit," I told her. "I love you dearly, but you can sell water to a dying man and lose on the deal."

Her mouth turned down in a pretty pout. We were blocking the hallway, but the others were busy. "Let me try, once more," she pleaded. "There's a captive audience. I can sell the spices." Her tone was reaching that certain harmonic that made my eye twitch. Amra could be very stubborn when she wanted.

"Come on, boss, let the gal do it." The voice floated through the metal siding of the transport. Bhon could hear us through the wall. "You can sell quickly, can't you Amra?" she said.

I hesitated, and Amra moved in for the kill.

"Please?" She smiled at me in a way that hinted at brain-melting rewards in the future if I let her have her way.

Mentally noting how my future self owed me, I threw up my hands. "Fine. We're going to lose on them one way or the other. Take the cargo section, but sell the spices as fast as you can. Kamuli can ride with me while I drive the rest of the transport to the meeting place." I gave her the directions the gentleman Sureri had written down.

"I'll find you soon," Amra promised, scooting past me.

"Take Bhon with you," I called after her. "She can at least threaten to shoot someone if they won't buy anything."

* * *

In the pilot's seat, I rumbled along the too-narrow alleys of the market port of Naiyul Montufal Desretre. It probably wasn't the real name, just what the Sureriaj told aliens. Saart was busy keeping the steam engines running smoothly in the next section, and Kamuli stood behind me, watching the bland and windblasted buildings flow by.

Amra headed off with Bhon some minutes before we started out. Both halves of the transport were traveling to the section of the city belonging to the Frente family. The Naiyul ruled the trading town, the only commercial entrance to their planet. Within the city of the disgraced, all but the most conservative of the upright families owned sections, acting like trading embassies.

Kamuli must have wandered down the same line of thought. "Remind me," she said slowly, her words even more precise than usual, "why we decided to travel to the most xenophobic of the ten homeworlds? Who thought this would be a good deal?"

"You know full well who thought it was a good deal," I answered. "This is the only place we could get enough from those spices to buy a portal to the next homeworld."

"The ones we are dumping for whatever Amra thinks is a good price."

I ground my teeth, ratcheting back one of the steering levers. The transport skidded on its wheels to the right, narrowly missing a Sureri mounted on lizardback, trailing a cart filled with red leafy vegetables. He yelled something at us and I waved back cheerily, purposely misinterpreting his intent. Amra had the cargo and living sections, so I had to be careful not to oversteer and ram the engine into any more buildings. There were not many people out today, likely because of yesterday's disturbance. I could move faster through the streets than normal.

"I had not heard of this epidemic," Kamuli said, gripping a handle to keep her balance. "We have been absent from Methiem too long, especially if it is so bad the authorities must import medicine from Sureri." Kamuli kept tabs on local medical news, but since we had arrived here from an isolated community on Loba, her information was dated.

"The Sureri have good medicine," I said. "And the contract insisted the cargo is expected on Methiem by tomorrow morning. It must be an emergency." I swerved again, taking a hard left. I was pretty sure this was the correct turn. The buildings here all looked the same.

A tinny voice emerged from the speaking tube next to my chair. The words were obviously shouted, but came out muffled. "We have an official following us, riding one of those tall beasts!"

"Just what we need!" I shouted back into the tube. "I'm speeding up. Keep the furnace going." Even if they couldn't kill all the aliens that came to their planet, didn't mean they wouldn't try to arrest them on the merest offense. The protest had everyone on edge. I was probably driving too fast, or they were upset about the building I might have nicked a few turns back. I ratcheted the speed lever up another notch.

"Fortunate then that you were contacted to fulfill this contract." The big woman took up her previous line of questioning without a break. Kamuli would never directly confront me. She just poked and prodded. I still wasn't sure how she and Bhon got along without killing each other. The one time I had tried to needle Bhon, I ended up with a handcannon about two fingers away from my nose. "Surely there were other more well-equipped merchants here. But that is why you lead us, after all. I would never have found such a contract as we are—" She grunted and shifted suddenly, countering the transport's hard turn. That *had* been the wrong street. "—*rocketing* toward. Fortunate indeed."

I had been trying to push down that niggling doubt within myself since I signed the contract. Why did they pick me? I was deciding what to answer, when the speaking tube crackled again.

"Do you want me to burn this engine out? You're going faster than a tree skater with its feet alight. I can only shovel so fast."

"Sorry Saart," I shouted back into the tube. "Almost there." I didn't slow down, though. The border between the Naiyul and Frente sectors was around one more turn, the warehouse not much farther. The disgraced Naiyul family might have been corrupt, but it was small compared to the major families of Sureri. They had no desire to start a fight they couldn't win, and I used that to my advantage. If a Naiyul made a stink within the borders of an embassy, there would be repercussions I was betting the disgraced family didn't want to deal with.

"How's our tail?" I interrupted the swearing coming from the speaking tube.

"Mine's about to catch fire from all this—" There was a pause. "Oh, you mean..." There was another pause, and I steered between two tall buildings. The streets were smaller here, barely wide enough for the transport. Lucky there was no one coming the other way.

"She's sitting about four buildings back," came Saart's voice, "making some gesture that—oh, now that ain't called for."

I moved the speed indicator lever back down a few notches, gradually bringing the transport to a stop outside a boxy adobe building, larger than most of the others surrounding it. A pipe hissed in the cabin, letting out a buildup of pressure as the old military transport came to a halt. A vent creaked in the other section, and there was a thump that rocked Kamuli forward as the section behind us settled into its final resting place. She took a moment to set her headwrap back to rights, and adjust her jacket.

We waited a few minutes, but I wasn't expecting Amra for some time yet. They would have to go through negotiations, come to a—hopefully reasonable—price, and then unload the cargo before coming here. Best to move slowly.

The weak Sureri sun was not quite fully overhead, and we scouted out the warehouse, looking for anything out of the ordinary. We kicked up small clouds of dust in the barren yard. There wasn't much plant life in this city, and I wondered what the rest of Sureri looked like. Had the great families given the least inhabitable land to their disgraced cousins, or was their whole planet poor in life compared to other homeworlds?

But the yard was empty, and we couldn't stall any longer. The Naiyul official hadn't followed us into the Frente section, so that was one positive. I jerked my head at the warehouse, looming in the empty yard.

"Time to go. Keep your eyes up and your feet light. I intend to be back on Methiem this evening with enough money to think about retiring."

We slid the warehouse door to one side with a screech of rusty skids. Kamuli grunted as she helped me, and I noticed her knives were loose in their sheaths. I waited while my eyes adjusted to the gloom, feeling Saart's fur bristle on my other side, and shivered. This was not the sort of contract I usually took on.

The warehouse was largely empty, skeletons of shelves towering to left and right. The center of the floor was open, but littered with blocky objects, pushed together.

"Anyone there?" I called out. "I was supposed to meet someone to pick up cargo."

A shadow detached from a far wall of the warehouse. I put a hand, palm out, to the others, telling them to wait.

"Eyah, we are here," a voice said in the Trader's Tongue. It had a lilting accent. "Yer just keep yerself cool there, alien, and we'll get the medicine ready."

"Why have they got medicine in this old dingy warehouse?" Saart whispered. "Don't make sense."

I shushed him. The Sureri supplied lots of medicine to the other homeworlds, though it usually went through more official channels. I didn't want to argue with the paycheck, but I had to check the seller's story.

"Medicine for what?" I hoped this Sureriaj would answer the same way.

There was rustling, and a lantern flared to life, making shadows flicker and illuminating five gangly and fair-skinned Sureriaj. They looked as if they had been waiting in this warehouse for months, not hours.

The one in front attempted to smile. I felt Saart bristle beside me. The Festuour and Sureriaj species were not close.

"There is a great epidemic in yer Methiemum cities goin' on. Yer did not know of it?" he asked. "The grand-dame asked yer to make a special run to Methiem, did she?"

"That's right," I said, trying to follow his lyrical accent. "Told me I needed to deliver this to Kashidur City in twenty hours."

"Seventeen now, it is," the lead Sureri said. "Very sensitive to the time passin'. Got to hand it off quick-like." His eyes narrowed. "The epidemic is growin' fast and yer own people are dying. Don't want any o' this gettin' lost before it gets there." Kamuli snorted. As if we would lose cargo.

I put one hand inside my vest pocket, where I kept the directions the well-dressed Sureriaj had given me. I saw the alien's hand twitch, and I pulled the paper out slowly.

"I've got the directions right here—"

"Lemme glance it with me own blinkers," the Sureri said, stepping forward. I tensed, but handed over the paper the gentleman had given me. The alien looked through it carefully, silently sounding out words. I guessed he was able to speak the Trader's Tongue better than he read it.

I hoped he didn't find anything wrong, especially considering the pistols I saw strapped to their thighs. The Sureriaj were even more enamored of the weapons than the Festuour, and unlike Bhon's handcannons, their pistols could fire more than once before being reloaded. If I could get my hand in that market, I wouldn't need to resort to deals like this to turn a profit. The Sureri snapped up projectile weapons from Methiem like a Kirian on a grub. But the circles those merchants moved in were far above my own.

"Eyah, tis right," the alien said shortly, and thrust the paper back at me, adding his own sheaf. "Yer bill of lading. Now pack these crates up nice-like and be off with yer and yer ilk. And make yer sure that fuzzy don't interfere too much, ey?"

He peeled back to the other four Sureriaj, ignoring Saart's snarl, and gestured to twenty large wooden containers—the objects gathered on the open floor of the warehouse. They were almost haphazardly arranged, as if they had been moved here in a hurry and dumped with little purpose or arrangement.

Kamuli and Saart picked up a crate each, and I tucked the paperwork away. Amra would check it later. I could understand the loading bills, of course, but hardly had the patience for it.

I coughed delicately, and the leader's head whipped toward me. I opened my hands to show I meant no harm, and stepped past the others, hoisting a crate. My advance hadn't been expressly clarified in the meeting this morning, so I would be relying on my negotiating skills.

"I must be able to get off-world quickly to deliver this cargo," I began.

"Aye," the leader growled.

"And thus I must schedule the portal to take me to Methiem. Those aren't easy to come by, last minute." I hoped he would take my hint.

"Unless yer plan to cross vasty unknown interstellar distances in some sort of flyin' steam engine, I would agree with yer. And I'm wagerin' ye'd not make it in time."

So that's how it was going to be. "I had to offload my cargo in a hurry to pick up this shipment for you." I told him. "I won't make much profit and I need funds to get me to the drop off point."

The Sureri scowled, looking even more like a grotesque on top of a building. "Me grand-dame did nae specify what to pay yer now," he grumped.

"No, she left that up to me," I told him. "This medicine is important. You said yourself people were dying." This particular member of their species seemed unlikely to be on an errand of mercy. Despite the claim this morning there were no illegal drugs, I wondered if those well-off Sureriaj could be scamming the desperate Methiemum governments about medicine for the epidemic. Were the crates actually filled with drugs like Fuzz or StepUp? I wasn't completely against the odd smuggling job, but that wasn't what I signed up for this morning, especially if my people were suffering from this epidemic. Besides, smuggling required extra planning.

The alien wasn't taking my hint, and I put hands on my hips at the lack of answer. "Do you want it transported or not? If you do, I need the money to move it."

The alien turned away from me abruptly and held a quick conversation with the others. They were certainly his family members—

probably all cousins, or maybe a brother or two. He spoke low and fast in the Sureriaj language, so I didn't get more than a few words.

When he turned back to me, he was even paler.

"Eyah, we have enough to cover twenty percent now, the rest-like when yer complete the run. I will have ter inform the grand-dame, yer ken."

I only raised my eyebrows at him. If they freely admitted to having that much, then they had more. They would have planned to give me a small advance. Their family would reimburse them. "Half—to at least cover my expenses."

"Thirty percent. No more for yer until proof of delivery." Oh, this was too easy. Never send a thug to negotiate with a merchant.

I tried on my best innocent-but-not-really face. "It's a question of pure logistics. If I don't get enough money to move these crates, I might have to open them up and sell to the highest bidder to cover my costs." I had intended to get at least get forty percent with this jab, but his eyes widened, his hairy ears coming to points.

"Yer may not open the merchandise!" he snapped. "They must remain sealed to keep the medicine fresh. If we find yer have tampered with any-like part of the crates, me family will find yer and yer other aliens."

I stepped back. I could see a couple of the other aliens reaching for their weapons, and I held up my hands. Threats on a medicine run? What was in those crates? I kept my tone level. "Then I had better have enough to cover everything, and more, don't you think?" I put my hands down, surreptitiously wiping sweaty palms on my leather leggings.

The obviously agitated Sureri turned away again for another *sotto voce* conversation. At least they weren't drawing weapons. Yet.

"Yer are a merchant, no? Yer know how to schedule a portal. We canna be responsible for all yer expenses. Thirty percent is final."

That would barely be enough. The portals were expensive. I signaled Kamuli, and she put down the box she had picked up. "Then I'm afraid we may have to cancel our business." Now the guns did appear, and I kept myself from moving, tense for the sound of a shot. Careful.

"Yer have signed a contract with me grand-dame," the Sureri said in a low voice. "I donna think yer want to be seen as a contract breaker, do yer?" His men fanned out, showing that they had five to our three.

This would be a fine time for Amra to arrive with Bhon to even the odds.

"There's no need for a broken contract," I said. "Give us the fifty percent up front, and all will go well. I'm sure your grand-dame will—"

"Yer donna talk about our grand-dame!" one of the other Sureri called out, and I swallowed. Seems I'd hit a nerve.

"Fine, fine. This is just business. Simple merchants, negotiating as friends." My hands were at my sides, where I kept a few knives hidden. Kamuli and Saart had stopped all pretense of moving the crates out, and stood on either side of me.

"We will give yer forty percent," the lead Sureri said suddenly. He was watching his brethren, evidently seeing where this negotiation was going. I don't think anyone wanted to try explaining bodies to the Naiyul constables.

And I would have taken that amount, too, a few minutes ago. Now, I was starting to get annoyed.

"I think we'll take the full fifty percent," I said, locking eyes with him.

"Why you—" He switched into his native tongue, and his face went almost white with fury. As he began to reach for his holster, there was a clang behind us, and the Sureri started back.

"Need any help, folks?" came Bhon's voice, and I sagged. She appeared in a stream of light from the open doorway, Amra behind her with a long iron pipe. Bhon had a handcannon in each of her furry paws, and the two flanked us. Five against five.

"Thank you Bhon," I said loudly, "but the nice man here was about to give us fifty percent of our fee up front to keep our delivery timely and *safe*." I watched him, challenging him to another move. He turned to his familymates with a snarl, and the group began handing small bags between themselves.

"Fifty percent," he spat at me, and produced a large bag. By the light chiming sound coming from it, it held the clear unbreakable chips used for trading between the worlds. Nether glass. "If me or me familymates find out yer tampered with the cargo, we will—"

"And who should I go to for the remainder of my fee, once I deliver everything?" I didn't want to know what threat he was going to make. The Sureri sputtered until he got his words going the right direction.

"Yer need to see...to see..." He paused, clearly collecting his thoughts. Sureriaj were touchy about giving out their names, or names of those in their families.

"Ask for...Frente Yatulnath," the Sureri finally managed to say.

I nodded, but by now, I was fairly sure this wasn't the Frente family. We were in the Frente section of the Naiyul trading town, in a run-down warehouse, with five thugs who obviously didn't know much more than we did. I knew the Frente family was fairly liberal in off-world trading— one reason I was willing to take the deal in the first place. These aliens seemed like they would rather trade with sewer rats. Whatever was happening, I doubted the Frente family would appreciate these five Sureriaj, whoever they were, being on their property. My thoughts flashed back to the Naiyul officer following us.

"I will find Yatulnath," I promised, fixing a cheery smile on my face. "I guess I should thank you for this deal, Frente...?" I left the name open for him to complete—an insult, though an uninformed 'alien' wouldn't know that—and watched carefully enough to see him stiffen at the word.

"Eyah, Frente...Masnaith, I am," the Sureri said, not entirely smoothly. He was as Frente as I was. He recovered, sneering. "Yer have seventeen more hours 'til delivery on Methiem. Be on yer way, then, all of yer, and donna let yer dogs mess the floor on the way out."

Kamuli had a hand on Bhon's arm, and from the number of her teeth showing, the Festuour heard the Sureri's last insult. I eyed the false Frente one more time, and guided Saart to the last few crates in the warehouse, making sure he didn't try to start an inter-species war on the way.

Once we were all out, I pulled the warehouse door closed with a screech. Let the false Frentes stew in the dark. I saw the rising questions among my crew and cut them off.

"All the crates into the transport now. We can talk when we have steel walls around us."

There was grumbling, especially from Saart and Bhon, as I helped them pull the last crates into the cargo section. It was full from floor to ceiling, only a small square left to stand in and a narrow corridor down the length. We would have had no room for the spices, and I wouldn't have gotten more than a pittance selling them on my homeworld anyway. I prayed Amra negotiated for a decent amount.

Saart banged the connecting pin to the two halves of the transport with extra vehemence, and Kamuli took the chocks out from the wheels.

When everyone was in—Saart in the engine compartment, Bhon and Kamuli in the living quarters—I closed the heavy steel door of the cockpit shut behind me and threw myself into the co-pilot seat. Amra already had her hands on the control levers, her wrap settled around her.

"Let's go."

We had barely left the warehouse compound when the speaking tube beside the pilot's chair crackled.

"You want to...huff...tell us...huff...why that felt as legal as a...huff...padam made of wood?" Saart was busily shoveling coal as he complained.

There was a wheeze from a second tube, placed above our heads.

"A dog, eh? If the next batch of gargoyles are as pleasant as these they'll be getting my hairy fist in their—" The voice was cut off by Kamuli hushing her mate.

"They do have a point," Amra said.

"Don't you start. Anyway, how did it go with the spices?" I searched the road ahead, but the Naiyul thug who had followed us had fortunately left his post. "Tell me you got something decent for them."

Amra gazed out the windscreen. "How do you do it?" she said, avoiding the question. "Stay so calm in negotiations? I get all flustered the moment someone tells me I'm wrong. I start to doubt myself. I don't suppose I could negotiate while I had my ledger open?" She looked at me with regret and apology on her face.

I sighed, but then wondered how my own negotiations might have gone without Kamuli's imposing presence. No it was better for Amra to have sold the spices, even if we did take a loss.

"I think having your nose in your ledger would take away a bit from your selling presence," I said. She turned the transport carefully around a corner, and tugged her red wrap closer with one hand. "I could never make the numbers dance to my tune like you do."

"And what was the price?" Better to hear the bad news all at once.

"Twenty drezels per ounce."

I tried not to wince, while the Festuour's argument died out over the speakers. "You did good. Next time pretend you're writing all those numbers down in your book rather than staring at the ugly mug you're selling to."

"Next time?" Amra's face lit up and I realized my mistake. I tried to backpedal.

"Yes, well, we have to save up for that little shop on Methiem somehow, don't we? And you have to keep up your habit of supporting whatever orphans and beggar children come our way. Just think, one day, you may even turn a profit! We might have enough to feed a child of our own!"

Amra poked me from the pilot's seat. "I'd give up trying to sell things and be content to write in my little book if you'd agree to marry me *before* we die of old age. We don't have to be stationary to live together. We've done well this far."

I must have looked pained again, because she rolled her eyes. But neither of us got to say anything further.

"There is another Sureri following us." Kamuli's tinny voice cut into our conversation. "He looks like an officer in one of the gangs."

I peered out the window to see the Naiyul official on one of the tall bird-things they favored. Not gaining on us, but just...watching.

Amra frowned. "We had one of the Naiyul constable thugs following us all the way from the market, even though we were doing completely legitimate business. I have all our merchant licenses in order. The protest has everyone acting nervous." She paused, biting her lower lip. "Though Bhon might have taken a little bit of a pot shot at him to keep him from getting too close." That explained the tail.

"Is there something you are not telling us, boss?" Kamuli asked. "What happened when you signed the contract?"

I described the well-to-do grand-dame and her gentleman family member, and how they had presented the contract. It was starting to sound too good to be true. Amra had been right not to trust them. "In any case, those Sureriaj were definitely not Frente." I finished.

"Then what's their game?" Bhon asked through the speaker.

"I don't know," I answered, "but let's get to the portal ground before anything else happens. With the advance they gave us, we can jump the line and get to Methiem today instead of tomorrow. We won't be able to deliver this in time otherwise." And the sooner we got off Sureri, the better.

I held on to my co-pilot's chair as the transport went over a rut in the dirt road with a clang. I heard a grunt from one of the speaking tubes, but other than that my crew was silent, likely contemplating the same questions I was.

The portal ground was on the edge of the trading city, and we lost our shadow by the time we got there. I gripped my chair's arms as Amra brought the heavy transport to a tenuous stop in the line queued at the roped-off square. The transport was good for hauling cargo, not so much for driving through a populated city.

The side hatch clanged open and Saart pulled himself up. "Do I have to say I don't like this?" he asked. He adjusted his glasses. I could hear the engine winding down in the section behind us.

"You just did. And I don't like it either, but it will make us a lot of money." I swiveled my chair, taking in Saart's soot-stained fur. "Or maybe you want to drive this transport back to the warehouse and tell those thugs we've thought better of their deal?"

"No, I want us all to understand what's going on, instead of jumping into a bad deal like a bear into a tar pit. You could have turned this down when you saw the payoff was too large. But you didn't see fit to consult the rest of us."

"I already apologized." I relaxed my grip on the chair, and fought to keep my voice level. "I had to take the contract then or not at all. The profit will cut down the number of new trades before we can look at a shop on Methiem."

Saart snorted. "You'll never settle down."

"Why do you think I took this contract?" I asked.

Amra was pulling levers, letting the transport roll forward in line. "It's a start for him, Saart."

Saart snorted again. "Remember when Prot was 'sick' with the 'Kirian maggot flu?'"

"Yes, when we were supposed to look at potential shopfronts outside Biharia..." Amra turned with a hiss of inhaled air. "Tell me you didn't lie to me."

"So I got cold feet." I raised a hand. "The brakes!" I said, trying to keep the panic out of my voice. There was a cart in front of us with two terrified-looking Lobath. They were gathering bunches of smushfruit in their arms to cart out of the way.

Amra jerked on the lever, and I barely got my hands up to stop myself flying out of the seat. Saart stumbled into the back of my chair, and I heard a series of grunts and bangs from the passenger section speaking tube.

"That took time and money to set up. If you're so interested in settling down, don't waste my time." Amra was fuming.

"What the hell is going on up—" Bhon began before I flipped the switch next to the speaking tube, cutting her off.

"I'll handle the customs officials," I said, extricating myself from the seat and ignoring both Saart and my accountant. "Get this thing ready to travel to Methiem." I left the cockpit before anyone could catch me and ask any more questions, banging the hatch shut on an enraged squawk from Amra.

I shook my head as I walked. We had to get the merchandise delivered. We had to get the money. We had nothing saved up without it. I pushed away the feeling of impending doom settling on my shoulders.

A few steps away from the transport, I checked the layout of the portal ground. There were four large merchant parties, each with several wooden cargo wagons pulled by System Beasts. One set—in the form of immense horses sparkling like glass in the cold sun—doubtless cost more than my transport and cargo combined. The maji-created animals ate grass to sustain themselves, but the cost to recharge the system that ran them was more than I made in a full cycle.

Another group consisted of a pair of Etanela, towering above everyone else, and carrying heavy packs on their backs. Four Kirian women, with short, wildly colored robes ending above wrinkled elbows and knees, talked off to the side. I could see their crests fanning and flattening as they gossiped. There was even one lone Benish, standing rooted to the spot like a particularly gnarled anthropomorphic tree. they carried an immense bag in one hand. All the parties here had surely booked weeks in advance.

I searched the Sureriaj guards, dressed in a combination of family regalia. I could recognize a few—Frente and Baldek, and even one of the Nara family. What I was really looking for was...there. Technically one of the great families, the Naiyul also had a right to put a customs official at the portal ground.

Sureriaj tolerated corrupt family members less than most would tolerate a corrupt employee. Imagine being dragged in front of your company owners and seven of your great-great-grandmothers—who happened to be the same people—to explain why you had taken the money from the nice man with the shiny transport.

As a race, they were loyal to a fault to their family, but the rare individual Sureri was willing to take a little extra on the side. The disgraced Naiyul had fewer ties to family, making them more susceptible.

I checked to make sure none of the other Sureriaj were paying attention before I slipped over to the customs official dressed in the navy and yellow of the disgraced Naiyul. "I need to go through the next portal to Methiem," I said. I took a quick look at the sun. "In the next hour or so, if one's available."

The customs Sureri hefted my proffered clinking bag of Nether glass—a sizeable fraction of the advance I had been paid— and evidently found it acceptable, as he tucked it away with a conspiratorial grin and bent to fill out paperwork. He checked a sheet with timetables, then checked around to make sure the other agents weren't watching before completing the form he gave me. The writing was all in the interconnected Sureri script, but I assumed it was legitimate. I had offered enough.

"Yer in luck, yer are. The majus is makin' a hole to Loba just now, but the next one for them," he threw out a long finger toward the group of Etanela, "is goin' to Kashidur City." He handed me the paper. "Lucky yer leavin' today. Grounds were closed yesterday, what with that protest by the Baldek." He cocked his head to one side. "I'm hopin' yer had a pleasant stay here, regardless."

"Many thanks." At least this Sureri didn't act like I carried fleas. I'm sure the bag of money helped.

I tried not to think of how much the bribe reduced my assets, but it did let us skip the line. Much of the rest would go to the price of the portal itself. I would be expected to share the cost equally with the group of Etanela, so at least they wouldn't complain at our jumping in line. Still, even what Amra got from selling the spices was a valuable addition to our savings at this point.

Without the portals that moved us from planet to planet, the ten homeworlds would have no trade. Just because the maji were the only ones who could open them was no reason to charge so much. Every majus I had seen was rich as a king with an ego bigger than Methiem.

By the time I got back, the others had prepared the transport to travel. I carefully stayed around the other side from Amra, watching Kamuli and Bhon bolt in the last panel to trim down the outline.

My vehicle had been a war machine, in its past life. Its kind had only been used once, more than twenty-five cycles ago, when the Methiem waged a short war against the Sathssn over their trading rights on Sath Home. Turned out preparing the machines for battle, once they passed through portals linking the homeworlds, took so long the Sathssn defeated the Methiemum easily. But we still got the trading rights in the end. That's war for you.

Saart found the transport right after we met, we bought it for a song-and-a-half at a junk yard from a rather eccentric majus, and Saart fixed it up. Physically, it was long and narrow, with low ground clearance. A majus could only open a portal so large, and the transport could only traverse one after modifications to reduce its overall height. The adjustments made riding claustrophobic while in transport mode, but it was worth it to carry cargo between planets. With its capacity, we could rise above many petty merchants, even if we weren't at the level of the larger, better-funded parties.

I sighed. I couldn't avoid things any longer. I stopped pretending to observe my transport, and came around the front of the pilot section at the same time Amra was pulling open the door to the cabin. We stopped, watching each other.

I broke first.

"I shouldn't have lied. I...I wasn't—"

"No, you shouldn't have." Amra interrupted. "If you don't want to settle down yet, tell me. Don't sneak off."

"I wasn't sneaking. I was trying to get our portal scheduled so we can actually make money." I threw a hand back toward the portal ground.

"Oh, and I'm not capable of making us any?"

I frowned. "I never said—" I wanted to tell her how much the money from the spices helped, but before I could, she broke in.

"You were thinking it," Amra accused.

Suddenly, I was angry. I didn't have time for this. "Look, I want you, I want children, I want our store somewhere. We just have to—"

"We've 'just had to' for nearly six cycles," Amra said. "When do we finally find the time to make it happen?"

"I don't know," I shot back. I took the door from her, climbing in. "Maybe when this delivery is finished. Maybe not."

Amra climbed in after me. "We lose money traveling from homeworld to homeworld."

"Then we need this last job to go right," I told her. And a few others. Amra snorted, and took the co-pilot's seat. "Then we can start looking..."

She held up a hand toward me. "I don't want to hear it now. Drive. I can't stand going through portals." Her segue only meant she didn't have a good answer either. But this argument wasn't finished.

I pushed any retorts to the back of my mind, and checked through the speaking tubes that everyone was strapped in. Driving to the front of the line, I saw the portal to Loba closing, the hole in the air compressing to nothing.

The majus standing in front of our transport—a red-skinned fishy-looking Lobath—went to the group of Etanela, asking a question. A bag of coins changed hands. She shivered in the cold, the wind puckering her rubbery skin. Her three long tentacles growing in place of hair were drawn close to shield her from the wind. Next she came to us, calling in the Trader's Tongue through the side door I had left open.

"You are going to Methiem, yes? You agree to split the cost with the other party?"

"We are, and we do," I called back. Amra counted out the fee in Nether glass we got from the Sureriaj, not looking at me. The amount was much bigger than that of the bribe. I eyed it with distaste, wondering where the money went. A bribe to smooth our transit was one thing, but the cost of traveling from one homeworld to another was far too high, in my estimation.

Amra handed the pouch to the majus, who hefted it with a practiced hand and gestured us forward. I kept the transport idling right behind the group on foot. Amra shut the door and, despite our argument, a thrill ran through me. This never got old.

The Lobath majus walked to the front of the line, but before she could do anything, there was a disturbance behind us, and I looked out the window near my seat. Four of the Naiyul constables pushed through the waiting line, each riding a tall bird.

"These aliens are not allowed to leave our world," the one who had tailed us said. He must have gone back to get reinforcements.

I didn't have time for this. I went to the hatch, rolling it back to argue, but the majus got there first.

"What is the suspicion?" she asked. "You have a warrant for them, yes?"

The Sureri faltered. "They've been hangin' 'round warehouses, and we think they mebbe have stolen goods..."

"We're merchants," I shouted. "We hang around warehouses for a living. Do you have proof or not?" I could see others in line starting to talk and shuffle. The Sureri constable was going to have another riot on his hands if he wasn't careful.

"They have already paid for portal," the Lobath majus said. "I must make it now, unless you have proof."

The Sureri made a horrible face at me. "We know yer involved," he said. "We'll track yer down soon, don't fret."

I traded looks with Amra, our argument swept aside for the moment.

The majus turned her back on the constables and waved vaguely in midair, doing her magic. The black oblong hole between worlds opened, and I climbed back in my seat. Unless the Sureri physically stopped the transport, there was nothing they could do. Anything to get off this world.

They *had* been watching us, but why? The cargo? We just needed to deliver it, get our money, and all would be well.

I drove away from the constables, away from Sureri, and past the majus. The Etanela we shared the portal with were a bit taller than the transport, and ducked to pass through the top edge of the portal. The majus had skimped on the height to make it wide enough for us. I kept the wheels turning slowly, aimed directly for the slice of utter blackness, barely high enough for the curved and aerodynamic outline of the transport. My arms broke into gooseflesh as I tried not to think about the two halves of the transport separated by the distances between homeworlds.

The cabin passed through the hole in the air, and in the briefest flash of black, the chill desert afternoon of Sureri turned to a warm spring morning near Kashidur City on Methiem. I felt something loosen in my chest. It felt good to be home.

PART TWO

Customs

Official portal grounds are tightly regulated by homeworld customs agents. However, it is impossible to tax all trading on each homeworld, which encourages smuggling. Most illegal goods are local to the world. Pertinent issue for discussion concerns small percentage of goods smuggled through portals between homeworlds. Goods not available or manufacturable on one homeworld will be worth more when sold there. Rare reports exist of maji bribed to pass goods through unofficial portals, though claims are not yet supported. If confirmed, would lead to heavy disciplinary action by the Council of the Maji.

—Summary of Great Assembly session topic, third gathering of the second quarter, 997 AAW

If I had my way, I would have driven out of the portal grounds and been to the city in a few minutes. But Methiem is the biggest trading planet of the ten homeworlds, and Kashidur City the biggest trading port. The customs officials were depressingly good at their job, as I had learned more than once when passing through my home planet with goods of a...delicate...nature.

This shipment particularly bothered me, and the assurances of the well-dressed Sureriaj and his grand-dame who had bought my services were starting to lose their ring of truth. But no matter how strange the circumstances of the transaction, I had to believe the time and effort of whichever family was pretending to be the Frente did not simply consist of a plot to land me in a prison in Kashidur City. I wasn't worth that much. I wiped at my forehead.

"Are you sweating?" Amra asked. We were at a standstill behind a line of travelers, and I had the parking lever crammed upward to keep the transport from rolling forward.

"I'm beginning not to like this delivery." If everything went well, they'd take a look at the cargo compartment, Amra would give them our bill of lading, and we'd be on our way. I prayed the Sureriaj had finished all their documentation.

"Beginning?" Amra asked. I could tell by her tone she was still angry. "I haven't ever liked it—what?" She must have seen me start. With our fight, and the quick ride to the portal ground, I had never given her the sheaf of paper from the false Frentes.

I patted the pockets of my vest swiftly, my shoulders slumping as I found the papers in my left breast pocket where I'd put them. By now Amra was staring at me.

"With everything that happened, I forgot to—"

There was a clang, and Kamuli opened the pilot section hatch to interject her very large, very dark, frame into the cockpit. "Boss, you should come see the cargo." Her rich, precise tones sent a shiver through me. Our time was running down and we didn't need any more upsets.

I thrust the papers at Amra with a growl. "Check these." I stood up and exited the transport with Kamuli.

Kaumli jogged past the engine and living compartments, her knives clacking as she ran, one hand on her headwrap. "Why are we running, and why couldn't you tell me this before I was in line to have my earwax inspected by Methiemum customs?"

"We only just found it." As usual, she betrayed no anger at my accusation. Kamuli was never a good target for my frustration.

If only I hadn't been in such a hurry to leave Sureri. If only I hadn't fought with Amra. If only I had all the riches of a majus.

I eyed the line for customs. There was a whole mess of Lobath merchants up front, head-tentacles tied in intricate knots, milling around a creature like an octopus mated with a circus tent. I'm not sure how it came through a portal, but the officials would be several minutes before they were through. Live animals were always troublesome to bring to other homeworlds.

There were several other groups behind them: Methiemum with carts filled with goods, a few wealthy Festuour and Lobath families, obviously on a vacation, the Etanela who came from Sureri in front of us, even a small group of Sathssn, dark cloaks showing no hint of their skin, leading a line of lizard-like pack beasts.

Bhon was in the cargo section, standing guard over the wooden crates. Her green-yellow fur was already drooping in the humid air on

Methiem, and I knew Saart's would be doing the same, though he was more used to it from operating the transport's engine. Their homeworld was more akin in temperature to the Sureri trading port in many places, though not as dry.

"What do you want to show me?" I asked, tucking my shirt back in after our brief exercise. A trickle of sweat ran down my back.

"It's smack dab in the middle of one of the crate panels," Bhon told me, her bright blue eyes sharp. "But that side was turned down when we loaded it up—I think those gargoyles planned it that way. I only picked up on it 'cause the crate didn't sit right."

The twenty crates were stacked up to the low ceiling, two by two. There was barely enough room for us to stand, Kamuli with one foot outside the hatch. The crate in question was pulled into the small open space of the cargo segment. My transport was spacious for what it was, but Kamuli's head brushed the ceiling, and it was barely wide enough for all three of us to stand side by side.

The crate, about one arm's length wide, had been turned with the offending side up. A flat hexagonal panel was attached to the surface.

"Any idea what it is?" I asked.

"None," Kamuli told me. "It is not a mechanism, nor is it biological in nature. I do remember the crates felt odd when we moved them into the train." Bhon nodded her agreement.

I realized I had tightened my shoulders again, and was grinding my teeth together. So much for the relaxing passage through the portal. I had an inkling of what the hexagon might be, but hoped I was wrong.

"Anything strange with the cargo?" I asked. At Bhon's bark of a laugh, I amended, "Anything *else* strange?"

"There's one more thing we found," she said, taking out her handcannon. I started moving the instant I saw what she intended, but too late. The crack of the shot was a physical thing in such a confined space, and I instinctively ducked to avoid a ricocheting bullet.

"Look, boss." Her voice cut through the ringing in my ears.

I raised my head at Bhon's words to see the projectile still traveling toward its target. The little lump of metal slowed to a crawl, covering the distance by halves and thirds, as if traveling through thick molasses. Several seconds later, the bullet gently touched the side of the crate and fell with a *tink* to the floor. I eyed Bhon, wondering how exactly she knew what the bullet would do.

"The customs crew isn't going to like this," I said, reaching out to hover my palm over the little hexagonal plate. It was giving off just enough heat to feel, as if it had stolen the energy from the bullet.

"Is it of the maji?" Kamuli asked.

"Unfortunately," I said. I realized I was still tensing my jaw and tried to relax.

Those who travel off their home planet know the maji create the portals allowing us to travel the ten homeworlds. The portals, and the maji enable us to have the Great Assembly of Species, which is the absolute authority on anything inter-species in nature.

But that is the least of what the maji can do. They're responsible for creating the System Beasts and many other magical constructs. They help out in times of disaster and strife, displaying awesome powers to change the nature of reality.

Each of the ten planets has their own small share of maji. Some are even minor celebrities, like the Etanela racer Mierla Utelu Tadeti, or the Kirian actor Havrasta Kyliner. Fewer people know the maji separated themselves into houses, each concerned with a different concentration of ability.

"You can't open any of the crates." I guessed.

Bhon's eyes widened. "How'd you know that?"

"Lucky guess." I was fairly sure the hexagonal panels were artifacts made by a majus of the House of Potential, but I didn't have time to tell the pair *how* I knew. I tested my theory, attempting to lift the lid of the crate. By the time I touched the wood, my fingers were tingling and I hardly had strength to pull my hand away. I rubbed my numb appendage. "All of them are like this?"

"Even with a crowbar," Kamuli muttered, and Bhon grimaced up at her. Bhon tended to get carried away sometimes.

Masnaith shouldn't have been so concerned about us opening the crates. There must have been a countering effect at the warehouse, allowing the crates to be loaded and moved. He probably hadn't understood what it did.

"Medicine," Bhon grunted.

"I imagine it *is* a particular kind of medicine," Kamuli supplied. "But not for the sickness on Methium. Instead, it is one our buyer does not want us to know about, or take any 'samples' for our own use."

"No, the grand-dame herself insisted this wasn't drugs, and paid us a lot to deliver them quickly." This wasn't sitting right with me. "She might not have been Frente, but I don't think she lied about that part. It can't be that simple." What was in these things? Now I was going to have to break into this cargo.

Unfortunately, that was when the transport began to rumble forward.

Leaving the two bodyguards with the boxes, I exited the cargo section and ran alongside the slowly moving vehicle, pulling myself out of the dust and back into the pilot cabin. Amra was in the pilot seat.

"We're up," she said, smoothing her red wrap. This morning on Sureri seemed like days ago. "You took too long back there, so I took the pilot's chair to not rouse any extra interest." Her voice was businesslike. She still hadn't forgiven me, not that I could blame her.

"Thanks," I said, without much enthusiasm. The Lobath and their octopus circus tent were gone, as were a few groups behind them. A selection of Festuour leading a string of fuzzy bovines were finishing up.

"Amra," I started, "I'm sorry I lied. I really do want to settle down with you. It's just—"

"It's always 'just,'" she answered, then shook her head, still concentrating on driving the transport. "Not now. We don't have time to argue about it, and we're *going* to come to an agreement this time, one way or the other." She flashed a look at me and I sat back. With that face, I could wait.

The line must have been longer than usual, as the customs officers were splitting up, checking on each group to make sure their transition would be smoother than the Lobath's. There's always that one unprepared group. I had a feeling we would be another.

Our transport caught the attention of an old and hostile looking woman in the green and brown of the Methiemum homeworld customs. Her light gray hair was pinned in a bun, and her mouth looked permanently stuck in a frown.

I kept my footing while Amra slowed the transport. She thrust the bill of lading back at me. "Everything looks official," she said. "I'm glad *one* of us took the time to read it. I assume there was nothing wrong with the cargo? Did Kamuli give a false alarm?"

I snorted a bitter laugh and took the documentation from her. "I'm sure we won't be thrown in prison at all."

"What's that supposed to mean?"

I ignored Amra, hopping down from the pilot's section and handing the bill of lading to the customs woman, who investigated it for several moments. She was waiting far enough outside the door to give me space to get down, but no farther. Keep the suspect from running.

"What are you carrying today—" she glanced down, "—Prot?"

"Cargo for delivery," I told her with as much confidence as I could muster. "Medicine from Sureri for the ongoing epidemic of the Shudders." The grand-dame and her family would have alerted the medical centers this shipment was coming. "I'm planning to take it to the storage facility as soon as I get out of customs."

The woman's frown deepened, her bottom lip in danger of climbing into her mouth. "We've already received the scheduled delivery of anti-seizing capsules. It was early today." She pulled a clipboard from under her arm. "And the inflammation reducing poultices are being delivered in two days' time."

My heart sank with every word. "It's an extra shipment? It was a rush job, very urgent." I tried to exude official-ness. Surely the grand-dame sent word ahead. The one who signed a false family name to the document. The one who wanted me to move the cargo as soon as possible, as in *before* the official delivery. I carefully kept my face neutral. I really hoped it wasn't drugs.

Her expression didn't change. "Either way I'll have to inspect the items. We'll figure out what those Sureri are sending, won't we, Prot?"

I winced. What could I do? I usually dealt with art, or foodstuffs, or furniture, not with sensitive and potentially harmful items. I gestured helplessly to my cargo section and the old woman limped toward it.

Kamuli or Bhon—probably Kamuli—had enough sense to turn the crate artifact side down. They had their best innocent faces on and I jerked my head for them to wait outside. The cargo section would be crowded enough without them.

The woman began her inspection, counting and touching the crates, but soon grunted in frustration. "I can't get any of these crates open, Prot. How are they secured?"

"I'm just transporting this, as I told you," I said. "My supplier was fairly adamant I not open the crates. I guess they locked them up well. Perishable maybe." I looked out the hatch, keeping my face neutral. "I hadn't checked."

The woman eyed me. Her hair was stark white at her temples, and her tanned skin as wrinkled as a Kirian. It was a marvel she was still working. But her eyes were keen as a well-sharpened blade.

"Were they," she drawled. "Hadn't you." She strode past me in the confined cargo compartment. "We'll get the majus to investigate this," she grated over her shoulder as she exited. "Move your vehicle to the side, and we'll pass you through as soon as she determines there is nothing of the maji tied to this cargo."

I held out a hand to the woman's retreating back, but let it fall as she disappeared outside the hatch. She moved fast for an old lady.

The willowy Methiemum woman serving at the portal grounds soon arrived. She took one look at the crates—or at something around them—and turned back to the customs woman, puffing up the ladder behind her. Kamuli and Bhon were still outside, undoubtedly listening, and I remained where I was, emitting beams of pure innocence.

"This is work of the House of Potential," the majus said smoothly in a fluid accent. She must have been from somewhere on the northern continent, possibly even from Ibra. I suspected most of what this majus said or did was smooth. Her actions were graceful, almost as if she was swimming. Her clothes were expensive, finely tailored and ornamented with silver inlay. About what I would expect from one of the elite magic-users.

"Which means what?" the customs woman asked.

"It is a complex arrangement of the Symphony, but that is all I can tell you." The majus pulled her long hair back over her shoulders.

"Whoever put you up to transporting this was concerned about keeping it secret, Prot," the official told me. I was getting annoyed at her continual use of my name. They were probably trained to do it to convey friendship. It wasn't working. "Anything with this level of security on it needs to be investigated."

"Can you open them?" I asked the majus. I could hedge to the recipients later, assuming I wasn't arrested. I just had to get these crates delivered in time and get my money. And never take a contract from a Sureri again.

"Of course not." She flicked a hand in my direction as if shooing a fly. "I am of the House of Grace."

"We'll have to impound your vehicle while we call for a majus from the House of—" The customs woman looked to the majus.

"House of Potential," the finely dressed majus said.

"Potential," the old woman repeated. "Right."

"My replacement is arriving in a few hours, but he is of the House of Strength, and will not be able to help," volunteered the majus uselessly.

"I have to deliver this cargo by tomorrow morning," I told them. "If you want someone to inspect it, it'll have to be now."

"Your supplier should have thought of that before they set this up," the customs woman countered. "Unless you can find a majus of the House of Potential, your delivery will be coming in late."

I stared back at them, remembering when Saart and I first bought the old war machine. Who we bought it from. I must have stood longer than I thought.

"Prot?" The customs woman looked vaguely worried.

I swallowed. "I may know of one, but he's retired." I hoped he still lived in the same place. I hoped he was still alive. I hadn't seen the man in years.

"I don't know of any maji living near here," the majus sniffed.

"You don't know everything, missy." The old customs woman mumbled something sounding like 'stuck up maji.'

The majus harrumphed and flounced out of the train and I smirked at the customs woman despite myself. There was more to this old bag than I thought.

"Will you let me fetch him?"

The old lady considered, but our mutual dislike of the pampered majus must have improved her perception of me. "Move your vehicle out of the way. Only you may leave." It was a start. We exited the cramped compartment and I closed the hatch behind us.

"May I unhook the pilot and engine section to get there faster? My mechanic has to keep the engine running." If she didn't let me, there was no way I could get there in time. I might as well wait for the official majus.

The woman's face scrunched up until I thought her mouth would disappear entirely, but she scanned the line of travelers passing through customs. Kashidur City had more visitors than any other city on Methiem, and it was a busy day. While we had been in the cargo section, five more groups had come through portals—one was a gaggle of Kirian schoolchildren, their robes a whirlwind of conflicting colors, crests fluttering and changing as they pointed excitedly around them. Their teacher, an older woman with the trademark wrinkled and liverspotted Kirian skin showing on her bare arms and legs, was trying to herd them. Her feathery crest looked as if was trying to go in all directions at once.

"I'll have to process more paperwork." The woman sounded as if she would rather cut off her own leg, but we both knew it would get me out of her hair sooner. "Wait here."

While she waded through the red tape of the Methiem customs bureaucracy, I filled my crew in on what had happened.

"And you know of a majus in the city other maji do not?" Kamuli asked. I had been hoping that question wouldn't come up.

"It's a long story," I said, and Saart nodded beside me, his eyebrows raised. "Suffice to say we bought the transport from him, a long time ago."

"Another story you haven't shared?" Amra suggested.

I sighed, but she was right. "I'll tell you when I get back, when we have that talk. Promise."

"Whenever you two want to stop bickering and get back to making us money is fine with me," Bhon said, furry arms crossed. I looked around my crew, seeing agreement from the other two. I took Amra's hand. She didn't pull away, at least.

"I will make this up to you, I promise," I told her. She didn't seem mollified.

By the time the woman came back with her paperwork, we had unhitched the front two sections and Saart was priming the engine. I signed the necessary documents, in triplicate, saying my cargo was forfeit if he and I decided to make a run for it. The thought only crossed my mind for an instant.

"Amra is in charge while I'm gone." I hesitated for an instant. "Unless some transaction comes up, then Kamuli is." I still wanted to make money, after all.

My accountant's eyes were alight when I climbed into the pilot's seat. "This had better be worth the money," she whispered as I went past her. Her voice had an edge.

"Enough to start us toward a storefront," I told her. Maybe with just one or two more deliveries. "Think of our little shop, a couple kids underfoot. I'll be back before you know it." She glared back, but at least didn't slam the hatch.

Saart and I rumbled out of a side door in the wooden fence surrounding the customs area, and turned to the city. Its skyline rose above me, the largest mercantile firms in the city center over twenty stories tall. Another huge building was in the midst of construction, scaffolding covering the metal exterior. Where the structure showed through, the polished steel gleamed in the morning sunlight. No other city I knew of had so much metal in once place.

"Did you have to tell Amra about the Kirian maggot flu?" I asked him.

The speaking tube between the pilot and engine sections crackled a moment before Saart's voice came through, gruff as usual.

"Boy, you've been tiptoeing around that girl for the last six cycles. Would you have ever told her if I didn't?"

I thought about that a moment. "Probably not."

"Then it's a good thing I did. I may not have a lady-friend myself, but I know how to treat one. If she leaves, our books are going to be as muddled up as they were when you were in charge of them, and no one wants that." Not to mention what it would do to me.

I blew out a breath. Saart stayed out of the money—and relationship—side of the business as much as possible. But when he decided to comment, the old Festuour was usually right.

"Fair comment," I said. And we left it at that.

The two of us consulted over the speaking tube as I drove and he shoveled coal. We bought the transport almost fourteen cycles ago, just after we met. I had been a fresh-faced teen, Saart older, but fed up with working in a repair shop on Festuour. We met in a bar one night, hit it off, decided to go into business, and never looked back.

Between the two of us, we figured out where the old junkyard had been, on the outskirts of Kashidur City. If it was still there.

It took the better part of two hours to find it, tucked away between a warehouse storing bins of minerals and ore, and a newly constructed store selling replacement parts for wagons and transports. The yard was smaller than I remembered. I could see the ridge of another vehicle like ours, but this one rusted beyond use, with a hole blown in one side large enough to run through. The transport we bought had been in better shape than most.

We pulled into the yard to a chorus of dogs barking. The junkyard mutts were all chained up, though well taken care of. I hopped down from the pilot's cabin. A few moments later Saart huffed down the stairs from the steam engine, wiping coal dust from his glasses off on his fur.

"Well, now what?" He adjusted his bandolier and glasses, though I saw he had unbuttoned a couple pockets to make sure his larger, heftier tools were within reach. He didn't have the same attraction to guns Bhon did.

"Now we hope the old coot is still alive," I answered.

We threaded a path through the junk. Someone was obviously here. The dogs would have been loose to guard the yard if they were out. Saart pointed to a little shack, hidden behind a stack of broken cartwheels. I had vague memories of finishing our business deal to buy the transport in there. The piles of broken parts and garbage had grown since then, almost covering the building. As we progressed, the path narrowed, until we were slithering sideways between stacks. I heard Saart grunt as he pushed through two piles of broken tile shingles, stacked on top of each other.

The entrance to the building was blocked by the huge, outreaching forelimb of a system beast carcass, evidently too run-down to be useful. The junkyard owner must have been working on it. This one was shaped like one of the predatory thrycovolars of equatorial Festuour, long drained of any magical energy and fallen on its side. I reached out to move the jointed forepaw to clear the doorway, but my hand went dead as I touched the beast. I pulled it back sharply, shaking it, holding it to my chest.

"What? What happened?" Saart was next to me in an instant, looking me over.

"We've reached the majus," I told him. The feeling was starting to come back to my hand. There was no way we could get to the building without moving the beast, or at least its forearm. "Help me shift this thing."

"Hey in there!" called Saart. "Do you want customers or not?"

No answer.

"Come on. Even if he doesn't, we have to see him." I put my shoulder to the bear-cat monster's foreleg. The feeling in my arm started to drain away, but the layers of clothing in between helped. Saart didn't have that luxury, and hissed through his pointed teeth as he pushed. Time was wasting, but by resting every few moments, the feeling would come back to our extremities, and the forepaw, as big around as my body, began to move with a shrill squeak. Once it was out of the way, there would be enough room to slip through.

"Almost there!" Saart said, and gave a final heave with his considerable bulk. With a screech, the paw jerked forward and I, one hand outstretched, fell face-first into the body of the thrycovolar.

I felt suddenly weak and sleepy, and blackness descended. Strange dreams invaded, of cold lands and metallic horrors, with a treasure guarded by magic and bat-faced shadows dressed in rags.

"Wake up." I swam toward the gravelly voice, and opened my eyes. I was confronted with a shaggy, none too clean face, surrounded by long unkempt hair—it was older, but familiar. As my head cleared, I saw we were inside the little shack. Had Saart carried me in?

"My little surprise traps most who try to find me," the bewhiskered man said. He was wearing a shaggy brown leather cloak, buttoned down the front, and not much else. Bare, dirt-encrusted feet poked out from beneath it. Even inside the shack, there were piles of junk. "But Prot, if you wanted to visit, you should have sent word ahead."

I thrust away the last of the dreams. Did the old majus actually remember my name from our one business deal fourteen cycles ago? I looked to Saart, sitting gingerly on a pile of broken tables. He shrugged. The man had been strange when we first met him.

"How is the war transport treating you?" The man was looking me over as if I was a long-lost son, not a customer. "Still running smooth? I see you lost a couple sections since the last time we met."

"I...no, we haven't lost..." I paused, gathering my thoughts. I pressed one hand to my left eye. The field on the broken system beast had been like those on the crates, sucking away energy. That convinced me we were in the right place, though I wished I hadn't fallen into it. "That's why we're here. We need your help."

The man looked confused for a moment. "With the transport? I have some spare parts, but..." He gestured with one gnarled hand at the junkyard in general.

"With what's in the other two sections," Saart said. His nose was wriggling as if he smelled something off. "We need a majus."

The man snorted. "I don't do that anymore. Gave up the whole pomp of it for peace and quiet out here." His words were punctuated by his dogs, barking at the transport.

"But—" I pointed a thumb back to the door.

"Yes, there are exceptions," he snapped, and just for a moment, I saw the regal bearing of a majus, before the man slumped again. "I don't have much of my song left. Spent too much when I was young and now I'm reduced to tinkering in my junk piles here."

"We only need your help for a few hours—" I fumbled for a name.

"Call me Colonel," he said. I remembered he had gone by his rank before. He had been in the Methiemum army, back in the war with the Sathssn. Probably how he came across so many of the ill-fated transports.

"Colonel," I agreed. "We need you to open some cargo crates for us. They've been sealed by another majus of the House of Potential. There are none who can be spared and the cargo is time sensitive. Saart and I wondered if you could help." It was how we knew so much about the House of Potential. The Colonel had still acted as majus then.

"Time sensitive, eh?" The Colonel scratched at his dirty beard with one hand, dislodging a small shower of dandruff. "As in expensive?"

I sighed, wondering how much this would cost me. "They're medical supplies ordered for the victims of the Shudders epidemic ravaging the southern continent," I told him, without much hope of it helping.

"So you're saying you'll be paid well by a government institution for delivering emergency supplies on time," he said. "We can discuss my price when we get there."

Saart threw up his hands and stalked out of the shack, grumbling. I signaled for the old majus to follow.

The trip back was uneventful, and much shorter, now I knew where I was going. Fortunate as well, as the Colonel had a rather unique odor. He gabbed on the whole time, remarking how well the transport was kept up, asking Saart keen questions about the engine, and occasionally poking at one of the buttons on the dash. I didn't even know there were shutters to close the front windows. It would have been more helpful if I had not found out while driving.

The same old woman let us back into the customs area, and I backed the cab and engine in front of the other two sections. As we emerged, the woman eyed the majus with her usual frown and one raised eyebrow. He was dirty, ragged, and hairy. Not in any way the upright symbol the maji liked to present to the universe. He nodded back, as if this was all familiar to him. It might have been—he could have been stationed here, long ago, to open portals. They might have even met each other.

"Let's get this...majus to open those crates, Prot," she said, pushing us toward the cargo section. "You're blocking up my area." She was at least willing to let the Colonel through, but I could practically feel her disbelief.

The others crowded around as we walked. "Is that the majus you bought the transport from?" Amra asked, tucking her wrap in close so no one would step on it.

"Pretty sure," I said. "Otherwise I'm going to have a dirty beggar I found in a junkyard inspecting my cargo. That and he knocked me unconscious with a magical trap."

"Are you—?" she started, and I waved the question away.

"Just...strange dreams." The images while I was unconscious unsettled me. This job was playing with my head. I looked to the sun, but it was far past where I had hoped. We arrived on Methiem in the morning, but had spent much of the day at a standstill. Of our original twenty hours, there was maybe half that time left. Could we deliver the cargo at night? Would we want to? I wasn't sure I wanted to be in a dark warehouse with whoever was supposed to receive this cargo.

The offending crate was still in the middle of the cargo section. Bhon and Kamuli had heavy wool gloves to protect their hands, one pair for three-fingered Festuour and one for Methiemum, and turned the crate so the plate was visible on top again. The customs woman grunted at this, but said nothing, as the Colonel creaked up the stairs to the rear hatch.

He bent over the box, fingers hovering a mere hairsbreadth away from the strange plate. I glanced down at my own hand, remembering the tingling when I touched the device and the system beast. The majus seemed to suffer no such setbacks, although his face fell.

He looked at me, and it was as if all the raggedness and dirt fell away. "I can open this," he said, "but I have a price."

Always maji, and their prices.

"What?" I said through gritted teeth. Our remaining funds were running low. The more I spent, the more Amra and I quarreled. Our little store was drawing away like a stone sinking to the bottom of a deep pool.

"You must do the right thing with this cargo, Prot," the Colonel told me. "It is imperative you succeed. Much more rests on your decision than you think."

We all stared at him, but his face was deadly serious. My heart lifted a little at the lack of monetary compensation, but there was such earnestness in his face. Well, hadn't I always done the right thing, minus a few smuggling runs? I would admit to occasionally taking advantage of a gullible customer, but somehow I knew the majus was not talking about that. I met his eyes.

"I promise," I said, and my crew looked at me as if I was speaking nonsense.

With a click, the little shape on top of the crate cracked in two, and we all jumped save the Colonel. He picked up both pieces and reverentially gave them to Bhon.

"Let's see what's inside of these here crates," he said.

With evening fast approaching, Bhon levered the top off the crate, the only resistance to her crowbar that of the nails.

We all looked in on the nest of shavings and little glass jars.

"Medicine," Bhon said.

Kamuli helped her pull the top away. "She is right, as far as I can tell." She dug one dark hand into the crate, shifting wood shavings aside, bringing out a jar filled with small pills.

The customs woman leaned forward through the hatch, clipboard and pen held ready. "Those are the anti-seizing drugs, though I don't know why there's an extra delivery," she said. "And the others?"

"We can't open all of them," I told her. "I'm liable to lose payment already for this one."

"I have to make sure," she said stubbornly. "This one could be a decoy."

I cast about, my gaze landing on the Colonel. "Could you open all of them?" It would take time we didn't have, but if the first crate passed inspection, the others should as well.

"No." The Colonel shook his head. "I don't have that much song left." I closed my eyes.

"But I can do one better." He pushed through Kamuli and Bhon, raising one old hand to trail along the boxes. He shuffled along the narrow path to the rear of the cargo compartment, turned, and came back the other direction, his other hand now making a rasp as it slid down the wooden surfaces. As he got closer, I saw his eyes were closed and his head was cocked slightly, as if he was listening to a faraway song.

"By their energy potential, the crates all contain the same thing," he pronounced. "Each is filled with containers, and each container has a supply of dense manufactured pellets." He took one more step forward and took the glass jar from Kamuli, considering. He closed his eyes again, his right ear next to the jar. Then he put his head to the nearest crate.

"Yes. As far as I can tell, they all contain the same objects as this one." He opened his eyes again. "Will that satisfy you? This delivery is as urgent as he says."

The old customs woman drew in her eyebrows, but agreed. "It'll have to do. It seems you are clear, Prot. I hope you are still in time." She gave the old majus a stern glare, ripped off a signed piece of paper from her clipboard, gave it to me, and exited the transport. I followed her, but the Colonel cleared his throat loudly.

I stopped, and exhaled, gesturing my guards out. "Take that jar with you," I told Kamuli. The majus nodded at my action.

"You want me to do something else with this medicine," I told him when we were alone, "and that's going to cut into my profits even more. What do you know?"

But the majus only smiled sadly. "I told you I'm out of that business. I no longer get involved in these things, Prot. Bad for my health." He scratched at his beard. "Speaking of which, my pension from the Council of the Maji has long since run out. Surely twelve percent isn't too much to spare for keeping you on time."

"Barely on time," I countered. "I can spare five percent, and that's it. More than that and my accountant will injure me greatly." How many more jobs would we need before we could stop traveling the homeworlds? After this delivery, staying on Methiem was starting to sound better all the time.

"Make it ten and we have a deal," the Colonel said.

"Seven, and I try to 'do the right thing' with this cargo." I stared at him a moment, trying to divine by sheer will what the old man had meant by that. For all I knew he wanted me to give the medicine away, but I didn't think so, based on his willingness to take my money. He stared back impassively for a moment, then spread one hand in agreement.

I turned away. "I'll get your payment," I told him, and went down the stairs.

Behind me, I heard him call to Amra. "Come help an old man down out of this thing." She went to him, and stood talking while I got my last pouch of Nether glass. He might tell her the story of how we bought the transport. He liked to talk enough.

When I returned, Amra gave me a funny look and went to the pilot's section. I gave the Colonel the pouch and he hefted it with one hand, a little grin on his dirty face. "What was all that about?" I asked.

He shook his head. "Simply imparting some advice to your lovely accountant. Good luck. And be careful. I can find my own way back."

I wasn't planning on taking him back to his junkyard. I turned away with a halfhearted wave, calling to get the transport ready to roll out of the customs yard. We had taken far too long, I didn't want to make the delivery at night, and now I had a mystery to follow up on.

While the others connected the sections of the transport, I investigated the jars myself. Each glass container was marked discretely on the side with the crest of the Sureriaj family that had made it: Nara, Frente, Baldek, Perchet. I sifted through the crate, taking one from each house, but counting up fractions in my head.

Three of the great families who had contributed to this shipment were fairly liberal with regard to aliens. The Baldek were not. What were they doing sending medicine offworld? I wondered what 'Frente' Masnaith's true name had been.

I took a few more of the Baldek-marked jars, just to make sure, one each from the other houses, set them aside, and closed up the crate. I heard the *thunk* of the connecting bolt between sections and took the jars with me.

"All ready?" I asked Saart outside.

He tucked a hefty wrench away in his bandolier and nodded, adjusting his glasses with his other hand. "We going to get these things delivered tonight? Don't have many hours left."

"No." By the lack of reaction, he wasn't surprised. His glance trailed over the jars I had tucked in my arms. "But the warehouse is on the other side of Kashidur city. Let's park on the outskirts tonight so we can be ready to deliver these Vish-cursed things at first light. We'll still be within our time limit." Barely.

Saart's bright blue eyes watched me behind his glasses. "Anything you say." He went to start the steam engine.

I secreted my collection of glass jars in a blanket in my bunk so they wouldn't rattle, and went to the pilot section. I let the others know we would be stopping for the night and making the delivery in the morning.

Saart kept the engine going, and Bhon and Kamuli rode in their usual place in the living section. Amra, of course, was beside me in the co-pilot's chair. We rode in silence as the sun dipped below the horizon, and the gaslights started to flicker on in Kashidur City, lighting our way. We had our own lamps on top of each section. Two more on the transport's nose spilled illumination before us.

Halfway around the city, Amra spoke.

"I've been noting down our expenses." There wasn't an overt question attached, but I knew what she meant.

"I gave the last of our upfront bonus to the majus," I told her. "Seven percent. You should add that to the total." I was contemplating numbers in my head, and I didn't like where it was going. I could be wrong.

Amra calculated for a few moments, peering at her ledger in the dim light reflected from the front lanterns. "Don't tell me the number," I said. "We don't have enough to even think about buying a shop."

"We wouldn't have enough even without these expenses. You keep going on about our shop. You know I'm happy to travel in the transport for now. Did you ever mean to buy a place?"

Saart's warning flashed through my mind. He was right. It was time to change things.

"No." I glanced over to see her mouth set, eyes fixed on her accounts. "Not at first. But I do now, Amra, I really do." She raised her face, but still didn't look at me.

I thought about my discovery with the jars. "I'm done with the traveling game," I told her. "After the last four months on Loba, and the week on Sureriaj, I'm done trying to scrabble for a living, taking what we can from the maji, and the homeworld governments, and their customs bureaucracy. Make the customers come to us, if they want what we have. We'll have a little garden out back of the shop, and grow our own food, and have a couple pigs, or some pulluus from Kiria for eggs. And a little girl." Amra finally looked up at that.

"What if I don't want a child? What if it's a boy?"

I shrugged. "Then just us, together."

"And what about Saart, and Bhon and Kamuli? If we invest so much into a shop, how can we pay them?"

"You know we can hear you." Amra's face darkened in a blush as Bhon's voice floated in the cabin, tinny and remote. I had forgotten to switch off the speaking tubes.

"They have a switch at the other end, too," I said into the air. Nosy interfering...

"We know," Saart said, and I sighed. The conversation was over, but Amra watched me for the rest of the ride.

We stopped on the other side of Kashidur City from the portal ground, the evening glow of the city overwhelming the stars. The taller buildings even blocked one of the rising moons.

There was a park we had used before, frequented by those with no permanent place of residence. We turned the transport into a 'U' shape to give us shelter. Tonight wouldn't be relaxing. We still had work to do.

Once we were set up, I found Kamuli Balion. The large woman seemed to know what I was thinking. She had the sample jar she had taken from the crate.

"There's more," I told her, and led her to my and Amra's bunk.

Kamuli had a small set of chemical reagents, a few beakers and testing vials, and a couple larger pieces of equipment including something she called a 'masseous spectrum-analyzer.' When we were in a friendly town, and she wasn't needed on guard duty, she would often help Saart with the coal mixture we fed to the engines, or cook up a few handy mixtures for when one of us encountered a local ailment we had not yet run across in our travels. None of us had expected to be able to catch the Lobath head-tentacle fever when we were on Loba, but the disease had proved surprisingly adaptable. Fortunately, Kamuli had been able to rework a local treatment into a reagent than worked for both Methiemum and Festuour.

Kamuli stared at the pile of jars on my bunk and then at me. "I will get my equipment," she said. "Meet me outside with these. I will need the campfire to help break down the pills into their components."

The others had finished setting up camp, and Saart had a healthy blaze going, seats from the transport placed around it, by the time Kamuli's equipment was set up—all polished metal rods and glass beakers. There were a few leather tubes and strangely shaped glass constructions, with a small pile of carefully labeled chemicals. I didn't know what the equipment did, only that it was among my doctor's prized possessions.

The sun set. We talked for several hours into the night while Kamuli worked. Saart made us a meal from whatever he had left lying around. I didn't taste it. I had shared my suspicion of the Baldek family's motives in sending medicine and we were all twitchy to discover Kamuli's results.

There was a gang of children who made their home in the bushes around the park. I'm sure they were thieves by day, but they came up to us openly as the night grew, their numbers larger than the last time we had been here.

Amra tsked. "There must be orphans from the Shudders epidemic joining them." She got up, gripping a change purse and reaching for the pot of Saart's stew. "They look like little crows, all skin and bones."

I didn't interfere, but I didn't help, while Amra doled out portions of stew and a small coin each for the urchins, her red wrap tucked in close. She had no problem helping others, but when it came to the uncertainty of raising one of her own, she balked.

Bhon held the pot as each child took a mouthful from Amra's ladle, and I tightened my jaw as each padam left her hand. I loved her generosity, even if I wanted to tear my hair out sometimes. Each of those children needed a good home, and a few coins wouldn't help that. I hoped the medicine in the delivery was clean. Maybe we could keep more orphans from joining this group.

After the children had departed to their leafy beds, the large doctor sat back with a sigh. Her headwrap was coming unpinned, though she didn't notice it. In the past few hours she had accumulated a pile of detritus around her—discarded jars and pills, samples of the crate packing material and even a small bit of the wood, and sheets of notes in her tight handwriting. Bhon had a cup of tea heated by the fire and brought it to her mate as she finished. Kamuli took a long draught of the hot liquid before she spoke.

"All of this medicine, despite which family manufactured it," she began in her round tones, "is anti-seizing medication which will work to reduce the effects of the Shudders."

I felt my shoulders relax a little, until I saw she wasn't finished.

"Each family has a slightly different chemical concoction in their pill, likely a formula each family's scientists have discovered and not shared with the others. All of them include only the basic materials needed to assuage the fever." She felt around for one of the jars, inspecting the side in the firelight for the tiny maker's mark. "Except for these, from the Baldek family." My shoulders tightened again.

Kamuli held up one dark finger. "For a pregnant sufferer of the Shudders, when taking certain other medications commonly supplied by the Sureriaj, this pill can cause stillbirth. Specifically for Methiemum, it also has the ability to cause permanent sterility, if one takes multiple doses." Her brow was furrowed tighter than I had ever seen it on the normally placid woman. "I would never make this connection if I were not looking for something wrong with this medication. Given the fraction of the jars from the Baldek family and how they may be distributed on Methiem, I doubt any scientist will be able to discover this connection once the effects are realized."

"That's appalling." Amra stood, looking as if she would throw down her ever-present ledger. She looked to the bushes at the perimeter of the park. "I won't be any part to this."

"They can keep their dirty money, I say," Bhon added, incensed. "I ain't gonna be sterilized!"

I involuntarily looked at her choice of life mate. So did the others.

"I still have a choice!" she defended grumpily. "These crazy Sureri have got to be stopped. I say we take the price of this out of their ugly hides."

"But was it deliberate?" I asked. It could still be a manufacturing error. Vish let it be so. Even with all the other strange setbacks in customs.

Kamuli shook her head. "The additional compound could not be a simple accident. This was purposeful sabotage. My mate talks sense, even if she may not have as much at stake as she thinks." She threw an apologetic glance at Bhon, who bared her pointy teeth at Kamuli. "However, the only affected people would be those with the Shudders, who take a pill made by the Baldeks and who have not yet reproduced." She also spared a look for the bushes. "It may even help combat certain...ah, unfortunate social conditions."

Saart was as practical as always. "So can't we just deliver it and take the money?" He was leaning against a padded seat, his furry three-toed feet stretched out to the fire. "No, no. Stay with me." he explained, as everyone stared at him in shock. "There's a limited amount of medicine. The Baldek's tainted a fraction of the cargo, right? This stuff's only administered to certain people who have the Shudders, Kamuli tells us, and it *will* still cure them?" He waited for the doctor's slow nod. "Whatever the greasy gargoyles are planning, it can't be that effective. This sounds like a desperate plot by one family trying to lash out wherever they can. They'll hit the rare individual—probably less than the infant mortality rate. Deliver it, and get our money. Alert the officials later if you want."

When he explained it that way, it made sense. I could see the others considering it—even Bhon. The Baldek's plan didn't seem an effective strategy. I looked to Amra, who was still standing. The money from this delivery wouldn't be enough to buy a store, but if we didn't fulfill the contract, who knew how long until we climbed back out of debt? We would be traveling from homeworld to homeworld for cycles to come, until we were both old and gray.

Amra's face hardened, and I knew she was thinking the same thing. She opened her mouth. Perhaps the best thing was to deliver it anyway.

"Could the ingredients that make us sterile be added to other medicine?" she asked.

There was silence.

Kamuli bowed her head in thought, then picked up a few sheets of her notes. She spent a few minutes comparing her results.

"From my chromatography data, I would say...yes." There was shuffling around the campfire as the members of my crew shifted positions nervously. Slowly, Amra sat back down in her chair. She looked pale.

"I had not thought of this." The sheets trembled in Kamuli's hands, casting flickering shadows. "You are correct. The Baldek family could have—might have already—appended this concoction to almost every other medicine they are known to make, with little effect save some lessening of the potency. It would be just as difficult to find in other pills or reagents. They may be able to affect thousands of Methiemum families, over time."

Even Saart was frowning now.

Do the right thing. The Colonel's words came back to me. His strange promise. Had he sensed the contaminant in the pills? Had he heard of other shipments? It still didn't invalidate the money we needed from the delivery.

"Well, what are we supposed to do?" I asked my crew. "Go after the grand-dame who contracted me?" I didn't even know her true family, though I could guess. "Go after the entire Baldek family?" That was like trying to attack an entire government. Were they all in on it?

"We...could just tell the authorities in Kashidur City," Saart suggested, but his heart wasn't in it.

"And then these ruffians we're supposed to deliver to scatter like cockroaches under a light, and we still don't get our money," Bhon said. She hit one furry paw into her other palm with a meaty smack. "I want to take them down."

"This isn't a smuggling run," Amra put in, "it's a war, in all but name. Can we alert the maji?"

I thought about the flouncy woman who had been running the portal ground. "We can't trust this to someone else," I said. My heart was hammering, my mouth suddenly dry. "We have all the information here, now, with the contact waiting to receive their medicine in a few hours. Once the medicine is distributed, who's to say the pills will stay in their original jars? Each hospital might divide them up into different containers, all signs of the Baldek family erased." I cut the air with the side of my hand. "We have to deal with this delivery ourselves. Later we can bring in the authorities—" I nodded to Saart, "—and the maji." This time to Amra.

"And when we capture those bastards, then they will give us news on their employers," Kamuli said. There was a disturbing gleam in her eye.

We made plans, and got a few hours of fitful sleep before the sun rose.

PART THREE

The Delivery

In the last five hundred cycles, more civil wars have been fought on the ten species' homeworlds than all the wars fought between species combined. I direct you to the census taken by adjunct to the Etanela Speaker recorded in 975 AAW. But have all wars truly been recorded? What defines a war taking place between planets separated by un-knowable distances? I propose to the Assembly to study our histories for those wars never recorded, or hidden as 'trade disputes.' I think you will find much more conflict between the species than previously indi-cated.

—Transcript of a section of a speech given to the Great Assembly of Species by Speaker Otuvari Thientect of Kiria, 982 AAW

The warehouse could have been a twin to the one on Sureri; similarly run down, dark windows shaded in the morning sunrise. No legitimate medical delivery would happen here.

I parked the transport in front, then sent Bhon around back to scout, her small form silent on her padded feet. Kamuli was with me, tucking her headwrap tight in anticipation. We made a show of checking the cargo to give Bhon time. I was sure there were eyes watching from the windows.

"We are not going to give them the medicine, yes?" Kamuli asked.

I shook my head. "I don't want these boxes to leave our hands, but we need proof of what the Baldeks are really doing."

Before long, Bhon returned, keeping to the shadow of the building. "I just about put my nose into it," she said, halfway out of breath from her jaunt. "I'm a frog if there ain't a whole herd of the hairy gargoyles out back, sitting around, playing cards and such. A couple new ones arrived while I watched. Looks like they put word out for reinforcements." She waved a furry paw to the dilapidated warehouse.

"Insurance if we've discovered their plan?" Saart asked.

"If they're even planning to pay us," I said. "We go in armed. Kamuli and Bhon in front, I'm in the middle, and Saart guards the rear. We need to capture at least one of them." I fixed my love with a steady stare. Her wrap was emerald green today, the bottom pinned up so she could move quickly. "We may need to leave this place in a hurry, and I need someone ready to pull the transport around if we come running with angry Sureriaj hot on our heels." I didn't say that this would keep her safe. She was not a trained fighter like Bhon and Kamuli. Neither were Saart and I, but we had been in our share of scraps.

Amra nodded, face serious. "Give those child killers what they deserve and get out quickly," she said.

Kamuli pushed the mold-encrusted doors open, her long knife at the ready. A mace and Bhon's crossbow hung low at her side. Bhon had both handcannons out. With their long reloading times, she would have to switch to a differently destructive weapon after a few rounds.

"Anyone here?" I called into the gloom. "We have cargo to deliver." I stopped behind a line of boxes and metal scrap. More piles lined shelves to either side. This warehouse was more crowded than the one on Sureri. High windows stained with dust let in limited light. A shape detached from the back of the warehouse, and came toward me.

She was Methiemum. My people.

The woman could have been from any of the cities on the southern continent. Three more men and a woman came forward to join her, just as unremarkable. All wore dark clothes, the better to disappear into unlit spaces.

Bhon raised her handcannons and Saart primed his contraption. What he held was technically a welder, or at least its ancestor was. What it did now—well, I wasn't completely sure. Kamuli was to my left, a little in front, her face stony.

I adjusted my plans.

"How much did they promise you for taking the medicine?" I asked. "Where are you taking it? To a hospital, or to some other dodgy warehouse?"

"You're not being paid to ask any questions," the woman in front growled. "And neither are we." She was large, with thick arms, probably from moving goods in warehouses like this. I saw hands drift to pockets, and put one of mine out to the side, palm down, to keep my crew from overreacting.

I held up my other hand, palm up, the broken pieces of the lock in it.

"But why would they need to secure ordinary medicine with one of these?"

The woman peered forward. "What is that?"

"An artifact prepared by a majus to lock the crates. How often have you seen one?"

The group looked at each other. A grumble came from the back. "I was only supposed to deliver a box, Wima. Weren't nothing said about the maji gettin' involved." The one who complained glanced over his shoulder, to the Sureriaj in back, no doubt. If I played this right, it might be nine of us against the Baldeks instead of four.

"I don't think your employers told you everything," I said, moving one step toward the woman in charge—Wima—hand still out in front. "Did they tell you which families the medicine came from? Did they tell you some of the pills could permanently ster—"

A report boomed in the warehouse, echoing around the large room.

Wima coughed. Red ran down her chin, and she slowly toppled forward. The others shouted, stepping away, and Bhon raised her guns, growling. My crew stepped back, nearer cover.

"I think that will be plenty o' yer rambling on," came another voice. Several Sureriaj stepped forward, guns at the ready. Their skin was pale, even in the dim light in the warehouse. He nodded sharply to his family members behind him, and there were four more loud gunshots.

My crew scattered as the bodies hit the ground. Kamuli and I dove behind a convenient stack of pallets, Bhon and Saart behind one of the taller shelves. Other reports followed, echoing in the large warehouse. Something whizzed and *thunked* into wood above me. I ducked, my gut tightening.

There was a silence. Reloading.

"Frente Yatulnath...or should I say *Baldek* Yatulnath?" I called from my hiding place.

"Eyah, yer've bodgered a right mess now, yer have," Yatulnath said. His head swiveled, trying to spot us. "Me employees donna need to know so much."

"They killed their delivery crew first," I whispered to Kamuli. "Why not us?"

"They would know too much of the Sureriaj soldiers," the large woman said. "Not enough guns for all, and we were the lesser threat."

"I have me familymates with me," Yatulnath called out. "Yer canna hide here. We will kill yer and take the cargo."

There was a burping cough from Saart's weapon. A line of flame disgorged from behind the shelves. Foreign curses sounded, and a lone shriek of pain. Good old Saart.

I peeked an eye around the corner of my pallet to see a Sureri rolling in the dirt, trying to beat out the flames on his clothing. A few of the others crept toward cover. I motioned to Kamuli, who had a knife up, tip held in one hand. The blade whizzed through the air and an alien clutched at his throat, sinking to his knees. The group moved faster, confused.

Two Sureriaj down, a whole bunch to go. I didn't like those odds.

Bhon's handcannons spoke, louder than the Sureriaj's small pistols. One shot went wild, but the other clipped a running Sureri in the shoulder, sending him spinning.

Behind cover, the aliens had time to finish reloading. More poured in from the back of the warehouse. Yatulnath, striding like a gruesome stork, gestured to either side, and his men spread out, flanking us.

I pulled a small pistol from my boot, and took a Sureri in the leg. He rolled, tripping one of his companions. I began reloading.

Answering fire. I ducked back, hoping the wooden pallets held. Kamuli loosed her crossbow, then hung it back on her belt. No time to crank it again. Another round of loud shots came from Bhon. Shadows flared as Saart flung gouts of flame, pushing the Sureriaj back.

There wasn't time to reload, and Saart couldn't keep them all away. I judged the distance to the door, the safety of the transport. Too far, out in the open. Doubtful any of us would reach the door.

"Run," I whispered to Kamuli. I hoped Saart and Bhon would see us and follow.

She nodded and faced the enemy.

I took one more look back, fumbling with my pistol—

With a shriek of tortured metal and shattering wood, the old war transport crashed through the front of the warehouse, sunlight bursting in behind it.

Splinters flew in all directions, and I fell back into the stack of pallets. A stake of wood buried itself in the ground between my feet. The transport rolled a few more feet into the warehouse, then lurched to a stop. The turrets Saart kept shiny and clean rotated to fix on the Sureriaj, and they cringed back. But when the transport's guns stayed silent—their ordnance long gone—the Baldeks grouped up, aiming their weapons at the new threat.

Projectiles began to clang off the metal sides of my transport with little effect. I gritted my teeth at the new dents, but the plating held. Amra was supposed to stay away from the fighting.

Before I could get up, a new sound, loud and thick, filled the air.

The transport bucked as the turret discharged a loud, glowing object over our heads and just behind the mass of Sureriaj. I covered my ears as the stack of pallets came down around me. The pressure of the blast dug into my skin. My sight went dark for a moment.

When I could see again, I peered dazedly into what was left of the Baldek troops, my ears ringing. A long-fingered Sureri hand twitched by itself. A leg, with no body. Blood. Worse. I swallowed bile, saw Saart prone, on the floor, blood around his leg. Bhon was holding a hand to her side, trying to drag him back to cover.

Kamuli must have been protected by the pallet. She bounded forward, mace up, and caved in the skull of the nearest Sureriaj. I yelled at her, though I couldn't hear myself. We needed one alive. My ears were ringing, noises indistinct. I stumbled to the left.

Staggering around the broken pallets, I went directly to the long-legged form of Yatulnath, barely upright. The mass of aliens in the back had caught the worst of the blast, shielding the others with their bodies. I caught him as I lurched past, swinging him around to rest between me and the three last Sureriaj standing.

"Don't try anything!" I shouted to them, and raised my pistol to Yatulnath's head. I needn't have bothered. The others were stunned, eyes blank. Even Yatulnath took a moment to respond, before calling to his family members to stand down. As they did, Kamuli and Bhon limped out to cover them. We were covered with tiny burns and scratches. Bhon had Saart's flamethrower, and my old friend was still lying motionless, glasses thrown to one side and cracked. Unconscious, or worse? I couldn't spare the time to check. Thanks to Amra, and whatever she made the transport do, we had the advantage. Good thing she at least was out of harm's way, behind the metal walls of the transport.

I needed information. "What's your plan?" I shouted to Yatulnath, and poked him in the head with my pistol. I hoped he didn't know it was unloaded. Sounds were starting to come back to me, but he only hunched his narrow shoulders.

"I haven't got much patience at this point," I said loudly, looking into his face so he could see my words. "Are those your cousins?" I thrust my chin toward the other Sureriaj, hands at their sides and guns on the floor.

"Two cousins. One brother," Yatulnath said. I could barely hear him, but I caught his meaning.

"Bhon?" I gestured to my most bloodthirsty bodyguard in case she was as deaf as me.

There is little love lost between the Festuour and the Sureriaj. Bhon almost leapt forward, raising the flamethrower to one of the captives.

"Shall I guess which is the brother?" I asked, and Yatulnath shuddered under me. Siblings were precious to them, even more than to Methiemum. They would gladly, eagerly, betray extended family for those closer to them.

The Sureri in the middle reached out with one thin hand, toward his sibling. Bhon shifted the glowing tip of the flamethrower to him.

Yatulnath began to speak.

"There will be more comin'," he said. "Yer canna stop this by killin' me or me brother. Shipments are goin' out all over yer planet."

"We'll deal with that," I told him. "Why are you trying to sterilize us?" I moved around to face the Sureri, still holding my gun up.

He grimaced as he saw me, his eyes gone cold as if he watched a poisonous insect. "We Baldek know what's really happenin'," he spit. "Other Sureriaj great families are weak. They let the Methiemum stay on our planet. Yer kind are the worst. See something, and yer take it. For ages, we barred the other species from our home, but yer and yer kind forced yer way in. The other species too, but yer are the worst. Yer breed like maggots, eyah? Just because me own don't grow so fast, yer think yer can take our own planet away from us!"

"That's insane. Why would we want to live there?"

"Eyah, so yer ask, but we know better." Yatulnath said. "Yer have people living on all the ten homeworlds. It's only a smidge o' time until yer start breeding like yer always do."

"Those are trading posts," I told him. "Those are so we can *trade* with you. Both of us win." I glanced at Bhon and Kamuli. They looked as confused as I was. I snuck a peek at Saart, still out. I wondered why Amra didn't come out to help him.

"That's how it starts, eyah," Yatulnath returned. "But the Baldek will keep yer kind from takin' over all of the ten homeworlds by stoppin' yer incessant breedin'. See if we won't!"

He surged to his feet, pushing my gun away from his head, and shouting orders in the Sureri language. His family members dove for their weapons.

Bhon shot a blast of flame at one and Kamuli blocked another, stabbing with her knife. Yatulnath's brother raised his gun and fired. Kamuli grunted, staggering off balance, holding her arm. She recovered quickly, punching her attacker, her left bicep showing a gash of red. As he reeled back, she hit him with the butt of her mace. The Baldek dropped.

But Yatulnath reached a dead alien, grasping the dropped firearm.

"Stop!" I cried, and he froze. "We can fix this!"

Yatulnath snarled wordlessly, and raised his weapon.

Bhon's blast of flame caught him full on, turning him into a torch. But before the blazing form fell, his gun fired, and something slammed into my shoulder. I staggered, tripped, and the world tilted.

* * *

Kamuli's dark face swam into view.

"How long?" I muttered.

"It was only a minute or two. You hit your head when you fell."

I tried to raise my left hand to feel my head and pain shot through my arm, overriding my massive headache.

"And you were shot, of course. You will need a hospital."

"Thanks." I grimaced. There was a cloth bandage wrapped around my upper arm, stained a blotchy red.

My mind replayed the last several seconds of the confrontation.

"Saart?" I gently pulled my head up to look around. The warehouse was lit by the dying light of the Sureri bonfire, the sunlight coming through the broken doors. It stank of fried flesh and spilt blood and I forced my stomach back down. Yatulnath's brother was trussed by the pallets, unconscious.

I caught sight of my Festuour chef and mechanic off to the side. He was sitting up, peering through his cracked glasses and pressing a matted bloody paw into his thigh. Bhon was ripping up a sheet of fabric beside him.

"It's fine," Saart grated, pinning me with his brilliant blue eyes. "Shrapnel nipped my leg. I'll be dandy in a few days." From his heavy panting and the amount of blood, I wasn't sure. I could see shredded flesh beneath his paw.

We were all accounted for, and mostly whole. We didn't have our money, but maybe, with our captive—

I looked around again, carefully. Two Festuour, one large Methiemum woman. I would have expected Amra to be out of the transport as soon as the fight was over, her wrap pulled around her, making sure everyone was alright.

I pulled myself to my feet. The other two were busy with Saart. I walked as fast as I could to the transport, wincing and cursing, holding my arm, and tried not to scream as I jerked the hatch open. I clambered clumsily inside.

Amra gazed at me, face tight, one hand over her abdomen. A crimson puddle was pooling beneath her. My head swiveled to the tank's windshield, where I saw the tiny hole the stray bullet had made.

"Kamuli!" I called. She was there in a moment at the panic in my voice, and bent over my accountant...my love.

"This is not good," she said quietly. Amra had closed her eyes, but I thought she still heard us.

"But you can help her."

"I...do not know," she replied. "This is worse than Saart."

"We're in a transport full of medical supplies, for Vish's sake! Find something! And get the others in here!" I pushed at her with my good arm and Kamuli leapt back out the hatch.

"Keep pressure on it!" she called.

Amra's eyes opened, a rictus of pain on her face.

"Don't worry," I told her. "Kamuli will take good care of you. She'll make sure—"

"Did you have any idea...what you were doing...attacking a troop of Baldek...soldiers?" she gasped, interrupting me. "Lucky I was here to...to rescue you."

"I'm sorry," I said, my voice a whisper. I tried to figure out where to press. How not to hurt her more.

"We'll never get the...money now," she said. "If you...plan our marriage like this, I'll shoot you...myself."

I looked down. There would be a wedding. I hadn't realized before how much I wanted one. I wanted to marry this woman, have children with her, and have our own little business on Methiem, selling trinkets from around the ten homeworlds.

"You will marry me, won't you?"

"Of course, you idiot," she grated. "Talk to me. Keep me awake."

Behind her, the base of the turret was still turned into the warehouse.

"How did you fire it?" I placed one hand on hers, shaking and white over her stomach. Crimson stood bold against her green wrap. She was too warm, feverish and weak. I helped her hold pressure on the wound. One hand I put on hers, the other I slid around her back, trying to keep my face calm at her cries of pain.

"The Colonel gave me...one casing before he left," Amra told me between gasps. Red seeped through her fingers as she spoke. It stained my hand too, hot and sticky. I couldn't feel any blood behind her. The bullet was still inside. "Old. Might not work. Said it was what the tank was built...to use. Couldn't...depend on it...working."

"So you didn't tell me about it. Not a sure strategy." Her accounting side, letting me plan for the worst case. My jaw tensed. "And he said he wouldn't get involved. Meddling maji." Otherwise we would all be dead. "It must use ordnance made by the maji of the House of Potential. No wonder these things aren't used any more. With a cost like that, you could never fund them." With this cost. I kissed Amra's forehead.

"The Sureriaj?" she asked.

"You got them. We left one alive to question. I need to find another buyer for our cargo, with the Baldek's portion removed. Even without this contract, we can turn a profit. People with the Shudders still need medicine. Then we can get married. Just—"

"Just a few more jobs...right?" my fiancé guessed.

Kamuli, sweating, with scratches on her arms, pushed through the hatch.

"I have painkillers, but the cargo section is a mess. The Colonel only opened the one crate. Ramming the building and firing the turret turned the jars to shards of glass."

She held out a handful of pills, some of her own making, and some from the delivery.

"The Shudders medicine? Will it help her?" I tried to get a better look but Amra grunted in pain and I kept my position.

"It will reduce inflammation and stabilize her metabolism until we get to the hospital. But..."

I counted the handful of little gray things in her hand. "You don't know which jar they came from."

Kamuli shook her head. "It is more than likely not the contaminated medicine."

I looked at Amra. "Are you sure she can't make it without—"

Amra's eyes tightened and she winced.

"She is losing too much blood," Kamuli said. "We will need to dose Saart as well."

"Do it," Amra croaked.

"Do it," I agreed. We'd sort things out later. We couldn't waste any more time.

"No more deliveries," she whispered. Kamuli shooed me out of the way to tend to Amra herself. We traded positions gingerly.

"No more deliveries," I agreed. I didn't have to think hard about it.

"Help me lay her down, get the others ready," Kamuli told me. "On three." Amra screamed when we moved her and my heart almost stopped in my chest.

I helped Bhon drag Saart and the last unconscious Sureri to the passenger section, then jumped into the pilot's seat, still slick with my fiancé's blood.

We left the bodies where they lay. Bhon stoked the engines and I drove full speed down narrow streets.

* * *

Kashidur City is the largest trading port on Methiem, and the capital city of the largest nation. One of the best medical facilities was not ten minutes distant, the way the cargo transport rumbles. The promise of medicine for the Shudders got us in quickly.

Saart and Amra were wheeled into the operating theater on stretchers. Kamuli came in as our personal doctor and Bhon came with her mate. All of us bore injuries to a degree.

As was the custom, the theater was open to observers and students of the medical arts, behind a line of glass windows. This early in the morning, the seats were empty, except for one person.

"What's *he* doing here?" The old majus was calmly sitting in a corner. I sucked in air as a masked nurse with her gray hair in a bun slid a needle into my arm. It started to go numb and I let out a breath.

"Thought you might need help wrapping things up," the Colonel shouted through the glass. I could barely hear him. "Those crates are still sealed, if I remember right."

"But how did he get here before us?" I asked a masked Kamuli, who was helping the nurse. Amra had a small crowd of people around her, and medicines and poultices vanished into the group. Saart had his own crowd, examining his leg. Kamuli ignored me.

Time passed, as it does in hospitals. They even forced Bhon down at one point to treat her burns and cracked ribs.

They told us Saart would lose the leg. The damage was too great, too much of a risk to his life. Saart was stoic; I complained more than he did. The amputation was quick, Saart rendered unconscious by a mask of ether. The first thing he did when he awoke was to ask for pen and paper to begin designing a prosthetic leg. And new glasses.

On Amra, we heard nothing definite. Doctors traded places, a steady stream of medicines arrived.

I must have been dozing, seated in an out-of-the-way chair, and woke to the theater door opening. A woman with olive skin and a long black braid entered, mask down around her neck. A white smock covered her, but I thought she was wearing a formal white dress underneath. Was she another doctor? She immediately went to the majus in the observation nook, a white bell tied to the very end of her braid chiming as she walked.

"Where have you been hiding?" she called through the window. The old majus had the grace to look embarrassed. "No matter. Deal with you later."

She looked around, and settled on me. I stared groggily back. The painkillers were affecting me.

"You're the one with the illegal medicines and the Sureriaj prisoner."

I almost answered her before I realized she hadn't asked. I propped myself up on my good arm and glared back from my chair, taking a moment to check Amra. She was sleeping, her chest slowly raising and lowering under a thin sheet. There was blood on it. "Who are you?"

"The one asking the questions." Her dark brows drew down. "The maji have an interest in how these medicines and the Baldek came to be here." Of course she was a majus. How could I have missed that haughty stare?

"You are of the House of Healing?" Kamuli asked. She had only just sat down, a dressing around her upper arm and headwrap near to falling off. "Can you help?" She pointed to Amra.

"I am House of Healing, but not that kind," The woman answered. She tapped her head. "I deal with this." Her glance swept the room, registering our faces, and she frowned. "But I'll see if I can do anything."

She walked to Amra, and stretched both hands out over her. Her head tilted to one side, as if she heard birdsong, or a sound the rest of us couldn't. For a silent minute, her hands roamed above Amra's body. Then she picked up a jar of medicine beside the operating table, investigating each one in turn. Finally, she faced us.

"The good news is that Doctor Chaptali did an excellent job," she said. "There is much internal damage, but I believe she will recover, in time." The majus picked up one of the bottles of liquid on the table. "The bad news is that I must apologize for the contamination in these vials. I don't know what happened to them."

"What contamination?" Kamuli asked, but my stomach was clenching. I knew the answer.

"A foreign compound, not supposed to be there. The poison is in her reproductive system already, reacting with the antibiotics."

I closed my eyes for a moment, then looked to Kamuli, her head in her hands. Either she guessed the wrong pills or Amra got contaminated medicine from the hospital. We would never know, and in either case, this was exactly the Baldeks' plan. We should have avoided the warehouse and gone to the maji to begin with.

"You can't...?" I gestured vaguely with my good hand.

The majus gave me an apologetic look. "She is still very weak. Any part of her biology I changed now would kill her."

"I hoped..."

"I'm very sorry, but," she scanned the room once more, "if everyone is out of immediate danger..." Doctor Chaptali, slumped in the background, signaled his agreement. "I'd like to discuss what to do with the crates and the prisoner sitting outside this hospital."

"You can have the Baldek, but the crates are my property, until they get delivered." My eyes went back to Amra. Bhon watched me, her face pained.

The woman tapped her hand on her leg, impatient. "They're your property...for now. Only because I am choosing not to confiscate the entire lot." She fixed me with her dark-eyed gaze again, and I blinked first. This woman had *hard* eyes. "Despite the question of who owns them, what are we to do with illegally imported medicines containing compounds causing sterility in Methiemum?"

I realized my mouth was open, and hastily closed it. How did she know?

"Not a healer. Still from the House of Healing." The majus wiggled her fingers by way of explanation. "The biological contaminants in the melody of the medicine are very similar to what I heard in this bottle." She lifted the vial used on Amra.

I narrowed my eyes. "Melody?"

"Never mind." She wiped the air with a flat hand. "The cargo?"

"I have a lot of expense in that manifest. Even more now." I glanced at Amra. "Plus, I'm recently out of work, and...saving up for a wedding."

The majus pursed her lips. "You're not the only one with expenses. We'll have to bring in maji and scientists to check all medical supplies recently imported to Methiem." Something relaxed in my chest. Others knew. Even if we did nothing, this...this majus would take care of it. It wasn't just us anymore.

"I have a thought," volunteered an old and scratchy voice. We both looked to the Colonel, as he entered the main theater.

"What if you turn this whole thing back on its ear? Keep the good stuff, and send our 'extra' poisoned medicine back to those who made it in the first place."

The younger majus looked thoughtful.

"Would they even use it? Would it have the same effect on the Sureriaj?" I asked.

"Not as much," she answered, "though that's not the point."

"Could you make the whole Baldek family die out?" I asked. For Amra. For those new orphans in the park.

The female majus shook her head. "No. Some Baldeks might end up taking their own medicine, but I will not continue this war." She contemplated a moment. "I *will* make them recognize their own handiwork. Show them we know. Teach them this is not the way of the Great Assembly. Our way is peace. Otherwise, one errant faction can give an entire species a bad name."

Her words made me look to my fiancé again. My vision of a little shop with children in the yard was fading.

"I think the Naiyul constables were investigating the Baldeks," Kamuli said, her eyes red. I remembered our tails on Sureri. "They may be able to help."

"But can they help enough?" I asked. "This took the influence of an entire *family* of the Sureriaj. Surely the Methiemum provinces are busy dealing with the Shudders epidemic?"

The woman smiled back, thin-lipped and nasty. "There are ways. The Council has the influence and finance."

"The Council of the Maji?" My eyes widened. This woman had connections. The Council answered only to the senatorial power of the Great Assembly. Here was a power that could rival that of an entire family of the Sureriaj—that of a multi-species senate with power bases on all ten homeworlds.

My eyes strayed back to Amra.

"You can't just take the cargo," I said quietly. "I have to make sure she's safe." My stomach clenched at the emptiness of my threat. One man against the entire Great Assembly. This one majus could incapacitate me by herself.

She followed my gaze and gave me another smile, this one understanding. "I think we can come to an arrangement."

"Which is?" Would they simply throw us all in prison? I still didn't trust the maji.

"For the services rendered in discovering what might have become an interspecies war, the Council can send a reward your way. With the other cleanup we'll have to do, a little more expense won't be noticed." That got our attention.

The majus named a price. My mouth dropped open.

It was enough to keep Amra and I comfortable for years, as well as Bhon and Kamuli. Saart would have enough left over to tinker with whatever old gadgets he liked, build a dozen steam-powered mechanical legs. Our little store was a reality. As many children as...except not.

The silence stretched out.

The Majus was waiting. I offered my good hand to shake. "It's a deal."

As we shook, she was already talking. "With the samples here, we can start a full-scale search for the rest of the contaminated medicine. We'll turn this back on the Baldeks in no time. And I'll have your payment drawn up officially as soon as I get back to the Council."

I froze. She didn't just know the Council, she was *on* it. This was the head of the House of Healing herself. If anyone could stop the Baldeks in their genocide, this woman could. Maybe the maji were not only out for themselves. The two here had shown honor in dealing with a small-time merchant.

Sometime later, I leaned over Amra as her eyes fluttered open.

"How would you like to have a place right here in Kashidur City?" I asked.

She grasped my hand, weakly. "Prot. We don't have—"

"We have everything we need," I told her. "And I have you." I took a deep breath. "After the wedding, what do you think about adopting a little girl? I've been told there are a lot of orphans, victims from the Shudders epidemic."

Amra looked back, confused, and I smiled at her. "It's an idea. You don't have to decide now. Rest up. We have a lot to plan." I would break the news—all the news—when she was a little better. I looked to Saart, Kamuli, and Bhon. No more deliveries.

The First Majus in Space

1003 A.A.W.

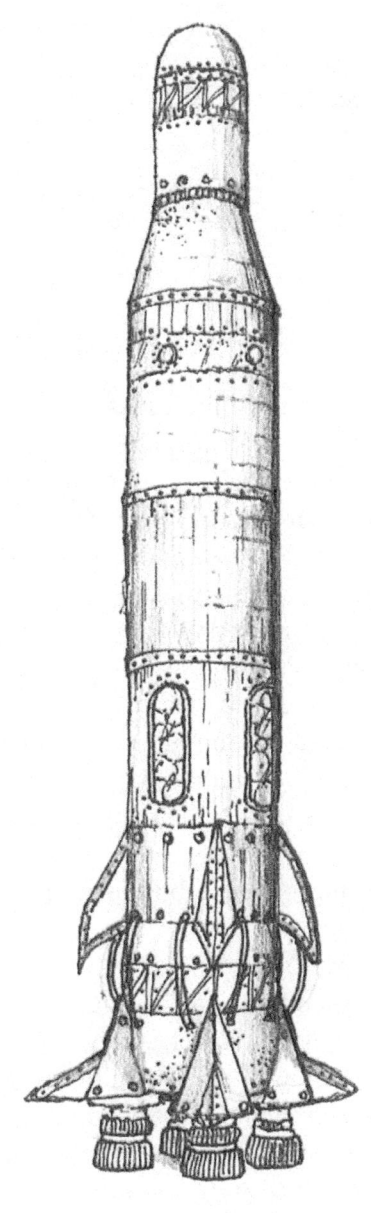

First Flight of the Vimana Aryuman

The Houses of the Maji are vastly different in scope, yet none are considered above the others. Each has a balance for the other five. The House of Healing may undo the House of Communication's change, one from the House of Strength could stand firm against the draw of the House of Potential, and the House of Grace can evade the House of Power's raw might.

—Fragment of a parchment, dated circa 550 B.A.W.

Origon pushed through the multitudes packing the arena on the outskirts of Kashidur City. A great shrouded hulk loomed in the distance at the far end of the crowded space, big as a building. If he remembered correctly, this used to be a forest at the edge of the city. The plain was flat compacted dirt now, soon to be baked earth, if the hot and sunny weather held. Odd to place a lone construction out here, then pack people around it. Methiem was already the most populous of the ten homeworlds, and members of other species had been arriving all morning at the portal ground from their own far-flung worlds or from the Nether.

Excited babble assaulted him on all sides, and air currents carried their intent in the trills of the Symphony of Communication.

"Look there, mama!" A child Lobath, her head tails not yet long enough to braid.

"They told me it was bigger than a building. They weren't lying." Two Festuour in conversation.

"What does it do? Why now?"

"How much did you spend on that?"

He could hear tension of alien species in the music, wondering at the presumption of the Methiemum. This latest proof of their technological arrogance grated on the slower and more cautious species. He was not so bothered. The trader species made a lot of interesting gadgets.

"Get yer fried keilbash!"

Origon's feathery crest ruffled as a hawker jostled past him with a tray of sausages that smelled overcooked and over seasoned. No sense killing it and wasting the meat with all that spice. Belatedly, he moved a long-fingered hand over the inside pocket of his colorful robe where he kept his coins. No one would dare steal from a majus, but in this crowd, a cutpurse might not even realize from whom he was stealing.

As he shoved closer, smoothing his moustache down, he eyed the structure at the front of the crowd, surrounded by ladders and scaffolding. The canny Methiemum had an open invitation to anyone and everyone to watch the unveiling of their grand invention. If they could have made a profit from it, they might have called the ten species here to reveal a giant block of cheese, but he didn't think that was the case. The thing was the presentation, and the Methiemum were masters of it.

He thrust forward, using his height and sharp elbows to create paths, and ignoring curses thrown his way.

"Oy! Watch yer bony arms, ye great robed buffoon!" The angry Sureri, like a furry, starved gargoyle sans wings, layered doubts upon his parentage, his furry face screwed up into a grimace. There were always those who were jealous.

Origon paid him no mind. The maji who attended should have prominent positions, and he was no exception. He finally reached the front of the arena, where a line of the Mayoral Guard stood at attention. The soldiers parted at a glare from him, recognizing him as a majus from the badge with his house colors, and Origon took a place by other important people—including at least one Etanela Speaker, half again as tall as he.

"Greetings, Majus," the Speaker said, her long fingers making a graceful curve through the air. From high above, her large pale eyes acknowledged him from a face surrounded by a mane of light hair.

"Speaker," he returned the greeting, settling beside her.

Beings of every shape and size stretched to his right and left, pushing each other, trying to get closer to the front, though the line of guards held them back. They were before a raised stage, the Methiemum's shrouded construct towering overhead. It cast a shadow across the crowd, now reaching back to the edges of the area. The dirt plain, stretching nearly as far as he could see, was even fuller than when he arrived.

A snap of material drew Origon's attention. With a cheer from the crowd, the immense sheet covering the structure dropped, folding in on itself. There was a round of gasps, and an immediate buzz of conversation. He barely suppressed his reaction, forcing his crest to lay flat. No need to look completely ignorant. He had been consulted—indirectly—on how wind currents would affect a smooth object at a great height. He was prepared for some sort of great balloon, perhaps launched from the top of a building, but this was...impressive.

It shone in the sunlight, bright enough to make him squint. The main structure was a cylinder of burnished metal, sleek and bright, rounding to a dome far overhead. The base and jutting fins were sparsely ornamented, as was the main shaft, but the filigree and hatching he could see was finely done. It looked like nothing so much as a giant finger, pointing to the sky. People were shielding their eyes, gesturing to the gleaming object.

One of the official-looking Methiemum on the platform spoke from behind a podium. Origon thought it was the mayor of the province of Kashidur, though he could hardly keep such people straight. The man's voice was amplified by a tube glowing with stored energy of the Houses of Communication and Potential.

"Welcome, all!" The man shaded his eyes with a hand. "I see people from every homeworld of the Great Assembly of Species here today. Good, good." The man swept a hand to the great structure behind him. "The capsule you see before you will shortly begin a monumental journey." There were exclamations, and questions from the crowd, asking how such a thing could move.

But the mayor was still speaking. "It will bring a crew of Methiemum, and one of our revered maji, up to our moon, Ksupara." The closest and smallest of Methiem's three satellites. Better to start small, if such a plan was to be believed.

"Once there, the crew will explore the new land, mapping and providing the first scientific study of Ksupara." To see what minerals were available, Origon mentally translated. The audience shouted and muttered at this pronouncement. Others had come to the same conclusion. Why waste so many resources to build this thing, when the ten homeworlds were connected by portals, an easy step from one place to another? Leave it to the Methiemum to want more than one homeworld.

The mayor continued his speech, detailing how the majus would assist flying the shuttle, establish the coordinates of a new portal ground, and bring the crew back from Ksupara 'the short way.' Origon of course knew all this. If maji could simply make a portal anywhere, he would have traveled over much more of the universe. Sadly, one could only make a portal where one had been before, thus the capsule. Otherwise, every species might have ventured to their moons and to other planets in their solar system.

While the mayor rambled on, telling of the construction and planning required, Origon examined the capsule. A majus was required to fly it, as in all great acts, but as far as he could tell, the vehicle was fashioned wholly by hand, and not by maji changing the Symphony. He marveled at how much wealth the Methiemum tied up in this mechanical venture. No wonder they invited everyone to see. They could at least make some of their money back with the increased trade. The Methiemum, after all, practiced usury with abandon, which no self-respecting Kirian would do.

As the mayor spoke, a group of people climbed a tall ladder behind him, connected to a walkway at the top of the structure. They reached the top when the mayor wound up his speech. "So we see the prowess of the Methiemum. Our species reaches out to the nine others, showing, and soon sharing, what heights can be achieved by the sweat of our hands. Without even the assistance of the maji, we have built this vehicle you see behind me." He gestured backwards again. "It will be the first to travel between the stars, built by the technology and ingenuity of my people. And thus, I set this great craft, the *Vimana Aryuman*, in motion, lighting the fuse to allow its passage to Ksupara." The mayor stooped around his prominent belly and pressed a button.

With a *whoosh*, flames banked around the capsule behind the stage, slowly building higher, to the appreciative cries of the audience.

It was a show for the gullible crowds. Origon could hear the Symphony of Power's strident chords deep in the melody of the shuttle. The visible flames were just a coal-fired pilot light to a great furnace stored in the belly of the capsule.

So why is it that I am standing down here in the crowd?

He was one of the best suited for this purpose, his abilities rare even among the ranks of the maji. Very few could hear the Symphony of two houses; only three other maji were members of both the House of Communication and of the House of Power. For this capsule to fly to Ksupara, a majus would be needed to control the fuel burn with the House of Power, as well as correct the shuttle's flight through the air with the House of Communication. He supposed two maji could try to coordinate their changes to the Symphony, but it would be much harder than one majus controlling both. The mayor only mentioned having one. Thus the capsule required the rare majus who could hear both Symphonies at once to function at peak efficiency. Like him. Yet no one had asked him. He squinted up at the walkway looking for which majus had been chosen in his place.

One of the figures, vaguely familiar, waved from the walkway near the top of the capsule. There were only a few thousand maji total, so many were known on sight, even to the common folk. What was his name? The mayor was speaking again, announcing the titles and names of the crew. Origon ignored the others until the mayor got to...ah. Teju. Origon had to admit the boy was a fitting choice. Teju was the one Methiemum out of the four maji in existence with access to the Houses of both Communication and Power. However, he was recently raised from the ranks of the apprentices, if Origon remembered correctly. A fitting choice, perhaps, but not a strong one.

The pretty show flames licked the bottom of the giant cylinder. The crew would be on their way shortly, the great capsule lifting high into the air. Just one more opportunity passing him by, given to a majus by far his inferior.

The air cracked overhead, and Teju stiffened. Shouts grew in the audience, arms rose, pointing. The line of guards pushed forward. Origon swung around, searching. A glint of reflected sunlight caught his eye, but the giant Etanela next to him motioned, and her elbow caught his head and knocked him sideways. Origon scanned the arena, trying to get his bearings. He rubbed his temple.

"My apologies," the Etanela Speaker said, stooping. "What do you see? What happened?"

Origon ignored her. *There.* A cloaked person, all in gray-green, wearing a wide-brimmed hat, surely sweltering in the hot Kashidur sunlight. Something flashed again, a reflection from a long metal tube, peeking out underneath the long overcoat. A projectile weapon of some sort?

Origon thrust ahead, aiming for the figure. "Move!" he called to those in front of him. They surged, not listening. He knew he was too late even as he fought the crowd. The cloaked figure raised the long metal cylinder to its face for a second shot, and Origon let the Symphony of Communication flow around him, catching chords representing air currents as they flashed by. He used his song to tune the chords, harmonizing, arranging them in a lattice. Crystalline yellow, the color of the House of Communication, outlined a tunnel before him. His alteration to the music shifted the air, magnifying his vision.

Origon got a brief glance of fine hair covering a gruesome face, a flash of an eye and thin, high cheek. Then the head jerked out of his tunnel vision by the gun's recoil. It was enough to recognize one of the Sureriaj, possibly even the one who had accosted him earlier. The xenophobic species was outspoken, but a rare sight on other homeworlds.

Belatedly, Origon grabbed at the notes of the bullet's course, but it was far too fast, the beat frenetic, and the notes of its music slipped from him. The bullet pinged off the walkway to the capsule. It was not right that a tube with powder in it could defeat a majus.

"May all your feathers fall out!" He cursed the shooter. The saying might not apply outside his species, but he felt better for it. Still, some attribute of the Sureri nagged at him. Eye color? Were brown eyes common? He thought most Sureriaj were orange or gray-eyed, depending on the family lineage. And the eyes looked too small. Large eyes in a gargoyle face made Sureriaj generally unattractive to the other species.

Yet another shot rang out. The Mayoral Guard were hopelessly bogged down, unable to get to the shooter. The crowd heaved against him and Origon held on to a railing to keep his balance. Three shots. If he was incredibly fast, the shooter might have reloaded between the first and second shot, but a third, so close? There must be another barrel to his rifle, or he had a second one, already loaded. This was no snap decision to sabotage.

He followed the path of the bullets, feeling the way they cut through the melody of the air, and saw Teju slumped against the rail of the walkway. A pit of fire rose in Origon's stomach. How dare someone shoot one of the maji!

When he looked back, the shooter was gone. Someone jostled him, then he was buffeted by dozens of people running. Clothing of all colors and beings of all sizes whipped past his view, blocking any hope of seeing where the shooter went.

"Ancestor's eggs," Origon cursed, and began running against the panicked crowd, back to the stage. He wrapped his robe close around his legs to keep it from getting stepped on. If he were high on the walkway, he might be able to see where the shooter was going. And he could help Teju.

It took longer than it should have to push through the crowd. Halfway through, he gave up and extended a hand. He caught at notes, readying his song to make a windy corridor. The air resisted, and Origon cursed again. The Symphony could not be changed in the same way twice in the same place and time. This was too similar to his magnifying glass.

He sighed, listening instead for the jangling chords of the Symphony of Power. They were harder to hear, discordant and irregular. People's connections in a crowd were not so easy to change as the wind. Orange light dripped from his fingers as he encouraged those in front of him to notice his importance and move aside. He ran through.

When Origon reached the stage, he reversed the change he made to the Symphony of Power and regained the rest of his song. Every person was defined by their own specific vibration. Invest enough of that song permanently in changes and what would be left?

Rilan was waiting for him, plucking and fiddling with one of the white corseted dresses she was forced to wear on official business. It set off her black hair and dark features. She was here as representative of the Council of the Maji, then. He wasn't surprised. Nor was he surprised she arrived before him. *She* had probably been invited to sit with the officials, being Methiemum herself. He nodded to her curtly and they both strode to the ladder leading to the walkway.

"Don't know if he'll survive," Rilan said, as if it hadn't been two cycles since they last spoke, this time. "The shooter was good."

"Teju is the only one here trained to set the shuttle on its way," Origon remarked casually. He shifted his eyes enough to see Rilan's wry expression. He had missed her. Had they truly known each other for more than twenty cycles?

"There's a good reason why you weren't chosen, Ori," she replied. "We all know you're one of the best at manipulating the Houses of Power and Communication when they're together. But you aren't Methiemum. The government was insistent."

"Teju is little more than a child. Now look what has happened," Origon remarked. If he had been up there, he could have deflected those bullets.

"And what if we had chosen you?" Rilan continued. "You'd be up there chewing those Sureriaj bullets right now."

Origon snorted, but ignored the jab. "You think it is their species as well?"

"Sure. Who else has trained marksmen who can hit a target that far away? Most people would miss their own foot with one of those things."

"Agreed," Origon said. Guns had only been around for fifty or sixty cycles, one of the nastier inventions of the Methiemum. The Sureriaj favored the weapons, though they had grudgingly accepted the invention at first. Most other beings still used swords and staves, trusty things with no need to reload, or crossbows for range. Origon wondered if that was where the idea for the capsule originated. It was in essence a giant gun, shooting at the ground, from what he could tell.

"In any case, that's the rumor from people who saw the shooter firsthand." Rilan added. "One of the cabinet members passed it on to me."

Another reason to be included with the important people. Origon opened his mouth to say he had seen the shooter firsthand as well, but stopped. Rilan would ask for more details and he honestly did not have any except for brown eyes. He was beginning to doubt himself on that account. Later.

They reached the ladder and began climbing. Origon kept the Symphony uppermost in his mind, listening to the notes and phrases of the complex construct flash by as they rose above the milling crowds. The Symphony of Power's glissandos and trills mirrored the holes and directions of the people below, many of them still running. The Symphony defined everything. What he saw was just the physical manifestation of it. The other four Symphonies were there too, but of course he couldn't hear them.

"Can you give us a shield?" Rilan called down to him. He shook his head, then realized she wasn't looking.

"Not now. We will not be able to reach Teju."

Once created, the underlying vibration would resist him creating a second shield until he was far away from this spot or much time had passed. He would have to hold it constant—unable to interact with Teju and the crew —or let it drop and be more or less defenseless.

Only now he felt just as defenseless, climbing the multiple-story ladder.

A few minutes later, they reached the top, without getting shot at. Up here the air currents were fresher, Communication's melody almost playful.

Rilan hurried forward to Teju, who seemed to be the only one injured. One of the crew, probably the doctor, was already there.

"Here, Councilor," the doctor said to Rilan. She crouched over the fallen man and pressed her hands to his abdomen, where blood ran freely. Origon saw the white and olive green glow form around her hands, sinking into the injured Teju's belly. He always thought olive was a strange secondary color to complement the white of the House of Healing, but then, one did not choose the secondary color—it grew naturally. He was secretly happy for the anonymity of having two house colors—yellow for Communication and orange for Power. It meant he had no secondary color.

"Shiv's toenails!" Rilan cursed at Teju. "Hold still! I'm a psychiatrist, not a surgeon. I'll do what I can, but you can't go dying on me." Origon saw the crimson flow lessen slightly, and the bewhiskered doctor pressed a cloth to the wound, but there was an awful lot of blood darkening the narrow walkway. Rilan had never been good at physically healing with the Symphony, but then, not many maji were.

"Is anyone else injured?" he asked the shaken crew, cowering on the carpeted walk. The whole thing trembled with the smallest breath of wind, and Origon was tempted to stabilize it, but that would take too much effort and time. He asked in the Trader's Tongue, the common form of communication between species. He and Rilan had not needed to use it, of course, being maji.

"No, Majus," answered one of them, an older woman with gray hair pulled into a severe bun. She looked only slightly less petrified than the rest. She and the rest of the crew were wearing matching heavy blue suits with gray piping, thick and all one piece.

After a moment's contemplation, Origon knelt down, too, behind the engraved metal handrail. He wouldn't be able to see as far, but he was taller than the average Methiemum and didn't want his topfeathers shaved off by another bullet.

"Did you see the shooter?" a crewmember asked.

Origon nodded. "From very close. It was to be one of the Sureriaj. Now quiet, while I find him again." He listened to notes from the House of Power, peering over the walkway's handrail. Far below, he heard trills of fear running through the crowd. There was a strange base line as well, which he ignored. The Symphony was as complex as reality and often more confusing. Origon traced the path of the shooter with the House of Power, reading the tremolos and vibratos of people shying away from the gray-green cloaked Sureri.

The path started where Origon first glimpsed the shooter, gun to his shoulder. It cut across the crowd, the spikes of fear in the melody decreasing farther from the source. And then it vanished. Origon scratched his head, then let his crest resettle. Surely the shooter continued to cause confusion as he moved through the crowded amphitheater. But there was nothing.

"Ori!" The shout intruded on his surveying, and he lost the thread of the music. The Symphony flashed by, leaving him with no sense of the shooter's path. Origon frowned. If he wanted to track the path again, he'd have to find another way. He turned to Rilan.

"What is it?" he asked, annoyed.

Rilan jerked her head toward the capsule, where the crew were scuttling toward the safety of the entrance. Origon's eyes widened as the strident base chords intruded again from the Symphony of Power. Smoke drifted past the edge of the scaffold, burning his nose. The dense fuel the pilot light would activate was heating up. The pilot flames had been going too long in the chaos. Soon the real fuel would start to burn, disastrous without a majus to control it. He stroked his moustache, thinking.

"Can the pilot flames be shut off?" he asked, again in the Trader's Tongue. The older woman—probably the captain, from the many bands of color on the sleeves of her jumpsuit—shook her head vigorously. She was hunched against the rail, only paces from the hatch leading to the interior of the capsule.

"It was designed to burn fiercely for a short time, Majus, to provide a power source for Majus Teju to use. If the real fuel catches fire too soon, it will burn out in an explosion the size of this arena. Many will be injured, and it will be multiple cycles before we can amass this much fuel again. Our flight to Ksupara will be scrapped. Can you direct the pilot flame? Could you fly the ship in Majus Teju's stead?" The woman must have been informed of his abilities.

"We're losing him, Ori!" Rilan called. She had her hands pushed tight against Teju, whose head fell back against the railing as if it were too heavy for him. The crew's doctor was trying to investigate the wound as she held pressure, but his hands were already soaked with blood, his doctor's bag next to him splayed open to reveal a variety of tools. "Even if we get him down from here in time, I don't think Doctor Chitra can save him. There's too much damage." Her eyes were wet when she stared up at him. "Ori, help me make my people proud. I don't want this day to be a complete failure."

Origon looked to the dying Teju, to the burning smoke, the crew on the shaky walkway, and to where the shooter had disappeared, far down in the crowd. Who had gone against the trading might of Methiem? Who had disobeyed the wishes of the Great Assembly of the ten species, and the Council of the Maji? Both organizations had given approval to this endeavor. Without a culprit, there was as much chance of sabotage if the Methiemum tried a second time. But if they were able to get to their moon this day, he could do Teju's job: create a portal back to the Methiemum homeworld. Once complete, the knowledge could be disseminated, and travel to Ksupara could be an everyday occurrence, protected by the maji. And from there, farther into Metheim's solar system.

If he did this, he would be the one to guide the capsule into the sky, remembered as the first majus to fly a space shuttle.

There was really only one choice.

Origon pushed up from his crouch on the walkway, running to the capsule's entrance, ears straining for the sound of another bullet whizzing past. None came. The crew followed. One of the crewwomen began closing the heavy door of the capsule behind them and through it, he saw Rilan dragging the body of Teju back toward the ladder. The doctor was shaking his head, wiping blood from his hands and packing up his bag. Origon could investigate the body when he got back, assuming he got back intact.

Origon stepped through the short hallway to let the doctor pass, then followed the crew to the one circular room at the nose of the shuttle. He reached out with all his senses.

I shall be the one to put this capsule on Ksupara! The thrill raced through him. *The first time members of the ten species are traveling in space!* There would be time to grieve for a fallen majus later, after he returned from the moon. Honor and ceremony would accompany the return, though he pushed the thought away. *For now, it is critical to concentrate on the task.*

Around him, the eight crewmembers scurried to various tasks, flipping levers and tallying up sums on chalkboards. Several checked gauges for liquids coursing along walls of the room and down into the bowels of the lengthy cylinder beneath them. Origon stood near a half-sphere of metal, detailed with ornamental filigree, thrusting up through the center of the domed room. The burnished ceiling missed his topfeathers by a handsbreadth, and the diameter was maybe four times its height. Polished riveted walls reflected the light of Methiem's morning sun through small portholes filled with thick lead glass.

Origon ignored the scurrying Methiemum, feeling the awe-inspiring verses of the Symphony of Power below him, like a thousand trumpets blowing at full volume. His mind recoiled from the roiling furnace of fuel attached to the bottom of the capsule. Surely this was too much? Once that melody was released to its full potential, it would consume the shuttle. But the Methiemum would not have designed it so poorly. He traced the racing lines of music describing the pilot flames, a candle to the sleeping sun in the tanks of fuel at the bottom of the shuttle. He could hear the shape of it in the languid Symphony of Communication. Air passed beneath it, blown through a tube by a slight breeze from outside. A small valve stuck closed, but a directed staccato trill, a burst of air, would be enough to switch the valve and let the pilot flame in. It would happen anyway, if he didn't control the burning pilot light first. It was designed for a majus to use.

"Is everyone to be ready?" he asked. There was little time before the pilot flame reached the main tank. Crew scurried around his unfocused eyes, and someone tugged on the sleeve of his robe.

"Please, sit, and tuck in your restraint," said the captain. Origon looked around. Everyone else was seated in reclining chairs around the periphery of the room, each stationed near a bank of dials and levers. They watched, eyes wide, firmly strapped in place. The captain pointed to one of two empty seats.

Origon sat, and the captain helped him buckle his restraints. His height made the seat uncomfortable—it had been designed for one of average Methiemum stature.

"Is this all to be necessary?" he complained.

"Quite so," the captain answered. "There. Done." She stepped back. "Please wait until I have restrained myself, and then feel free to start our journey, honorable Kirian." Quickly, the captain strapped in, then nodded to Origon. "Our lives will be in your hands."

He realized the captain and crew were terrified to have him here, rather than Teju. He assumed the younger majus had trained with them. Well, Origon had many more cycles of experience using the Symphonies of Communication and Power. There was really no need to worry. They would all be back by dinner.

He relaxed, letting himself float back into full absorption of the Symphony, feeling the chords surrounding him. The two Symphonies were separate, yet connected. Most maji only heard one sixth of the full music of the universe, but he was fortunate enough to be able to hear two Symphonies—one third. Each expanded in his mind from a single chord to individual symphonies to fractal themes swirling within each other, defining the interconnected phrases of Power and the multi-layered themes of Communication.

The capsule faded into the background. He found the catch again, air swirling around it, the opening for almost unlimited potential power. He sensed the tempo of potential and force with the House of Power, saw the restraints that would direct the liquid fire. Yes, that would most certainly lift the ship. He took a deep breath, changed one gracenote in the Symphony of Communication with his song, and flipped the valve open.

He was pushed back into his seat, neck straining to hold his head up.

Fire surged, more than he could bear. The tempo was a military drummer beating to quadruple time. Notes slipped through his mental grasp, far too fast to handle, much less change. He clawed through both melodies at once. This was the reason he was here, for Communication and Power had merged into one; burning air and a hurricane of fire.

The capsule was rising into the air, gaining speed, listing. Soon, it would veer to one side and then back down to the ground, digging a hole and smashing him and the crew into a paste.

The air outside the ship. He listened to that comparably languid music, felt the way the ship moved. If he could redirect where the burning air went, he could propel the ship the other way.

Notes slid by him, too fast to change, and he had the sensation of hanging. They were moving sideways. The crew might have been shouting, but he could afford no concentration for his physical ears. There *was* a pattern to the relentless beat of the fuel. He didn't have to catch the notes to change them. He instead saw their pattern, made the new musical phrase, crafted from his own song, ready to insert it...*there*.

The ship righted abruptly, but Origon felt his invested song ripped out of his grip, flying out far beneath them. The ship began to list to the other side.

Gasping, his stomach threatening to jump out of his throat, he realized what he should have before. He no longer envied Teju his place here. There was no chance to reverse any of the changes he made. Every change to the Symphonies on this trip would be permanent. The shuttle was flying so fast that the surrounding music was in constant flux, notes changing. It would strip each application of his song from his being. If he was not efficient, the flight would drain him to something insubstantial, his song stripped of its notes.

His body hung to one side and Origon made another construction from his music, inserting it into the breakneck beat, wincing as a small portion of his essence was lost. This could only buy time.

The flight would be several hours long. Ksupara was small and near to Methiem, compared to moons of other species' homeworlds, but would serve as a gateway to extensive exploration of the Methiemum system. He would have asked for chalkboard and chalk to make notes, but he could not move under such pressure. This would be by instinct and experience, guiding the ship the smallest amount while keeping to the most efficient path to space. How much *had* Teju trained for this?

He listened for the outer cadenzas of the Symphony of Communication, hearing the air currents far up into the atmosphere above the capsule. Below the tank of fuel, swirls of power and force made the music too discordant to follow. While his mind rode the vibrations of the air currents, planning their course, he wondered if Teju *would* have been able to handle this job, no matter the training. It was nearly beyond even Origon's grasp. The ship listed again, and he redirected the flow of the fuel with another change, a bit of his song thrust into the Symphony at the right instant. He felt weaker already.

For a small eternity, Origon molded the Symphonies around him, sweat dripping from his brow. His pointed teeth ground together with each jarring rip as his song disappeared into the air. Time flew by almost unnoticed as he put his full concentration into fighting his way through the air, a small sun strapped to his back. He *was* the capsule. They were moving fast enough that each change to the Symphony was distant from the last. It was oddly liberating to repeat the same composition again and again. Yet every time he did so, the song defining him became more a skeleton than a sonata.

At some point, the acceleration lessened, and his arms began to rise on their own. His robe billowed out like a multi-hued balloon. Sounds— aside from the internal music of the Symphony—intruded on him, like one or more of the crew being violently sick. He would never shame himself like that. He stifled a burp.

The melody of the tank of fuel was lethargic now, nearly empty, and he had little need to use his song to effect changes. Origon opened his eyes, blinked, and licked his thin lips, realizing he had not moved or spoken for—how long?

"What is—" He stopped at his croaking voice and swallowed. The captain twisted fluidly in his direction, no longer pressed down by the great weight of acceleration. A lock of her long gray hair had come free from its bun, drifting like a halo around her head. She was highlighted by shielded carbon arc lamps, throwing great swaths of harsh light around the cabin. A chemical heater protruded from the center instrument cluster, warming the cold interior. Engineers must have installed the newer lights rather than relying on candles—too hazardous in space—or energy stored by a majus of the House of Potential. The crew fiddled with switches near them. Some had small lanterns to see detail by.

He tried again. "What is the time?"

"We've been traveling for nearly five and a half hours, honored Kirian," the captain said. "We were worried when you did not answer our calls, but our capsule did not falter after the first few minutes, so we assumed you were busy in your work."

Had they called to him? He searched his memory, but could not remember. "I am named Origon Cyrysi, Captain. What is to be done when the fuel tank is empty?"

"There is a way to detach it with your magic, Majus Cyrysi," she answered. "If all has gone well, you can begin our deceleration with the secondary tank. The hardest part will be landing."

Origon didn't bother to correct the woman's use of 'magic.' He was too tired, and even a few maji thought what they did was supernatural, not a science. He bent his head in concentration, seeking through the Symphony for the mechanism the captain spoke of.

There. Four large catches on the side of the empty fuel tank. Origon could feel the latent power, a slow steady beat, behind the explosive bolts. With another wince, he changed their tune in the Symphony of Power, building the melody to a snappy crescendo with his song. The bolts exploded and the empty fuel tank sliced away behind them, no longer on their trajectory. Of course the change was not reversible. The explosion disintegrated the bolts and the music describing them.

He knew the Methiemum built this capsule by menial methods, but had the designers not consulted a majus on how to control it in flight? Every little thing seemed planned to use up his potential. It would be a simple thing to modify the architecture.

Origon sighed. When he got back, he would track down the designers and have a long talk with them. The melody of Communication and Power between the crew—the little solos and trills that manifested in their body language—told him they were over their terror and growing more efficient at their jobs.

In the depths of the Symphony, there was a glimmer of a building theme so strident it would overpower the rest when it was louder: Ksupara itself. The House of Communication was weaker here, as there was little air, but the capsule was sealed well. He added his own cadenza to the melody of the air in the capsule, freshening it. That at least was not permanent. He retracted his song and the breeze died down.

The strident theme was getting louder. "Captain," Origon said. "Is there a way to be viewing our destination?"

"Certainly, Majus Cyrysi," the captain answered. She pressed a button and a section of metal slid aside, revealing thick glass. A neat piece of engineering. Through it, he saw a milky glow beneath them—Methiem. Above, a deep swath of black extended in every direction, sprinkled with tiny points of light. Several of the crew gasped, and his breath caught in his throat.

Shivers ran up his arms as he fixed the picture in his mind. He would remember it for the rest of his life. Wisps of clouds raced below. Ahead, an irregular round object shone, reflecting light from Methiem. It had to be Ksupara. One of the other moons rose behind it, larger, and farther away. But the rocky surface of Ksupara was closer than it should be. Origon said nothing. No sense panicking the crew.

"That will help immensely," he told the captain, who nodded back.

Origon focused on the shining object and the heavy, rising theme which would direct their course. He would have to land the capsule, or rather crash it with everyone intact. The capsule did not need to fly back to Methiem. Those who came through later portals could hack it up for scrap for all he cared. He no longer had any interest in the fine design of the capsule. He let one shaky hand float up, imagining he might be able to see *through* his hand if he spent any more of his song. But he wasn't done yet. He took a deep breath in through his nose, resettled his crest, and blew the air out.

The Symphony of Power outlined the secondary tank, trills of blocked power humming. The tank had exit ports on all sides of the capsule, controlled by small nozzles, each with a lightweight valve. Once the fuel passed the nozzle, it would catch fire and push the capsule in the opposite direction. It was simple in principle.

There was only one problem.

Origon raised his head to scowl at the captain. "Did your engineers consult at *any* point with one of the maji?" he asked. She visibly paled under his gaze.

"We did, Majus. Is there a problem?"

Origon waved a hand irritably. "Never you mind. I will be addressing the problem myself."

The subtle vibrations making up the universe could only be pulled and changed so far and for so long. Once he grasped control of the valves to make adjustments, he could not let his focus lag from any of them, lest he could not move them a second time. He would have to maintain a focus on—how many were there?—*eight* separate valves all at the same time! Teju would never have held the capsule together. He wasn't sure *he* could handle it, and he had been out of apprenticeship for forty cycles, not newly raised from apprentice.

Origon sighed noisily, and the captain raised her eyebrows at him. The other crew watched too, but Origon ignored them. Their calculations and buttons did not regrow his song. Why hadn't the Methiemum designed a lever for *this* job? Eight people could pull levers, guided by a majus for the correct timing. By the great winged ones' beards, he would personally rend the designers of this capsule when he got back. *If* he got back.

"I wish for absolutely no one to disturb me until this capsule is resting upon Ksupara," he commanded. He glared around the room. "The less noise the better." Without waiting for a confirmation, he tightened his straps and clasped his long-fingered hands together, concentrating. He heard a chorus of fabric-on-fabric sounds as the crew followed his example, then silence. Origon stared out of the glass at the approaching moon, listening.

With the House of Communication, he could control the eight valves. Only a glissando was required to turn them on or off, but the notes wavered as if he heard them underwater, and he slumped in his chair. He found the first valve, clutched at the notes. Then the second, and the third. His breathing became ragged. Four. Five. He shook, just a little, then reached out and grasped the notes controlling the last three valves. The Symphony buffeted him, as the capsule sped ever nearer Ksupara. He had to keep a connection to each valve to adjust any one of them in time. If he lost the connections, he would not be able to get them back.

Their speed was the first problem, and he invested his song in three valves pointing the direction they were traveling. His hands clenched at his chair's arms as liquid fire rushed past the valves, randomizing the air currents. Sweat popped out all over his body. But the ship slowed.

It skewed off course the other way. Ready this time, Origon opened two different valves and closed the first three, correcting.

Decelerate. Correct. Stop the twist. Sweat. Breathe. More deceleration. Repeat.

Ksupara was massive in the front view, and he ignored the captain's plaintive stare. They were going too fast. He wished he could close his eyes as he did for the flight into space, but he needed to see the moon through the glass. That meant more distraction from the crew's twitches and scared faces.

Decelerate. More. More. They were going into a twist, but he couldn't correct it at the same time and stay conscious. Some loose object whirled about the capsule. All the force must go forward to stop their movement. Another crew member was sick, and Origon fought down his own gullet. He closed two valves, opened two others. He had counted on more help from the air itself, resisting their movement, but had miscalculated. Not many realized how much air weighed, and the medium of communication here was much thinner than he expected.

With the small bit of rational thought left to him, Origon considered his options. Overshoot and they might never land. Crash directly down and they would most certainly die. What else was left? What could resist their movement? He watched Ksupara's ground coming closer at startling speed. From here, he could see valleys, short, eroded mountains, and large flat plains.

The surface itself. The insight put a pointy smile on Origon's face, making the captain's whiten in response. He ignored her and gently aimed the capsule just below the horizon.

"Prepare yourselves," he told the capsule in general. He heard rustling.

The impact jolted through him, his head bending forward, and his chair rattled in its bolts. He felt one of the valves crush, its music ceasing. It was a relief to hold only seven. He eased the capsule up from the surface, but there was a persistent vibration that shook his bones. A range of hills sprang up as they soared over the landscape and Origon gritted his teeth, opening all the valves on the right side of the craft. They veered left. The capsule trembled and twisted as one corner brushed the side of the highest hill.

Still not slow enough. Origon aimed the capsule down at a plain dotted with circular marks, keeping the forward valves open.

The capsule bounced off the plain, the impact shaking his chair like a leaf. Something bent with a screech that made his ears hurt. He rocked back and forth, lighter than he should be, as he readjusted their flight upwards to clear a hill. The ship was slowing.

One last time he touched the capsule to the surface of Ksupara, smashing another three valves. He heard the captain grunt. Then there was a crash from his left and a form flew across his vision. His was not the only loose chair. He did not have time or attention to spare for the occupant.

The capsule plowed through the dusty ground of the moon, cutting a groove. He could see a huge valley coming up fast, many times deeper than the capsule was tall. They were rotating sickeningly, and Origon felt for the correct orientation of the remaining valves. Waiting, waiting.

Now. He opened all of them and the ship rose, listing to the left. The valley sped by underneath them, reaching far into the moon. Someone screamed.

The reserve of fuel was nearly depleted—most of it had gone to decelerate the capsule. He could force them to the ground a final time, using the still intact valves now on the upper side of the capsule, but they would not rise again. He strained to see the edge of the valley, which seemed to take up half of Ksupara. Finally the far edge came into view— thankfully a plain, and not a mountain. Origon hoped he had cut enough speed to keep them all from dying.

"This is it!" he cried, and let the last remaining fuel guide them forward and down.

Violation of Natural Law

The exploration of the sky above our worlds is a journey we will eventually take. Though ten species at least have found the Nether on their own, we are separated physically by uncharted distances. Certainly there may be other neighbors, closer. If we were able to explore the sky, might we find others and bring them knowledge of the Nether?

—From the first Methiemum proposal to the Great Assembly on the subject of space flight

Origon awoke to a flickering light. It was a store-fire lamp, an artifact of the House of Potential, storing the song of fire from a majus of the House of Power. It showed the captain's face, close to his. There was a large bruise on her cheek and her gray hair had fallen out of her bun, draping her face.

"Majus Cyrysi? Are you well?"

Origon blinked wetness out of his eyes—blood?—and mentally checked himself. There were points of pain all along his back and neck, and his shoulder seemed twisted, but nothing broken. He nodded slowly, narrowing his eyes at the pain in his head. He was sideways, and the captain was standing on the rounded wall of the capsule.

"Are we landed, then?" He barely remembered to use the Trader's Tongue.

"Yes, Majus, and the crew all accounted for. Dipara has a badly broken leg, but thankfully nothing worse, for all she flew across the length of the capsule." Origon looked to the other side of the capsule at a sharp cry. A young woman was lying down, two other crew around her. He quickly averted his eyes from a shock of white protruding from her leg, glistening in the low light. "In addition, Doctor Chitra has suffered a concussion and is not able to ply his trade. Numerous other bumps and bruises among my crew. I will be speaking to the engineers on the condition of those seats when I get back." The captain folded her arms.

"You will wait for me to finish with them first," Origon told her, rubbing his neck. "I may not be leaving anything to complain to. Help me out."

The captain undid his restraints and Origon nearly fell from his chair, rolling in the light pull of Ksupara. He stood on the former wall and stretched, barely catching himself before he stretched straight into the air.

"Be careful," the captain warned. "You are far lighter on Ksupara. Lighter than on any homeworld—even Etan." Origon let out a short laugh. His arms and legs were barely able to hold him up, even here. If he had been standing on one of the homeworlds, he would have fallen over from fatigue.

Chairs and equipment hung sideways in the capsule, unlatched buckles dangling like hanging vines, casting shadows from the chemical lights on the center hub, now to his right at head level. One lamp was cracked and sputtering, but the others threw out harsh orange light. They had landed partially capsized, the flat bottom of the capsule in the air and the base of the rounded dome planted in the surface of the moon. The other side of the floor was now a peak far overhead.

Cabinets on the far side of the capsule hung open above them and Origon saw a jar fall out of them, curiously slow, to land next to one of the crew. Supplies were tossed about and underfoot and the crew was separating them into piles, useful and not, broken and whole. The thick glass viewing window had not broken in the crash, though there was a crack running its length. It was vertical, now, the lower edge buried in gray-green dirt and the upper portion higher than Origon's topfeathers.

"Well, captain," he said, slumping back against his horizontal chair, "what is to be the plan? Are we ready to go back to Methiem? I believe I may be managing a portal, if you are giving me some few minutes to build up my strength." He could barely hear the Symphony. He had used up more of his song in the flight than ever before. He knew he should be angrier at what the capsule designers did to him, but was too tired to summon the emotion. His crest sagged in exhaustion.

"Oh no," the captain replied, sounding scandalized. She brushed her hair back, trying to make it lie straight in the light pull of the moon. "We will be the first inhabitants of the colony on Ksupara. All supplies are included to turn this capsule into our base of operation. The plan," she looked around sadly at the ruins of her upturned capsule, "was to have the station function as it landed, but since things did not go, ah, quite as expected," she gave Origon an apologetic half-grin, "we will make due. The tanks of air are planned to last us two days, though my mechanic tells me one developed a leak in the...landing. Likely we will have a day or so before they will need to be recharged by a majus."

"One of the House of Communication," Origon added automatically. They were the only ones who had the ability to achieve such a task. The captain looked confused and Origon dispelled his words with a wave of his hand. "It is not mattering. I will be leaving shortly, so anyone wishing to come back to Methiem should accompany me."

"Dipara will have to go with you, of course," the captain said. "And probably the doctor. The rest of us will stay here, and hope a replacement physician can come up with the next majus."

"Fine," Origon told her. He looked around at the crew. There was another cry as a crew member set the unfortunate Dipara's broken bone. He recalled he didn't know any of the other crews' names, nor that of the captain. He was more interested in getting back to Kashidur City, and seeing the look on Rilan's face. And taking a nap. His eyes were ready to close as he stood, and his breathing was labored, as if he couldn't pull enough oxygen into his chest. He listened to the Symphony, intending to use his song to refresh the stale air, but the music flashed by faster than he could concentrate. The beat was indecipherable. He flailed at the notes, and they slipped away from him as if greased.

He walked slowly across the curved side of the capsule, hoping the movement would refresh him. The thought of Kashidur City reminded him of the cloaked figure, running through the crowd. The assassin—the reason he was here. He hoped Rilan had uncovered more evidence. Maybe enough to capture the assassin himself when he returned to Methiem. He stood a little straighter, his crest righting itself. His eye caught the featureless plain through the window, a rounded mountain rising in the distance.

But to pluck another feather, how many days of one's life were spent standing on the surface of a moon? He stroked his moustache. It was the first space exploration of any of the ten species. And he was the first majus in space. There was time to revel in his accomplishment.

He stumbled the rest of the way toward the viewport, his feet bouncing off the floor with every step, skirting a pile of salvaged supplies fallen from the cabinets. His long and colorful robe, not as handy here as on the surface of a homeworld, swirled around his legs as he moved, showing a nearly indecent amount of ankle. He pushed it down, but the robe caught something and nearly sent him tumbling into the banks of controls. He grasped at a panel in a clatter of supplies, glaring around, daring the crew to comment. Most looked quickly back to their work. An urn of some sort clattered out behind him with a heavy *crack*, but he ignored it, striding slightly too fast to the window, catching himself on the wall to stop his forward motion. He flashed another look at the crew, dutifully minding their business. They would watch him as soon as he looked away. If he had not been falling-down tired...

And why would someone want to bring that dreadful urn he tripped over? Perhaps it carried dried foodstuffs. He shook his head and peered out the newly vertical viewport.

The surface of Ksupara was bleak; uninteresting. It was gray rock, pitted with crevices, stretching to the slopes of the eroded mountain. Dust stirred up by their landing clouded his view, but he could glimpse the stars above, clearer here than on any homeworld. His father, an impossibly religious Kirian, always told him each star was the soul of an ancestor who had gone before. Origon never believed it until now. The pure glory of each dot of light was hypnotizing. The patterns of stars were far different than on Kiria. There was no Ploughman here, nor Philosopher, nor—

"Majus!"

Origon turned irritably to chasten the errant crewmember. He stopped short, mouth still open.

There was a dirty, uneven ball, like skin stretched around pus, floating higher than his head above the pile of supplies. It was directly over that ancestor's-cursed urn, broken in shards. Origon watched the ball slowly expanding, unaffected by Ksupara's light pull, though everything else in the capsule was.

The surface touched a bag, hanging by one strap from a chair bolted to the floor, and with a crackle of energy, the cloth disintegrated, pulled into the pale skin of the ball. Origon heard a gasp from someone, and realized he had pushed back against the window, trying to get as far away from the thing as possible. He forced his crest flat, forced his shoulders to unknot. The maji were always to be seen as calm in the face of the unexpected. He reached for the Symphony of either house by instinct, but it was still faint, like music played in a different room with the door closed. The notes were slippery and he ground his teeth as he tried to catch even one.

The growing ball intersected the chair next. There was a screech like metal being torn and the chair distorted, pulling like putty into a swirl around the thing.

"Holy Vish!" someone cried, and Origon pulled back, his eyes widening. There were tiny bits of leather and cloth floating on the ball's opaque surface. It did not move but for its slow expansion. It was as if the sphere was planted in the air, grown from the size of a child's rubber ball and inflated like a balloon. Now it was almost half the size of a man. The crew crowded toward the walls of the crashed capsule, trying to get as far away as possible. Origon shivered.

"What is it?" the captain called.

"I do not know," Origon called back, his voice thin in the chill air. He eyed the wall above where the chair had been. "But it may be eating through the capsule wall as easily as it did the chair." He had to contain it, stop the threat. He had to change the Symphony. Such a thing should not be a struggle.

He shook again, rubbing his fingers together. It had been cold inside the capsule from the very beginning, yet the heater in the center hub gave out warmth. Now it felt as if the air itself was freezing. A knife of cold sliced up his back and he turned to the window behind him to see ice crystals condensing on it, blocking the view of the moon's surface. They spread to the metal walls like spiderwebs.

"Can you stop it, Majus Cyrysi?"

What did the captain think he was doing? Origon gave only a grunt in return. His pointed teeth chattered violently and he bit his tongue. The shock of copper and cold gelled his thoughts and the Symphonies of his two houses grew in his mind.

Origon strained harder than at his test for majus, forty cycles ago. Harder than when he first heard the beautiful music of the universe. A single note rose up in his mind and he brought it to his attention. It fractured into a second note, then a trill, then exploded into a Symphony of its own. He slid down the icy window, concentrating, trying to separate Communication from Power. The Symphonies of the capsule sprang up, giving the musical equivalent of the crew's hushed words, the dead air in the capsule, the still fizzing remnants of fuel in the lines, the connections from the banks of switches and levers, the dimming chemical lights and dying heater.

Around the irregular ball there was discord. Notes frayed, veered off pitch, and became dissonant. It was the counterpoint to its slow consumption of the capsule.

Investing so much of his song into their flight made changing a single note an effort. He might recover his old potential eventually, but it would be many cycles. A person's song could eventually return to full strength, defined by their every moment in time. He pushed aside the thought. Complaining about it would not change what happened.

"I shall be shielding it from doing any more damage," he called out. One of the nearer crewmembers nodded nervously in agreement.

He adjusted as few notes as possible, a couple each in the Houses of Power and Communication, putting just a little of himself into the change. He would compress the air around the floating thing. It left him breathless, but at least those notes of his song could be reclaimed when he let the air decompress.

Only a few scholars and maji appreciated the weight of air, and even fewer appreciated it could be compressed hard as rock. Simple air, with the correct transfer of heat, could be a powerful shield or even a prison. He reached out, applying his change, and bright yellow and orange light burst forth around the ball in a cage, squeezing inward. The heat of the action melted ice on the walls. There were calls of appreciation from the crew, watching the physical effects of his change.

But when the color touched the ball, the crystal yellow and orange lattice, visible only to him or another majus, shattered and dissipated. The changes he crafted in the melody fluttered and tore as the hanging mass' discord shredded through the Symphony.

Origon staggered, slipped sideways, and felt bile in his throat as the ice climbed upward again. The captain called out wordlessly at the obvious failure. That part of his song was gone, sucked into the thing before him. He could ill afford it.

A hand caught his arm. "Majus, are you well?" Worry was all over the woman's face. "Where did this thing come from?"

Origon could not summon the will to speak for a moment. He gasped on thin air. Then: "I am fine. I must try again. And I do not know." He waved the crewmember off, but noted the Methiemum woman stood close, ready to catch him if he fell again. Several others inched closer, pressing around the circumference of the capsule to get to him while staying away from the mass. He did not complain. The effort was not worth it.

Each person's song—that portion that intersected the Symphonies of the universe—was connected to everything. There was nothing it could not touch. But the ball had eaten his changes to the melody. Impossible.

He grasped for the Symphony of Power, not attempting to change, but only listening, for anything to tell him what the sphere of destruction was. There was nothing. Origon blinked, slumped against the freezing window. There was never *nothing*. Music fractured and died as the ball ate the console attached to the wall of the capsule. But that music was the decaying energy of the objects. Inside the ball, there was no energy, no melody. This sphere did not exist, as far as the Symphony was concerned. It was a void in the universe. It took the energy around it, breaking it down, and...what? What could it do with the energy it took if there was nothing inside it? Energy could not be created or destroyed— that was fundamental.

Origon grasped for both houses, their harmonious fractal of Symphonies, blended perfectly with every particle of the universe. With his entire composition of his existence, he reached out toward this thing that violated natural law...and failed.

He could not touch it.

Origon, for the first time in many cycles, was truly afraid.

This thing was more important than the assassin and the landing on Ksupara together. How had it come here? Was it made by an intelligent species, or could it be natural to Ksupara? What if it grew forever, eating its way through the universe? He had to bring this information back to the Council of the Maji.

The crew was staring in horror. Several clutched together for warmth, and one might have fainted. Origon shivered again. The ice had nearly covered the viewing window and the chemical heater was sputtering, though it was not in the path of the void. It was as if...as if the void were draining energy from everything surrounding it.

"A Drain, that is what it is."

"A what, sir?" the woman next to him asked. She had her hand out again as if to catch him. He struggled upright.

"It is draining energy, so I shall call it a Drain," Origon said. He discovered the thing, so he should get to name it. It bore down overhead, filling a good quarter of the capsule and growing. Soon it would reach them. Or would it reach the wall first? Either way, the capsule was claustrophobic. He hunched down, seeing the crew doing the same.

"We must all be going," he called out. "This, this *Drain* will be destroying the capsule very soon. I am afraid none of you will be staying here to build a base on Ksupara." He hoped he could hold the notes still long enough to make a portal. Otherwise none of them would be going anywhere.

"Majus Cyrysi," the captain called, halfway across the circumference of the room. The woman looked frustrated, her voice plaintive. It was obvious there was nothing to be done. Origon held up a thin hand, forestalling her.

"Unless you are able to breathe the cold vacuum of space, and survive *that*," he pointed a finger upward at the swirling pale mass, still growing—a second chair disappeared with a screech and the captain winced, "you will go with me. I am unable to alter this Drain. It will be destroying the wall of the capsule in moments. You all must accompany me through a portal back to Methiem." He drew in a lungful of thin air. The anomaly above them must be eating the very atmosphere.

"But...can't you do anything?" another of the crew asked. He was a young Methiemum, barely more than a teenager. He trembled, but held his back straight under the looming menace. Good lad.

Origon shook his head. "This is to be a matter for the Council of the Maji." There were mutters from the crew. To non-maji, the Council, each member the head of a house, was almost a thing of fantasy.

The captain bowed her head, then looked around the remains of her capsule. She spoke in a carrying voice. "Take only essential items with you. Calculations, observations, and mathematical equations have the first priority. If we are scrapping this mission, then by Vish, we're going to know how to do it better next time."

A shudder ran through the capsule. The void—the Drain—had reached the wall, converting it to non-existence. Origon pushed the woman next to him and she started moving. The rest of the crew bustled at the captain's orders. Origon aimed up-slope, to what had been the dome of the capsule, where there was slightly more room to make the portal. They ducked as they walked, the mass ahead reaching down for them.

The crew scrambled to gather supplies and notes, leaving the dead weight of rations and clothes. The captain was holding the concussed doctor up with one shoulder and three more of the crew hefted a tarp holding the prone Dipara.

A horrible whistle grew, like a giant teapot coming to a boil. Origon looked up at the mass of the Drain. It had breached the wall and air was escaping into vacuum. Then the whistling stopped suddenly, as the Drain plugged the hole, eating both hull and air. They had moments left.

Origon set his feet, closed his eyes and strained to hear the Symphony again. The single chord rose up, duplicated, and split into the Symphonies of Communication and Power. He fumbled for the notes he needed, almost falling with the effort. The female Methiemum—one of two not supporting the wounded—caught his shoulder and held him upright. He let her.

Portals—one way holes from here to there—were one of the first lessons every majus learned. Yet there was resistance here. The Drain was taking his energy. He grabbed the notes, like lifting lead weights, and forced the measures and phrases to alter, blending his song with the melodies of this place and of the portal ground on Methiem until they were the same melody.

Sluggishly, a pitch black hole swirled into existence, ringed with yellow and orange. It pressed against what had been the top of the capsule, as far away as Origon could get from the Drain. The portal was just large enough to admit his height, but he would have to turn sideways. For all his song in the portal, it should have been half again as high and wide enough for three. The room tilted before him, and he leaned heavily on the woman. He could not faint. Not yet. It would be the death of them all.

"Orderly through the portal!" the captain called. She was at the back of the clump of Methiemum.

"I must go through last," he slurred. "Move." The crewwoman left him and he fell hard against what used to be the dome of the capsule, a curved surface not quite a wall. It was crafted of finely burnished steel, worth more than many wealthy members of the ten species would see in a lifetime. He didn't know why that was important. He gasped for air.

The improvised stretcher with Dipara and the three who carried it went through first, turning awkwardly, then the two free crewmembers, holding bundles of supplies. The captain paused to survey her capsule sadly, a small pack slung over her shoulder, and Origon would have cursed her for the wasted effort if he could have. The Drain was not even two body lengths away. It must have eaten most of the far wall and the floor by now. Finally, the captain nodded to him, then pushed the doctor through in front of her. She disappeared through the portal. Origon's head turned slowly to the malevolent ball. There was only one feeble light left. So cold. So dark. The Drain buzzed in his mind, deconstructing the Symphony, threatening the portal—

His head turned, so slowly, back to the patch of blackness next to him, ringed with his colors. There was something he had to do. Reverse the change he made? Yes. He began to unknot the melding of this melody, his own, and the one at the portal grounds, but it felt like untying cobwebs with heavy mitts. His eyes drifted shut.

"No." The word was soft. He must have said it, for there was no one else here. He had to be on the *other* side of the portal. His shoulder slid along the steel, and he stumbled into the blackness. As he lost consciousness, he felt the portal come undone and his song flowed back into him.

* * *

"Ori."

Someone poked him and Origon sat up, the Symphony of the room springing into his head. The notes slipped away as he tried to craft a shield of air.

He realized who had called his name.

"Where am I?" he asked Rilan. She was still wearing the formal white dress she used for Council business. This close, he could see the olive green scrollwork highlighting its contours. She saw him looking and gave an ineffectual tug at the garment.

"Finally awake," she mumbled. Then, "I've managed to hold the questions off to let you rest, but they're getting insistent."

"How long have I been sleeping?" Origon smoothed back his crest, ran fingers down his moustache.

"Most of a day." Rilan crossed the room and pulled a window shade open. Morning light from a sun still low made Origon wince. When they had left in the capsule it had been almost lunch the day before. When had he last eaten?

"One of the Mayoral Guard was waiting for you at the portal grounds. The crew shared their stories, and how you saved them. Ksupara is still there, so evidently a giant...ball...didn't destroy it. All their stories agree, or the mayor and the other officials wouldn't have believed them." Rilan frowned. "Also, Aditit's asking for you." She completed her summary as Origon pushed himself up from the bed. He hastily grabbed for his robe on a nearby chair and yanked it over his head. Not that Rilan hadn't seen it all before, but it was just indecent to show off so much arm and leg. He stuffed his feet into his boots, lying by the bed.

"Yes, yes. I will be going to her first," Origon said, and yawned. He still felt lightheaded, and hadn't had nearly enough sleep or food. The Symphonies of Communication and Power were still there, flowing through his head, but he dared not try to change the music. He pushed down a stab of fear at the thought of his song failing, and that he might never make a complex change again. He kept his face neutral. Rilan followed him out the door, to make sure he didn't fall over, he suspected.

"We're in the Mayoral Hall," Rilan told him as they exited the room. Origon looked around. A guard stood on either side of the door, one female, heavyset but muscular, the other male and skinny almost to unhealthiness. Both were dressed in suits, but he could see the bulk of leather armor underneath the cloth. They each had scimitars at their sides.

The hall was decorated in the prominent architectural style of the wealthy Kashidur province, tall, fluted columns and glistening marble and quartz everywhere. Just as in the capsule, the Mayoral Hall was lit by carbon arc lamps, dim in the morning light. Normal bland Methiemum architecture. Could have used a splash of brighter colors.

Origon followed Rilan for a few steps, then looked back. "Why the guards?" No one would harm the hero of the first space flight. And they seemed familiar for some reason.

"The assassin," Rilan said, still walking. He could catch up to her easily with his long legs, so he watched the guards a moment. They looked steadily straight forward. He had almost forgotten about the assassin.

Something was bothering him about them, and he caught up to his old friend quickly. "Who are the guards answering to?" They made their way across the immense entry foyer of the Mayoral Hall, headed to a side room.

"Only the mayor," Rilan answered. "Nandara spared no expense in making sure the entire crew was protected when they returned. A couple are still in hospital, but the rest have retired to their homes, each with their own Mayoral Guard members to protect them." She threw a thumb over her shoulder. "One of these two was waiting at the portal for you." That explained the familiarity. "Old Nandara's a skinflint, but he's not taking any more chances with endangering his space-faring crew. He wants to show them off at all the award ceremonies Kashidur province will be holding. Can't do that if they're dead."

"He is to be a model of avuncular concern."

Rilan snorted. "You'll see."

Ten maji of the House of Communication were waiting for him in the side room, all Methiemum, of course. The species would have their own monopoly on traveling to their moon, at the start. Eventually, the location would get around to maji of other species, but the Methiemum might well construct a barrier by that point, to keep anyone with the location of the shuttle's landing spot from traveling farther into Methiemum space.

Origon nodded to Aditit Baska, a particularly old Methiemum female he had known socially for several decades, clothed in a boring dun colored dress. Her black hair had long since turned to a silvery gray, and her wrinkled and liverspotted face made her look more like a Kirian than a Methiemum. She and the others greeted him and Rilan politely. She was obviously the one in charge.

"Councilor. Thank you for retrieving Majus Cyrysi," Aditit said in her old, dry voice, then turned to him. "I'm glad you will finally share with us."

"I would have earlier, had I not left enough of my song in that ancestors-cursed capsule to nearly kill me," Origon told her. "I have been...recuperating since I returned. You must be cautious. There is to be a disturbance—a Drain—in the capsule. I am not knowing how big it is now, but I could not touch it. It had...it had no Symphony." He pulled on the end of his moustache, nervous. It pained him to even say that much.

Aditit pursed her lips. "This is hard to believe. I heard as much from the crew, though in layman's terms, of course."

"Of course," Origon agreed. They probably spouted off something about his magic being weak. Those who had not heard the Symphony did not understand.

"Astronomers have been searching Ksupara with their telescopes, but they cannot see the capsule, or its remains." Was that emphasis on the state of the landing? He wished Aditit had tried piloting that disgrace of a spaceship. "They must take the word of the crew."

"The Drain will have emerged from a hole in the capsule," Origon said. It must have somehow stopped growing after they left, or it would be eating into the surface of Ksupara, surely visible by telescope.

"There is nothing," Majus Baska repeated. "Our scientists postulate it was an effect of the differing conditions on Ksupara."

Origon looked to Rilan, who shrugged. "I heard the same." A few of the maji in the background were whispering together, shaking heads.

He suddenly remembered the urn he tripped over, so out of place. The Drain appeared directly over it. Could it possibly have...? Certainly not. For that to happen would mean some person or agency knew about the launch, had resources to sabotage it, and had the means to create such an anomaly. Such a conspiracy would have attracted the attention of the Council of the Maji by now, if not the Great Assembly of Species itself. Better by far if it was a strange natural phenomenon. If they could only get near it again, protected this time, they could study it. Aditit and the gathered maji were watching him expectantly, and he frowned.

"I am not knowing what happened to it, but it was a Drain, I tell you. The Symphony did not touch it. I will show you, though there is to be danger in opening a portal." Once they could see the thing, their disbelief would vanish. Fortunately the House of Communication could bring their own air supply with them. Majus Baska nodded in agreement.

He stepped close, pressing his long fingers to the woman's temples, and felt through the Symphony of Communication. The notes were shaky. Origon took in a deep breath, letting the wash of music pass him by for an instant. Then he snatched at the phrases, barely catching hold of the notes defining this place. They would not slip away.

His rest must have refreshed him enough. Yellow light dripped from his fingertips as he summoned the memory of the surface of the moon: the dusty landscape, the musty smell of used air, the equipment laying helter-skelter in the capsule, the feel of being light as a bird, and lastly, the menace of the Drain. He rolled the melody over to Aditit, not making changes, simply using his song to show the way the music would be arranged to bring both sides into accord. It was a complex set of coordinates, half mathematical and half intuition. That was why it was left to the House of Communication to disperse the location of new portals to the maji population.

Origon stepped back, regaining the portion of his song he had used, and felt the room spin. Rilan's strong hand caught his arm, and he clutched at her to keep from falling. He heard a couple of the other maji gasp, and let go as soon as he could. Majus Baska was staring at him.

"The capsule took much from you, didn't it?" she said.

"I will be better in a few days," Origon lied. "I simply am needing sleep." He couldn't stand in front of the group of maji any longer, not in his state. "If you will excuse me, I am sure there are to be many more questions coming from the inquisition into the failure of the capsule. I hope to get more rest soon. Do not be forgetting the scarcity of the atmosphere on Ksupara." Once they saw and believed, then they could discuss the phenomenon of the Drain.

"Of course," the older woman said. Origon made for the exit in a hurry, trying not to lean on Rilan. The embarrassment.

He was almost to the door, Rilan surreptitiously supporting him, when Aditit called out, and Origon turned tiredly to see what else she required. The old Methiemum was staring ahead of her, brows wrinkled more than usual.

"It doesn't work," she said flatly.

"What?" Origon almost forgot his weariness. His crest surged upward in surprise. It wasn't possible. He had translated coordinates for close to forty cycles, in remote and unexplored regions. He did *not* translate them incorrectly. That was a mistake apprentices made, and not more than once. If a portal even opened with incorrect instructions, it might be anywhere. The complex mathematics involved were in no way linear, and a small change could result in a portal opening on the other side of the universe.

"Were you compensating for the difference in pressure?" he asked, more for words to say than anything else.

Aditit gave him a withering look. "I have been doing this since before you were born, Majus. I have opened portals to vacuum before. There is a reason I am the senior Methiemum in the House of Communication."

"Of course, Majus Baska," Origon said, placating, raising a tired hand. "It is not my intention to imply any disrespect." He was her equal in the House of Communication, even if she was the senior Methiemum. She was probably upset about the loss of Teju, as was he. "We have both been working with portals for many cycles."

He took a deep breath, and let it whistle out through his pointed teeth. He gauged the stress of opening another portal, while holding a pressure difference in the air around him. How much more of his song could he spare? But he owed it to these other maji to check his own portal. He knew the location was not incorrect.

He closed his eyes, but Rilan grabbed his elbow, swinging him around to face her. "Transfer the location to me," she whispered. "You can do that much, but Shiv desert me if you can do more without collapsing. I'm not letting you open a portal in your state."

Origon thought about arguing, and gave up. Rilan was far too stubborn, and furthermore, she was right. Rilan was House of Healing, so she could not change the air density, but the other maji in the room could easily hold the pressure difference at bay. He planted his feet to keep from swaying and grasped at the notes again. He was only showing how and where to make the portal, not actually making it. Otherwise the Symphony would not have let him do the same thing twice in such a short time. Wearily, he passed the location again, yellow light flaring, then leaned back against the wall to recover while she tried the portal. He was weaker than the newest apprentice.

Rilan had her eyes screwed shut, one hand out. No portal opened. A halo of white and green buzzed around her hand.

Her eyes snapped open. "It won't work," she said. "There's too much resistance."

Origon considered, following to the one possible conclusion. It must be the Drain. Ancestors only knew what the landscape looked like on Ksupara after the Drain stopped eating. His coordinates, what he experienced, was no longer accurate.

Once before, many cycles ago, an earthquake marred a portal ground on Kiria, plunging half of it underground. He had traveled there over land to re-establish the melody of the place for the maji. The Symphony was forgiving, with respect to portals. Rain would fall, plants would grow, air and earth would move slightly. Still the portals opened. The only way they would not was if the location of the portal changed beyond recognition. The capsule must be completely destroyed. And that meant any evidence of the urn was destroyed as well. He would have to start investigating it somehow else. At a later time.

He explained his thoughts, leaving out any mention of the urn. That would be his private investigation.

Aditit *humphed* after he was finished. "Unlikely," she said. "But possible. Still, I trust your skill enough to know you would hardly give us the wrong coordinates. I must take this to Councilor Freshta."

Rilan raised an eyebrow. Origon knew she was sick of other councilmembers pushing her to the sidelines. If it had spread to the maji population as well...

"*I* will take this to the entire Council, not simply the head of the House of Communication," she said. "Unless you've forgotten my own place on the Council."

"No offense meant, dear," Aditit told Rilan. Origon could see his friend's back stiffen through the white dress. "Of course you should take this to the Council."

"I will come with you," Origon said hastily. It was his discovery—he should get the credit for it.

"After we meet with the mayor and the city elders, of course," Rilan said.

He grimaced. "Of course."

Aditit tapped her fingers together. "Then I will work here on Methiem. I have many tempers to soothe." She turned to the group of maji around her, assigning orders.

* * *

Origon watched the room full of well-dressed Methiemum dignitaries, bankers, and politicians. They watched him back; a sea of gray and black. They had been in the midst of a vigorous discussion when he and Rilan entered. Fortunately, they stopped so he could address them. He smoothed down the bright orange and yellow striped fabric of his robe, picking small bits of dust out of the blue scrollwork. The other species never had enough color in their clothes. He was standing next to Rilan at the center of a vast crescent of bench seats, occupying most of the area of the Mayoral debate chamber. Hanging scrolls and banners glittered with gold and red, and the walls shone white in the morning sun through a line of windows.

The Methiemum were primarily traders, and Origon gathered many had wagered significant amounts of their wealth on the success of the venture. No self-respecting Kirian would be caught dead gambling money on such a profound and philosophically important event as exploration of space.

"We heard you were taken ill after your voyage, Majus Cyrysi," a corpulent figure in the middle of the sea said. His voice was loud, used to public speaking. It was the same person who had "launched" the capsule—Mayor Nandara. "Still, Kashidur City owes you a large debt of gratitude. You seem much recovered. Maybe enough to give us your account?"

Origon glared at the assembled Methiemum, trying not to sway on his feet. The arrogance! "I am not much recovered at all," he countered, "as your capsule nearly killed me on the way to Ksupara. The design was to be so terrible it could only have been purpose-built to suck away the ability of a majus."

As he expected, the sea of gray and black began muttering and gesturing to each other. He looked to Rilan, who had a long-suffering expression on her face.

"You could at least try to make this easier instead of harder, Ori," she said. The noise of the room was enough that no one else would be able to hear her. He ignored her, waiting until the clamor died down.

"At least your noble sacrifice results in a new state of affairs for the Methiemum, and indeed for all species of the Great Assembly," Mayor Nandara said. It was all political bluster. Origon gave the room his best toothy smile—the one most Methiemum found disturbing. He did not like this mayor. Not that he liked many individuals who led power-hungry groups.

"Alas, I just discussed this with your Majus Baska. It seems the calamity which was to be endangering your crew is also preventing a portal to be made to Ksupara. You will have to commission another space capsule, I am afraid."

This time he heard Rilan sigh before the uproar swept away the sound. She leaned close to his ear. "This is why you don't get invited to share your new findings with the Council."

The mayor finally managed to intimidate the others into silence. "Our best majus," Origon raised an eyebrow at that, "was killed before he could even get in the capsule. We have heard reports it was one of the Sureriaj who killed him, perhaps simply an individual, but possibly with other interests behind him." Origon watched the sea of hungry faces closely. He had never seen the Methiemum as xenophobic, but as the sole alien in the room, he felt as if he was being judged, and found wanting. "The Sureriaj may be jealous of our technical abilities. Others may be as well. No offense meant to you, Majus Cyrysi, but you have seen the guards I must post to keep us safe. Isn't there any other magic you can do so we do not have to go through this effort again?"

"There is not," Origon told them, now wary. "The location was irretrievably lost. I, or some other majus, would have to again be walking on Ksupara. However, surely now the species have seen such a capsule can be built, they will be willing to help build another? You have paved the way for them." He didn't mention the Drain. That was a matter for the maji.

He looked around. Even Rilan beside him was quiet, her mouth pursed.

The mayor laughed—a stage laugh, meant to carry to others, but a laugh nonetheless. "The Sureriaj will not help us, as they have already sent one to stop us. Yes, there could be others of the ten species who wish to help, but as you yourself say, majus, none of your community would wish to pilot such a ship again."

"You may be correct," Origon said, but his mind was spinning. There was something wrong here—off. The mayor was making too many connections, too quick to point a finger at the Sureriaj. The emaciated face of the assassin popped into Origon's mind. The figure had been shooting at Teju. What had he thought at the time? The eyes. Could it even be possible? Was the mayor so corrupt? He barely kept his crest neutral. "And you must be excusing me now. New information has come up."

He ignored Rilan's grunt of surprise as he took hold of her arm and towed her from the chamber. The mayor's voice boomed behind him to stop, but he paid no attention. The guards at the door stepped in front of him, but Origon let Rilan's arm go long enough to grab at slippery notes defining the air currents in the room. The day was warm, and he took a little heat from all over the room with the House of Power, adjusting notes so that heat and air built a barrier between the guards and him. As he used his song to craft the change, he stumbled forward, spent, turning the movement into a headlong run from the room. He plowed into the wall across from the chamber, using it to change his direction as Rilan caught up to him.

"What are you doing?" she hissed, but he didn't answer. He reversed his change to the Symphony, sighing as his song flowed back to him and his strength grew slightly. He might be able to make it to his room without collapsing.

"Ori—what?" Origon stumbled on, up a spiral staircase, leaning heavily on the carved wooden bannister. "Shiv's kneecaps," he heard her mutter behind him, but she followed. He knew how to spin a mystery to keep her attention. He needed her for this.

Origon was breathing like a lathered cartbeast when he reached his room. He wouldn't even have been winded a few days ago. He was weak, and it was Nandara's fault.

The two guards were still there, and he gestured to them as he came closer, gasping before he was able to speak.

"It is to be...an emergency. Come...with me quickly." He opened the door, feeling the guards turn in behind him. Rilan must be in the rear. Perfect.

He reached his bed and turned, resisting the urge to fall into it. Indeed, the two guards were in front, Rilan in back. "Close the door," he told her, and she reached for the handle. Origon felt for the Symphony of both his houses, gauging if his song was strong enough to make the changes. He tried for the notes of the music of Communication, failed. He would be no help here.

But he could hear the connections between the two guards with the House of Power. They knew each other, comrades in arms, but there wasn't the close connection he associated with good friends or close family members. More evidence.

"Ori, what in the name of all the gods are you doing? You blew off the mayor of Kashidur, by Shiv's holy nose! I know you like to make sure you're in the middle of everyth—"

"Do you still trust me, Rilan?" he cut in.

"—ing." She stared at him a moment. "Yes."

"I am knowing where the assassin is." He carefully watched the guards as he spoke. They both reacted in surprise. The larger of the two only looked ready. The skinny one, the guard who must have starved himself to be that unhealthily thin, took a very slight step back, hand straying to his scimitar. Good.

Origon looked back to Rilan, straight in her eyes, then flicked his glance to the skinny guard. Back to her. "The assassin hid in the crowd because he was not to be Sureriaj. He was Methiemum."

He saw Rilan's eyes widen as she understood him, at the same moment the skinny guard drew his scimitar in a slice toward Origon's throat. Rilan, head of the House of Healing, youngest member of the Council, was even faster. One hand flew out, olive green and white flinging from it like droplets of water. Origon stood firm. He couldn't have dodged if he wanted to. Rilan's hand touched the guard's shoulder just as the scimitar connected with Origon's robe. The expression on the skinny guard's face changed from determined to pained as his arm gave out, dropping as if he had no control of it. The scimitar skimmed down Origon's robe and clattered to the floor at his feet. The guard followed, crumpling. Origon brushed away the wrinkle of fabric at his shoulder where the sword had started to cut.

"We still make a good team," he told Rilan. The other guard had her scimitar half out of its scabbard, but slowly eased it back in place with a metallic hiss, taking care to make sure both of her hands were in view. Origon nudged the limp body at his feet with one boot.

"This is one of the Mayoral Guard," Rilan told him. She looked to the larger one. "You wouldn't do anything without the mayor's approval, would you?"

The guard looked torn for a moment, her eyes taking in the body on the floor, then back up, mouth firm. "No, Majus. All the Mayoral Guard are of the highest character." She looked to the body again. "Almost all. He was a new hire."

Origon felt once again for the Symphonies of both Communication and Power. Observing the notes took much less strength than changing them. He could hear the connection between the two guards fading, notes of Power dwindling to piano, then silent. A whisper of the guard's last sentence still echoed very quietly in the music of Communication. The notes had the feeling of truth in them, the tones harmonious. Not a certainty by any means, but a good indication.

"Are you willing to be staying here and keeping your former associate from leaving?" he asked the guard. The woman nodded once, sharply.

"Good." He turned to Rilan. "I believe we are to be due a meeting with Mayor Nandara."

Rilan tugged her white dress straight. "I believe you are correct."

They found the debating chamber emptying of officials and representatives. Origon pushed through the flow, wishing he could spare a little of his song to force a path of air through them.

Mayor Nandara was there, talking to members of his cabinet. When he saw them coming, Nandara dismissed his advisors, who quickly exited the room.

"I see you finally made some time for me, Majus," the mayor said, disapproving. Origon felt his crest ruffling in annoyance.

"I have made time. Now I am finished with the assassin who killed Teju, I have plenty of time for you." The cabinet members were out of earshot by now, leaving the vast hall.

Mayor Nandara's heavy face drew down in a frown. "What do you mean?"

"I think you know," Rilan said. "The Mayoral Guard answers only to you."

"It does, but what does that have to do with anything?" Nandara pulled a handkerchief out and mopped at his receding hairline, where he was beginning to sweat. His other hand went to the small of his back, as if it ached.

"*Your* Mayoral Guard, that one who was dressing as a Sureri to hide, was just trying to kill me a few moments ago."

Nandara's eyebrows went up in surprise. "How awful! I shall be sure to investigate this shocking—"

"Stop it, Nandara," Rilan cut in. "We know it was you. I, a Council member, know it was you. What was the reason for sabotaging your own space program? Money? A rival?"

"Why, for Shiv's sake, would I sabotage—" the mayor started.

"You are knowing I am of the House of Communication, Mayor," Origon said. He spared a glance around. The room was empty but for them. "I can tell a lie when I see one." Not completely true, but the mayor didn't know that.

"I will be taking this to the Council," Rilan added. "I witnessed firsthand your guard attack Majus Cyrysi."

The mayor slumped, his heavy shoulders sagging. He wiped his forehead again, then stared off toward the door of the debate chamber, probably wondering if he could escape. Origon was about to add to their accusations when he finally spoke.

"You maji hold us back from progress. If it wasn't for you, we would already be traveling through space instead of through your portals."

"Yet I was to be the one to—" Origon began, but Nandara cut him off with a swift motion of the handkerchief in one hand. The other came out from behind his back with a small pistol. Origon felt his crest rise in surprise. Rilan straightened.

"The maji are helpful in limited ways, but more often than not they are relics. Oh yes, stepping through a doorway of blackness to another place is easy, but you people also take away the challenges that force us to advance. Thirty cycles ago, I would never have thought to threaten one of you, let alone two. But with this," he motioned with the gun, making sure his arc covered the two of them, "I have the advantage in any negotiations."

"You can only take on one of us with that," Rilan gestured to the weapon with her chin. "You'll have to reload in between shots, and the maji will still have the advantage." She seemed calm, but Origon knew that was a mask over the furious storm raging in her.

"Wrong again," Nandara said, taking a small step forward, pressing them back. "Progress and new technology, remember? With this weapon I can fire up to five times without having to reload. Imagine how far through space we could travel, without you holding us back." Origon's mind raced to the assassination. There had been three shots in quick succession. More proof they were connected, as if he needed it.

"Now, let us proceed to this supposed assassin, and take care of the matter." Nandara waggled the gun for them to walk ahead of him.

The short walk up the stairs to Origon's room was nearly devoid of people. Now the meeting was over, the other members had scattered. A few servants ghosted through the corridors, but when one passed, Nandara stepped in, hiding the gun he used to push them onward. But not too close. The House of Healing functioned best by touch. Origon thought Rilan might still turn and grab the Mayor by his cravat, whatever the consequences.

The female guard was still there, watching over the skinny one, who was just regaining consciousness. The larger guard straightened to attention as she caught sight of the mayor.

Nandara shot her.

The gun was strangely silent, and Origon, shocked, absently noted the long cylinder attached to the muzzle. A dampener of some sort? Yes, the melody of the Symphony of Communication agreed with his assessment. The explosion's sound waves were not nearly as high in amplitude as they should be.

He watched, helpless, as the guard crumpled and the mayor turned the gun back on them. The guard fell as her former fellow rose to his feet.

"Forgive me sir," the assassin said to the mayor. "I was not able to take out the second majus, as you commanded."

"And see what a mess you have left," Nandara said. He gestured sharply to Rilan, who was creeping closer. Origon had hoped she would be able to affect the mayor on the way to the room, but no luck. He moved with her, close to the assassin.

"Kashidur province went practically bankrupt from funding the shuttle," the mayor said. "We had to make sure it paid back our investors in time."

"You would be getting many new minerals from space," Origon told him.

Nandara waved a fat hand—not his gun hand. "Too late, too late. The banking guild wanted real money, and soon. They've gone to adjust their accounts already. We had to guarantee the success of the mission."

"By shooting the majus in charge?" Rilan stepped forward, but stopped as the gun's muzzle settled on her torso.

The mayor had a strange smile on his face. "Either success, or have the mission fail so utterly that it must be someone else's fault. No one was supposed to live to tell tales. It would have gone smoothly if this idiot hadn't messed up." Nandara nodded toward the assassin, whose face was slowly falling, as if he just now realized on which side of the gun he stood. "I could have gotten the Sureriaj back for that business a few years ago. We still have outbreaks of the Shudders, and a low birth rate in four cities."

"Shiv's spleen," Rilan swore, turning to Origon. "Ori, I *told* them you would be watching. That you were like Teju, but more experienced." She eyed the mayor. "And how did you know about the Sureriaj? It was supposed to be a secret."

Origon frowned at her. He had no idea what they were talking about. But the mayor ignored Rilan. "The Sureri assassin was an extra benefit. The design of the shuttle would show how the maji hold us back—"

"You egg-sucking son of a turtle." Origon glared at the mayor. Only his exhaustion kept him from changing the Symphony of Communication to squeeze this excuse for a person like a grape. That and he wasn't sure he was faster than the gun. "The shuttle was meant to be taking away my song. You were to be keeping me from interfering."

"And *he* was waiting for you, alone." Rilan flicked a finger to the assassin, next to her. "Ori, he would have killed you, weak as you were. And if he missed Teju, if Teju flew the capsule and returned, the guard would have been waiting for *him*, instead." She stabbed a glare at the mayor. "You have conspired to kill at least two maji. The Council *will* hear about this, Nandara."

The mayor raised an eyebrow. He wouldn't dare shoot a member of the Council of the Maji, would he? Better to distract.

"The only reason I was to be saved was the Drain," Origon said. "It threw a mallet into your works, did it not? The crew was not supposed to be coming through with me."

"A mess, as I said," Nandara told them. "I don't know where the damnable thing came from, but fortunately, you have found the assassin, who, in the resulting confusion, managed to shoot and kill two more maji before turning the gun on himself. Never fear, I can still set this all back on track and get rid of the interference of you maji."

"That is not—" was all Origon got out before the next shot took the assassin in the chest.

He grabbed the opportunity presented. He had recovered enough energy to control a gust of air. As the gun swiveled toward Rilan, it went farther than the mayor expected, pushed aside.

The rest was up to his friend's exceptional reflexes. Rilan saw the opening, as he knew she would, and lunged forward, knocking the mayor's arm aside, the bullet discharging with a *pop* into the wall of the room. The mayor's suddenly nerveless arm dropped the contraption and it clattered to the ground. A knuckle to his temple and Nandara dropped like a sack of grubs.

"I'm getting slow," Rilan complained. "Ten years ago, I would have disarmed him with no problem."

"Must be all the time sitting around with the Council," Origon observed innocently. "Dulls the reflexes." He bent to the assassin, who was gasping feebly. The man was choking words out—Origon heard whispers of it in the Symphony of Communication, but couldn't quite make it out.

"The holy...holy ves...vessel...made its...voyage." The light went out of the man's fevered eyes. Well, Origon was not one to judge others' beliefs.

"Now what?" He was exhausted.

"What in Shiv's holy earlobes was Nandara planning?" Rilan asked. "Keeping the maji out of the picture? Who does he think will open a portal to get to his new resources?"

"Taking the challenge out," Origon mused. "Rilan, do you suppose it is to be possible the maji do *too* much for others? By the ancestor's eggs. I was knowing the Methiemum were crafty, but this—"

"Why would they not want help from the Council and the maji?" Rilan countered. "The other species would jump ahead of us if we had to build a new shuttle every time we wanted to go into space."

"Unless the mayor planned to woo other species to be joining him in removing maji from space travel." Origon could almost, *almost*, see why. It was the same reason he traveled the homeworlds—the challenge of doing it himself. But surely not the right way to go about it.

"Whatever the reason, Nandara will not be so easy to take down, even with this evidence," Rilan told him. "His solicitors will argue this case before the Assembly and the Council of the Maji." Rilan growled. "*Idiot.* He could have done this cleanly. The Methiemum economy is already the biggest of the ten species. With the new minerals from space and the new trade agreements, it would have been unstoppable, and they would only have paid a few tariffs and fees to the maji to create a new series of portals. But now..." Rilan's expression promised retribution. "Even my own people must be held responsible for assassinating one of the maji. No amount of profit is worth it."

"This is not to be just the mayor's plan, is it?" Origon asked.

Rilan shook her head. "Sometimes I'm not proud to be a Methiemum. Believe me, they meant to do this, exactly this. They wanted a new source of wealth, but thought they could take the maji out of the equation at the same time, and even coerce other species to do the same." She shivered. "Maybe we are becoming outdated."

"Not completely. The Drain foiled their plan," Origon mused. "A positive result, for an object so destructive. Without a majus, the crew would never have escaped." He pounded one fist into his other hand. "I must be studying the phenomenon more. Where does it come from? Was there some catalyst on Ksupara?" He nudged the assassin's leg with a boot. "If only this 'holy vessel' had not made its voyage yet."

Rilan looked askance at him. "What's that supposed to mean?"

Origon shrugged. "His last words. I assumed it was one of your religions."

"Not one I know of." Rilan was silent a moment. "You don't suppose he meant—"

Origon looked down at the body. "The mayor as much as admitted the Drain was not to be his doing. But what if the assassin had other orders?" He ran his fingers down his moustache in thought. A holy vessel? Unholy, more like.

"Rilan," he began, "there is one more thing." He described the urn, and how out of place it seemed with the rest of the supplies. His old friend listened, her face tightening.

"The very act of creating this void in the Symphony keeps us from traveling to its location by portal," Rilan said. "As if the thing was designed to prevent maji from investigating it. Where did it come from? How do we study something like that?"

"We do not," Origon said. "Not until we return to Ksupara." He paused, as an awful thought occurred to him. Where *had* the urn come from?

"What is it?" Rilan must have seen his expression change.

"Or unless another Drain forms, elsewhere." Now her face mirrored the horror he felt.

"Vish preserve us, I hope not," Rilan said quietly. "Let this be an isolated event. Are you sure it was the urn that created the void?"

"Ah...no," Origon admitted. "It could have been a natural event, or perhaps it was to be a reaction to what was in the urn." No way to tell now, with the sole person who might have been connected lying dead at his feet.

"There will be a second capsule built, now it's proven possible." Rilan gestured vaguely with one hand, encompassing all of Methiem. "We will discover more evidence the next time we get to Ksupara."

"Then I am supposing we must include a majus on the flight," Origon told her. "Though it will not be me." He looked out the room's lone tall window. He could not see Ksupara in the day, but it was out there, waiting to be explored, as were the moons and solar systems of the other homeworlds. Even if the maji did not help, the ten species would go there eventually. And he would learn more about the Drain, one day.

"Then we must leave the mystery of your void for now, and hope there's no need to explore it further." Rilan grunted as she began to heave the corpulent mayor to a sitting position. "For now, we have to deal with him. Help me out. We'll bring him to the Council before he wakes and runs to his solicitors."

"Can you do that?" Origon tried to remember the councilor's powers in an emergency situation.

"I have some privileges, even if the other councilors ignore me as often as not. Come with me back to the Nether, Ori," Rilan told him. "We'll take the mayor and his plot to the Council now, today. And you could stay with me while you recuperate. It's been a long time since we had a real chance to talk, and your apartment is probably full of cobwebs and spiders."

"Too long," Origon agreed. "And what of the Drain? Shall we be discussing it with the Council as well?"

Rilan hesitated, holding the unconscious mayor's form up. "They'll learn of it," she said. "But maybe best not to press the issue for now. We have to hope this is an isolated incident."

Of course she was correct. Rilan's position with the Council was tenuous enough without wild stories about voids that lacked the Symphony. She had been busy on the Council while he had been traveling the homeworlds. He could aid her out now he was back. Origon helped her lift the mayor. They would alert others to the mess in the room, make sure none of Nandara's associates arranged the evidence against them. Origon would let his song regrow, and with that new music, discover what, or who, was behind the Drain.

The Symphony Eater
1003 A.A.W.

Nara Reyhorer, known to his friends as Rey, trudged through the House of Potential. It was his second ten-day here, but Majus Kheena had set him manual labor every day he had been in the Nether, in addition to his studies as an apprentice. First it was moving boxes out of his room, then painting and cleaning the apartment until it nearly shone. *Not what I was expectin' to learn. I want to change the Symphony, not cart gadgets around and do housework. If I wanted more chores, I could have stayed home pullin' the spines out of the garden for the parents.* The Sureriaj people didn't often leave home without a good reason, and he wished he was back with his mother and fathers. Again.

Majus Kheena was in his living room, poring over a set of papers filled with calculations. As far as Rey could tell, most of what Majus Kheena did was calculate. His Sathssn mentor had his hood back, as usual, displaying the tufts of fine dark hair poking between his scales. The Majus was muttering to himself, something about energy nets and flow coordinates. Rey cleared his throat.

"We're supposed to be havin' a lesson shortly?" He had discovered it was best to interrupt Majus Kheena at his work if he wanted to learn anything.

"Three measures more than the last iteration." Majus Kheena pointed a gloved finger toward the other seat at the table without looking up. "In a moment, we shall begin."

The Majus bent back over his papers, scribbling something with a fine pen. Every few moments, his disturbing slitted eyes would flick to one side or the other, staring at nothing. He tapped the dark green scales around his mouth with the other end of the pen, then his eyes flicked to Rey.

"Today, I will get nothing else done on this proposal. We may as well begin," Majus Kheena sat back. "Energy transfer is the basis of the Symphony of Potential, but our house, it is different from the other houses of the maji. It can even manipulate the other Symphonies to some extent. We hear how energy moves from place to place. This, it is not as limiting as hearing the music defining the realm of communication or strength. I think only the House of Healing comes close to our, ah, potential, if the phrase will be pardoned." Majus Kheena hissed laughter.

Rey just kept from rolling his eyes. He was used to the majus going on about how brilliant the House of Potential's aspect of the Grand Symphony was. "Yer've said as much before. We take the music from one place and transfer it elseways," he gestured from side to side with his hands. "I've had this lesson before."

The majus was already shaking his head. At least Majus Kheena was one of the Southern Coalition Sathssn, which meant he was a bit freer with his clothing. He often wore his hood down, and sometimes went without gloves. It meant Rey could make eye contact with his mentor, and see the Snakey's expressions.

"This, it is not so simple as you make it." He picked up his pen, rolling it back and forth between his hands. "I see as much from the calculations you have performed for me. You do not think of complexities."

Rey grimaced. He could do his sums, but Majus Kheena manipulated equations with a finesse that made everything seem so simple. "It's the Systems. I don't yet ken 'em. We canna hear the music of the other houses, but yer say we can still move along their melodies, whether it be the House of Power, or Strength, or Grace. Then we somehow bodge together a System out of 'em, holdin' things in place."

The majus waved one of his papers in the air. "Exactly. There are even ways to change the music of the other houses—no, do not sigh, the correct calculations define such processes..."

"If I could just see what the blasted things mean," Rey interrupted. He hadn't meant to speak out of turn, but scribbles and equations had little relation to the beautiful symphonies in his mind. Ever since he was young, listening to the classical operastanzas of Grand-Dame Moreya, he knew he could manipulate the Grand Symphony that underlay the universe. Instead he was writing out numbers and symbols.

Majus Kheena hissed to himself for a moment. "So. Maybe in this, I have catered to my skills rather than yours. To learn energy transfer properly..." He trailed off, looking upward. Rey leaned toward his mentor. "This task, I was saving it for myself, merely for nostalgia, but I believe you need a practical application to further your training."

Rey blinked. "Practical?"

"Would you rather more equation work, then?"

"'Course not." Something practical was exactly what he needed.

"Good," Majus Kheena dropped the pen and thumped the table with a gloved thumb. "This moment, we can go down to the cellar."

"The...cellar?" Rey had envisioned somewhere further afield.

"Yes. We have a rodent problem."

* * *

Rey hadn't even known the House of Potential had a cellar. They left the apartment, and traveled farther into the maze of corridors between maji residences. The low, sprawling house was connected by a series of backdoors and corridors to Imperium University, which was built on the back of the house like a shell on the back of a desert crawler. But rather than going to the university, Majus Kheena led Rey down a set of passages he had never seen before. The normally austere corridors turned even more utilitarian; numerous pipes and cables crawled up the walls, many softly glowing with the rust brown of the House of Potential. Rey examined the cables disappearing through the ceiling. Many supplied the Systems that ran through the houses of the maji and even out into the Imperium, supplying things like water, light, and stored motion—used to power geared devices. The transfer of phrases of the Symphony was integral to his house.

"The cellar, it is down here," Majus Kheena said. His all-black garb made his form hard to follow in the sputtering light from the overhead tubes, but at least it reflected off his scaled head. The Southern Coalition—a small free nation—eschewed the most rigid traditions of the Sathssn theocracy and the Cult of Form. Even so, Rey would never understand why the Snakeys all wore the same thing. It was blasted hard to tell them apart when they kept their cowls up—and most of them did.

"I didnae know this was here. What do yer keep in yer cellar?" Rey peered down a shaky set of wooden stairs.

"Down there, we have the large energy transfer System. It funnels many of the notes contributed by the maji to those Systems the notes power. The musical phrases play in contrast to the harmonic filter the House of Potential installed to break the phrases into component diatonic scales. They intersperse with the chromatic measures that keep the music from—"

"And that's where yer little trouble is," Rey broke in. The majus would go on all day about scales and musical efficiency if Rey didn't butt in.

Kheena humpfed, but changed topics. "Some of the notes, they are not making the transition to the new melody they are to integrate with. We have had complaints from the other houses about interruptions of power and water." He paused. "And supposedly, the voice amplification system cut out during one of Speaker Humbano's speeches about her new arts funding proposal."

At least I know the reason this is suddenly a problem. "So yer need a plumber, is the basics of what yer sayin'," Rey said. *First a handyman...*

"I have a proposal that needs finishing," Majus Kheena corrected. "Lots of tricky phase transformations to do. These, they could also be good practice for you instead." ·

Rey waved one hand in the air, eager to avoid more sums. "No offence meant to yer. Plumbin' is a noble occupation."

"Good. Then your job, it is to find out why the transfer of forces is being interrupted and fix it."

"Yer think rodents are stealin' yer notes?" Rey asked. "Majus rats?"

Kheena wobbled a gloved hand at him. "Yes. Not exactly. This, it is something a bit rarer, if I am correct. As I mentioned, I was planning to take care of the problem myself, though last time..." He broke off, and Rey narrowed his eyes at his mentor. "This task, it requires one who prefers solutions of a physical nature. You will see. Go on now, and me, I will get back to my calculations. Let me know when you finish." He gestured down. Rey sighed and entered the dim staircase.

* * *

Rey wasn't sure what he expected to see, but it wasn't the mechanical construct down the stairs. It was taller than him, covered in a mass of interconnected gears and spindles. Rey had heard of computing machines, of course, though they were rare. This one looked old—older than him—and was buzzing and clanking to itself in the glow from an overhead light.

Rey reached a hand out, hesitantly. Contrary to what he expected, there was no shock from the machine, though it was warm to the touch. It glowed with the rust brown of the House of Potential—something only folks who could hear the Symphony could see. Pipes ran off in all directions, smelling faintly of ozone.

He listened to the chords of the Symphony. The music was intricate, with scales layered in ascending complexity until the result was an incomprehensible block of notes. They carried the music he couldn't hear—that of the other houses. Like many Systems, the melody was thrumming, regulated and mechanical; an artificial piece of music rather than the naturally occurring rhythms that made up everyday objects.

Then the glow, and the volume of the music, dipped. Rey jerked his hand back. Had he bodged something up? But he hadn't changed anything. If it wasn't him, then...Rey looked around the machine.

There was something organic in back, a mass of multicolored fur and scales hanging from one of the pipes that left the machine. There were legs, dangling in the air. The head was fastened to the pipe in some way. Rey poked at the thing with one finger and it dropped off, screeched, and scurried away.

Well, that was flippin' easy. Rey was slightly insulted, not that he hoped the critter would try to bite him or some such. "Solutions of a physical nature" indeed. As soon call an exterminator. He peered in the direction the thing had run off. The creature must sense the dense layers of the Symphony—Majus Kheena said they were rare—and the notes passing through the machine conduit acted as what? Bait? A tasty treat for the critter?

He picked his way around the clanking machine, but the thing was no longer in the room, as far as he could tell. If he failed to stop it from returning, and one of Speaker Humbano's speeches got cut off again, she might come down personally to the House of Potential, and then everything would simply slide downhill to him. Even he had heard of the respected Etanela Speaker. She had been around forever, and some folks said she could get an audience with the Effature in seconds flat. Could he get drummed out of the maji? He had heard of maji leaving, but that was a rarity. *Best tie this little knotty problem up tight.*

He'd not yet caught the method to create a System—that arrangement that held musical phrases in place even when a majus wasn't messing with them. His calculations always equaled out on paper, but that was nothing like changing the chaotic fractals of the Symphony.

If I want to keep that furry blighter away, it's got to be a System. Nothing else would last long enough. Rey rubbed suddenly damp hands along his pants, trying to dry out the little hairs that covered his fingers.

He listened to the melody passing through the chamber, then waved an arm across a wall. Sterile. He looked around. The machine's gears created kinetic energy, reflected in the buzzing chords of the Symphony.

Cannae take so much from the machine, though. From what the old Snakey says, it supplies half of High Imperium's Systems.

There was nothing to fall, or create a source of energy where he could transfer the notes from that musical phrase to another. The House of Potential had to have a pool of notes from which to transfer, especially for creation of a System. He was practically at the base of the Nether. If the cellar was any lower, the machine would have rested on crystal instead of the wood planking under his feet. He stamped one boot, listening to the short echo.

Rey shook his head. He supposed he could jump up and down for a time, and build up heat in his body. Technically, he could use that chaos of notes as a source, but that might be a permanent change, and he had no wish to lose his notes, if he could help it.

He looked around the room again, including behind the clanking machine. There was a hole in the wall, presumably where the critter was getting in, and in front of it was a small wood crate, as if someone had tried to block the hole. It was pushed out at an angle. *Not doin' any good here.*

It would have to do. There was one source of potential energy in the room—the stairs. If he lugged the crate up the shaky steps leading back up to the world of the living, he could at least throw it back down and steal some of its notes as it fell.

Rey humphed the bulky crate along behind him, hearing the sparks and trills of the friction between the crate and the floor. Not enough notes yet. He climbed the stairs, and the song of the crate's potential gained notes with every step. At the top of the stairs, he paused, and dove into the Symphony.

It was a riot of music, as usual. The clanking machine was the major player of course, dominating any and all melodies nearby. Rey dug down, ignoring the main theme until he found the source of high velocity eighth notes that was in the crate. Then he threw it across the room.

As the crate tumbled through the air, Rey took notes from its song, using a few of his own to guide the transition of the energy. Grace notes and trills dissolved, and the pounding beat slowed to a steady thrum. The crate fell in an abbreviated arc. His throw should have carried it across the room, but it tumbled to the floor less than halfway across. Those extra notes buzzed in Rey until he thought he would burst. Multiple keys played in his head at once, measures overlapping each other.

Now came the hard part—converting that chaos of notes to a System. He attempted to arrange the extra notes from the crate into a new pattern, transferring the energy to a new form—in this case a barrier of force that would cover the hole in the wall—and keep anything from getting through.

The equations were not so hard, but they didn't take into account reality. Rey fought the tide of music, using a few of his notes to translate measures into linked musical phrases. Each System took one of the majus' notes to anchor, a permanent investment from a member of the House of Potential. Rey tied the buzzing energy from the crate into a sloppy package and ran down the stairs, thrusting one hand toward the wall before the thing could collapse into dissonant notes. He didn't make it.

With a bright flash, his anchor, the notes used to guide the melodies, and the melodies themselves dissipated into energy in its most primal form—heat and light.

"Bah." Rey covered his eyes against the tiny explosion, clenching teeth against the unpleasant pulling and tearing as his notes were lost. They'd take a few days to grow back, fueled by his experiences.

Rey leaned against the wall, breathing heavily. "This is what I get for days of calculatin' rather than practicin'." The old Snakey did love his equations.

Nothing for it but to try again. The critter's hole wasn't going anywhere and now he wanted to make this System work.

Rey retrieved the crate, lugged it up the stairs, and tried again. This time he wove his notes *through* the music defining the kinetic energy leeched from the crate. The resulting music was tighter, more even, but as he reached out to tie the anchor note to the wall a measure slipped and slid sideways, making a hash of dissonant scales.

"Oof." Rey blinked away the afterimage of the eruption. When he lifted a hand, it shook slightly. More of his notes lost. He'd sleep well tonight.

Maybe he could just put the crate back against the hole—that would keep the little thing out for a time, at least. He bent down and peered into the hole. It was deeper than he expected, and somewhere in the back, something glassy caught a glint of reflection. A faint chittering echoed from inside the hole.

"So yer not far off, are yer?" The crate would only work for a few minutes against the determined creature. Were those claw marks on the bricks? So, even if he boarded the hole over, he had a feeling it would be back in a few days.

Rey thought. What was making the System go unstable? He looked toward the clanking machine, listened to the confusion of melodies arranged over each other. Of course. He hadn't factored in how the machine processed incoming music. The wall was close enough for the machine to strip the notes guiding his barrier of energy. *Mayhaps I could spend a few more notes, preventin' the Systems from overlapping.* If it didn't work, he'd lose even more notes, but if it did, he'd be finished up with the majus' little task before mealtime.

Once more, he lugged the increasingly battered crate up the stairs, threw it, and took the notes describing its energy. This time, he knew how to form the measures, how to smooth out the tempo. He took more notes from the core of his being, formed them into a solid wall of sixteenth notes, a repeating motif around his System. *I hope by the Greatmother this works. If no, the majus might find me passed out down here, if he even remembers to take a break from his calculatin'.*

Back behind the machine, Rey reached down, taking the anchor note from the song that made up his being. This time, when he pressed his fingertip to the floor in front of the hole, the music stolen from the crate attached—raw and vibrating like a plucked string—to his note. It formed a ward of pure energy blocking the hole, suitable to shock that little furry critter, should it decide to show its face. It would last for quite some time.

Rey dusted his hands and went back upstairs.

* * *

It was another lightening or so before he went back to the majus. His hands were still shaking and he felt as if he had run the length of the Imperium. He slipped back into the apartment for a quick wash and a nap, which helped him recover a bit.

When he dared the living room again, confident he wouldn't fall over if he walked too fast, the majus was standing in front of the communication System tucked into one corner of the room, scaly hands propped on his hips. A hazy Etanela face with a frizzy halo of hair was barely visible in the projection.

"This situation, Speaker, it is one my apprentice is currently investigating...Yes, I realize that last time... No, of course not. That, it was an isolated...Certainly, Speaker."

Rey froze. Something was wrong. Was that Speaker Humbano herself, come to drag him from the maji? He started to turn away. *Mayhaps I can pack and be gone before anyone notices.*

"Reyhorer—there you are." Rey's shoulders tensed, and he pivoted, as if on a spit. "This creature, I was thinking you were getting rid of it, not inviting it to take up residence." Majus Kheena was staring at him now, the communications System dark behind his cloak.

Rey tried to shrink into the floor. "I did fix it, sir, meanin' I thought I did. That wasn't Speaker Humbano, was it?"

The majus' scaly brows drew down in confusion for a moment. "Humbano? No, this was not her, but one of the junior Speakers. A row of lights, they just went out during an Assembly session. An annoyance, but I am thinking one with the same core problem. What did you do, in the cellar?"

"Then she's not going to throw me off the maji?"

"What are you speaking of? What of the distribution machine?" the majus had his arms crossed now—never a good sign.

"It's...er...it's all clammed up, Majus Kheena," Rey said. "That wee beasty's not to get to yer machine again."

"Then why is a Speaker calling me directly?" Majus Kheena waved a sheet of parchments, forgotten in one hand. "This, I think, has more to..."

The light overhead winked out, then back on, reflecting off the majus' dark green scales.

"You were supposed to create a deterrent."

Rey slumped. "I thought I did, sir. I made a System meself, to block 'im."

Majus Kheena strode forward, his dark cloak swirling around him. No word of praise for Rey's first success at a permanent System. His mentor's scaled lips compressed. "Then this field, it is already gone. These creatures, they are not so easy to get rid of. I set you a task, and I expect you to complete it. A skilled majus, they will know how to adjust said notes for the properties required. Find a lasting solution."

Rey scratched at one of his ears. He felt the tips curling in confusion. "So, yer want me to kill it then?"

Majus Kheena hissed something inaudible. Rey could have sworn the majus muttered something about his own mentor. "No. Even with this damage to our infrastructure, it does not mean we should exterminate rare creatures, favored by the Symphony. Even if this were some sabotage of the Imperium's networks, I would not allow you to kill such a unique animal. The object of this lesson, it is the preservation of the Imperium's ease of living; a demonstration of how we subsist along with our fellows. Off with you, and do not make me do this myself. I do not want to hear from a Speaker again." He made a shooing motion.

Rey turned back to the network of halls leading to the cellar. Unique creatures, favored by the Symphony? Sabotage? What was this critter? *Should have stayed on Sureri, pulling spines out of the garden.*

* * *

When he got to bottom of the cellar steps, Rey could sense his barrier was gone.

"Where'd the blamed thing go to?" *Did I set the System wrong?* But no, he had felt the connection between his note and the surrounding Symphony that last time. The barrier should have stayed there for ten-days before degrading.

Chirrup?

Rey spun, almost tripping down the last stair. He caught a flash of something brown and white. "Did you have sommat to do with this, yer little bugger?"

Cherrp. Krr?

He could see it, peering out from behind the clanking conduit, its call an interruption to the constant repetition of the machine. It shared the long snout and scales of the scurries that ate the bluefins around his parents' garden, but the rest of it was furred and sleek, made to dart in and out of holes in the infrastructure. It looked bigger than the last time. Could it have grown in a couple lightenings?

Krup? It unfolded two sets of flared—ears? Yes, he could see the earholes beneath. The tips had tufts of white fur.

"Ach, yer cute, then, are yer?" Though Rey had heard his standards didn't often match up with the rest of the ten species. The critter cocked its head to one side.

Cherrup. Krup? The wide mouth opened as it made noise, revealing lines of barbed suction cups instead of teeth. So that was how it had been hanging off the machine.

"Shew, then, yer bugger." Rey flapped at it with his hands. It didn't move. "Right. Sorry about this, but yer cannae stay here, suckin' the notes out o' this clanker." He gestured to the conduit machine, gears grinding along contentedly. The critter looked at the machine, then back at him. "How did yer get rid of me System, in any case?" He could tell more of his notes were missing. The nap helped, but he felt a weariness as if he hadn't slept much the night before.

Rey let the Symphony overtake him. There was energy all around, though concentrated in the machine, the mass of jangling notes overpowering anything else in the room. "The majus surely won't mind if I nip a phrase or so out o' the flow." Not enough to shut down any more lights, hopefully. He took a measure of notes from his song as well, each one irreplaceable, grown from his own experiences, and used it to bridge one of the higher register themes that flowed through the conduit. Music transferred outside the machine.

"This may sting, but yer havta go," Rey said. He extended a finger to the critter, still watching him, and used a few more notes to bridge the music directly to the creature. An arc of static leapt from his finger, not enough to kill it.

Instead, the creature shook itself, then opened its suckered mouth wide. Rey's notes disappeared with the phrase, and the critter cooed. Feathers suddenly curled around its head, growing rapidly.

Rey staggered back, the notes jerked from him to feed that little beast. "Yer *are* eatin' the music, that's why you were hanging around here. Yer got a taste for the notes of the Symphony."

The furry scaled thing crept a few steps closer, its ears unfurling again. Looking for a more food. It didn't look as cute any longer.

Cherp Cherp. The call was insistent, demanding, and its eyes opened wide. There was a...gap in the Symphony now, a suction as if the notes were gravitating toward the creature.

"Ach—no yer don't." Rey let the melodies in the room flow through him. Could he use his notes to tether it? He linked phrases from the Symphony of Potential to his own being, bracing his stance as if he could pull the very music into his body.

The machine's clanking faltered, gears grinding as the block of music flowing through it strained. Rey gritted his teeth.

"Yer cain't have it," he told the creature. It was braced too, its mouth still open. A long tongue protruded from its suckered maw, growing forward, closing the distance to the machine.

Krup? Krup? The critter's fur was brighter, and it shook itself. More feathers unfolded between the fur and scales, curling around its shoulders and haunches.

Rey was...*stretched* was the only word, his song latched to the Symphony of Potential. Its main theme in this place was the computing machine, and that was in danger of being sucked into the little abomination.

"Yer metabolizing the notes," he said. "Why? What's it givin' yer, besides more feathers than a Kirian?" He couldn't hold the songs in place for much longer. He could hear his notes tearing away, becoming one with the Symphony of Potential, then fated for the mutating creature's craw.

KrupCher. It was a call of battle, and Rey lost control with the will the creature exuded. A block of notes slid from the computing machine, and Rey heard gears grind. The room went dark.

When the lighting came back a moment later, the creature was closer, and bigger. It had a hairy mane now, and paws spread wide—seven toes apiece. A distended belly nearly dragged the floor.

ChupKrup. Even its voice was deeper, and it eyed Rey as if he were another snack. He fell back against the stairs, breathing hard, one hand propping himself up.

The Speaker will be back on the line with the majus, no doubt. He wondered how much energy it had stolen, and from where. Water systems? Lighting? Heating?

"Yer not gonna' drag me off, are yer?" The notes that made up his being stretched again, musical phrases becoming legato as they expanded. It was going to eat him, or his notes, at least. He had to do something.

Change the music. Rey dived into his own melody, clutching his notes to him. He focused on the music stringing out toward the creature—no, the beast. *Can I change my own song?*

Taking notes from elsewhere in his melody, he changed the pitch of the phrase the beast tugged against, then the tempo, adjusting it from a waltz to a jig. His heartbeat sped in response, and he grew oppressively warm, as if his body was running far faster than it should.

Cheeeerp. The beast shook its head, flicking its long tongue side to side as if trying to spit out something distasteful.

"So yer have a preference in music," Rey gasped, as the beast turned back to the clanking machine. "Go on then, take another bite." He pushed up from the stairs, listening to the block of layered notes in the conduit.

The hairy, feathered thing took a step forward, opened its mouth, and pressed the barbed suckers to the side of the machine. Rey listened.

It was impossible to hear the music from another house, but those in the House of Potential were used to transferring things they couldn't hear. How else could a majus like him put music from multiple houses into a System, like the one that ran the air circulation, or the water?

The Symphony of Potential flowed through the geared computing box, ushering notes to different places with a martial beat. Some part of that music slowed, and Rey looked to the critter. It was shaking, its swollen belly growing, and nubs of new wings poked from its back.

As the base beat of the Symphony of Potential faltered, Rey thought furiously. He knew what the beast ate, and that meant he could affect it.

"Alright yer critter," he told it. "Yer gonna have to find another place for yer meals." He took notes from his song again, though the action was a burden, his music resisting more interruption. But Rey forced them into the flow of music from the computation machine. He wouldn't get these notes back, and he used the least amount necessary to bump the beat of the machine into a higher register, changing the key of the harmonics, and polarizing the physical energy that passed through this junction.

The beast choked and coughed, its new wings fluttering. It backed away from the machine, and gave him a scathing look. It stepped forward and again tried to fasten its mouth to the side, but squirmed as if touching something hot.

Cherp. It glared up at Rey. It was the size of a pet diggerhound from back home, now.

"Nope," he told it. "Can't have yer disruptin' any more transfer points. Yer can find a tasty melody somewhere else in the Nether." There were sure to be other objects resonating at this same frequency. He hid his shaking hands behind his back, and stood as straight as he could manage.

The beast yawned at him, snapping its barbed suction cups in what was obviously a gesture of contempt. It turned slowly, belly scraping across the floor as it squirmed between the machine and the wall. Rey heard tortured bricks grinding together as two quick swipes of its paws opened the hole in the brick wall to something its new bulk could enter. It squeezed through with a final *Krup.* A brick tottered out of place and thumped to the floor in a plume of plaster.

Rey coughed away dust, then studied the large hole in the wall. *That could have been me.* Then something caught his eye. A scratch on the wall's sublayer, like graffiti, revealed by the beast's passage. He pulled himself closer.

It was Majus Kheena's name.

* * *

The majus was waiting for him at the top of the stair, arms crossed and a deep scowl on his face.

Rey dragged his feet up the last stair, then leaned against a wall. "That weren't no rat," he said.

"By your appearance, I am assuming I will see no further interruptions to the Imperium's power grid? Me, I am tired of fending off angry diplomats and maji."

"Like the last time, eyah?"

At his words, Majus Kheena's eyes opened wide. "I...well, yes."

"It's gone. Broke a hole in the wall and dragged itself off." Rey waved a dusty hand at his mentor. If the majus refused to teach him any longer, then that was fine. Just let him get some rest. "But I saw yer name down there. This ain't the first time this has happened, is it? Did yer change the frequency too, when yer fought it? If so, it's adapted."

Majus Kheena's face relaxed, into his usual glower. "Interesting. No. My own mentor, he was of the mind to kill the creatures and keep them from becoming a larger problem. I intervened to save the last one that had propagated from the previous batch."

"Tha's why you wouldn't let me off this one."

"Indeed. We maji should not so simply interfere with creatures native to the Nether."

"Native?" That caught his attention. "I thought nothin' was native here. The species bring their own critters when they arrive."

Majus Kheena nodded, and turned down the corridor, gesturing Rey to follow. "My hypothesis, it is that these are native creatures, or at least have been here so long they have evolved to be in symbiosis with the Nether's peculiar existence."

Rey didn't really care one way or the other, as long as the thing wasn't sucking him dry of notes.

"To answer your question," Majus Kheena continued, "Me, I did not change the frequency of the transfer System. Instead, I crafted a modulating set of scales which changed their pattern so quickly the creature could not "bite" it, if you will." He sighed. "Alas, I was too late. Today, I assume it has again gathered enough of the Symphony to gestate?"

Rey nodded, keeping pace with his mentor. "You failed too?"

"I did. Had six different Speakers contacting my mentor to complain." He gave Rey a rare smile. "Speaker Humbano, she was one of them."

"Greatmother, she's that old?"

"Older," the majus confirmed. "Perhaps you or I will discover a permanent solution to keep the creatures from feeding on our systems, in time. For now, it is enough to know that the Symphony Eater will sleep and gestate for another thirty or fifty cycles, until it births a new generation. Us, let us hope we have a better way to live alongside these rare beings then. I will call in workers tomorrow to repair the damage."

Rey dusted his long fingers against each other, his shoulders held higher. If Majus Kheena hadn't found an answer to the beasty either, he didn't feel so bad. Maybe he'd make a decent majus one day. Better than going back to pulling up spines out of his parents' yard.

"If nothing else," he said to himself. "This'll make a right swell story to tell over a dinner and a drink."

The Feastday
1001 A.A.W.

"I've never seen the Bazaar like this," Prot said to his wife, Amra.

"You've never seen the Bazaar," Amra retorted, smacking Prot in the shoulder with one hand.

"Yes, but you know what I mean," Prot said. He shifted the box under his arm. "In paintings and postcards, there are stalls everywhere, with Mid-Imperium looming behind it, and you can buy anything you can imagine. Now it's just...food. As far as you can see."

"I'm just glad we could buy passage here," Amra said. "I have a list of places I want to see in the Imperium. It's the best place to find those rare items that aren't for sale on the homeworlds. We should be able to make a tidy profit out of this trip."

"Thank Saart for it," Prot told his wife. "If the old cook hadn't entered the Feastday contest, we wouldn't have had to buy passage here."

"How *did* you get such a good rate on a portal?" Amra asked.

Prot still hadn't told her, but now he threw his chest out, just a bit. "I have connections in the maji, I'll have you know."

"Are you still milking favors out of that councilor we helped? It's been, what, two cycles? You'd think she would tell you 'no' at some point."

"Hey—if she wants to keep helping us, I'm not going to complain," Prot said. "Now, which row is Saart down?"

"He's with the rest of the Festuour entrants," Amra said, counting off rows. "The Methiemum are over there, and the Kirians are the next row over. I have no idea why they would put those two next to each other. Do they want to turn people's stomachs?"

Prot wasn't listening. His nose was in the air, taking in the scents of the festival. "Is that fried goat's cheese?" he asked.

"We don't have time for—" Amra broke off. "Oh, it is. With some sort of..." she closed her eyes and inhaled. "It smells like a roasted mountain pepper sauce."

"Let's stroll down the aisles," Prot suggested. "We'll get to Saart eventually, and the actual contest doesn't start until tomorrow. The old bear can wait a few minutes for his 'secret ingredient.'"

Prot linked his free arm with his wife's and they turned down the first aisle. The once-a-cycle Feastday contest had started with one person judging the best flavors of each of the homeworlds, or so the story went. Now it was a five-day event, with each homeworld trying to out-compete each other for the tastiest, most unique food on their homeworld. During that time, the Bazaar was turned into a stew of mouthwatering flavors, and people came from all over to roam the stalls and pick their favorite foods. The actual judging event was almost an afterthought, to everyone but the entrants.

The Methiemum row was familiar to Prot and Amra, even as well traveled as they were. They rarely moved around now, since they had bought their shop on Methiem four cycles previous.

"Mmmm. Smell that?" Prot asked. "Dried and roasted dates." He angled toward a stall where a plume of smoke erupted around a large-bellied man who held a cast-iron skillet over an open flame.

"With fish fillet," Amra said. She pointed to the side, where samples were laid out. "Fish stuffed roasted dates. That's a new one." She snagged a small piece with a nod to the chef and popped it in her mouth.

"Wow," she said when she could speak again. "It practically melts. Think we could get some of them to sell at the shop? I bet it stores well."

"We'll start a list," Prot said, and pulled a length of paper out of his pocket. He shifted the container under his other arm and produced a pen from a different pocket of his long coat. He wrote down the kiosk description.

The next stall they stopped at was run by a woman in a wrap the same color as Amra's. While they traded information about what cloth was best for a wrap, Prot tried some of the woman's fruit curry. Definitely another keeper. He wrote her name and the town she was from down on his list.

The third Methiemum who caught their interest was a baker. She was nearly as large around as her stall, but whirled and sidestepped to transition from her small clay oven, to her cutting counter, to another station stocked with spices, vegetables and fruits.

"Stuffed bread?" Amra asked, pulling Prot closer.

"Try a piece," the woman told them, thrusting a quarter section of a slice toward them. The middle of the bread sagged with an orange and green paste, and Amra divided it in two and gave half to Prot.

"Kiwi and carrot, baked in a sourdough crust."

Prot hesitantly tried a bit, and his eyebrows shot up. "This is good!" he said.

"I also have cucumber and basil, fish and onion, and horseradish and pepper in pumpernickel, if you like more spice," she said, pointing out samples. Then she twirled and took another loaf from her clay oven.

Prot and Amra got her name.

The Kirian aisle was next, and the two dutifully walked down it, but there were few places they stopped, and fewer people in the aisle.

"Well, those mealworms were fresh," Prot managed. He felt a little nauseous, especially after the bread.

"The vendor said they were," Amra said. "We could add some fly larvae to our stock, just in case we get any Kirians passing through."

"I suppose." Prot considered. "Have the featherheads *ever* won the contest?"

"Not that I know of," Amra said. She slowed, looking at a case filled with water. Wriggling white maggots the size of her thumb swam around, and she shuddered.

They moved to the Lobath aisle, giving the Festuour one a miss until the end. They were familiar with many of these dishes as well, as Lobath spice sold well on almost all the homeworlds. The cooks here put it to good use, flavoring pastes, stews, raw mushrooms, breaded, fried, and baked mushrooms, and fungi in all shapes and sizes.

At the end of the row, Prot was licking his fingers from his eighth sample.

"You're going to fill up before you reach the other side," Amra told him.

He patted his stomach. "I've been training, with your cooking," he said. Amra poked him in the side.

"At least we know the 'secret ingredient' of about half of those stalls," he said.

"*Ibora labat*?" Amra asked, naming the spice hardest to find on Loba.

"Exactly," Prot said. "Though I especially liked what the cook from Mushroom and Spice did with it. I've never had candied shelf fungus before. The *Ibora labat* pairs with the sweetness quite well."

The Sathssn aisle was not as bare as the Kirian one, but close. No cook fires gave off smoke here, however there were many stands with vibrant plantains and leafy greens as tall as Prot.

"I've heard a lot about Sathssn veggies," he told Amra. "Never had one fresh from the plant." He wandered to a stall with ten or more buckets filled with dirt. Vines sprouted from them, running up trellises and dotted with hundreds of little orange fruits, like tiny jewels.

"These, they are the freshest starcress on all Sath Home," the attendant called out. She had her cowl back, bright green scales glistening in the light from the Nether walls. "Try one."

Prot plucked an orange fruit off the vine and popped it in his mouth. The skin cracked as he bit down, and erupted in a gooey, tart mass inside his mouth. Prot stood still, trying to take in all the tastes in the little berry. First tart, then a sweet flavor, like a strawberry, but fading into a spicy aftertaste that gave off hints of cinnamon, and cloves, and pinesap.

"Can I buy one of these vines?" he asked the attendant. Amra gave him a raised eyebrow, but the Sathssn shook her head.

"This, it only grows in soil native to Sath Home. Very carefully bred for the best yield, most resistance to disease and best flavor, but the downside is, the starcress, it only grows in this soil, and only from the southern latitudes." The vendor tapped a bucket. "This flavor, it is not as strong as it would be, growing in a field."

Prot wrote down her mailing address anyway, just in case. If he could import a starcress vine, he'd make back the cost easily. It couldn't be that hard to order a few buckets of dirt. He had a few connections with Sathssn who lived near the equator.

"Come on," Amra told him, pulling him to the next aisle. "It's been a lightening already, and Saart won't like us keeping him waiting."

The Etanela aisle was next, and Prot found himself looking up, at bluish faces with manes of hair standing out like small bushes. The Etanela largely lived on the coasts of the small islands dotted through their world, and were the best source of sea-based food of the ten species.

"Oooh, is that boiled firesea taligrani claw?" Amra made a beeline toward a shop with a display of sharp pincers, their sides burst open and dripping with oil and salt. This stall didn't have samples, but Amra bought one anyway, sucking the tender meat out while they walked.

"What about the budget you keep going on about?" Prot said, only half joking. He reached for the claw of meat, but Amra pulled it away.

"Maybe your councilor friend will lend you the Nether glass to pay for another one," she said, and sucked the meat out through an opening near the pincer.

Prot rolled his eyes, but went to a stall selling seaweed-wrapped bundles. They were Etanela surprise bundles, usually given out around the day of Sea Mother's Rise on Etan. The Etanlea looming over the display must have thought there were enough people here willing to chance the delicacy.

"I'll take a gamble," Prot told the attendant, and flipped her a small piece of Nether glass. He moved his hand over several seaweed-wrapped bundles before choosing one of them. He raised it to his mouth, closed his eyes, and bit down.

Prot chewed thoughtfully.

"Well?" Amra said. "Good or bad luck for the next year?"

"Not sure." Prot swallowed. "It's not a sea slug, so that's good, but it's still an...interesting flavor. I wouldn't say *bad*, but maybe an acquired taste?"

"Ah, you probably got the Sea Mother's ovaries," the attendant said. "Only one in the whole batch! Traditionally, it means the next year will be filled with new and intense experiences, bad or good."

"Let's hope it's only tradition," Prot said as they walked away. He looked for a place to dispose of the rest of the seaweed bundle.

The next two aisles were each split between two species. The first was mostly filled with buzzing Pixie venders, but before Prot and Amra got there, they stopped at the two lone Benish stalls.

The first had a selection of hard-looking objects sitting on a polished metal platter.

"What are these?" Amra asked the Benish attendant, who cocked their head with a crack of splitting wood.

"Traditional, hmm, staples of Aben. Meant to, hmmm, sustain one for many cycles while on knowledge journeys."

Prot tapped one brown and orange striated object. "Are they nuts?"

The Benish seemed to consider. "They, hmm, *were* nuts. Now they contain many minerals and salts vital to long days of walking. One must only, hmmm, keep the journey seed in one's mouth while walking. It will, hmm, keep one moving for days at a time."

"I'm sure it will," Prot said.

The next booth held bowls of liquid so viscous they barely ran when Prot tilted one toward him.

"Try a taste," the attendant said, holding out a silver thimble of the liquid. Prot stuck one finger in and put it in his mouth.

He sucked in a breath. "Try this, Amra," he said.

Amra stuck her pinky in the same thimble. Her eyes widened when she put it to her tongue.

"Tree syrup, but powered by a majus, right?" Prot said, and Amra nodded. "What's in it?" he asked the attendant.

"There are over, hm, two hundred and thirty different saps, nectars, extracts, spices, and roots in each vat of syrup," the Benish said. "The process starts with drums as big around as, hm, this stall. They are boiled down to this concentration." The Benish held up the silver thimble.

Prot got the name of the substance. It was sure to be expensive, but they could sell this for as much as liquid Nether glass.

The Pixie area was a riot of scents and colors, and a sickly-sweet aroma filled the row. There were fruits of every size and color: blue and orange and green and red and purple, and every shade and stripe in between.

"I've never seen so many kinds," Amra said.

"No wonder their wings buzz so much," Prot answered.

They tried a few here and there, and the fruits' taste was just as varied as their colors. They stayed away from the fermented ones, though the Pixies who were combing through the rows of food flocked to those stands.

"Popular with the locals," Prot said.

"I'm still not trying them again," Amra answered. "Last time I tried a fermented Pixie drink I was on the toilet the entire next day."

They turned a corner into the last row, where dour Sureriaj—mostly male, of course—glared at customers suspiciously.

"Ugh—we can give this aisle a skip," Prot said, glaring back at the vendors. "I had plenty of their salty, spiny food while we were stuck on their homeworld."

"Oh come on," Amra said, and towed him to a stall at random. "What's this one?" She asked the vendor, a particularly ugly Sureri who looked like he was from the Perchet family.

"Eyah, it's mushed turp root with spices. Traditional recipe." He thrust out a small cup. "Try yer a mite."

Amra ate some, made a small choking noise, and gave the cup back. "It's very...well preserved," she said.

"Ach, yeah. The rock salt keeps the mush from dryin' out. Terrible, ain't it?"

"Um, yes," Amra said.

"Dunno why the families keep makin' us come out here," the Sureri grumbled. "Only the Kirians win less'n us, and they eat maggots."

"At least he's honest," Prot said.

The last third of that row was given to the Lobhl, who had one long table with several of the silent beings milling behind it, their large hands in constant motion as they spoke to each other and their customers.

"It's all liquids?" Prot asked, and Amra nodded.

"Looks like you get your own straw to taste all the different concoctions," she said.

The first Lobhl handed them a straw, her other hand signing, <Try each one. Please let us know at the end which you enjoy the most.>

Prot and Amra tried each vase of fluid. They were all different, sweet, bitter, pulpy, spicy, and so on.

The Lobhl at the end spread his hands when they reached him, fingers crossing over each other in a question. <Which one did you most enjoy? We are eager to find out.>

"I liked the third one down," Amra said. "It was sort of like a good curry, but the aftertaste changed to something like a roast."

Prot counted the vases. "I liked the one four down from that. Sweet and hot at the same time. What's it made of?"

<That would be telling,> the Lobhl signed, fingertips twitching to show he meant no offense. <These are all special recipes, made for our Festival of Light. If you visit our homeworld, you will be able to taste them again.>

Prot and Amra finally headed back toward the entrance. Prot juggled the case under his arm. "Now the Festuour row."

"I'm stuffed," Amra said, but she lifted her head to sniff the air. "The Festuour food is always so rich, too."

They passed displays of red meats, dripping with juices, and plates of soft white and yellow cheese, starting to melt in the midday air of the Nether.

"I would stop if I thought I could eat *anything* else," Prot said, eying a fried concoction of fruit, cavarra cheese, and thrycovolar belly bacon.

Saart's stall was about halfway down the row, and the old Festuour spread his hands wide when he saw them.

"Prot! Amra! Finally. Did you bring what I asked?"

"Pure Rooflin flower honey," Prot said, setting the cask down with a *thump*. "Now why would you need so much of it? This costs a bit of shiny Nether glass to import."

"Ya'll are just in time," Saart said, and pulled a pan of golden brown dough from a small oven. He put the pan on a mat on a table, then opened the cask with one twist of his thick furry paw.

Prot sniffed the air. "That smells fantastic. What is it?"

"My granny's recipe," Saart said. "Chorin skin pastry. You have to get the thinnest skin of bark from the tree, and layer it up until it makes this crust," he gestured at the golden top of the pan. "Throw some nutmeat and spices in the middle, and bake the blazes out of it." He lifted the cask of honey. "But this is the most important step." He upended the cask over the pan, and it crackled and hissed like molten metal hitting water. The honey became more viscous, flowing into cracks in the Chorin bark.

Prot closed his eyes, breathing in the hot, sweet, and crusty aromas. "I think I know the winner of the festival," he said. "Now when do we get to try a piece?"

The Society of Two Houses
953 A.A.W.

PART ONE

The Body

Maji in the Great Assembly of Species are rare, born at a rate of, hm, one per five million individuals. Most hear only one of the six aspects of the Grand Symphony, but one in every sixty maji, or one in three hundred million individuals, can hear two of the Symphony's aspects. It is one's belief these few—the, hm, ones gathered here—have the ability to drive innovation in the Great Assembly, bolstered by a sensitivity to the underlying rhythms of the universe. For this group's final entrance into the Society, please, hm, step forward for the geas to be applied.

—Private address by Moortlin, Benish Head of the House of Heal-ing, on the induction of new members into the Society of Two Houses

I stared down at the body of Speaker Thurapo, willing my frozen feet to bring me further into his study. I was supposed to be presenting the prototype model I held, not discovering his corpse.

I clenched my hand involuntarily, then yelped and released my fingers as the scale model of the System Beast dug tiny sharp hands into my palm. The delicate construct, made in the form of a Festuour—like my colleague Gompt—had taken days to build. The pain unlocked my feet and I hurried forward to set the model on a side table—just a little too tall for me, like everything in the Speaker's study.

Though my first instinct was to go to the Imperium guard, I instead closed the study door. I had a few minutes during which the deceased Speaker and I were supposed to meet, before his secretary announced his next appointment. My mind flew through what questions the guard would ask if I alerted them.

Majus Mandamon Feldo, is it? Why were you here to see the Speaker? Why does a majus need approval from the Assembly? Shouldn't this be going through the Council of the Maji?

Even thinking of telling the authorities about the Society of Two Houses made the jingly earworm of the geas threaten to derail my thoughts. The guard would quickly become suspicious when I further choked and fainted instead of telling where my prototype System Beast came from or under whose patronage I worked.

I shook my head, dislodging the music that kept the Society safe. Because of our...unconventional methods, Society maji went through a roundabout process of getting approval from the Great Assembly to introduce our new and disruptive inventions.

Per our usual methods, the head of the Society had 'convinced' the late Speaker not to ask questions about where my colleagues and I got our resources. Even I didn't know how the Society provided so many high-quality metals and logical gearing ratios.

Once available, our System Beasts would be the perfect servants and secretaries. They could haul loads, act as butlers, deliver mail, remind owners of engagements, and much more. However, without a sponsor, Gompt, Kratitha, and I would never be able to supply them to the inhabitants of the Nether. If this murder even hinted at our organization's existence, it would also compromise and taint our research by association. I'd be left with nothing, and the Society could no longer develop innovation without those in power asking severe questions. My heart sped, just thinking about it.

Now, the Speaker who would have sponsored us was dead. I let myself really look at him, sprawled out on the floor. He was an Etanela, half again as tall as me, hence the furniture.

What had happened to him? One hand rose to my mouth, then down to the small beard I was growing out, pulling at the hair in thought. Something in my head was silently screaming, though I had been near violent death before. *Stay calm.*

I had to concentrate—use the few minutes available to figure out what happened. Then I would at least have a way to defend myself against questioning authorities. Otherwise, they would detain me as a suspect, no matter what I said. Any questions would lead to the Society.

There was a pool of blood, slowly seeping into the carpet, and still dripping from the deep cuts which nearly severed the Speaker's neck. His head was at an unnatural angle, wide glassy eyes staring out from his faintly blue face. Though his mouth was open in shock, the blue coloration was natural to the Etanela, not a symptom of asphyxiation. He wouldn't have had time to suffocate before the blood loss to his brain killed him. I tried to push away the nausea threatening to bring my breakfast back. Adding to the mess would only complicate solving Speaker Thurapo's death.

The Speaker and I had corresponded through the Imperium's mail service just the day before, and he'd invited me to show him the model my colleagues and I had created. Introducing innovations developed by the select group of maji I belonged to had to be handled delicately—a dance of avoiding names, places, and methods of experimentation.

Was the Speaker killed to stop me from showing him the little System Beast? Did someone find out about the Society and its methods?

No. That was paranoia bordering on my mentor's level. No one outside of my unique Society even knew what the System Beasts were.

Was this self-inflicted? I couldn't see how. There was no implement here with which the Speaker could have cut his own throat—not like that.

The Speaker's secretary would check on us soon—maybe even open the closed door without knocking. I had perhaps ten minutes—the time in which I would have presented my proposal—before someone else called for the Speaker's attention.

The defining quality of maji belonging to the Society of Two Houses was that each of us could hear two of the six aspects of the Grand Symphony, rather than just one, like most maji. Each combination of aspects had its own label. My title in the Society was 'Investigator.' Until now, I thought the titles merely convenient masks for those members not wanting to be identified by name. Now it seemed more ironic.

So—I would investigate, and if I could clear any trace of the Society from Speaker Thurapo's death, then I would go to the authorities. If not, well, I'd deal with that when I got to it.

Wood paneling made the office comfortable, and a dominating Festuour-made rug covered the tile floor. There was one desk, clean save for a writing mat, with a chair on either side. Beside me was the side table where my prototype sat. Both side walls held rows of bookshelves, dusty and obviously little used. The Speaker's body took up most of the floor, splayed across the center of the rug.

I looked at the chronograph—an older invention of the Society— chained to my vest, marking time until I estimated I would be discovered with the corpse. I knelt by Speaker Thurapo's body, careful to avoid putting the knees of my tailored suit in the pool of greenish blood seeping into the rug. I could feel the heat from the blood, and from the body, though the sticky liquid was already coagulating. He had not been dead long, whatever happened. I swallowed bile and leaned in.

Aside from the deep gash in the Etanela's throat—certainly fatal— there was no other sign of a fight. I looked from the body to the closed door of the study, gauging where the Speaker would have been standing.

Falling back on the rug like this meant he was facing the door. Along with his killer? It was pure luck the body hadn't hit the chair pulled out on this side of the Chorin-wood desk. I held one hand out, measuring. Speaker Thurapo's frizzy mane of auburn hair was less than the width of my hand away from one leg of the desk.

I pushed my glasses up my nose, and tried to forget how Thurapo would have been the sponsor for our new company selling System Beasts, and a façade to remove interest in where and how my colleagues and I had developed the idea.

Many of the experiments occurring behind the walls of the mansion where I lived would not sit well in the public eye, yet the Society was a generator of progress. It also had connections—under false identities, of course—to many of the Speakers for the Great Assembly, using its members' reach to exploit potentially embarrassing knowledge. I didn't know what Speaker Thurapo had done, but I hoped his indiscretion had nothing to do with his death. The Society's direct involvement would complicate things greatly.

From information gathered over the short time I had been a member, I knew the Society's efforts had saved people's lives and ended wars quickly and efficiently. Its members had added comforts to our lives like freezing and heating technology and remedies for bacterial infections. If, in the process, a few unknown persons suffered, or a few highly prized resources went missing, what was that against the good of all? Yet I was sure the Great Assembly or the Council of the Maji would not see it the same way.

Time was wasting, and I reigned in my thoughts, looking up to the desk. Someone must have been sitting on this side, speaking with the Etanela before pushing away. The Speaker had come from behind his desk before he was killed. I clenched my jaw. What prompted his death, and why did it have to happen this morning, of all mornings?

A non-majus might have difficulty discovering more in the brief time before they were found. But as an 'Investigator,' I had two advantages: the Symphonies I could hear.

I let the Symphony of Healing fill my mind with faint rising and falling scales. It told me Speaker Thurapo was definitely dead, his complex trills and glissandos degenerating into steady and uninteresting eighth notes.

Conversely, the Symphony of Potential dealt in transferring energy, and as I listened to the fundamental music underlying the universe, I heard residues of people's actions, reactions, and movements. Each one was a traceable resonance, though some were extremely faint.

As I got to my feet and went to the desk, the musical themes of energy became clearer. Speaker Thurapo *had* come around the desk—a glissando and dipping trill in the music—following another body, who was speaking with him. I crossed the rug on the other side of the Speaker's body, stepping over his large boots, pointed out at angles. I looked away from the ghastly wound.

Sifting through the Symphony of Potential, I found another fading theme. Thurapo had been standing just here, and...I listened carefully, trying to separate out one rhythm, like listening to a single string playing in an orchestra. I *thought* his assailant had stood in the doorway, ready to leave, but it was hard to say. Closing the door had partially written over that music. I checked my chronograph again—I had found nothing yet, but there was still time.

Did this other person murder the Speaker? They must have. Could it be connected to showing the System Beast prototype model? The geas protected the Society and—some would say—its unethical practices. It was supposed to be foolproof. I didn't want this extra complication. Just creating the System Beasts had been challenge enough.

Need more information. My eyes, almost of their own accord, were drawn back to the body, my subconscious registering something I'd missed. I wiped sweaty hands on my vest and stepped closer, pulling the hem of my pants away from the ruined section of rug, and Thurapo's throat. The fingers and thumb of the Speaker's right hand were together, as if he had held something. Going by the corpse's open mouth and wide eyes, he had been surprised when he died.

The House of Potential revealed a fading jangle of discordant notes—tight muscles in the Speaker's hand, now loosened in death. The House of Healing repeated an intertwined duet—he'd been holding something made from organic material, like cloth or paper.

I knelt down by his right hand. Another trait of an Investigator was to hear the past energy and biology of an object—like seeing a short way into the past. I listened to the pattern of harmonics between the two Symphonies.

The music of Healing was regular, overlapping chords weaving into a rigidly defined structure. The music of Potential held the fading change in beat that meant the object had been cut or torn from another source. It was probably a piece of paper, taken from a larger source of information—maybe something the Speaker had written? *Finally, another clue.*

I let the Symphony of Potential take the upper hand, retracing the descending melody. It led toward the closed door. So, whoever had killed the Speaker had taken what he held into the hallway and beyond. I checked the timepiece on my vest again. About half my interview time gone.

I opened the door, peering both ways. The short corridor was empty for the moment and I surged outside, closing the door silently behind me. The intersection of Healing and Potential rose out here, the notes more recent. Whoever had taken the paper went this way.

I turned left, following the melody. This hallway was in the lower level of the Dome of the Assembly, where each of the sixty-six speakers had their own rooms, and, unfortunately, their own secretary.

I had only gone a few steps when a face under a bob of golden hair stuck around the next corner. The Etanela who had let me in must have heard my steps. She was wearing the kind of makeup many female working Etanela adopted, with tiny red dots above and below her eyes, her lips tinted deep purple against the faint blue of her face.

She came fully around the corner, putting away a tube of lipstick, and I stopped dead, my mind whirling. Something about her movement looked suddenly familiar, as if I knew her from somewhere, but I couldn't place it.

"Anything I can help you with?" she asked. "Are you finished with your interview? I'll just pop in and see what the Speaker—" Her hands clasped together in front of her, each massaging the other.

She must have seen something. She couldn't have killed him.

I interrupted her flow of words. "Ah, no. We're not done yet." What if...? "You haven't seen anyone come past, have you? Perhaps with a piece of paper?"

The secretary considered me, looking down from shoulders and head above me. Her eyes were watery, and still puffy from sleep. They would have been comically large on one of my species, but in her faintly blue, freckled face, they only looked earnest. "I haven't, but I got here just before you. You're the Speaker's first appointment." She shrugged. "He works odd hours. Sometimes early in the morning, sometimes late at night."

So whoever had killed him had left with the list just in time. I still needed to clear the Society from this mess, and somehow keep the Imperium guard from arresting me once this secretary figured out I'd been having an interview with a deceased speaker.

Perhaps a little misdirection. "The...the Speaker asked if he had another five minutes in his schedule." I shrugged. "He seems to have lost some information necessary to my presentation." I tried to keep my face neutral.

"Just a moment. I'll check." She sniffed, then ducked back around the corner, presumably to her desk. I let out a slow breath, trying to keep my hands from shaking.

In the few moments available, I focused on the fading musical traces of the paper's thief. Whatever happened had been very recent, or I wouldn't have been able to still hear the notes. It went right by her desk, and unless I wanted to run past and alert everyone to the body, the musical trail would fade away before I could follow it. The way the music was dropping notes into inaudibility, it wouldn't be long until it was impossible to track.

The secretary popped around the corner again, her hands tracing elegant paths through the air. "He can spare another five minutes. I'll come tell you when the time is up."

She looks tired—must have been late coming in this morning. That will only make her feel worse when she finds the body.

"That will do nicely. I'll let him know," I said as I backed away, then threw a glance down at the chronograph. A few more minutes to search. Once I left, the Speaker's cooling body would not stay secret long. My only chance was to find a clue inside the room.

I paused at the door to make sure the secretary wasn't watching, then closed my eyes, separating out the bubbly, anxious music that defined her person from the rest of the Symphony of Healing.

Taking notes from my being, mimicking her chords and melodies, I tied them to a note keyed to the House of Potential. An aura of white and brown grew around me, visible only to maji—the physical results of changing the Symphony. I pressed my fingers on the doorframe, and the aura transferred to that spot. The new construct—a System—would send me an alerting tone if the secretary came down the corridor. Losing a few of my notes was worth the extra warning.

Inside the study, I closed the door, frowned at Speaker Thurapo's body, and scanned the room. The desk was the only other place to look, and the fading music pointed in that direction, though it was nearly inaudible.

The Speaker brought the paper from his desk. Why? To give to the killer?

I positioned myself where Speaker Thurapo would have sat, though my legs dangled as if I were a toddler, and spread one hand across the writing mat on the desk. It was leather, dyed green, with filigree around the edges. The Symphony of Healing held a last leitmotif woven through the writing mat, swirls of notes corresponding to the swirls of writing. The source of the paper's trail was here, maybe copied from another place. I only had a few more moments before it faded completely.

I closed my eyes, tracing the most recent indentations in the mat with a finger as I followed the music along a measure. I could *almost* make out what was written. It was a list of some sort, with names and...titles? Translating notes of the Symphony into writing was not something I had done before, and I hoped the tactile input from my finger would help me decipher the script.

My eyes flew open and the Symphony left me in a crash of noise. I was tracing my own name.

My finger continued its path, unaided now by the music in the back of my head. It would be even harder to catch hold of that particular sequence of notes before it disappeared. The Symphony did not like maji fiddling with it overly much.

Mandamon Feldo – Investigator

Why would this contain the name the Society used for my combination of houses? Only a member should know of them. I traced the next line, now more familiar with the indentations.

Tethan – Overwhelm

The name was vaguely familiar—another member who worked in chemistry, I believed—and I felt farther down.

Timpomitnob Gompt, Watcher – Archeologist

It was the name of my friend and colleague, working on the System Beast project. The little prototype was modeled after her. That meant the next line was probably...

Kratithakanipouliteka – Engineer

Yes, Kratitha, our project team's third member. It was conceivable the Speaker had all our names, likely even, as I had been scheduled to speak with him. But why and how were our Society titles included? What had this Tethan to do with it? The list went on.

Plithin A'Tyf – Psychiatrist

I knew him socially, a boorish Lobath.

There was one more indentation I could make out, below Plithin's name.

Moortlin – Biologist

No, this was no list of appointments. This was a list of the members of the Society of Two Houses with our internal titles, which no one outside our group should have. My heart sped at the implication. *The Speaker is not a majus, thus not a member of the Society. How did he get this? Someone else knows, but* what *do they know?*

I knew exactly who I needed to see.

Moortlin wouldn't like this. The Benish was paranoid about anything hinting at the Society's existence. Could I get proof for them?

I ran a hand over the desk drawers to search for paper to make a copy of the names, but a sustained tone rang in the back of my mind, and I held my chronograph to eye level. My time was up.

I sprang from behind the desk, grabbing my prototype model and then the extra chair as I went. The Symphony of Potential's beat grew louder as I dragged the legs across the rug beside Thurapo's corpse, creating friction. I flung open the door, stepping out into the surprised secretary's path, and left the chair teetering behind me, grabbing notes from my being and sliding them between measures in the music. I redirected the energy of friction and the movement of the falling chair into slightly different rhythms.

The door banged shut behind me, covering the noise the chair made as it reversed direction and hit the handle. "Just in time." I smiled at the secretary. "Thank you so much for coming to get me. The Speaker asked not to be disturbed for a few minutes, to write up a report."

I listened as I babbled, hearing the syncopation of the beat as the chair fell slowly, then stopped, fell *up,* and wedged under the door handle. That should keep prying eyes away for a short time.

"That is no problem at all," the secretary said. She flashed me a wide smile—she seemed more composed than she had been before, and I attempted to stretch my face into the same expression. "I was going to pop out for some tea anyway, to wake me up." She matched pace with me as we walked down the hall, away from the bloody mess in that room. My mind raced in the silence.

Just leave it alone. It's to your advantage. But no, I couldn't stop myself from asking the question.

"I...thought he had another appointment?" The secretary had checked his schedule.

"Oh...no." The Etanela's face creased in confusion for a moment, then cleared. "The Speaker is very busy, but it's not all meetings, naturally."

"I see," I said, trying to keep the anxiety from my face. We reached a branch in the corridor, and I listened for any hint of the musical trail I was seeking. It was gone, the music erased by new actions. "Well, enjoy your tea."

The secretary nodded and turned in the other direction. I picked up my pace. I would surely be implicated in this murder, once someone found the body. With the Society involved, I could not go to the Imperium guard. Fortunately, the Society had a lot of practice cleaning up embarrassing messes. Was it possible to fix this before the secretary returned from her tea?

* * *

The Spire of the Maji was a good few minutes' walk from the Dome of the Assembly, but my feet ate up the cobbles. I barely looked at the people I passed. Any of them could be the killer, and I had to work quickly. I was used to the alleys of the Imperium, the largest city and capital of the Nether, even if I didn't live here.

I circled one of the immense crystal columns—reaching higher than I could see—that dotted the enclosed, planet-sized interior of the Nether. This was the central hub for the ten species of the Great Assembly, rather than a homeworld, which meant there was a lot of traffic, with representation from every species. It also meant my list of suspects could have been quite long. However, it was reduced to those who knew about the Society of Two Houses—a very small number.

Inside the Spire, I passed the chamber of the Council of the Maji. The Council wasn't in session at this hour of the morning, but the one member who knew about the Society was nearby. I found Moortlin in their lab three levels higher in the Spire.

"Mandamon, hm, come in. None have followed this one, yes?" I shook my head at the question my mentor had asked every time I visited them in the Imperium over the last two cycles. Moortlin's paranoia was as healthy as ever.

Councilor Moortlin stepped away from their current project—a hybrid species of sticky trap tulip, meant to reduce the scritling population in the lower levels of the Spire. They were getting into the flour stores. "Then what is this one's, hm, question?"

The Benish was old, though how old they'd never shared. All I could do was compare with the others of their species I had seen. Moortlin's rough skin was no longer continuous, but peeling in fine strips, lighter patches showing beneath the walnut-colored exterior. Their unblinking yellow eyes stared into me.

"I have some unsettling news," I said, though my shaking hands and the sweat running into my beard showed that was an understatement. Not all of it was from my pace getting here, and I took a moment to straighten my suit. I had worn my best one to see Speaker Thurapo.

"The request for an audience with the Assembly? This one did not get a, hm, time to present?"

I paused. My presentation was such a small part of this. The Society might be able to arrange another speaker to sponsor the System Beast project, but this murder had to be tied up in a neat knot before then.

"That isn't it," I said, "but no, I could not schedule an audience."

Moortlin cocked their bald head with a creak like a teak tree shifting in the wind.

"Speaker Thurapo is dead." I let out the revelation in a breath, but then held up both hands, warding off my mentor's questions. "That is still not the extent of things. I did a little...Investigation."

Moortlin's pupil-less eyes flashed at my phrasing—a sign of concern in Benish.

"The Speaker had a list of Society members' names—potentially all of them," I said. "I think whoever killed him took it."

Moortlin crossed to the door of his lab—quickly for one of their species, which meant an odd straight-legged gait, sounding like someone snapping kindling into pieces. They closed it with a *click*.

"*Killed* then not, hm, *died*? And how does this one know what was on the list if it was not there?"

"The...*incident* must have happened moments before I arrived," I said. "There was still fading music in the Symphonies of Healing and Potential directing me to where the list had been. I found indentations on the Speaker's writing pad." I pressed a shaking hand to my pants leg to still it.

"This one came here first, yes?" Moortlin questioned. "Not to the, hm, Effature's guard?"

"Of course." I was slightly offended my mentor didn't trust me to keep our organization secret, and tried to remember they had seen many more cycles than I had. "I couldn't have said much with the geas, could I? I knew you would want to know first." My mentor's paranoia when dealing with the Society knew no bounds—warranted, in this case. I had absorbed some of those fears in the last half cycle I had been a member.

"It is good this one did not," Moortlin said. "Not even the Effature could prevent, hm, retribution against Society members if certain actions were discovered. There are...costs to how the Society brings new opportunities and conveniences to the public." They shook their head to another chorus of creaks and cracks, and I felt more justified in not going to the authorities.

"The Great Assembly must be protected from, hm, dangers it does not realize. That task falls to the Society." Moortlin's eyes held me. "What of the body?"

That was the more immediate problem. "I barred the door to the room, but I don't know how long it will hold," I replied. "Speaker Thurapo's secretary was going out, but will break into the room eventually, and call the Imperium guard." The energy I put into the chair would keep it snug to the door for several minutes—maybe up to a full lightening. "We need to clean up the body."

"One will manage that task soon," Moortlin assured me. "The Speaker will be discovered to have had a natural, if sudden, hm, death. *After* this one left."

What then? A speaker of the Great Assembly was still dead, and there were only sixty-six speakers among billions of inhabitants of the ten homeworlds. It would cause an upset, though the Assembly had procedures to replace a speaker who suffered a sudden death.

But procedures would not extend my time available to find the killer. Moortlin was on the Council of the Maji and also the head of the Society of Two Houses, but even they had only so much power to impede an official investigation if foul play was suspected.

"Could the names this one found be, hm, coincidence?" Moortlin asked.

"No." I wished they could be, but five, or more, names were a pattern. "Our Society titles were listed as well. Whoever wrote the list knew details about us, or copied them from another source. Someone has gotten around the geas."

I had only been in the Society for a short time, though long enough to see why our methods had to be kept secret. Many would condemn how we achieved such a rapid pace of innovation. During my six months in the Society, albeit with some diligent searching, I learned of those experiments involving sentient beings—voluntary and not, and others that included stolen and sensitive materials. Moortlin did not give out information easily, and the geas kept us safe. If someone got around its security, half our protection was gone.

"Then the Speaker's killer knows of this group," Moortlin said. "If word gets to the rest of the Council and the Assembly, the Society's days will be, hm, numbered. One will not allow this. Aegrino will be the best choice for these ones to talk to. The Society's record keeper will arrange things."

Moortlin took a key from a pocket in their loose vest. Benish rarely wore pants, as they were much more resistant to cold than the other species, and had no genitals to hide away.

They locked their door and creaked back to the middle of the room. "Stand back. These ones will go there directly."

"By portal?" I asked, surprised. The nearest portal ground—the one I used for my usual commute—was outside the Spire, not more than a few minutes' walk. Making a portal outside designated grounds was illegal, for reasons of safety, and even the Society mostly followed that rule, save for transfer of materials that might generate too much notice.

"These ones do not need more, hm, eyes making connections, especially so soon after Thurapo's murder. This one knows the Spire portal ground activity is recorded." I looked down. I should have remembered that, but the events of the morning had rattled me more than I thought. "All travel can be reported to the Council. Even though one is Head of Healing, one can, hm, only divert so much."

An oval of blackness rotated into being in the center of Moortlin's study, ringed by green and white—the colors of the Benish's two houses. I heard the music of the House of Healing changing, since I shared that house with my mentor. The melody of their lab in the Spire—tranquil phrases looping in repetitive chords like a chiming clock—mixed with the familiar melody of the mansion in Poler, all the way on the opposite corner of the Nether. The music there was in another key, slower tempo, and lower pitched, but the two phrases melded together as the portal formed.

Moortlin gestured for me to step into the blackness. They would be last through the portal, as it would close when they reached the other side.

As I exited the portal, the musk of Moortlin's study in the Society of Two Houses made me wrinkle my nose. I could see flakes of their skin dusting the floor around the place where the Benish usually stood behind their desk. Their species was not well-equipped to sit.

Moortlin followed my gaze as they exited and the portal closed in a splash of white and green. "It is nearly time for one to return to one's homeworld of Aben and bud. This life has been long, and one has, hm, seen much. Perhaps this breach of the Society is a sign."

I frowned at my mentor. "Don't say that," I said. I had worked under Moortlin for a little over two cycles, ever since my original mentor in the House of Potential passed away. Majus Abarham Garhuk had led me through apprenticeship, though I had been close to him since I was a child. I let the usual tug of emotion wash through me at the memory, and my right hand rose to finger the scar around my right eye. I had almost lost it in the accident. But now was not the time to wallow in Abarham's death—even if it had caused me to become a member of the Society.

My breathing came easier with the great distance from the Imperium, and the murder, but the incessant beat of the chronograph in my vest pocket urged me to action. "How can Aegrino help us with the body?" Clearly, the Society's record keeper held a lot of information, but I hadn't known he also cleaned up the Society's messes.

Moortlin's yellow eyes flashed again, deep emotion from the Benish, then they turned for the door, which was closed and locked. They were not one to let others see what they did not wish revealed.

"Aegrino will likely be in the library. These ones must let the record keeper know of the breach, and the Speaker's, hm, death, of course," Moortlin said. I felt that was second in their thoughts, only relevant by the threat to the Society. I followed them down the carpeted hall, doors lining the walls.

Hallways branched off at intervals in the sprawling structure. The Society of Two Houses was a mansion in Poler, the city on the opposite side of the Nether from its capital, the Imperium—where the Effature, the Council, and the Great Assembly were all based. Without a portal made by a majus, it would take a very long time to traverse the distance between the two.

We passed members of the Society along the way, some familiar, and some not. Even though the murder pressed me onwards, I slowed and stared at a strange being strolling by. I knew the individual must be a Lobhl, though I had not seen one of their species until now. They had only joined the Great Assembly a cycle ago.

My eyes naturally fell away from the Lobhl's face and down to their hands, which were extravagantly tattooed, with five fingers and two thumbs each. They gave me a quick twirl of their fingers in greeting and I waved back.

"Touching Digits is our newest member," Moortlin said. They must have heard the hesitation in my step. "One gave that one the geas not three days ago."

Down two more hallways and another three turns was the library, the repository of information the Society collected over the cycles and deemed too revealing to give to the larger maji community. It was put to better use furthering the Society's contributions to the Great Assembly.

Aegrino was the current record keeper, and the Etanela had been at the job for over twenty cycles, so I was told. There were still many secrets in this place, as Moortlin had only decided I could be trusted with the Society's existence after a cycle-and-a-half training under them.

Majus Aegrino Plumera Lunigi met us a few steps into the library. Aegrino was tall, even for an Etanela, reaching nearly half again my height, and I couldn't help but make comparisons to Speaker Thurapo. They might have been of an age, though Majus Aegrino had a mane of golden hair tied back in a severe bun, revealing the thin blueish planes of his face. His eyes were bright and large as his hands waved in the air. Something tugged at my thoughts, but his next words blew the feeling away like a cloud on a windy day.

"Moortlin, thank the Sea Mother you're here. I must speak with you. Something terrible has happened," Aegrino's ever-moving hands described fluid arcs by his sides, his words slurring together in his excitement.

"Another, hm, problem?" Moortlin rumbled. "Today seems a stimulating one."

"I was revising the list of Society members yesterday," Aegrino continued over Moortlin's words. "Adding our new members from the last half cycle—" Here a hand waved in my direction, "—and I left it on my desk for the night. When I came back this morning, it was gone."

I exchanged a look with my mentor. Moortlin's yellow eyes were flashing.

"Foolish of you," they chastised. "One has cautioned all the, hm, members of the Society of leaving important information where others can find it. This one knows better." Aegrino grimaced and waved an apologetic hand. Moortlin continued. "Nevertheless, this is not, hm, a new problem, but the same one of which these ones were to speak."

"Speaker Thurapo is dead," I told the record keeper. "He was to be our sponsor for the System Beast project, but when I got there, I found him on the floor of his room at the Dome with his throat cut." I drew in a breath, pushing up my glasses, which had slid down my nose again. "He had a list of the Society's members." Considering how closely we guarded that information, the list could only have come from Aegrino's desk. *Who had taken it?*

"Speaker Thurapo?" The majus blinked several times at me, fingers waving languidly. "Oh my. Oh Sea Mother. He spoke for my home district on Etan. I must tell my sister, if she doesn't already know. She...will be very upset." He searched around, as if one of the records would reverse my words, then spared a glance at Moortlin. "No, not now. Later, of course, after this is over." His eyes found me again. "Oh, but the list! You have it? Quickly, give it here." He made a pulling motion with both hands. "We are still in danger of others finding out—"

"It may be too late already," I broke in. Aegrino was normally a little scattered, but the news about the Speaker's death seemed to have hit him hard. "The list was stolen. I only know the Speaker had it by using my houses to track the paper's history. More importantly, we must clean up the body before the Imperium guard finds it."

Majus Aegrino paled to a light blue, then pivoted in place, gathering a few slips of paper and a quill. He crossed the room and slipped between two bookshelves. I heard rustling, as if he was searching for equipment. His disembodied head poked out over their tops. "I will handle it myself directly," he called back. "My sister is in the Imperium in any case."

"This one will not share any sensitive information, naturally," Moortlin cautioned, and Aegrino answered with a grunt. "Additionally, the Speaker's body must be found in, hm, natural death."

"There is a chair wedging the door closed from the inside," I added. "Symphony of Potential."

At least the geas will keep him from blabbing about the Society to his sister. I'd tested the limits when I was first inducted, which was how I knew of the further debilitating effects, past the distracting music. The geas was sometimes applied to family, so it was conceivable his sister was included, though usually it was only for those who lived at the mansion, and when absolutely necessary.

Aegrino nodded and his head disappeared as I turned to the councilor. Even if Aegrino concealed the murder, that left the list, and I had no idea where the culprit was.

I checked my chronograph. The secretary was surely back from her break. Would Aegrino be in time to stop her entering the room?

And what is it that feels wrong about this situation?

"What if the Society is revealed?" I asked Moortlin. "The geas will make us look guiltier if we cannot defend ourselves in court. Would the Council even let us rejoin the rest of the maji?" I tried to think of what raw material and equipment I had used. How much had we stolen? From where? At least I had not done experimentation on live subjects.

Councilor Moortlin regarded me for a moment, their eyes dulling, deep in thought. Maybe all the secrecy was based on their paranoia. Maybe losing the list was not so bad.

Don't delude yourself.

"This one has been with the Society for less than a cycle, Mandamon," Moortlin finally said. "One rarely shares the Society's secrets for, hm, many cycles more, but with this development, one judges it necessary for this one to know more of this group's, hm, history. These ones can spare a few minutes while Aegrino cleans up the Speaker's office—even with other pressing matters."

The Benish creaked, shifting from one gnarled foot to the other, as if still unsure whether to let any more information go. Then they reached for the doorknob with a sound of snapping branches. As I followed them back into the corridor, I heard the *pop* of a portal opening. Aegrino was on his way.

"Does this one know how old one is?" Moortlin asked as we walked down the Society's halls.

I frowned, thrown by the question. I knew the Benish were long-lived beings, perhaps the longest lived of the ten species of the Assembly. They were secretive about how their kind reproduced and how their parents— progenitors—taught them.

How will this help me find the list?

"I do not, Councilor," I answered.

"One is nearing the three hundred and seventy second cycle of existence," Moortlin said. I must have stopped, because they did too, half-turning in my direction.

"It is long even for one's people." They brushed a flake of skin from their arm, revealing a lighter surface underneath—the Benish had a dense, hard flesh, more like aged wood than muscle and meat. "But one's time has been, hm, busy, keeping the Society a secret from the Assembly while promoting new technology and social change. Otherwise beings would live shorter, uglier lives."

They took a rasping step forward and I followed. "One has watched this one's progress for many cycles, even before this one's, hm, second house emerged. It was such a tragedy to hear of this one's mentor, and family—" They broke off abruptly as I stiffened. It was still a tender subject. "—but, hm, leaving that aside, this one's inventions were what first attracted one's attention."

My second house—Healing, like Moortlin—was only beginning to show when the Benish contacted me, a few days after the accident, my wounds still fresh. I had recently passed my test to graduate from apprentice to majus, and was flattered one of the Council thought so well of me. I'd assumed such a catastrophe would doom my chances of amounting to anything in the ranks of the maji.

However, the councilor urged me to downplay my second house so others would forget. They offered tips and training, helping me find my strengths in the House of Healing. Those ran to inert organic materials, and despite the name, actual healing was an effort for me.

We reached Moortlin's study and entered. The councilor glanced both ways down the hallway before shutting and locking the door.

"This one's inventions are the talk of the Society," Moortlin continued. I made some feeble protest, my mind straying to the cooling form of Speaker Thurapo, but the Benish spread a thick hand out in negation. "No, there is no reason for, hm, false modesty. This one will be a force in the maji for cycles to come."

Flattering, but how does this help me find the list? Yet Moortlin continued, as if we had all the time in the Nether.

"Mark these words. This one's work on replicating a picture over long distances was perhaps ahead of its time, but focusing harmonic resonances into physical form and recording changes to Systems can surely, hm, be used in a cycle or two, once the issues are resolved. Finally, there are the System Beasts."

"Those still need fine tuning, before the big presentation to the Assembly," I objected, "and really, it is a combined effort with Gompt and Kratitha. They have each done at least as much as I on the project, if not more." However I *was* proud of the automatons. They could be incredibly helpful assistants, once they were approved for sale.

"Yet the original idea was this one's." Moortlin gently poked me in the chest with one thick finger. "Such ingenuity is important to encourage and develop, and the Society is the best place to, hm, do so."

I stared at Moortlin, realizing the Benish was much more worried than I had previously thought.

"This one asked about the repercussions of the Society becoming widely known. One has witnessed this firsthand," Moortlin said. "In the past, the Society was shut down and its members prosecuted."

My face must have reflected my astonishment. I pushed my glasses back up my nose. "Shut down? When? How? What happened to the two-house maji?" I smoothed my beard as my stomach tried to turn a flip. "It can't have been recently. Majus I'Ban's work with visual communication was made public ten cycles ago, and Majus' Juut, Thinker's work with pistols was twenty cycles before that."

"Precisely the issue," Moortlin answered. "This one has lived in a privileged time for the, hm, Society. One has kept our members safe, with plenty of resources. Everyone knows the maji provide new scientific advancement, and, hm, no longer question how such technological leaps arise. The Society becomes complacent." Moortlin's eyes flickered and they stumped to their desk, rooting through a stack of papers nearly the height of their head. Their motions were sharp, like twigs popping in a fire.

They're...furious. I'd never seen the Benish truly angry. They shoved papers aside as they searched, quicker than I'd ever seen them move. The controlled power of their movements frightened me more than their revelation of the prosecution of Society members.

Moortlin pulled a sheaf of papers out, cocked their head, and put them aside. "When one was very young—perhaps, hm, 630 A.A.W.—one was an apprentice, ready to become a majus." They pulled aside another section of the stack. "The Society then was run by Councilor Fortilath, head of the House of Communication, though that was, hm, not revealed until several cycles after the Society was shuttered. The geas was not in effect, then."

That's over three hundred and twenty cycles ago!

"Did one of the members let the secret out?" I asked.

Moortlin shook their head and thrust a sheaf of paper at me—very old, and with writing scribbled in the margins.

Society of war maji shut down!

It has come to the attention of the Assembly of Species, the Council of the Maji, and the Effature, that the clan of maji named the 'Society of Two Houses' has been practicing forbidden energies of war, for the express purpose of fomenting outrage and rebellion within the eight homeworlds of the Great Assembly. Not since the Aridori war of old has such an affront to the sovereignty of the Assembly been perpetrated. These maji, even more powerful in their sound magics than the rest of the maji, have used live subjects to research ways to incapacitate armies, reduce buildings to rubble, and connect portals in tandem in order to transit from homeworld to homeworld in the blink of an eye! Fortunately, the suspected maji were discovered by a group of Kirian private agents before any further damage was done. Several have been sent to Gloomlight Prison, and their place of work torn down.

I handed the page back with a frown.

"The facts are distorted," Moortlin said, their eyes' intense glow dimming along with their anger. "The Society was, hm, researching defenses against inter-homeworld conflict, brought on by hostilities between the Etanela and the Festuour over trading rights for a type of, hm, luxury fabric." "The methods for discovering defenses required, hm, *volunteers* from the war to test said defenses. Councilor Fortilath was caught on the battlefield by that one's own people. The public feared the Society would, hm, pull down their homes and take them as test subjects. Completely unfounded, as the two-house maji were, hm, trying to protect others."

"We're not in a war now," I said. "People would act differently."

"And what would they say if information was shared about this one's, hm, device focusing sonic energy?" Moortlin asked.

Is that a threat? Or merely to remind me I'm complicit as well? As if I needed another reminder.

"After the accident, I stopped working on sonics immediately," I said, then swallowed. My hands were in fists at my sides. I clenched them to keep from touching the scar on my face. The accident was not my fault. *It wasn't.* I'd spent the last two cycles wrestling with myself over it. I thought I had gotten rid of these feelings of guilt, but Moortlin's casual reference brought them back full-fold.

"That is of little import." Moortlin gestured back to the pile of papers with one hand. "The Society of Two Houses has formed, and, hm, been destroyed, at least four separate times since the Aridori war. Possibly more. Each time, fifty or sixty cycles must pass before the Assembly and the Council forgets the 'danger' and the Society can reform. Always, much knowledge is lost—knowledge that, hm, should be used to help the species of the Great Assembly."

Moortlin paced the room, creaking like branches in a storm. "This is why a member of the Society—the head, preferably—is also a member of the Council of the Maji, by election or, hm, trickery. One has been on the Council twice over the course of one's life." Moortlin looked at me. "One will do whatever is necessary to keep the Society from the notice of the other maji."

What is Moortlin capable of? The Benish had lived a long time and was crafty. Could this all be a sham? Could Moortlin themself have killed the Speaker and taken the list? Then why go through this ruse of alerting Aegrino? Were they *that* paranoid?

I shook my head. I'd worked with them closely for two cycles, and my instincts said Moortlin couldn't be involved.

"What if we brought the matter to the Effature privately?" I asked. "He's a reasonable man—he would surely see our side."

Moortlin laughed—a mirthless bark. He gestured to me. "This one is still young. One has known the Nether's caretaker far longer, enough to know the Effature is, hm...chameleonic, changing with the times." Moortlin paused, then cocked their head again. "Nevertheless, it would not help. The Effature is under the same geas as the Society."

I goggled. "The Effature knows?" The self-styled caretaker of the Nether influenced much of the finance, business, and lawmaking between the Imperium and the other cities in the Nether. He presided over the Great Assembly, though only rarely lent his voice to the debate.

"A directive from the post of the Effature originally began the Society," Moortlin said. "Has this one heard of maji born to three houses?"

My face certainly showed my confusion. That was a night-tale, told by nursemaids to children.

"It is no made up story. The Society keeps records on such rare, hm, cases." Moortlin turned to another corner of their desk, where a neat stack of papers sat under an enormous volume of plant species native to the Nether. "They are very, very rare. Rarer than, hm, two-house maji are to one-house maji. Those who are born show symptoms immediately, so in tune with the Symphony are they. None with the potential ever survived past two cycles of age, in any records one has discovered," their pupil-less eyes fixed me in place, "and which one has concealed from the Council." They patted the volume of botany protectively. "The overload of so much of the Symphony causes madness, and eventually death. This one knows the, hm, instability of some of the two-house members."

I hesitated, then nodded. Living in the mansion afforded an easy opportunity to see that many two-house maji were eccentric at best. Moortlin's paranoia was a prime example. Many of us, myself included, sometimes struggled to connect with others.

"The original directive was for those with two houses to protect against the potential threat of those with access to three houses," Moortlin said.

"That makes no sense," I said. "If none with the ability to hear three Symphonies live to use such abilities, then why is it a problem?" I tried to imagine hearing three of the aspects of the Grand Symphony. The combinations multiplied exponentially. *They could change half the music of the universe at will.*

"One sees the risk is understood," Moortlin said. "No such beings live here, but what if another civilization were to find the Nether, as the Lobhl did a few cycles ago? What if they have, hm, a militarized maji corps, and have harnessed those with three houses? The Great Assembly frowns on martial use of the Symphony. And so, the Society must guard against such an incursion. This group's other inventions are a fortunate offshoot of the core directive."

What other subjects were researched behind closed doors, and what forbidden resources did they use, even past those practices I had already discovered? I had been caught up in the rush of new scientific study, and meeting Gompt and Kratitha—realizing there were others like me who yearned for more knowledge than available within the Great Assembly of Species. No doubt it was precisely what Moortlin intended, to keep new members busy.

They crossed close enough I could smell the musty resin of their flesh. "There are much worse things out there, hm, in the wide universe," the Benish said. "Which ones are to say the next species contacting the Nether will be benevolent?" They shook their head and I winced at the crackling sound. "The Society of Two Houses is necessary as a first, but, hm, secret line of defense against the unknowns of the universe. It cannot be shut down without great loss of knowledge. It leaves the Great Assembly undefended until its resurrection."

They turned away, making their stiff-legged stride across their study, pacing once more. "This one is the Investigator one most trusts, though this one is new to the Society."

Moortlin stopped before me. "One is known far too well in the Assembly. One's placement on the Council of the Maji means one's moves are, hm, tracked closer than one would like."

They took in a deep breath, their chest creaking with the effort. "Mandamon, investigate this missing list of Society members. While Aegrino, hm, cleans up the murder, this one must find who took the list as quickly as this one can. Keep the Society alive."

"What about the System Beast project?" I protested.

Moortlin raised their hands to stop me. "It will wait a few days if needed. There is no other choice. Include this one's colleagues, but this is, hm, not to go farther that this group's small circle."

They breathed out, a gust of exhalation like the groan of a great tree. "One must return to Aben soon. The time to find a group to plant with is coming. One's memories will be passed down to the next generation of Benish, but one's work with the Society?" Their eyes dimmed. "It must remain with the two-house maji. This one—" they poked my chest again, "—is the best choice. Solve this mystery and keep the Society active for another hundred cycles."

I rocked back at the enormity of the task Moortlin had just entrusted me with. *Surely there are others better suited?*

"I will figure out who took the list, Moortlin," I said. I clenched my hands, pushing away memories of my first mentor, now dead. If the Society was closed down, I had nowhere else to go—my own actions had guaranteed that.

The Mansion

The Society, it has been my home for over forty cycles, accepting me when the maji ridiculed my ideas about the new chemical substances I have devised. Altering the chemicals the brain produces can be danger-ous, yes, but could also prove invaluable to help those with social and behavioral differences such as myself. The other two-house maji, they helped push my discoveries into the main body of majus work, but I fear my ideas will never be fully utilized without backing from the Council, and that would require revelation of my situation in the Society.

—Personal Journal of Tethan, Sathssn majus of the Houses of Strength and Power, titled "Overwhelm."

Thoughts of undiscovered species of martial beings with maji in chains followed me as I walked down the corridors of the mansion in Poler. Moortlin was paranoid, but I suspected they were also correct to worry about the fate of the Society. They could not have been involved in the murder—not with such passion for two-house maji, and for so many cycles. The original Society even had a blessing from the Effature at the time, hundreds of cycles ago.

I thought back on my twenty-and-six cycles in the Nether. Moortlin had lived for nearly fifteen times that long. What secrets would the Benish take with them when they returned to their homeworld?

My feet led me to the lower floors of the mansion. As I had not designed my inventions alone, so I could not solve this mystery alone. I had not met many Society members—by nature, we were secretive and antisocial—but the two I worked with were skilled, intelligent, and I trusted them. Their fortunes were bound up in the success of the System Beast project, which was threatened by Speaker Thurapo's death. Maybe the others could help me discover who killed him, and who had the list of Society names.

I could hear Gompt and Kratitha arguing before I entered the laboratory. I couldn't leave those two alone for even one lightening of the Nether's walls before they were off again, debating the best method of calculating efficiency. They shared the ability to hear the Symphony of Grace, and both had opinions on the best way to reduce the effort required to power the System Beasts.

We shared a spacious area in the Society mansion, cluttered by the results of our work. Kratitha was the worst, for she flitted from project to project even faster than she spoke. Gompt was slower, more deliberate, but she was as young as the rest of us, and still prone to flights of fancy. I preferred to at least get a prototype working before I moved to a new project, but I was certainly guilty of abandoning my share.

I edged past a massive construct of pipes and hoses—a failed attempt to harness performed music and compare it with the Symphony—and around stacks of books to arrive at the heart of our workshop. I was surrounded by our many iterations of System Beast design, each crafted in a different form of creature from across the Nether and the ten homeworlds.

"—find the screw for my glasses, Kratitha?" Gompt was asking. "I've been trying to fix the actuator on the new prototype without them for half a lightening." The Festuour was gesturing expansively with one furry arm, and I stepped back to avoid being hit.

"Speaker Thurapo is—" I began, but Kratitha cut me off.

"Yes, yes, found screw and fixed them just now, but had idea," she chirruped. Her wings were a blur and she held her small body at table height, peering through Gompt's glasses first with one, then another section of her compound eyes. "Need to see windings on motor. Too many for magnetic ratio. Glasses magnification most helpful. Though could add another lens to glasses to account for distribution in Pixie focal lengths."

"I calculated the ratio yesterday," Gompt said. "We wound it too tightly before. Take off six rotations and it should work. And calm down—your wings are going faster than I've even seen. I swear, you're jumpier than a pelt flea on fire today."

"The Speaker is—" my teeth clicked together as the Pixie spoke over me.

"One moment. Done!" Kratitha looked up in triumph. "Mandamon. Appointment with Speaker was successful? Was anticipating you back sooner." She buzzed to another table, half walking, half flying. "See the new motion control for the System Beast? We think it may provide better autonomy when—"

I barely got my mouth open this time.

"When it has to switch interaction targets," Gompt interrupted. "I also thought it would fit in the casing better and provide better control." She followed the Pixie a few steps. "Kratitha, my glasses, remember?"

Kratitha held the lenses in front of her multifaceted eyes once more, then gave them absently to the Festuour before peering into the interior of our largest prototype System Beast, created in the shape of a Kirian Ethulina pullbeast.

Gompt thrust her glasses back on her snout, blinking through them with bright blue eyes. They were slightly askew from Kratitha's ministrations, and Gompt tried to straighten the frame. "Now how did the interview go? Did Speaker Thurapo agree? By what date do we need this ready?" She thumped the casing on the Ethulina, causing Kratitha to jump in surprise. Her head had nearly been enclosed in the pullbeast's interior. "Kratitha, did you do something to my glasses? They work...better."

"Ground left lens slightly," Kratitha said. "Focus was off. Also adjusted focal length with—"

I drew a deep breath, then shouted, "Speaker Thurapo is dead!"

There was silence, as both Gompt and Kratitha stared at me, open-mouthed.

I took the model Festuour from my vest pocket. It was the first working System Beast Gompt had made. She'd come straight to the maji from her friend group on Festuour, at an early age. They had moved with her to the Imperium, but she still didn't get to see them often. I think the model may have been a subconscious attempt to give her another of her species she could relate to. The three of us had grown closer since then.

I handed the model back to Gompt.

"Worse than that, the Speaker held a list of members of the Society. We could be shut down if the Great Assembly finds out about us and our...resource acquisition." I frowned. "Or some of the experiments other members have performed."

"Who would kill Speaker Thurapo?" Kratitha asked. Her wings were buzzing in agitation—an emotion I could easily agree with. "Must have just happened."

"That's what I'm trying to discover," I said, and briefly described the scene I found in the Speaker's study, the missing list, and how I left his body.

"What is Moortlin doing about this?" Gompt asked.

I drew another breath. "They have tasked me with finding the killer and returning the list of names. They said they were too well known to do it, and you know how paranoid they are." I waved a hand in exasperation. "They didn't want to tell anyone else about the problem."

"Well, they are head of House of Healing," Kratitha said. She tapped a wrench into one blueish hand. "When do we start?"

"Right now." I nodded to the Pixie. She was a rarity among the small beings, as most Pixies belonged to the warrior class. The other species looked down upon them as being less intelligent. Kratitha was one of the declining scientist class, and made sure others knew it. The slow death of her class resulted from some world war fifty-odd cycles ago—a lifetime for the short-lived species.

"Aegrino is cleaning up the mess in the Speaker's study," I began, "but Moortlin wants me to search out the killer."

"Because you are Investigator, yes yes." Kratitha was nodding along.

Gompt had one furry finger raised, mouth open, as if about to make the same point. She glared at the Pixie.

"We must start at the beginning then." Gompt said. "Why was the Speaker killed? Who has cause to know about the Society? Who benefits from giving away the list of members? Are they being paid by someone, or working for themselves?"

I didn't miss Gompt's accusation, and neither did Kratitha. "Assume two-house member was paid to give it away?" she asked.

"Or was blackmailed. Who else would even have known, with our enforced silence?" Gompt replied. "How would they get around the geas? That jingle is enough to drive anyone mad—even before it incapacitated them—if they tried to bypass it to show off a list of Society names."

Kratitha's hands clasped tightly together. "Might be circumvented. Two-house maji have many resources." She scuttled to the prototype, absently checking torque on the System Beast's bolts.

I watched her, tugging my beard in thought. The Ethulina pullbeast was a work of art. We'd formed the mane of crested feathers from crystal slivers that reflected light, and the claw-hooves were of solid steel, etched with filigree. Kratitha and Gompt had spent a ten-day attaching wooden representations of the scales along its body, hiding the service hatches—one of which the Pixie had open now. She flipped several switches and the pullbeast raised one forehoof, which split into separate digits. Even though the System Beast imitated a draft animal, we had increased its dexterity to allow for grasping and holding.

The creature was starting to look as impressive as we first imagined, and its mannerisms were almost entirely lifelike, with the latest adjustments to the gearing ratios. The model I would have shown the Speaker was a toy compared with our masterpiece. We had to bring this to the Assembly, and demonstrate how the System Beast project could help our culture. They could be used as servants, and recorders, but also as a way for physical invalids to interact with the rest of the Nether. Our customers would think of many more uses once our creations were public.

That meant we had to find the killer, and the list.

"The geas hasn't failed in nearly three hundred cycles, to hear Moortlin talk," I said. "I'm sure they've tested it extensively." *What am I missing?* "Did someone find the list by accident?"

"And give it to the Speaker? And then kill him?" Gompt asked. "Why? The list would be meaningless to one who doesn't know what the Society is—just a list of names with words after them."

"Important point," Kratitha said.

"So only a Society member would know what the list meant, but would have to get around the geas to give it to the Speaker," I said. "Someone outside wouldn't have access to the list, but would have no trouble transporting it to the Speaker. I still don't see the motive to kill him."

"You didn't send any information on ahead of your appointment, did you?" Gompt asked. "The list could have been stuck to another page like a suckerfish on a whale."

"Now you think *I* did it?" I raised my eyebrows at the Festuour.

Kratitha tsked from where she was studying a selection of springs. "Not suspecting. Could have been an unfortunate accident. Maybe no one guilty. Or could have been coercion. Ah!" She picked a coil of wire out and fluttered back to the prototype, fitting it in the head cavity. "Might fix the head stutter issue."

Gompt's attention was diverted. "Does it match the calculations on the harmonics in the House of Grace?" she asked. "I've been looking for the right tension constant for three days."

"If we could attend to the murder and the Society being shut down?" I suggested. Gompt and Kratitha both turned to me, looking chagrined. "I sent the proposal to the Speaker myself last ten-day. There were no extra papers included. Even if we limit our search to Society members, and I think that's a better guess, we can't just ask everyone whether they're plotting to shut us down."

The two considered, and I looked around the workshop for inspiration. The numerous small automatons—previous attempts at System Beasts, on a lesser scale—stared back. The full-size prototype was the first of its kind. Others had exposed gearing, or no coverings at all. The skeletal face of a rodent-shaped beast peered at me from one shelf, its lidless eyes frozen in a glassy stare. Its beat in the Symphony of Potential was mechanical, a representation of the System's artificial construct. "Is there a way to use the prototypes to gather information?" I asked.

Gompt followed my gaze. "I suppose I could alter the gearing in some of the old ones to record waveforms, and leave them around the mansion," she said. "We might happen on important information."

"Too long," Kratitha argued. "Need quick answer, before killer gets too far with list." She waved her wrench vaguely, taking in the Nether as a whole.

"I can adjust a few," Gompt protested. She held up the model I'd taken to the Speaker's office this morning. The little figure held a tiny drum, which disguised a wax cylinder, where the figure could inscribe sums. "I can change the gearing to make it write sound waves rather than mathematical figures."

Kratitha, drawn as ever by a challenge, drifted forward. "Will have to account for sound wave distortion," she said. "House of Grace can help in cutting out noise, but will need to tune System powering it."

"The smaller scale can be used to filter the lower register," Gompt said, lifting the figure out of the Pixie's grasping fingers. "There are a few others I can adjust the same way."

"New algorithm must be altered for differences in size and shape—" Kratitha was already searching the standing, half-disassembled prototypes. "Ah. This one." She pointed to a System Beast in the form of a sticky lizard, with adhesive feet made to climb walls. It was missing its tail and lower jaw, but it carried a similar wax cylinder on its back, a stylus positioned nearby. We had played with replicating animal sounds with this one. It would work even better than the one Gompt held.

"This will require what, two or three lightenings to adjust?" I asked. "Moortlin wants this tied up as quickly as possible—today, if we can."

"If we get the gearing right the first time," Gompt said. She played with her glasses thoughtfully. "What do you think, Kratitha?"

"Two lightenings, maximum," Kratitha said, still tapping sections of the lizard. "Can finish while you investigate Society members." She looked back at us, compound eyes reflecting many facets of the room. "Go, go. Will work here. Talk to others to save time."

"I guess that's our dismissal," I told Gompt. In truth, I was having trouble keeping my hand from drifting to my chronograph. I wondered if Aegrino had intercepted Speaker Thurapo's secretary in time. *Or did she find the body?*

"Remember to account for the waveform distribution of the System Beast so we don't pick up any echoes this time," Gompt called as I propelled her out with a hand on her furry arm. Kratitha waved a hand in acknowledgement.

We strolled out of the workshop, picking a direction in the mansion largely by happenstance. We had only gotten a few paces down the hall before Gompt began a rumbling hum, thinking.

"You're right. We can't ask every member of the Society where they've been and what their motivations are."

"I don't even *know* half the members," I said. "You've been here longer than me."

"Only by a few ten-days," Gompt replied. "Kratitha was here several months before me, but I doubt she's gone to any lengths to meet others. Keeps her head down lower than a racing canis on the scent."

I added combinations in my head. "Six houses, fifteen combinations of two-house member abilities—"

"Though not all equally represented," Gompt added.

"True, but with a hundred and some members in the Society, there must be at least two or three of each type. Could a specific combination affect the geas?"

"Maybe," Gompt adjusted the bandolier that held her favorite selection of tools. Festuour liked accessories—hats, glasses, scarves, belts, and bandoliers—more than clothes. There was little point with all that fur. "But I'm nigh certain I've heard Moortlin say the geas was built up from all six houses. Hard for one majus to get around that."

"So you're saying it could be more than one?" I wasn't ready to dig a conspiracy out of a secret society. That felt like one too many layers.

Gompt waggled a three-fingered paw as we turned into the next hallway, where some of the Society's clinical studies took place. "Possible, but I doubt it. What about the section of the list you found? Whose names were on it? They might be ones the Speaker was paying more attention to."

In the interest of time, it was a good place to start. I thought back. "The three of us," I began. "That would be the Houses of Potential and Healing for me, and Potential and Grace for you—"

"And Kratitha would be Grace and Power." Gompt was nodding along.

"Moortlin was on the list as well, and they're a Biologist—Houses of Strength and Healing." *That's odd.* "In fact, I'm surprised Moortlin was not more concerned about their name getting out, considering their place on the Council."

"I'm sure they've got the politics of this all tied up. Have you ever heard Moortlin sound unsure about anything?" Gompt peered at me over her spectacles. "How inept would the Council be to let a scandal take down its members? Anyway, as secretive as the friendless old root is, I can't believe they had anything to do with this. What about the other names?"

"If we discount us and the Benish..." I searched through my hazy memory. Both names had been familiar. "One was Tethan, of the Houses of Strength and Power."

"So an Overwhelm," Gompt said. We walked up a staircase, passing a Lobath talking with another Festuour in hushed tones. Gompt watched the one of her species as we passed, but the Festuour didn't notice her.

"What are their strengths?" I asked. I hadn't seen an Overwhelm in action.

"Strength and Power give some ability to push others to do what they want, and to pry objects apart into components," Gompt said. "If anyone could take apart the geas, an Overwhelm could. Sounds fishy to me."

I had to admit my friend was right, but my memory of Tethan was of a small, frail Sathssn. "Have you seen her recently?"

Gompt shrugged. "I went up to her room to ask her a question once about the System Beasts responding to chemical signals."

"I doubt she's murdered more than a hot meal in cycles," I said.

"Still prudent to follow every lead, and this is all we have right now," Gompt said. The maji who lived here would have apartments in their primary House back in the Imperium, but I had found most in the Society preferred the obscurity of Poler, desiring to follow their own studies without interruption, or any distracting ethical questions.

We found Tethan on the third level, tucked into a corner of the mansion. The sprawling house was big enough for new members to get lost in. I'd lost my way frequently in my first few ten-days.

I knocked on the red painted door of the majus' room. Gompt and I traded glances at the chorus of thumps and complaints coming from inside. There was another clatter, as if a stack of plates had fallen to the floor.

"Maybe later?" Gompt suggested, and I almost stepped away when the doorknob rattled.

The red painted wood opened a crack and a slitted red and yellow eye, surrounded by gray-green scales peeked out.

"Yes? You are here about the pipes?"

"Ah—Majus Tethan?" I asked, somewhat at a loss.

"Yes. That is me. I have been sending messages about the pipes for ten-days now. You, come in."

The door rattled closed, and Gompt frowned at the sounds of metal latches being unfastened. Then the door opened again, showing an ancient Sathssn, gray of scale and shaky, with white wisps of hair floating around her head. I was nearly as surprised at her age as I was at the lack of coverings. Tethan wore no cowl, had on short sleeves, and her tunic was dark blue—something I had never seen on a Sathssn.

"I thought they all wore black?" Gompt whispered. Tethan peered at us as if she had heard something, then shook her head and gestured with a scaled hand for us to come in. A short black skirt covered the majus only halfway down her legs, and below she wore open sandals rather than the more common enclosed boots.

We followed the old Sathssn inside and Tethan hobbled around us to close and latch the door again.

"Now, my pipes, they have been squeaking for months, but Moortlin refuses to send anyone up here." Tethan shuffled around to look at us, then away, leading us farther into the apartment. "At least until now."

The room was uncomfortably warm, and I pulled at the collar of my shirt as Gompt opened her mouth in a pant. Books were stacked everywhere, with trinkets, statues, and little plates piled on top as if the books were plinths. It was a collection of plates that had tumbled to the floor by the door.

Something squawked by my foot and I hastily looked down.

"Don't worry about Scampers. Him, he complains all the time," Tethan said. A scaled creature with six legs rubbed against me, leaving a white smear on my best pants. "Especially right now, as he is molting."

I shook off the thing and glared at Gompt, whose tongue lolled in silent Festuour laughter.

"The sound, it is right back here." Tethan waved a wizened arm, and I could barely stop myself from staring at the loose scaly skin.

I don't think I've ever seen—or want to see again—so much bare Sathssn flesh.

She knocked at a wall and I jumped at a chittering whine that grew louder, vanishing to a shriek. It sounded almost organic, but I had heard all sorts of sounds from these old walls.

"We—we wanted to ask a few questions," I attempted, but Tethan was shuffling along, not paying any attention.

"The pipes, they run along here." She traced a finger along the wall. "Nothing in the Symphony of Strength, but me, I hear a repeating arpeggio in the melody of Power." She looked to me and I looked to Gompt, who shrugged—neither of us could hear the House of Power.

"What about the House of Potential?" I suggested. There might be an overlap. Gompt sighed, but her blue eyes took on a faraway look, even as I tuned into the music that echoed though my head.

"Yes, I hear it," I said. "There's a chord progression like something…"

"Something blocked. Energy is building," Gompt said.

I nodded. The rhythm was natural, like that of a wind tunnel. What did those pipes transmit? Not fluid. Maybe they heated the upstairs. If so, then Tethan must have requested her vents opened all the way for the apartment to be so warm.

Gompt walked down the hall, knocking on the wall. I took the chance to corner the old majus.

"What do you work on?" I asked.

"Oh this and that," Tethan shrugged. "Now, not so much as before. But twenty cycles past, I was making some of the best psychotropic chemicals available. The remedies, the Assembly decided they were too dangerous, even for those who needed them, so here I sit." She spread scaled hands to the messy apartment.

Mind altering chemicals? My thoughts raced. Like something that could make a speaker cut his own throat? "Can you tell me where you've been the last several days?" I asked.

"What now?" Tethan cupped a hand around one earhole. The wattle of scales under her chin wobbled as she did.

I repeated myself louder. "Have you been out of the Society mansion in the past few days?"

"Oh, Great Forms no." Tethan shook her head, mouth slightly open. "My rooms, I don't leave them. They bring my dinners here. Who would feed Scampers while I was gone?"

I looked back to find the little beast following me, sniffing at my pant leg. The majus' words and the state of the apartment triggered a connection in my mind. The plate by the door probably contained some of her breakfast. If so, she would have been here eating about the time the Speaker was murdered.

"Found it!" Gompt called from the other room, and we both went to her. My colleague was holding a glistening orb nearly the size of her hairy paw. "This was stuck in the pipe. The cover was loose."

I looked at Tethan, then down at Scampers. "I think your pet may be a female," I suggested.

"Naughty Scampers!" Tethan shook a finger at the beast, who whined, then chuffed at her sandal. "Yes, yes, the egg, we will put it somewhere safe. I wondered where you went that time you got out."

Gompt gave Tethan the egg and followed my crooked finger back to the entrance of the apartment. We left the Sathssn cooing to her pet and the thing's offspring, but before leaving her front room, I ran my finger around the topmost plate in the fallen pile by the door. I listened to the harmony between Healing and Potential, letting the Symphony guide my sense of time. It confirmed my suspicions.

Outside, Gompt blew out a breath. "Hot enough to cook an egg in there, not just hatch one."

"At least we can mark one name off," I said.

"We may have fixed her pipes, but we're no closer," Gompt protested. "Tethan's old, but she could still have broken the geas and sent a list of names to the Speaker. You should have seen the set of chemicals and beakers in her bathroom."

I shook my head. "She said she hadn't been out of the apartment in days. All those little plates? They're the remains of old meals, sent up from the kitchen. I think Tethan is a shut-in. She could have done it, possibly, but until there's something more concrete, I think we should search elsewhere."

"I suppose she'd be terrified of the Society closing down," Gompt said. "Then there's Scampers, and Scamper's egg." She let out a sigh. "You're right. Any more names?"

I thought back. "Plithin A'Tyf. A Lobath belonging to the Houses of Communication and Healing."

"A Psychiatrist," Gompt said. "There's some definite potential to mess with how a mind's affected by the geas." We turned down another corridor.

Are there any combinations of houses that don't *have a way that might undermine the geas?*

"Isn't he the one that made the speech at the last big Society symposium where members shared their inventions?" Gompt asked. "There were more members than I've seen in one place before."

I rolled my eyes. "On the subject of 'Cooperation within the bounds of the Society'? It sounded like generic noise. Uninspired. I guess belonging to the House of Communication doesn't guarantee good oration." We stumped down a set of stairs.

"We still need to visit him," Gompt said. "You know, just to make sure he isn't secretly plotting to overthrow the Nether."

"If he isn't, then we're back to the beginning," I said. "Speaker Thurapo isn't getting less dead, and the list of names isn't getting less lost." I looked down at my chronograph. All this traipsing around was wasting time, though I wasn't sure what else I could do. If the Society was shut down, where would I go? Technically, I had access to an apartment in the House of Potential, but everything I knew was in Poler, including what remained of the home where I grew up.

All this is assuming the two-house maji aren't put on trial once the records hidden in this mansion get out.

Majus A'Tyf was on the second level, near the front of the mansion. I straightened my coat, now some of the sweat from Tethan's apartment had dried, and we placed ourselves in front of a white door with a granite lintel.

This time Gompt knocked, and we heard a conversation cut off before someone opened the door.

Plithin A'Tyf, was short even for a Lobath, in a maroon jumpsuit, his head-tentacles wrapped up in a neat bun. He stared back with wide, surprised eyes, though that was normal for his species.

"Yes? Can I help? You two are from the workshop, aren't you? With all the new Systems? What can I do for you?" His voice was low and bubbly.

"We have a few questions—" Gompt began, but the Lobath cut him off.

"And I have answers. I remember when all the new members of the Society used to come to me. 'Unity,' I'd tell them. The Society must be a cohesive unit. Together we can go far." He stepped back. "Come on in. Meet my spouses. Always a pleasure to meet the new folk around here."

"Athera, Mieru—we have guests," he called out, and I raised a hand to stop him, but too late. Gompt and I followed, stuck in his wake.

Oh well.

Where Tethan's quarters had been warm and close, these rooms were cool and distinguished, vases on stands and artwork on the walls. Athera was taller than her husband, but a little shorter than Mieru—the wari spouse, who was of the third Lobath gender. Cups of fishy-smelling tea sat on a little table next to bowls of mushroom paste, and it was obvious we had disturbed them while they were relaxing.

"You want something to eat? We have plenty."

Refusing was futile, and we soon had our own bowls, with stiff mushroom caps to scoop out the contents. We learned neither of Plithin's spouses were maji, though they had lived in the Society for cycles.

"We accompany him to all the major functions," Mieru told us, patting hir husband's hand. I don't know what he would do without us." Athera nodded along.

Plithin laughed good naturedly. "Now what did you young ones want to ask me about? Some philosophical question about the Symphony, I suppose? That's what it usually is. You two must be about my daughter's age. She's not a majus, of course. Out at university in the Imperium. The best money can buy for our girl!"

Now Athera patted his hand. "Let them ask," she chided.

"Certainly! Ask away! Don't be afraid to come to your elders with any problems you have."

"Majus A'Tyf," I said, in a desperate attempt to stop him before he trampled all over our words. "We have some disturbing news. I recently found evidence of a list with names of our members and Society titles, in a speaker's office. We are trying to discover how it happened."

Plithin puffed up like an angry squid. "As well you should! My spouses and I are well known to the higher societies in the Imperium, and if information about the Society got out—"

"This isn't about those volunteers you requested last month, is it?" Athera asked, and Plithin deflated.

"I don't...think so. They were all, er...compensated for the tests we ran." He turned back to us. "The geas has always been sufficient for me and my spouses to avoid any unfortunate—lapses, even when I've maybe had a few too many. That infuriating tune is quite enough to break anyone's concentration, even before it gets nasty. Surely the Society is safe?"

"Your name specifically was on a list Mandamon found," Gompt said. "And the Speaker who held it was found with his throat cut." The majus' spouses stared in horror. "We think it may be an attempt to expose the Society, and rouse public opinion against us."

"Oh." Plithin was quiet for a moment. "Oh, I see. No that would not be good at all." He stared at us with large silvery eyes. "Our friends in the Imperium know my spouses and I, yes, but not about the Society. They think we live in a nice house in Poler, not—" he trailed off, waving a long-fingered hand at their home. "You say my name was on this list? Any idea why?"

"That's what we were planning to ask you," I said. "Are you familiar with Speaker Thurapo? He was the one killed."

Mieru clapped a hand over hir mouth, stifling a gasp. Plithin looked to his mate. "Zie knows the Speaker, but only socially. I have never met him myself. How do you know my name was connected to the Society? We are all very careful with any correspondence we send, even with the geas' warning melody."

I briefly outlined the murder scene I found, and the impression of the paper I had found in the Symphony.

"Tracing it with the House of Healing—very clever," Plithin said. "I have done similar things in my time. I would love to discuss the methods you used. Did you have to change any chords, or merely listen? You hear the House of Potential too? The harmony between the houses would—" He waved Athera off. "Yes, yes, I know I am straying. I may have a moment to indulge my curiosity, even in the face of this dark news. It is the right of philosophers everywhere."

I kept my eyes firmly forward, though I desperately wanted to roll them at the Lobath's words. I had met other maji like this—who thought because they could hear the Symphony they could expound on theories of the universe better than regular people.

"We will leave you to your contemplation, majus," I began, "if you can tell us where you were yesterday night or this morning?" It was late in the afternoon by this point and I was despairing of discovering any useful information today.

The list is getting farther away.

"We were here," Athera said. "Both Mieru and I can corroborate that." The wari Lobath nodded hir head.

"And you have sent no correspondence in the last few days that could have given away this information?" I was convinced by this point, but felt I should ask.

"Certainly not." Plithin drew himself up. "If I find the miscreant who did so, I'll come to you directly. I cannot abide one who would undermine the Society and what I have with my family."

I rose, and Gompt rose with me. "Thanks for your time, majus," she said. "We'll let you know as soon as we hear anything."

"I should hope so," the majus said, leading us to the door. "The life I have built here is dear. We raised our daughter in this home. Please find whoever did this and stop them." He showed us into the hall. "Unity. It's what the Society needs, at this point more than any other. Stay safe, young ones."

Gompt and I walked down the front hallway of the mansion in silence.

"He can't have had anything to do with this," Gompt finally said. "Not with so much to lose if the Society falls."

"The daughter?" I suggested, with little conviction.

"Possible she could rebel against her parents," Gompt said, "but there's still the problem of the geas. I feel like the culprit must be a majus."

"I agree," I acknowledged with a tip of my head. "Then we are back where we started. There's no connection between the names, save ours. All six houses of the maji are represented—Strength, Communication, Power, Grace, Healing, and Potential. Who else can we go to?"

We turned into the east wing of the mansion. "Aegrino should be back," Gompt said. "Maybe he'll have more information about the Speaker."

"Good idea," I said. "He might know other members with motive, too."

"His title is 'Dancer,' yes?" Gompt asked. She wasn't as familiar with the Etanela as I was. "Strange for him to be the record keeper."

"Communication and Grace—fluid in mind and body." I shrugged. "Helps to keep all those records in mind, I suppose."

"If he knows the names of all the members of the Society, then he's a weak point." Gompt adjusted her glasses. "There's one in every group of friends."

A valid argument, though a strange way of saying it. I knew Gompt didn't see her friend circle nearly as often as she used to. She'd complained about it while we worked with Kratitha on the System Beasts.

I brought my mind to the present. "But he couldn't possibly have given the list away. He was the one who told us about the theft."

"A good way to throw off your suspicions." Gompt tightened her bandolier of tools. "And if he is innocent, he can help us narrow down the list of members. The geas doesn't keep people from lying to us, after all." She pointed back the way we came. "Either of those maji could be spinning us a yarn, though I doubt it."

"I know." I had been thinking the same thing, but I couldn't help believing Tethan and Plithin. "Then it'll be good to ask Aegrino about the situation in the Imperium." We turned our steps toward the record room, passing other maji deep in conversation.

Now everyone looks suspicious. Why are those two whispering? Who would want to do the Society ill?

In short order we reached the records room, near the center of the mansion and Moortlin's office. I would have updated the Benish on what we'd found, but they had gone back to the Spire of the Maji in the Imperium. They were busy, being on the Council.

The record room seemed empty, and I wondered if Aegrino was still in the Imperium, too. It should be easy to spot the tall Etanela.

"He made a portal back in the shelves when we left," I said, turning a corner into a tight path between bookcases. They were higher than my head, stuffed with books, rolled papers, ideas, contraptions, and other, less identifiable objects.

I stopped short. Aegrino Plumera Lunigi was lying face down on the floor, a puddle of greenish blood pooling beneath his chest.

PART THREE

More Than One

When I applied to be the record keeper for the Society, little did I realize the extent of the accounts Moortlin collected over the cycles. I have piles of notes on wartime uses of the Symphony rendered illegal by the Council, forgotten inventions, and secrets that could tip the politics of the Great Assembly to the benefit of a single species. It is little wonder our leader is paranoid about others finding us out. The Society may have more dangerous information stored than the rest of the maji combined.

—Aegrino Plumera Lunigi, Record Keeper for the Society of Two Houses

"Gompt!" I called. My friend came running, then skidded to a halt, bracing herself against a bookshelf to keep from stepping in the puddle of blood.

"Oh no! Is he...?"

I knelt by the body, pressing a hand to the back of his neck. Still warm, but there was no rise and fall of breath, no movement.

"It must have been recently. It's only been a few lightenings since Moortlin and I spoke with him. If he cleaned up the Speaker's study, he can't have been back for long either. Help me turn him."

Gompt came forward, one paw over her mouth, but hesitated. "Shouldn't we go to someone—?" She looked around as if one of the Poler Civic Watch would materialize out of the woodwork.

"Who are we going to tell?" I asked, sitting back on my heels. "We are in a mansion filled with suspects, in an organization with a geas keeping it secret. We can't let anyone outside know, and we can't trust anyone on the inside. Now come help."

Gompt grimaced, but reluctantly came forward. She was obviously uncomfortable, but together, we lifted Aegrino's corpse, bluish arms flopping lifelessly.

The body had not stiffened yet, and our actions revealed the method of the record keeper's death. There were vicious slashes across the front of the Etanela's robe, parting both fabric and flesh. Gompt hissed and covered her mouth again, and I barely kept from jumping to my feet. The cuts were to the bone, vitriol and blood dripping from fierce lines of violence.

"What could cut a body like that?" she asked. "It's like the killer was in a rage."

"But there's no sign of a struggle," I said. "At least not from what I can see. Just like Speaker Thurapo." I forced myself to stay over the body, though my mind screamed at me of what happened this morning, and two cycles ago.

"What about the Symphony of Healing?" Gompt said, and I nodded, already listening for the strains of music. *Losing myself in the music is always calming.*

The melody of Healing around Aegrino's body was ragged, almost doubled, arpeggios cutting off and resuming in a different key like two pieces were playing at once. The usual forte measures of exertion were not present.

"He didn't fight, or even move much before getting gutted," I said. "What could have done this with such speed?"

"Maybe the Symphony of Potential can tell us." Gompt's eyes were far away again behind her glasses, and I could tell she was listening to our shared house. I transitioned from the music of Healing to Potential, like changing from a wind quartet to a drum solo.

The melody of Potential was a different thing from Healing, from warm to cold, organic to artificial. Potential was the song of logic and forces.

"There," Gompt said. "That repeating cadenza, with the descending fourths." I waded through the music, searching for the same part of the arrangement. It was situated around the wounds, like the broken measures in the Symphony of Healing.

"What does it mean?" I asked. Gompt was better than I at deriving history from Potential alone.

She mimed a path at head level through the air, in time with the beat of the music. It would have been at chest level for the Etanela. The same place his wounds were centered.

"It's like he was slashed by a bunch of blades, all at once," Gompt said, screwing her snout up so her canines showed. "I keep our metal and woodworking tools that sharp, and there are other rooms in the mansion where corpses are dissected. The implement could have come from any of them. It's ghastly."

I opened myself to both Symphonies, the organic rhythms of Healing meshing with the syncopation of Potential. I blinked in surprise as I realized the disruptions in one piece of music matched the spirited sections of the other. The Symphony of Potential had literally cleaved the Symphony of Healing in twain.

"Interesting. This is not a normal injury." *I just can't understand why*. I pushed my glasses up. Something was nagging at me, begging for connection with some fact I knew intimately, but it made no sense. "This must have been done by someone Aegrino knew."

"Did Aegrino let the killer come to the mansion through a portal? Did he even finish cleaning up Speaker Thurapo's body?" Gompt put her paws on her furry hips and looked away from the mess. "It makes no sense. There's no way Aegrino invited the killer here, but they were able to get from the Imperium to Poler just as quickly as him. I'd bet Nether glass it's a Society majus. It's got to be."

"But why?" I stroked my beard. "There's little reason for one of the Society to betray their own. Here we have safety, freedom to research and escape from persecution, others who think as we do—what's the motive?"

"Too much ambition? Jealousy? Just not satisfied with something?" Gompt shrugged. "Could be anything. Finding the perpetrator is the quickest way to the motive."

I wasn't convinced. If we knew the *why*, that would lead us to the *who* and the *how*. There had to be a solid reason a second person—a second Etanela—was killed on the same day. I moved back from Aegrino's body, feeling like I should do something with him. *If we can find another clue here, it may lead us to the killer.*

"What about his records?" I asked. Gompt looked around as if they would appear out of the air. "What if he had another copy of the Society names? Could the killer have lost the first copy somehow?"

"Let's look around." I was grasping at ideas, distracted and half expecting officials to come knocking at the mansion door. Whoever had the list could have gone to anyone in the Assembly, especially since this person knew where the mansion was and how to get past the complex System installed at the front gate. Normally, it caused others to overlook the mansion, in a similar manner to how the geas kept us from speaking of the Society. Maybe it wasn't working anymore.

We looked around the records room, led by dips and trills in the Symphony of Potential to follow Aegrino's path. It was almost random, as if the majus was not familiar with his library.

Gompt called out, "Aha!" a few minutes later. I ran to where she was bent over in front of a small cabinet, stuffed with records so ancient they were more dust than text. She had a roll of parchment in her hand with recent writing at the end of a long list of names.

I took the sheet gingerly, tuning a few chords of the music of Potential to a lower key to prevent my fingers from causing any more destruction to the ancient list. I read from the bottom up, noting names of some older members I recognized, leading back in time. Tethan and Plithin were both on there. I rolled the scroll backwards, noting Moortlin's name about a third of the way up. There were cycles noted for many of the names, with substantial gaps in places. The oldest reached into the single digits.

"Gompt," I breathed, "The oldest of these names are almost a thousand cycles old. They reach all the way back to the Aridori war."

Gompt shivered. "I don't need any more nightmares. Growing up, my friend group would tell us tales of Aridori, sneaking about and making off with naughty children, taking their place and causing chaos. Stick to the present."

I rolled the scroll to the end. Neither I nor my two friends were on the list. It was an older copy, but likely one Aegrino had used to make a new version. Indeed, the Symphony of Potential had a soft chorus drifting into silence: the action of copying information from this place to another, but the music was too faint to determine where the new list was located.

"This is useless," I said. "It's not complete, and the new sheet is missing. Even if we found it, we're back to sifting through however many members of the Society there are at the moment."

I sagged back against a bookcase. I couldn't do this. If the Society was shut down, I had no place to go. My family was gone, and our old house had been sold last cycle. I put the scroll on a nearby shelf and held my head in my hands.

Gompt was there in an instant. "What's the problem?" she asked. "What can I do?"

I shook my head. "It's nothing."

"It's not nothing," Gompt told me. "The Society can't be shut down so easily. The Council has to know something about us. I can't believe Moortlin—and over a hundred maji—have kept this place a complete secret, even with the geas. Some shred of evidence must have gotten out before now."

I looked up at my friend. "But where would we all go, if the mansion was closed? Think about Plithin and his family. About Tethan and Scampers." *That's not the only reason.*

I hadn't told Gompt about the accident with my family. Moortlin was the only one who knew.

"Every majus has an apartment in the Imperium," Gompt said. "If the Society closed, we could live there."

"I've never lived in the Imperium," I said. It came out almost by accident and I closed my mouth. Gompt looked at me strangely.

"How—" her brow drew down behind her glasses. "What about classes in the Imperium? Living with your mentor while apprenticed?"

"I...we commuted," I said.

"That would take a lot of money, even for a majus," Gompt said. "Using a portal to arrive in the Imperium every day? Leaving at night for home? Did you come from Methiem?"

I was already sweeping my hands side to side, negating her words. *It's not like that. Not anything like that.* A memory intruded—my mother watching while my future mentor stood beside me, the rusty brown of the House of Potential visible to us both. Abarham was leading me through my first attempt at changing notes in the Symphony of Potential. We were in my house, after a lunch with my parents' good friend and his husband.

Abarham Garhuk. The thought of my old mentor—practically another father—made a lump rise in my throat, and my hand rise to my scar. The emotion was stronger than my reaction to either the Speaker's or the record keeper's death, and I was still in the same room as the latter's corpse. Poler was a large, but quiet town, and an insular community; relationships were long-lasting. When my mother's childhood friend discovered we could hear the same aspect of the Grand Symphony, a bond formed between us instantly. There was no doubt I would apprentice with him.

"I grew up in Poler," I said. "Right here in this town. My family—" My hesitation only lasted a heartbeat. I pushed away the feelings climbing up my chest. "My family knew the person who later became my mentor— Majus Garhuk."

I waited for the realization to catch up to Gompt. It always took a few seconds, when people heard his name.

She blinked furiously behind her glasses. "Wait...you mean Majus Garhuk, who was killed in Poler two cycles ago?"

I nodded. "The same. Most people pay attention to the high profile name in that story, but not much else." *Not to the other names.*

"What do you mean—" Gompt broke off, looking to the ceiling of the records room. This was not the first time I had been seated only a few paces from a rapidly cooling corpse.

My Festuour friend looked back, concern on her ursine face. "A local family was with the majus when he died, in a strange disturbance. No one could ever figure out how one room had collapsed when the rooms next to it were whole. That was—that was your family?"

I knew the look on my face was confirmation enough.

"Oh, Mandamon, I'm sorrier than you can imagine," Gompt said. She reached out, putting a paw on my shoulder, and squeezed. I placed my hand on her paw, feeling the fine fur on her three wide-spread digits.

"I've only been out of the Nether twice," I admitted, "both times to my grandparent's villa on Methiem, in Ibra." I took in a deep breath, breaking the bubble of memory that surrounded us.

I can't break down now.

"But that's in the past. If the Society is shut down, I suppose I'll get an apartment in the Imperium, and find out what the big city is really like." I made an effort to stop my mouth from turning down.

"Hey, you're welcome to stay with me!" Gompt said. "My friend group has a set of apartments in Mid Imperium, and there's always room for one more." Her furry brow creased. "At least there was the last time I was there."

"Maybe I will," I said, and wiped at my eyes behind my glasses. "Though the first thing is to prevent anything happening to the Society."

Friend group. Always one more. The thought brought something that had been lurking in my subconscious to the fore.

"Wait—we listened to the music around Aegrino's death," I said, and Gompt nodded. "So why didn't we hear the notes of whoever *killed* him?"

Gompt stood up straight as I pushed away from the bookcase. "You're right. I should have heard some music around those knives that killed him. Who wielded them, and how? Rot and claw, I can't believe you trust me to help you designing complex Systems for these automatons." She fished the little Festuour System Beast out of her bandolier.

I contemplated Gompt's little figurine as we approached Aegrino's corpse. "I missed it too. That's why we're working together."

Gompt saw where I was looking and held it up. "Mechanical," she said. "Sort of like the music, isn't it?"

"Just what I was thinking," I said. I listened to the System behind the little model. The beat, the key, even the tempo was like the faint echoes of the slashes on Aegrino's body. Systems did not occur in nature, but were created by maji. They never had the same beauty as naturally arising music—the Grand Symphony.

"This was done with a System," I said. "The murderer has a weapon made by a majus, or stolen from one." There was some part of this that still felt too familiar, but I couldn't place it.

Gompt cocked her head from side to side, tapping her fingers to some beat I couldn't hear. It must be the House of Grace.

"Aegrino was a Dancer—Communication and Grace. Someone who could change the Symphony of Grace could waltz right out of the reach of whatever slashed him." She waved her paw holding the figurine at the corpse, keeping it out of her sightline. Her other hand was tapping at the air, as if touching points on an intricate diagram. "There's no residue in the music. None of the scales are interrupted and all the chords are in place. If Aegrino had used the Symphony to move out of the way, I would still be able to hear it."

"Maybe another aspect can tell us more." I braced myself, and bent over the body. The Symphony of Healing was a faint whisper. The body's mechanisms were breaking down, even in the few minutes we had been here. I stood. There should be music here describing another person, but all the phrases seemed to define Aegrino's body, ragged and fragmented as they were. Gompt's and my measures were forte and in the foreground. It was unnatural. There was something we were both missing.

"If I had some part of the weapon the attacker used," I mused, "I could trace who held it with Potential and Healing combined." *Just like when I traced the paper the Speaker held.*

"What about the...the wounds?" Gompt suggested. "There may be a piece stuck...inside." She looked away, and I think if Festuour had less fur, I'd have seen her turning green.

"Good idea." Physical contact was helpful for both my Symphonies. I took in a deep breath, then ran a finger down the tattered strip along Aegrino's chest. As I touched the jagged flesh, several themes popped to the forefront, first a spiraling chord progression in the house of Healing—the identifier every being held within them. The music bled to everything a person touched, and was unique.

Second was a martial beat in the music of Potential, decaying from a high register to a lower one. As seconds passed, the rhythm evolved in a regular manner. Try as I might, I could only hear one spiraling chord, with some minor variations, though that could have been an artifact of Etanela biology. There was only Aegrino here. Had he somehow killed himself?

I wiped my fingers on a clean section of Aegrino's coat, used a few notes in the Symphony of Healing to burn away any other contamination, then straightened.

"There is nothing else." I let my face show my puzzlement. "Maybe Moortlin will have another idea. We have to tell them what happened, anyway."

Gompt agreed, and we made our way out of the record room and down the hall, leaving Aegrino's body behind. Hopefully Moortlin would have a way to clean it up. It wasn't like there had never been death in the mansion.

It was late in the afternoon, and the head of the Society spent their evenings in the mansion. We knocked on Moortlin's door, but even with repeated knocking and calling out, there was no answer.

We were about to leave, and bring Kratitha up to date on our findings instead, when a small noise caught my ear—the liquid *pop* of a portal opening.

I held one finger up to Gompt and knocked again.

This time there was rhythmic stumping, and Moortlin's burnished face peered out at us from the opened door.

"Yes? These ones have caught one, hm, between meetings. One has little time for—"

"Aegrino is dead," I cut Moortlin off. Their solid yellow eyes flashed bright for a second, and they pulled the door open.

"Come in then, and, hm, tell one what has occurred."

We quickly told the Benish about Tethan and Plithin, and how we found Aegrino, plus the lack of information on the killer.

"It has to be a majus in the Society," I finished, "but they have hidden their tracks too well. Neither Gompt nor I know what else to do. And, someone will need to deal with Aegrino and the mess in the records room."

Moortlin paced to a chorus of creaks. "One cannot accept anyone inside the Society would do such a thing. One has, hm, personally interviewed every two-house majus over the last several hundred cycles. Care was taken to avoid any personalities with attributes leading to a situation such as this. This is very disturbing."

"If it wasn't someone in the Society, then who was it?" Gompt asked. "If someone got in here, easy as you please, that means this place isn't as secret as you make it out. Is the geas not working? Is the System at the gates broken? You can't have it both ways."

"This one is correct that there is more happening than on, hm, first inspection." Moortlin's eyes dimmed. "Was there anything to suggest another avenue of investigation? Both victims were Etanela. Is this a, hm, specist crime?

We all looked at each other, but I shook my head. "It doesn't...feel like it," I said. "Why go to all this trouble to invade the Society? There are other Etanela members who haven't been harmed, and the Speaker wasn't a majus."

"If it was about Etanela, then why that method of murder? Why steal the list?" Gompt asked.

"Perhaps one could accompany these ones back. With four of the six houses accounted for, surely these ones must discover—"

Moortlin broke off as Gompt jumped, clapping a hand to her belt. "What in blazes?" she cried, fumbling with the buckle. "The friendless thing is trying to stab me!"

"What is?" I asked, as Gompt drew the System Beast model from her pouch. The little hands were waving in all directions, tiny fingers stabbing in the air. The Symphony of Potential around it was spiky with glissandos and trills. Gompt almost dropped it as one little hand gouged her finger.

"Ow! Little thing is haywire!" She juggled it from one paw to the other, trying to keep it from stabbing her.

"If this is how these System Beasts function, one does not have high hopes for the proposal," Moortlin said, stepping away.

"It's never done that before," I said. "What could possibly make a System Beast act like this?"

That was when the screaming started.

PART FOUR

System Beast

System Beasts will form a new type of service to the members of the Great Assembly of Species. They can be geared in a number of roles, from laborer or draftbeast, to social secretary or aide for those with disabilities, or even items of luxury. The possibilities are nearly limitless, as the constructs can be quite intelligent and take orders well. I look forward to seeing how the people of the Nether receive and apply System Beasts to make their lives easier.

—From a proposal by Mandamon Feldo, majus of the Houses of Healing and Potential

The three of us rushed into the hallway to find lights blinking, and rumbles echoing through the walls of the mansion. A majus ran past, carrying a bucket of water.

"The kitchen is on fire!" she yelled over her shoulder.

It wasn't just Gompt's System Beast that was malfunctioning. All of the Systems in the mansion had gone crazy. In this place full of maji, I hardly thought about how many Systems were hidden in the walls to drive water uphill, heat rooms, and even light corridors when the walls of the Nether had dimmed for the night.

Moortlin stumped away down the hall in the opposite direction from the running majus. "One will recruit all maji who can hear the Symphony of Potential," they called in a voice like splitting wood. "Those are the only ones who can deactivate the Systems."

"We'll help anyone we can," I called back, but then Gompt took my arm, and I turned to her.

"Kratitha," she said. The fur on her shoulders was standing on end.

My eyes widened, and I ran after my colleague. The Pixie was surrounded by the most advanced Systems ever made in the Nether, and couldn't hear the House of Potential. The System Beasts would tear her apart!

Our workshop was down several flights of stairs and in a different wing of the mansion. While we ran, scenes of chaos intruded on us—burst pipes spewing water from walls, broken and sparking lanterns, and several rooms filled with the roar of flames. But maji were everywhere, battling the mayhem. All six colors of the Symphony glowed around walls, ceiling, and Society members like a mad kaleidoscope.

I listened to the Symphonies of Healing and Potential as I ran, but the music was dissonant, with too many changes happening at once. I could do little to help those who already fought the chaos, even if I wanted to. The Systems weren't only turning off or malfunctioning. It was as if their notes were being released in the most chaotic manner possible.

Finally we arrived at the workshop, and Gompt worried at the doorknob before thrusting it open and rushing in.

It looked as if a hundred people cluttered the room rather than just one, and all were clambering to get to the little Pixie in their midst. Light glinted from moving limbs, and my eye was drawn around the workshop, colors flickering in and out of existence as different Systems moved our constructs around.

In the middle danced the Ethulina pullbeast we intended to show to the Great Assembly, striking out with its front hooves and snorting clouds of steam, though Kratitha wove and danced away from it, avoiding a confrontation. Every bit of damage we did taking it down meant that much more work in repairs. We'd be destroying our own days of labor.

Kratitha was a blur of motion, her wings keeping her just above the floor and away from the smallest, reaching System Beasts. Her body glowed blue with the House of Grace and bright orange with the House of Power. She coordinated every move perfectly, and the Pixie hummed along with the music she heard, so deep in concentration was she. Her complicated voice box picked off paired chords and harmonics, and despite myself I paused a moment to listen.

I think that's the closest I've ever come to hearing the Symphony of Grace.

Gompt also flowed into the Symphony of Grace, insinuating her thick body between two strutting peacock-shaped Beasts who lashed out with filed metal talons. Neither touched a hair of her pelt.

Kratitha was the only one of our trio who couldn't change the Symphony of Potential in order to shut down the Systems. Instead, a spear of orange accompanied her tiny hand, showing she was adjusting the Symphony of Power. She inserted her hand between the head and body of a bulky dog-like automaton, twisting at just the right angle, then jerked and the head popped to one side. The clanking Beast listed and plowed into a wall. Not a big loss, as that design was meant to test the walking mechanisms.

A metal claw struck the doorframe a handbreadth from my ear and I jolted back. The malfunctioning System Beasts were angling toward me and, I belatedly realized, toward Gompt. They weren't just attacking Kratitha, but any person within range.

Or any majus?

I fell into the music of Potential, hearing an overlapping stream of clanking, whistles, and shrieks. The music associated with Systems was artificial, lacking the beauty of the natural music of the universe. That meant it was easier to disrupt. I laid a hand on the head of a crawling lizard System Beast that came to my knee, keeping away from the wooden hinged jaw full of teeth.

Why did we ever put teeth in these things?

The foundational beat held the Beast's mechanisms together—the cognitive gearing tied to the movement actuators tied to the structural frequencies. I dropped the beat to a lower register and the lizard Beast jerked to a halt. One down, and—how many to go? We'd made over a hundred of the things in the past five months.

Gompt reached Kratitha and powered down one of the larger prototypes as I had. Its mouth sagged open instead of sinking into the Pixie's flesh.

I moved forward, avoiding clumsy thrusts, slashes and even attempts by two or three System Beasts to gang up on me, disconnecting the Systems as I did. Some part of my brain rejoiced, realizing our creations were working in concert, though we had not yet programmed that level of sophistication.

The Ethulina seemed almost to be coordinating the assault. Every time it tossed its head toward us, or kicked out a leg to strike, smaller System Beasts would swarm in around it.

The three of us moved together, each familiar with the others and overlapping in aspects of the Grand Symphony. Gompt and I shut down Systems, leaving a trail of System Beasts in mid-stride, or crawl. Kratitha moved with a butterfly-like grace, flitting between smaller opponents and the pullbeast, taunting it away from attacking while making thrusts augmented by the Symphony of Power. She left orange auras washing over the other colors of the Systems, disrupting how they interacted. She did the least damage she could to each construct, while leaving it incapable of further function.

I quickened notes in the Symphony of Healing, toning muscles in my legs. They would ache later, but doing so allowed me to keep up with Gompt, who flowed—a furry dancer—through the thick of our creations, stopping each one with a deft touch.

It took minutes, or a whole lightening, I wasn't sure which. But finally, only the Ethulina prototype—the ringleader—still moved. None of us wished to damage it, or disrupt the fine-tuned System keeping it running. We'd been circling it, deactivating the simpler System Beasts first.

We'd created the Ethulina pullbeast with fantastical materials instead of the flesh and feathers of the native Kirian fauna, but it pranced and cavorted like a real creature. It shook its crystal mane with a chime of glass as its haunches—reflective metal above ranks of wooden scales—bunched and caught the overhead light. Gompt and I flanked it carefully while Kratitha buzzed in the background, calling out unhelpful admonitions not to injure the thing.

I dodged a flailing front hoof, its joints expanded into a dexterous hand, while Gompt stepped in from the back. She tried to lay a paw on the automaton long enough to sort through iterations of music formed from our notes and the Symphony of Potential.

"You'll have to use both houses," I called to my friend, and I fell deeper into both the House of Potential and Healing. Keeping both Symphonies present in my consciousness was like swimming against two currents, each trying to drag me down.

I doubled the chords of melody in my skin, then tripled them, taking notes from the core of my being and making my skin temporarily much thicker, covered in a sheen of white from the House of Healing. Gompt used the House of Grace to dodge the System Beast's quick slashes, as evidenced by the aura of blue surrounding her.

An iron hand-hoof grazed my arm, impacting my hardened skin. More bruises later to go with aching muscles, but at least the strike hadn't broken anything.

Finally, Gompt grasped a forelimb firmly enough to keep it from another strike, and I moved in close, both hands on its metal and wood flanks. I flinched as a back leg kicked at my shins, but held my contact against its side.

The Symphony of Potential was a riot, with what should have been an arrangement of ordered solos and duets corrupted and tangled together. It would take time to sort, and would cost Gompt and I more notes from our beings. Without damaging the System more, I searched for the connecting node in the midst of it, buried between five louder pieces of music clamoring for my attention.

I grasped the notes that connected that System to the others and yanked them free. They had originated from my music in the first place, and the notes settled back in my core like old socks stretched past their original use. The creature stuttered and came to a halt.

The workshop fell quiet, save for the rustling of wooden limbs against wire mesh. A System Beast in the shape of a turtle clamored against its cage, still making its bid for freedom.

I let out a long breath and turned to the others.

"Will have to rebalance all servos before taking it to Assembly," Kratitha said. She dabbed at several cuts on her arms, which dripped a brownish blood.

I took back the notes I had added to the melody of my skin, rejoining them to the core of my being, like cool water poured on a burn. I rotated one forearm, watching a blotch of green and purple that was forming. *That will hurt later.*

"I think that's the least of our problems," I said. "This was obviously some sort of attack or distraction related to the two murders."

"Two murders?" Kratitha looked up from tending her wounds.

"Aegrino is dead, too," Gompt said. She looked unharmed, but there were several places where her fur was matted and mussed, and she held one paw to her side. "Someone is trying their hardest to make sure the Society crumbles in on itself, both emotionally and physically," she gestured to the ceiling by the doorframe, where a steady drip of water was beginning in one corner.

"Then what do we do?" I asked. "We have very little to go on, no suspects, and whoever is doing this seems to have more control over our

Systems than we do." I paused, frowning. There was still something nagging me about that.

"Help Moortlin?" Kratitha suggested.

"We should see how many others of the House of Potential they found to help," Gompt said. "We can assist in shutting down other Systems in the mansion if they haven't finished."

I shrugged a shoulder in acceptance of her point, but it felt like giving in, somehow. *The head of the Society is counting on me to figure out what happened.*

"Yes. I have cleaning to do here, and servo recalibration," Kratitha agreed, shooing us with one hand. Then she twitched, mouth tightening, and placed her fingers over a particularly wide and shallow cut on the other forearm.

"Will you be all right here?" I was not very good at regenerating flesh with the Symphony of Healing—it was a rare talent—but Kratitha waved me away.

"Others with worse. Tend to them. Find out who did this. I will set things right in workshop."

I looked to Gompt, who shrugged. "Let's go find Moortlin, then," she said.

On the way there, Gompt helped tie a sling on an older Methiemum while I listened to the trills of pain running through his music. I turned a few from sixteenth to eighth notes, dimming the worst. He thanked us both, then went back to his job of keeping water flowing through this section of the mansion, despite a large crack in one pipe. The blue of the House of Grace and the green of The House of Strength surrounded him.

Near the stairs to the next level, we helped a Sureri woman with an elegant coif of hair. Auras of green and yellow—the Houses of Strength and Communication—kept the ceiling from totally collapsing, though a portion had already fallen in. Two Sureriaj males—her partners, I supposed—were picking pieces of plaster off her. I knew her by name, though the species was stingy with sharing that information.

I listened to the Symphony of Healing. "Majus Zuege, I don't hear any bones broken, though you'll have bruises more impressive than my own. Is there anything else we can do?"

"Well, I thank yer, but no," she said gravely. "Go off an' bodge together some aught folks with ills. There's plenty injured more than meself."

We found Moortlin on the highest floor of the mansion, brushing wood and plaster dust from their rough hide. Much of the shedding skin that told of their age had been scraped away. We confirmed they had found others in the House of Potential, and deactivated most of the other Systems.

"The damage is, hm, extensive," they said, "though the worst is under control. The time to repair the mansion will be, hm, lengthy. One has not seen such chaos in one's time as the head of the Society." They let out a great gust of breath, like wind through branches, and slapped more dust from their skin.

"There is something more going on here, obviously," I said. I hoped Moortlin would have some other information for us, despite the chaos.

"There is," they agreed, and their unblinking yellow eyes stared between Gompt and I. "Before recent events, one was going to suggest this group, hm, attend to Aegrino's body. Now is not the best time, but this one believes it is necessary to learn more."

I traded a glance with Gompt, not sure what more we could learn from that source, though we could at least give him some dignity. *Poor Aegrino. No one deserves that fate, and he was a good record keeper.*

When we got back to the records room, Moortlin stumping along behind us, we were confronted with an empty patch of hardwood floor. Aegrino's body was gone.

I spun to the others. "Where did he go?" Gompt's eyes were wide behind her glasses and even Moortlin stood stock still, dazed.

"These ones are, hm, *certain* Aegrino is dead?" Moortlin ventured.

"I'm certain." I said, as Gompt said, "He's definitely dead."

"We listened to the Symphony around his body," I added. "I've seen death before. The melodies were breaking down in the same way."

"Then who did this?" Gompt asked. She paced around the spot where the Etanela's body had been until a short time ago, peering at the jointed oak floor. "Were the haywire Systems just a distraction?" The pool of blood was gone as well, and the space had been cleaned and tidied, as if nothing had happened, despite water dripping from a burst pipe overhead.

My Festuour friend bent until her snout almost touched the wood planks. "There's still a stain here, but it's faint. Whoever cleaned was faster than a racing thrint in heat."

"The confusion would have covered much," Moortlin rumbled, and I checked my chronograph.

Another lightening-and-a-half gone dealing with haywire Systems.

"Still, what one would have the, hm, ability to do such a thing?" My mentor took their own turn around the place where the record keeper died. "To affect so many Systems at once, and to do things they had not originally been composed to do—it is as if one majus has been multiplied into several." They turned back. "This reminds one of the work this one conducted on harmonic resonances, Mandamon."

I froze, my palms tingling, then sweating. *That's what has been nagging at me.* It acted similar to one of my first inventions—the most dangerous. Similar in method, yes, but there was no way it could have affected an area this size. Plus, I had torn the thing apart!

It was also what caused Moortlin to invite me to the Society, despite the accident. Despite me losing all I held dear.

I leaned against a bookshelf. It was *not* the same. 'Harmonic resonances' was just a fancy way of saying different actions were amplified by each other. I had the idea to link Systems people used into one big mechanism. Imagine being able to control heat, water, and power sources in one System. People could even have carried the resonator around with them, turning Systems off and on with a simple switch.

However, mingling so many Systems proved unstable. Every time I used my invention, at least one of them failed. I thought I could fix it. I thought I could accommodate the fluctuations in the Grand Symphony all by myself.

Right up until the day Abarham and my family died.

I'd recycled some of the safer ideas into the concept of the System Beast, but I'd never touched the harmonic resonator again. I'd purposefully tried to forget it, after dismantling the device.

"The resonator can't have caused this." My voice was weak, barely more than a whisper. I forced my hand away from fingering the groove below my right eye. "No one else knows how to use it, and it could never affect the whole mansion, unless modified greatly."

"One is not suggesting anything," Moortlin said. "One knows this is a, hm, delicate subject. Merely that the mechanism is, hm, comparable." My mentor was contrite, their eyes dim. "One is confident this one did not cause this disruption. All invited to the Society are personally interviewed, and one holds them in highest regard. That includes Mandamon Feldo."

"It had to be someone inside," Gompt insisted. She was watching me, warily. "But Mandamon has been with me. I don't think he took the list of members, and he certainly couldn't have moved Aegrino's body."

"It wasn't me," I said, my voice a little stronger. "But I may have enabled whoever did this." Gompt stepped back, but my mind was not on her.

Where did I leave the pieces? When was the last time I saw it? I could not bring myself to completely destroy it, no matter what it had caused.

"Then these ones must continue to investigate," Moortlin said. "One must direct the maji in cleaning and repair of the mansion, and move those whose apartments have been affected." They sighed again and unfolded thick fingers toward Gompt and I. "Please inform one the moment these ones find anything."

With that, the Benish stumped from the room, leaving me to stare at the spot on the floor where a dead body no longer lay. Gompt was watching me.

Finally, I stared back. "It wasn't me," I repeated.

She nodded. "I believe you. But Mandamon, you've had something that could cause this much destruction, just lying around?"

"No. It couldn't have done this." I shook my head. "This would have required heavy modifications, by someone who knew what they were doing. It was supposed to help people." My words were helpless.

"Come on then," Gompt said. "Let's see if your gadget is still there before you work yourself even deeper into a funk. Maybe you're keying yourself up for nothing."

We walked in silence to my room, on a lower floor, not far from the workshop. Broken wood, pipes, and people surrounded us. A plank from the ceiling had fallen in front of my door and my hand shook as I reached for it.

So similar to the destruction in the accident, but on such a greater scale.

Inside, I stared around, digging into the memories of where I'd left the resonator. I went to a cabinet on one wall, jerking open the doors and reaching for a lower drawer, kept closed since I had arrived in the mansion. There was dust inside the drawer, outlining two long shapes where there should have been pieces of my invention.

I sank to the floor.

PART FIVE

Homebrew

What is the relation between a majus and their family? Would-be maji are often recognized early in life, as I was, and encouraged to live at their House in the Imperium. For maji who are still very young, the Council allows guardians to live with them. However, there is always a drive to separate the one who can hear the Symphony from those who can't. This is counterintuitive, as maji are also encouraged to marry and have families. If a family or friend group such as mine becomes too large for the small apartments in the Houses of the Maji, that group is given a stipend from the Council to find a place to live nearby. This setup both insulates maji from the rest of the Great Assembly of Species, and incorporates them as progenitor of new family lines, setting the status of "majus" higher than other beings.

—Part of an essay on the social impact of the maji, by Timpomitnob Gompt, Watcher, of the Houses of Grace and Potential

Gompt stood over me, paws on her hips, below her bandolier of tools. "It wasn't you, Mandamon," she said. "You didn't do this. I don't think you killed the Speaker, and I know you didn't kill Aegrino. Someone stole your invention, and they made it do these horrible things. It must be someone inside the Society, whatever Moortlin says."

I shook my head. *Could I have fixed the resonator and then blocked it out?* I didn't remember my studies for the ten-day after the accident. But that was two cycles ago, and it hadn't happened again. *At least I don't think so.*

"Even if it wasn't me, this couldn't have happened *without* me," I told my friend. "I am responsible, in some manner. Just like I was responsible when my parents and Abarham—" I cut off, my throat refusing to speak the words. Gompt was silent, and I thought she would agree with me. I looked up.

Her face was scrunched, almost into a growl, her brows pulled low behind her glasses. I don't know if she'd even heard me. "What is it?" I said, fearing her words would only be a condemnation.

"Which person is liable to tinker with inventions that aren't their own, make things work in a new manner, or neglect to tell others about their changes?"

I didn't even have to think. "Those are all things Kratitha does if...oh." I rubbed my suddenly cold hands together. It made a sick kind of sense.

The three of us had all been in each other's rooms. We shared thoughts and designs constantly. I'm sure I'd mentioned my research on harmonic resonance at some point. *Did I ever mention the controller wand?* I looked to the empty drawer, where the lines free of dust sat like an accusation.

I kept most of my work in the shop with the others. Aside from the cabinet, a writing desk with one stack of paper, my bed, and my closet, my room was empty. It would be easy to find something hidden, especially for an inquisitive Pixie good at getting into where she didn't belong.

"Back to the workshop," I said, and Gompt gave a sharp nod. It still didn't make any sense. *Why would Kratitha modify my resonator, then set it on herself?* I couldn't believe the Pixie could kill someone, and she abhorred destruction like the resonator caused.

A few minutes later we were back in the chaos of our workshop, broken System Beasts lying as if they had fainted. Kratitha was not there.

"Again? What is going on?" Gompt paced ahead, auras of brown and blue surrounding her. I was not sure what she was looking for in the Symphonies of Grace and Potential. From what I gathered about the combination we called an Archeologist, the House of Grace augmented patterns in music, revealing objects out of place or sequence in the House of Potential's notes.

"Here," Gompt said, pointing to a small patch on the floor. She was near the inert Ethulina pullbeast, one hoof still raised. "I think this is Kratitha's blood."

I moved closer. "She was bleeding from fighting against the System Beasts."

"This is different." Gompt walked a few paces away. "Those drops start here, and spiral out as she fought." Her furry fingers traced a spiral of brown droplets spread around the room, flung like a dance partner spinning around their mate. Now Gompt pointed them out, it was a beautiful pattern, in a way. I traced arcs and swirls with my hand, imagining the Pixie slipping impossibly between attackers, while delivering perfectly timed strikes.

"But here," Gompt drew my attention to the original spot, "this breaks the pattern, and there's only one spot. It happened after everything else, probably after you and I left."

I let the Symphonies of Healing and Potential fill me, listening to notes curling around the brown stain. The measures were changing key, organic compounds oxidizing. The notes defining the energy quieted as the blood cooled, and there was a definite difference between this spot and others around the room.

"I agree," I said, frowning. "This blood was shed after the rest. She exerted herself and made her wounds bleed again."

"Or something was done *to* her?" Gompt suggested.

"First you say Kratitha took my device, now someone else is responsible?" I crossed my arms. From the moment I saw Speaker Thurapo's corpse this morning, nothing made sense. Had Aegrino cleaned the scene before he was killed in turn, or were Imperium guard on their way, even now? There was something missing.

"I can't believe she did all this, Mandamon," Gompt said. She played with the frame of her glasses where Kratitha had fixed it. "She was fighting the System Beasts when we got here. Why would she have caused this chaos only to be attacked?"

"Maybe she didn't think it through. This is Kratitha we're talking about." But my words had no weight behind them.

"Think what through?" Gompt asked. "Bringing down the mansion and the Society? Why would she do that? Her caste is dying off, Mandamon—you know that. This is the last place she has."

Just like me. I knew the Pixie was at odds with her people, but Gompt was closer to her than I was. I hadn't known she was in exile.

"So let's find her," I said. "Maybe she went to her room."

But Kratitha was not in her room, or in the medical facilities, or anywhere else in the mansion we could determine. Gompt and I met back in the workshop half a lightening later.

"Was there anyone else in here?" We searched the workshop, with our eyes and the Symphonies, but the music of her passage was fading, and Kratitha seemed to have been the only one present.

"She is of the House of Power," I said. "Good at showing connections between places and things. Perhaps she realized something about the murders."

Gompt raised a finger. "Could she have linked the attack to someone removing Aegrino's body?"

"From down here? No idea." I shrugged. "But she's not in the mansion, and if she found something, then it's more of a lead than we've had the whole time." *Maybe we'll catch this killer today, after all.*

"How do we track her?" Gompt looked at me, and in concert, we turned to the pullbeast.

"It's made to follow orders," I said. "I could adjust some of the gearing to process a 'track' command—it will only take a few minutes."

"And I can change the input System to accept a sample of Kratitha's blood." Gompt found a clean rag on a table, and gently mopped up the newest blood stain, absorbing as much as she could into the cloth.

We worked for a time, both engrossed in our respective Symphonies, hearing the overlap in Potential as we changed notes of the same piece, but in different places. Occasionally, the Symphony would resist when we both tried to change notes the same way.

It took another few minutes to restart the Ethulina and align its components, and I felt as if the time added to the weight of my chronograph. It pulled against my vest pocket. Outside, light from the walls of the Nether faded as, inside, lights grew brighter. Each illumination was surrounded by a glow of orange and brown—Systems created from the Houses of Potential and Power.

"Just need to tighten the servos on the neck a bit farther," I told Gompt as I made a half-turn with a screwdriver. "There."

We stepped back. The System Beast had marks on its flanks that hadn't been there before the attack, and Gompt had installed a device of metal and wood at the pullbeast's neck that could process the music in the cloth containing Kratitha's blood. It wasn't pretty, and we would have to remove our additions before showing it to the Assembly, but it would work.

"I was hoping she'd be back by now," Gompt said, "waltzing in here like a giant honeybee, halfway through our work, telling us how we were wasting our time." The Festuour fiddled her glasses straight again, and wiped oily paws on a rag. There was a streak of grease matting the fur in a line across her chest.

I looked down at my own clothes—still the same ruffled shirt, cravat, and vest I had worn to my interview with the Speaker this morning, though there was a streak of grease across my front where I had leaned over the Ethulina. *I might never get them clean again.* At least I had removed my coat while I worked. I retrieved it from a nearby chair.

"Then we'd best hope this can find her." I reached for the access panel on the neck and flipped a toggle. The System supplying energy completed its circuit, and I danced back as the Ethulina pullbeast sprang to life, snorting and pawing as a real creature would. Neither of us had deactivated the System that made the Beast imitate the genuine animal.

The pullbeast flicked its mane of crystal and snorted dust, then lifted its head as if it smelled something, and trotted out of the room.

Gompt and I scrambled to follow, she tugging her bandolier of pouches tighter, me shrugging into my coat. At least it hadn't attacked us again.

The Ethulina trotted down the corridors, metal hooves clumping on the wood planking. Other maji, still trying to fix broken walls, pipes, and ceilings, shifted to let us past. Given the day's events, it was little wonder a few of them stared.

Our creation led us to the front of the mansion, sniffing at cross-corridors, then through the front doors and down the path to the street. Outside, birds sang quietly in the evening air. The trees on either side cast faint shadows from the dimming walls of the Nether, which stretched far overhead, purple and blue and semi-translucent. I took in a deep breath, grateful for the freshness of the air. The destruction in the mansion had kicked up dust older than I was.

So she did leave. What did Kratitha find?

From outside, the mansion appeared as any other residence belonging to the elite of the Nether, who often chose Poler as a home away from the bustle of the Imperium. Poler had never achieved the greatness of its cousin, though it was in as favorable a position, nestled beneath two of the massive walls that both boxed in and lit the Nether.

The wrought iron gate at the end of the cobbled path separated the mansion from the street, and the Ethulina paused impatiently, one hoof pawing, for me to unlock the gate.

"Gompt, look here," I said, pointing to the carved teak ball, wide as my two hands together, hung from a hook on the central arch above the gate, nestled in a little cup. Metal inlay swirled around it, some hanging just *above* the surface of the object.

The home of the Society was protected from notice by a complex System that influenced anyone approaching into rethinking their path. It had been designed hundreds of cycles ago by a particularly gifted member of the Society. I once spent a ten-day researching it, but gained little insight into how it worked.

One had to turn the sphere off briefly to exit the gate, but the sphere was already dark, inert. Usually it shone to a majus' eyes with all six colors of the houses of the maji.

"Someone's been through here, and one who doesn't care about the secrecy of the Society," Gompt growled.

People will notice a sprawling mansion rising from nothing in a day.

A movement caught my eye. An elderly Lobath was out for a stroll, but he'd dropped the leash to his tentacled pet and was staring toward the mansion.

Oh no. "We need to get the sphere working again, and quickly," I said, rising up on my toes to reach the dull sphere. My hands froze a finger width away from the surface. *That's odd.*

Gompt peered around me. "What is it?"

"The System is still activated," I said.

"But it's off."

"Exactly." I unhooked the sphere entirely from its stand. The Symphony of Potential floated around it, but the music sounded like someone had forgotten to play part of the piece. I couldn't detect the Symphony of Healing, either. I held it out to Gompt, raising my eyebrows in a question.

She cocked her head, as if listening. "The House of Grace isn't a part of the System any longer."

"Something is very broken in this sphere, and it's the only thing keeping out the neighbors." A chill clawed at my chest. *If we can't turn it back on, I don't know who could recreate its protection. Does Moortlin know how? The Society will be exposed even if we find the list!*

Gompt's brow was knotted behind her glasses, and she ran her paws down the pockets of her bandolier. "We need to hurry," was all she said, and my other hand went to my chronograph. A Methiemum woman joined the Lobath in staring at the mansion.

At least it's almost night. Tomorrow morning would be interesting if we couldn't reactivate the sphere, but there was nothing else we could do right now. I put the teak carving back on its perch.

Once the gate was open, the Ethulina sprang forward, making the two spectators leap back. The Lobath tugged at his pet's leash.

"Watch where that thing is going!" the woman yelled.

Now they'll have tales of a mansion rising from nothing, and a mechanical beast that nearly ran them over.

I gritted my teeth, and Gompt and I followed the Ethulina into the quiet city of Poler. Could we fix the sphere before word got too far into the community? Even if we could, the list was still missing, the murderer was still loose, and even if we found them I might be implicated as an accessory.

We jogged around one of the immense columns holding up the ceiling of the Nether, stretching up into the distance. The column's crystal sparkled with the same dim light of the walls. Street lights were coming on, some powered by notes of maji, others simple kerosene lamps. They lit quiet houses, most of their residents already at home. Poler was not known for its nightlife.

These dwellings were familiar. My parents' house was not far away, slightly at an angle to our current path. Walls of stone, and brick rose to both sides of the street. No carriages were in sight, but I doubted we would see many this late.

The Ethulina snorted again and turned down a lane between two large homes. This led to the less affluent sections of the town, and also toward my family's old house. I clenched my fists at my sides. *It belongs to another family now.* I had not been back since a ten-day after the accident, when I removed my family's possessions to a storage facility. They sat there still.

Reaching the end of the lane, the System Beast turned onto the street *toward* my old house, and a surge of something like hot ice rose in my chest. My hands were sweating, though the night was cool.

"Are you well?" Gompt asked. "You're puffing more than the pullbeast."

"It's nothing," I panted, but my eyes were drawn to the stone cottage fourth in a line of similar residences. There was the chipped tile on the roof where I had slipped while climbing when I was seven. There was the branch of the flowering mushfet tree where I used to sit and read.

The damage to the side room has been repaired. There's no reason to look for it.

Gompt restrained the Ethulina and turned to me. "You're white as a ghost. Do you see Kratitha?" Then she followed my gaze. "What's special about that old house—oh."

Suddenly Gompt's paw was on my shoulder, pulling me close to her. The Festuour came from a civilization based on friend groups instead of families. It was natural to her to comfort others when needed.

I'm fine. I don't need anyone else. This pain should be behind me.

I folded into my friend's embrace. The softness of her fur, her firm grip, her musty scent—all pushed reason from my mind, and I felt tears run down my face.

I struggled to reach one hand under my glasses to wipe the offending liquid away, all while Gompt held me close.

"There, there," she said, the nothing words offering far more comfort than they should have. I drew in a deep, ragged breath. Gently, she pushed back to regard me, strong paws gripping my shoulders.

"I'm better," I said, my face hot. The Ethulina was pawing and inching forward despite Gompt's instructions to stay put. "We need to keep moving. Find Kratitha." Gompt nodded and stepped away to let me compose myself.

When we began again, I half expected the System Beast to turn toward my house, as it was where I first came up with the idea of the resonator, but instead it trotted past, as if there were more important things than the end of my youthful innocence.

I looked back several times until we rounded the curve and my parent's home was lost to sight. Why had Kratitha chosen to come this way? Did she know this was my old house or was it just coincidence?

I'll go through that storage facility when this is over.

The Ethulina led us into the heart of Poler, and around another giant column. It supported a market built against the column's side, though the kiosks were empty this time of day.

Finally, with a stamp of what seemed like satisfaction, the pullbeast nosed toward a residence I didn't recognize: neither extravagant, nor poor and tumble-down.

"Kratitha's in here?" I asked, despite knowing it couldn't answer. It stamped a metal hoof again.

Well, maybe it can.

At the door, Gompt shrugged, then raised one paw and knocked.

The door creaked open, and I realized I was staring into the depths of a cowl like those the Sathssn species wore. I was reminded of Tethan, one of those few who eschewed the traditional garments.

"Yes?" The voice sounded female. "This night, there is something you want?"

"We—we're trying to find a friend of ours," I said. *An odd summary of two murders, the chaos at the mansion, and the danger to the Society.* "She's a Pixie, about so high," I put my hand beside my hip. "We have reason to believe she may have...visited this house." I hoped my hesitation wasn't noticeable. I didn't want to accuse every person we talked to of kidnapping.

"Who is at the door, Harha?" called a voice from farther inside the house.

"We're maji, on official business," Gompt put in behind me.

"Maji, they are here from the Imperium," Harha called back.

"We're not—" but I let the words die. I could feel the geas climbing in my mind, stifling any intent to tell them of the mansion or the Society. "We just need to find our friend, and we'll be on our way," I said.

To my surprise, the door opened further. "My mate Slitho and I, we always welcome maji to our home."

"You've met others, then?" Gompt asked.

"Certainly," Harha said. "Though not the one you describe." She wore the usual black boots and gloves of the Sathssn, her cowl pulled forward so only the glint of yellow eyes could be seen. "Us, we are friends with several maji. Usually, we meet them in the Imperium to discuss theology."

Theology? Had we stumbled upon a pair of those who revered the maji as blessed by a divinity? There were groups who still believed that, no matter how much the Council discouraged such thought.

I looked to Gompt, who once again shrugged, though her blue eyes were wide. We would have to be cautious.

"Your...animal...it will have to stay outside," Harha said, looking between us to the Ethulina.

"Not a problem," Gompt said, and flipped the switches for the System Beast to go into an inactive mode. I was confident no one would steal it, as it weighed more than Gompt and me combined.

Inside Slitho and Harha's home, the construction was very plain, the walls consisting of barely-worked wood, with stone blocks set together to make a floor. There was no mortar between them, and several rocked as I stepped on them.

Sections of tree trunk served as chairs, and a slab of wood on another stump was a table. No paintings graced the walls, no rugs on the floor. The hair on my arm lifted in a cool breeze and I realized there was no glass in the windows.

"I have never been in a house...like this," I said. "Is this how people live on Sath Home?" Few who were not Sathssn visited their homeworld. *Why did the Ethulina bring us here?*

"This, it is a style little used," Slitho said, as the other resident came through a doorway with no lintel. He held a small bundle of black cloth, which wiggled and gurgled happily. "Only by the Most Traditional of those who serve the Form." I could hear the capitals as he spoke. Slitho had a deep voice for the diminutive species, and I guessed he was used to public speaking. "Please, have a seat. We enjoy conversation with other species and ways of thought."

"'Blasphemers,' he means," Gompt whispered in my ear as we found seats on the unfinished stumps. Mine was of some heavy purple wood, and Gompt chose one that was dull orange with rings of green. We introduced ourselves to the couple.

"We unfortunately have little time for conversation," I said to the two black-cloaked figures. A giggle came from the bundle Slitho held. "Though we would welcome any information on the maji you've spoken with." The openings of their cowls followed me, but aside from that I could tell little of what they looked like. *Have they talked to someone from the Society?*

"This, we understand," Harha said. "Would you care for refreshment while you are here? We have pure water, and a selection of greens from our garden."

"No thanks," Gompt said before I could speak. She was looking at a corner of the room and I saw a bundle of leaves, half separated onto two crude pottery plates.

"I apologize if we've disturbed your meal," I added.

"In this, there is no offense," Slitho said. "We do relish talking with maji. It is our belief they are instrumental in making the Great Assembly a place of happiness and life." He lifted the wiggly bundle he held and I saw two little black footies stick out from underneath. "We wish only the best for our son Essra."

"A noble concept," I said. *Who would disagree with that? Yet why are we here?*

"Me, I am glad you agree." Slitho lifted his son up to stand on one of the Sathssn's thighs. "There is a group of our people who have strong beliefs likewise, and even a few in other species. Too much, we are sick of people rushing around, with no respect. There is murder and crime in the big cities, and people, they are just unkind to each other."

"We wish to celebrate life," Harha said as I fidgeted, wishing to go already. "The maji, they would be a valuable addition to the coalition of likeminded people we know. Devoted, what was the name of the one who came to our house recently? A local majus, I thought." Harha gestured vaguely at her mate.

"The tall fellow, yes," Slitho said, then spoke to Essra in a sing-song voice. "What was his name, now? Lanera? Luni--?"

"Ah, Majus Lunigi," Harha supplied. Both Gompt and I sat bolt upright.

"Majus Aegrino Plumera Lunigi was here?" my friend asked. I leaned forward as if I could pull the answer from them.

"Why—yes," Harha said. If a blank cowl could show surprise, hers did. "You know him? A pleasant Etanela, if a little scattered."

"We are familiar with him." I tried to keep the excitement out of my voice.

"A friend—or was it relation?—of his brought him to one of our meetings," Slitho said. "Majus Lunigi, he found a simple comfort in the things we said. We met with him a few times afterward, as we both lived in Poler. I believe he lives somewhere nearby, though we could never learn quite where."

"With you, we would be happy to share some of the literature our coalition has created," Harha said.

I stood. "Would you mind terribly if I used your facilities?" I asked. "We have been looking for our friend for some time. I'm sure Gompt would be interested in your pamphlets."

"This, it is the least we can do to assist," Slitho said. "Just through there." He pointed to a nearby door, little more than a slab of wood.

I gave Gompt an apologetic grimace as I passed. She showed me her teeth. That was not how Festuour smiled.

I heard her making sounds of agreement as I slipped into the Sathssn couple's bathroom, which was as simple as the rest of their house. The toilet, as I suspected, was merely a hole in the floor covered with a piece of stone.

Kratitha hasn't been in that room, but Aegrino has. So why did the Ethulina track Kratitha here? What's Aegrino's connection to Slitho and Harha? Do they know about Speaker Thurapo's death?

I opened myself to the Symphony of Healing. The melody defining Kratitha's blood was still fresh in my mind. Like any tune, it was simpler to remember a specific section than the whole piece. I found a roll of coarse paper near the toilet, and drew a small knife from my belt.

I winced as I pricked my finger, then squeezed out a single drop of blood onto the paper. The frenetic tempo of my blood slowed as the droplet cooled, and I recreated what I remembered from Kratitha's melody with my own notes, then imposed that refrain over the music in the drop of blood. It was inexact, but until I took my notes back, this droplet would act as Kratitha's blood.

I paced the small room, holding the paper and trying to match the simple tune I constructed with another strand of the Symphony. Outside the door, Gompt's robust tune rolled underneath the counterpoints of Slitho and Harha, with a few trills from Essra. I saw no reason for the pair to lie. They seemed earnest folk, if a little strange.

So why did the System Beast insist Kratitha was here?

There was a little window in the bathroom, also with no glass. I went to it, and a harmony formed with the bloodied paper I held. *Did she only pass close by? If it was close enough, the Ethulina may have been fooled.* I leaned as far out as I could, and the matching music was stronger, down in a curly-leafed bush growing beneath the window. I suspected if it had not been so dark, I might have seen droplets of her blood.

Now I listened to the Symphony of Potential, stroking my beard. The bush had resisted a weight, and I could hear a subtheme playing slower than the rest. Kratitha had been outside this window—for what reason?

Had she been alone? I closed my eyes, listening for where the two Symphonies intersected—where music of biology complemented the energy of bodies. I could almost visualize a corridor of music—Kratitha's path. No...there was another! Someone larger than the diminutive Pixie and me. The music of the other body was quieter. Had she been following the killer?

"Feeling refreshed?" Gompt locked eyes with me as I exited the bathroom. There was a small pile of papers on the stump where I had sat, and the two Sathssn were leaning forward excitedly, while my colleague was turned slightly away. Essra was sitting in her lap, a trail of greenish drool making a slick down his black tunic and matting the fur on Gompt's paw.

"Much better." I looked to the Sathssn. "And I'm sure we've taken up enough of Slitho and Harha's time."

Gompt got to her feet in a flash, handing the little wiggling bundle back to his parents. "Yes. We need to continue searching for Kratitha."

She tried to give a piece of paper back to Slitho as well, but he waved her away. "This information, keep it. If you feel inclined to come to one of our meetings, we are always accepting of new members."

We made our farewells, and exited. Gompt reactivated the System Beast, and we walked down the front path. I could see Gompt's furry ears quivering with the effort of not saying anything.

"Kratitha passed by the side of their house," I said. "We should be able to pick up her trail the next street over."

"Then maybe listening to that gibberish while you played around in the bathroom was worth it," Gompt growled. "'Coalition who believe in life' indeed. I wouldn't be surprised if they were trying to gouge maji out of their money. It all sounds very inexact and fluffy." She shook her head disgustedly.

"Many religions sound like that," I countered. "Though I can't say what Aegrino saw in it. I thought he was a logical individual. It feels like this should be connected to the Speaker's murder, but I have no idea how."

We turned a corner, the pullbeast trotting along behind us. "On top of that, Kratitha stopped by their bathroom window."

"Why?" Gompt asked. "Did she figure out Aegrino went to listen to those two fanatics?"

I shook my head, then pushed my glasses back up. "Unknown. Maybe she saw a chance to bandage her wounds."

Gompt shook her head. "The way Kratitha's mind skids like a cub on ice, she'd probably forgotten she was bleeding by that point. She must have been looking for something, or someone."

I acknowledged the point with a wave of a hand. "Then what did she know? Why did she leave, and why didn't she tell us about it?"

"The mansion *was* exploding at the time." Gompt rested a hand on the pullbeast's flank. It was pulling ahead, leaning into the next turn. The System Gompt had attached to its throat must have picked up Kratitha's trail again.

"What is the connection between Kratitha and Aegrino?" Gompt mused. "I don't know if they'd even talked to each other." I could just see her questioning blue eyes in the twilight from the walls of the Nether.

"She was following someone," I repeated. "Or was it the other way around? Kratitha might have been captive, and tried to call for help at that house." The pullbeast was slowing, and we slowed with it. "If the killer has my invention, they can cause catastrophe with any Systems they encounter." I paused. "What is it?"

Gompt was peering into one of the System Beast's hatches, one paw scrabbling for a set of gears. "It's stopped. Something must be wrong."

"Uh, Gompt," I said. *I hope that isn't...* "Gompt!"

My colleague jerked up. "What? Oh—is that—?"

We ran to the entrance of a nearby alley, where a small lump of clothes and wings lay in a pile.

I put one hand under Kratitha's neck, staring into her face. Her compound eyes never closed, and Pixies rarely slept—a product of their short life cycle—so if one was unconscious, it was a bad sign.

"Is she still with us?" Gompt put a paw on the Pixie's arm, her neck, then let out a frustrated snort. "No circulatory system, or at least no pulse to feel. How do you tell if a Pixie's alive if it's not running around?"

"By how much talking they do," Kratitha said in a weak voice, and Gompt and I exhaled in relief. She pushed up on one hand, her wings starting to buzz. We scooted back to give her more room.

"Why did you leave the mansion?" I asked. "What happened to you?"

Kratitha waved one hand at me, the other running over the chitinous ridges that decorated the top of her head. "Must have hit me harder than I thought." She got to her feet, wings lifting her.

"Someone hit you? Who?" Gompt had her paws out to catch the Pixie if she fell.

Kratitha looked between us. "Thought you were smarter than that. Aegrino, of course. He stole your invention I fixed, Mandamon."

PART SIX

Harmonic

Many think Pixies are dumb beasts, hardly worthy to be allowed entrance into Great Assembly. This is false. Pixies are varied and individual as other species, though we come from hive mind mentality. Few visit Mother Hive to see firsthand. This is part of reason warrior-descended hives can wage war without oversight from Great Assembly. First to go were philosophical and religious-descended hives, dating back from original five-mother split over twenty-five hundred cycles previous. Warriors needed scientists and engineers for many cycles, but now think they can get progress from trading with other species. Instinct to kill off cousin hives grows overwhelming in warrior hives. I fear my generation may be last of forward thinkers on Mother Hive.

—*On the genocide of Mother Hive, by Kratithakanipouliteka, Pixie majus of the Houses of Power and Grace*

"Aegrino's alive?" I asked, aghast. I had listened to his Symphony degrade, felt his dead wrist, and seen the bloody wounds in his chest.

"Can't be," Gompt said. "We both checked him out. Deader than a furry scrounger in a trap."

"Saw him come out of records room," Kratitha said. Now she was upright, her wings were buzzing like a swarm of insects, lifting her shoes up off the pavement. She brushed mud off her shirt. "Brought the Ethulina with you? Gompt modified the initiative System to replace with tracking. Could fix that so it does both, with time." Kratitha half-floated toward the pullbeast. "Had your invention when he left the records room. Must have caused all the System input errors in the mansion."

I took a moment to process her stream of information. She must have been feeling better. "Wait—you saw Aegrino with the harmonic resonator? My resonator?" My mind raced. "Then did he kill the Speaker after all? Did he clean up the body or not? If not, Thurapo's secretary must have found the body by now." *Or did Aegrino kill her too? Another Etanela murdered?*

"Was very much alive." Kratitha had reached the System Beast and opened a hatch. "Hm. Gears in back left flank are blunted. Probably from shock, walking on cobblestone. Or maybe from fight in mansion. Need stronger heat treat for production models." She turned back. "Followed him for a while, but figured out I was there. Ambushed me in alley." She raised one thin finger to the dark side street where we had found her. A single streetlight illuminated her face.

"Hold on just a dang moment," Gompt said. She squinted down at the Pixie. "You said you *fixed* Mandamon's invention?"

I blinked and reviewed Kratitha's stream of words. She talked so fast it was sometimes hard to keep track of everything. "So *you* stole it out of my cabinet?" I asked.

Kratitha's feet landed firmly on the ground, her wings drooping. "Thought I could increase efficiency, make use of it in System Beast project to coordinate different sub-Systems. Increased operating range, but, ah, you know that."

Gompt snapped her furry fingers. "That's how Aegrino could affect the entire mansion at once."

"After he was dead, I might add, which is the more impressive part of it." I looked up at the single streetlight, its light glinting off the metal of the Ethulina's hooves. It was one of the majus-fueled ones. *There's still something that doesn't add up.* "How did Aegrino get hold of the resonator wand, if you had it?" I asked.

Kratitha shrugged. "Found it in the workshop? Meant to tell you about it, but kept slipping my mind."

"He must have picked it up before last night. The Speaker was killed early this morning." The messy cut through the Speaker's throat was similar to the slices in Aegrino's chest. "But then how did he fake his death? Those wounds were lethal."

"He was...is a Dancer—Communication and Grace," Gompt said. "Both houses can be subtle. Maybe we didn't actually see what we thought we did."

Kratitha's wings were buzzing again. "House of Grace could couple with Communication to mask signs of life? Breath?"

"Could be." Now Gompt looked thoughtful. "Neither of us hears Communication, but I've heard talk it's good for messing with what others hear or say."

"Grace musical component acts as helping component. Increases efficiency. Smooths flaws." Kratitha suggested, the light reflecting off her compound eyes.

I put my hands on my hips. "So, he dulled his vital signs with the House of Grace, and interfered with us detecting them with Communication," *Why pretend to be dead in the first place?* "Could he have conjured up great slashes in his chest? Those looked—and felt— pretty fatal." I looked at my hands. "If I hadn't sterilized and cleaned my fingers after touching the body, I could test for fakery with the Symphony of Healing. Too late now."

The others were silent.

"You're sure it was Aegrino? Not another Etanela?" I asked Kratitha. There were a suspicious number of the tall species involved.

She buzzed her wings, lifting off the ground for a moment. "Had the harmonic resonator, very tall, came from records room, saw blood on front of shirt, golden hair, yes? Who else?"

I stroked my beard. "Aegrino was very convincingly surprised when we told him Speaker Thurapo was dead. He even seemed to know Thurapo. Said he had to tell his sister."

"House of Communication again?" Gompt asked. "So, Aegrino's better at lying than being a record keeper." She pushed up her glasses and glanced around the dim intersection. "Though that still doesn't explain why he would steal his own list, give it to the Speaker, then kill him."

Kratitha's wings trembled above her head, a sign of nervousness. "Two Etanela victims. Some species rivalry? Or blackmail to steal list." She turned away from us and toward the pullbeast, running a hand down its flank.

Why is she nervous? Is she scared she followed a murderer?

"Moortlin mentioned a specist crime." Gompt ran a hand across her belt of tools, as if to check they were all there. "It's right weird. I can't see how murder has anything to do with a missing list of Society members."

"Maybe Aegrino found way around geas by communication with another member of species?" Kratitha suggested. She was still turned away.

"I've never been able to do anything like that," I said, "and I've talked to plenty of Methiemum."

"Also not House of Communication," Kratitha said.

"One way to find out." I stood beside the Pixie and opened the hatch at the Ethulina's neck. I set it to follow us. If Aegrino was the murderer, we'd need all the help we could get against another two-house majus. I also took the time to watch Kratitha. She was trembling, but I'd only caught it because I was looking for it.

What is going on with her?

"We need to find Aegrino quickly." I said. "If he's found a way around the geas, and wants to bring down the Society, it will ruin any chance we have of bringing the System Beasts to market."

"And any other inventions after," Gompt added. "Might even harm other products invented in the Society."

"Didn't see where he went after was hit." Kratitha gestured around the dim streets. "Which direction?"

The single streetlight overhead went out with a crack of glass.

"Gompt? Kratitha?" Their queries greeted me, and I heard the scrape of metal on rock as the Ethulina moved a hoof. The Nether's walls, towering over Poler, provided faint light, but only enough to see shapes, once my eyes adjusted.

Wings buzzed, and I felt a gust as Kratitha flitted by. "Saw movement over here," she said. Pixie eyes must adjust to light changes quicker. Aegrino might not have gone that far after all.

Gompt and I groped after our colleague's voice. "Can't see a blamed thing," Gompt muttered. The *ping* and *clop* of hooves sounded behind. The pullbeast was following.

"Gompt, number four spanner," Kratitha called, and I heard the Festuour fumble in one of her pouches. There was a *whizz* in the air in front of us, and something clattered, farther down an alley.

"Kratitha, did you throw my *best spanner*?" Gompt's voice was a low growl.

"Missed him too," Kratitha said. She seemed unaffected by the growl that put the hairs on my arms on end. *Maybe Pixies don't have a large evolutionary predator covered with fur.*

"We'll get it back," I said quickly. "Won't we, Kratitha?"

"Yes yes," she said. "This way. Might be good time to listen to Symphony?"

My eyes were adjusting, stone walls passing on both sides as we rattled down the streets of Poler. I heard Gompt grunt and sweep something from the ground.

"The shaft's nicked," she grumbled at Kratitha's wings.

"Will buff it out later," Kratitha called back. "Trying to listen to connections in House of Power. Might be trying to flank."

The Symphonies of Potential and Healing were a chaotic arpeggio of changing energy. Kratitha was a fugue of notes—a master belting out a constantly changing stream of rhythm. Gompt was a lower, solid beat with a rumbling base line driving forward. I tuned out the mechanical repetition of the pullbeast, as there was another theme, buried underneath the top layer of music. This contained long, languid sweeps of melody, increasing and decreasing in pitch. Was that Aegrino? I tried to remember what I had heard around his body, but it had been too long ago.

"He's going left," I called, and we swerved onto a side street where a few lights still shone. These were kerosene, not powered by maji.

We pulled to a stop, but the Ethulina sped past, as if seeking revenge for being made to fight its creators. At the end of the street, back to a wall, was a tall figure, certainly an Etanela. He was holding a long object.

My resonator!

The resonator flashed in the air, and the pullbeast jerked, its feet tumbling over each other. It sprawled in the grass, just a pile of connected limbs. Rage built in me. There was too much time invested in the System Beast for Aegrino to destroy it.

"Don't let him hurt it more!" Gompt cried. She must have been thinking the same as I was. "Careful—he's got Communication and Grace."

"Can handle Grace," Kratitha said, flying forward toward the prone pullbeast.

Below her, the street ruptured, throwing cobbles in all directions. I shielded my face with an arm, but could hear the deep *thump* of the stones hitting grass, and the patter of water falling down in a shower.

When I looked again, a blue glow surrounded broken clay pipes, poking up from the street. Water puddled around it. Aegrino had used my invention to make the System in a water pipe go haywire. My teeth ground together at the misuse, the casual destruction.

Kratitha was on the ground, one wing bent back, a ragged piece missing from the top. A cobble must have grazed her. She reached an arm behind her to assess the damage.

Gompt and I rushed forward together, but skidded to a halt as the air flashed like glass, reflecting dim light back toward the walls and streetlights. Gompt yelled and clapped a hand to her side.

"What was that?" I called. The glass-like reflection in the air was gone, and I swiveled side to side, trying to see if there was anything left. There had been a sting of sound in the Symphonies—both Symphonies—when it happened.

"Don't come closer," Aegrino called out, his voice was nervous in the clear night air, higher than the record keeper's usual timbre. His mop of golden hair wavered like a cloud above his head as he checked the dead end behind him. There wasn't much light, but I thought I could see dark blotches on his shirt. With the wounds I'd seen, I had no idea how he was standing.

"Give me back the harmonic resonator," I called out "And the list of—" my mouth rebelled at me and that annoying jingle of music played, scattering my thoughts. "The names you have." *He'll know what I mean.*

"I'm afraid I can't." Aegrino's words slurred together, as Etanela's speech did when they were excited. "This is the only way to keep you maji from doing more harm. This is an excellent weapon to reveal your secrets."

Kratitha yelled and dove forward, but she was slow. What was left of her left wing membrane trembled, not in concert with the right. Aegrino turned the wand toward her and pushed a button. Another splash of sound played through my head.

"Stop, Kratitha!" I called, but it was too late. The slivers of light appeared again, right in front of the Pixie and she screamed, falling back.

Brown blood splattered on the Ethulina, and trickled down Kratitha's arms and front.

"Best not to rush in here," Gompt said, to my left. "Aegrino's a trained majus. He's skilled in the Symphonies of Communication and Grace, so why ain't he using them? Why is he talking about the maji like that? Wasn't his shirt a different color when we found him 'dead?'"

It's not Aegrino?

"I'm getting past you," the figure said. "Don't follow me, or I'll carve you up, maji or not!"

"Don't know if even the House of Grace can avoid those spikes of nothingness," Gompt said. "Do you hear that resonance in the Symphony too?"

I stared back. "I thought it was just me. It must be creating a feedback loop between the notes—"

I broke off. *Just like the accident.* In a split second, the memory pushed through my mind, as my hand went to the scar around my eye.

It was after dinner in my parent's home. I showed my mentor, Abarham, how the resonator created a connection between different Systems, causing them to work in tandem. But the harmonics multiplied out of control. Walls caved in. I smelled blood and dust as a chunk of the roof crushed Abarham in front of me. A rafter nearly put out my eye.

I crawled from the wreckage, but my parents didn't. When the Poler City Guard and the Fire Brigade arrived, they found lacerations on all three bodies. I had cuts all down my arms.

The resonances my invention made in the Symphony were so concentrated, they intruded into physical space. I'd never made the connection before, but now I did, my mind flashing through the wand's construction.

"I know how to stop the resonator," I told Gompt. I looked to Kratitha. She was holding hands over her arms, and blood was running down her front. "But it will take all three of us."

"Move aside! Leave me in peace!" the figure yelled. He was trapped, with the stone wall behind him, but he'd stopped our attack with almost no effort. We couldn't let him leave. "My friends and I won't bother you."

"Friends without *two houses*," Gompt called back, getting around the geas' restraints.

"Not maji at all." Aegrino/not-Aegrino backed up, my wand held in front of him. "Just a coalition of likeminded people. We're trying to make the Assembly a better place, but you people had to bring Juristo into this—blackmail him!"

"Who?" I had no idea who this Juristo was, and I met Gompt's eyes, then Kratitha's multifaceted orbs. Had they heard the same thing?

"On the way here," Kratitha gasped out. She was crouched low. The top of her left wing was a mess of crumpled tissue. Like butterflies or bees, I didn't know if Pixie's wings ever healed. "Heard things while Aegrino—or this person," she jerked a thumb toward our antagonist, "spoke to weird Sathssn."

"We found the place," Gompt said. "Slitho and Harha, right?" The Pixie cocked her head at us, then nodded.

"It was to protect Juristo! You didn't even know his name?" Aegrino/not-Aegrino called. "Back away and we can all leave in peace." The figured shuffled his feet back and forth, as if he were about to run between us. I wasn't going to let that happen.

"You've murdered another Etanela," I shouted back. "Maybe two. We'll track you anywhere you go."

A shift in the figure's stance told me he'd decided to attack again rather than run at us, so I was ready this time when he pushed a button. He knew how to use the resonator, but I guessed he didn't know everything, especially if Kratitha had tinkered with it.

The wave of harmonics was like a pipe organ overriding the Symphony, all notes tuned to the same key, playing concert. It pushed into the Symphonies of Healing and Potential, and disturbances in the air reflected the faint light from the streetlight and fading walls of the Nether, traveling toward us like shards of thrown glass.

They'll slice us to ribbons. Don't have time to explain the change using all three of us.

I did the best I could with an instant's thought.

The notes in the Symphony of Potential were overwhelmed with the harmonics, and I took notes from my being to change them, bridge the gaps, and let those powerful chords become part of my being. I absorbed the energy into myself, knowing it would rip my bones apart and shred my muscles. Fortunately I had more than one house.

The Symphony of Healing was a riot of disruptions, Gompt and Kratitha's notes unraveling despite me taking the brunt of the attack. As if in slow motion, I could see fur separating on Gompt's torso, skin tearing.

I took more notes from my being, and altered the monoliths of noise, bridging from melody to melody in the Symphony of Healing, dispersing the harmonics between different branches of music.

I was dimly aware that I was on my knees. The energy I had taken in with the Symphony of Potential threatened to shake me apart. I stole yet more notes from the melody that made up my being, dispersing the energy. My fingers felt like they were on fire, my heart hammering. Kratitha screamed, and out of the corner of my eye I saw a line of brown open from her forearm to wrist.

I won't let what happened to Abarham and my parents happen again.

I took more of the resonance into myself, breaking it into component notes, changing tempo and key so they could no longer harmonize. I could not reclaim these notes, and it would take many days to rebuild my song.

I shook, pitching forward, then realized the wall of sound had ceased.

I raised my head. My eyesight was blurry, my hands trembling, as if I had touched one of the live wires transmitting electricity to the new lights in the mansion.

"What? You should be dead!" Not-Aegrino was adjusting settings on my device. "It was an accident before, but I remember. I remember."

I waved my shaking hands at my friends to come closer so I could explain. Gompt was bleeding from her chest, but the cuts were shallow. Kratitha was in worse shape, but the little Pixie limped over, her head high.

"Must keep resonant harmonics from—ow—from forming," she said.

"That's right." My shaking was subsiding. "The harmonic resonator combines available melodies into a harmony. If prevented, I believe the energy will feed back into the device."

"You believe?" Gompt said. Her voice was raw.

"It's the best chance we have," I said, watching the figure standing at the end of the street. "Listen to your Symphonies. Keep the melodies from harmonizing. It will be hard, but we only need to hold the changes for a few seconds. We can try—" I broke off, seeing the other figure look up. "No time. Get ready."

The others spun around, as not-Aegrino raised the wand. I could already hear strands of the Symphony of Potential wavering, tones speeding or slowing to fall into a rhythm. I took more notes from my song. *It's so bare of music.* The notes would return over time, but it would take many more experiences for me to grow back to my full potential.

I inserted my notes like bookmarks between pages, keeping them from sticking together. This was not a carefully crafted change, but creating music with no theme, stuffing notes into both Symphonies that did not belong in the beautiful, natural music of the universe. I could hear Gompt doing the same thing in the Symphony of Potential.

Auras surrounded the three of us in the colors of our houses, visible only to another majus, blue and brown for Gompt, white and brown around me, and blue and orange around Kratitha. Sparks filled the air, dancing off motes of dust, and blinding me for a moment. I heard a crack of stone, and a twisting, splintering noise of wood exploding. Seconds later, I turned my head away as tiny slivers pelted my face, dropping away harmlessly.

When my vision returned, a line of cobbles in front of me was fractured. The streetlight danced with flame, the entire globe around the light engulfed in fire. A nearby bush was wilted, dropping leaves, and Gompt's fur shone with ice.

"It worked!" Gompt called, and I looked up. The figure was braced against the wall, my invention a shredded mess. Even from this distance, I could see splinters of wood and metal imbedded in his bluish hands. More blood dotted his shirt, where slivers had driven into his chest.

Gompt rushed forward, past the prone System Beast, and I followed, puffing as if I had raced across Poler. Kratitha came behind, but she was slow, obviously hurting.

Our antagonist struggled up, but Gompt got there first, checking the other person with a massive shoulder. He staggered against the wall and Gompt clamped both furry paws—strong from months of crafting in the workshop—on his arms.

I looked up into the Etanela's face. It *was* Aegrino, except it wasn't. The face was subtly different, but also familiar. The hair was the same shade, and in the same style.

I know this person.

This was a dominate female of the Etanela, while Aegrino had been a subordinate male—two of the four divisions of Etanela gender.

Bloody slashes marked her chest as they had Aegrino, though in this case not fatally. Had it happened at the same time? I imagined the resonator between the two, creating deadly energy and slashing at both Etanela. Slashing at the Speaker's neck.

She was wearing makeup before. That's why I didn't recognize her similarity to Aegrino.

"You're the secretary!" I said. My voice was like sandpaper. I might have screamed while the resonant notes coursed through my body. "How do you know about the...the Society?" The geas let me whisper the word. This person clearly knew more than she should.

"I heard a lot, as a secretary to one of the Assembly's speakers," she muttered. "I just needed to get you out of the way so I could clean up. I knew you wouldn't go to the Imperium guard."

The Etanela's hands did not describe fluid patterns, as normal for the species. Instead she held them in front of her, trembling as she tried to prize shards of wood from where they punctured her palms. Greenish blood dripped, and I could see the tips of several splinters poking all the way through the backs of her blue-tinted hands.

"Did you kill Aegrino?" Gompt said, still holding the Etanela's arms. Kratitha stared up to meet our prisoner's eyes.

"My name is Bethaya Plumire Lunigi," she said. Her voice shook, the words slurring together so much it was difficult to understand her.

"Related to Aegrino, by the name," Kratitha croaked, and Bethaya nodded, her mane of hair waving.

"He was my brother—great Sea Mother, it was an accident!" Bethaya wailed. "Everything went so fast. We were just supposed to disrupt the geas with this—thing." She lifted her hands, where the shards of the resonator pierced her.

Aegrino said he had to tell his sister about Speaker Thurapo's death. But she already knew. His sister was the secretary...

"Then you are aware of the Society," Gompt rumbled.

"I've known for cycles," Bethaya said. Tears were flowing down her face. "Slitho and Harha were the ones to finally understand, of all the people my brother and I have tried to tell." Words flowed from her, as if from a deflating balloon. "We used your accident as an example of the dangers of the Society. Aegrino learned about the resonator wand from his records, then glimpsed it in your workshop one day." Kratitha hissed in air at that.

What are those two Sathssn up to? "Was Speaker Thurapo an accident too?" I asked. "Were you trying to recruit a speaker to your cause?"

I did not expect Bethaya's next response, which was to crumple to the ground. Gompt barely kept hold on the Etanela's limp arms.

"Sea Mother. It had just happened when I heard you coming. I had no time to take care of Juristo's body." Bethaya looked at me, seated on the cobbles of Poler, face wet with tears.

Juristo is *Speaker Thurapo.* It was like a sheet of cold water washed over me. I hadn't known his given name. Bethaya must have been with the Speaker before I got there this morning. *Her eyes weren't puffy from sleep this morning—they were puffy from* crying. Things began to fall into place.

"More than a secretary to Thurapo, yes?" Kratitha asked.

Bethaya sunk in farther, and her response was almost inaudible. "Juristo and I...became intimate. That Benish councilor pressured him to listen to your proposal, or they would tell Juristo's mates about us." Bethaya's words trailed off in a sob.

"Then...*you're* the leverage the Society had on the Speaker." I said. "Finally, some motive to interfere with the System Beast proposal, and the Society."

"He had been studying that accursed list of names all night," Bethaya said. "I thought this was finally the chance Harha and I talked about, to show someone in power how our Life Coalition thought."

"Wait—you didn't give him the list of Society names?" Gompt asked, and I stared at our captive. Something *still* didn't fit. Kratitha hunched in, and her compound eyes took in everything.

Bethaya slowly pulled a splinter from her palm, hissing in pain. "No. Juristo said someone delivered the list the night before—a Pixie. I saw the chance to show him what destruction two-house maji can cause." She looked up at me suddenly, venomous. "Even if you make people forget about the explosion you caused in Poler, others won't. But they don't know about the Society. I do. I can show how its members play with forces beyond their control."

"That was an—an accident," I choked out, mirroring Bethaya's excuse. "My parents *died*, as did my mentor. You have no right to—" I stopped at Gompt's hand on my arm.

"We'll figure that out later," she said.

Had I been yelling? My hands were in tight fists.

Bethaya was talking about how the Speaker wanted a demonstration, and how it went wrong, but I had seen those effects for myself, and Thurapo had paid the ultimate price.

My eyes were on Kratitha, hunched beside me. She was no longer looking in my direction.

There were plenty of Pixies in the Society. Fewer than my species, but a good handful. It could have been any of them who delivered the list to the Speaker. But Kratitha had already admitted to adjusting my invention. An invention which Aegrino thought could remove the geas.

"Did you—" I started, but as usual, my colleague was ahead of me.

"Did not anticipate these events," Kratitha said, still hunched over. Her right hand cradled her left arm, tracing around the sliced skin running the length of her forearm, still slowly leaking blood. "Had separate reasons to talk to the Speaker. My caste needs protection. Few scientists left, even now. A genocide, by the warrior caste, and Speaker had...requirements. He suspected Society existed and wanted independent proof. Found a way to accommodate. Promised would not go farther than him."

"You little maggot," Gompt spat. Now it was my turn to put a restraining arm out. "You could have told us at any time where the list of members came from, but you let us wander around like fools."

"For our good," Kratitha said, and her voice gained strength, and speed. "For the good of the System Beasts. The Speaker would approve vote—get other Etanela to vote our way. Would send support to family on Mother Hive. Didn't know about this one when I did it." The Pixie waved a languid hand toward Bethaya.

"Too many secrets," I said. I pulled Bethaya to her feet, keeping a tight hold on her. I trusted Kratitha to come along with us. She may have been misguided, but I knew her well enough to know her loyalties aligned with ours. There would be...complications. "Where is Aegrino's body?" I asked our prisoner.

"Burned," she said. "As is Juristo's. Sea Mother, what have I done?" She sank again, but Gompt and I supported her.

"She's in shock," I said. "Let's get back to the mansion, and figure this out properly."

"It was *your* weapon that did this," Bethaya snarled, and I deflected a half-serious swipe at my head.

"An *invention*," I replied, "and one that has constructive uses. There was a reason I broke it."

"Apologies," Kratitha mumbled, shuffling along beside us. I could tell she was in pain. It might dull her hyperactive nature until Gompt and I reached Moortlin to tell them what had happened.

I went to the heap of the Ethulina, and was surprised to find the Systems still intact, but jumbled. I used a precious few more of my notes to knit the aspect back together, and our creation wobbled to its front hooves, then up on all fours. It followed us, favoring a rear leg.

At least the System Beasts are innocent in all this. We still need to get their production approved, somehow.

"How much do these Sathssn know?" I asked Bethaya as we walked. "Will they be a problem for the Society?"

The Etanela grunted as she pulled another shard from her hand, leaving the splinter beside the road. I watched it fall behind us. *Maybe I can make a version that works as intended.*

"Slitho and Harha are innocent," Bethaya said. "Leave them out f this."

"They know about the Society," Gompt said. A line of red marred her chest fur.

"So do I," Bethaya said. "So do the families of the maji who are members. Leave the Sathssn's Life Coalition out of this. It's a small collection of like-minded people who merely want the universe to be a better place."

I snorted, and Gompt rumbled a growl. That didn't match what Bethaya said about maji having too much power. It was also a common complaint, and I'd endured enough of the Sathssn's trite nonsense to know it was a fad like other intersections of religion and philosophy dotting the Great Assembly. If the Life Coalition was so concerned with making everyone happy, and with recruiting majus members, the little group wouldn't do anything against the influence of the maji.

PART SEVEN

The Society of Two Houses

My great-grandfather Slithen, you know him as 'the Dreamer.' This, it is a title given after his series of still-unexplained visions, thought to be sent by the Ideal Form itself. Our coalition of believers, who celebrate the beauty of life perfected, came into existence over fifteen cycles after his death, when I was an infant. For cycles, we have languished, slowly growing our membership, and recently even reaching out to blasphemers outside our species. Me, I am happy to report plans for a new invention delivered by one of these outsiders. I hope this will put to rest discord of whether other species should be included. Information about this invention will speed the work of our scientists and maji in discovering the method to pierce the shroud between our universe and the beyond.

—Notes of Harha to select members of the Most Traditional Servant sect of the Cult of Form, 953 A.A.W.

We reached the mansion as the light of the walls brightened. I had been awake a long time, starting early yesterday morning when I found the Speaker dead.

Bethaya came along quietly, neither trying to escape nor fighting our guiding hands. She had lost a brother and a lover in one day, by her own misguided hand.

I lost parents and mentor in one day, too. She will remember this for the rest of her life.

Kratitha trudged along, her damaged wing unable to carry her weight. She spoke little—a sign of how cowed she was.

We passed the gates of the mansion, and I looked to the sphere containing the inert concealing System. It was yet another problem the Society would need to fix, along with the damage to the interior of the mansion.

We must have been a sight. Even amidst the chaos we drew the gazes of other Society members as we climbed the mansion's main staircase. Plithin A'Tyf and his spouses were cleaning fallen ceiling plaster, and the trio of Lobath nodded to us gravely. Plithin looked as if he might speak, but we hurried past.

Moortlin was in their study, and at our knock, I heard the click of multiple latches being drawn.

The door creaked open and the head of the Society took us all in with one sweep of his unblinking yellow eyes, then gestured into his office. We crowded in, and Moortlin bolted the door again, ensuring we would not be disturbed.

"Bethaya," he said to the Etanela, with a creak of his head. "One remembers there was a ban in effect to keep this one from entering the mansion. Does this one need to be escorted out again?"

"Then you know her?" Gompt said. She took a step toward the Benish. "You could have mentioned she was Thurapo's lover."

Moortlin raised one thick hand out to the side. "One was not aware that one was, hm, even involved, nor could enter the mansion. Bethaya is, hm, the one this group searched for? How would that one get the list, and what of Speaker Thurapo? One visited the Dome of the Assembly, but Aegrino had already, hm, cleaned up the body and the Speaker's office."

"Bethaya was the one who took care of both bodies—burned them," I told the Benish. I spared a look at Kratitha, who must have caught my movement, though her head was bowed. Her assent was a quick twitch of her head. "Though it turns out Bethaya was not involved with the disappearance of the list of Society members."

It was the closest I had seen to Moortlin being surprised. Their eyes blinked dim, then back to their normal luminescence, both hands coming up and out, as if reaching for the answer. "There are more here who wish to see the, hm, Society gone?" they asked. "One suspected the Society would fragment again—one's enemies have increased over the last two hundred cycles."

I was saved having to explain by Kratitha. "Was a matter of family," she said. "Of caste and pride, and—and Speaker Thurapo asked for much in return for support from Etanela fighters. He suspected Society existed."

Moortlin's head turned from side to side, creaking like a door in need of oil. "The Council of the Maji has been concerned with the recent hostilities between the warrior and scientist classes on Mother Hive. One was surprised when the latest reports said the warriors were beginning to, hm, lose battles." They reached a hand out toward the little Pixie. "This one had an involvement in that situation?"

Kratitha raised her head. "Was birthed in the new scientist queen's first brood. Only majus among them, and close to queen mother. She insisted something be done. Wouldn't agree to any truce with the warrior mother. Reached out offworld through me. Speaker Thurapo insisted on information in return for help."

"This one could speak or write of the Society?" Moortlin's words were quiet, but I could discern the edge of tension—or was it panic?

"Turns out Mandamon's invention could disrupt the geas, with a little tweaking," Gompt said from where she was helping Bethaya remove more splinters of my wand from her hand. The two were leaving green bloodstains on Moortlin's carpet. "Kratitha got her hands on it before Bethaya stole it. Aegrino must have given it to her to try to disrupt the geas around them, too." The Festuour held up one of Bethaya's hands as the Etanela nodded, confirming Gompt's theory. "It won't be a problem any longer."

Moortlin shook their head with a dull creak. "No. Once a secret has been breached, hm, it is far easier to breach again." They made a fist. "One has already had an inquiry about the mansion, now the System at the gates has been damaged. One assumes this is also Bethaya's work?" The Etanela didn't answer, and Moortlin continued.

"Mandamon knows the construction of the instrument, Kratitha a way to modify the Symphony attached to it. If a dire need arose, could any of this group swear not to make another object to, hm, render the geas inoperable?"

None of us could meet the Benish's eyes.

"One thought not." They watched Bethaya picking at the shards of my invention, and their voice lessened from sandpaper over wood to a file on leather. "Bethaya. Bethaya!" The Etanela looked up, obviously still in shock. Her eyes did not focus on the Benish. "This one has the, hm, copy of the list of Society members? This one took it from the Speaker's study, yes?"

Slowly, Bethaya nodded. "I did," she said. "But after what happened to Aegrino, I...I," she stopped again, staring into the distance.

"What did you do with it?" I urged her, and she watched me as if she didn't remember who I was. "The list?"

Her head came up, looking to the ceiling of Moortlin's study. "I burned the salt-soaked thing, with their bodies."

Moortlin made a low noise; the creak of an oak settling after a hurricane. "Not ideal. One would like to, hm, have the list in hand rather than supposedly burned and gone." They sighed. "If this is the situation, then this group will make the best of it." They turned to Gompt. "Please take Bethaya to the clinical ward. That one's wounds must be treated before, hm, a trial is attempted."

Gompt looked like she might say something, but Moortlin's stern expression cut her off. She nodded, and helped Bethaya rise, still picking wood and metal shards from her hands. Gompt unlocked several clasps and chains on the door before it would open. Moortlin locked it behind her. They put their back to the door. "Kratitha, this one made no other copies of the list?"

The Pixie shook her head. "Stole the one Aegrino copied, then took it to the Speaker. Only because Mother was in danger. Would never hurt the Society otherwise."

I cocked my head. *Something isn't right.* "But the Speaker copied at least part of the list. I picked up the indentations on his writing pad. Neither list was in the room."

"As one said," Moortlin replied. "When a secret is, hm, revealed, it is very difficult to conceal it again."

Kratitha looked between the two of us holding her arm. Her stooped stance spoke of bone-deep tiredness. "Delivered the list to Speaker very early in morning—previous night, really. Speaker copies list. Then Bethaya shows invention to Speaker and Speaker shows her copy?" She swayed just slightly before her intact wing buzzed to support her. "Yet Bethaya only takes copy, burns it, and Mandamon finds nothing." She paused as if we should be able to fill in the missing information. "Only two solutions. Either paper still hidden in Speaker Thurapo's study, or another person took it."

Moortlin clenched their hands with a creak like wood about to snap. I took an involuntary step back. "It may be impossible to save the Society from the breach, as, hm, one has already stated." They opened their hands again, and their eyes brightened.

They stepped away from the door. "Kratitha, follow the others. This one also needs medical attention, and has a presentation to show off the, hm, System Beast. This group will need to be fully healed."

"But the Speaker—," I started.

"Presentation not yet approved," added Kratitha, even as she loosened latches. It was a sign of her discomfort that she didn't protest the Benish's order.

"One has made, hm, other arrangements." Moortlin said. "It is not preferable. It leaves a trail connecting the System Beast to one, to the Society, and to the mansion. At this point, the truth is perhaps, hm, unavoidable."

"What of punishment?" Kratitha ventured.

Moortlin waggled their fingers. "Much has been done in the Society by suspect means for the good of the whole. One is glad this one's caste has a chance to survive. The Assembly needs more scientists, and fewer warriors."

"Thank you," Kratitha whispered, before pulling the door closed behind her.

As soon as we were alone, Moortlin creaked to the door, pulling latches locked once again. I wondered if they could save time and dispense with the action, but they finished quickly, and took three straight-legged strides to their desk.

"Moortlin?" I asked, but the Benish fished something from deep in a pile of paper on their desk with a grunt, and passed it over.

It was a list of Society members.

But this was lost. Someone took it. "Is this—? Did you—?"

"Buried in the bottom, locked drawer of Speaker Thurapo's desk." I was almost certain Moortlin's craggy face showed a smile, though I don't think I'd ever seen that expression on them. "Bethaya thought the copy was the original, and though one did not find the Speaker's, hm, body, one found this."

I had missed it too, in my original haste to discover what happened to the Speaker. I remembered nearly looking in the desk before Bethaya knocked on the door. *If I'd only had a few more seconds, this all would have been easier to unravel.*

My thoughts went back to the dusty scrap Gompt and I found in the records room. "And older versions...?"

"May now be, hm, conveniently lost."

Then the list would not be revealed to the larger majus community after all, or to the Assembly. We still needed to fix the front gate, but tightness melted from my shoulders.

I tried to hand the paper back, but Moortlin crossed their arms. I frowned. "Why?"

"The Society will be disbanded, and likely sooner than later. One feels the event, hm, happening even now. There is too much damage to the mansion, and the deaths of a speaker and a majus will not go unnoticed."

I still don't understand.

"One will go back to Aben soon, and plant with a suitable group. One has said as much. The Society must be seen as dissolved for many cycles—hm, until all have forgotten about it." Moortlin paused. "Save perhaps the Effature. That one forgets little, though is also, hm, bound by the geas."

I was slowly coming to realize what Moortlin meant. "You want me to keep this secret. For a long time."

Moortlin nodded with a crack of a branch snapping. "Until this one deems the time is right for the Society to, hm, re-emerge. It will be many cycles. This one will be the new head of the Society when that happens. Do not tell the others. One fears a larger group would only, hm, complicate matters."

"Surely there are other, more senior members who are better equipped—"

"Senior, but also, hm, older. This one is one of the youngest, and most capable, members. One can see this one's future will be...interesting."

"I...I don't know what to say." I fumbled with the list, unsure whether to fold it and put it in a pocket, or keep it unbent and frame it, or just lock it in the safest place I could imagine.

"Say nothing. Watch and record the events of the Great Assembly of Species. Decide when the Society of Two Houses should reform to, hm, face the threats of the universe."

Moortlin stepped around me to unchain the door.

* * *

Three ten-days after Moortlin gave me the list, I stood, with Gompt and Kratitha, in the rotunda of the Great Assembly. It was my first time on the crystal floor, below the seats of the maji, diplomats, and representatives.

I was surrounded by the sixty-seven chairs of the speakers. Several were empty at any time, and my eyes strayed to the bank of five Etanela speakers, led by the imposing form of Rabata Liinero Humbano. Speaker Thurapo's chair was vacant, as his districts of Etan had not yet picked a replacement.

"You may begin." The voice drew me back to the moment, and I heard the chime of the Ethulina's hoof against the crystal floor. I looked to the Effature, who had said the words. His face was expressionless, the circlet of crystal on his brow reflecting a beam of light shining through the dome.

Don't throw up. Gompt shifted from foot to foot, and even Kratitha was preening her right wing. The left had been amputated last ten-day, but she was already working on a System-based prosthetic to lift her weight off the floor.

"Gathered representatives," I began, trying to keep the prepared words straight. "Today we are here to demonstrate what a System Beast can do."

When Gompt spoke I could barely hear the tremble in her voice. "I am giving the System Beast a few commands," she said, lifting a hatch and flipping several levers. Kratitha wrung her hands as she watched. "In light of the recent tragedy, we thought the creature that helped bring a killer to justice could also give its condolences." Gompt closed the panel and said, "Give your package to Speaker Humbano."

The Ethulina stepped forward, metal hoofs clicking. The glass in its mane caught the light from the dome. There were gasps and conversation as the Ethulina walked across the circle of speakers, stopping in front of Speaker Humbano. Its mouth opened, and from the mobile lips emerged a handwritten note. One hoof split into fingers, took the note, and gave it to the Speaker.

Speaker Humbano frowned, but took the paper, unrolled it, and read it silently. I tried not to mouth the words I had labored over for a full ten-day.

Speaker Humbano rolled the paper up and, surprisingly, addressed the System Beast. "Thank you," she said, "for delivering these heartfelt words. I will see they get to the Speaker's family on Etan."

Her words were the floodgates. Over the next three lightenings—nearly the entire afternoon, we paraded the Ethulina through its paces, and the speakers, the Council, and the Effature debated.

At the end of the demonstration, the Effature addressed us, his warm voice too large for his small frame and balding, elderly head.

"This Assembly agrees to the production and use of what you call System Beasts."

Gompt grabbed my hand in a bone-crushing grip, and my shoulders relaxed for the first time since I had found Speaker Thurapo's body. *We did it. Our concept will be used throughout the ten homeworlds and the Nether.* After all the destruction, there was one bright point.

"But—" Kratitha whispered to us. "Will be a 'but.'"

"But, we would like to see the following adjustments before the speakers all agree to let System Beasts be sold on their homeworlds," the Effature continued.

Kratitha let out a labored sigh. I shook Gompt's paw off before she squashed my fingers.

"The homeworlds of Festuour, Loba, and Methiem wish the displayed intelligence of the System Beast to be reduced. They suggest their homeworlds' citizens will be afraid to use the devices if they perceive them to accommodate their requests too easily."

I heard Kratitha's low-pitched grumble, and tried to ignore the leaden lump growing in my belly.

"In addition, the homeworlds of Mother Hive, Sath Home, and Sureri wish the ability to locate individuals removed or reduced. They fear potential for abuse."

Now Gompt scowled. "So they want a shiny packhorse, is what they mean."

The fine gearing loops of thought, the cognitive functions we'd labored over? Were they all a waste of time? The System Beasts could be so much more than what these speakers wanted, so much *bigger*.

I grasped my thigh with one hand to keep it from balling into a fist, and addressed the Effature. "We can make these changes," I said.

There was still an upside, and I kept it forefront in my mind. Gompt, Kratitha, and I could make System Beasts with all their abilities. The Assembly only restricted us from selling them publicly.

On the way out, Moortlin caught my eye, and waved a wide hand toward themself. I left Gompt and Kratitha with a promise I would meet them at the celebration that evening.

"There was another, hm, decision made today, by the Council of the Maji," Moortlin rumbled when I came close enough. They swung their bald head side to side with a grinding creak as they spoke.

A weight settled in my stomach. "The Society?"

Moortlin nodded with a snapping sound. "It will be disbanded, the mansion condemned. This ten-day."

"What of the—" I broke off as a Lobath speaker strode past. "—of the members and their families? Some haven't been to the Imperium in cycles." *Tethan might not survive moving from the mansion.*

"One has spread the word to the members of the Society. Several families will go into hiding, as those groups chose not to, hm, rejoin the mainstream maji for personal reasons."

Meaning, news of questionable experiments they performed won't be well received.

My hand rose of its own accord to the inside of my fine brown wool jacket, which I had specially cleaned and mended just for the presentation. The list of Society members was tucked inside. *I have the only record of everyone, when they disperse.*

"All this is because of the murders?" I asked.

"Bethaya was, hm, very direct in that one's tale," Moortlin answered. "Though that one listened to one's request to leave certain...others out of the recounting." They raised one finger to my chest.

"And the geas?" I asked.

"There is no *known* way to reverse it, is there?" One of Moortlin's eyes dimmed and brightened in a slow wink. "This will keep unwarranted information from, hm, spreading—a happy side effect."

I watched the Benish's straight-legged stride toward the other members of the Council, wondering at the tightness in my chest. Gompt had already offered me a place to stay with her friend group. We would have to find a new place to work in the Imperium, but the Assembly's agreement to produce the System Beasts also came with a grant of funds.

I silently thanked the Society for helping me. It was disbanded, but not forgotten, and I suspected my knowledge would guide all my future actions in the world of the maji. Someday, the Society would be needed again, be it ten cycles or fifty, and I promised myself I would keep track of its members, both existing and those who could join in the future.

The conviction rose in my chest. The next time the Society of Two Houses emerged, it would be in the open.

Changing State

632 A.A.W.

Moortlin felt their sap rising, heating their chest. *Councilors are not known to make mistakes.* "One does not believe one heard correctly."

Councilor Fortilath smiled briefly, feathery crest flaring upward, then relaxing. The other species of the Great Assembly had such expressive faces, compared to the thoughtful, solid, Benish. Moortlin felt every move their body made, pulling matter and connecting tissue into new configurations. Those Benish who chose to leave Aben were warned the universe moved faster than they were used to. Moortlin was still adjusting. They had made it through apprenticeship, graduating to full majus the previous cycle.

"The Council believes you are to be uniquely qualified for this task," the councilor said, ignoring Moortlin's complaint. "Hearing two houses is unusual among the maji, and the Houses of Strength and Healing are exactly what we are needing. The Council has received strange reports of unnatural creatures, such as a pullbeast to be walking on its front legs, then collapsing into a pile of leaves. Other sightings are of walking flowers, or creatures that are morphing as soon as they are seen, shifting into some new shape."

"And this one believes it is the, hm, Aridori?" That had been the word that made Moortlin disbelieve. *If that species has returned, there are larger problems than one Benish can handle.*

Councilor Fortilath held up one finger, ending in a thick, curved fingernail. "I was not saying that. *Some* are to be conjecturing this is the work of Aridori, but as the species is to be six hundred cycles extinct, this seems more likely a rumor growing out of hand."

"But this one, hm, feels a majus is still required?" Moortlin asked. *Why did Councilor Fortilath recommend one for this task?* It made no sense. Moortlin felt their joints shift as they moved from foot to foot, and the councilor politely didn't mention the snapping sound. The other species were so quiet when they moved. "This one wishes me to confront these potential Aridori, hm, alone?"

"Call it a special assignment from the Council," Councilor Fortilath said. "We are not believing the stories, but there may be something else sinister at work, and the combination of Symphonies you hear means you are to be well suited to inquire into issues with plant and animal life."

The old Kirian had, for some reason, taken an interest in Moortlin, now they were a majus. More testing of the slow Benish. Why did everyone assume that simply because one thought about an answer, one did not know it? But then, Moortlin was considered reckless, instead of reflective, among one's own kind.

"Then one will do one's best to satisfy," Moortlin said. *If this is no Aridori, what else could cause such chaos? The councilor must have some idea, but why choose one instead of another majus?* Moortlin rubbed their left thumb across their fingers, thinking.

As if reading Moortlin's thoughts, Councilor Fortilath's crest ruffled, as if that one had a secret to tell. "I am also to be able to hear two Symphonies, young majus," the councilor said. "Those of us with such abilities must be supporting each other."

So that was the hook. The councilor was giving a simple job to one who could benefit from its success—a welcome advantage for a new majus with few connections. *The notice of one of the six council members is nothing to ignore. A success could increase one's standing greatly.*

"One will, hm, be happy to help, Councilor," Moortlin said.

* * *

A few lightenings later, Moortlin's gnarled toes gripped the cobbles of the street, pulling them forward in a steady pace, while passersby twitched at the *snap* and *crack* of their movement. It was a rare occurrence to see a Benish in the Imperium—the group memories from Moortlin's progenitors told them that.

Well, Moortlin wasn't planning to return to Aben soon. They were just beginning their career. There was plenty of space to rise in the hierarchy of the maji—if nothing unpleasant happened, like botching a personal assignment from the Council. Their associates back on Aben warned Moortlin would come to a bad end, making such a quick judgment about leaving the homeworld, but Moortlin was willing to take that chance. And now Councilor Fortilath—another maji with access to two houses—had presented an opportunity.

The disturbances had been reported near the docks on Lake Thaal. The lake was on the other side of the capital city, and Moortlin could tell when they crossed into Low Imperium. The cobblestones grew scarcer until the street was reduced to packed earth. Pedestrians tried to avoid the main avenues, where an occasional freight cart rumbled past, pushed by ten to twenty people followed by an overseer. This close to the docks, there was a lot of cargo moving through the streets, but Moortlin doubted much of it belonged to those who lived here.

They stopped as a flicker in an alley caught their eye. There had been something...off about the scurrying creature crawling through the gutter. It might have had too many legs, or perhaps...was its fur moving independently? *Is this one of the strange creatures?*

Moortlin hurried after the animal, listening to the Symphonies always playing in the core of their being. Yes, there were odd chords present in the music that underlay the universe, in this place. Most combinations were natural, despite their oddness. The universe was a big place, and there were many strange things living in it. These notes, however... Moortlin tapped the side of their head with a thick finger, as if that would make the music fall into a more pleasing rhythm.

They wound through the close corridors near the lake, following the trail of discordant notes first from the little scurrier, then to an odd growth of buds peeking through an open slat in a building, then to the corpse of something that looked a month dead. Moortlin couldn't tell what it had been when alive, or even how many legs it had. They were glad they didn't have as refined a sense of smell as some of the other species boasted. Benish were better at listening than smelling.

None of the music they followed was *wrong*, as such, but there were sections of notes sounding as if an inept majus had dismantled them, then put them back in almost the right order. The councilor had been correct. This must be a majus' doing, not an Aridori. Rumors and panics arose every few decades about the extinct species, of how they would return to infiltrate the other species once more, but the rumors always turned out to be false. This situation was the same—something else caused it. But what?

As they continued down the street—it was more of an alley between houses that had grown next to each other—Moortlin could feel they were getting closer to the source of the disturbance. A new theme was growing in the Symphony of Healing. The music that thrummed and vibrated through this part of the city sounded as if some person had wrung out the music.

Their body creaked and snapped—there were no other species in this dark alley to stare—and Moortlin pushed the music of Healing aside and listened to the House of Strength.

Where the Symphony of Healing was high and melodic, sometimes even shrill, the Symphony of Strength was solid and low. Vibrating strings, matched chords, rhythms built upon each other until the result was a massive chorus.

Some of the voices were just out of sync, as in Healing.

Moortlin stopped near a cross-street, where a vine crawled up an abandoned building. The oddness in the music was stronger here. They raised one hand, thick fingers surrounding the leaves of one tendril.

The vine was bleeding—thick purple blood.

What is this?

Moortlin drew their hand back and wiped the mess on the open tunic they wore—an affectation to keep away questions from other species more than for its protection from weather or its comfort.

The vine writhed, the blood flowing, then dripping, and an aura of white, and green, and orange grew around it. Those were the colors of Healing, Strength, and Power.

Moortlin cocked their head and stared as a section of the stem sprouted little green fingers and pulled its way up the wall. It ripped away from the stem sustaining it, as if the youngest portion of the vine rebelled against the rest of its being.

No, this is no Aridori. This was of the maji.

As the vine continued to mutate—fingers to claws, leaves to wings, until the section which had separated was an emerald green flying thing of lace and steel—the two aspects of the Grand Symphony Moortlin could hear shifted to another key. The top of the vine left a smear on the wall, and another section with newly sprouted fingers shredded its skin against the rough wood.

Auras rotated around the plant and its flying offspring as the Symphony of Strength—the aspect more closely associated with plants—bled notes into the Symphony of Healing. Lace wings blurred and the creature buzzed at Moortlin, making them duck with the snap of breaking branches as razor claws grazed the top of their head, leaving curls of hard flesh behind.

Moortlin sucked in air, and ran fingers across the wound. It was not bad, but also unexpected. Foolish. Things were moving fast. Too fast? No. They would prove their worth to Councilor Fortilath.

Musical phrases were staggering across key and tempo, disappearing for a few seconds, then overlapping and playing again as if a slow band had thrown down their instruments and performed an opera.

Movement.

Moortlin turned their head as fast as they could, to where the dirt street crossed another. *Someone passed by.* If there was a majus actively making this change—certainly not Aridori—that one must be close. Moortlin creaked after the unknown person, but when they got to the intersection they swung their head left, then right. No one was there.

Wait. There was a furry scrounger, snuffling along where wood planks were buried in the dirt.

Except. Hm. There was a feeling in the air, as if a thunderstorm threatened. A tremor in the Symphony of Healing quavered like a string being tuned to the breaking point. Moortlin tilted their head against the painful notes.

Colors only a majus could see erupted around the creature.

The scrounger stopped, shook, and its back bubbled as little yellow flowers sprouted from it. The petals dropped, and the flowers grew into buds, which opened to reveal tiny versions of the scrounger. The offspring swarmed down and followed their parent, which seemed unaffected by the stems still waving on its back. The creature scuttled along, followed by its new brood.

Moortlin strode forward. They could not afford to stop, though the instinct to study, and learn, was almost overpowering. They had never heard such changes in the Grand Symphony—ones that did not respect the boundaries between houses. This was a new occurrence, and possibly dangerous.

Down another street, Moortlin stepped around an abandoned board, still studded with the nails that previously fastened it to a home. It was writhing as if alive, colors of the Symphony around it. Moortlin shifted to one side as a length of grain ripped free, creaked upward, then drooped to the ground as if it were not wood, but elastic gum.

A tortured wail split the air, and Moortlin stared at the next house. *Lumber does not hiss and screech.*

The entire house glowed, and the Symphony transformed faster than Moortlin could track. It was music conducted by a mad genius, in three different keys at once.

Moortlin had little time to think, but knew this was very dangerous—a rogue majus, or more than one. They were powerful to change the Grand Symphony so. The warnings from other Benish crashed through their memory. *This one moves too fast. This one will be killed by something not understood. Aben is the only safe place for Benish.*

The slats of the house were bubbling, as if too close to a flame, but with no heat. Moortlin stepped close, though they wished to back away. At a touch, a pustule on the wood burst and crumbled to dust. Underneath was blue flesh, rubbery and wet.

All around, the wood was shedding its outer layer like caked dirt, revealing the jiggling surface beneath. Benish anatomy had similarities to wood fibers. *Will one also slough one's skin, revealing moist nastiness beneath?* Something clenched in Moortlin's gut, but they pushed forward. No one else close could handle this menace, and if they left, who could say how fast the unknown maji would disrupt the Imperium?

The door was unlocked, or the lock no longer functioned as such. The wood bent and flexed under their thick hand, and the door bowed inwards.

Inside, a parent cried, and an infant played, surrounded by song and color.

The parent was of the Methiemum species, fleshy, thin-skinned, with a mop of hair on top of that one's head. Watery eyes, white with blue centers, unlike Moortlin's small yellow orbs, watched in horror.

"I can't stop him," the Methiemum pleaded, ignoring Moortlin's intrusion. "He's been doing this for a ten-day now. Things around him change. I don't think he knows what he's doing, but it's getting worse!"

The Methiemum held up one shaking hand. Rather than the brown color of the rest of that one's skin, the hand was blue and green, sprouting thorns on one side and tendrils on the other.

"Oh Brahm—no! I would have told someone, but they'll take him away. I could distract him before, but now—"

The parent turned to them and Moortlin saw the person's hair was waving and curling, turning to thin spidery fingers rather than individual strands. "Can you help us? What is wrong with my child?" The parent was shaking, tears streaming from that one's eyes.

Moortlin pushed away the hollow feeling inside, like worms gnawing through one's stomach. This was very wrong. So many adjustments in the Symphony, so quickly, was like a cascade of noise in their mind. The Symphony resisted too many changes, and the infant was barely old enough to stand. *How can that one be so powerful?*

"One is a majus," Moortlin told the parent. "One will do what is, hm, possible to set this right." They tried to sound more confident than they felt. A mere child had created so much chaos that others thought the Aridori had returned, and the Council of the Maji had become involved. *Should have listened to the others on Aben.*

The infant played with toes, and fingers, then grabbed at the air. Three colors spun out from it—green, orange, and white, and Moortlin heard the bizarre harmonies between the House of Strength and the House of Healing. There must be more notes they couldn't hear, in the House of Power—the third color.

The infant can hear them. This undeveloped person could change three of the six Symphonies that created and sustained the universe. Half of all existence.

This is impossible. Keeping track of two Symphonies was a challenge Moortlin had barely started in their fifty-odd cycles. To influence both at once was incredibly difficult. To do so with three Symphonies must be exponentially harder. *It will lead to madness.*

Moortlin gazed around the room, at the weeping walls, the distraught and mutated parent. *Madness is already here.*

Then the infant looked at Moortlin, and their world changed.

Threads of music assaulted them, seeking to play with the notes that made Moortlin's being like a hunting beast played with its prey before eating it.

Yet Moortlin felt no sense of harm from the infant—that one was merely curious. Moortlin's flesh burned, their fingers clenching into claws. They did not feel pain in the same way other species described it, but the discomfort of their insides rearranging made them draw in a thick breath. *That one likes to make plant into animal and animal to plant.* They were naturally attracted to a Benish's anatomy. *Must restore one's notes, quickly!*

"That one must not, hm, do this," Moortlin rasped. Their words were calm, easing the child, but Moortlin grabbed for the notes at the center of their being, blocking the measures changing key in the Symphonies of Strength and Healing. There were more notes in his music than there should be. Placed there by the child? The parent was no help, quivering in fear in one corner.

Moortlin hoped the changes in the House of Power would falter once they blocked the aberrations in the other two Symphonies. They rushed through decisions, making judgements other Benish would consider rash. *Can one teach the child? Not so quickly. Punish? That one may strike back by instinct. How does one communicate with a child so young?*

While their thoughts raced, a waltz became a march, a thrumming string becoming the snap of a drum. Moortlin threw their notes against the child's changes, but the Symphony resisted them, flexed already to its breaking point. The toes of their left foot curled up, then stretched out, as if seeking to plant themselves in the floorboards, which bent up to accept them.

No! Moortlin searched through the Symphony of Strength, which connected physical objects together. The notes around their leg were twisted through and around the House of Healing, the music that told of biology. The resulting rhythms were a mangle of notes and timing, reflecting the twisting reality. Moortlin tried to change the notes back, but as soon as they did, their work was undone, the notes swept from their grasp. *That one is too strong!* The infant could hear more of the fabric of reality, giving that one a terrifying power.

Moortlin doubled over as the change grew from their toes, to their foot, then up their leg, their joints cracking and shifting, yearning to form a new configuration. Moortlin slumped to one side, discomfort radiating up into their torso. *If one had been another species, one would have collapsed in pain.* Benish, fortunately, were hardy. The parent was not, and that one was curled in a ball. Moortlin could see something unnaturally twisted in that one's face.

The child could pick the exact notes needed and bend them to another aspect of the Grand Symphony, while Moortlin desperately tried to keep the new melodies from modulating into unnatural masses of notes.

Then, the infant's attention shifted and Moortlin's changes gained traction, reversing some of the damage done to their body. Their foot, however, was fixed to the floor in a way they couldn't hear clearly in the Symphony. *This is more than one can handle.* Disfavor by the Council was bad, but Moortlin had to be alive to receive it.

Around the three, the house flexed, swaying planks weaving into gripping limbs, floorboards mating and dividing into pelts of fur, or flower buds wider than a person. The plaster ceiling dripped down around them, and there was a hiss and a scream as a dollop of the mutable substance fell on the infant's parent. Moortlin shrunk away with a series of creaks and pops, pulling at their foot. It was welded to the floor. *Will one have to cut it free?*

They shifted around their fused appendage as another arm of ceiling-matter plopped to the floor and began ripping tendrils of fungoid stalks free with newly-formed pincers. Moortlin lifted their other foot, wobbling, as a claw snapped. *That would have severed one's other leg, dense Benish flesh or no. One must leave!*

By the orange auras surrounding the room, much of what the infant did was in the House of Power. That symphony dealt with connections, and the infant must intuitively understand how biology and structures could be pulled and restructured like putty.

And Moortlin was pulled along with the changes. They came far too fast and thick for them to even contemplate reversing them. Moortlin dove deep into the House of Strength, pulling the constitution from what little was left in the house, building a web of harmonizing choruses around them to rebuff all but the strongest of changes. The notes making up the core of their being were thinning, the score of their experiences growing quiet.

Moortlin felt it before they saw the change. The infant had made the melody of Moortlin's foot strange and dissonant, and it interacted with the notes they were pouring into the music. In a puddle around their toes, the wood was rippling with spiky purple crystals. As they watched in horror, the crystalline formations grew up and inside their foot and ankle. They could feel the pointed protrusions spreading through the interior of their leg, and curled around the pressure and discomfort.

This is how three Symphonies can interact under one influence. And there is nothing one can do about it.

They hunkered down, certain the room would soon collapse and bury them forever. They needed to get their leg free.

However, the infant's attention was on them again, and Moortlin could feel the Symphony almost as a physical presence of music, drums beating a dirge against their skin, pressing in with the child's attention. Their leg spasmed as crystals broke through their skin, trailing greenish sap, growing a cocoon around their leg. Moortlin roared, in real pain.

Then the crystal solidified, and as if satisfied with the rest of the chaos, the infant pulled the orange and green and white auras close, spinning them in a sphere. Squishy and naked, the little child sat in the middle.

The young Methiemum held up one hand and Moortlin watched as that one's flesh purpled, then shook, then hardened. The appendage lost color, becoming gray, then white, then perfectly clear, as if it was made of glass.

Or crystal—like one's leg. Did that one discover some truth hidden in the Symphony? Was it music concealed from those with only one, or even two houses? *Can it change one's leg back to normal?*

Moortlin tried to grab for the change, but the rhythm was too fast, the notes too intricate. The infant looked down and a leg morphed, like Moortlin's, until it was the same transparent substance. The new material, whatever it was, passed in waves along the infant's body, the floor and walls showing through it in stripes, then crosshatched.

"No!" came a gurgle from the corner of the house. The creature that once was the infant's parent was transformed. Eyes stared from melting ooze, fixed on the child, though no longer recognizable as a member of the eight species. Moortlin, trapped in the bubble of solidity they had constructed, crystalline leg fastened to the floor, could only watch. *One no longer holds one's own survival.*

The infant, seeming spun of pure glass, spread both hands wide as if grabbing for a treat. What once was living flesh, now hardened crystal, shook to a rising pitch, so powerful Moortlin was sure it would be audible even to a non-majus.

Come with me.

The voice was thorns in Moortlin's mind, and they bent in agony, while the parent cried out in pain.

There was sound like a sculpture of ice dropped on hot iron, and the infant disappeared in a splash of orange and green and white.

Moortlin sagged, dropping the bubble of constitution they had created. The notes it returned to them was like water after a day in the scorching heat. Around them, the house sagged as well. With a sigh, the parent sank into a puddle of goo, that one's body separating into a mess of proteins and acids. Where had the infant gone? Had that one discovered something from Moortlin's condition? Simply collapsed in repeating musical phrases? They could hear nothing in the Symphony that gave a clue.

Their Benish nature pulled at them to study this phenomenon, find out what happened. Their acquaintances back on Aben would have. *But one is not part of that group, as was repeatedly said.*

Moortlin looked down at their leg, fastened to the floor planks. They could no longer feel it.

Time to go. Limbs will regrow, over the cycles. Though that much of their leg, almost to their knee, might take a decade. They reached into both Symphonies, rearranging measures across the two houses. Strength and Healing, plant and animal, biological and structural.

Above the crystal, Moortlin's leg separated with a *snap* and they limped on the stump, leaking sap, half crawling through the pulsating maw that used to be the house's doorway.

* * *

"You are certain it was to be a three-house majus?" Councilor Fortilath questioned. That one was standing, fists on hips, crest sticking almost straight out. "Not Aridori?"

What else fits these facts?

"It was, hm, Councilor," Moortlin said. They still felt the raging Symphony inside them, as they leaned awkwardly on a crutch in front of the Kirian. The leg would grow back, over the cycles, but not all had been restored internally. There were balls of matter inside, no longer their flesh. Moortlin thought they could reverse those changes, with time, and might even learn a few tricks of the Symphony from them. *As the child learned from one's accident? One must investigate how the Symphonies interact.*

"One has never seen such a, hm, display of raw power. One thought only mature persons were fully able to tap into the Grand Symphony."

"There are to be many aspects of the Symphony not yet understood," the councilor said. That one's crest fanned, then drooped, showing the Kirian's worry. "However, I have...friends who also wish to study rare phenomena like this. You were surviving a complex and unstoppable force, and it is showing your constitution."

Quite literally. One should meet these friends.

They shifted on the crutch, creaking with the effort. "One was not the real target," Moortlin told the councilor. "But thankfully the problem has solved itself. The child is either dead or transformed somewhere which does not intersect this place."They had not shared that the child likely got the idea for that one's transformation from Moortlin. They thought it would not be well-received.

"Has it?" Councilor Fortilath asked. That one's crest made a sweeping question. "Even in another plane, a three-house majus could cause problems. What if it returns?"

"Then these ones will, hm, suffer the consequences," Moortlin said. "There was nothing one could have done to affect what the child did to the Symphony. That one was, hm, too strong."

"For one majus alone, yes," the Kirian said. "For even a majus with access to two houses. However, with time and research, we may be able to fight back. This is to be fitting with other, rare reports I have seen." That one paused, considering, crest slowly raising. "It was why I was proposing the Council send you. I am to be needing more maji with two houses, who have experiences such as yours."

"Needing maji for, hm, what?" Moortlin asked. They caught the undercurrent of caution from the Councilor. *What is so secret one of the six most influential maji must hide it from peers?*

"For researching, and protecting," the councilor said. "There are to be many more things we have not yet discovered, nor understand. The maji, at their core, stand between the lives of the Great Assembly and the wider, uncertain universe. You have seen a hint of that today."

Moortlin thought back to the twisting music, far more powerful than anything they had experienced before. *One imagines there are many more secrets of the Symphony to discover.*

"One is eager to learn more of this one's offer."

Journey to the Top of the Nether

1003 A.A.W.

The Ground

To my dearest daughter:

On the front of this postcard you will see my latest rendering of the Imperium. The hot air balloon is aiding my research greatly. Fortunately for me it was a clear day for viewing.

I think we may be able to travel even higher than I can in my balloon! I have a surprise to show you when I return home. Are you looking forward to your first adventure with your mother?

With Love,

Mom

—Postcard from Morvu Francita Januti to her daughter.

I stared up at the giant, glowing wall of the Nether, stretching up above us. I made sure I closed my mouth before Mom saw me. *It's higher than I can see. It just...fades into the distance.*

"Come on, Natina, we need to pack the balloon," she said. I rolled my eyes at the wall.

"Mom, when you asked me to come on a climbing expedition, I thought it would be the haunted cliffs on Sath Home or something," I said. "Not a wall of crystal *no one* has ever seen the top of. Are we really going to try climbing this?"

"We are," my mother said, and I turned to watch her. "Others have tried to reach the top of the Nether before, but no one ever made it. We'll be the first. Just think of it!"

"I think someone else could be first. Let them fall off and find out what *not* to do." I shuffled one shoe through the green grass and weeds thriving where the crystal wall met dirt. I imagined a body landing here with a *thud.* "We can try later, when it's safer. Or better yet, study what they find from the comfort of our own home." I was missing my room already, and we'd only been gone eight days from Etan, with preparations and travel time.

My mother—the famous explorer Morvu Francita Januti—spread her long arms wide, taking in the sheer face of Nether crystal in front of us. It stretched to the left and right as well, an immense glowing sheet. "Where's your sense of adventure? No one has even gotten past the cloud layer in a balloon."

"There's a reason for that," I said, looking past her at the strange hunk of metal and crystal behind us. "You seriously think this crystal beetle thing will do it?"

"My excavation team calls it the Nether drill. It's not actually a beetle, even if it looks like one," Mom corrected. "We tested it out at Broken Column where we found it. It can drill holes in Nether crystal—hence the name—and it climbed all the way to the gap in the column."

"Which is not, in fact, as high as the clouds," I reminded her.

"Well, no, but we know the concept works," Mom told me. Now she was frowning, her cheeks turning a darker blue. I was starting to annoy her. Good. "I discussed all this with the Effature himself and the Council of the Maji when they approved my expedition. I don't need to explain it to you."

"No, you just needed a fourth body for the ascent," I said. Fortunately, I was good at rock climbing. Our family had been going on mountaineering trips since before my little brothers were born.

"It's good for you to research in nature, not just at home," Mom said. "The drill will make everything a lot easier, anyway. Now come on."

"I still like 'crystal beetle thing' better," I muttered and crossed my arms. Something chirped in the bushes that grew near the base of the wall, but I ignored it. I'd seen enough 'native specimens' on the trip in from Gloomlight already.

It does look like a beetle, all hunched over like that. Especially with the black shell and those jointed legs. It even has crystal mandibles. I took in the two shimmering spikes that stuck out of the 'head' attached to the metal shell. *They look like melted glass.* The device was pretty amazing, even if I thought the plan to kill ourselves climbing a sheer, slippery, indestructible wall was kind of terrible.

"Let's finish the packing," my mother said again. "We can debate all you want on the balloon ride, while you still have the energy to do it."

I wouldn't let her off that easy. "Why are we taking the balloon again? If this...drill...can climb the wall, why not save the effort of getting the balloon ready?"

"It's quicker. The beetle isn't strong enough to carry us all at once," Mom said. She pulled her dark hair back and tied a ribbon around it so it was out of the way, like she did when she wanted to work on something complicated. "We'll rise as high as we can with the fuel on board, then attach the drill to the wall, and climb behind the drill from there. I told you all this already, or weren't you listening?" She turned away.

"I was listening," I said, but quietly. I shook my head and trudged after her. When she wasn't looking, I gave the crystal beetle thing a pat on its side as I went past. *It* wouldn't have forced me to come on one of Mom's expeditions of hardship and drudgery.

Good girl. Its jointed legs were tucked up underneath the shell, but it was almost taller than me, and Mom and I were taller than a lot of the other people in the Nether, since we were both Etanela. I didn't know how the other nine species survived, being so short. The majus traveling with us would have trouble keeping pace while the other three of us were climbing.

I took another look back at the wall, as I followed Mom. I had been in the Nether before, but not often. Mom was the one who spent all her time here, rather than at home with my other mother and father.

The wall of the Nether stretched left, right, and up, as far as I could see, casting the light that lit this place. These walls enclosed the whole Nether, but it was hard to imagine, on such a massive scale. It was like we were at the bottom of a giant box, almost as big as my homeworld of Etan in land area. It would be dark in the Nether except for the light of the walls, and the columns, of course.

At the pile of luggage that would somehow accompany us up the sheer face of the wall, I poked at the bundle of wafers, jerky, and water—rations for our journey. The faint fishy smell was a comforting reminder of home. We'd catch more to drink when it rained, but we had enough to start.

I'm hungry enough to eat a whole package of wafers by myself. I held back, though. No one knew how high the top of the Nether was, and if the wall was this sheer and bare the whole way up, we'd need to watch our food carefully to make sure we didn't starve.

I let my hand trail off the seaweed wafers, counting what Mom brought. *Looks like enough for about twenty-five days.* I looked up at the wall again, then had to catch myself before I fell over. *I really hope Mom knows what she's doing.* She said the return would be quick, and we wouldn't need to worry about supplies. Were we going to rappel the whole way down? I...might not have listened to *that* part when she was explaining.

My hand fell onto another box, bulky, and made of squishy wood I'd never seen before. *It's like the big seaweed stalks that dry out on the beach on Etan, with the hollow insides, but harder.*

When I saw what was on top of the box, my hand drifted toward the metal hexagon. It had a strange pattern carved into it.

"Don't touch that, girl," a harsh voice said. I looked up into large, silvery eyes. A set of three head-tentacles were wound in a bun on top of Majus E'Flyr's head. She was a Lobath—the only other of the ten species of the Great Assembly with what Mom called 'an aquatic background.' I wrinkled my nose at her musty scent. She didn't smell like the ocean at all, not like an Etanela.

I let my hand fall to my side. Maji were important, and no one messed with them.

"Well, go on." Majus E'Flyr made a shooing motion with one long-fingered hand. The other was perched on the hip of her blue jumpsuit. Her skin was so red it was almost purple, and incredibly wrinkled. She was *ancient*. "That System took notes from many maji to create, and if you break it, all that effort will be wasted. It's supposed to protect what's inside."

I gave the majus a skeptical look. *I'm not a child.* Mom brought home plenty of artifacts and breakable fossils, and the whole family helped her sort them. I helped analyze the strange, new discoveries. I just didn't like risking my neck *finding* them.

I sighed and gave Majus E'Flyr a friendly nod and what she would think was a smile. I'd have to deal with her while we were climbing, and I didn't want to make a bad impression right at the start. I might end up helping her up the wall.

At least I could talk with her normally, in the Nether. I'd learned the trader's tongue in school, and a little of the Lobath language, but the

Nether helped translate when people were inside it. It meant I could speak my own language, and the majus would still understand me.

Mom was staring daggers at me from the basket. Behind her, the mass of orange fabric was stretched out over the grass at the base of the wall. Mom would need to fully inflate the balloon before we could take off, so I had time.

I checked the little watch Alondri—my father—gave me for my last birthday. *Fortunately, it measures Etan hours as well as lightenings and darkenings. No converting to figure out what time it is, and I don't have to ask Mom.* She had made sure to tell me all about how there was no sun in the Nether, as if I didn't already know. It was weird seeing the walls and the columns dim and brighten at the same time every day, but I'd adjusted.

It was about half past fifth lightening—early morning—and I hadn't had any breakfast yet. My stomach growled. *Maybe I could sneak a couple wafers from the stores if I help Partino load them.* But I'd let him handle that big box the majus was guarding. I could see her silver eyes watching me from here.

Under Mom's gaze, I went to the last member of our party, another Etanela like Mom and me, who was lifting heavy boxes into the basket of the balloon. *She won't look away until I lift something. First dragging me along, now forced labor.*

"What are you loading, Partino?" I asked. Partino Jusare Okala had been my mother's porter—a research assistant really—since before I was born. He was a lot more fun than she was.

"Oh, just cases of your mom's scientific gear," he said, with a wink. He lifted a case as tall as me up over his head and into the basket of the balloon with a *thunk*. He was the strongest person I'd ever seen.

His arms might be bigger around than Majus E'Flyr's waist. But I wasn't staring.

"That better not have been my spectrum analyzer you just dumped like a sack of old squid chum," Mom called out from the other side of the basket. The balloon was inflating, and the basket was big enough around that she couldn't see Partino wince. Or me.

Partino held a finger up to his lips, and I bit back a laugh. *Might as well do something.* I went to the pile of luggage and pulled at the sack holding the books and necessities I'd packed.

"Oh, this is heavy," I said, and now it was Partino's turn to laugh.

"Maybe shouldn't have packed so many books, little one," he said, and poked my nose with a wide finger. But he took the sack from me and put it in the basket as I scrunched my face up.

I'm not little anymore. He had called me that since before my two younger brothers—five and six cycles younger than me—had been born.

"Stop fooling around and get the rest in," Mom called. Partino and I both sighed, and then laughed at each other. "We've only got another lightening before the balloon is ready to take off, and I want to be far up the wall by evening."

She kept muttering as Partino and I turned back to the pile of luggage. "Other naturalists mocked Alondri and Kayla for cycles about their theories on the top of the Nether," I heard her say. "Well now we can prove them right."

So that's why she's so fired up about this expedition. I pulled my hair back out of my face—the same dark bushy mop as Mom. *She's worried about our family's reputation.* I shouldn't give her a hard time, but with all the papers she'd written with my other parents, and all the awards she'd won for being first at this and the best at that, I thought she could take second place for once.

Let someone else discover what was at the top of the Nether. We'd be there to make the important scientific connections later. It was always easier to see how things fit together when you could look at them in your own time, rather than in a rush. That was the main place where Mom and I differed.

I picked up another box of rations and carried it to the basket. My father and other mother were busy back on Etan with my little brothers, and taking care of our house. They did a lot of research into the artifacts Mom brought back. *And we're going to bring back more from this trip.*

Mom said my other father died before I was born, but people said his theories were even crazier than Alondri and Kayla. *Is this all to prove he was right, too?*

Despite the grief I give her, Mom and I have a special connection. It's why I'm named after her—my name is Natina Morvu Januti, and hers is Morvu Francita Januti. She got her middle name from her favorite parent, just like me.

I call Alondri and Kayla by their names. I don't love them less—I just connect more with Mom, most of the time. It's why she forced me to come along when I complained I never got to see her anymore.

Time to do some work, Natina. I picked up another box. *If I don't fall off this wall, I can at least bring back proof Alondri and Kayla are right about...whatever theory they have.*

* * *

"All in?" Mom shouted over the roar of the vent on the burner as she held the valve open. I held my nose as the oily smell of gas filled the air, and looked around with her. Partino nodded back from where he leaned against the side of the basket. Majus E'Flyr raised a long-fingered hand from where she was settled like a pet sea slug between two large carrying cases.

"Then we're off! Partino, Natina, release the cables!"

I went to one side of the basket, feeling it jostle and tilt as I did. *Hopefully this thing won't tip me out.* It was floating just above the ground, and the woven floor flexed as I walked across it. I slowed down when I got to the edge. The top of the basket was right at my head height—as tall as many other species got. *I'm already taller than the majus.* And I wasn't even full grown.

Because the sides of the basket were so high, there were openings so we could look out. At one of them, I leaned out and fumbled at the knot tied around a metal spar fixed to the side of the basket.

"It's stuck!" I called back. *Dumb balloon.* Then the balloon jerked and I lost my grip. "Ugh!"

"One away!" called Partino. He was already moving to the second knot, and I growled and grabbed the rope again. *Come here, you!*

I barely got mine undone before Partino finished his second one, but I was ready for the basket to jerk this time, and he wasn't.

"Aha!" I yelled, and half sprinted, half slid to the other side of the basket. Majus E'Flyr tsked at me as I passed, but I ignored her, reaching through the window. I felt Partino come up behind me. He was so big I could feel his presence like a big ball of heat. *Getting slow in your old age, huh?*

"I got it," I said, wrenching the knot apart.

Partino's hand on my shoulder tightened as the basket gave the biggest lurch so far, and I would have fallen if he hadn't held me up. I got my balance as the tops of nearby trees sunk beneath the sides of the basket.

We're moving!

"That you did, little one," he said. He gave my shoulder one last pat and let go. I scowled at the name and turned away.

Just have to prove I'm not so little. Mom was at the central mast, which contained tubes and equipment and the burner. The majus hadn't moved from her perch, even through all the jostling.

Despite misgivings about climbing an unclimbable wall, and Mom dragging me out here, a thrill of excitement ran up my spine as the ground fell away beneath us. The land stretched out to either side, growing smaller by the second. It was my first time in the balloon Mom used to map the Nether.

I caught my breath, starting to understand what I was in for. *My first adventure with her.* Above us, the wall stretched up and into the clouds. *At least I'll have something to tell all my friends back home. If we don't all die.*

The basket gave one last lurch, and I clutched at a nearby sack. "What was that?"

"Just the drill," Mom said, and I stuck my head back out the window. I'd almost forgotten about the crystal beetle thing. It had been tied beside the basket while we were on the ground. Mom said she'd switched the normal envelope of balloon fabric to a larger one to be able to lift it.

The beetle's hunched back swung beneath the basket, and there was a little lurch every time it switched direction. As I watched, the motion lessened and it stopped directly beneath us, its two gleaming mandibles facing toward the wall, as if it was waiting to dig into the rolling expanse of crystal. Its jointed legs were folded beneath it.

While my head was out the little window, I stared at the ground, getting farther and farther away. I wished I could have seen the Imperium—the capital of the Nether. Mom made a sketch of the city from her last test in the balloon, right after the deal with the Life Coalition and the Imperium.

But we were far away from the Nether's capital—and any other sort of civilization. All I could see were farm lands, like someone had sketched out squares and circles on the ground. We'd traveled through the fields on the way here, but they didn't look so regular from the ground. Several were divided up by a river, and it made them into triangles instead of squares.

Will we get high enough to see the Imperium? Probably not. It was half the length of the Nether away, though the Nether was flat, instead of a ball like Etan. I looked up instead. The clouds were high and thin, but I still couldn't see the top of the walls. It was like they fuzzed out in the distance, farther than I could see.

* * *

I watched the ground for a long time while the balloon rose. Then, when I couldn't make out fine details, I watched the great crystal wall. The balloon was rising so close to the expanse of crystal that the orange fabric was in danger of brushing against it. I hoped Mom knew what she was doing. If we poked a hole in the fabric, the balloon would deflate and plunge us all to our deaths.

Mom tended to rush into things, but Partino didn't seem concerned, so maybe we would be fine. The wall was pretty smooth. In some places it swelled like a wave caught mid-break, the light it cast broken into all the colors of the rainbow as it reflected through the facets buried under the surface. Back on the ground, I'd tried to mark it with a rock, but I couldn't even make a scratch. *I guess that's the beetle's job.* The metal hulk was steady in its harness beneath us.

I moved to the other side of the basket to pick out the giant crystal columns rising in the distance. At least they didn't get farther away, like the ground. I could see lots of them if I squinted, but there were four close enough to see clearly. We'd passed a lot of columns on the way to our launch site—they grew out of the ground in the Nether, in no real pattern I could see, and went straight up, disappearing like the wall did into the distance above. They were big enough that it took a few minutes to walk around one, and Mom said they held up the roof. *Though if no one's ever seen the top of the Nether, how does she know?* Like the walls, the columns gave off light, but not as much.

"How's your first time out on an expedition?"

I hadn't heard Mom approach, and turned around quickly, ready for more chores, or to be told I was doing something wrong. Instead, she held a little book folded in her hands. *A peace offering?*

"I didn't know there would be this many hours for relaxing," I said.

"Lightenings, not hours," Mom corrected. "And it's only been two. It's not even time for lunch yet." Then she scowled, watching my face. "I'm sorry. That was patronizing. If you're old enough to come with me, you're old enough for me to treat you like a young lady." She smiled. "Even if there is a lot of complaining involved."

"I don't *need* to be out here like you do," I said. "I like to study the artifacts you bring home, with Alondri and Kayla. Why can't I just do that?"

"It's not the same—believe me," Mom said. "You've got the same spark of adventure I do. Alondri and Kayla are...theoretical, like Jonduri was."

I never got to meet my other father.

"And anyway, I won't be doing this forever," Mom continued. "Etanela live longer than most of the other species, but we still have limits. This life isn't easy on the body." She shook her head, her large green eyes fixing me in place. "But that's not what I came over for." She held out the book. "Here. This is for you."

I took it from her, and flipped through the pages, then brought it up to catch the scent of new pages. The paper was thick and white, but there was nothing written on them. As I ruffled through the pages, a pencil fell out, tied to the book by a ribbon.

"It's empty." *What does she want me to do?*

"It's for you to fill," Mom said, "with the observations you make. Sketch things you see. Find out what it means to be a naturalist, like me, instead of a researcher, like your other parents. See if you like it."

I stared back at her for a moment. *That's actually kind of cool.* This was why I had a special connection with Mom. Every once in a while, she knew how to reach me.

"Thanks. I will." I clutched the book, and turned back to the window so Mom couldn't see my slow grin forming. I wasn't so quick that I missed her smile.

* * *

"That's certified salvage," Mom said. "I have the receipts to prove it, just like my other artifacts." Her voice rose in volume, making me look up from where I was trying to draw one of the columns in my new book. Sketching halfway transparent crystal was hard.

I watched Partino look over the side of the basket, his big arms behind his head. He turned, as if he could feel me looking at him, and gave me a shrug.

"—one signed to say we're officially sanctioned by the Effature," Majus E'Flyr was saying. The Lobath's voice rose too. She pointed to the bottom of the page she held. "The Council is very interested in your expedition as well, which is why they were willing to partially fund it, and to let you keep the drill. For now."

What are they talking about?

"It's still mine, no matter who funds the expedition," Mom told her.

"Yes, but your other artifacts can't bore into Nether crystal. You're lucky the Council—or what's left of it—didn't confiscate it after you found the drill." The majus' head-tentacles twitched as she spoke.

Is the majus excited, or angry, or what? I got to my feet. Our whole family treated artifacts with the respect they deserved. We made sure the pots and bottles and skeletons Mom found were all properly dated and stored. We even returned a portion to the species they originally belonged to. Mom's discoveries were in museums all over the ten homeworlds.

"I'd be surprised if they managed to take it from me," Mom said, her hands waving toward the majus. "The Council isn't even close to operating properly. Half its members are dead, missing, or traitors!"

"They at least filled one seat," Majus E'Flyr grumbled, but then she looked back up to Mom, her silvery eyes catching the light from the wall. It was near midday and the wall was bright. It made me squint to look straight at it.

Mom opened her mouth, holding up another paper, but there was a sizzle and a *thump* from the center of the balloon. We all looked up. The flame that had burned since we started, keeping the bright orange balloon above our heads filled with hot air, was gone. I wrinkled my nose at the smell of gas.

"Partino," Mom called. "We need a new canister of kerosene." I could already feel the balloon falter and slow.

Changing out the canister took several minutes, with Mom popping levers on the rack of controls in the middle of the basket. I helped Partino lug a cylinder almost as tall as me from one section of the basket. There were twenty canisters altogether, tied into the spaces between the windows. *Were they this heavy when I helped lift these things into the basket?*

"Quickly now," Mom said, gesturing with both hands. By this time, the balloon had stopped its ascent and was beginning to fall under the weight of the metal beneath us.

"We're dropping! Do you usually fly the balloon like this?" I shouted as I wrestled the canister forward with Partino. I didn't know if the jolt traveling up my spine was from the work, or from feeling the balloon descend. *Come on, push!*

"It's the weight of the drill," Mom said. She wrestled the empty canister from the station in the middle of the balloon and traded with Partino, hooking the full canister to a tube made of shiny golden metal. She flipped a few switches and with a *foosh* the flame re-ignited. The whole balloon gave a little jerk and we stopped falling.

"You knew about the weight before you started." I put a hand to my chest to feel my heart slowing.

Will it be like this every time?

Mom dusted off her hands and looked at me. "We can't always cover every possibility," she said. "This is the difference between theory and the real world. Things act differently than we think."

"I think I like theory better." I coughed as smelly fumes came from the new canister, and we began rising again.

"Toss this one?" Partino asked, holding up the empty canister. We both stared at him as if he'd just popped into existence.

"Yes—over the side," Mom said, and gestured toward the edge of the basket. "The weight will slow us down."

Partino shrugged and lugged the cylinder to the side of the basket, then tossed it overboard. I followed him and watched it fall, tumbling end over end. When it faded from sight, I turned back.

"What if it hits someone?" First the balloon dropping, now heavy canisters tossed over the side. Mom was usually more careful than this.

"Low chance of that," Majus E'Flyr said. "We specifically chose this area because of the low population density. It's all farmland, out here by the wall. It's the best light to grow crops, and it's not harvest time. There will be very few, if any, people underneath us. We can drop anything we want."

Anything? I looked out one of the openings again, several new games to pass the time running through my head.

Then I looked back to the canisters. It had taken two lightenings for the first one to empty. Ten lightenings and ten darkenings in one day. I frowned, calculating.

"Only two days in the balloon?" I asked Mom.

"I did some calculations," she said. "This is the most weight the balloon could carry with the drill, and still rise fast enough to be worthwhile." Her eyes were bright. "After that, the fun begins."

I hoped she did those calculations correctly.

* * *

Time passed, with Mom and the majus talking about things in low voices. Partino and I played about twenty rounds of Take-My-Ship with a deck of cards, and I made more sketches of the balloon, the clouds, and the beetle, hanging beneath us. We all watched the walls and columns out the windows. Mom made sketches too, of the different swells and ridges we could see in the walls. About every two lightenings, by my watch, the gas in the canister would fizzle out and the balloon would lurch to a stop. Mom and Partino and I rushed to change it out each time before we lost too much height. The majus was too old to help, obviously. If Mom had taken a little more time figuring out how much the balloon could carry, my heart wouldn't jump out of my chest every time the fuel ran out.

Every time, I watched the cylinder tumble end over end, falling back toward the ground. *Is there a pile of canisters stuck in a farmer's field?*

We didn't open the supplies for lunch—those were for the days to come. This morning, I'd helped Mom pack a bag with fried fish, and kelp soup in little glass containers. We warmed them up by putting them near the flame in the middle of the basket. Majus E'Flyr had brought food of her own—a container of the mushroom paste Lobath liked to eat.

By the time the third canister of fuel fizzled out, I couldn't hold it any longer. My bladder was really full, but I couldn't figure out what I was supposed to do. Mom hadn't explained that part of riding in a balloon.

"You look like you're about to start a dance," Partino told me. He was sitting on a locked chest, long, strong legs stretched out.

I rolled my eyes. How hard was this to get?

"What is wrong, little one—"

I interrupted before his stupid name could make me angrier. "I have to pee!" I yelled.

Mom looked up, a sketch under her hand. "Time to try out the facilities."

Partino stood. "I'll show you how, Natina."

Finally, no name-calling.

Even the Majus looked on with interest as Partino moved a case of equipment to one side, revealing a covered bucket built into the floor of the basket.

"Behold the wondrous commode!" he said with a sweeping gesture, and removed the lid.

I looked down through the bucket. *That's more empty air than I want to see right now.*

"We even have a special barrier," Mom said, and pulled a section of basket out. It unfolded section by section until it surrounded the bucket.

"Thank the Sea Mother," I said. They still stood there. "Well, go on!" I flapped my hands at them. *This will be embarrassing enough as it is.* I didn't relish what I knew had to happen while we were climbing the wall.

"Good luck!" Partino chuckled, as he and Mom retreated. I threw a dark look at him, but he only grinned back.

Thanks.

I really hoped Majus E'Flyr was right that there was no one below us.

* * *

Sometime in the afternoon, I moved Partino's discarded coat out of the way to get to my books, and a piece of paper fluttered out of the pocket. It landed open on the sack of supplies and my eyes widened as I read. I snatched it up and stepped across the basket to where Partino lounged against the wicker barrier that kept us from falling.

"When were you planning to tell us about this?" I asked.

The porter looked confused for a moment, then I opened the note. He popped to his feet, put one hand to his mouth, then let it fall back down.

"Tell us about what?" Mom said. She was by our side in an instant, and took the note from me. "When did you get this?" she snapped.

Partino paled, and clasped his big hands together. "Oh, I'm so sorry. I received it right before we left Gloomlight, ma'am. Very sorry. In all the rush, packing and making sure we had calculated the rations correctly, it plain left my mind until just this minute when Natina found it."

The heat in my chest cooled a little. *He only calls Mom 'ma'am' when he knows he's done something really bad.* Like when he forgot to check the traps for a whole ten-day one time, and he and I had to clean up stinking fish guts.

"That was days ago, Partino," Mom said. "Who knows what else they've done since then?"

"What's happened?" the majus asked. She'd finally gotten up from where she'd been sitting.

"According to this note from the dig site, there was a break-in," I said, pointing to the flap of paper Mom held. "It was the site where Mom found the crystal beetle thing. They might have stolen something!"

"I got the note before we left," Partino said with a grimace. "If you read it carefully, nothing was stolen, *technically*. They had a license for that area."

"It's stealing to me," Mom grumbled. "I had a license good for the *whole area* around Broken Column. Those Kirians only swooped in for the last month, after word leaked when that layabout Dusty Dunderdink got drunk in town and blabbed about it. Made up a song about the drill and everything, as if talking wasn't enough. By rights all discoveries should be mine, no matter what competing license the Kirians have."

"And what might have been discovered?" Majus E'Flyr asked. The last time someone tried to interfere with the relics Mom found, they'd ended up in jail in the Imperium. She didn't mess around with archeology. I didn't envy that other team, when she caught up to them.

"We think there's another drill buried, right at the boundary between the two licensed areas," Mom said, "but there's no way to be sure without another letter from the workers at the site, and we're not liable to get that, this high up." she had one hand on her hip, the other waving back and forth with the paper.

"Right before we left, the team discovered the tip of another metal case, like the drill below us." Partino pointed down. "They'd only excavated a little, but we thought it wasn't in as good shape as the one we found."

"That's why I went ahead with this expedition," Mom said. "Using the drill first makes it my discovery. But without me there, I'm certain those Kirians have found a way to claim the other." Mom crumpled the letter in one fist.

"They can't have claimed it so quickly," Partino said, though he took a step back from Mom. "Surigran Wailimani and his team are sloppy."

Even I had heard of Wailimani. Mom talked about him every time she came home, how the Kirian had desecrated this holy site, or sold those artifacts off to the highest bidder rather than giving them to a museum.

"Partino's right," I said. "That Kirian doesn't have the experience you do. He's no match for you." Mom and I had our differences, but on the subject of preserving the sites she studied, we agreed.

"He's competent enough to get around our security," Mom said, then took a deep breath, held it, and let it out. She was calming down, which was good because we couldn't do anything about it up here, and I didn't want Mom trying to drag the rest of us under the rudder just because she was angry.

"We can't confront Wailimani about it now." Mom echoed my thoughts. "We're a quarter of the way through our fuel, who knows how far up, and I'm *not* turning around. I'll deal with it when we get back, though by that time, they can most likely claim ownership of the whole site!"

Majus E'Flyr leaned forward, and I saw the ends of her head-tentacles twitching. "If there *is* another drill, then the Council will be *very* interested in it. Maybe I can pull some strings when we return."

"That would be much appreciated, Majus," Mom said.

* * *

Seeing the Nether in the dark from this height was something new. The air was crisp and cool, a wind playing with my bushy hair. There was a soft glow from the walls and columns, though the rest of the land was plunged into darkness. I thought I could see a faint glow of lights directly behind us, and a long way off. I pointed it out to Mom.

"That's Gloomlight," she said.

"Traveling in the balloon really puts the distances in perspective," I said. It had taken several days of constant travel to reach this edge of the Nether, and that was using fast, expensive, System Beasts pulling our carriage day and night. If we had used regular pullbeasts, it would have taken a couple ten-days, but Mom wouldn't wait that long.

"It's very clear tonight," Mom told me. "It looks like just a little ball of light because we're seeing as far as from our home to the Yulati Harrowan archipelago on Etan."

I frowned, looking out one of the basket's windows and calculating distances. "That's halfway across the Sea of Light. I hadn't realized the Nether was so big." I'd only been here a handful of times, passing through a majus' portal from Etan to this place. The Nether wasn't like the homeworlds. It wasn't a planet, and it didn't orbit a star. In fact, no one was sure *where* it was. Maji found it long ago, and that's how the ten species found each other.

"You'd think someone else would have figured out how to climb the Nether's walls before now," I said.

"Good thing they didn't," Mom said. "Then I wouldn't have this opportunity with you."

"I'm still not convinced this is better than staying at home and studying what you bring back," I told her.

"Give it time."

"What if I want to go home?"

"That's too bad." Mom's voice gained a little of the harshness that said she was getting annoyed again. "Try it out, Natina. I think you'll like being a naturalist."

We watched out the side of the basket for a while longer, silent. Besides the glow in the distance and the columns and walls, there were only a few spotty lights near us, a lot closer than Gloomlight. Majus E'Flyr had said they were probably houses of the farm owners and workers who lived on huge tracts of land near the wall.

"I bet if I spit over the side and aim just right, I could hit one," I said, after a while.

* * *

I didn't sleep well that night. All my parents liked camping and long sailing trips, so my brothers and I were used to sleeping outside. Still, there was something about trying to sleep on a mat woven from thin strips of wood, floating so far above the ground I could barely see anything more than colors and shapes.

In addition, we still had to change the fuel canister every two lightenings. Every time the balloon sank, it woke us all up. The next morning we were tired and cranky, but at least the balloon was still rising.

"How tall is this dumb wall, anyway?" I asked. I watched the wavy crystal to my right, and the nearest column to my left. If I was at home, I wouldn't need to pee in a hole in the floor, or lose sleep when the balloon tried to fall out of the sky.

"A lot taller than this," Mom said, her tone sharper than usual. "Just...draw a picture. Write about how I made you come on this expedition. Or you could help me take measurements of ground features."

Mom had some of her equipment out, her telescope resting on the side of the basket. She leaned back to the eyepiece, her other hand sketching. "I don't just pick up ancient skeletons off the ground and discover sites anyone can walk to. There's work involved."

"Just like at home," I told her. "So why did we come all the way out here?" It wasn't fair and I knew it, but I was tired.

Mom looked back up. "Can you get a view like this from our house?" she said, her voice getting a little bit louder. She gestured over the side. "Can you measure the Nether's width from our little cove on Etan? No. You can't." We both looked to the central mast at the familiar sizzle and *thump* of the canister emptying. I set my mouth in a frown.

I'm getting real tired of changing that.

"There's only one more canister change before we tie up to the wall and start the Nether drill." Mom crossed her long arms, fingers twitching with frustration.

"I...we're going to start the crystal beetle thing?" My anger melted away.

Mom opened her mouth, probably to tell me that boring name she had for it instead, but then she stopped. She smiled. "Yes. We're going to start the 'crystal beetle thing' soon. Partino will go down there with the majus. The quicker we get the luggage sorted and lined up, the quicker we can get it attached to the bottom of the drill—the crystal beetle drill."

I nodded at Mom's name. It was a good combination of mine and hers—she was trying. My tiredness was gone, or at least pushed to the side for now. But then I thought of something else.

"What will we do with the balloon?" I asked. "Do we let it fall back down the wall like the canisters?" I imagined the giant orange sheet of the balloon tumbling end over end.

"We'll disassemble the whole thing!" Partino called from where he was pulling at the controls, releasing the empty canister. I watched his long arms work the levers. "The balloon can be folded up. Then the fabric and any supplies we don't really need can be stored where we start climbing."

Partino jerked the canister free, muscles in his arms and legs bulging. "We'll take the basket apart, and part of it will make individual sleeping mats for climbing the wall. The mats, the rest of the luggage, and the four of us will all be tied to the drill—excuse me, the crystal beetle drill. That's what will be doing the real work."

He lugged the canister to the side of the basket and tipped it over. While he did that, I unhooked another full canister from where it was tethered. But not the last cylinder...

"Wait," I said, counting. "We still have five canisters left. Can't we go farther up in the balloon?" I braced as the balloon began to sink.

Mom shook her head as she adjusted valves beneath the central hole in the balloon. "We'll leave those behind, hanging from the wall, in case there's an emergency and we can't go any further."

"An emergency?" I gave Partino the canister and he installed it. "Like what?"

Something else Mom didn't account for?

"Like if one of us falls," Majus E'Flyr said, and my head whipped around. She had been watching us talk.

Does she know I've been thinking about that since we left?

"Or if someone breaks a limb, or gets sick, or *all* of us get sick, or worse," the majus continued.

"Don't scare her," Partino said, and for once I didn't mind him talking about me like I was still eight. The majus only snorted and returned to watching the wall drift past.

What's she done while we've been working, anyway? Sure she had helped me with a few canisters, but only because Mom and Partino were sleeping. My mind went back to the box I'd found in the luggage. *Is she just here to guard it, and watch us?*

Soon, Partino unfolded another strange contraption from the middle of the balloon and cranked a winch with long movements of his arms. I came closer to watch.

"Careful there," he said in between rotations of the crank. "Don't get too close to the blades." He pointed with his chin. The mechanism he had unfolded was a propeller, propped over the side of the basket. The crank turned them until they were a blur. Partino's mass of dark hair floated around his head, waving in the wind.

Wind?

We'd drifted away from the wall over the last day, and the propeller corrected that. The balloon was steadily drifting closer to the massive wall. My heart beat faster as I realized we would really climb the unclimbable walls of the Nether.

* * *

Over the next half a lightening, according to my watch, we drifted closer until the orange balloon fabric just touched the smooth, glowing surface of the wall. The columns behind us were off in the distance, the entire Nether stretched out beneath us like a sea of green light. The illumination from the wall made us all cast long shadows.

Mom throttled the current canister down to a low flow, so the balloon barely moved, hanging like a fly against the crystal sea beside us.

The excess fuel that wasn't burning stank, and I had a moment of vertigo as I saw the wall as *down* and everything else as *up*. My eyes swam, and I clenched the side of the basket to keep from falling out and away, to drift out over the expanse of the Nether.

After a moment, the feeling receded, and I loosened my grip, breathing fast. I looked into the wall.

It was...beautiful. At the basket's edge, I reached out as far as I could. My fingers couldn't quite touch the surface, because the curve of the balloon overhead held us too far away.

The wall was clear, but the deeper I looked, the more the crystal went on forever. How thick was it? What was behind the wall? Space? Another planet?

Bands of purple and blue and green passed along the glassy surface, with orange reflecting from our balloon. It was almost too bright to look at. The wall gave off enough light to make the whole Nether bright. I felt like something that big should smell, or hum, but it just sat there—larger than any other object I could think of. I was looking at only one little piece, like if someone was staring at one pore of my skin.

"That will do it," Mom said, and I jumped. How long had I been staring at the wall? Her fingers were tracing patterns of excitement in the air. "Partino, can you get the drill—" She shot a look at me. "—the crystal beetle drill started up?"

"Will do," Partino said with a mock salute.

Majus E'Flyr stumped up next to him, half his height. "Hold on there, you pile of muscles," she said. "I'm going with you. I won't miss starting up an ancient artifact like that. There are all kinds of Systems created by maji involved. I'll want another look." She began retying her head-tentacles into a tighter knot to get them out of the way.

"You do know Partino will climb underneath the basket?" I asked. The porter was pulling at straps on the basket's floor. After learning how the toilet worked, I'd left them alone. I wanted as much support between me and the ground as I could.

"What do you think we'll be doing when the balloon's disassembled?" the majus asked me. "I was a champion mountain climber in my youth, or did your mother not tell you that?"

"In what cycle?" I asked. She must have been twice Mom's age. *She's just been sitting there, the whole time.*

Mom frowned and opened her mouth, but the majus got there first.

"Never you mind." Majus E'Flyr whipped her head around at a snort from Partino. "I'll wager my arms against yours any day, porter."

"I may take you up on that, Majus," Partino said. "Would be nice to have extra Nether glass to spend when we get back down."

The majus' rubbery lips turned up in a smile, though her surprised silvery eyes made the expression less challenging.

What can she possibly do better than Partino? I'd seen the porter lift things twice his size, and even pull in an adult shellshark while fishing.

Mom and I knotted the rope around the central mast of the balloon, then stood far enough away from the hole Partino opened so I wouldn't accidentally stumble and fall through. Even though the balloon was almost still, a breeze whipped past the opening, and the basket shook more than normal. There was a noise like the wind over the surf at night.

Partino looped the rope around his waist, and then Mom looped the rope around the mast again so we could lower him down carefully. Any Etanela worth their weight in seaweed learned how to tie knots soon after they started walking, and I was no exception.

The porter was tall enough that he probably could have touched his feet to the back of the crystal beetle drill while still holding onto the basket, but better to have the safety of the ropes.

"I'm down!" he called back up as I felt the rope go slack. There was a tug and I looked over the edge of the hole. Partino was standing on the shiny black back of the drill, holding onto the cables that connected it to the bottom of the basket—one to each of the beetle's legs, folded underneath. He'd made a sling of the rope, knotting it around the cable he held onto.

Before I could do anything, Majus E'Flyr gave the other end of the rope, tied to the central mast, a quick tug to make sure it was tight, then vaulted over the side of the hole.

"Watch out!" I cried. *The old fool is going to lose her grip and fall to her death!*

Majus E'Flyr's long fingers gripped the rope as if they were carved from old wood. I could see tendons straining beneath her dark red, wrinkled skin.

Like a chirruping tree fish, she descended, hand over hand, until her feet touched the surface of the drill and she settled. One hand dusted the front of her jumpsuit.

Partino had his mouth open like a deep sea gulper waiting for a meal. I made sure mine was firmly closed.

"Still want that bet, Muscles?" Majus E'Flyr asked Partino.

The porter's eyes were wide, but he nodded his head.

Together, they knelt over the crystal beetle's back, and Partino opened a small hatch I hadn't seen before, fiddling with something. The two of them took up a good portion of the beetle's back, especially with the hatch behind the head open.

A strange surge of excitement rose at seeing this relic work again. *Is this what Mom feels like?*

"Can I go down too?" I asked.

"Let them get everything started up and us anchored to the wall first." She turned to me. "You *want* to go down there? This is new."

I shrugged. "They did it." I could hear the majus muttering as Partino moved a lever in the insides of the beetle. I avoided the grin on Mom's face.

"Ah—that's what the System does." The majus' voice faded away, then came back. "I could hear the notes repeating from outside the drill, but now I can see the colors inside, I know what the House of Strength is working with." Another pause. "This is using all the aspects of the Grand Symphony in its design. Definitely something made by early maji…"

"What's she talking about?" I asked Mom.

"I'm not entirely sure," Mom said. One hand waved through the air as her other checked the rope. "You know the maji hear what they call the Grand Symphony?"

I nodded. My brothers and I had played majus back at the house, before I got too old for it. It largely involved waving our hands around and pretending we were making trees grow, or throwing fireballs, or changing our shapes. Now I was older, I wasn't sure if real maji did any of those things.

"Well, as far as I know, the maji can change the notes of that Symphony and make…things happen."

Maybe she doesn't know much more than I do.

"They say each house of the maji is a different color, but of course only the maji can see them."

I went to my hands and knees, peering over the edge. There were no extra colors around the beetle.

Just then, there was a grinding sound and Partino gave us a wave. "Got it working!" His other hand still gripped the cable.

Majus E'Flyr rubbed both hands together and stood. She wasn't gripping a cable, but she looked as solid as if she were standing on the beach rather than on the curved back of an ancient artifact, as high as the clouds.

* * *

Partino hooked a winch between the cables suspending the crystal beetle drill from the balloon, and he and the majus pulled ropes through it. While they stood on its back, almost like they were surfing, the beetle gradually drew closer to the wall. Its shining mandibles were spinning now, and they looked even more like melted glass.

I went to one of the openings in the side and looked down, my new notebook in one hand. I could just about get the shape of the beetle's head right, as the spinning mandibles came closer and closer to the wall. Nothing could break, destroy, or even scratch Nether crystal. Until now.

Mom appeared beside me to watch, her fingers moving even more than usual, showing her excitement. With a hiss, the rotating glass-like mandibles touched the face of the wall and...bit in.

"Yes!" I looked over in surprise and saw Mom with both hands clasped in front of her. Then they relaxed, fingers moving gracefully again.

"You said you tested this, right?" I asked. Below us, Partino and Majus E'Flyr pulled on cables and guided the beetle's mandibles until they drilled their full length into the wall, stopping where the spinning glass-like mandibles met the beetle's head.

"Yes, we tested it at the Broken Column site, and it made holes in the column, then used them to climb up," Mom said, then looked away. "The wall is thicker, and maybe something would change this high up and—" she shrugged. "That's why we call it an adventure. We're discovering new things."

"You didn't know this would work?" My hands clenched. "You dragged us all up here, just to be first at climbing the wall, whether it worked or n—"

"First anchor holes done!" Partino called up. I looked down, away from Mom's surprised and hurt expression.

The porter was drawing the drill back. The mandibles left two neat holes in the crystal, each a little bigger than my fist. Majus E'Flyr was perched out on the head, as steady as she could be. She had a couple pieces of twisted metal in her hands, and inserted one into each of the holes.

"Ready for the next two," the majus called, and went back to the body of the drill. They both pulled on cables and the drill rose closer to the bottom of the basket.

Partino and the majus repeated the process, while Mom regulated the fuel into the envelope so the balloon rose a little. I kept silent, intrigued by the beetle, but still mad at Mom for risking so much. The spinning mandibles plunged back into the wall, making another pair of holes.

When they had several pairs drilled, they drew the beetle back and Majus E'Flyr bent back down to the hatch on the back. I could hear her clearly now she was closer.

"It's amazing the System has lasted this long," Majus E'Flyr said. "You sure this thing can climb?"

"It did when we tested it back at the column," Partino said. "It's that lever there."

I watched through the hole in the bottom of the basket as the old Lobath messed with controls. "Well, right you are. This must be a creation from before the Aridori war. We lost so much back then."

I leaned closer, my anger leaving me. *The Aridori war? That was over a thousand cycles ago!*

"I'm still surprised the Council let you keep this artifact," the majus muttered. "They're as interested in what's up there as you are." She pointed a long wrinkled finger upward. "Ah, that's got it."

"Bring us back up," Partino said, and Mom and I hauled them up with the rope pulley around the central mast. While we did, the beetle moved its head side to side, and then up and down. The legs that had been tucked under the beetle's shell unbent and waved around, as if it didn't quite know what to do with them.

The legs were long and black, and each had three round joints, so the little feet could move in all directions. The ends of the feet were small, and shaped like a series of bells stacked on top of each other.

Nether glass was just as slick as the regular kind, even if the wall waved and undulated. *There's no way it will work. We'll have to float back down to the ground, and I'll tell Mom she should have let me stay home.*

The crystal beetle drill waved its joined legs at the wall, like it still didn't know where it was. But then a foot found one of the holes the beetle had drilled, and all six snapped forward, grasping around.

The beetle got all its feet in holes it had drilled, and slowly put its weight on the wall. The ropes holding it went slack and the balloon rose, released of the weight of the metal beetle. Mom throttled the gas canister until it was barely putting out any heat and the balloon steadied.

While that happened, the crystal beetle drill used the holes to climb up the wall, until it perched at the last set. It was right next to us, its head searching like it saw, or smelled us nearby.

I could touch it—no, *her*—black metallic back through one of the windows. I was almost certain she shivered under my touch. Then the head bent forward, plunging the mandibles into the wall once more with a hiss like a storm through the seaweed forest.

"Looks like it will hold," the majus said behind me and I turned to her. "Now comes the hard part." She held me with her large silvery eyes.

* * *

It took us another two lightenings to disassemble the balloon, the basket, and transfer the things we were leaving to a set of permanent anchors set in the bottom set of holes we'd drilled. We stood on a platform made from one side of the basket, suspended far above the ground. At least there was a bit of a rail keeping us from tumbling out into nothingness.

We filled three giant nets with everything we were taking along: food and water in one, the few clothes and personal items we brought in another, and Mom's scientific equipment in a third. We attached the equipment and clothes to the beetle, only leaving the food down with us, along with a few necessities.

Majus E'Flyr then took the longest coil of rope I'd ever seen, and looped the end around the body of the beetle. Partino made a bowline knot to make sure it wouldn't come undone, and tied the other end to the platform we stood on.

The majus gave the back leg of the beetle a whack, and she began climbing, plunging her mandibles into the wall and leaving behind a series of handholds.

"Wait—where's she going? What's she doing?" I said. "Catch her!" I looked for some way to get up to the beetle, but it was impossible.

"Calm down, girl," Majus E'Flyr said. I clenched my hands around the woven fibers of the platform until they creaked.

Don't call me girl. Anyone would be concerned if our way to climb the wall left.

The majus continued. "I discovered a little more about the System powering it when I had my hands down in there. The music that makes it run is incredibly elegant. It hints at cooperation between maji like I've never seen. Of course, I can't hear the other houses, but I hear where they interact with the House of Strength and—" She took in my clenched fists and scowl and looked up into my eyes. "It will blaze a path for us, leaving holes in the wall we can use to climb."

I took in a deep breath, then let it out. *I'm not a little girl. Mom wouldn't have invited me if that's what she thought.* "Couldn't we ride the beetle up the wall?" Then it wouldn't need to blaze anything.

But Majus E'Flyr shook her head. "We're too heavy, along with the rations and the equipment. The internal mechanics and leg joints in the beetle would never survive the stress. We've got to climb after it." The majus grabbed the rope, spooling out beside her. Her head-tentacles were twitching, probably with anticipation. "This rope will be our safety line so we don't fall. Unless the drill does."

Partino leaned over. "We'll need to support ourselves on anchors set into the wall, but if we get too tired, the beetle should be able to pull one or two of us up at a time."

"I can help with that too," the majus said. "It's why I've been resting up during the balloon ascent. I was saving my notes for the real challenge."

"Speaking of which, the climb will start tomorrow morning," Mom called. "Let's get a good sleep tonight. We'll need it."

My watch said it was the sixth darkening. We got dinner from the ration net, moving carefully along the little platform we'd set up. While we ate, we watched the little city-shaped points of light in the Nether brighten as the wall dimmed.

Low Country

Broken Column is the only place I've found in the Nether where the crystal shows damage, except for the Dome of the Assembly. I don't think it was a coincidence that when I started the excavations around the base of the column, one of the first things we found was the drill. I believe both drills—the whole one and the damaged one—were used to drill into the column for some purpose. Maybe the creators of the drills wanted to use columns as storage, or houses, or water reservoirs.

—From the journal of Morvu Francita Januti

We began the climb the next morning, leaving the balloon parts and unneeded supplies hanging below. I'd slept better than in the balloon, even though I'd been wrapped up in a woven hammock, hanging from a metal anchor, my legs dangling out over infinity.

The beetle, far ahead, pulled the rope tied to our platform taut, and the majus explained the beetle could tell from the tension when she should stop for us to catch up.

"Make sure your harness is snug," Mom called from a few anchors above. I nodded and tugged on the clasp, just to make sure. I was familiar with climbing gear, from adventures with all three of my parents, though never off Etan. The harness was sort of like a big diaper with holes in the sides, and a rope went through a metal hook at the front, so all my weight was supported right at my center.

The crystal beetle drill left us pairs of holes in the wall, each set about as far as my wrist to my shoulder. Because of its unusual nature, this climb required four people to work best. Partino and Majus E'Flyr led the way, taking turns to fit metal hook-like anchors in the holes. It was an exhausting job, which was why it took two people. Mom and I came behind, taking up the anchors we'd used, and bringing the net up with us.

We're building a ladder as we climb.

The majus was as fast as Partino, despite her age. I stared up at her, glad she was a good distance ahead of me. I didn't need any more condescension—the climb was hard enough. *She must be using the Symphony to help her.*

I watched the expanse of crystal glittering above me, wondering exactly how high it went. The beetle was a speck, nearly out of sight, save for the rope trailing down. With only the wall stretching to either side and above, there was nothing to give a scale to the view. I glanced down, past the supply net dangling, to see the Nether's floor—a slab of green and blue far below. It was beautiful. *I'm glad I'm not afraid of heights.* But it was enough to give anyone vertigo, and I looked back up. *Only afraid of falling. Trust the harness.*

We climbed with our noses practically touching the smooth glassy surface, and it only grew brighter as the day progressed. I started to squint.

Mom swung over on her harness, during a break. "Try these on." Leather goggles with heavy, dark lenses obscured her eyes. I studied the pair she gave me, then put them over my head. The wall dimmed and everything went slightly purple. I turned around, hooking my legs around an anchor.

"Wow."

"What is it?" Mom said, and we looked out over the Nether. There were low clouds a little above eye level, reflecting the light from the wall. With the goggles, the clouds were purple, shading to dark maroon. The nearest column pierced one, scattering wisps of water vapor like a pen through a wad of cotton. A halo of light hung around the column, bouncing up from the cloud in rays of amethyst light.

"You couldn't have seen this at home," Mom said. "In fact, we might be the first to see such a sight."

"It is beautiful," I said. That's all I was willing to admit for now, but I took in a deep breath, then let it out, trying to fix the sight in my mind. I shook out my arms and legs. I'd make a sketch of this tonight in my notebook. I needed to remember every detail.

* * *

Partino and Majus E'Flyr had to pull themselves up by hand while they set the anchors, using the holes the crystal beetle drill made as grips. It was the most dangerous of our tasks, and they traded off who went first every lightening, while the other climbed the set anchors, or rode the line trailing from the beetle and rested.

I looked down, counting the anchors below us. It was my job to retrieve them from the holes. We only had a certain number of anchors, and we had to reuse them. That was where the other half of our four-person team came in—Mom and me.

Mom slipped a pulley wheel over the end of an anchor, then looped the rope connected to the food net around it. "Ready?" she asked.

I tied the other end of the food net rope to my harness and took a deep breath. *This never gets any easier.* "Ready." I let go of the anchors, my weight bringing the net up as I rappelled down to the bottom set of anchors.

At the bottom, I yanked the lowest bent metal pieces out of the wall with a grunt, hooking them on my harness for safekeeping.

"Got them!" I called, and Mom hauled me upwards, the pulley multiplying her strength, as I plucked each anchor out of its hole. Before long, I was next to Mom and the food net, my harness stuffed with anchors.

"I'm still not sure how these anchors work," I said. It felt like they should fall out of the holes.

"The Council of the Maji gave them to me," Mom said. "They said they have Systems in them, and the maji who made them sized the anchors especially for the holes the beetle drills. Something about how climbing higher with them gives them the notes to stay in the holes." She shook her head. "I didn't really understand it, but they work."

"Weird," I said. They didn't do anything when I held them.

Maybe they activate when they're in the wall. Maji weren't like what my brothers and I used to imagine.

"Are you two planning on climbing any more today?" Partino called down, and I realized the rope to the beetle was drawing tight.

"We're coming!" I shouted back up, and reached for the next anchor, but my arms were already shaking.

* * *

The day turned into repetition: climb up with Mom until the food net was a good distance below, then set up the pulley and bring up the food net and collect the used anchors at the same time. Mom and I switched off, though I was better at rappelling down, and she was better at hauling me up.

I looked down, surprised to see how far away we were from the supplies we left behind. I could barely make out the woven mat and the remains of the basket. Everything looked the same up here except for the waves and swells in the wall. It was like we were climbing a vertical ocean. *My arms are burning, and it's only a little way into the afternoon! How many days of this can I take?*

"I'm out of anchors," Partino called down to us. We were climbing over a small bulge in the wall, which meant we had to support more of our weight while climbing up the anchors.

"I'll get it," I called to Mom. She'd handed up the anchors the last time, anyway. My arms were burning, but I wasn't going to give Mom the satisfaction of seeing me back down.

As long as I'm here, I'll show her a researcher can do just as much as a naturalist.

I was used to the spacing of the holes by now, and climbed hand over hand, angled backwards over the abyss, my feet finding each metal rung between us and Partino and Majus E'Flyr.

"Here they are," I said, fumbling at the harness. I had probably thirty of the anchors hanging there, ready to use again. Mom had more with her.

Partino reached down, his strong arm seeming as long as I was tall. I pulled out a handful of the anchors—at the same time the one I was holding onto loosened, just a little. Time slowed, and the smoothness of the metal flowed under my fingers as they peeled away from the anchor.

I'm falling! Sea Mother break over me!

The anchors tumbled from my other hand as my heart hammered, and my vision narrowed to a tunnel. Wind whistled past my head. I screamed.

"Ooof!" The rope jerked me to a stop, but the anchors kept falling, end over end. I hung from my harness, gently twirling, until the anchors disappeared from sight below.

They're gone. Just like that. We only have so many anchors, and I lost these. What if I lost more? Will Partino laugh at me? The majus will give me that look she has. I'm only a dumb researcher. I should have insisted Mom take someone else.

"Are you all right?" she was at my side, her hands on my shoulders, stopping my spin. "Anything broken? Does anything hurt?"

"No, and...ow...just my body," I said. I wiggled my fingers and toes. Nothing seemed broken, but I would have bruises from where the harness caught me.

I have to tell her. If I don't, I'm only a kid.

"I lost some of the anchors, Mom," I couldn't look up at her.

I messed up. She trusted me and I'm already wrecking the expedition.

"I don't care about them," she said, and I looked up at the quickness of her answer. "I care about you," she said.

"But—" I let one hand drop out over empty air, where the metal pieces had disappeared. *Maji made them. How expensive were they?*

"But nothing," Mom said. "Hm. Did you know I lost all of my team's rations on my first expedition?"

I met her eyes. "You never told me that." I grabbed the rope above my head and heaved myself back to wall, hand over hand. My arms tingled and it took three tries to get upright, hanging on the rope. I hadn't realized I was so tired.

"Well I did," Mom said. "Lost them in the middle of the Sea of Fire on the third day out. Had to spend a whole day fishing for food. Explorer Harthena was furious with me, but that didn't stop him from letting me take over his business when he retired, did it?"

"You mean Uncle Harthena?" I asked.

"The same. That's not the only stupid thing I've done, either."

I felt a grin tugging at the corners of my mouth. "Strange how he's never told me those stories. I need to ask him when we get back." *I bet he's got a whole boat of salty water on Mom.*

"Yeeess." Mom drew the word out. "We'll see. For now, I think we need a little help from the majus. It's about time, anyway." She waved a hand up at where Partino and Majus E'Flyr were watching anxiously. "She's all right," Mom said. "But she needs a little boost."

Majus E'Flyr's head-tentacles were unbraided today and they twitched in what I thought was concern as she came down the rope that connected us, hand over hand.

"Let's see what we can do," she said when she was closer, her large, surprised eyes looking me over. I could smell her, musty earth mixed with oil and rope. Her wrinkles reminded me how old she was. How had she been climbing all day, and only sometimes using the anchors? I looked at her long hands, purple and wrinkled. They were covered with dust from climbing.

"How do you do it?" I asked.

Majus E'Flyr must have figured out what I meant because she chuckled, gripping an anchor to keep her from swinging.

"How much do you know about the maji?" she asked.

More talking down to the 'girl?' But then I saw she was serious. I waggled my head side to side. "Not a lot. My brothers and I used to pretend to be them, but now that I see you..."

"The Grand Symphony underlies the entire universe," Majus E'Flyr said. "It exists everywhere, but maji can hear its music and change the notes." She reached out with one dusty hand and took my arm, skin to skin. Her hand was warm and dry, with a vigor that ran to her bones. "I belong to the House of Strength, which means—"

"You can make me stronger?" I interrupted. Mom made an irritated noise, and I sighed, pushing my irritation down. *The majus is trying to be nice. Don't fight her.* Or at least I thought she was. It was hard to tell with the Lobath's surprised-looking eyes.

The majus was in a better mood than when I first met her, maybe because of all the climbing we'd done. "That's a part," she said. "But the House of Strength affects a lot of things, like plant growth, and keeping you from getting cold, or sick. I can even adjust the melody of your skin so it can't be cut—for a short time."

"Oh."

That's actually pretty impressive. Helpful for a long climb. I could see why Mom wanted her on the expedition. Then I looked to the glowing surface of the wall. We'd been climbing all day. "Why—"

"Why haven't I helped you out yet?" Now Majus E'Flyr was the one interrupting. I swallowed the flash of heat that rose in my chest, and nodded. "We maji use the notes that define us to make changes. If we use too many—" she gave a one-armed shrug, "what's left? I didn't get this old by using my notes up."

I frowned. *She has to give up part of herself to change the Symphony?* "I didn't realize it cost you so much to do your magic."

The majus' head-tentacles twitched again, this time as a laugh. "It's not so bad. For a lot of changes we can reverse what we do and take our notes back. That's what I'll do to you now. I'm going to make you a little stronger, so you don't get tired as easily. I'll take it back before we sleep tonight. Is that acceptable?"

Is it? Of course it's acceptable. My arms are about to fall off.

"Yes," I said. It was still afternoon, and the wall was only beginning to dim. We had a lot more climbing to do today.

Majus E'Flyr grasped the anchor, and tightened her grip on my arm. Her eyes were looking far away, and her head-tentacles twitched in time to music I couldn't hear.

I gasped. The pain where the harness chafed me suddenly faded away, and I felt like I could climb for days. As the majus took her hand back, I reached out to the nearest anchor, raising myself up with one arm.

"How's that?" the majus asked. She was panting, and the wrinkles in her face seemed deeper. "You'll feel more tired at the end of the day when I take back the changes I made to the music." She looked up to Mom, and then farther up to where Partino hung, listening in.

"Much better," I said. "I'm ready to go!"

* * *

The view on our second night sleeping on the wall was like the first—the wall and columns didn't change, and the ground was so far away that our climb today didn't make it any smaller. It was peaceful, like I was one little speck of dust on the face of a god. Partino and Majus E'Flyr tied a bunch of ropes from the topmost anchors, and we unrolled the mats we kept in the supply nets. Each of us had our own hammock, tightly bundled up so we didn't slip out in the middle of the night and fall. The rope up to the beetle trailed down, and I assumed she would climb through the night until she'd drilled as many holes as she could.

I looked up, nestled in my hammock. The wall undulated above me, like the sea on a calm day. How high could it be? We had enough rations for several ten-days, but I couldn't imagine the wall was that tall. We were at the first layers of fluffy clouds that broke around the columns like waves around a buoy. We'd covered a lot of ground—or air—in the balloon. What was above the clouds? More of the same, or something new?

* * *

The next morning, we found the crystal beetle drill stalled.

"I could barely make it out, now the wall is bright enough," Majus E'Flyr said, when she came down to talk to Mom and me. "It's not moving, and looks like it hasn't since sometime last night. The rope up to it isn't taut."

"Any idea what's wrong?" Mom's voice was tight with anxiety.

If the beetle can't drill holes, we can't climb. We're stuck! Could we climb back down, replacing all the anchors? I swung my harness closer to listen.

"Don't know yet," the majus said. "We'll have to climb up to it and find out."

"Hold on a moment," Mom said, and lowered herself down to the nets with our rations. She searched around the wafers and jerky and water before I heard her make a noise of triumph. When she climbed back up, she held a long cylinder.

"I should have been using the telescope before now to keep a watch on the drill," she said, opening it up and holding it to her eye. She stared up, then growled, and shielded the end of the telescope with one hand. "Stupid wall is too bright," she said. "Ah, now I can see it. It's right below the cloud layer. The drill is stuck in the wall and it's just hanging there."

"What's wrong with her?" I asked. "Can Majus E'Flyr fix her with the Symphony?"

Partino chuckled at that. "The majus' music can't fix everything, little one."

The majus held up one long finger. "I might be able to do more than you think," she said. "The House of Strength can't do what the House of Healing can, but the mechanical components of the drill far outweigh the organic ones. I can do a lot to increase the constitution of—"

"How did they get up here?" Mom cried. We all turned to look at her. She was looking down, not up.

"Who? Where?" I asked. We were so far above the ground I couldn't even make out the individual shapes of the farm plots anymore.

No one else could be up this far.

Mom shut the telescope with a *clack*. "It's that hack, Surigran Wailimani and one of his thugs. I *knew* they ransacked my dig site. They're...they're *riding* the other drill!"

"The broken one?" Partino asked. He reached for the telescope and looked through it. "It was still buried when we left. How did they get it out and working so fast?"

"They must have pulled it out and started right after we did," Mom said. "If I'd been using the telescope, I would have seen them before now, and we could have climbed faster." I doubted that was the case, knowing how hard it was to climb the sheer wall. "Wailimani has always been as crafty as he is ruthless. Whatever he did, it worked. The point is they're gaining on us. We need to get started, quick!"

My muscles were aching from the day before, but Majus E'Flyr went around to each of us, and did something, her head nodding to music I couldn't hear. Again, I felt ready to climb the wall with no ropes. *But the majus looks tired.* Her wrinkles were more prominent, her skin dark and dull. I made sure she had a good grip on the anchors before she climbed to the front of our group. She couldn't even rest and ride the rope from the beetle, since it was stalled.

"Pack up that mat, Natina, now," Mom said, her fingers twitching toward me. "Get your things stowed in the net so we can leave."

I glared at her. *She of all people should understand climbing safely.* My mind jumped to the clump of anchors I'd lost down the wall. "Mom, I'm going to drop something else if we keep rushing," I said.

Mom tsked at me. "Then drop it on his head. The last ones must have missed." She pointed down. "We have to stay ahead of Wailimani. This is *my* expedition. The Council approved *me*, not that Kirian scum." She pulled herself up to the next set of anchors.

* * *

It took a full day of climbing to reach the crystal beetle drill, and it was too dark to continue when we got there. Mom had pushed us all day, and even Partino was drooping. The majus was barely awake, but when she took back the change she made to us, she visibly straightened. *She's losing a lot of herself to keep us going.*

"What's the problem?" Mom asked, almost before the majus got a chance to look at the drill.

"Give her a chance, Mom. She's exhausted."

It's like she's got a giant squid swimming after her. Maybe she did. It was obvious Wailimani and the other beetle were catching up.

Majus E'Flyr ignored us both, sticking long fingers inside the black shell of the beetle as Partino held one of our few torches over her head. She took a long time to respond, and now both Mom and I fidgeted in our harnesses. Partino glanced down every few moments at the other beetle and the Kirians.

I can see them clearly now, even in the dim light. They were lying on the back of their beetle, riding it lengthwise, since there were only two of them. That was how they had caught up. Wailimani was obviously the one in front. He was pointing things out to the other Kirian with him. Both had the feathery hair like the rest of their species. The beetle was moving jerkily up the wall, using the holes ours had already drilled. *That's cheating!*

The mandibles seemed wrong on that one—was one of them broken?

"It's the main drive shaft," Majus E'Flyr said, and I looked back up to where she and Mom were hanging over the beetle.

"Sounds bad, doesn't it," Partino said, and I nodded.

I haven't gotten to talk to him much the last couple days. He'd been climbing up above with the majus most of the time. I looked down at the other beetle limping toward us. *It must have been climbing day and night, with those Kirians strapped on tight.*

"Mom will blow a gasket," I said. "Or maybe throw the Kirians off the wall."

Partino chuckled. "Or both. Let's see if we can help the majus out."

I realized Mom and Majus E'Flyr were arguing. "What do you mean, you can't fix it?" Mom asked.

"What I said," the majus replied. "I can't just throw notes at a problem. It doesn't work that way." She pointed into the beetle. "Look there—the driveshaft for the left drill is stripped, and the one on the right doesn't look great. Probably hit something inside the wall that didn't agree with it, though I don't know how. This crystal all looks the same." She flung her other hand out toward the shining wall, while gripping the beetle's shell. "Whatever happened, I can't fix it."

I looked down at the other beetle again. At the rate they were going, they would catch up before morning.

* * *

We camped for the night, once it was clear Majus E'Flyr couldn't do anything with the beetle. She managed to get the mandible drills backed out of the wall, but when the majus tried to start the beetle climbing again, the metal construct let out a high-pitched whine when the crystal mandibles hit the wall, and the metal construct skidded to one side, grappling for the holes in the wall with her six legs.

"Watch out!" I yelled.

She's going to fall off the wall!

Majus E'Flyr moved faster than I thought possible, and put one hand on the beetle and one on the wall, grunting with the effort. Mom and Partino swung out to each side, their arms out. Partino's strong arms might be able to hold the beetle for a few seconds, but not Mom's. Then the beetle found the holes she had drilled and clung. The majus slumped.

"I didn't need to spend those extra notes," she complained. "This wall resists any change to the music around it. Everything I've done so far, altering the Symphony, has been harder."

"What did you do?" I asked.

I wish I could hear the Symphony. But that would never be.

"I increased the connection between the music of the drill and the wall," she said, then looked at me when I didn't say anything. "Like when I stood on top, under the balloon, without falling off."

How does that sound? I tried imagining the Symphony. What music did the drill make?

"That's all I will do tonight," the majus announced.

"But what about—" Mom gestured downward, but Majus E'Flyr cut her off.

"Let them catch up. I won't risk my neck trying to climb at night, and climbing with six will be easier than climbing with four."

At least I'm not the only one she interrupts.

The four of us didn't speak as we went to our hammocks. I heard Mom shifting around far into the night.

* * *

In the morning, we woke to the second beetle stopped a short way down the wall, within easy climbing distance.

Mom was fuming. *Did she even sleep last night?* About once a minute she would push all her hair back and away from her head. It sprang right back, each time. I had the same hair—all curly and poofy, and unless you tied it tight there was nothing you could do with it.

The rest of us stayed out of her way, as much as was possible when we were all strung together like stingers on a jellyfish. I watched the two Kirians stretch and eat something, as if there were nothing unusual about the metal hulks perched by each other on the huge expanse of the wall.

Majus E'Flyr and Partino studied the wall where our crystal beetle drill was stuck, as Mom hovered over them. *As much as anyone can hover while hanging in a harness. She still manages it.*

I watched the Kirians and the other beetle. It was shaped mostly like ours, except where ours had two long crystal drills in front that looked like mouth parts, this one looked like it had horns, one over the other. Or it should have. Where our beetle was nice and helpful, theirs looked mean. *Definitely a boy.* The top horn was missing completely, leaving a hole.

"Are you to be having trouble with your contraption?" the Kirian I thought was Wailimani shouted, as if we had met while out for a walk.

His voice is really squeaky. I almost laughed at the strangeness of it. He was big, even for a Kirian, which meant he was taller than me, though nowhere near as tall as Mom, and certainly not Partino. His assistant was busy in the back of their beetle, tightening straps on the provisions attached to the back. *It looks like they threw a bunch of stuff together in a hurry to catch up with us.* I shook my head. *Don't they know how important it is to plan out an expedition? Even I know that.* We'd spent several days in Gloomlight, planning and buying our provisions.

Both wore the colorful robes Kirians liked, Wailimani's with yellow and red stripes, and his assistant with green and gold and purple. The robes didn't seem practical for climbing, but then, they were riding their beetle. Unlike them, Mom and I had tied back our sleeves, wrapping them around our arms so they wouldn't catch on anything. We'd wrapped the flowing split pants we liked to wear around our legs in the same way.

I stared at the bag I thought must hold their food. *That's not nearly big enough.* It should be about half as big as our bag of rations, but it was less than a third the size. *Were they planning to use ours when they caught up? There won't be enough.*

"What are you doing here, Wailimani?" Mom called down. She was using the same voice as when my brothers or I did something we weren't supposed to, and I tensed without meaning to. Even Partino jumped a little, and I smiled.

Glad it's not only me.

"My assistant and I were to be thinking an expedition of such magnitude should not be witnessed by so few," the Kirian answered. "Such a momentous occasion calls for assistance, so we came as quickly as we were to be able, to make sure no disastrous events befell you."

I've met other people who like to use big words because it makes them sound important. I decided I didn't like Surigran Wailimani. I gripped my rope and glared at him.

"You thought wrong," Mom said. "And you stole that drill. That's *my* salvage. You couldn't have gotten up here without us." Then she narrowed her eyes. "How did you get up to where we started drilling, anyway? We came by balloon."

"I am to be well aware of this fact," Wailimani shrilled in his high-pitched voice. He gestured to the single blunted horn on their drill and his robe's sleeve swept out like a wing. "I am afraid this drill was not to be designed for operation with only one of its fascinating crystal extrusions. When we pushed our contraption to, ah, be making up time, the extra exertion wore down the drill. We were barely making it to your graciously offered handholds."

"They weren't meant for you," Mom said. She crossed her arms, but that meant she swung in her harness. She uncrossed them again and held onto an anchor.

Wailimani bowed his head, his crest of feathery hair spreading out in what was meant to be apology, but I knew it wasn't. "Nevertheless, this contraption was available, with simple repairs, as your permit for the area around Broken Column is not exclusive, despite what you think. My team was able to—"

"If you all quit your arguing for a few moments," Majus E'Flyr interrupted, "we could fix this problem and be on our way." Both Mom and Wailimani fell silent. The assistant even looked up from the back end of the beetle. Both Kirians were pale-skinned with brownish spots, like some older people got. It was just how Kirians looked. They probably thought my blueish skin and the majus' head-tentacles were strange too.

"The problem is right here," Majus E'Flyr said. "Partino found it." The big porter had been silent, frowning down at the Kirians, but now he held a hand out to the last hole our beetle tried to drill.

We all peered closer. Wailimani shaded his eyes from the glow of the wall, but I didn't think he could see from where he was. *They didn't bring goggles either.* I climbed up the anchors until my nose was almost pressed to the smooth crystal.

Is that a crack?

"The drill hit right between two shear lines," Majus E'Flyr said. "I don't know how Nether crystal forms cracks if nothing can break it, but one starts right here."

"And continues up there," Partino said. I followed his finger straight up. We hadn't seen it because of the light. The crack got bigger and bigger the higher it went, until it ended in the first real sharp edge I had seen on the wall. It would take a lightening or more of climbing to get up that far. There was an indentation, and I could see something dark against the glowing surface.

"Is that a *tree*?" I asked. I had seen no other plants on our climb. There weren't even birds up this high. At least I didn't have to worry about insects biting me.

Partino nodded. "Dirt and seeds must have gotten up here somehow. Maybe it was a freak storm."

"It's also not helping us climb," Majus E'Flyr said. "Wailimani—you arriving here might be a blessing in disguise."

Mom actually growled.

I would have picked another way to say that.

"I am to be very pleased we could be of service," the Kirian said. He gave a little bow, but I wasn't fooled.

The majus waved her long fingers at Mom, her head-tentacles twitching. "I don't care what's between you. The Effature and the Council of the Maji are interested in getting information on what's at the top of the Nether. We couldn't complete that task with this drill broken. Now we can."

"How?" Mom sounded reluctant.

"I assume the two machines are compatible, since they were found together. If these fools haven't burnt out their driveshaft too, we should be able to combine the two machines and continue up the wall," the majus answered.

"With us included, of course," Wailimani said. "Since we are to be contributing parts to your noble enterprise."

Mom took in a deep breath. "And taking some of the credit. It might be better to go back down." Even I could see that wasn't a choice—she was just angry at the Kirians for poaching her expedition.

I was too. I frowned at the two newcomers. *They dug up Mom's site.* I knew how much pride she took in keeping her expeditions neat, and if the way the two packed their beetle was any indication, I didn't want to see how they got the machine out of the ground. Maybe *they* broke off the other horn.

I haven't come all this way to go back.

Majus E'Flyr shook her head. "You could. I'll stay up here."

"What about a portal?" Mom asked. "We could go back to the Imperium, get rid of these two, make repairs, and come back here."

I cocked my head. Portals were the only way to get from homeworld to homeworld, and to the Nether. Only the maji could open them.

Majus E'Flyr shook her head. "We could get down, yes, but how would we get back up here? Just walk through the portal and hope we catch an anchor while falling? I don't think I can place one that exactly—I need a larger area."

The majus pulled on a head-tentacle. "In fact, I'm not sure I can make one at all this close to the wall. As I said, its music resists changes, and a portal needs a big change to open."

"Wait—could you have opened a portal to the top of the Nether this whole time?" I asked her. *Why are we doing all this climbing?*

"No, girl." The majus turned her wide silvery eyes to me. "At least one majus has to have physically been to both endpoints of a portal. No one's been up there," she pointed above her head. "That's one reason I'm here. It's why the Council is interested."

I tried to keep my face from showing my irritation at the majus calling me a child, again. *Though she's probably about six times as old as I am...*

"Yes, who is to be saying what treasures may be above the clouds?" Wailimani put in, and we all stared at him. "There is to be no reason to stop now."

"Treasures *you* want to claim discovery of? Like you got a permit for the same dig site?" Mom thrust one finger down at the ground.

"Surely there is to be enough credit for all," Wailimani whined. "Six people discovering what is to be above the Nether's clouds is not so much different from four."

Is that all he wants? My anger at Mom for dragging me all the way up here had faded, now I'd seen such incredible sights. Even if my arms ached. But I hadn't even thought about making money off our climb. *Isn't the achievement enough? We'll be the first people to reach the top. I might even be as famous as Mom!*

That thought ricocheted through my brain and suddenly I wasn't so sure. *Will my friends want my autograph? How will I be sure they want to be with me, or if they just want to be near a famous person?* I gripped my ropes tighter, unsure of what would happen when—if—we returned from this expedition. *What did Mom haul me into?*

Mom made an annoyed noise, interrupting my flailing thoughts. "We're wasting time. If it's the only way, then that's what it is." She jerked her head to the Kirians. "We'll keep an eye on these two and combine the drills."

"Doesn't anyone want to be asking for my permission?" Wailimani said. "After all, my team was responsible for excavating this drill—"

"No!" said Mom and the majus together. Partino cracked his knuckles menacingly.

"Be grateful we're letting you climb up with us," Mom told the Kirian. "It's a long way down."

* * *

The repairs took the rest of the day, and while Majus E'Flyr and Partino worked on the two beetles, Wailimani and Mom stayed out of each other's way as much as possible while combining our supplies.

I glared daggers at Wailimani *and* his assistant, who still hadn't said anything. *He's just as shifty, though.*

The other Kirian was short, nearly as short as the majus, and moved with quick, little motions. *It looks like he's always trying to make sure no one sees what he's doing.* But I saw. Even when he slipped some of our rations out of the netting and ate them.

"Hey!" I called, but he scampered away in his harness back to their beetle. I tried to get Mom's attention to tell her, but she was too busy avoiding Wailimani.

I'm watching you, buddy. Assistant Sneaky gave me a pointy-toothed grin, and I shivered. I looked around quickly, but everyone else was busy. No one else had seen.

The wall had dimmed by the time Majus E'Flyr and Partino started up our crystal beetle drill. We all looked up at the familiar hiss of the crystal drill mandibles.

"She's working!" I yelled. *Finally!*

Mom's face relaxed for what might have been the first time that day. "Let's start it climbing while we sleep," she said.

"What if it hits another crack in the wall?" I asked. I doubted another party would ride up on a *third* drill with convenient spare parts.

"We've got to make up for lost time, Natina," Mom said, and I slumped in my harness.

I see how much my opinion is worth.

Unexpectedly, it was Majus E'Flyr who spoke up. "The girl has a good point. I want to keep an eye on the drill while we're climbing, from now on. We're too high up for anything else to go wrong, unless you want to cut this expedition short with an emergency trip to the ground by portal. We'd have to climb back up, without the drill."

"We were to be climbing through the dark without trouble," Wailimani offered.

I rolled my eyes. I guess he didn't know Mom that well, for all their arguing. He was helping me without meaning to.

"There are only two of you, and you evidently don't care if you fall and break your neck," Mom shot back. "The crystal beetle drill can't hold the four of us and climb, and it certainly won't hold six. You're right, Majus. We'll have to wait until morning to start." She looked like she couldn't decide whether to be more upset at the Lobath majus or the Kirian explorer.

"The crystal beetle—?" Wailimani's crest rose in surprise.

Nope, you're not going to argue with that too.

"It's *my* name," I said before he could finish. "If you think it's stupid, then tell me." I gave the Kirian my best frown, like when I bossed my brothers around.

Wailimani stared at me a moment, then his crest settled back down and he bobbed his head at me. "I would not be dreaming of doing such a thing. We shall gladly spend the night here and start tomorrow well rested."

I glared back. *None of us will get much sleep with that squeaky Kirian and his creepy assistant.*

Mom and Partino talked quietly while we were getting our mats ready, but I saw a lot of looks toward the other party, who were planning to sleep tied to their non-working beetle, which still gripped the wall, unmoving. Its back was opened like some larger beetle had emerged from its shell. Its one, blunted, horn pointed straight up.

My muscles pulsed with weariness and, even though I wanted to watch what happened, I could barely keep my eyes open. I fell asleep while Mom and Partino were still bickering.

* * *

A sound woke me in the middle of the night.

What was that?

Maybe it was a dream. My eyes were closing.

Hsss. Tump.

My eyes opened again, and I leaned out over the edge of my hammock, moving quietly so the mat wouldn't shift under me.

There was a dark shape moving beneath me, visible against the low glow from the wall, which was never completely dark. The shape was too small to be Mom or Partino, or even Wailimani. *Is it Majus E'Flyr? Why would she be out?*

I looked over to the majus' hammock, to my right and above mine, but I could see the dent her weight made in it.

I looked back down. *So it's Assistant Sneaky.* The only other person that size.

If I wake everyone up, they will ask a lot of questions, and Assistant Sneaky will shrug it off and give us one of those creepy grins. I've got to catch him in the act this time.

I watched for several minutes, ready to call out, as the little Kirian moved around the camp. He touched nothing, though he climbed all the way up to our crystal beetle and all the way down to the nets holding our supplies.

I still couldn't wake everyone. *He'll say he woke up and wanted to stretch his legs.* Or Wailimani would, since the little Kirian was as silent as he was shifty. Then everyone would be even crankier tomorrow.

Assistant Sneaky made no other noises like the ones that had woken me. It had been when he passed close by, probably because my hammock was the closest to their beetle. He soon returned to the beetle and strapped himself back in. Despite trying to watch him, I soon fell back to sleep.

* * *

"You're grumpy today," Mom told me after I complained about the harness being uncomfortable. For the fifth time. It didn't help that it was cloudy and chilly. The cloud layer had dipped lower in the night and surrounded us. I couldn't even see the nearest column.

"So are you." I wasn't in any mood to be agreeable. *You've only told us about twenty times how the crystal beetle drill isn't moving as fast as before.* The beetle was visible a short distance above, contentedly drilling holes in the Nether wall. The rope that connected her to us was like a limp length of seaweed, hanging nearby. I took my purple goggles off to clear the condensation away. The anchors were slick, too.

I looked down and saw the small tree nestled in the crack, now far below us. We had stopped for Mom and I to make a quick sketch, but mine got smudged.

I hope my notebook isn't getting wet. I'd wrapped it in oiled paper and put it in the food supply net after I finished. I'd drawn a few sketches of the repair job yesterday, but unless we stopped for a while, it was impossible to take any notes while climbing, especially in the damp.

"Partino and I didn't get much sleep," Mom admitted. "We were both trying to keep watch to make sure Wailimani didn't try any tricks."

"So you saw him then?" *Maybe I won't have to prove anything.* I hadn't mentioned Wailimani's assistant, hoping I would spot something out of place, or a piece of equipment missing. Nothing.

"Wailimani?" Mom asked. "He was asleep all night."

"No, Assistant Sneaky," I said.

How could they have missed him?

"Assistant Snea—" Mom cut off with a chuckle. "Well, I suppose that is fitting, and he hasn't said one word. He is kind of strange."

"This is serious, Mom," I told her. *Don't just laugh it off.* "He was sneaking around the whole camp in the middle of the night."

Mom sobered, holding onto an anchor. She looked up to where the two Kirians were climbing in the middle of the group. Their robes were flapping around their legs, even though they'd tried to tie them back like Mom and I did. *They must be heavy with all that water soaking in.*

We'd decided it was best to keep them where we could see them. Our original team could handle placing the anchors, so Mom and I took up our positions hauling them up, while Partino and Majus E'Flyr placed new ones up above.

"What did he do?" Mom lowered her voice. "If he touched anything..."

"I...I don't think he did," I said. "That's why I didn't wake everyone up. He just looked around, then went back to sleep."

"Probably trying to decide what supplies the two of them could steal," Mom said. "Thank you for telling me. I don't know how Partino and I missed it last night, but we were all tired." She sighed. "I don't trust either of those Kirians. Even if the drill hadn't broken, they would have caught up to us."

"And passed us," I said. "This way, you still get to be the first to the top." I realized I hadn't been mad at her dragging me our here since the Kirians showed up.

Mom gave me a nod. "That's true. However, following us so quickly smacks of inside knowledge from the Imperium. Someone near the Council of the Maji or the Effature sold information about our expedition."

"They'd do that?" I asked. "For what?"

Is this part of exploring? Watching for crafty rivals? I wondered if Mom dealt with this sort of thing all the time. If so, I'd never heard about it.

"For money, or for a share of what we might discover up there," Mom told me, jerking her head upward. "There's a lot more to the real world than studying artifacts. It's one reason I wanted you with me. I just didn't think you'd get such a close-up example."

"I'm a quick learner," I said. "I'll figure out what he's doing." I pondered ways to catch the Kirians while they were doing something underhanded.

"We'll all have to try harder." Mom took the pulley from her harness. "Time to bring the anchors and food net up. Get ready." Her fingers waggled toward the bottommost anchors and the netting that hung beneath us.

We set everything up. "I can help," I said. "We can take turns watching."

Mom was silent as I rappelled down, got the anchors, tucked them into my harness, and climbed back up.

I grimaced at the ache in my arms. The majus had done her thing to all of us again this morning, but it was clear it took a lot out of her, and it felt like it wasn't working as well as it had been. *How long until we can't climb anymore? How high is this wall?*

When I got back, Mom had made a decision. "We need you rested," she said. "Partino and I will keep watch, but tell me if you see anything. It will be easier after we get through this cloud layer."

I watched Wailimani and Assistant Sneaky the rest of the day. It helped break up the monotony of the climb, surrounded by gray clouds. *It's like climbing through cotton. Wet cotton, that sticks to my clothes and hair.*

* * *

I didn't sleep well that night either, my mind churning as I listened for sounds of the Kirians doing something funny. Mom and Partino's hammocks were both occupied, and I wondered which one was watching.

I must have fallen asleep at some point, because the same sound awakened me.

Hsss. Tump.

I shifted carefully to peek over the edge. With the clouds around us it was nearly impossible to see anything, even with the faint light from the wall. *Where is Assistant Sneaky? What is he doing?*

Try as I might, I couldn't see him moving around. I thought I heard a faint buzz, like rope rubbing against an anchor, but neither Mom nor Partino cried out. It could easily have been hammock ropes rubbing against each other. I fell asleep, still trying to listen for movement.

* * *

It was raining the next morning.

"Blaugh!" I cried, waking to droplets falling on my nose. I was twisted up, my head hanging out one side of my hammock. The others were already packing up. I shook my hair and clothes out as best I could, but everything was soaking wet.

What did I hear last night? Or see? Everything was jumbled up in my memory. I opened my mouth to say something, but Partino spoke first, making the thought flee like the remnants of a dream.

"Be very careful climbing today," he told us. "If you feel like you're going to slip, depend on your harness. You'll need to tighten it up. It will catch you, but you might fall a little further than normal. The ropes are wet. That means they're heavier, and if you fall, your harness will jerk you around more than usual."

"At least we can fill up the water jugs," Mom said. She held one out as an example, catching the rain. We'd filled them once before, holding the jugs out on long poles during a quick shower in the balloon. "We were getting pretty low." She looked up to Majus E'Flyr. "Can you help us out one more time today? I promise I'll let you rest tomorrow."

The Lobath majus sighed heavily. Her head-tentacles were drooping, and she looked even more wrinkled than usual. "I can do it," she said, "but I'll need a good rest tonight. I can't keep spending my notes like this. I can get most of them back when reversing the change to the Symphony, but there is degradation over the course of a day." She came around to me first, then Mom, and then Partino.

"What about me?" Wailimani squeaked in his high-pitched voice. His assistant nodded vigorously, but said nothing, naturally.

That voice is really starting to get on my nerves.

"Yes, even you," Majus E'Flyr said. "Can't have you lagging behind and holding us back. We'll be climbing slowly enough as it is." She clambered over to the two Kirians, whose robes were soaked. Their crests hung limp in the rain.

Good, I thought at them viciously. Something nagged at the back of my brain, watching the Kirians. Had I seen or heard noises the night before, or was it a dream? *What was it?* I couldn't remember. Maybe events during the day would bring it to mind.

Climbing before had been monotonous, but climbing in the rain, inside the clouds, was *exhausting*, even with Majus E'Flyr making us stronger. It was so common for someone to slip off an anchor and swing around in a circle that I stopped paying attention. We'd tightened up the rope to the beetle so it could act as another failsafe.

I had my fair share of slips, but each time my harness saved me. We were very careful to tie our ropes well whenever we had to adjust them. The metal of the anchors was slick when wet, and my hands grew so tired I could barely grip them. Everything stank of wet metal.

Sometime in the afternoon, Partino had one hand in a bare hole, ready to put in a new anchor, when he slipped off. It had happened before, and I didn't even look up at his cry.

"Your harness!" At Mom's shout, I looked up. Partino was dangling, half out of his harness. I froze, my hands locked around anchors. I could see the tear, right by his hip.

Then everything happened in a blur. There was a *riiiip* and Partino was falling, long arms and legs stretched out to catch something, anything.

No! I threw out my arms, heedless of how it made me swing out from the wall. Maybe I could catch him as he went past.

Instead, Partino caught on Wailimani's arm, pulling the Kirian off his own anchors, and swinging them into Assistant Sneaky.

"Get off me, you oaf! You are to be pulling me down!" Wailimani squeaked at Partino. He pushed the porter, and Partino grabbed at the assistant instead.

I don't know if Assistant Sneaky had been lazy with fastening his harness, or the rain made it looser, or Partino was too heavy, or what.

In a flash, both Partino and the Kirian were free, away from the wall and tumbling, down, out of sight.

"Partino!" I screamed. I could hear the others shouting too, but there was absolutely nothing we could do. The two figures vanished into the clouds in a matter of seconds.

"Partino!" I screamed down the wall. "No! Come back! Partino!" I don't know how long I called for him—it felt like hours, and my voice was a rusty squeak by the end.

I hung in my harness, numb. I could hear Mom crying above me. The majus and Wailimani were whispering back and forth urgently.

Partino had been Mom's porter since before I was born. I had grown up with him around—his strong arms throwing me and my brothers up in the air and catching us. He was there when Alondri and Kayla, my other parents, taught us how to sail. He'd accompanied Mom all over the Nether. He'd shared half credit for some of her discoveries.

He's gone.

* * *

We were very quiet the rest of the day.

Even Wailimani had lost his bluster. "Haribrana was the best assistant I was ever having," he said, his crest almost flat. "And I pushed your porter right into him. I was only trying to keep from falling myself, you are seeing..."

None of us said anything to the other explorer, though he looked around as if someone would tell him everything was all right. I couldn't even really say it was his fault, though I wanted to. It happened so quickly. I wanted to shout at him, to throw something, but I didn't have the energy.

At least I have a name for Assistant Snea—for Wailimani's assistant. Haribrana. I said a short prayer to the Sea Mother for both of them. Maybe they had survived? I felt tears running down my cheeks. They were saltier than the rain.

Mom spoke with the majus, and even with Wailimani, about climbing down below the cloud layer to see if Partino or the assistant had managed to catch onto something. I mostly stared at the wall, thinking about what I could have done differently. I couldn't come up with anything. When Partino fell into Haribrana, they had fallen away from the wall.

"It's a long way down," Mom finally decided, "and it's very unlikely they were able to grab one of these holes." She put her fist out beside one of the holes the beetle had drilled.

Trying to catch onto one of those, with no anchors, in the rain, while falling...

Impossible.

We began to climb again, each lost in our thoughts.

That night, we rested, still wet, still silent. Mom had brought both harnesses with us, in order not to waste extra supplies if another harness broke. She inspected them while Majus E'Flyr went to each of us, reversing the strength she had given us that morning.

I drew in my notebook, with a sheet of canvas above my head to keep out the wet. I was trying to get the curve of Partino's face just right.

Why can't I remember what he looks like better than this? He can't be gone. Surely he found a way to survive.

When the majus touched me, removing the change she made, I slumped. *I feel like I haven't slept in two days.*

"I'm sorry about everything," Majus E'Flyr said, her voice quiet. "I could tell how much Partino meant to you." She fell silent, her wide silvery eyes catching the last glow of the wall. It reflected off the dark clouds around us, like we were in a giant cave. "He told me a lot about you and your siblings while we were climbing together."

I was trying to think of something to say when I heard Mom cry out. The majus and I were instantly alert, and I was climbing up to her before I knew it.

Is she hurt too? What happened?

"This harness was *cut*," Mom said, holding it out toward Wailimani as if it was a spear. From the size, I knew it was Partino's.

Wailimani's crest stood out in shock, like a grey and blue mop on his head. "Cut? I do not believe it!"

His voice is even higher than normal. Like some sort of little rodent.

"No need to believe it—it's right here," Mom said. "I want an *explanation*." She was using that voice again.

"Well, I can be telling you it was not me," Wailimani said. For once, all pretense was gone from his voice. "Haribrana was always being a crafty one. I...I did not ask how or where he was getting his information from. Every expedition he was on was simply turning up in our favor." The Kirian shrunk into himself. "I should have been asking. I would be asking him now if it was possible..."

Everything from the past day boiled up inside me. "He *cut* Partino's harness?" I shouted. "What kind of an idiot are you, not to know that?" Haribrana—no, Assistant Sneaky had done this on purpose? Why?

At least he fell, too. Good riddance.

"Give me a reason not to toss you off this wall, too," Mom told Wailimani, and he curled in further, his crest crumpling.

"I can be helping. You must be having four members, to climb. I have been paying attention. Less and you will not make it. The majus will be fatigued from bolstering your endurance."

"Not good enough," Mom said, and started climbing down. I tucked my sketchbook away, ready to follow her, but the majus stopped me with one remarkably strong arm.

"*No one* is getting tossed off this wall," she said, and her voice echoed like thunder around us. Mom stopped climbing.

"No one *else*," I hissed at Majus E'Flyr.

She stared at me a moment, like her wide eyes could bury me in the crystal of the wall.

"No one *else*," she finally agreed, then turned away. "Come back up here, Morvu. The Kirian is correct. We *do* need four to climb, despite what we all want to do to him."

Mom came back up to us, grumbling, and we glared at Wailimani. He made his hammock as far away from us as he could.

I'll be watching you.

* * *

I watched Wailimani until I fell asleep, and throughout the next day, while we climbed through the damp clouds. I was wondering how we could leave him behind, and I think Mom was too.

Just as she said, Mom didn't make Majus E'Flyr use the Symphony to help us out, and all of us felt it. We climbed slower than ever, with lots of rests. Mom had to help the majus place the anchors and Wailimani helped me use the pulley system to bring them and the food net up. We needed him, after all. Mostly, he let me do the work, except for bringing me up, and that was fine with me. It meant I could make sure all the lines were tied correctly. I wasn't going to trust anything he did.

Days passed this way. We would get up in the morning, stretch out kinks from the day before, then keep climbing. Majus E'Flyr used the Symphony on us every other day, but she still looked more tired than the rest of us, her skin so dark purple it was almost black.

Slips were common in the never-ending wet. I began to long for the sky, and a sight of the Nether, but there was nothing but clouds. I tried to draw in the evenings, but I was too tired.

Joy had left our group with the loss of the two climbers. There weren't any jokes, or even much talking, except for Wailimani. That Kirian could *complain*. And he did—about everything—In his high and squeaky voice. The harness chafed. His robes were wet. His hair was wet. Everything was wet. His hands had blisters. The wall was too bright. It was cold.

With his wet, bulky robes, it was common for him to slip and hit an anchor. I relished every single time he did. None of us were quick to give him a hand.

I also fantasized about the clouds growing so thick that I couldn't hear his shrill voice.

The third day, I tried shouting at him, but that only made him complain more, and then whine to Mom about me 'not showing the proper respect to one of his station.' Mom shouted at him, too.

The fourth day I ignored him completely, but that didn't stop him griping. I was also getting sick of seaweed wafers and squid wafers. Wailimani complained about those too, and loudly—the lack of good food.

"The squid in these hasn't been alive in *cycles*," he piped, while we paused to eat a midday snack. "How I am to be yearning for something wriggling between my teeth, just a little." He bared his pointed teeth and I shivered. Kirian teeth were scary. I could only think of the smile Assistant Sneaky had given me.

By the fifth morning of climbing in the endless clouds I was ready to throw him off the wall, whether we needed him or not.

Then, halfway through that day, it began to get brighter. I felt something rise up, as if the ghosts of Partino and Haribrana were drifting away.

The rest of the day the clouds lightened, and we heard a distant rumbling, as if someone was beating a faraway drum. It vibrated the clouds around us.

Soon, the crystal beetle drill became visible. She had been hidden since the accident because the clouds were so thick. She trundled above us, the rope dangling down.

The clouds became white instead of gray, then misty instead of white. A giant presence loomed a little ways from the wall, and with a start, I realized it was my old friend the column. I could see its siblings, too. *How long since I've seen them glistening in the wall's light?* The rumbling had only increased, until now it was louder than the surf in a hurricane.

As the last wispy bits of cloud blew away, we stopped. Wailimani even trailed off in the middle of a complaint about his sore shoulders.

Wow. That explains the sound.

We could see the Nether wall again, glistening with water. It rose until it was obscured by a waterfall, rushing down the wall toward us. It was incredibly tall, and as wide as a sea. It would have plowed straight into us, and knocked us off like Partino, except the sheet of water crashed into a giant ridge in the wall, and was diverted straight out into the air. The noise of it rang in my ears, driving everything else away.

The torrent of water thundered over our heads, like all the waves in the world breaking on the beach at the same time. Water glistened in a graceful arc as it hit the bulge in the wall, cascading out into open air, separating out into millions of tiny droplets, each reflecting the light from the wall and the columns. The globes of water glistened like jewels suspended in midair, striking the top of the cloud layer, grown thick enough to absorb the immense amount of liquid.

"I guess we know why there's always such a heavy cloud layer here," Mom shouted. We could barely hear her. "It must be a separate ecosystem up here!"

Rainbows were everywhere, arcing from droplet to droplet, and piercing the waterfall. They split the sky into a maze of color. One arc, larger than the rest, made a path between the waterfall and the white cottony layer.

Something loosened in me, and I felt tears running down my face.

We're above the clouds.

TEN-DAY THREE

High Country

The atmosphere above the cloud layer is different. It is wetter here, most likely from the great waterfall, while it is relatively dry below. I see tiny patches of moss here, though I don't know how it is attached to the Nether crystal. Below the cloud layer the wall was completely smooth. It seems like there has been more damage to the crystal this far up, probably from the damp. I have no idea how many cycles such decay would take. I will have to investigate the tiny white spots I've seen, in the next few days.

—From the journal of Morvu Francita Januti

We stopped early that day, taking time to wring out our clothes and shake out the ropes.

"It's nice to see the walls fade again," I said to Mom as we sat together in one hammock, chewing on seaweed wafers. The light from the walls was turning orange and deep red. "Partino would have enjoyed seeing it." We had to sit close to each other to hear over the constant noise of the waterfall.

Mom put her arm around my shoulders and squeezed. It was hard to have any contact when we were climbing, and I leaned into it. I sniffed.

"Yes, he would have," she said. "I wish he was here too."

No. Hold it back. Not now! It's been five days!

I sobbed into her shoulder. I heard her sniff too, and that made me feel better. If Mom was crying about it, then it was worth crying about. We sat that way for a long time, but both of us felt better afterwards.

The walls slowly turned dark, and Mom and I watched the waterfall arc over us—droplets falling into the clouds below.

* * *

The next day, we climbed as close as we could to the bottom of the waterfall, right where the wall swelled out into the largest curve I had seen. It was like a giant ripple, or a cresting wave stuck at the midpoint, and it spread out as far as I could see to either side, above our heads. It gave a little protection from the water.

We hadn't been using the goggles the last couple days inside the clouds, because it was too dark. Now we all had them back on, except for Wailimani, who was squinting, and occasionally wiping water out of his eyes. None of us offered him a pair.

I stared up at the bulge in the crystal where the waterfall splashed outward. The swell in the wall had a little overhang.

Like a nose on an immense face.

"Can we call it the Wall's Nose?" I shouted over the noise.

Mom shrugged. "Fine with me."

The majus nodded. "You have a way with words, girl," she called.

Still with the name. I'd have to find a way to show her I was more than a girl. I was Mom's eldest child. I'd be following in her footsteps someday.

Wait. When did I decide that? I'd been angry at Mom for dragging me on this expedition. I wanted to stay home with Alondri and Kayla, studying the artifacts Mom brought back. Except I didn't, anymore. I wouldn't have missed this sight for all of Etan.

"If I had *my* way, I would be calling it the Waterfall's Annihilation," Wailimani piped up. His shrill voice cut right through the noise of the water.

We all glared at him, and Mom went so far as to climb down and get the map of the wall out of the net. She had been tracking our distance each day. Now she made a note on the graph she had drawn, marking 'The Wall's Nose,' in large letters.

The Kirian glowered, and his crest stood up straight in frustration. "I am seeing how much I am contributing to this expedition."

"You weren't *invited*," I told him. Since the water was so loud, that meant I could shout at him and pretend it was just so he could hear. *If you weren't here, then Partino would be.*

"Now I am present, I can be helping publicize any discoveries we make." Wailimani waved a hand. "I am seeing the sketches you draw, and the notes Morvu makes. I have been making notes too. There is plenty of fame to be going around."

"It isn't all about fame!" I shouted at him. "It's about learning about where we live, and why the Nether acts like it does."

"An apt summary of being a naturalist," Mom added in a loud voice. "Which you, Wailimani, are not. You are only an opportunist, plain and simple."

"*Though I agree, bickering won't help us climb*," Majus E'Flyr said. I stopped with my mouth open, ready to support Mom. The majus' voice had gained...strength, I suppose, bellowing over our argument. She must have done something with the Symphony. Her head was tilted up, her silvery eyes fixed on where the beetle hung stationary, right below where the Nose swelled from the rest of the wall. "I need to give the drill new commands." Her voice was still loud, but no longer overwhelming, now she had our attention.

"I...yes, you're right." Mom said. "I was wondering why it had stopped again, but I was afraid to ask."

"She isn't sick again, is she?" I shouted.

"Machines cannot be getting sick," Wailimani put in. He had no trouble being heard.

I rolled my eyes at him. I think we'd established how much his opinion mattered.

"It must have detected it could go no further," the majus said, ignoring both of us. "As far as I can tell, there is no problem. I just need to get closer."

We made our way up the last few holes and tied our ropes to the beetle. If she had gone farther, she would have had to climb almost upside down. That was probably why she stopped.

"Can we get over the Nose and climb up the current?" Mom shouted as loud as she could. I could see the tendons in her long neck sticking out, and her face was darker blue with effort, just so we could hear.

"We could, but we'll hit the waterfall, and I don't think even the drill could hold on in that deluge," Majus E'Flyr said, pointing with a long finger to where the spray jetted out nearly horizontal, not far above us. "I might be able to strengthen the connection between the drill and the wall, so it can climb over, but it will take a lot of my notes." She was speaking at a normal volume, as far as I could tell, but her words were clear.

I wish I could do that.

"Can the beetle climb sideways instead?" I shouted, looking from Mom, to the majus, to Wailimani.

"That would work better. Your daughter has a good mind," the elderly Lobath said. She pulled her head-tentacles back and tied all three in a knot. "Let me see what I can do."

Well, I guess 'your daughter' is better than 'girl.' I'd take the upgrade. I felt my lips twitch up in my first smile since the accident.

We waited while Majus E'Flyr stuck her head inside the hatch in the metal shell of the beetle. Wailimani hung to one side in his harness, frowning at nothing. His crest was wiggling like he was deep in thought, though.

"Should be able to do it," she said finally. I let out a breath I didn't know I had been holding.

"We'll lose time, but it looks like the only way is to go around. This waterfall must have edges," Mom shouted.

The sheet of water cascaded from above, breaking on the Nose. The ridge in the wall went on as far as I could see in either direction, making a kind of overhang sheltered from the torrent. Surely the ridge had to smooth out somewhere, so we could climb over.

"Which way?" Wailimani asked. His crest was under control now, and he showed no trace of remembering our disagreement.

Mom brought out her telescope again and looked left, then right, then up. "I think I can see the Nose get smaller to the right, but I'm not certain."

"Right it is," the majus said, and stuck her head back in the hatch.

"Why did you look up?" I called to her.

Mom bent her head close to mine, holding our harnesses close together. "I was trying to see if the roof of the Nether is visible yet." She shook her head before I could ask. "I can't see anything with the waterfall and the Nose in the way. I'll have to look again when we're out from under it."

It took most of a lightening for the majus to make the changes to the beetle, and while she did that, Mom and I fashioned earplugs out of the wax that was keeping the rations from getting wet. We had to stuff them in pretty good to deaden the noise of the waterfall. The majus waved us away when we tried to give her earplugs. The Lobath didn't even have any folds on the outside of her ears—just little holes in the side of her round head, under where her head-tentacles started.

Finally, Majus E'Flyr signaled the crystal beetle drill was ready. Mom and I hooked our food net to the shell of the beetle with the rest of the supplies this time. It would already be hard to climb sideways. The pulleys we'd used to hoist the net up wouldn't work going sideways.

We were almost done when I realized Wailimani was waving an arm at us so fast he was twisting around in his harness. We took our earplugs out so we could hear him. "Why do we all not simply ride on the beetle?" he shouted.

Mom and I looked at each other. "We're too heavy," she shouted back. "The drill can't hold all of us. We tried when we first discovered it, back in Broken Column."

The Kirian raised a finger. "It *could not* be holding you all before. But I am to be much lighter than your porter, and you have been eating your rations. We are weighing less now."

Mom frowned. I could tell she wanted to argue.

That's all right, Mom. I want to argue too. Any time the Kirian mentioned Partino, I wanted to hit him. I took in a deep breath, then let it out. *And hitting him won't do anything, will it?*

Unless he falls off the wall and then the beetle has to carry even less. Then we won't need four climbers.

Majus E'Flyr considered our group for a long time, then went to the nets hanging from the beetle, touching each one. I saw her head-tentacles twitching in rhythm, like when she was doing something with the Symphony.

Finally she came back to us. "We can try it. The strength of the drill seems to be a little higher than the weight of the party, but it's close."

The majus opened the hatch on the beetle's shell again and flicked a few switches. "I'll try it first, and we can add more people, one at a time."

Majus E'Flyr tied her harness to the intersection between the beetle's legs and body, and hung underneath while the metallic body rotated sideways, legs scrabbling. The beetle caught the holes she'd already drilled, and turned her head so it was pointing horizontally under the ridge of the Nose. She scuttled forward, then plunged her mandibles into the wall. I couldn't hear the hiss over the waterfall, but I knew the sound the crystal beetle drill made as she worked. Majus E'Flyr waved a long hand to us so we would climb after the beetle.

It was *really* hard climbing sideways. Mom and I had to support our whole weight while reaching out to install the next anchor in an open hole. Then we'd transfer our harness to the new anchor.

I'm so glad I have earplugs in. I looked back at Wailimani. His mouth was open, and I'm sure he was complaining about, well everything. *He's going to catch a mouthful of water. If he drowns, I'm not going back.*

After a few minutes, Majus E'Flyr climbed up and stopped the beetle, then gestured me join her. We arranged the ropes so I was tucked in, like we were both riding sideways piggyback on the crystal beetle drill. My legs dangled out over the white and frothy clouds below us. I was glad I couldn't see the ground from here.

After a few more minutes, Wailimani joined us. I saw Mom rolling her eyes as he passed her, obviously talking about how he should get a place before her because his shoulders hurt and he was so pitiful, blah, blah, blah.

Soon after, Mom joined us too. The beetle creaked a little when she got on and we all froze. We and the three nets were all hanging off the side of the beetle, nothing under us. If she fell off, we would fall like Partino and Wailimani's assistant. My heart skipped a few beats, and an image of a body, arms outstretched, flashed through my mind. I gripped the black metal of the beetle's shell.

Don't fall. Don't fall. You can do it! You're the crystal beetle drill! You're old and strong and you can do anything.

The beetle shifted, tipping out from the wall.

I yelled, and Wailimani yelled with me. *We're going to fall!*

But then she pulled herself back straight, putting her jointed legs in different holes. She reached out to drill the next set of holes, and her legs creaked forward, dragging us along, each step tipping us out over nothingness until the jointed leg found a hole and gripped it. We hung there while she continued to drill, and walk, drill and walk.

My heart was hammering, my breathing shallow. I wiped water from my goggles as the beetle kept moving.

"She's working!" I called out. Mom must have barely heard me, because she turned and gave a little grin.

* * *

We spent four days and three nights riding on the back of the crystal beetle drill, underneath the ridge of the Wall's Nose, wiping spray off our goggles, and listening to the roaring of water. There were little spots of moss on the underside of the Nose. Maybe dirt had somehow collected under there. I wanted to stop and get my notebook out so I could do a couple sketches of how the little patches of green grew. Could I figure out how they attached to the wall?

When did I start wondering about things like that?

I kept the earplugs in the whole time, mainly to block out Wailimani's whining. None of the rest of us did much talking. We slept where we were, in our harnesses.

At lunch on the third day, I saw Mom looking through the rations before returning with seaweed wafers and squid jerky. I was sick of them by now, and we'd been eating them long enough I knew exactly how much everyone got. There was a little less jerky than the day before. I looked a question at her, but she only shook her head.

We could see an edge to the curtain of water now, and it got closer, lightening after lightening. It was near dark on the fourth day when the bulge of the Nose began to fade back into the wall. The rushing water wasn't nearly as strong here, and stopped entirely a little further ahead.

Majus E'Flyr let the beetle run sideways until she crossed the last surge of water. Out here, without the Nose, the flow ran straight down the wall and into the clouds. The beetle didn't have much problem wading through this sheet of water. She just dunked her head underneath to drill, then moved her legs carefully to find the hole.

"Look there," I called. The waterfall was still loud, but we didn't have to shout so much, and I took out my earplugs, moving my jaw around to loosen things up.

"I see it too," Mom said, as she took out her own earplugs. There was another crack in the wall, where a sharp hunk of crystal jutted out like a thumb. On top of it grew a massive tree, its trunk sticking almost straight out from the wall.

"That is to be better," the Kirian explorer said, as soon as the earplugs were out. "I was worrying we would not be able to converse for the rest of the journey."

"How sad," I muttered. I caught the edge of a smile from Majus E'Flyr, but then she pretended to re-braid her head-tentacles.

"Are you not to be glad I was having the suggestion of riding the beetle?" Wailimani continued. "You see I am to be a benefit to the team."

We stared at him, and finally Mom said, "This doesn't make up for anything, you know."

"Give it time," the Kirian said with one of his pointy smiles.

Was that what the sneaky coward was up to, with all that frowning and thinking? Trying to make himself useful to us? Well it's not working!

The beetle climbed through the water to the tree, clambering up on the pedestal. The tree's base covered the thumb of crystal, spreading out and clutching with long dangling roots. Somehow another seed had grown up here, so far above the ground even the clouds were below us. It must have been hundreds of cycles old, branching into multiple gnarled limbs that formed a sort of platform, the leafy canopy sticking almost out to the nearest column.

The trunk was wider than the beetle, and she clambered up to stand on it. We could sit upright for the first time in days, and decided to stay the night there. While we made camp, the majus fiddled with the insides of the beetle, to make her climb straight up again, rather than sideways.

Mom looked up the expanse of the wall above us, the waterfall now to our left. "Can we ride the drill rest of the way up rather than climbing?" she asked. "We can attach the harnesses around the neck so we hang down its back."

Majus E'Flyr waggled one long-fingered hand. "Probably, but there was a lot of stress on the legs while we were climbing sideways. I don't think it was meant to do that."

"Could you make her legs stronger?" I asked. I had my notebook out, trying to get the long curving trunk of the tree just right.

The majus' silvery eyes looked even more surprised than normal. "Another good idea, Natina. Especially considering I will need to strengthen the whole party each morning if we do not ride the drill." She tugged on one head-tentacle. "I will think on it tonight while we sleep. It will require finesse with the Symphony."

I carefully did not jump up and down and cheer, partly because the tree was not *that* wide.

From 'girl' to 'daughter' to 'Natina.' I have to keep coming up with good ideas.

We hung our hammocks between the tree's branches that night. It was ancient, and its roots curved and gripped the jutting crystal like a vise. It was much nicer than getting jostled around as the beetle climbed. With the waterfall, the noise, and the motion, I hadn't slept well the past few days, but at least my arms and legs had rested. The majus was looking better too—not quite as purple and wrinkly.

The beetle stood motionless at the base of the tree, jointed metal legs stuck in holes among the tree's roots. I imagined she was sleeping too. *About time she rested.*

* * *

The next morning, the majus was up before I was, climbing over the beetle and examining her legs. Mom and Wailimani were at the supply nets, looking through the rations. I went to see the majus.

"So can you make the crystal beetle drill carry us without hurting her legs?"

Majus E'Flyr wiped grease on her orange jumpsuit. She had two suits—the orange one, and the blue one—but while we'd been climbing, both had become covered with grease and dirt. Mom and I had wrapped our flowing pants tight around our legs so they couldn't get in the way, and now there were stripes of dirt down them where they had touched the wall.

"Yes, I can make the legs stronger. The weakness is mainly in the side of the knee joints. I had to find the right melody to figure it out. Right there, see?" The majus pointed to the nearest leg with a long wrinkled finger. There were three round joints between the parts of each leg, which let them reach in all directions. I looked closer.

"It looks like the metal is curved outward. That joint won't bend very well. Is it supposed to be like that?" I asked.

The majus shook her head. "Our weight hanging off the side of the drill for four days caused the deformation." She straightened, then set her stumpy legs on the trunk of the tree, leaving her hands free. "I'll have to try something complicated. This will take a lot of my notes, and it will be permanent." Her large silvery eyes watched me. "That means I can't get those notes back. I will be tired for a few days, but hopefully we'll be climbing while that happens. Now watch."

I stared at her as she reached both hands out, and clutched two of the beetle's six legs. The majus tilted her head to one side, fingers tapping a slow rhythm on the metal.

At first I didn't see anything, but then I noticed the color changing. Usually the beetle was dark, almost black. But around each leg joint, her color was lightening a little. As I watched, it turned from black, to grey, to silver with a sheen of blue on top. I looked at the other legs. All of them had changed color.

Majus E'Flyr let go with a sigh, leaning back in her harness, which was still clipped to the tree. I caught her arm, which was dark purple again. Her skin was cold and clammy. She might have fallen off the trunk if I hadn't held her.

After a moment, the majus shook her head. "I am well, Natina," she said. "Just tired."

I straightened a little at my name. "What did you do?" I asked.

I'm helping a majus, discussing changes to the Symphony like it's a normal day! No one back home would believe this, even if they accepted that we'd climbed up the wall of the Nether.

"It's complicated," she answered, "but in simple terms I made the metal stronger right around the joints."

"Why did it change color?"

Something from the Symphony?

"It's a side effect," Majus E'Flyr said. "The metal alloy composition is a little different now, because I took some tiny bits of metal from around us, and in us, and from the surface of the wall. When I added them to the joints in a certain ratio, it made a stronger mixture of elements."

I nodded my head. Even if I didn't completely understand, I wouldn't let the majus know that. I'd be back to 'girl' in a moment.

Mom and Wailimani came back soon after, and we showed them what the majus had done.

"So, we no longer need a four-person climbing crew?" Mom said, giving the Kirian a very direct stare.

"If we leave him here, he can gnaw on the tree for food," I suggested. I showed my teeth to him. Mine weren't pointy, but I hope it got my attitude across.

Wailimani's crest rose and spread, and his eyes grew wide. "I have already showed I am to be helpful." His hands rose too, fingers with curving nails spread wide as if to ward us off. "I am having many good ideas. I can be helping you tell others about your adventures, and returning valuable artifacts to their owners. Whatever you are wishing."

Mom growled, then turned away. "No, we can't just leave you here, whatever you've done. That wouldn't be ethical."

I grimaced and looked to the majus. "We can't?" She hesitated, then shook her head.

"Whatever help you are needing," Wailimani said. "Only be telling me what—"

"Shut up," Mom said, whipping back around. The Kirian closed his mouth with a click of pointy teeth. "Just. Shut up. You'll come with us, but one more wrong move and..." she raised a finger, pointing out over the abyss beneath us.

Something else Mom didn't tell me about being a naturalist.

We tied ourselves onto the beetle, Wailimani with his head down, not saying anything. Our mount drilled new holes in the wall, making her way from the trunk of the tree to bare crystal again.

We'll have a fresh supply of water as long as the waterfall is nearby. I tried not to look at the Kirian.

Climbing was a lot smoother now the beetle was going straight up rather than sideways. She seemed to have no problem with our weight, maybe because of her orientation, and maybe because of what the majus did to her joints. We hung in our harnesses, tied to hooks and joints on the beetle.

My arms almost felt rested from the days of climbing. *I bet my muscles are twice as big as when we started.* I felt my upper arm when no one was watching. *Feels bigger. Not as big as Partino's arms, of course...*

I sighed, and turned to watch Mom, who was tied in on the other side of the beetle. Her brow was creased like when she was trying to do calculations, and not getting the answer she wanted.

"What's wrong?" I asked her. Then I remembered her and Wailimani looking through the rations.

"It's been about twenty-five days since we started from Gloomlight," Mom said. "I wasn't thinking the climb would last this long, or at least that we might come across some other food source. But it's been bare crystal, the whole way up."

"Except for those two trees," I reminded her. "And the moss."

"Yes, I was hoping to find more like that," she said. "However, I'm pretty sure that moss was toxic, and anyway, there weren't enough patches to be worthwhile."

"What about Wailimani's food?" I asked. I remembered the small bag they carried. I narrowed my eyes.

Wait, I don't remember seeing it for a while.

"Haribrana was to be carrying much of our supplies when he...fell," the Kirian explorer said. His crest was flat and spread out in sorrow. "We were not calculating to be climbing so long either."

"So our rations are getting low," Majus E'Flyr said.

We all fell silent for a moment, jolting around with the movement of the beetle. I heard the *hiss* of her mandibles drilling another pair of holes.

"We have another four days," Mom finally said. "Six if we stretch it out." She shaded her eyes and stared up the length of the wall. "I can see a haze up there. If it's the top, we can go a little light on meals and should be fine."

"If nothing else goes wrong," the majus said, and Mom acknowledged the comment with a shrug. "What if it's *not* the top?"

"Then you can make a portal to get us back down, right?" I asked. I could see the haze, too, and hoped it was the top of the Nether. I could be a little hungry for a few days, if it was the difference between reaching the top and *almost* reaching the top.

"If we absolutely have to, we can bail out early," Mom said, and grimaced. "But the original idea was for Majus E'Flyr to make a portal once we reach the top. It would let others travel directly there, now we've blazed the trail. Then we could explore more of the Nether's ceiling."

"Which should have been the real objective of this expedition," Wailimani piped up. "Who is to be knowing what awaits up there? I am to be looking forward to traveling back up once the portal is stable, with whatever we are finding. You will see I am to be very good at publicizing such adventures."

As good as he is at missing the point.

"That's the question, though," Majus E'Flyr said. She'd been quiet while we discussed the portals only she could make. "*Where* can I make a portal? I've told you, resistance from the wall interferes with big changes to the Grand Symphony." She concentrated for a moment, the ends of her braided head-tentacles twitching, then shook her head. "It is still harder than I anticipated, changing the melody up here versus on the ground."

"What does that mean?" I asked.

"It's how portals open," the majus said. "I am not sure if it's the height, or the lack of other melodies. I even went out as far as I could on the tree's trunk. The resistance grew less, but it still will not let me open a portal. We must find a platform away from this crystal surface."

Where are we going to find something like that? I looked up the expanse of the wall.

"Then we keep climbing," Mom said.

* * *

"Can you make out the top yet?" I asked on the third day up from the tree and the Wall's Nose. We were all still hanging off the beetle's back while it trundled upward.

Mom had taken her telescope out, and hooked her harness nearer the beetle's head as the wall dimmed. She was looking straight up. The waterfall was a curtain of rushing water to our left, and if I looked down, I could see the giant spray where it hit the Nose and turned into the cloud layer. There were still a bunch of rainbows down there.

"No—" she fell silent.

"What is it?" I asked. The majus and Wailimani also waited for her to answer. *At least he isn't complaining about his arms since we started riding the beetle.* Only that his harness wasn't comfortable, and that he was cold, and the ride was too bumpy...

"There's a big hazy mass of light up there." Mom panned the telescope left and right. "That might be the top, if it's made of crystal like the walls, but there are little bits interfering with the light. I can't make out what they are."

"Can I try?" I asked. She handed the telescope down and I was careful not to drop it, with the beetle bumping along.

I looked up.

Yep, it's a bunch of light. I moved the telescope left. *And there's the waterfall. It just keeps going, all the way to the top—* I looked closer, trying to adjust the little focus knob on the top of the telescope. *There's something at the very top of the waterfall.* I couldn't figure out what it was, so I moved the telescope around. *There are more things like whatever's at the top of the waterfall.*

"See anything interesting?" the majus asked.

I lowered the telescope. "Yeah, there's an object up there, but I don't know what it is. The same thing is at the top of the waterfall, too."

"It is?" Mom took the telescope back. "You're right, Natina. You have sharp eyes. I missed that."

So what is it?

* * *

We climbed through the night again, since the beetle had no trouble carrying us, especially with the dwindling weight of our rations. I slept off and on, waking up when my harness swung, each time she hit a section of the wall that curved out. She had to scrabble to get a good toehold in the holes she drilled. When I slept, I dreamed that the light from the top of the Nether had descended and was all around us, leaking out like water, sprouting tendrils that reached for us. The beetle stayed just beyond their reach, but they were coming closer...

* * *

"Huhhh! The lights," I said as I awoke with a start.

They were going to get us! Except, I didn't remember who 'they' were. The dream was fading like mist. I rubbed my eyes and looked around.

Is everyone else still asleep?

They weren't asleep, just silent—even Wailimani. The only sound was the hiss of the beetle's drill and the creak of her jointed legs.

Part of my dream came true. There were little white lights all around us! The beetle climbed through them.

"What are they?" I whispered.

"We don't know," Mom said. "Wailimani saw them first, a few minutes ago."

I looked to the Kirian, whose crest was wide and flat in astonishment, his mouth hanging open. He must have felt me staring at him, because he turned his head to look at me. "They are to be *beneath* the surface of the wall."

Beneath? That's impossible.

I looked over the side of the beetle, careful not to interfere with her steadily churning legs. I was lying along her back as she crept vertically, and the little white lights were all around, right under the reflective surface of the crystal. They were like little worms that had somehow dug into the wall, but none of them were moving.

"They're pretty," I said. I climbed up as close to the front of the beetle as I could, just behind her head, and connected my harness into a hook on her shell.

"Could you hand me my notebook, please?" I asked mom. She dug around and produced it, then handed it up. "I want to sketch this."

* * *

We watched the little white lights until midday, and as we got higher, they only got bigger.

By now we had all tired of watching them, though we appreciated the glow they gave. We hung in our harnesses, and I munched through my small lunch of wafers and jerky, almost happy we were running out. I was really starting to hate those things. At least the lights would guide our way at night, so we'd have fewer problems traveling.

Suddenly Majus E'Flyr jerked upright, grabbing at the beetle's shell for support. We all looked at her. "I can still see the glow," she said.

"Well, yes, if you look close enough," Mom replied. She looked around the side of the beetle.

"No, I can see the white glow clearly, even with the wall at full brightness. Even through these." She took off her purple goggles, her silvery eyes reflecting the wall's light. "It's the Symphony. They're alive."

"The Symphony? How is music supposed to be white?" I asked. Majus E'Flyr had told me about the different kinds of music she heard while we climbed, and how she changed it. This was something new. I couldn't hear anything, of course—*I know I'll never be a majus*—but I could still imagine the music she described.

"The Symphony isn't white," the majus explained, "but changes to the notes appear as colors to us maji, one color for each house."

"How is that to be helping us?" Wailimani asked.

"Well, changes made to the notes of the Symphony of Strength—my house—are surrounded by a green aura, to a majus."

"And? What about white?" I asked.

"That's the House of Healing" Majus E'Flyr said. "It deals with living things, and with biology."

"What is that having to do with you seeing white light?" Wailimani waved one hand at the wall. "We are all to be seeing white light."

"I'm seeing it all the time, and even through the light of the wall," Majus E'Flyr said, her head-tentacles twitching in excitement. "I see it *in addition* to the white light you see. The auras created by changing parts of the Symphony are different colors, but they're not light, exactly. They don't illuminate things. We can't use the auras to see by." She held up a wrinkled purple hand to stop my question. "So what that *means* is that these little things are very much in tune with the biological aspect of the Grand Symphony—enough to affect its notes."

"Which may be why they can burrow into the wall," Mom said. The majus nodded.

* * *

The majus might have been the one to figure out the little white things were alive, but I figured out what they really were.

"Roots!" I called out as the walls began to dim for the evening.

"Root of what?" Wailimani asked.

"Plants! Up ahead." I pointed above the beetle. I was strapped in closest to her dark metal head, which dipped down regularly to drill new holes.

Am I the only one who can see them? Maybe I do have sharp eyes.

"They're growing out of the wall—growing up from the white things," I said.

Now Mom came up next to me. "I see them," she said. "There's a whole field of stems and buds."

Soon the beetle was in among them, brushing through little green and blue and purple shoots growing out from the surface of the Nether crystal like grass. Their leaves were glossy and dark.

Mom reached over the side. Her arms were just long enough, as she rode on the length of the beetle's back, to touch the wall. She was the tallest of us, now Partino was gone.

Don't think about him.

She brushed her hands along the leaves of the plants, then she leaned even further out, and I caught her harness before she twisted off the beetle's back.

Mom came back up and presented a handful of black stuff to us. "Dirt," she said. "It must collect here, on the top side of the sprouts. That leads to another question though—"

"Where is the dirt to be coming from?" Wailimani asked.

* * *

We kept climbing through the night, and the beetle crept around the small plants, occasionally testing the bushier ones to see if they would hold her weight.

"Get some sleep," Mom finally said, when the wall was almost completely dark. I was looking around the side of the beetle, as the white roots of the plants gave off about as much light as the moons did back on Etan.

"I want to watch," I said. "How can you think about sleeping, with this forest sticking out of the side of the wall? It's so...*weird*." I'd given up sketching a few lightenings ago, when I could no longer see the lines I put down, but I couldn't stop peering at the plants.

'Forest' wasn't the right word, but there were larger bushes and even a few short trees, their trunks gradually curving up so the tallest ones were vertical. Their roots were a mass of light, reaching out in a great spider web of white beneath the surface of the wall.

"It will still be here in the morning," Mom said. She grasped a chink in the beetle's shell to steady the swing of her harness and peered up ahead of us. "As far as I can tell, the plant life only gets thicker. Now, go to sleep. You'll need your rest for whatever comes tomorrow."

I did eventually sleep, but it took a long time for my mind to quiet down.

* * *

The next day, the plant life was even thicker, and the beetle was rarely drilling holes. Instead, she climbed from tree to tree, and her jointed legs held onto bushes and large clumps of grass.

"Maybe we'll be able to have something different for breakfast," Mom said, pointing to a tree that grew right in our path.

"Are those toka fruit?" I asked. *I can't believe my eyes.* The fruit was found only in the Nether, but it was considered one of the best tasting fruits of all ten homeworlds.

"Looks like it to me," Majus E'Flyr said. She pointed to the trunk. "See the bark? It's got to be the same species. And in season, too."

I reached up as we passed between the branches and the wall, picking one of the purple globes that hung from the tree. These were some of the biggest toka I'd ever seen. I peeled the rind and bit into the ridged blue fruit inside.

"Mmmm." I let my eyes roll up. "Delicious!" *And not squid wafers.*

Mom, the majus and I all had plenty of fruit for breakfast, but when we offered one to the Kirian, Wailimani shook his head, crest up and pointy.

"Fruit is not to be something I like," he said, then made a quick motion with one hand. "The bugs that are accompanying fruit, however..." he raised a small flailing thing to his pointy teeth. I grimaced and went back to my toka.

No accounting for taste, at least not in Kirians.

I think that was the best breakfast I'd had in several ten-days. We all hung, relaxed, in our harnesses after we were done, resting along the black shell of the beetle.

"I'll have to pick extras and store them in the nets for later on," Mom said. "I'm not sure I can move yet."

"Better do it before we get out of this grove," Majus E'Flyr said.

"Maybe I can be catching extra flies along the way," Wailimani mused. "I was packing a jar somewhere in here for such an occasion."

I pulled myself up, grimacing at how the harness squeezed my full belly, then froze. *What is that attached to the trees?* Tied into the larger trees were long beams, cut square. I followed them with my eyes, out from the wall, where they met up with other beams in a crisscrossed array. The structure was like a giant treehouse, but on the edge of a forest, the last row of trunks supporting it out in open air.

"Mom!" I called, and pointed. She followed my finger, and frowned.

"Trellises," she said. "Those *can't* be natural, and look there! That one's still green wood—new construction. Someone *lives* up here."

"Uh, you can say that again."

I was staring at a face peeking out from behind a toka tree.

* * *

Majus E'Flyr climbed up, opened the hatch, and flipped levers to make the beetle stop climbing. I was the first off, making sure my rope was tied to one of her legs.

"Be careful. We can't tell for sure if it's a person or an animal—" Mom had one hand out, but I was already out of her reach, climbing from trunk to trunk. This was easier than climbing with the anchors—the trees grew so close I could step from the branches of one to the next. I swarmed up closer to the face.

Can't she see the way they're looking at us? I took in the big purple eyes that were flicking between me, Mom, Majus E'Flyr, and Wailimani. *That's a person, like us.*

"Hello?" I called. "We won't hurt you. We want to meet you. Can you tell us where we are?"

I kept calling out questions as I climbed toward the face. I passed from bush to tree, finding handholds easily. The face had ducked behind the tree, but slowly came back out as I kept talking.

Only a little bit closer. A little more...

"Hi there," I said, as I grabbed the trunk of the toka tree. The face was close now, and I saw the eyes watching me, the mouth working.

"Uh...hi," the face said in a low voice. "Who are you? You look...different."

I smiled back, thankful the Nether let us all communicate with each other. This would be harder if I had to learn a new language, or was on one of the homeworlds.

I put a hand on my chest. "I'm Natina Morvu Januti." I snuck a look down at the beetle. Mom was climbing closer, through the foliage, but the majus and Wailimani still hung from the beetle's shell. "That's my mom, Morvu Francita Januti, and on the crystal beetle drill are Majus E'Flyr," The majus waved a long-fingered hand, "and Surigran Wailimani." I tried not to scowl as I said his name. Then I looked back at the face, hoping this person would show us more of themself. "What's your name?"

"Avi," the person said. "That's short for Avi Iva Vana Vinai Aivi." One hand crept around the trunk of the tree. The fingers were brown, with skin stretched between them, and had green fingernails.

"Avi," I said. Hopefully I could learn the rest of their name soon, but it had all come out in a growling rush, the words echoing off the wall and nearby trees. I only caught the first part. "We're part of the Great Assembly of Species. My mom and I are Etanela, and the majus is a Lobath. Wailimani is a Kirian." I held my other hand out, showing my bluish skin. "You can see us. Can you come out so we can see you?"

Avi waggled their head, which I thought meant 'yes,' and slowly came out from behind the toka tree. The face was long and pointed, with a beak below large purple eyes. Avi had something not quite like feathers, and not quite hair, that extended backwards from their head. Their body was short, with stumpy legs that gripped grasses and plants. But their arms were longer than mine, and I could see the flaps of skin that connected their hands to their sides. Avi was wearing a white smock that covered their shoulders and legs, but had holes for the excess skin.

I took in a deep breath. "You can fly, can't you?"

Avi nodded. "Can you not?" Their purple eyes shifted behind me. I looked down as Mom's hand patted my leg. Wailimani was off the beetle now too, his eyes roving over my new friend.

Like he's hungry.

"No," I answered. "We all have to climb if we want to go somewhere high up. That's how we got up here."

"What do your people call themselves?" Mom asked quietly.

"We are the Grumv Vugm Mugv," Avi said. Their language was a growl, deep in their throat, and it echoed. Anyone nearby would be able to hear them clearly. "My family farms the grove for the city. I can take you to meet them, if you want."

"We'd like that very much," Mom said.

* * *

Avi's family lived in the treehouse, supported by wooden beams tied into the strongest toka trees on the farm. As we got closer, we could see there were steps and grooves cut into the top of the beams, so that a person climbing through the trees growing from the wall could step directly onto the trellis.

Majus E'Flyr led the beetle to the base of the platform and then flipped a bunch of levers that told her to stay put until we got back. The beetle gripped two trees, folding her legs in around them. The trees creaked as she did.

I helped Mom and Wailimani untie the ropes attaching us to the beetle, while Avi looked on, their head cocked in curiosity.

"Why do you tie yourself up?" they finally asked.

"It's so we don't fall," I told the Grumv. I had my legs wrapped around a tree trunk and waved one of my arms in the air to show I didn't have the same webs of skin Avi did.

Avi cocked their head the other way. "You mean like this?" They summersaulted backwards, wings unfolding into giant triangles of skin connecting their body and hands.

"What—" I saw Mom's eyes widen in surprise even as my heart caught in my throat. I could only see Partino, tumbling end over end, until he disappeared into the clouds.

Don't cry. Not in front of Avi. I'm not just a silly girl.

But Avi didn't fall. Instead they glided out from the wall, away from the trees in a slow spiral. We watched as the Grumv made a lazy circle, then turned back in our direction. They didn't flap their wings, but drifted up, maybe catching a patch of hot air. They landed a little below us, then came back to our level with great leaps from tree to tree, their wings unfolding with each jump, strong short legs propelling them upward.

Huh. Well, that's a good reason for being shorter than an Etanela, I thought. Mom and I couldn't have made those leaps, even if we had wings. Our legs would have gotten all tangled up in the branches.

Avi was panting when they got to the beetle and us.

"You don't actually fly, do you?" Mom asked. "You glide."

Avi tilted their head back and forth. It seemed like they didn't see a lot of difference between the two.

"Well, if you are to be done giving us all attack of the chest muscles," Wailimani complained, "perhaps we can be entering your home."

Avi unfolded a hand to a step carved half into a toka trunk and half into a beam. I glared at the Kirian.

You didn't need to be so harsh. I carefully unclenched my hands from where I'd grabbed onto my rope.

We transferred from the toka tree trunk to the broad trellis, crafted from several overlapping wooden beams tied into separate trees with what looked like thick white rope.

There was no rail to hold onto, as we moved through the trees and away from the surface of the wall, but there were many branches to catch hold of.

I suppose the Grumv don't need to worry about falling.

"Careful," Mom said, as the branches thinned. She must have been thinking the same thing I was. "We should tie our harnesses together."

"So we can all be falling off if one does?" Wailimani asked, his crest spiky in fear.

"I will not fall," Majus E'Flyr said, from behind us. Her boots made solid smacking sounds on the wood beams, and where the rest of us were hunched over, trying to stay as close to the beam walkway as we could, she walked upright, confident. She must have changed notes of the Symphony so she had a stronger connection with the wood, like she had when she stood on the back of the beetle. "Avi can lead us, and I will follow. The rest of you tie onto my harness, and if anyone falls, I will bring you back up."

The branches here were not big enough around to support my weight. We were emerging into open air, away from the wall and the canopy of the vertical forest, but the trellis continued. We passed by other beams connecting to trees farther away, and above and below. They gave stability to the bare stretch of thin trellis—no branches and no rails—

leading from us to a low rounded structure of wood—Avi's house. Below us I could see giant beams, and even trees trained to grow straight out from the wall, supporting the structure.

"All well and good, but shall we be walking all the way back there so you can be getting in front of us?" Wailimani pointed back to the wall.

"Not a problem," the majus said. She grasped the Kirian's robed arms with her long fingers, and spun in place, so he was behind her. I forced my lips together so I wouldn't laugh at the expression on Wailimani's face—it managed to be offended and amazed at the same time. Avi didn't have the same restraint and made a bubbling, coughing sound deep in their throat.

I was next and Majus E'Flyr lifted me up as easily as if I was a bag of groceries, then spun and plopped me down behind her. It was like being lifted by a rock. She didn't even wobble. I watched in astonishment as she even did the same thing to Mom, though she was half again the majus' height.

"Well, I guess that will work," Mom said, a little breathless.

We passed our ropes forward, tying onto Majus E'Flyr's harness, and continued after Avi.

The Grumv looked back to see we were following and continued their loping pace across the trellis, using both webbed hands and feet.

"You are like the holy one," they called back after a moment. "The one who changes the music only he can hear."

The majus paused in the middle of a step, just for a moment, then continued walking. "You have a majus?" she asked. Her voice was tight and controlled.

She's as surprised as we are. I'd gotten to know her well over the past few ten-days.

"If that is what you call the ones who change the music, then yes," Avi said.

* * *

Avi's house was very open. The outer structure looked like a lot of cylinders, made from stacked and curved beams. Inside, woven mats were suspended between the walls to make the floors. The mats hung down in the middle, so each room was shaped like a bowl with a springy floor. The center of the bowl dipped as we entered, stretching so low my chest was about level with the beams that divided this room from the next. Wailimani put his hands out to his sides, balancing on the shifting mat.

Will this hold us all? Thoughts of falling sped through my mind, but as I put out a shaking hand to the nearest beam—at head level—I realized the mat was quite thick, and didn't look unsteady at all. *They're supposed to act like this!* I pulled my hands in, getting my balance.

Above, more trellises acted as ceilings, but they weren't covered. I saw rolled up mats attached to some beams, so maybe they could roll them out like awnings if they needed to. *I need to sketch this house when we get settled. I've never seen anything like it.*

"Mater, Pater, I've brought new friends," Avi called out, though anyone in the house must have seen us coming from the wall. Overhead, I could see more thick beams and the trunk of one particularly tall tree, tying the house into the top side of the vertical farm.

I could just see farther into the house, and the nearest woven bowl wobbled as if someone was inside. Then a head, like Avi's, poked over the side.

"Avi! You are well?" Avi's mater sounded uncertain, as I'm sure I would if three new species had appeared at our house on Etan.

"I'm fine, Mater," Avi answered. "They're from below the white sea. They're explorers. They say there are many more who live down below."

The head poked out again, then swiftly down. "I always thought those stories were made up," Avi's mater said. "But if you are certain you are well, then bring your new...friends here, and we will learn about them, and get them something to eat."

Avi spread their wings and vaulted over the side of our bowl into the next, then popped her head back out.

"Over the side to enter." They cocked their head. "You will have to climb, like an old one with holes in her wings."

Majus E'Flyr went first, and her long fingers clung to the mat as if they had been glued there. She vaulted gracefully over the top, then tugged on the ropes connecting us to let us know we could follow.

We climbed over, Wailimani complaining the whole way.

"This is to be undignified," he said. "Falling over woven grass, my legs and arms to be waving in the air for all to see!"

Not again. I rolled my eyes at Avi, whose head was cocked to one side again. It seemed like the Kirian didn't like it when his ankles or wrists showed.

Isn't that pretty much impossible to avoid while climbing? What did he think would happen?

After we pulled Wailimani all the way in, still grumbling, we turned to Avi and the larger Grumv who stood behind them, arms protectively around them. Avi's mater's eyes were wide, her wings drawn in tight around Avi.

"Hello," Mom said to the other Grumv. "I am Morvu Francita Januti and this is my climbing crew. We come from the ground of the Nether—a journey of many ten-days. We represent three of the ten species that live below, and we are very excited to meet you and your species." She gave a little bow, like when Etanela greeted old or respected members of society.

The other Grumv gradually uncrossed their arms, then spread wings out to their full extent. Their voice shook, then gained strength. "I...I welcome you, on behalf of the Grumv Vugm Mugv. My spouse will be here momentarily."

"Spouse?" Mom confirmed, and the Grumv tilted their head in agreement. "Are you...female? If you don't mind me asking?"

"I am," the Grumv said. She was calming down, though her eyes darted between the four of us—no doubt marking the differences in our species. "I am called Mira Arim Rima Rait Mairi, but you may call me Mira."

Mira was like Avi, but larger, like Mom was larger than I was. She had the same brown and green skin, the same hair/feather plume on top of her head—if a little longer—and even wore a tunic like her child, though Mira's was pale green.

That's strange, I thought. *Is this what Mom thinks about all the time, being a naturalist? How you classify the new things you discover?*

The same way the Nether helped us all communicate with each other, it also usually gave us hints about what gender a person was, since it wasn't always easy to tell between species. But I couldn't tell if Avi was a girl or a boy. They were just...Avi.

I was about to ask, but there was a rustling from the next bowl over and a huge...*stunning* creature vaulted into our bowl.

Mom caught her breath, and Wailimani took a step back. Only Majus E'Flyr stood still, considering the new creature.

He's beautiful. There was no doubt this was a male Grumv.

Where Mira and Avi were brown with green patches, This Grumv's upper body and head were bright blue and green. Instead of a simple plume of hair and feathers, he had a crest that draped down his back, white, but tipped with blue and orange in little patterns that reflected the wall's light when he moved. This crest flitted and flapped as his eyes pinned each of us in turn.

His wings were folded closely to his sides now, but when he had been crossing between the rooms, I'd seen circles of blue, orange, green, and purple on his wings. I couldn't tell if they were natural colors, or some sort of tattoo. Beneath his deep maroon tunic, even his legs were bright orange and deep black. He was a full neck and head taller than his wife.

Remember this too. I have to draw them tonight before I go to sleep.

"Welcome to our home, strangers," he said. His voice was a deep rumble I could feel through the woven mat. There was a threat in it, if we did not obey the hospitality of the house. "I have heard your introductions. Excuse my lateness. I was setting our table with toka and other fruits from our farm. I am Hria Airh Riha Rani Hairi. You come from far below?"

"Hria," Mira said, wrapping one long brown arm protectively around her husband. Her wing fell like a blanket around his shoulder, highlighting the differences in her drab coloring and his brightness.

"Very far," Wailimani said. "We were not knowing there were people like you up here."

"We did not know of you either," said Hria. "I think we were all surprised." Then his crest settled. "But I must admit, we are interested to meet—three is it?—new species. You must tell us more of what exists below the white sea."

I felt the tension in the bowl-like room ease as Avi's family accepted us. With our initial surprise and hesitation over, I turned to Avi, more comfortable with someone about my age, while Mom and the majus and Wailimani talked with Avi's parents. I couldn't help comparing Avi to Mira and Hria.

"Sorry for asking, but are you...more like your mom, or your dad?" My new friend looked a lot more like Mira, but didn't have the same kind of softness their mother had.

That sounded so awkward. I hope Avi knows what I mean. I hope I didn't offend them. There were a lot of differences in the genders of the ten species of the Great Assembly.

Fortunately, Avi seemed to understand exactly what I was talking about. "I haven't decided yet," they said, "but I've always thought it's better to be smart and sneaky, like Mater." They leaned in close, gesturing with one webbed hand. I put my head close to Avi's. "I love Pater a whole lot, but you know what men are like, all loud and colorful. Can't help but spread their wings."

I chuckled. I think I knew what Avi meant.

"Plus, there are a lot of men in the town right now, so it's probably better if I become female when I molt."

I nodded like I understood what Avi meant. *Something else for the notebook.*

"Did you already choose to be female?" they asked. "Some kids do that earlier than me. My friend Luna did."

"I—choose?" I stuttered. "Uh, it works a little differently with my species. I've always been female, like Mom."

Technically, I'm a dominate female, like Mom, instead of subordinate, like Kayla. But I could already see Avi's eyes widening, and figured now wasn't the best time to explain the little differences between my two mothers. Even species familiar with the Etanela had a hard time telling our different genders apart.

I wanted to talk with Avi more, but the grown-ups were looking like they had agreed on something. I listened to what they were saying.

"...welcome to eat with us tonight. Avi told us you like toka fruit," Hria was saying, stretching his arms out to display the colors on his wings.

I traded a look with Avi. *Men.*

"It's just this way," Mira said. The two adult Grumv hopped over the dividing beam holding the two woven bowls up. Mom, the majus, Wailimani, and I climbed over. We were still tied together. Avi helped us, curious to see how we worked without wings.

In the next bowl, we untied ourselves from Majus E'Flyr and set the harness and ropes in a pile to one side. We'd be safe from falling, as long as we stayed inside the house.

There were little hammocks, strung between sides of the bowl, filled with purple toka fruit, and others I didn't recognize. Avi showed me how to grasp the top of a hard white berry, and pull the insides out like an ice pop.

Wailimani looked concerned, his crest drooping, until Hria pointed out a pile of wriggling worms in a little hammock by themselves. Wailimani's crest rose quickly, and he patted Hria on the back, before picking a particularly hairy one up and sucking it down. I shivered.

At least the Grumv have a little bit of everything. They're very kind, especially to three completely new species. I don't think I'd be this calm. Maybe it was just their way.

I looked up. Now we were out from the wall's light, I could see more detail, and caught my breath. "Look, Mom, Majus E'Flyr! It's the ceiling of the Nether!"

They looked with me. The top of the Nether was visible without a telescope, a mass of light, crystal like the walls. The nearby column rose to meet it.

"Finally," Mom breathed. "I wasn't sure I'd ever see this." She reached out and grasped my shoulder, and I sniffed back a sudden lump in my throat.

Against the lit crystal were other shapes, like this house, but much bigger, if I judged distances correctly. It was beautiful.

We stared for several more minutes, Avi's family pointing out different features to us.

Finally, I turned to Avi. "Does it ever rain up here?" I asked. "I mean, we climbed through the clouds on the way up from the ground."

"Clouds?" Avi tilted their head, then clacked their beak. "Oh, the white sea below us. No, there is none of that above, only the light from the ceiling." They waved one hand upward, stretching out their wing. "Sometimes the ceiling gets drippy, but if it does, then we can pull those mats overhead to make sure nothing gets too wet." They indicated the rolled material hanging from the beams above my head.

I looked out the other way, while peeling a toka fruit. The waterfall was just as big up here, a rushing mass of water that passed close to Avi's family's farm.

"What about that? Where does all the water come from?"

I'm asking questions like Mom does. I always thought it was rude that she skipped around to so many topics when she talked to people. Now I see she just wants to know everything.

"My mom says our ancestors made the great water happen, a long time ago," Avi answered. I looked down at them. "The town gets a lot wetter than we do down here, since it's closer to the ceiling, and so people directed all the wet away from them. Pretty soon all the water connected up and became the great water. I hear the other towns do the same thing."

"There are other towns up here?" I asked. *Mom will want to know this.*

"Several," Avi said. "But I've never been to one. Mater and Pater stay busy on the farm. They say we might go to visit—"

A shout from the other side of the room interrupted Avi's words. "What is that to be?" Wailimani said. He was on his tiptoes, crest spiking out to all sides. At his feet was a big hairy creature with a mass of eyes and a beak at the front, and at least eight long black legs coming out from its bulbous body.

I jumped back too. *Did a creature from outside get in?*

At the Kirian's yell, the creature had scuttled across the floor, away from him, with surprising speed.

"Churi Iruhc—there you are!" Avi met the creature halfway across the bowl and ruffled the black hairs behind its eyes. "Did you eat all your leaf fleas? Did you? What a good boy!"

The creature snuggled up to Avi's hand and made a chirping noise.

"This is your...pet?" Majus E'Flyr asked. Even the normally unflappable Lobath was having a hard time not moving away from the little monstrosity.

"Yep!" Avi said, leading the creature forward. "Mater and Pater said I could keep Churi Iruhc here with us, rather than with the rest of the herd."

"The herd?" Wailimani's crest was trying to escape his head. I took a little bit of guilty pleasure seeing him squirm.

"Another part of our livelihood," Hria explained. "The toka trees are our prime crop, but we also grow several other types of fruit, and milk the Arach Hanar for their silk, which we sell to the tailors in the town, who make our clothes." Hria picked at his tunic with one hand.

"Speaking of the town," Mom said, "I would greatly like to see it. Could one of you take us there? We'd like to learn more about your people, and offer a gift from our government to yours."

My mind went to the sealed box Majus E'Flyr had shooed me away from the day we started climbing the wall. It had slipped my mind on the climb, buried at the bottom of the net with the scientific equipment.

But that would mean Mom, and others, thought there was a chance we'd find people up here. She was prepared for this.

Mira and Hria exchanged one of those glances like Mom did with Alondri and Kayla when they were trying to decide something.

"The crops," Hria began, but Mira flipped a wing out, and he fell silent. Then she tilted her head in Avi's and my direction, and Hria took in a deep breath, the colorful plume on his head perking up.

"We must stay here to harvest toka tomorrow," he said. "They are at their full ripeness, and we will get the best price for them." Mom's shoulder's drooped and she opened her mouth, but Hria kept speaking. "However, I think we can get by without our Avi for a few days. They need to bring a crate of silk to the town anyway."

Mom straightened. "That would be quite helpful. Avi has already been a superb guide."

"The town has no doubt seen you already from the telescopes in the holy one's home," Mira said. "It will be good to arrive with an escort of one of our own people."

"Thank you," Majus E'Flyr said.

I looked back and forth between my group and Avi's family. They had promised we would be watched.

Surely they don't think we'll hurt their child? But we were strangers. I wondered what I would do if a new species appeared on the beach near our home on Etan. *Could I lead them to the nearest city?*

"For now, please, finish your meal," Hria said. "We will give you hammocks to sleep in, and you can begin your journey early in the morning, if that is acceptable."

TEN-DAY FOUR

Top of the Nether

This species, far from being the poor community I was imagining upon finding a people living in isolation at the top of the Nether, were actually to be quite rich. They were having access to several types of material that cannot be found anywhere else in the ten homeworlds and the Nether. I was trying my best to create a lasting trading partnership, but alas, my efforts were to be stymied by my accidental traveling companions.

—From "Remembrances from the Wall of Light," A memoir by
Surigran Wailimani

We left early the next morning, accompanied by Avi. Once out of the house, we attached our ropes to Majus E'Flyr, and made our way back down the main beam which connected the Grumv's house to the wall.

It was nice walking upright for a while.

At the wall, Majus E'Flyr reactivated the beetle, and we tied our ropes to her shell again and got on board. Avi carried a net filled with white fiber—the silk delivery for the town, and hooked it to another leg. It weighed almost nothing.

Churi Iruhc skittered along beside us, clambering from tree to tree, and Wailimani kept well away from the creature.

"Will...he come all the way to the town with us?" I asked Avi. I watched the way the little beast hooked his hairy legs over the plants, climbing as quickly as I could walk on the ground.

The way his legs can support his weight is fascinating. He's sort of like the beetle. I wonder if the people who made it watched creatures like this.

"Only to the rest of the herd," Avi answered, spreading their wings to hop over a few bushes and cling to a tree. "He likes to see his family every couple days, but he always comes back to the house."

558 William C. Tracy

"We will be seeing more of them?" Wailimani asked. His crest was spiky and I tried to hide a smile.

Yes, Churi Iruhc is pretty scary, but he's not as devious as you, once you get to know him. I reached down with one hand to gently pat the coarse black hairs on the Arach Hanar's head. He bumped his head up into my hand and I drew it back quickly, then realized he wasn't going to bite me. I rubbed his head again, and he made that chirping noise.

"Aw, he likes you," Avi said.

I glanced back to Wailimani, whose lip was curled up in a sneer, his crest straight back in disgust. "Don't pay any attention to that Kirian," I told Churi Iruhc. "He's just a big baby." *And maybe a murderer.* Wailimani had been on his best behavior since Mom threatened him at the big tree by the waterfall, but I felt like the warning was losing its effectiveness. We could give him another reminder, but it wouldn't work as well with all the trees around us to catch onto.

Wailimani grunted, but the majus chuckled, from where she rode in front of us. The sweet scent of toka fruit was everywhere, like a coating of jasmine and marzipan.

Along the way, we passed Hria, already out among the toka trees, his brilliant coloring standing out even among the green and brown and purple of the trees, and against the early morning shine from the brightening wall. He was lobbing ripe fruit into a net strung between two trees, and waved to us as we passed. We waved back.

"How does he get all that fruit back to the house?" I asked Avi, who was hopping along beside us, from tree to tree to bush. Mom turned around, interested.

But I asked the question before she did, didn't I? That's what comes from knowing how to research, not just stumbling on things out in the world. I sat a little straighter.

Avi hopped near the beetle and grabbed on so they could talk to us. I froze, remembering the beetle tipping out from the wall, under the waterfall, but Avi must not have weighed much. The beetle kept her steady crawl upward, jointed legs wrapping around the plant life that grew from the wall.

"See right there?" Avi pointed with a finger of one webbed hand, and we all looked up and to the left. There was a pulley system, attached to a particularly large toka tree. I followed the smooth white ropes out into the distance, where they intersected the house.

"Do you carry everything by pulley?" Mom asked. "I can't imagine you can hop or fly, holding a bag full of fruit."

"We use the pulley for most things," Avi said. They scratched at their chin. "For long distances, we hook up one of the bigger Arach Hanar with nets, like you're doing with this mechanical beastie." They thumped one hand on the beetle's shell.

I made a mental note to write down my theory about the beetle's designers the next time I had my notebooks out.

It was most of a lightening later when we got to the herd of Arach Hanar. I could feel Wailimani and Majus E'Flyr both tense up beside me when the mass of webs came into view, crossing from tree to tree, but Mom leaned forward.

The creatures saw us coming too, and swarmed along sticky strands, hissing and chittering. The creatures seemed offended by the beetle's slow lumbering climb up the wall, as if she was going to invade their webs.

"Quiet down!" Avi shouted, and the chittering lessened. "Pater will be along soon to get your silk, so be good."

As we came closer, one Arach Hanar, with silver spots interspersed in its coarse black hair, came off the webs, and approached us, front legs waving in the air at the beetle.

"Hm. A defensive posture similar to the small arachnids on the floor of the Nether," Mom said, leaning out over the side of the beetle. "I wonder if they are related species?"

Well, maybe finding stuff out in the middle of nowhere can help as much as research, sometimes.

"I can study them when we get back to the floor," I volunteered. Now I took my notebook out and jotted down a note, as well as the other things I'd thought of. I tucked it tight into my harness, in case I thought of anything else.

"Perhaps now is not to be the best time to play scientist?" Wailimani said. He jerked one foot back under his colorful robe, away from the hissing Arach Hanar.

"Oh that's Mater Rutha Ahtur," Avi said. "She runs the herd, but don't pay her any mind." The Grumv leaned out and thunked the big creature just above her beak and under her mass of eyes. The Arach Hanar chittered again and backed away. "Get back now. Back to your web and leave these nice people alone."

I heard Wailimani let out a long breath as the big creature moved off.

I hope he didn't wet himself. We have a while until we get to the town. I carefully kept the smile off my face, and watched the herd as we climbed past, wondering if there were creatures like this anywhere else among the ten species.

* * *

It took the rest of the day to climb up the wall to the Grumv town. We had plenty of time to talk with Avi, and learn more about their culture, as the beetle trundled upward. We watched the bright haze of the ceiling gradually coalesce into a sheet of crystal like the walls. The wall itself was hidden by the vertical forest, but now the top of the Nether hulked over us, stretching out into the distance as if we were in a giant cave. It was bright enough I could pretend it was the sky on a cloudy day, but it still made my shoulders hunch.

As we got closer to the city, the mass of beams and woven mats got clearer. The individual buildings had curved walls like Avi's home, giving the town an organic feel. There was a low wall around the whole thing, and I could see a huge system of pulleys around and below the town, with goods being carted back and forth along them. There were even a few other Arach Hanar, climbing along the pulley lines or on the underside of the great woven bowls. Some had riders, and their coarse hair was painted in patterns and stripes. I made a sketch in my notebook so I could study it later.

Word of our arrival had traveled ahead of us, and I saw other young Grumv, brown and green with short plumes, looking over the edge of the bowls, or hanging from plants on the wall. Avi waved to one of them.

"That's Luna. I'll introduce you later."

We reached the edge of the city near evening, and Majus E'Flyr brought the beetle to a halt. There were three Grumv waiting where a wide trellis was tied into the plants growing from the wall. We transferred our ropes to the majus' harness, climbing the last distance to where wooden trusses tied into two giant trees, arcing sideways from the wall.

The delegation stood on carved steps, and posts behind them bore lights on top. The lights, which we hadn't seen at Avi's family's house, were all through the city, making it sparkle in the waning light from the walls. With the dimming ceiling close overhead, it felt almost like we were in a huge building, with smaller, circular, houses built inside.

The leftmost of the three winged people was an ancient and stooped male, his once bright colors muted and faded. His crest was limp and fell to one side.

Next to him was another male, much younger. This one reminded me of Avi's Pater, with bright green and blue around his head, and short yellow and black legs. He spread his wings as we approached, and I could see a pattern of hexagons mixed with what I thought were letters and numbers of the Grumv language.

So they are tattoos on the wings. I wonder if any of the coloration is natural? I looked behind the three to where other Grumv stood, waiting for us to come closer. There was less coloring on the younger males, when they opened their wings. I'd have to discuss the markings with Mom later.

"We welcome you to our city," the third of the trio said, and I brought my attention back to the group. The female was the one who had spoken. She was just as drab as the other females, her skin bland brown with green striping. But she held herself upright, her hair and feather plume sticking straight out. Her large blue eyes shifted from Mom, to Majus E'Flyr, to Wailimani, and finally to me and Avi. "I am Kita Atik Tikka Akan Kaiti, the mayor of this town." She gestured to the two males. "This is Gami Imag Maig Agga Gaima, our city's announcer, and Shura Aruhs Hara Raaka Shiare, our holy man." The younger man bobbed his head at the first name, and the older one swept one wing in front of him at the second.

"We have been traveling for many days and are being honored to meet you," Wailimani said, pushing in front before Mom could introduce us. We all glared at him. "We represent the people from far below, living on the floor of the Nether."

He's going to try to take advantage of these people like he did to us. But this wasn't the place to start an argument with him.

Fortunately, Mom edged around the Kirian. "Yes, *I* put together this expedition to explore the wall." I heard the emphasis in her tone. "We wanted to be the first to find out what the top of the Nether looked like. We could not guess your city was here, but we look forward to our future relations."

Wailimani tried to step forward again, but I stamped on his toe and he glared at me, his crest all spiky. *Not so fast.* Meanwhile, Mom took the chance to introduce us.

"You stay out of this," the Kirian hissed at me in a low voice. "I am having one chance to make an impression on these people. They may be having unknown kinds of wealth."

"Which is *theirs*," I whispered back. "Remember what Mom said? You don't have any more chances with us. We're meeting a new *species*, for the Sea Mother's sake! They may not want to even come down to the floor of the Nether."

Wailimani glared at me, but said nothing.

He'll find someone to talk at, the first chance he gets. I need to watch him.

"...and we met young Avi at their parents' farm yesterday. They volunteered to bring us to meet you." Mom was still speaking to the mayor.

"I am most interested to talk to a fellow majus, or holy man," Majus E'Flyr said to the old Grumv—Shura. "Which Symphony can you hear?"

The old Grumv perked up at that, speaking in a scratchy, but resonant voice. "I hear the Symphony that interweaves through all living things, playing the notes of their heartbeat and growth."

"We call that the House of Healing," Majus E'Flyr said. "I hear the House of Strength—the Symphony that binds and strengthens living and nonliving objects." She tilted her head to one side, her head-tentacles twitching. All I noticed was that she planted her feet more firmly on the beam supporting us, but the old Grumv's eyes widened.

"Yes—the emerald green of your changes is familiar. I have heard our city far to the other end of the Nether has a holy one who can hear the same song." He spread one wing, pointing along the dimming wall back toward the waterfall. "My teacher heard the song that connects all things and creates heat. An orange aura."

"The House of Power." Majus E'Flyr nodded. "We have much to talk about."

"As do we," Kita, the mayor, said. She pointed behind her. "Please, come into our city."

* * *

We had an evening meal with the Grumv mayor and a few others who helped run the city. They had to push some other Grumv out of the door of the cylindrical building, and roll down one of the mats they used for doors. This species seemed generally friendly, and they were all eager to meet us, or at least stare at us. I probably would have been the same. The ten species had been together a long time, but there were Etanela who hadn't ever left their homeworld. Even though I'd traveled a lot with my family, I still found some of the other species strange.

As the mayor spoke, I let the string of names wash over me, and watched the ceiling of the Nether above us slowly darken, through the building's open roof. I let out a breath. *We made it*. Except our goal felt like second place, now we'd met the people who lived within sight of it. I thought it was a fair trade—I liked the Grumv.

I went to a hammock of toka fruit hanging on one side of the massive bowl serving as town hall. The open area was as wide as our house back on Etan, and ripples moved through the mat as people walked on it.

I looked down at the floor as I chewed the blue fruit. *How did they weave so many fibers together and keep it from breaking?* There were white strands running through the mat, like the ropes Hria used to pass his produce back to the house. Come to think of it, all the pulley systems had the same white rope.

Oh! Arach Hanar silk! It must be very strong to support the biggest creatures. White strands ran all through the mat, most of which was made of plant fiber. I would have bent down to look closer, but Avi approached me.

"Pater said I could stay with you while you were in the city, if that's all right," they said. "I don't have many friends here, except for Luna, since Mater and Pater's farm is so far away." They looked down at the mat, then back up.

"Of course it is!" A well of relief rose in my chest. *I was hoping Avi would stay with us.* "I have a few friends back on Etan. Maybe I can introduce them to you sometime." I gave an overdramatic sigh. "And I suppose you'll have to meet my two younger brothers, even though they can be pests."

Avi laughed at that, a deep grunting. They reached out and put their arm around me. It was like being wrapped in a cozy blanket, with the skin of their wing draping down my back. The Grumv all had a warm, spicy smell, strong but not unpleasant. "Come on," they said. "The toka fruit is good, but I bet you don't have any yuka akuy where you come from."

"I don't think so," I said, and followed them to the other side of the room, through shadows cast by more pillars with those strange lights on top.

Mom was talking with the mayor, and Majus E'Flyr was deep in discussion with the old holy man, but Wailimani was off in another corner, three male Grumv standing around him, their heads close together. The Kirian's crest was spiking up and then relaxing as he talked, and he gestured up and around, and then down below his feet.

I'll be keeping an eye on you, Wailimani.

* * *

We were given rooms in the city, which consisted of cylindrical walls and flexible floor mats, like at the farm house. The ceiling of the Nether was wet that night, and this close, I could see drops falling all over town. It was like a slow, but steady rain. Other Grumv were in the beams above the city, rolling out the mats that were normally kept stored to one side of the rooms.

Avi was staying in my room and we both rolled out our ceiling mat to keep off the rain. It was lighter than it looked, and I got a good chance to see the Arach Hanar silk running through it. While the other fibers ripped if you put too much pressure on them, the silk was much stronger—I couldn't even break the thinnest strands.

This would be great for climbing ropes.

"What a jewel night," Avi said, as we finished rolling out the mat.

"A jewel night? What do you mean?" I looked up as we attached the other side of the mat to hooks on a beam. "Oh. I see." The ceiling was almost dark, but the water collected on it reflected the last bits of illumination, bouncing the light in all directions until it looked like a sky full of stars back on Etan. It was a relief from the hemmed-in feeling I'd had all day.

"Isn't it beautiful?" Avi said.

"It is," I agreed. We sat there for a few minutes, taking in the vast ceiling of the Nether. Not far off, I could see where the nearest column— the one I'd kept an eye on the whole climb—met the ceiling. Around its edge, there were even more shining water droplets, like hanging bunches of grapes that glowed green and blue and purple.

"Come on," Avi finally said. "We should get to our hammocks. I'm sure your mater and the others want to explore the town tomorrow."

I agreed, and we climbed under the roofing mat.

"How do we make those lights stop glowing?" I asked. I looked at the five wooden posts placed around the circumference of the bowl-like mat. On the top of each one was a small glowing object like I had seen around the town.

"Oh, that's easy," Avi said. They went to a post, and picked up the little object. Its light faded away, and they put it back. "Just think about the light going off."

Just think about it? That's strange. But I walked to the nearest light post and picked up the rough object sitting on it.

"This is like the Nether wall!" I said. After climbing up it for so many days, I knew exactly what the smooth, almost slippery crystal felt like.

"That's right." Avi went to another light. "We sing to them to harvest them. Don't you have them on the floor of the Nether?"

"Harvest them? No, we don't. Wait—sing?" I stared at the crystal. *Turn off,* I thought. The faint light faded from the crystal and my eyes widened.

I need to tell Mom about this. Before Wailimani learns about it.

"Avi, your people can break off parts of the Nether wall? I thought that was impossible!"

Avi shrugged expansively, opening their wings. "Sing, not break. That *is* impossible. And the singing takes a really long time to learn. It's not like we can do whatever we want with it."

I placed the lump of Nether crystal back on the lamp post. "It's still something special. None of the ten species can do it."

In the dim light, we climbed into our hammocks, made of more Arach Hanar silk, and despite my excitement, the comfortable bed lured me to sleep.

* * *

The next morning, I found Mom as soon as I could. She was in front of the building we'd slept in, running a hand over the trellises that made up the streets of the city. The planks were set in a mesh, just far enough apart so we had to watch where we stepped. We couldn't fall through the holes, but we could certainly slip a foot through if we weren't careful.

"Where's Wailimani?" I asked.

"He went off with those new friends of his," Mom said, pointing toward where the nearest column stretched up through a section of beams. The Grumv's city extended past it, all the way to the next four columns. There must have been thousands of Grumv living here to take up that much area.

There was a stairway winding partway around the column, reaching toward the ceiling, and I could just make out mesh strung around it, as if to catch something—like crystals sung from the Nether wall.

I bet he already knows. That Kirian was devious, cowardly, and would take any advantage he could find.

I told Mom what Avi and I had talked about last night. Fortunately, the Grumv was off getting their breakfast, so we had a little privacy.

"I think Wailimani wants to make a deal with the Grumv, but he will make sure he gets a lot more out of it than they do."

"Hm." Mom bit at the end of one of her fingers. "You might be right, but if he makes a deal with the Grumv, I can't stop him. As much as I dislike him, and...what happened, he has a right to negotiate on his own."

"Partino would still be here if Wailimani and his assistant hadn't joined us!" I said, louder than I meant. I'd thought about him less and less each day. *Does that mean I'm a bad person?*

"What happened to throwing him off the wall? We never found out what really happened." I tried to lower my voice. "What if Wailimani told his assistant to cut Partino's harness?"

"First, we're not on the climb anymore," Mom said. "We're in civilization, and I'm sure the Grumv have rules for people who don't fit in with regular society." She passed a hand around, taking in the buildings. "Second, he's done nothing since I gave him that warning. He's been good."

"Wailimani hasn't done anything because he *needed* us," I said. "He practically *told* me when we entered the city that he would take as much from the Grumv as he could."

Mom's lips tightened. "Then we'll both watch him. I trust him just as little as you do, but if we tell the Grumv they should lock him up—or whatever they do here—with no reason, we may lose any chance we have to trade with them. They have things here the rest of the ten species could use. Did you see the Arach Hanar silk? It's stronger than anything I've seen before."

I nodded. "I noticed it last night at dinner."

"I'm going to do tests on it today. Kita is letting me set up my equipment in their medical clinic." Mom looked up as Majus E'Flyr came toward us from one of the other cylinders.

"Have you asked her about the portal back home?" I asked.

Mom shook her head. "I didn't have a chance last night. The majus was talking with the holy one all evening."

The Lobath stumped up to us, the ends of her head-tentacles twitching around her shoulders, unbraided. Her surprised-looking, silvery eyes took us both in.

"Before you ask, no, I can't make a portal back," she said. "That strange interference from the wall is still too great, and the ceiling being so close only makes it worse. We have to get farther out. The holy one and I will visit the edge of the city to see if it will work out there."

My shoulders slumped. *I don't want to climb all the way back down.*

"We need a portal *somewhere* if the ten species are going to trade with the Grumv." Mom said. "Don't they go back to their homeworld, or visit the other Grumv cities up here?"

Majus E'Flyr lifted a long purple finger. "That's the interesting thing. Their holy one didn't know about portals. The Grumv travel the long way from city to city. They have waystations along the path, reaching between cities. Gami the city announcer is responsible for calling to the next waystation. It's a position of high status."

"Oh!" I said. "That makes sense. Did you notice how deep the Grumv's voices are? That must be so they can hear each other across long distances."

Mom was nodding along. "That's a good observation." She put a hand on my shoulder and squeezed. "Remember when you thought being a naturalist and explorer was a silly thing to do?"

I dipped my head. "I kind of got to like taking notes while we were climbing," I told her. "And it's better exercise than sitting at home. I've almost filled up the notebook." Mom looked surprised. "I can show you what I have."

A big smile crept over Mom's face, and I felt like there was a little fire in my chest. "I'd like that," she said. "Perhaps we can write about what we've found up here together."

I felt my eyes widen. *My name, on a scientific paper like Mom publishes?*

"Touching," the majus said, drawing our attention back. "But you missed the other important point. The Grumv don't *know* about portals." She waited, eyes flicking between Mom and me.

Both of us drew in a deep breath at the same time.

"They don't have a homeworld!" I said.

"That's right." Majus E'Flyr's head-tentacles flopped as she nodded. "They're isolated here. Maybe they came from a homeworld originally, or maybe they somehow evolved here. We don't know enough about the Nether to say for sure. In any case, they've been here for centuries. They don't remember any other home."

* * *

Later in the morning, Avi's friend Luna came by. Luna Anul Nulu Nali Luina was Avi's best friend in the city, and had already gone through her molting. She had chosen to be female, and I could see the small differences between her and Avi, like more curves and a slightly shorter beak. Luna was friendly, but more aloof than Avi. She only stayed a short time, more to see the strange new species, and report back to her other friends. Avi promised to tell Luna all about our first meeting, once they were finished helping us out.

I spent the rest of the day with Mom and Avi, setting up her equipment in the medical bowl. This space had its roof rolled out all the time, because there was equipment in here the Grumv didn't want getting wet. We saw a lot of other faces peek in through the windows, and the mayor came by a few times too. The Grumv were as interested to find out about us as we were of them.

Everything in the city was made of wood, and that made a lot of sense now. They couldn't mine for metal up here, and couldn't go to a homeworld to do so. They used the Arach Hanar silk for binding things together, and even had a process using an acid made from an insect living in the trees to turn the silk into resin.

They also used the Nether teardrops for many things other than light, like lenses and focusing devices. Avi told me there were ways to sing the crystals into different shapes while harvesting them. It took cycles to do so, by Grumv trained their whole lives to sing in a certain way. The shaped crystals were some of their most prized possessions, traded with other cities and handed down as heirlooms.

I wrote all this down in my notebook, and even showed Avi a small coin of Nether crystal—the money most of the Nether used. Mom had given me a piece before we started and I'd forgotten about it, tucked in a pouch in my clothes bag.

"This has been sung," Avi said, holding the small triangular piece of money, "and to a very precise shape."

"It's what the people down below use for money," I told them.

"Then you *do* know about crystal singing!" they cried. "You lied, last night!"

I held up my hands. "I didn't—I promise!" I took the triangle back. "All the money for the Nether comes from the Effature's palace and the Council of the Maji. No one knows how it's originally made."

"This Eff—Effature must know," Avi said, still peering over their beak at me suspiciously.

I nodded. "Probably, but there's nothing else made from this material, not like what you do. If the people down there could make other things out of Nether crystal, they would have. Maybe there's only a fixed amount?"

Avi lost interest soon after that, but I drew the triangle in my notebook, just in case, and then one of the unshaped lights, and a crystal lens one of the Grumv doctors let me hold.

Wailimani had snuck out that morning, before any of us realized where he was going. We didn't get a chance to find out what he was doing until that evening. He had found out about the crystals on his own, and I could tell from his pointy-toothed smile that he thought he had an advantage over us. I glared at him as he passed by the medical cylinder.

The majus came back that evening, after walking all around the edge of the town.

"I think I can make a portal, but it will take a few days," she said.

"A few days? Why?" I asked.

"The Grumv will have to build a special platform," Majus E'Flyr told me. Then she looked to Mom. "The edge of the town is far enough away from the wall and ceiling's interference to make a portal, but the streets of the city are not quite low enough. I could hang down on a rope and open a portal back to the Imperium, but when I tried to return, it would be as risky as opening one halfway up the wall."

"We've had enough of falling on this expedition," Mom said, and I shivered.

"That's what I thought," the majus said. "So I explained the situation and the holy one agreed to have a special platform built, but it will take a few days. He's keen to learn about portals. He's been to the Grumv city on the other side of the Nether in his youth, and believes he may be able to open a portal there, once I show him how."

"We'd be able to trade with all the Grumv, not only this city," I said, and the majus nodded.

"Then we'll use that time to study," Mom said.

* * *

The next day, the Grumv began working on the extension to their city, under the supervision of the majus. There was a quick-growing tree they harvested and sawed into beams to form their trusses. The wood was soft, but the intersecting planks of the trusses made their walkways very strong. Without metal, the trusses were bound together with clever joints and resin made of Arach Hanar silk.

Mom and I did a little research that day, with Avi's help. My new friend showed off their wings, and how little their body weighed, compared to us.

"Hollow bones, like a bird," Mom said, using the little portable scale she brought. It wouldn't have been able to hold my weight, but Avi was much lighter.

"If you're so light, why haven't any of your people tried to come down to the bottom of the Nether?" I asked them.

"Cross the white sea?" Avi asked, then shrugged. "There's nothing to grab onto, below where the plants stop growing."

"Without portals, it would be a one-way trip for them, much as for us," Mom said. "Though they would be much less likely to be hurt, since the Grumv glide." She peered at Avi, as if considering her size. "Do you have a cemetery, or museum, or someplace you put your ancestors who have died?"

"There is the temple of the honored dead, except no one is allowed in there but the mayor and the holy one," Avi told us.

"Maybe you could ask them," I suggested. I wasn't sure what Mom was getting at, but she probably had a reason for asking to get into somewhere off limits.

"I'll see what I can do," Avi said, but they looked dubious.

That night, when Majus E'Flyr came back from helping with the new construction, Avi was still off talking to someone about getting us into their temple.

"Tomorrow, you think?" Mom asked her when the majus had finished washing sawdust off in the bathing bowl, woven of tight silk fibers coated with wax.

The majus looked even more surprised than usual, her wide silver eyes reflecting the wall's evening light, then counted on her fingers. "Tomorrow's the fourth day again, isn't it?"

Fourth day? What's that mean? I looked at my watch. I'd gotten out of the habit of using it, while climbing, and stuffed it into my carry-bag. Only now, when we were on relatively stable ground, had I started wearing it again. I counted back in my head. It was the thirty-fourth day since we began preparing the expedition in Gloomlight.

"What's that mean?" I asked, and both Mom and the majus looked at me.

"I was meaning to tell you," Mom said. "I honestly thought we would reach a place to rest before now, but we've barely had a chance to stop."

"Tell me what?" *I thought I knew everything she did about this expedition by now. Am I still too young, after all that's happened?*

"It's in here somewhere," the majus said, and went to a bag still partially packed with Mom's equipment.

"What are you hiding?" I asked Mom, and she looked away from me.

"I did really mean to tell you, but it was decided before I asked you along and...it's complicated."

I opened my mouth to ask her *again*, but a shout from the majus interrupted us.

"Got it!"

Majus E'Flyr pulled out the box of spongy wood with the strange hexagon on top. I'd completely forgotten about it. She poised one hand above the hexagon, the other holding the box up. "The majus from the House of Potential tuned this lock to the House of Strength so I could open it," she said. Her hand didn't touch the metal, but something inside clicked. She must have changed the Symphony.

We all peered into the box. The walls bent under Majus E'Flyr's fingers, like the wood was from a mushroom instead of a tree. The inside was filled with shredded pulp, and I hesitantly reached a hand out to draw some of it back.

"Go ahead," the majus said.

I pulled the fiber back. *Now I'm allowed.* I remembered the majus' reaction when we started the climb. I must have impressed her along the way.

Inside was a perfect sphere of Nether crystal, bigger than both of my hands together.

"What...?" I said.

What reason is there to ship even more crystal up here?

"It's from the Effature himself," Mom said. "He gave it to us when he approved the expedition. We were alone with him at the time. I don't think even the Council of the Maji knew about it." She looked to the majus.

"I didn't tell them," Majus E'Flyr said. "The Effature has reasons for doing what he does, not that I know what they are."

"It's so smooth," I said, tracing my fingertips across its surface. I could barely feel it—only as coolness under my hand. There were no imperfections and almost no friction to the surface. Colors rippled in the wake of my touch. "Oh—I didn't mean to—" I took my hand back quickly.

The majus chuckled, and put the lid back on the box. "It won't connect properly until I make some adjustments. I'll probably need the help of the Grumv's holy one as well."

"Connect?" I was still lost, and looked from the majus to Mom, who shrugged.

"I still don't completely understand it," Mom said, "but the Effature says he has a matching one down there." She pointed.

"Another of his toys locked away where the maji can't find it," Majus E'Flyr said, with a frown. "I've told the Council more times than I can count that the maji should have free reign to explore the Effature's treasure trove, but somehow my request always gets lost going from them to him." She shook her head. "We should be able to talk to him directly with this. He gave us a window every fourth day when he would be available."

"Talk—with the Effature?" I had only ever seen the old man a couple times, and from a distance. He presided over the Great Assembly of Species, when it met in the Dome of the Assembly. People said he ran the Nether, but I wasn't really sure what that meant.

"Tomorrow night," Mom said. "We'll have to get the mayor, the announcer, and the holy one to attend." She paused. "And let's try to keep this between us. No Wailimani."

"No Wailimani," Majus E'Flyr and I agreed.

* * *

The day after passed in a blur—I could barely wait for the meeting that night. I tried to help Mom out with her experiments, but hardly remembered what I'd done minutes after I finished.

"Did you prepare that slide yet?" Mom's voice cut into my thoughts.

"Oh...uh, yes." I looked down to the piece of glass in my hand. It was smudged, but I thought it would still let Mom see what the Grumv's hair looked like under magnification.

Is it time yet? The light of the walls seemed to creep toward darkness, and our meeting with the Effature. *Will he be there? Did he remember us? Will the sphere even work?*

"What's hanging on your wings today?" Avi asked, when we were alone for a few minutes, but I could only shake my head.

"I made Mom promise you could come too," I told them, "but she said I couldn't tell you yet. We're not supposed to tell Wailimani either, because he's—"

My words died as a shadow darkened the door of the medical cylinder. Wailimani's feathery crest was spiky with interest.

"Be telling me what?" he asked, showing his pointy teeth. His high-pitched voice grated on my nerves. "Thought I was still to be talking with my new associates? I have concluded those negotiations, and I am thinking your mother will be cursing her ancestors that she did not take the same opportunity I was." His crest expanded in triumph. "Not all here are liking the idea of ten new species to deal with, but with a little carefully applied negotiation, I am to be bringing their leaders around to trade possibilities."

I stayed silent, frowning at him. Avi's eyes were wide. The Grumv wouldn't know much about relations among the ten species, however, I'd read my history. There had been pretty big fights between the species in the past, some started for less than this.

"Fine, do not be telling me. I will simply be staying nearby until time for this secret." He plopped down in a corner, staring at his long, curving fingernails.

When Mom got back, she stared daggers at the Kirian, but there was no way we could slip away without him following.

* * *

That night, eight of us met: me, Mom, Majus E'Flyr, Avi, the mayor, the holy one, the city's announcer...and Wailimani. If the Grumv noticed our discomfort with the Kirian, they politely didn't say anything.

We were all in the mayor's home, sitting in hammocks strung together in a circle so we could speak. Majus E'Flyr set the open box down between us, on a little table. "This is a gift from our government to yours—a way to communicate from the top to the bottom of the Nether."

The Grumv peered forward. "More Nether crystal?" Mayor Kita asked. She didn't seem upset by the gift, just confused.

"It's not just any crystal," I told her. "It's tuned." I wiggled my legs in the hammock, wanting to get up and walk around. I'd spent the whole day thinking about this. I'd seen Nether crystal do amazing things.

"It took most of the day," the holy one said in a shaky voice. I thought he might be even older than Majus E'Flyr. "I heard melodies I have never heard before. It is an incredible piece, touched by many holy ones, all changing the music at once."

"Tuned to do what?" the mayor asked.

Mom cleared her throat, I think trying to control the flow of the conversation. I watched Wailimani. Unlike his usual manner, he had been silent the whole time, fingers touching in front of his robe, his long, thick nails curving over each other.

"You will be able to speak with the Effature," Mom said. "He's our— well, not our leader, exactly. He is a caretaker of the Nether and its people. He presides over the Great Assembly of Species, which is a place where representatives from all ten of the species who live at the bottom of the Nether come together to discuss."

"Like a moot of the village mayors and holy ones," Mayor Kita said, and Mom nodded. "There has not been one of those since I was a child. The distances are very great."

"They will become shorter, once we can create portals between your cities," Majus E'Flyr said.

Gami the announcer rustled his wings at that. "This will be a change for all of us, my profession especially. I am happy for the benefit these other species will provide us, but there are others here who are not as certain. I hope this Effature can reassure our people."

Mom looked to me. "What time is it, Natina?"

I held my watch up so it reflected one of the crystals set around the room. "Seventh darkening, just now," I said.

Majus E'Flyr carefully raised the sphere so it rested on top of the padding in the box. "It's time," she said. "Holy one, if you would care to assist?"

Both maji stared at the sphere, Majus E'Flyr's head-tentacles twitching in a rhythm, and the holy one nodding his head to a tune.

The rainbow of colors began again, like it had when I touched it, and there was a creak as everyone leaned forward in their hammocks—even Wailimani.

The colors mixed, and crossed, and made new colors, until I realized I was looking at the back of a red, stuffed chair. The sphere gave out a sharp chime, and I heard two voices, one deep and warm, the other higher and younger.

"Ah, I believe I will have to cut this meeting short, Sam," the warm voice said. "There is other business I must attend to."

"That's...um...fine, sir," said the younger voice, and I saw a shadow of dark hair and a green vest rise up and out of view. "Should I shut the door on the way out?"

"If you don't mind, Sam." The warm voice said. There were footsteps, and the gentle click of a door handle.

Then the view in the crystal tilted crazily. Avi and the other Grumv started back, and I tilted my head, trying to make sense of the change.

The scene came to rest looking upward into an old man's face. He was Methiemum—the trader species, and most common of the ten. The face was kindly and wrinkled, a contrast to Wailimani's. This man was mostly bald, and there was a circlet of crystal on his forehead, a simple curve.

"Greetings, Morvu, Magara. I take it this means you have met with success in your expedition?" The voice from the sphere sounded smaller than ought to, but the words were clear.

I looked to the majus. I hadn't heard her familiar name the whole time we'd been climbing.

"We have," Mom said. "And we have someone to introduce to you, if you will come around the sphere." She opened her hand over the ball of crystal.

The Effature's figure moved around the edge of the crystal, as if he was walking around it, and then disappeared, but the mayor and the city announcer sat up. Gami the announcer spread his wings just a little.

"Greetings from the Grumv Vugm Mugv," Gami called in a deep echoing tone. "We are told you have an assembly of different species— ones who are willing to meet and trade with us for benefit of all."

"It is a pleasure to meet you," I heard the Effature say, though I couldn't see him anymore. "You are correct. We have welcomed several new species in the past few centuries, the newest only fifty cycles ago.

The Great Assembly is ruled not by any one species, but by our common interests, building a better society for all. We look forward to learning from the Grumv Vugm Mugv."

"Then you have no conflict?" Gami pressed. "There are some here with concerns that such a large population, with so many different types of beings, may take advantage of our people."

I frowned. I supposed that was true, but didn't the Great Assembly make rules that helped everyone? I'd have to ask Mom about it later. Beside me, Avi was tilting their head back and forth, perhaps thinking the same thing.

"It is true we have disagreements." The Effature sighed. "I will not lie. We even make war between us. But the vast majority wishes to welcome all to our society, and learn how those with different opinions can add new and beneficial possibilities. Our progress depends on the species working together, not taking advantage of others."

"That is reassuring," Gami said.

"Plagi's group will resist, of course," the mayor told Gami. "But I think we can talk them into joining this Great Assembly. They like their profit, after all, and so many different people will have a lot of new skills and tools to trade."

I snuck a glance at Wailimani, whose eyes had lit up at the mayor's remark. I was sure he already knew this Plagi.

The talk went on far into the night, but through it all, Wailimani said nothing, his crest rising and falling, his fingers clasped together.

What are you thinking about?

* * *

"Five days until we see your home!" Avi repeated for maybe the tenth time that morning. "I can hardly believe we'll be able to travel instantaneously to all these places. So many new people to meet!"

"It will take a little longer to get to my home," I told them, but I was counting down days in my head as well. "We're going to the Imperium. It's a city where a lot of rich folks and the maji live. I live on Etan—it's a completely different planet, and not like the Nether."

"But you know what I mean." Avi bounced up and down on their short legs. "I want to see your planet too—everything! Can we help the builders cut the logs, or bind them together? Anything to make it go faster."

"Then they won't be ready down there," I said, pointing at the bowed mat of the house we stayed in. It had become our gesture to refer to the floor of the Nether. "The Effature is planning for our group to arrive in five days, not before. That's as long as Majus E'Flyr said it would take to build the new platform."

I thought of my brothers, and of Alondri and Kayla. It had been a long time since I'd seen my other parents, and to be honest, I was ready to go home too. But that would have to wait until after all the festivities about a brand new species joining the Assembly died down.

I peered out the window of the cylindrical house. As always, there was a group of Grumv on the trellis street outside, hoping to get a glimpse, or talk to us. Most of them were really friendly, and seemed to be looking forward to meeting the other species, but there was always a small group who stood apart, glaring at us when we walked around the city. I hoped they wouldn't cause trouble.

* * *

We were granted entry into the temple of the honored dead on the second day after meeting with the Effature, but only while escorted by the holy one.

The old Grumv led Mom and me almost back to the wall, where a pyramid of six long, crossed beams were covered with a shroud of woven Arach Hanar silk.

The majus wasn't interested in bones, and Wailimani had disappeared again after crashing our meeting, no doubt trying to seek out Plagi and the others who only wanted a profit. The mayor said she wouldn't stop any of her people from making private agreements with those from the ground, and I was sure Wailimani was getting a head start while Mom and I learned about the Grumv's culture.

Avi wasn't allowed in the temple, and had to wait outside, their wings wrapped close in annoyance. They glared at a couple Grumv who had followed us—a brightly colored male and a female who looked like some of the ones who weren't sure about us being here.

"Only the most revered of our people are laid to rest in the temple of the honored dead," the holy one said. "The others are cremated, and the ashes help to fertilize the forest grown from the wall."

I traded looks with Mom and wiped my hands on my pants while the holy one wasn't looking.

At least now we know where the dirt comes from.

The temple was small and smelled musty and stale, as if—well, as if something had died in here, but a long time ago. A few crystals were placed to light the inside.

Many of the bodies still had skin, and hair. The coloring on the males was faded until it was hard to tell the difference between them and the females, except by size.

"Back here, you will find what you are looking for." The holy one hobbled forward on stumpy legs, flaring his wings out every few moments.

I don't think he's thrilled we're here.

In the back were the skeletons. They were smaller than I thought they would be. The Grumv were not large, but without the webbing connecting their arms and legs, the skeletons were tiny.

"I wish I could take a sample of the bone, but I promised the holy one and the mayor I wouldn't," Mom whispered.

"It would help if we could at least touch them," I said. The long skeletal arms were wrapped around the bodies, making it hard to tell which bones belonged where.

Mom leaned closer to a particularly old set. "Wait a moment." She looked back to see the holy one staring at us, and put her hands behind her back, bending so her nose was almost touching the skeleton. "I've seen these before."

"Seen Grumv skeletons? Where?" *Avi said they didn't go past the clouds.*

"I've dug some up, in remote sections of the Nether, near the wall." She straightened, and went to another skeleton. "Yes, I'm certain. They were very broken and disjointed, but I was able to reconstruct most of one, about ten cycles ago." She straightened, and looked at me. "I thought it was an extinct species of bird."

"It is, sort of," I said. "Falling all the way from the top of the Nether would break anyone's bones—" I stopped, looking at Mom, who stared back at me.

Flailing arms and legs, reaching out to catch him...

I shook the thoughts away, and Mom put a hand on my shoulder. We stood there for a moment.

"I wish I could take just one skeleton back," Mom whispered as we left the temple. "It would prove Alondri and Kayla's theory right."

"None of you ever told me about this theory," I said, pushing down my irritation. I'd helped my parents with their research since before my little brothers were born, and this expedition was the first time I'd heard anything about it. "Why didn't I know?"

Mom sighed. "It was nothing to do with you. Your other father, Jonduri, originally came up with it, but he was ridiculed, and after he died, we kept it secret that we still worked on his hypothesis. We never told you about it because Alondri and Kayla wanted you to have a chance at a fresh start, if you chose the same career we did. There was plenty else to research." She looked around the temple at the decaying bodies and the skeletons, as if building up courage. "Jonduri thought there had been meetings between those who lived on the Nether floor and beings who lived near the ceiling, many cycles ago. Even the idea there *were* beings up here was controversial."

"And that's why the Effature gave you the crystal spheres?" I asked. Mom nodded. "Well, we can prove now there are people here. But if there really were meetings, wouldn't the Grumv remember?"

"Not if it was a one-way trip," Mom said. "Maybe not all those skeletons fell to the ground. The Grumv are gliders. It's possible some could have survived the fall, and met members of the ten species."

"Then why don't *we* know about it?" *I can see why people thought this idea was crazy.*

"It could have happened before the Aridori war," Mom said. "That was a thousand cycles ago, and many records were destroyed then. There might be lost stories of the Grumv, hidden somewhere."

I could find them, one day.

"Did you learn what you wanted?" Avi asked as we exited. They tried to peer around the holy one as he closed and sealed the timber hatch over the entrance. Thankfully the other Grumv were gone. Maybe they'd gotten bored.

"I think we might have," I said.

* * *

As anxious as I was about finally getting to go home, the next two days passed quickly. Avi helped Mom and me out with the tests she was conducting on the crystals and the Arach Hanar silk.

"You'll get to do this later," I told Mom. "Why are you rushing to do so much? Whenever I do that back home, I make mistakes."

"I know, I know." Mom pulled her hair back. The moment her fingers left it, it sprang forward. "But anything I discover now is *mine*." She looked at me. "Ours. Once we get back to the Imperium, there will be hundreds of other naturalists and explorers who want their own discoveries."

"But you're the most famous of them all," I said. *That's what I was always told, growing up.* The idea that my mother might *not* be the best explorer the ten species had ever seen ricocheted through my brain.

Whether or not it was true, it calmed Mom a little. "Thank you, Natina," she said. "However many discoveries I've made, there's still Wailimani to contend with. He's a powerful voice in naturalist circles, and he can legitimately claim partial credit to everything we've discovered."

"Not this stuff," I passed a hand around the crystals and silk strewn about the medical bowl. "Anyway, the majus will probably back up your claims. I don't think she likes Wailimani any more than we do. The Grumv will help too, won't they?"

"Most will," Mom admitted. "Save for those who don't want to join the Great Assembly."

"It's a small group, and growing smaller," I said. I'd watched the unhappy crowds shrink over the last few days. I'd tried to talk to as many Grumv as I could, so they would get used to at least one new species.

"That Kirian might even help, while snatching as much support as he can," Mom said. "I haven't had time to talk to the group following him around, but it would help him *and* us to have Grumv willing to join the Assembly. His goals can't be too different from ours."

I wasn't as sure. "He's up to something. I know it."

"We only have one more day until the platform is completed and Majus E'Flyr can open the portal back." Mom picked up a sung crystal. "He can't possibly do much more in that time, can he?"

It turned out, he could.

* * *

Finally, it was the day the platform would be ready, and I felt like little jolts of lightning were running up and down my arms. Mom was rushing to do some last research, but I couldn't pay attention. This whole journey had been *amazing,* but now thoughts of my house near the beach on Etan kept running through my head. Mom finally kicked us out, grumbling about us messing up her results, so Avi and I went to check with the Grumv constructing the platform.

There were crowds of the winged people out on the trellises connecting their cylindrical buildings. Everyone in the town knew what time it was, and even the ones who didn't want to join the Assembly would be watching. They made space for me to pass, like a sort of minor celebrity, and the ones riding Arach Hanar moved the hairy beasts out of my way.

I can't believe I didn't want to come along when we started. Who wouldn't want to climb the walls of the Nether? Who could have imagined we'd find a species up here who wants to join the Great Assembly?

"What are you thinking about?" Avi asked. Their head was cocked and they looked at me over their long beak. It was around tenth lightening—midday, and it was almost time.

"Just about what will happen when the portal opens," I told them, chewing a nail. "Everything will change—even more for your people than for mine. I'll miss you Avi, when we have to go back to our own homes."

Avi opened their wings, like I'd seen the males doing. It was a strange gesture for them. "What if I come with you, and live down there?" They cocked a finger at the ground.

I stopped in the middle of a trellis stretching between two houses. A group of Grumv went around us, jabbering about the platform in deep voices.

"You mean for good? What about your parent's farm? Don't they need you to help with the harvest?"

Avi rolled one shoulder, making their wing half-open again. "A lot has changed since you came here," they said. "Someone will need to go with you, and find out what the people down there do and how they live," they spread their hands. "I'm close to my molting. I can feel it like an itch in my wings."

Now it was my turn to cock my head. I'd picked up the gesture from Avi over the last ten-day. "What does molting have to do with it?"

Avi clacked their beak, the equivalent of a grin. "See? We need people to figure out the differences between us. When the Grumv Vugm Mugv molt and choose whether they want to be male, or female, or something else, they also choose what vacancy they like best in the city, and tell everyone how they can fill it."

"That seems...limiting," I said. *What if I'd chosen to always stay home and help Alondri and Kayla research at the house, right before Mom asked me to come along?*

Avi shook their head. "It's what we do, and there's a big vacancy appearing. I want to fill it. I want to meet all the different people living on the floor of the Nether, and on the homeworlds, and tell them about the Grumv Vugm Mugv."

"You know, that's a good idea," I said.

* * *

"We're putting in the last planks," the lead Grumv working on the new trellis told us. "We want to make sure this area lasts for a good, long while, so we can have visitors from down below. The mayor wants trade with you people." The Grumv pointed one colorfully tattooed wing toward me. "Give us another lightening or so and it will be ready."

"More waiting," I told Avi, and they nodded. "Where's the majus, anyway? I thought she was supposed to be supervising the construction?"

The new platform wasn't big. There was a set of stairs leading down from the main trellis street running through the city. The stairs connected to another trellis, supported by strands of Arach Hanar silk attached to the one above, and ending in a bowl-like mat. The majus had given specifications how to make it big enough so any good majus could open a portal without it appearing over open air.

But Majus E'Flyr was not here, and Avi and I went back up to the city. We found Mom, both hands full with sacks of clothes and equipment. She set them down with a sigh.

"Have you seen Majus E'Flyr?" I asked.

Mom frowned at us. "I haven't. I thought she would be out here. Maybe she's getting the beetle?"

I smacked my forehead with one hand and Avi jumped in surprise. "I almost forgot about her!" I said. "How could I do that? Of course the beetle has to come back with us. She'd think we'd forgotten about her!"

"It might be more that the Council wants it," Mom muttered, but I waved a goodbye to her and took Avi's hand. I still had way too much energy, and needed to work it off.

"Come on," I said. "Let's go see if the majus is there. We can ride the beetle to the new platform!"

But when we got to the other edge of the city, puffing and gasping, the beetle was still silent, sitting beside the bridge that connected the city to the Nether's wall.

"Where *is* she?" I asked.

"Mater! Pater!" Avi called, and I looked down the wall. There were Mira and Hria, hopping from tree to tree. Behind them trundled the big silver and black Arach Hanar that had hissed at us as we left the farm. Mater Rutha Ahtur towed a huge net of white silk, filled to bursting with ripe purple toka fruit.

We met Avi's parents at the edge of the bridge, and both of them embraced their child, wrapping wings all the way around Avi.

"We wouldn't miss this for every crystal tear in the city," Mira said.

Her husband puffed up his crest and stretched out his wings. "Yes, the mayor's been sending messages down the silk lines to let us know what you were doing, Avi. We're very proud of how you're helping these people."

I looked at Avi, who was tilting their head nervously and clicking their beak together. I nudged their shoulder. "Well, go on," I said. I knew they wanted to ask about going to the floor, and a warmth rose in my chest at the thought of Avi and I exploring the Nether one day.

Avi curled their wings in close. "Mater, Pater, I have something to ask. It's about my path in life."

Mira and Hria traded glances, and I thought I could see sadness, but I looked away. It seemed like prying to watch them.

"Go on," Mira said.

"I...I'll molt soon. And...and I want to be the city announcer, except from our people to Natina's people." All the words came out in a rush and then there was silence, except for Mater Rutha Ahtur shifting position between two trees.

"Your Mater and I have actually been talking a lot with the mayor," Hria told his child. Avi sunk down, their wings folding even closer. They looked small.

"Mayor Kita is impressed with you bringing them up to the city, and showing them around," Mira said, with a tilt of her head to me. Avi began to unfold. "I think—" Mira clacked her beak. "I think if we were to speak with the mayor, we would all agree you're a great choice to go down to the floor of the Nether."

Mira lunged forward and wrapped her wings around Avi, and Avi clasped their Mater back, hard.

"Thank you," they said, then looked to their Pater. "What about the farm? The toka harvest?"

Hria waggled his head, making his crest wobble. "We've finished this harvest, and it will be a while before the next. I can talk to the mayor and see if we can get help. Otherwise the city will be in want of toka fruit." He opened a wing toward the Arach Hanar, which scuttled a couple steps away. I glimpsed his geometrical tattoos again. "Mater Rutha Ahtur has enough lazy children. Maybe I can train them to help me pick the fruit."

We all laughed, but I had to swallow a lump in my throat. *How long until I have to find my own place, away from my parents?*

* * *

Back at the platform, Mom was ready with our luggage, and a pang of guilt flowed through me because I hadn't helped her. I rushed over to take the last bags and walk the short distance to the pile, feeling stupid the whole way. Mom watched me with her hands on her hips and a half-smile.

I set down the luggage. *Mom must have finished cleaning up the equipment in the medical bowl, too.*

"Did you find the majus?" I asked.

Now Mom frowned. "No—I thought she was with you." She twisted, taking in the city in all directions. "And where's Wailimani? I know he's been skulking all around the city, but I'm certain he also knows when we're leaving."

"I don't know," I said, "but I think we'll have one more person traveling with us."

That got Mom's attention, and she looked to me, to Avi, and to Avi's parents, standing nearby, their wings intertwined.

"Your parents are all right with you coming with us?" she asked Avi, and all three of the Grumv nodded.

"Not only that," I said, "Avi will be the new—"

"Ah, then we are all to be gathered in the correct place after all," a shrill voice broke in over mine. I felt cold, invisible fingers climbing up my spine.

"I was to be worrying I would need to collect all the pieces in one place, but instead they are coming to me," Wailimani continued.

I clenched my fists, and turned with the others to see Majus E'Flyr walking toward us, her face like a thundercloud about to erupt with lightning. Behind her walked Wailimani, flanked by five male Grumv, tilting their heads and flashing their wings.

"What's going on, Wailimani?" Mom said. She sounded as angry as the majus looked.

"What is happening is that I am brokering a much better deal than any of us would be getting once the Effature and the Imperium get their hands on the resources laying out here to be used—traded for, that is," Wailimani said. His crest was raised in triumph.

"What's that supposed to mean?" I asked. I barely restrained myself from leaping forward and punching his smug face. My fingers creaked together in my balled fists. Everything had been going so well, and now he had to mess it up. Again.

"My friends here are speaking for those Grumv who do *not* want to join the Great Assembly." The Kirian waved a robed arm over the group behind him. "They would much rather be working through one contact, than deal with all the politics of ten new species. We are only needing the wing-print of the mayor and the city announcer. We've provided a little encouragement, just in case." His crest spread out as he smiled his pointy smile.

"What is this encouragement?" came a booming voice, louder than the waterfall below. I ducked down in reflex. So did Mom and Wailimani. The Grumv only looked to where the mayor and the announcer stumped up on short legs.

I understand why he's called the announcer now. That voice was loud enough to reach halfway across the Nether. My heart was pounding.

Wailimani turned, sounding calm, though his crest was spiky in surprise. "My associates have told me you will be joining the Assembly— a mistake, for the different factions there will be clamoring for your resources, and give you little in return. We are having a much better option, as long as you are agreeable," Wailimani answered.

"Plagi, Rhala, Usara," the mayor snapped at three of the Grumv following Wailimani. "Is this true? Have you gone against the majority of Grumv here *again*? We are joining the Great Assembly. I thought you learned your lesson the last time, when you lost your standing in our city meetings."

One of the Grumv flapped his brightly colored wings. "The method this Kirian suggests is much better, much safer. Many of our citizens don't agree with your views, Kita. Enough to ensure you lose your post in the next vote."

Avi gasped, and I looked between the Grumv. Mom and I had learned some about their culture, but not enough.

"What does he mean?" I asked my friend.

"Plagi has been trying to take the mayor's post for a long time," they said. "He's never had a good way to do it."

Can I do anything? I didn't see how. This was a Grumv matter, except Wailimani had put himself in the middle. Maybe those groups of angry Grumv hadn't gotten smaller after all. But why wasn't the majus doing something? She was hunched, not standing tall like usual.

"Your opponents are finding a new voice," Wailimani said. "You can either desist from the notion of joining the Great Assembly, and be letting all your trade with them go through my associates here, to me, and then to the Imperium, or the rather disagreeable majus will quickly cease to remember how to be making a portal back to the ground. We will be stuck here."

Wailimani raised his hand from where it had been hidden behind Majus E'Flyr and I saw the gleam of a metallic shaft.

He has a gun? How?

"Stop him, Majus E'Flyr!" I called. "Change the Symphony!"

But the majus only shook her head, her head-tentacles twitching furiously. I saw then she was holding her left hand in her right, as if it was hurt. Blood dripped from her fingers.

"The majus has found what several other maji have, recently," Wailimani said. "Even skin made tough by the House of Strength can't stop a bullet." He waggled the gun slightly, keeping the end pointing toward the majus. "I may not have prepared for every eventuality, but I knew you would be bringing a majus."

"You had that the whole climb?" Mom said, and I could feel the anger in her voice like little waves of heat. "You always planned to take the credit for yourself, didn't you? You *did* make your assistant cut Partino's harness!"

"Of course he did," I spat. I took a step forward, but Majus E'Flyr shook her head again. I growled, but I couldn't do anything, like a sea slug in a strikerfish's jaws. "You're a disgrace to the ten species," I yelled.

"It is to be of no importance now." Wailimani said. He addressed Mom. "But if you are asking nicely, I may be cutting you in on a fraction of my profits. You were setting up the expedition, after all." Mom's hands were clenched as tightly as mine, but she didn't move.

Then the Kirian nodded to one of the Grumv following him. "Just the signature, Mayor Kita. We will all be going home, and you will all be rich, minus the portion me and my friends here are keeping. No dealing with the troublesome Great Assembly."

"Do it," Majus E'Flyr growled, and I could hear a quaver in her voice for the first time since I'd met her. It made my stomach tighten. "If he shoots me again, no one is getting down. It will be cycles before another group gets up here, and both beetles are stuck on the wall."

I had to do something. *There's more than one majus here!*

"What about the holy one?" I asked.

"Knocked unconscious, back there," Majus E'Flyr said. "He doesn't know how to make a portal anyway. I'm the only one who can get us down to the Imperium."

"Very reasonable," Wailimani said. "Mayor and Announcer, your prints please on this declaration not to join the Assembly, and the promise to be dealing only through me and my associates. You will be proud protectorates of the Kirian Union, once I alert my homeworld."

Slowly, as if they were dragged forward, the mayor took the sheet of paper Wailimani offered. I was screaming inside, but I could do nothing, as the mayor dipped the tip of one wing in a pot of ink Plagi held, and marked the paper. Then the city announcer did the same, clacking his beak.

"Perfect," Wailimani said. He took the paper, blew on it, and tucked it inside his robe, the whole while holding the gun on the majus. "Now, I believe you are having a portal to create?"

"I need the holy one," the majus said.

"And we need the beetle," I said through clenched teeth. Maybe we could think of something in the delay.

Wailimani opened his mouth, his crest spiking and falling, and then he shrugged. "I can wait a few more minutes."

Several more Grumv came forward, loyal to Plagi and his group. They soon found the holy one and brought him, and Majus E'Flyr told me which levers to pull on the beetle to make her walk through the city. More Grumv escorted me, and even more stood around Mom so she wouldn't do anything.

I wish I could say my first time controlling the crystal beetle drill was fun, but all I could think about was the party waiting at the new platform. The Grumv would never be a species in the Assembly, so Avi could not be their announcer. Mom and I had proved my other parents were right, but no one would pay attention to that with what else happened today.

I followed the beetle down to the new construction. It creaked under her weight, but held.

"Now, Majus," Wailimani said. I dared to hope someone had taken the gun away, but no one had. The Grumv still stood guard over Mom. My eyes roved over the platform, but I couldn't find any way out, and I felt a burning lump in my throat.

The majus sighed, and stepped to the center of the new bowl. Her silvery eyes looked far away for several seconds, her head-tentacles twitching to a rhythm I couldn't hear. The holy one stood next to her, his head tilted.

Then in front of her, a disk of pitch black whirled in the air, growing big enough to fit even the beetle. The majus gestured to it with one hand.

"I must go last to close the portal."

"And I will go second to last, with my friends," Wailimani said.

I drove the beetle, and one by one, all of us walked through that black disk, back to the Imperium.

TEN-DAY FIVE

The Return

The ten species have not always numbered so. There were six, or maybe seven, who first settled the Nether and built the foundations of the Imperium, but that was long ago. Despite the loss of one species, others have joined the Great Assembly as the cycles passed, bringing the total up to ten. It is interesting to note that the time between a new species finding the Nether has grown less each time. It has only been fifty cycles since the last species found us, and now we have the Grumv Vugm Mugv. How long until the next species arrives?

—From the writings of the Effature

I stepped out of the portal behind Mom, Avi, and the beetle, into a hall in the Effature's palace. Wailimani and the Grumv came after, followed by the majus. Despite my still shaking hands—shocked at the change in our fortunes in only a few minutes—the multi-colored wall hangings and expensive looking sculptures scattered around caught my eye. I recognized a vase from the time of the Fourth Rebellion on Etan. That was a priceless piece!

Majus E'Flyr stepped forward and opened a little gate separating the end of the hallway from the group of people waiting for us. She hid her other hand behind her back, and I saw it was bloody, but not bleeding. She kept it held tight to her side.

The area was big enough for me to have the beetle trundle to a wall, and fold up her legs. She drew a lot of looks from the people waiting for us.

The Grumv were captivated, their heads tilting back and forth, taking in everything. There were twelve of them all together—eight of Plagi's people, the mayor, the announcer, the holy one, and Avi. My friend wrapped their wings close around them.

I went to them, and placed a hand on their shoulder. "Don't worry," I said. "We'll figure this out." But I wasn't so sure. My hands were cold with sweat. Could the Effature simply tear up the contract? A bunch of

Grumv supported Wailimani—there were more in this hall who did, than did not.

Avi clacked their beak.

"Welcome," said that same deep, warm voice I had heard through the sphere. The Effature was here, along with a bunch of other people. He was dressed in a green and purple robe that looked like it was made of tiny scales. On his head was the piece of curved Nether crystal.

I've seen the crystal lights and the sphere. I wonder what that can do. Can the Effature help us? He's responsible for the Nether, isn't he? I was very aware of the Kirian behind us, and his gun. This was supposed to be a first meeting between species. No one would suspect Wailimani had already taken control.

I watched the Effature's guards, placed at points around the hall. Would they come running if I screamed? But the Effature was already speaking. *I have to do something about Wailimani. Think, Natina!*

"The species of the Great Assembly welcome the Grumv Vugm Mugv to the floor of the Nether," The Effature continued. "We hope you will enjoy your stay."

I watched the others behind the Effature as he continued to speak, looking for any avenue of help. They were of several species, with a Festuour in front, big and furry, holding a sheaf of documents and wearing a tricorn hat. He looked down at his papers through glasses perched at the end of his snout, as if trying to find the form for a new species arriving in the Effature's halls. I wanted to yell at him that he was too late.

To the side, a Methiemum woman stood next to another Kirian. He was older than Wailimani, but I still glared at him. Beside them were two more Methiemum. One was a young man with a mop of dark hair, wearing a green vest. He folded his hands together anxiously. A short woman with long dark hair rested a hand on his shoulder.

Is that nervous man the one who was speaking to the Effature in the sphere? Who would be important enough to have a private meeting with the Nether's caretaker?

I shook my head. I doubted they could help. The Effature spoke more words of welcome to the Grumv, and on his other side, four members of the Council of the Maji stood. I recognized the Etanela who led them.

We can climb the walls of the Nether, and lead the maji. What can't the Etanela do?

I could feel Wailimani growing restless behind us as the speech went on, like someone staring at the back of my neck. We all stood stiffly, even the majus.

Gradually the Effature's words slowed, as he looked from person to person. He opened his mouth and I heard the flip and snap of wings opening and closing. Wailimani pushed to the front, his hands hidden in his sleeves.

"The Grumv are to be accepting of your welcome, but not the Assembly's. They wish a different approach than the other species." His voice was like claws down my spine. Wailimani bowed quickly and produced the contract from a voluminous sleeve—the one that still hid his hand with the gun. He handed it to the Effature, who frowned at the paper.

"Not joining the Assembly? Protectorate of the Kirians? *All* of the contact with the Grumv Vugm Mugv is to go through you, Surigran Wailimani?" The Effature's warm voice was skeptical. He handed the paper to the Festuour, who took it with one furry paw and pulled his glasses down with the other, reading it over.

"That is to be correct." Wailimani's crest rose and expanded. "All transactions will be going from me to my friends." He gestured to the group of eight behind him with his free hand. "There may be a change in the Grumv's political structure, soon."

"This seems an unusual arrangement." The Effature looked to the other Grumv. "You say you signed this, Mayor Kita, Announcer Gami?"

The city announcer flapped his wings once, then folded them around him. "That is correct." His head tilted from one side to the other, obviously unhappy.

I scanned the people here. Everyone knew something was going on. *If no one will do anything, then I will.*

"He's got a gun," I blurted, and several of the people behind the Effature gasped and stepped back. "Wailimani threatened the majus to make the Grumv sign the contract! He hurt Majus E'Flyr!"

"Hush, girl," Wailimani hissed, and lifted his hidden hand that held the gun.

The guards were already closing in even before the Effature signaled them, but Plagi and his associates moved in front of the Kirian, keeping the guards from him.

"You do not want to create an incident between our people, just as you meet us, do you?" Plagi said. "He showed us the weapon, but we had the idea. We take responsibility for injuring the holy one. Wailimani is blameless." The Effature made a small motion and the guard stopped moving, though they stayed close to our group.

Mom was there in an instant, looming over the smaller Kirian. "You may have gotten monetary gain from this, Surigran, but I dearly hope you are not planning to threaten *my daughter*."

Wailimani took a step back, looking up at Mom. "It is to be signed," he whined in his high voice. "The contract is to be official and unbreakable."

"It was signed under duress," Mom said. "It's not even valid to begin with."

"I disagree," Plagi said, opening his wings. "And so do those who wish not to join the Assembly."

"Nothing is unbreakable," the Effature said. He seemed calm, but I noticed a muscle in his jaw clench. "May I have that back, Burris?" he asked the Festuour. After he got it, the Effature held the contract between both hands as if he would rip it apart. "It seems this contract is not as binding as we thought. Are you well, Majus?"

Majus E'Flyr nodded her head. She had been silent and subdued since Wailimani brought her to the platform. She showed her bloody hand. There was a nasty gash in one side, but she wiggled all her fingers. "A flesh wound. The Symphony will keep me from feeling the pain." She glanced at the Kirian, her head-tentacles twitching. "The Grumv speaks the truth. They urged Wailimani to violence, but it was merely...an effective demonstration. He could have done worse."

The Effature shook his head and brought the contract higher, beginning to rip the paper. Before he could do so, Plagi pushed forward. "The mayor will not be the power in the city for long," he said. The Effature paused. "If you destroy that agreement, none of the Grumv will trade with your Great Assembly."

"Step back, Plagi," the mayor said, opening her wings threateningly. "We'll speak of this privately."

"No!" Plagi came forward farther. He was bigger and brighter than the mayor, flashing the orange and purple tattoos on his wings. "Other merchants believe the same as we do. We've been speaking with many who want no part of these ten species." He pointed a finger toward the Effature.

I stared at Wailimani. *There has to be a way out of this.* The Kirian's crest rose and spread in triumph, and he gave me a pointy-toothed grin.

The Effature sighed, a deep sound. "Then you agree to the conditions of this contract?" he asked the mayor.

Slowly, Mayor Kita nodded her head. The city announcer did too. The holy one, who had been silent, looked away, his wings crossed in front of him. "There is more division in my people than I thought," the mayor said. "Perhaps later we will be able to renegotiate this agreement."

I have to do something! This was the worst way possible for the Grumv to come to the Great Assembly. They couldn't be represented by that sea slug Wailimani!

Avi poked me in the back and I leaned down to them. "With these new portals, we can travel to all the different cities of the Grumv Vugm Mugv in minutes, can't we?" they asked. "It is a new way of thinking. It used to take many months to get word from the other cities, and I'm not certain the mayor has realized yet."

I stared at them a minute, until my brain caught up with what my friend was saying. I straightened, and my eyes widened.

"You're going to be a good announcer," I told them.

The Effature was speaking again. "—for now, I have no other option but to honor this contract, despite the situation—"

"The Grumv Vugm Mugv have lots of cities!" I shouted. *Sea Mother, I interrupted the Effature.* My heart beat wildly in my chest. "You'll be able to reach all of them by portal, not just the one these people live in!"

The Effature looked directly at me for the first time. I blinked under the weight of his gaze. It was like the Nether wall staring at me.

No wonder people listen to him.

The Nether's caretaker turned back to the mayor and the announcer. "You speak for your people, yes?"

"We do," the mayor answered. Plagi clacked his beak in agreement, too.

"You speak for *all* of your people, even in other cities?" the Effature clarified.

Now the Grumv paused. After a moment, the city announcer spoke in his deep, booming voice.

"To speak for *all* of our people, we must hold a moot with the other mayors and city announcers. Such a thing has not been done since before I was hatched."

"I see." The Effature carefully folded the contract in thirds, and gave it to the Festuour official. "Matthiawi Burris, Reader is my legal minister. Burris, please make sure this is marked, signed, and sealed, this day," he said. "*This* city of the Grumv Vugm Mugv, at this time, will not join the Great Assembly. All their trade will go through Surigran Wailimani."

"I'll have it done quicker than a hopper jumping on a griddle," Burris said, his mouth open and tongue lolling in a Festuour grin.

"Wait. I am thinking that—" Wailimani reached out a hand, as if he could take the contract back.

"What does this mean, Wailimani?" Plagi asked.

"It means Surigran here has negotiated for all trade with *only* your city to go through you and him," Mom told the Grumv. "*Only* your city has decided not to join the Great Assembly. However, it will be an easy matter for us to open a portal to any of your *other* cities."

"I think it may be time for another moot of the mayors and announcers," Mayor Kita mused.

"Yes," Announcer Gami said, "I will discuss with Announcer Oala how our trade may pass through their city to reach the Nether floor. We will have to settle for a lesser percentage of the profit, but then, Plagi and his crew have been increasing prices."

"I'm sure it will be a small difference in cost," the mayor said. "But it may bring some who do not want to join the Assembly to our side. We will have much to discuss with the other cities."

The Grumv who had followed Wailimani began to talk quickly, in low voices, and Plagi went back to join them.

"Wait. Come back," Wailimani told the Grumv. "We can be discussing our contract again. I have many friends in the Imperium. I can be—"

I tuned out the Kirian and smiled down at Avi. "Mayor Kita," I said. "Could we continue with our introductions? We should let the Effature talk to the new announcer between your city and the floor of the Nether.

They will be very important when you discuss whether you want to join the Great Assembly of species."

The mayor tilted her head at me, and I brought Avi forward, a hand on their shoulder.

* * *

In the days that followed, there were a lot of meetings with important people, and food, and more talking, and more eating. Wailimani got involved in a lot of legal issues, especially with whether it was the Grumv's fault or his fault he shot the majus. I didn't care either way. I'd never forgive him for what he did to Partino, but with his time and precious money tied up fighting to stay out of jail, I didn't have to hear his squeaky voice.

Majus E'Flyr disappeared with the holy one, off to introduce him to the rest of the maji. I'm sure the old Grumv would learn a lot of new tricks with the Symphony.

The Grumv did not immediately join the Great Assembly, even after contacting some of the other cities. Mayor Kita said their people would talk about it for a long time, but she thought they would come around eventually.

I cornered Mom after five days of this. "I'm ready to go home," I said. Mom nodded. "I am too, Natina."

* * *

It was seven days after we arrived in the Effature's palace when Mom and I finally got back to our house on Etan. Avi came with us.

Avi had a good head for talking with new people, and figuring out what they really wanted. It was no mistake my friend figured a way around Wailimani's and Plagi's attempted coup. However, *she* got a little irritated with the ones who called her a child, especially since she had started her molt during the meetings. I knew how she felt. It was time for a break—for all of us.

The three of us walked down the pebble beach where my house stood. I wished the beetle could have carried our luggage, but the majus had taken her to the maji, after a strict promise to Mom that the discovery and salvage rights were still linked to our family.

There was another hole in our little group, one that should have been filled by Partino's strong arms and easy laugh.

I miss being called 'little one.'

Mom and I told stories about his pranks to Avi, as we walked to the house. We'd have a service for him later, on the beach.

When we got close, I could see the silhouettes of Alondri and Kayla in the doorway of the big, angular house, which stood just back from high tide. They had painted the top deck while we were gone, a cool peach color that was the same as the sunset over the ocean.

"You brought us to your family, Avi," I told my friend. She was goggling at the ocean, like I had at the waterfall "Finally, we get to introduce you to ours."

Avi placed her hand in mine as my little brothers came running across the beach to meet us.

Mom smiled down at the two of us. "A long rest with our family will be welcome," she said, "but after that, I need some help with planning the next expedition."

Both Avi and I stood straighter. "Oh yeah?" I said. "Where are we going?" It was no longer a question of *if* I would accompany her.

"Have you heard of the Crystalline Sea?" Mom asked.

I shook my head.

"It's where the floor of the Nether dips down far lower than anywhere else," Mom said, making a giant bowl with her hands. "All the water in the Nether gathers there, but it never overflows. No one's ever gotten to the bottom."

"Yet," I said with a smile.

If you enjoyed this book, please leave a brief review at your online bookseller of choice. Thanks!

Want more Dissolutionverse? There's a whole trilogy to read, tying all the stories in this volume together. Get your copy of the first book, *The Seeds of Dissolution* today!

For behind-the-scenes articles, deleted scenes, and previews of upcoming works, sign up for my newsletter at http://williamctracy.com/newsletter-signup!

Appendix: The Houses of the Maji

For uncounted cycles, the six houses of the maji have worked together to uphold the Great Assembly of Species. They control the only means of transportation in and out of the Nether and between the homeworlds, and thus have a great responsibility to the non-maji members, who far outnumber them. As such, every majus has a say in the Assembly, a concept some non-maji are not comfortable with.

—Houses of the Maji, often attributed to Ribothari Tan, Knower, later of the Council of the Maji

Each house of the maji can hear and change one section of the Grand Symphony and thus affect reality, by the individual applying the notes that make up their own song. This application can be seen by other maji in a visual representation of color, often accompanied by a secondary color, personal to the individual majus. It is said each house's Symphony is based on a certain frequency or note.

—From "Memoirs of Yaten E'Mez," Highest of the House of Communication and Speaker for the Council, 379 A.A.W.

House of Strength

The color of the House of Strength is bright emerald green, and the areas of the Symphony it affects often have to do with constitution, defense, strength, and growth, as well as soil and rock. A large portion of these maji have jobs as herbalists, veterinarians, or naturalists, though as with any house, the possibilities are nearly endless. Their Symphony diverges from the sound of a baritone resonant string.

House of Communication

Members of the House of Communication are the most common councilmembers chosen to become Speakers for the Council of the Maji. Their house color is pure yellow, and they affect quick thought, speech patterns, as well as air pressure, weather systems and avian creatures. Many of the House of Communication serve as diplomats of the maji, working less with the physical changes in their Symphony than those of interplay between the species. Their Symphony's fundamental tone is that of a low reed.

House of Power

The House of Power deals with the play of politics, movement of societies, personal relationships, as well as power generation, and simple heat. Their house color is fiery orange. They can as easily be found in the industrial districts of the Imperium and the homeworlds as in clandestine meetings and national assemblies. Their Symphony's base melody is of a sounding horn.

House of Grace

Those of the House of Grace are often subtle, with their control of liquids and ice, as well as efficient movement, cooperation, and coordination. Their house color is sapphire blue, and they work around transportation systems, food distribution, diplomatic intermediaries, and engineering positions. Many members are fond of kinesthetic movements such as dance, athletics, and martial arts. The founding tone of their Symphony is a passionate tenor.

House of Healing

The members of the House of Healing are best known as skilled physicians and surgeons, as the brilliant white of their house color seems to indicate. However, there is much more to the specializations of the house, including plant and animal breeding, psychology, profiling information on individuals, and even archeology through residue of living creatures on ancient artifacts. Their Symphony's fundamental tone is a high ringing of struck metal.

604 William C. Tracy

House of Potential

The House of Potential is the most directly tied to science and engineering. Its members are responsible for many of the technological improvements of the ten species made in recent cycles. Their house color is a rich rusty brown, and they are, at the very simplest, concerned with energy transfer. They are known to work with the House of Power on fuel and work generation and the House of Healing on ancient history, describing energy paths of artifacts. They deal with kinetic movement as the House of Grace does, transfer of force as the House of Strength, and energy of the weather with the House of Communication. Their members can also create Systems, or long-lasting changes in the Symphony, driven through a store of energy. Their Symphony starts with the shriek of whistling air.

Appendix: The Species of the Great Assembly

The number of species in the Great Assembly varies over the cycles. Currently it resides at ten, including the recent addition of the Lobhl. The founding members are those who, according to tradition, started the first Assembly when the maji of their species discovered each other in the Nether.

—From the notes of the Effature, Bolas Palmoran, 983 A.A.W.

All members of the Great Assembly share basic similarity in form and function, though the species are physically spread far across the universe. The Nether helps to form connections despite differences, to the point where some scholars wonder whether the Nether has some impact on the species that find it.

—From "Assumptions on the Nature of the Nether" by Festuour philosopher Hegramtifar Yhon, Thinker

Methiemum

The Methiemum homeworld is known as Methiem, and hosts a species well known as traders and decent scientists. They were one of the first to discover the Nether, as they are entrepreneurial and prone to adventure, though perhaps at the expense of long-term planning. However, this cannot have affected them greatly, as the common trading tongue of the ten species is derived from one of their dialects. In addition, they were the first to suggest an Assembly of all species who discover the Nether, probably to secure trading rights with the others. They are the most prevalent species of the ten, of medium height and coloring ranging from a dark mahogany to very pale peach, even with cases of albinism. They often have fine hair restricted to the tops of their heads and sporadically over the limbs and torso, more so on the males.

Kirian

The inhabitants of Kiria are known for their philosophy, debate, and ancestor worship. They were another species to discover the Nether early and became a founding member of the Great Assembly. They make fine statesmen, though they have a convoluted natural dialect in many of their nations, which does not translate as well inside the Nether as other species. Kirians do not let this stop them from expounding on any subject they know of, and some they do not. The males of the species favor long colorful robes in many cultures, while the females prefer to leave their arms and legs bare to show off their fine feathering and delicately curved nails. The species is generally tall, with wrinkled, liver-spotted skin, and feathers creating expressive crests on top of their heads. Males may also cultivate moustaches and thin beards, and both are sparingly feathered on the torso. Their pointed teeth can be unnerving when bared in smiles, though their dentation is mainly for gripping in their diet of grubs, beetles, and other slippery creatures.

Lobath

The Lobath are often looked down upon by the other species as dull and uninteresting, much like the prevalent mushroom farms on their rainy homeworld of Loba. However, Lobath are found at every level of society, from the menial to the most intellectual, and are one of the founding members of the Great Assembly. Consistently, they are defined as hardworking, compared to the other species, and tend to fill more physically demanding jobs. They are usually savvy with technology, especially new inventions. Other species may joke of the permanently surprised expression on the Lobath face, arising from their unblinking silvery eyes. They have a large range in coloring, from yellow, to orange, to red and brown, but are more easily identified by their squat neck-less bodies and three head-tentacles sprouting from the crown of their heads. The tentacles are often braided or tied together in certain styles. Males may have small rubbery growths above and below the mouth, while females have thinner head-tentacles and wari, the third gender, are generally of slighter, taller, build.

Sathssn

The Sathssn are unusual in that over eighty percent of the culture of Sath Home subscribe to various sects of the Cult of Form, based on perfection of the physical body. This invades every aspect of their society, from dark cloaks, robes, and gloves, to marriage rites, where the participants must be examined by other family for any illness or disfigurement, to livestock, bred to only descend from the most reputable lineages. The inhabitants of Sath Home are especially prone to cancers and tumors, and their winnowing practice began as a necessary response. Like many such things, it became religion. A notable exception is the Southern Coastal Coalition, a nationality where scales are allowed to be shown, and some may even go about without cowls and gloves and in short sleeves, to the dismay of the rest of their species. In the rare occasion flesh is shown, the Sathssn body is covered in tiny scales, ranging from yellow to green. Sparse hair may be present on the head and face, and eyes are red with yellow slitted pupils. Some Sathssn antisocial tendencies have caused interspecies conflicts in the past, yet they remain in good standing as a founding member of the Great Assembly. Despite their almost worldwide religion, many become scientists or statespeople.

Etanela

The long-lived Etanela are described as inherent pacifists, though the planet of Etan provides its fair share of malcontents, adventure seekers, and revolutionaries to the Great Assembly, of which they are a founding species. The Etanela typecast comes from their love of music, painting, sculpture, and literature. Many accepted great works were either created by an Etanela, or funded by one. Lots of educated Etanela are gifted speakers, and love to argue. Physically, they are the tallest of the ten species, with the largest individuals rising head and shoulders over even Kirians. Their skin tends to light blue, revealing aquatic origins, also noted in their large eyes and long fingers, and small, streamlined noses. The only hair the species exhibits is in a mane surrounding the head, often left to trail to the shoulders. The species is largely divided into four genders, with both dominate and subordinate versions of those who carry young and those who do not. Their mating rituals are often obtuse to those not of their species.

Festuour

Festuour can be hard to pin down to a stereotype. They thrive in the variability of professions and are well known for their philosophers, gourmands, mechanics, scholars, tailors, and explorers. On their homeworld of Festuour, once a member of the species finally discovers their chosen path in life, it is appended to their name permanently. Their inclusive friend-based society encourages members to do anything they set their minds to, with cheery acceptance. Children are reared communally to give the best options for advancement of themselves and society. Physically, Festuour are stout, covered in coarse greenish-brown hair. Their faces have long snouts with large noses, and nearly all members of the species possess piercing blue eyes, though a common failing is nearsightedness. The hairy Festuour do not often wear clothes, instead preferring accessories such hats, glasses, gloves, and belts and bandoliers with many pouches. They were the last of the founding members to convene the Great Assembly, though they have the distinction to be one of two species to share a galaxy, the other being the Methiemum. The two are often staunch allies politically and many of the Methiemum's customs and idioms have bled over to Festuour culture.

Benish

Even longer-lived than the Etanela, the Benish were the first newcomers welcomed by the newly created Assembly of Species. Most still live on their homeworld of Aben, and they are the least populous members both in the Nether and in the Assembly of Species. Cautious by nature, Benish are studious to a fault, often observing a situation from all sides before making even a preliminary decision. Little is known about their home cultures, save that the species is genderless, and propagates by a form of budding, where the parents, however many, share and mix memories, arranging parts of their history before dying to produce a new child or children, who inherit the progenitor's memories. Physically, the Benish are one of the most different species, with flesh made of a substance closer to plant than animal. They have no well-defined bone structure, and each member is varied in coloring, skin tone and roughness, and placement of internal organs.

Sureriaj

The Sureriaj are the most xenophobic of the ten species, surpassing even the antisocial tendencies of the Sathssn. Their culture is entirely founded on the concept of family, going so far as to have, instead of independent nations, major family lines that matriarchally govern their homeworld of Sureri. There is also a large group consisting of the disgraced—those who have lost their right to their family name—known as the Naiyul. Names are very important to the Sureriaj, and each individual has a hierarchy of names, the most secret known to progressively closer family members. Physically, the Sureriaj are tall and gaunt, with proportionally long legs. They have fine hair covering the entirety of their body, through which the skin can be seen. Their faces are not always appealing to other species, and that, with their aloofness, is the basis of the species slur "gargoyle." Their society is two thirds male, and two males and one female are required to create a viable offspring. The Sureriaj have the second lowest birth rate of the ten species, just higher than the Benish.

Pixie

This warlike and competitive species was the second to last to join the Assembly. To others, some of their members seem less intelligent to the point of an animal intellect, though this may be explained by their descent from a hive mentality, as well as their careful breeding of a fierce warrior caste, at the expense of progression in other areas. For each sufficiently courageous deed a pixie completes, a letter or syllable is added to her name, and many go by shortened nicknames. Pixies are short, blue to gray in coloring, with black compound eyes. They are capable of short flights with their gossamer wings, though often they will lift from the ground when speaking to another species, as if in recompense for being the shortest of the species. There are reports of members of another gender, hidden deep in their enormous city-hives, but all individuals who interface with other species are identified as female.

Lobhl

There is no proper spoken name for the Lobhl homeworld, so it is titled as the members name their species. The Lobhl have been members of the Great Assembly for only fifty cycles, and caused controversy when they joined for the amount of money spent on social restructuring, especially in the rotunda of the Assembly. Because the Lobhl have no vocal chords, they communicate entirely with complex hand gestures, and expensive visual displays were added in many areas to cater to them. Lobhl faces and heads are nearly featureless, leading to small problems in communication, even in the Nether. Lobhl hands are the points of reference for the species, widely different between individuals, and often tattooed. Each hand has seven digits, two of which are thumbs on opposing sides of the hand. Generally the Lobhl species is talented visually and mathematically. They also have a great love of what they define as music, though most is visually experienced. Their names are translations of actions they routinely perform, and their gender roles vary with the individual and the social situation. Their young are raised communally, and are neither carried in the body, nor in eggs. Many Lobhl worship the god of music, an incorporeal concept of light, like a personification of the Symphony, and most of their other religions focus on vision over sound or language.

Aridori

Little is known about this extinct species. They were rumored to be one of the founding members of the Great Assembly. However, many records were lost in the Great Aridori War, when the entire species suddenly turned on the others, often taking the forms of old friends, or even close family members. They were eventually eradicated, with many renegades hunted by teams of trained Sathssn commandos, but legends of their shapeshifting prowess and patient, long-term deception have provided generations of nighttime stories to scare children.

Appendix: Timeline of Major Events:

A.A.W = After Aridori War

0 A.A.W. – End of Aridori War

632 A.A.W. – Events of Changing State

726 A.A.W. – Pixies Species Enters Great Assembly

927 A.A.W. – Mandamon Feldo Born

939 A.A.W. – Origon Cyrysi Born

952 A.A.W. – Lobhl Species Enters Great Assembly

953 A.A.W. – Events of The Society of Two Houses

962 A.A.W. – Rilan Ayama Born

964 A.A.W. – Events of The Five Hive Plateau

984 A.A.W. – Events of Tuning the Symphony

985 A.A.W. – Sam van Oen Born

989 A.A.W. – Events of Thorns and Fur

999 A.A.W. – Events of Last Delivery

1001 A.A.W. – Events of The Feastday

1003 A.A.W. – Events of The First Majus in Space

1003 A.A.W. – Events of The Symphony Eater

1003 A.A.W. – Events of The Seeds of Dissolution

1003 A.A.W. – Events of Journey to the Top of the Nether

ABOUT THE AUTHOR

William C. Tracy writes and publishes queer science fiction and fantasy through his indie press Space Wizard Science Fantasy (spacewizardsciencefantasy.com).

His largest work is the Dissolutionverse: a space opera with music-based magic, including ten books and an RPG. He also has a standalone epic fantasy with seasonal fruit-based magic through a LGBTQ+ small press.

William is a North Carolina native and a lifelong fan of science fiction and fantasy. He has a master's in mechanical engineering and has both designed and operated heavy construction machinery. He has also trained in Wado-Ryu karate since 2003 and runs his own dojo in Raleigh NC. He is an avid video and board gamer, a beekeeper, a reader, and of course, a writer.

You can get a free Dissolutionverse novelette by signing up for William's mailing list at http://williamctracy.com

Follow him on Twitter at https://twitter.com/wctracy for writing updates, cat and bee pictures, and thoughts on martial arts.

Please take a moment to review this book at your favorite retailer's website, Goodreads, or simply tell your friends!

Made in the USA
Monee, IL
26 May 2024

58832481R00360